MW01054871

A Small World of Our Own

We had our own
little government
in Oregon territory,
made our own laws
and executed them;
Uncle Sam was a relative
we scarcely realized
the existence of;
it was a small
world of our own.

David Shelton
Pioneer of 1847

*Authentic pioneer stories of the Pacific Northwest
from the Old Settlers Contest of 1892*

A

Small World of Our Own

———————— *ROBERT A. BENNETT* ————————

Pioneer Press Books
Walla Walla, Washington
U.S.A.
1985

Library of Congress Catalog Number 85-062415

Pioneer Press Books
37 South Palouse
Walla Walla, WA 99362

Cover art by Norman Adams

This book is dedicated
to
the Reverend Myron Eells
who
faithfully collected these stories

Acknowledgements

Thanks to the following people for their help in producing this book: Candace Pierce, L.L. "Larry" Dodd, Marilyn Sparks, Norman Adams, Scott Mayberry, Dyann Swanson, Bea Bowers and Susan Adams. Also, thanks to the Penrose Memorial library at Whitman College and the Washington State library at Olympia. Finally, special thanks to my family for allowing me the time to do these projects.

Table of Contents

Conflict on the Sound

Revenge and Reprisal

Fraser River Gold Rush

Northwest Wanderings

Epilogue

Tantalizing, that's what the sentence was, downright tantalizing. The alluring headline, just seemed to hypnotize me and demand my further scrutiny. Has this ever happened to you? Innocently, you are reading along and suddenly without warning, a certain word or phrase leaps into your mind and all your attention is riveted to that small section of the page. This frequently happens to me. I suspect that these engrossing tidbits are purposely put there to catch the reader's attention, so I call them "catchers." A lot of people call them grabbers, but then I guess that I'm not like most people.

All my friends play games for relaxation like raquetball, golf or tennis, sports that require a lot of physical activity. Myself, I enjoy hanging out at archives and museums. None of that grunting and groaning for me, thank you. Just plop me in a comfortable chair, in a temperature controlled environment, while I search for long hidden treasures, now that's recreation. That's what I was doing one warm Wednesday afternoon in the Eell's Northwest room at Whitman College's Penrose Memorial library. Washington State's upcoming Centennial celebration, which takes place in 1989 recently has focused my attention on the state's formative years, and I was trying to ferret out a few enthralling pioneer stories from the early days of the Pacific Northwest.

That afternoon at the library, my archivist friend, L.L. "Larry" Dodd guided me through the inner room's large vault door and steered me towards a large collection of scrapbooks which had been assembled by the Northwest room's patron saint, the Reverend Myron Eells. He pointed out three that were labeled "old Settlers stories," and it was in the front of the first volume that the provocative headline caught my attention. Win Two Roundtrip Railroad Tickets to the 1893 Chicago World's Fair, the headline invited.

My curiosity sufficiently piqued, I began to explore the rest of the old, yellowed advertisement. I found that it was announcing a contest which was being sponsored by a newspaper, *The Tacoma Ledger*, in order to promote the formation of an old settler's association. The rules of the "old settlers contest" were quite simple. To the man or woman judged to have written the most accurate and interesting story about the early days of the Pacific Northwest or during their westward journey would be awarded the grand prize trip to Chicago.

The newspaper's invitation must have reached a very receptive audience in those who first tamed this great land as each of the three one hundred page scrapbooks was filled with the fascinating and informative accounts which were entered in the contest. Needless to say, I felt like an old prospector who had just struck bedrock and uncovered the mother lode!

Without any reservations, I knew after reading the exciting stories contained in the Reverend Eells' scrapbooks that they would make a very valuable book. Who wouldn't thrill to these wonderful true life adventures written by those who had been among the first to come to this great land.

Collectively they formed a kaleidoscopic image of pioneer life in the early days of the Pacific Northwest. In a host of different roles, the old settlers explored, fought, dug, cut and finally won over the rich new land they now called home. In the days of their youth, when they had cast their fortunes to the wind and made the long and perilous journey to the west, they learned to be resourceful and self-reliant; those who didn't usually perished.

If this sounds interesting and you're looking for many hours of pleasurable reading, then I invite you to don your Judicial Robes so that you can select your favorite pioneer story. The contest's three judges' decision is found in the epilogue of this book. Get ready to embark on an exciting adventure where the hands of the clock have been turned back to a time when life was simpler but ever so much harder, a time when the Pacific Northwest was A Small World of Our Own.

Robert A. Bennett

THE OLD SETTLER

I'd wandered all over the country,
   Prospecting and digging for gold—
I'd tunneled, hydraulicked and cradled,
   And I've been frequently sold.
Chorus—
   And I have been frequently s-o-l-d,
   And I have been frequently sold;
   I'd tunneled, hydraulicked and cradled,
   And I have been frequently sold.

For one who gets riches by mining,
   Perceiving that hundreds grow poor,
I made up my mind to try farming—
   The only pursuit that is sure.
Chorus—
   The only pursuit that is s-u-r-e,

So rolling my grub in my blankets,
   I left all my tools on the ground,
And started one morning to shank it,
   For a country they call Puget Sound.

Arriving flat broke in mid-winter,
   I found it enveloped in fog,
And covered all over with timber
   Thick as hair on the back of a dog.

As I looked on the prospect so gloomy,
   The tears trickled over my face,
For I felt that my travels had brought me
   To the edge of the jumping off place.

I took up a claim in the forest
   And sat myself down to hard toil;
For two years I chopped and niggered;
   But I never got down to the soil.

I tried to get out of the country,
   But poverty forced me to stay;
Until I became an old settler,
   Then nothing could drive me away.

No longer the slave of ambition,
   I laugh at the world and its shams,
As I think of my present condition
   Surrounded by acres of clams.

And now that I'm used to the climate,
   I think that if ever man found
A spot to live easy and happy,
   That Eden is on Puget Sound.

Chapter 1

Ho! for the Land of Fish and Clams

M.P. Dougherty

Mr. Dougherty came to Oregon in 1843 where he was elected the Provisional Government Justice of the Peace. Later he was an Alcalda *in the California gold fields in 1849.*

Tacoma, Washington — September 30, 1892

I here give a synopsis of my journey and what induced me, with other persons, from the east and west, to cross the plains and Rocky Mountains to Oregon. Senator Linn of Missouri prepared a bill granting 640 acres of land to each emigrant to Oregon, and, together with his views with regard to the settlement in said country, submitted it to congress. The bill passed both houses, and received the signature of the president of the United States. A great excitement among the people, east and west, causing them to prepare for the land of promise, followed.

A company, composed of the following named, William Martin, William Shelden, M.P. Dougherty, Linsday Tharp and Parson Reading, started from Platte City, Platte county, Missouri, on the 15th day of May, 1843, and arrived at Fitzhugh's mill, on the Missouri river, a place of rendezvous for those who wished to go to Oregon. The party camped, put up a tent, and turned the oxen out to graze, intending to remain until the tide of emigration concluded to move. During our stay on the ground Kit Carson and Captain John Gant came over to our camp to see their old friend, William Martin. Carson was an old Indian fighter. During the conversation among the old friends, Dr. Marcus Whitman came over to our camp and had a talk with Carson and Grant relative to his journey from Oregon to Washington city and his return to Oregon. He started from Oregon in 1842 in the presence of Rev. Eells, Rev. Spaulding and W.H. Gray, for Washington city. He crossed on horseback in midwinter, the great desert, on his road to Washington, for the purpose of saving one of the finest countries on the Pacific coast from the grasping power of Great Britain. The doctor gave every encouragement to the emigrants with regard to the feasibility of the route across the plains for wagons, and instilled into the people connected with the emigration that spirit which God had endowed his mental and physical system with, enabling him to endure a great many hardships. The emigrants commenced moving on the 23rd day of May, 1843, from Fitzhugh's mill, in two divisions. Captain Perry Applegate had charge of the first division, Captain John Gant, an old officer of the army of the United States, in charge of the second division. There were 293 persons over the age of 16, capable of bearing arms. There were 111 wagons and vehicles of different kinds. The greatest number of teams consisted of oxen. The company passed Fort Laramie and arrived at Fort Hall and stopped a short time to give our oxen rest.

The following persons left our train at Fort Hall for the purpose of going to California: J. Atcheson, M. Boardman, Joseph Childs, Mr. Dawson, Captain John Gant, Milton Little, Captain William Martin, Julius Martin, T. McClelland, Mr. McGee, John Macintire, John Williams, James Williams, Squire Williams and Parson Reading. The following persons died at different points on the route: Mr. Stevens died on the Sandy; Clabornpain died on Sweet Water. The following named persons turned back on the Platte river: Nicholas Biddle, Alexander Frances, F. Sugar, John Laughbouraugh, Jackson Moore. Including those who went to California and those who turned back with those who died on the road left the actual number of our train 267.

Peter H. Burnett was placed on the division of No. 2. We proceeded on our route under strict discipline, Captain Burnett being assisted by James W. Nesmith. I was informed during the party's sojourn at Fort Hall that the emigrants of 1842 did not go through with the wagons to Oregon, but left them at Fort Hall. It was reported that Mr. Grant, who had charge of the Hudson Bay fort at that time, stated to the emigrants that the best thing they could do was to leave their wagons and pack through to Oregon. He told them it was impossible to go through with wagons, and under these impressions the emigrants of 1842 packed through to Oregon.

Notwithstanding the forebodings at Fort Hall we proceeded on our route without any difficulty. The advice of Dr. Marcus Whitman, whose character stood high, and his charitable feelings were appreciable. The impressions of such a character were a guide to the party and led them to their destination. We arrived safely at The Dalles, on the Columbia river, in the month of October, on the 17th day, 1843. The Indians did not trouble us on the route. Miles Eyers and C. Stringer were drowned in the Columbia river. William Day arrived sick, and died at Fort Vancouver. We took our wagons apart and shipped them on canoes from The Dalles to the Willamette falls in Oregon, the falls being the principal place of business at that time. The oxen and horses were driven by the Mount Hood trail to Clackamas valley, a short distance from the Willamette falls. The number of emigrants at our arrival was 267.

The distance we traveled from Fitzhugh's mill to The Dalles was 1800 miles. We found in Oregon many persons exclusive of missionaries, (who should be included in the general term of settlers), who had found their way from different points, some crossing the plains or Rocky mountains from the eastern states, some of them sailors, who had abandoned the sea; others were trappers, who had exchanged their uncertainties of a Nomadic life for farming, while others had found their way from California. The following named persons were found:

Armstrong Hearent, Mr. Brown, Hugh Burns, William Brown, Jonas Bales, J.M. Black, Dr. Bailey, Mr. Brainard, Madoram Crawford, David Carter; Samuel Campbell, Jack Campbell, William Craig, Amos Cook, Aaron Cook, Jim Conner, Allen Davy, William Cannon, William Doty,

Richard Eakin, Squire Ebberts, John Edwards, Philip Foster, John Force, James Force, Francis Fletcher, George Gray, Joseph Gale, Mr. Gistman, Philip or Deacon Hatch, Thomas Hubbard, Henry Huett, Jeremiah Morgan or Horegon, Joseph Hartman, Davit Hill, W. Hoxhurst, Mr. Hutchins, William Johnson, Mr. King, Mr. Kelsey, Reuben Lewis, G.W. Lebriton, Jack Larrisson, Joseph L. Meek, F.H. Matthews, John McClure, Sidnew Moss, Robert Moore, Mr. Fadden, William McCarty, Charles MacKay, Thomas McKay, John Morrisson, J.W. Mack, Mr. Newbanks, Robert Newell, James A. O'Neil, F.W. Pettygrove, Dwight Pomroy, Walter Pomroy, Mr. Perry, Mr. Rimmick. Oslam Russell, James Robb, Robert Shorters, Sidney Smith, Mr. Spence, Jack Sailor, Joel Furnham, Mr. Turner, Hiram Taylor, Calvin Tibbetts, Mr. Trask, C.M. Walker, Jack Warner, A.E. Wilson, David Winslow, Caleb Mikins, Henry Wood, B. Williams.

The following is a record of the names of different missionaries sent out to Oregon:

Marcus Whitman, Rev. W.H. Spaulding, Rev. Mr. Eells, W.H. Gray, Harvey Clark, W.H. Ramond, J.S. Parish, Jason Lee, L.B. Judson, David Leslie, A. L. Miller, Hamilton Campbell, W.H. Wilson, George Abernathy, Mr. Walker, A. Beers, Gust Hines, Mr. Perkins, Mr. Brewer, Dr. Babcock, Dr. Elijah White.

Upon my arrival at the falls of the Willamette I concluded to locate for a short time. During my residence at the falls the boys were anxious to have a provisional government. A notice was posted, calling for the citizens to assemble at Salem for the purpose of adopting some form of provisional government. In 1844 the citizens met at Salem and adopted a form of government and placed George Abernathy as governor. A paper called the *Oregon Spectator* was put in operation and John Fleming, a printer was put in charge of the press. Under the provisional government I was elected justice of the peace, being duly installed into office, and required to do the duties as such officer. The following cases or complaints came up before me.

Upon the complaint of Nathan Eaton, July 20, 1844, who being duly sworn, says that Alexander Staughton struck him on the forehead with a mallet, which Staughton was using for punching holes in shingles, and that the said complainant had been working for Mr. Staughton, and finished work and asked Mr. Staughton for his pay, and without any provocation on his part, Staughton struck him, causing a deep wound; therefore would respectfully request the justice to cause the said Staughton to be arrested and brought before the said Justice, to answer for an assault and battery on the deponent. Warrant issued and served by Constable Moss, by bringing the said Staughton before the justice, the case within his jurisdiction having been considered by the justice and causing bonds to be required of said Staughton for his appearance before district court in order to answer for the charge of assault and battery on said Nathan Eaton. The bonds required were given by Deacon Hatch and David Lesle, and as bondsmen, July 24, 1844, personally appeared before me, Charles Eaton, brother of Nathan, of Clackamas county, Oregon, and acknowledged a breach of the peace on the person of Alexander Staughton. The said Charles Eaton, after deliberation was fined $5. Payment was made thereon.

M.P. Dougherty,
Justice of the Peace.

Upon the affidavit of L.H. Judson, July 27, 1844, who stated that an assault was made on the person of the deponent and also uttered many awful oaths and accompanied with imprecations and threats at the home of F.W. Pettygrove, in the town of Willamette Falls, in Clackamas county, July 27, 1844. Warrant issued and served on said Betty Matson by Sidney Moss, constable, by bringing the said Matson before the justice. By the arrest of the deponent and defendant, the case was left to the justice.

The parties being ready for trial, no jury required, witnesses being sworn and examined relative to the case, it was decided by the justice that the said Matson pay a fine of $5 and costs — justice fees, 75 cents; constable fees, 37 cents. The fine and costs being paid the defendant was discharged.

M.P. Dougherty,
Justice of the Peace of Clackamas County, Oregon.

During my stay at the falls Dr. White was informed that Jim Conner had established a distillery for the manufacture of whiskey, or blue ruin, as it was named, out of molasses. The doctor concluded to search for the distillery. Some of the boys, as they were called, offered their services to the doctor and started from the falls down the Willamette river to the mouth of said river, and discovered the distillery, but no Jim Conner. They took possession of said apparatus, and came up to the falls beating on an old iron kettle in great triumph.

On the 19th day of September, 1846, I was married by Andrew Flood (a magistrate of Clackamas county) at the house of Judge Chambers, to Mary Jane Chambers, a daughter of the judge. The gold excitement in California in 1849 caused a number of us to go to the mines. We arrived in or at the mines and worked all winter, and returned. During my sojourn at the falls of the Willamette, now called Oregon City, W.F. Pettygrove and A.L. Lovejoy located a claim at the mouth of the Willamette river, and laid it out in town lots. The site was called Portland. Pettygrove named it Portland City, after his native place, Portland in the state of Maine.

A charitable feeling was shown by Dr. McLoughlin, McKinley and Dr. Barclay, members of the Hudson Bay company, towards the emigrants on their arrival in Oregon, in supplying some of their wants by furnishing provisions. On our road to California to the mines, in 1849, the party stopped at the base of the Siskiyou mountain. A party opened a road over the mountain for the wagons to pass. While here an incident took place during a shower bath. It was customary during winter and summer for me to use a cold shower bath. A.L. Lovejoy, one of our party, was sleeping soundly in the morning at the time of the bath, hence the excitement from noise of water on the nervous system of Lovejoy was so great that he sprang from his place of sleeping and kicked the coffee pot off of the fire. The boys had a great deal of sport with Lovejoy about his cold bath. During my sojourn in the mines there was a great excitement among the miners relative to the Mexicans, or peons, taking or occupying the best mining grounds. A meeting was called for by the miners, at a place designated, in order to ascertain the feelings of the boys relative to these peons. By acclamation I was put in as alcalda for that district, hence the wishes of the boys were enforced by the peons leaving the mines. One of the Mexicans offered me $200 to allow him to stay. I told him the order was given, and he could not stop for mining purposes.

The proceedings of the miners reached San Francisco. The flagship of Commander A.J. Jones was lying at the bay at, or during the time the order was given. The friends of Jones requested him to go to the camp and ascertain the cause of the disturbance. Commander Jones arrived and came over to my tent, and wished to know if I was acting as alcalda. I told him as such I was acting or officiating in the mining district, as the laws of the United States government had not been extended over the country at the time. The commander requested me, as alcalda, to relate to him the cause of the disturbance. With due deference to your position, I here state that the Mexicans, or peons, were occupying the best grounds for mining purposes and refused to allow the American boys to mine on the same ground.

Allow me to say to you, Commander Jones, your position and knowledge of the character of the Mexicans, with the gold of California would not lay it out in this country, but take it to Mexico. The American boys are a class of people that will not be imposed upon, they did not travel 1800 miles across the desert without looking forward in the future to be compensated and improve the country hence arises this feeling which has called forth this proclamation. The views, or feeling of the American boys, or miners, are here expressed through their alcalda to you, Commander Jones, in order to make a full report of the same. Commander Jones, in reply said the alcalda acted in accordance with the position and wishes of the miners, hence your official course could not be considered as aggressive under the present state of society. P.C. Stewart, the father-in-law of Dolph Hannah, was in the mines and a miner at the time, at our camp. P.C. Stewart is now a resident of the city of Tacoma.

Mr. Thomas O'Fallon, a wealthy citizen of California, was confined to his tent in what was termed a comatose condition. O'Fallon's friends thought it best to send for me to come and give him medicine that would cause a revulsion of feeling. I complied with their request and administered a dose that gave immediate relief. He manifested a feeling of thankfulness by offering me a farm in his section of California if I would come down there and live. I thanked him for his good feeling and said to him that my circumstances were of that cast that I could not receive the gift. From information, Thomas O'Fallon is still in the land of the living. It was a great satisfaction to know that I done my duty. My attention was generally called when any of my partners were sick.

Upon my return to Oregon I made preparations and moved with my wife and eldest son, George, to the Puget Sound country, September, 1850, at that time under the control of Oregon and called Lewis county. A claim of 620 acres of land was located by Judge Chambers (who preceded myself and wife two years) as a donation claim. Ezra Meeker, now a resident of Puyallup valley, surveyed our donation under a contract. The papers relative to the survey were transmitted to the seat of government at Washington and a patent issued on the 27th day of August, in the year 1871, with the signature of U.S. Grant, president of the United States of America attached thereto.

The Sound country was called Lewis county. Judge Chambers and myself were elected to serve as county commissioners for the county. The county seat was located at Jackson, on the Cowlitz, hence the commissioners had a long distance to travel in order to hold court. It was a difficult matter to get jurymen to serve as such during the sitting of the district court, for a number of years. I here state that when Pierce county was duly organized, I was elected and served as probate judge for a number of years. My native place is Washington, Washington county, Pa.

Since my arrival on Puget Sound, forty-two years ago, the development has been very great. Railroads have been built; populous towns and cities have developed rapidly of late years; extensive forests of timber are being converted into lumber; factories are becoming numerous; extensive coal fields with the mines are being developed; the city of Tacoma almost surrounds my farm where once I was monarch of all I surveyed, and yet there is room for great development in the future for the State of Washington. My age is now 80 years and I am as active and vigorous as most men of 40. I attribute my health to regularity of habit in obeying the laws of health, in regard to exercise, diet and cleanliness. I still continue to use the cold sponge bath every morning upon rising, which I continued from my youth.

I was a charter member of the first Masonic lodge organized on the Pacific coast, at Oregon City, Or.; also in the state of Washington while it was still a territory, at Steilacoom. My wife was the first white woman that settled in Pierce county. Our family consisted of eight children, four boys and four girls; two are dead. All but two were born and raised at my home near Tacoma.

Mrs. James Hartman

*The McAllisters, her family, were among
the first settlers on Puget Sound. They lived at first
in a huge hollow tree stump. Mrs. Hartman tells about
the love/hate relationship with the Indian
Chief Leschi and the death of her father
at the hands of the Indians.*

Sherlock, Washington — March 24, 1893

In the year 1843 James McAllister and family left Kentucky for Missouri in order to make an early start for the far west in the spring, his object for coming being his health. This being before my birth I cannot give details of the journey.

They were nine months from the Mississippi to Whitman mission, and remained there eight weeks on account of sickness, my oldest sister being sick with the mountain fever. They were treated with kindness, but were discouraged by finding the country different from what they had expected. When they started they thought they would find settlements, but alas! there were none. News was very difficult to get in those days, and, like a snow ball, grew as it went and just about as fast, so you see a small item soon grew to be a large one. Father was anxious to reach a settlement on account of schools, and he heard that there was one on the Sound and another on the Cowlitz river, and he started for the Sound in company with five other families: Gabriel Jones, wife and three children; George Bush, wife and six sons; David Kindred, wife and son; Michael Simmons, wife and seven children; three single men, Samuel Crockett, Reuben Crowder and Jesse Nurgerson. They got as far as Sophia island, in the Columbia river, when, winter overtaking them, they camped there. In the spring they started for the settlement and found that it consisted of a Hudson bay trading post without a white woman in it. There was one man named Burnier who was married to a half-breed lady. It has been stated that her son was the first white child born in the state. I do not think the lady claimed this to be the truth.

Still anxious to reach settlements they started to the Sound country, making their own road from the Cowlitz to the Sound. While waiting at the Cowlitz they were met by the chief of the Nisquallies, Leschi, who had heard of the white squaws coming. He met them and welcomed them to his country, making each family a present, and inviting them to join his tribe, saying that we might be annoyed by roving Indians, and if we did not belong to his tribe, he could not protect us. Some of the party joined, some did not, fearing to trust them. Leschi took them to what is known as Bush prairie, each family taking a claim near each other. Their claims were about twelve miles from Fort Nisqually, which consisted of a trading post with five or six men. These two trading posts were the only settlements here, hence those five white women were the first white women on the Sound and the first in the state, excepting three or four at Whitman mission—Mrs Spaulding, Mrs. Whitman and another woman whose name I have forgotten, and I think that Mr. and Mrs. Eells were there.

The English did not receive the first Americans very cordially, refusing at first to sell them anything or to have very much to do with them, but they afterwards became reconciled to them. The Sound Indians were always very kind to us. When we first came we had a little difficulty with them on the Columbia river, but were victorious. Nearly all the men were absent from camp, when a roving band of Indians came along, and seeing the emigrants unprotected they began to help themselves to whatever took their fancy, but, unfortunately for them, they began at the wrong camp, that being mother's. Father was gone, leaving her sole defender of her brood, so she jerked up a tent pole and laid it about her right and left with such good effect that she had her squad of Indians going on the double-quick in a very short time. The others, seeing them going, took to their heels, leaving the camp forever.

Father, finding the soil rather light for farming, came, by Leslie's advice, to Nisqually valley and selected his farm at the junction of the Shnonabdaub and Squaquid creeks, on the council ground of the Nisqually tribe. We were destined to witness many a wild and horrible scene that other settlers were spared. Our first wheat was planted on Bush prairie. Father secured half a bushel, the kindness of an old English gentleman enabling him to get it. The other families got the same quantity and were obliged to plant and replant the third year before they dared to use any, and during those three years the five families never saw bread, let alone tasting it, but they always had plenty to eat, such as it was, and more than people would think possible. We had all kinds of game, which was more plentiful than the tame stock now, fish and clams, dried and fresh, the Indians showing us how to prepare them, but we never succeeded in learning the art of drying them. We were successful in drying fruits, the Indians' mode requiring no sugar. There was no salt in the country. For vegetables they had lackamas, speacotes and numerous other roots. We children learned to like the Indian food so well that we thought we could not exist without it. We kept a supply as long as we could get it, but I have not seen any for many years.

Father was the first white man ever in Nisqually valley, going in canoes, embarking at Tumwater and following the Sound to the mouth of the Shnonabdaub creek. That was the only road for years except Indian trails.

In 1846, mother disliking to stay alone while father was building, he laughingly told her that he had seen two big stumps side by side, and that if she would live in them he would take her with him. Mother told him she would go, so father scraped out the stumps and made a roof, and mother moved in with her six children. She found it very comfortable, the burnt out roots making such nice cubby-holes for stowing away things. Mother continued to live in her stump house until father built a house, the work being necessarily slow, for father had but a few tools.

The council ground was a natural opening in the woods, about half a mile long by a quarter of a mile wide, lying southeast by northeast. Father built our house on the north part of it. Our stump house was about three hundred yards southeast of my present home. After coming in to Nisqually we began to live in earnest. We soon had plenty of everything. Father bought vegetable and fruit seeds which he planted as soon as he could. He had driven two yoke of cows across the plains. We were in the Indian country indeed. There were twenty Indians in the valley to one on the prairie. We soon learned to speak their language. Mother being a southern lady and being used to negro servants adopted three Indian maidens, Sateo, Wallah and Hettie, to train to house work. Two boys were taken, Clipwhalen and Mondesh. She found them apt scholars, and they remained faithful to us during the Indian trouble. One of them, Clipwhalen, gave his life to save our family. People had now began to come in to the country. In 1848 Mr. Packwood and Mr. Shaper came to the valley, living on one farm until such times as they could select claims and build on them. The California gold fever broke out and Mr. Packwood taking it went to California, but was soon cured, and he returned, settling on the same claim he had left. At this time the gold excitement was very high about Queen Charlotte islands. Father, with several others, took the fever; so twenty-seven of them formed a company and bought a schooner and started in high hopes, but they only got within a few hundred yards when the vessel struck the rocks. The men had to get ashore the best they could. They had an interpreter, with them and they succeeded in making a treaty with the Indians (the northern Indians are much more savage than the Sound Indians), who stood in great fear of them, and gave them all the wreck except the tobacco, reserving that for their own use. They remained prisoners three months, and were rescued by Captain Balch, the founder of Steilacoom. The British government furnished about $1000 worth of goods, which was repaid by the United States government.

They told many a good joke on one another when they got home, but there was one they tried to keep from their wives, which the bachelors told. On every new moon the Indians had a feast of a certain dish, which the men were very fond of, and which consisted of roots. Vegetables being very scarce it was a great treat to them, so the married men thought they would get the recipe for their wives, and asked the Indians how it was made, but they refused to tell. Not liking to be outwitted by an Indian they set men to watch, and this is what they saw: A rude stone furnace with a rude crock, and about a dozen old squaws around it as close as they could get, each one with a lap full of different roots which they would bite in huge mouthfuls, chewing it to the proper consistency and dropping it in the crock to be made into chow-chow, as the men called it. Strange to say, every man lost his appetite for that dainty dish!

Another story they told was about father. His teeth being very poor he could not eat the dried fish they gave him, so the chief called an old slave woman and bade her sit down and chew it for him, which she did not appear to think anything out of the way, but he failed to appreciate such kindness. When father returned he had lost a great deal of good money but did not bring so much as a bad penny. While he was absent some one sent an order for shingles. Mother would not lose the order, so she hired a crew and filled the demand, making about $500.

The Indians generally adopted the white people's costumes very readily, but some social habits they failed to observe, and knocking at the door for entrance was one of them. Some of them good naturedly complied with mother's request to announce their coming by rapping on the door. Mother explained to them that it was the custom of the people to do so. They replied, as she was in an Indian country why could she not adapt herself to their customs. As many of them objected to rapping she kept the front door locked. One day a strange Indian, who had never seen a white woman, came to visit these Indians, and was very anxious to see a pale face. They had explained our queer custom of rapping at the door. He said anybody was a fool to stop and rap; the idea of any one going to a door and having some one open it for them; he could open all the doors he came to. So he came to pay his respects. The other Indians declining to accompany him, he came alone, tried the door and found it fast, so he bravely attacked the door with his war club, a few blows bringing it to the floor. Mother, not knowing what to make of it, grabbed her horse-pistol and fired as the door fell, hitting him in the calves of both legs. She was alarmed at what she had done, not knowing how the other Indians would like it. As none of them appeared, she went to their camp and told them what she had done, and also what the Indian had done, but instead of being angry, they laughed and told her of his brags. Mother showed them how to make a litter to carry him to the camp. She dressed the wound, removing several buckshot, and nursed him until he was well. He was her best friend afterward.

One day mother and my oldest sister were gathering cranberries. They heard a slight noise, and looking up beheld an Indian covering them with his gun. Not knowing his intentions, and not liking to ask, mother drew her horse-pistol and made him lay down his gun and go away backwards. She captured his gun and took it home. She soon discovered that the gun belonged to a slave who was hunting for his master. He had heard a great deal about white squaws being more brave than the red ones, but said they were not any braver, but that it was their strong house that made them bold. This old Indian, Momluchion, is yet living. He tells the story himself, and will laugh very heartily about it. He was always friendly to the whites, and sent rescue to several families.

One day as mother was cooking hoe cakes by the fire some Indians came in. One old fellow squatted down as close to her Dutch oven as he could get. Mother stepped out for a moment, and when she returned she missed her cakes. She noticed the old fellow holding his arm out in a suspicious manner. Suspecting the trouble, she stepped up to him, took hold of both his arms and pressed them to his sides, holding them like a vice, and burning his arms to a blister. The old rascal had stolen mother's cake and hidden it under his blanket. He was always known afterwards as old "Hoe Cake". Another time some Indians reclined by the fire by which mother was cooking, and one of them, just to show his contempt, spat on the Dutch oven. Mother stooped forward, and without a word, took a stick of wood from the fire and knocked him down.

The wild animals annoyed us very much. We had to keep all the small stock very closely confined. One evening, judging by the actions of the dogs, we knew that animals were around, so the older members of the family went out to confine the stock, leaving we smaller children in the house. The dogs started the animals, pressing them so close that they took to the house instead of a tree. We little ones heard a scrambling over the top of the house, and were so frightened that we did not investigate the matter. The door was open and we were afraid to close it, and while we were planning how to close it, a huge panther thrust his head and shoulders in the door from the roof of the house. What to do was the question that we asked each other. It must have been Providence prompting us, for we did not know that it was the best thing we could do, but my eldest sister seized a flaming pine knot and ran up and shut the door.

I presume that my friends think that we did nothing but fight Indians and wild beasts, and indeed I could write a large book full of just such stories, but we had amusements as well. We had church oftener then than now in rural districts. We had no district school, but father hired a teacher by the month and I think that we were as happy then as now. Like Nasby, I often long for those good old days. Since arriving in the valley father had cleared quite a farm, built a saw mill, blacksmith shop and started a general store. He served two terms in the state legislature, and was a man that was first among everything.

The Indians now began to complain, and not without cause, about a great many things. Father had built a nice house two and one-half stories high, with ten rooms on the ground floor, but never finished the upper floor. He had everything to insure his comfort and happiness, but poor father did not live to enjoy his well-earned comfort.

In 1855 Leschi came to our house, bringing both his wives. How well I remember it! It was the last time we ever saw Leschi. He told us that he was going to fight. Father and mother both tried to persuade him to remain peaceful, and really thought they had done so. The women talked and cried together. He told father if he would remain on his farm and not join the army he should not be hurt nor his property destroyed. Leschi said: "I never will raise a hand against you or yours, but if you join the army I can not be responsible for what others do, for the other Indians are going to fight." And I firmly believe he would have done as he said. Shortly afterward he and his family withdrew to the mountains, and thus hostilities began. The white people raised companies of volunteers and built forts to take the families into. Father and my oldest brother, George, who was then only 17 years old, joined Company I, Puget Sound volunteers. Mother begged him not to do so, and said that the Indians would surely kill him, then or some other time, if he went. He laughed and said that he would take his cane and cane every one of them home. I think he only said that to quiet mother, but he thought he could persuade Leschi not to fight, and told Captain Caton so, if he could get the authorities to substantiate his promise. So they gave him a peace commission and he started to Leschi's stronghold in the mountains. Mr. Caton was captain and my father first lieutenant of the Puget Sound volunteers. The company consisted of eleven men, including three from our home, father, George and Clipwhalen. The company started from one house, going as far as Montgomery's the first day, reached Van Ogle's place the next day and camped there in a small house. Father, Lieutenant Connel, Clipwhalen and Stahi, the traitor, all departed from the company and went forward to make a treaty with Leschi, going to the White river, crossing Fannell's prairie (not Connell's), going into the wood about a quarter of a mile, when they were fired upon by the Indians in ambush. The Indians had hidden in three different places and five in a squad. The middle squad fired upon them. Father fell forward from his horse, shot twice in the breast, the balls entering about an inch apart, killing him instantly. Stahi gave a warhoop and joined the hostiles. Clipwhalen and Lieutenant Connel turned their horses back, and Connel was shot in the arm, breaking it. He did not fall from his horse, and rode down the road, of course right into the other squad of Indians, who killed him and cut him to pieces, scattering the pieces of his body in every direction. Clipwhalen's horse, being young, became unmanageable and took to the woods, thereby saving Clipwhalen's life. The Indians fired at him and grazed his body with the bullets. Clipwhalen started for home, arriving there about sunrise the next morning. About sundown Captain Caton was out looking for the men to return and stepped upon a log so as to see better, when he saw the muzzle of a gun pointing from behind a stump. He jumped from the log and started to the house, the Indians shooting at him as he ran. From that the firing became general, the Indians keeping it up all night. Three or four men were hurt, but none were killed. My brother was shot, a portion of his upper lip being carried away. The Indians were very saucy, calling out to the men, cursing and demeaning them. They fought all night and in the morning Captain Caton asked for a volunteer to go for reinforcements. My brother offered to go. The Indians had stolen all the horses except Caton's. It was tied in a slough and they did not find it. So George took the captain's horse and started for Steilacoom. After starting help to Captain Caton he came home, arriving about 3 o'clock. As he was crossing the Nisqually he was hailed by an Indian but would not stop, but his horse being very thirsty, he could not prevent it pausing to drink. When it had done so the Indian sprang forward, grabbing his horse by the bit, and my brother converted him into a "good Indian." When last seen he was floating down the river. Arriving at home he found us surrounded by Indians. Clipwhalen was talking to them, coaxing and threatening them by turns. He had sent my younger brother to the field for the horses, but they were all gone. They then started to the prairie for the oxen and secured one yoke. Meantime the Indians were making free with everything. We did not know friend from foe. They seated mother and us children on the stairs, took our dinner from the stove, wrapped themselves in our patch-work quilts. Sister and I, child-like, became tired of the restraint and left our seats, but we were put back again by an Indian called Ascon, who pointed out of the window. We looked and saw a number of Indians grinding their knives and tomahawks on our grindstone. They had moved the grindstone in front of the house so that we might witness their fiendish procedings. We had some friends among them, Clipwhalen and Ascon, who held the Indians at bay until the boys returned with the sun. We took what we could carry in one wagon, besides the family, and started for Fort Eleuma, and George returned to his company. Clipwhalen and one of the boys accompanied the family, the other going another road. The wagon had to cross the reservation in order to reach the fort. With one boy driving the oxen, and one ahead and one behind us, we started, beating the oxen into a run. The road was fearful, only the large logs having been taken out. The logs that would admit the wagons passing over them were notched for the wheels to pass through. Imagine a ride of two miles over such a road, with the oxen in a run. We were looking for the Indians to be on us every moment. Generally when a person is looking for something to get scared at it is very easily found. We saw an Indian on horseback and were frightened, not knowing how many more were behind him. We also saw a bear walking up hill on its hind-legs, which gave us another fright, as we first thought it was an Indian. We reached the fort safely. The building was a barn with a stockade built around it. It had stock sheds divided by partitions, which made quite a nice place, compared with other places that had to be endured.

Mother was prostrate with grief. After lying in the woods fifteen days father's body was brought home to her, and was buried from the place with both military and Masonic honors. Trouble never comes singly, and a few days after father's funeral my sister, Mrs. Thomas Chambers, left her babe asleep in its cradle and went out to care for mother, requesting brother George to care for it and we little ones. While she was gone the stove accidently was upset, overturning a teakettle full of boiling water into the cradle, scalding the babe to death.

We remained there several months, and meantime Fort Ragton was built, on the Nisqually, about two miles from our home. In order to be close home mother moved to this place, and then our hard times began. There were nine in our family, and we had rations for three men. We were there one year and I don't remember having a substantial meal during that time.

While there my younger brother went to the farm to get something for the family to eat. John, while trying to shoot some ducks, shot himself in the hand, crippling him for life.

We had some very bad Indian scares in that place. My blood used to run cold when the order came: "All children must sleep in the blockhouse." We were packed like sardines in the upper floor of the blockhouse. On account of my brother being shot mother could not go with us, so we had to go alone, lying on the rough puncheon floor, with only a blanket over us. The lower part of the place was occupied by the soldiers, and if we made any noise they would swear at us.

One day an Indian came up the river. As he neared the fort he put a white rag on his paddle and was paddling past. Some young men spoke to the commander of the place about it, saying that the Indian was carrying ammunition to the hostiles, but he would not permit them to interrupt him, and several young men started in pursuit. One of them had been very recently married, and his poor bride could not see him go, so she locked him in their room, locking herself outside to be away from his persuasions to be released, but nothing daunted, he kicked the door down and started after the other men, overtaking them before they got to the drift where, sure enough, there sat three Indians waiting for the fourth. The men waited too. Presently he came and began to unload his ammunition, when the boys proceeded to convert them into "good Indians."

The sentinels were often firing off their alarm guns, thereby raising a terrible excitement. One time a company of soldiers were coming for reinforcements. General W.W. Miller, commanding. Some over-anxious sentinel fired his gun, thinking it was Indians coming to attack the fort. Some one in the fort gave a warwhoop, and those coming up answered it. This caused alarm, each party thinking the other was Indians. To make matters worse they had let us children out on the island to gather berries, sending a guide with us. As soon as the women heard the warwhoop they started outside for the children. The officers ordered them to return, but they didn't feel obliged to return, so kept on. The officers charged them with their horses, but several got through, mother among them. Meantime we children were being sent across the slough with only two small canoes. They put the small children over first, making us stand still. There we stood while the Indians (as we thought) were charging and about to cut us off from the fort, both parties yelling like mad. We little ones stood there until the others got over. I think I can tell very nearly how the soldiers feel in battle. All across, they then placed a little child between two larger ones and started us on a run across the sand bar, where we sank ankle-deep every step, the men riding behind, crowding us on. The nearer the (imaginary) Indians came the harder they pushed us. Seeing that the little ones could not make it they began to pick them up on their horses. Being rather stout, my feet were soon pulled from under me by my two leaders and I was being dragged along, when an old man named Weabeaux made a grab for me but missed me.

Wheeling his horse he tried it again with no better success. He then thought to frighten me and drew his sword and was thrusting it at me, but I could only fall and scream. Then he would make another grab with the same result. Becoming provoked, he began to scold me something after the following manner: "Geet up, geet up, you leetle fool; geet up, I say. I cuts your legs off with mine sword," making a slash at me. "Get up, you lettle tevil. I cuts your head off next time;" another slash "Gone right off and leaves her, and let the Injuns eats her up alive; you lettle red-headed tevil geet up." The old man was scolding at the top of his voice, he being a little deaf and thinking every one else more so. Some one picked me up on their horse and carried me to the fort. I never knew who it was. This is a fair specimen of the scenes in the worst place I was ever in. As soon as mother considered it safe to go, we moved into Olympia, and remained there until it was safe to return to our home.

About this time those who had relatives killed began to arrest the murderers, bringing them in to trial. The law cleared every one but Leschi, whom they hung. The Indians who killed father were cleared by law, but they did not escape justice. "Little pitchers have big ears," and one night when we were living in town I was awakened by the deep baying of our faithful hounds. Presently I heard a tap on the window and it softly opened and a voice from the darkness said, "I am going to kill the old dog." A voice replied, "Kill the old dog but don't kill the young one." Then a hand came in at the window and picked up a pistol that lay on the stand, as it generally did. The window was then closed. In a short time (I had not yet gone to sleep), the window opened and a voice said, "I shot the dog." The hand entered and laid the pistol on the stand. I worried about the old dog, he being the favorite. The next morning I arose early to see about my dog. While I was in the yard one of our neighbor's boys came down the street throwing up his hat and catching it as it fell, shouting as he ran, "Good, good! Old Quiemelth is dead and in his shell." Quiemelth was the Indian who shot father, and he was brought to town to stand his trial, being promised his freedom if he would come. (Quiemelth, Leschi and Stahi were brothers.) Owing to his guilty conscience, Quiemelth would not come to town in daylight, and they brought him in at midnight, promising to take him out 3 o'clock in the morning. So he came and stood his trial. During the trial he confessed that he and another Indian, Topitior, killed father. He gave up the pistol and knife he had taken from father's body, and the judge pronounced that Indian "not guilty." The lights were extinguished, and a shot was heard. When the lights were relit, Quiemelth was shot and stabbed. I regret to say they did not take him out at 3 o'clock. They cleared those Indians who killed father, but they tried every way to hang those who killed father's murderers. Topitior was killed while resisting arrest, but it was no fault of the law that those Indians received their just dues.

Clipwhalen, who was a Similokeen Indian, was captured from his tribe when a child and made a slave. His master died, and he was allotted to be starved on his master's grave. Father and a chief, Weltikneke, interceded and saved his life. He remained with us until his death, in 1864, when he was killed on our farm by hostile Indians. They were afraid to fire guns, and brutally beat him to death with clubs. His murderers were cleared. He was killed out of revenge for saving our family, giving his life for those who had saved his life. He was known as Charlie by the whites, and was trusty, honest, kind and brave.

Before closing my story I will describe the habits and customs of the Indians. Clipwhalen married a Chehalis girl, and for the benefit of newcomers, I will describe the wedding ceremony of that tribe. The young Indian selects his bride elect and goes to his people and tells them whom he has selected. His people then send an agent to her parents to learn the price asked for her, and to jew them down if possible. Having settled the price they return and send invitations to all the tribe and often to others. They then begin to gather at the bride's parents, each one bringing them a present, great or small. As each one brings their own bed and provisions, the old folks are not put to much trouble or expense. The groom and his bride camp a few hundred yards away. Both parties feast three or four days, winding up with a grand procession. All march single file. Heading the procession is the bride seated on a pile of mats, carried by as many of her friends as could get hold of the mat, to the tent of the groom, the procession following, and each one throwing a return potlatch, or present, right and left, all having a grand scrabble to get their present. A squaw will store presents from her cradle, or rather, her backboard, to her wedding day, and from her wedding day to her grave.

As I have described a wedding I will now describe a funeral. When a friend dies all are summoned. They have a great respect for the dead, and all come bringing a present for the deceased. The corpse is dressed in its best, and laid in a canoe and the canoe is filled full of their choicest things. They turn another canoe over this one, lashing them together, and making a snug coffin. If they intend to go any distance, they tie each end to a horse, an Indian riding the horse, thus carrying the corpse very comfortably to some resting place. They then place the canoe containing the remains as high in the crotch of a tree as they can reach. They hired mourners when they did not have enough volunteers to go ahead of the corpse, and just behind, with a goodly number scattered along the route, howling and singing the praises of the departed. Some sing their deeds of daring, and some their virtues all at the same time. Imagine such a procession passing through the woods, where each voice will echo and re-echo. After placing the corpse in the tree they proceed to decorate the grave, often putting hundreds of dollars' worth on it; their favorite horse was killed, to ride in the happy hunting ground. Also their dog and slave, often starving the latter to death. The howlers still kept their positions, redoubling their cries as the Indians returned. They would go out and howl night and morning for several months afterward. For grandees they would have a still greater time.

The Indians have a great many queer customs. It would fill a volume to tell all of them. The one that puzzled the whites the most was the tomanomus, which is spiritualism pure and simple. I will now describe the Indian mode of dining. They eat a light meal morning and evening of dried salmon, clams or meat boiled on the fire, with dried herbs or roots and berries fresh or dried. They ate lying on mats. Their dinner was more elaborate, and was their principal meal. A good cook was quite an important person, who squatted by the fire, never leaving her seat, the slaves bringing her everything. She had a rude stone furnace, about twelve feet long by one foot wide, which was her sole convenience, and was only provided in the best families. She built her fire on top of the oven and inside. When properly heated she removed the fire and rolled her meat up in leaves, putting it in the oven and closing it tight. Fish cooked in this way is delicious. When done she removed the fish or meat, laying it clear from the bone with a skillful movement, breaking it in small pieces. She then gives it to a slave, who carried it around to those lying on the ground, each one having a small quantity of roots or berries on their mats. In season they have salmonberries, blackberries, raspberries and maple sprouts, with watercress and parsley for salads. Their dishes were made of different material, and were round and oval, while for plates they used spoons, each holding about a pint. The cook filled these, the slaves carrying them to the persons on the mat. They had a small spoon to eat with. They roasted meat before the fire, and they had a water-tight basket in which they boiled their food. They were very clean about their eatables. They have a number of medical herbs whose virtues are unknown to the white people. I have used a number of their herbs in my family with success.

I will now say a few words about Mount Tacoma. I have always heard it called Tacoma by the natives. It was called Rainier after an English admiral. The name Tacoma means "nourishing breast." I think that the name Rainier should be discarded and that the Indian name should be kept when possible. I have called our farm by an Indian name, Chilcoma, meaning raspberry. The creek called Shonabdaub by the Indians was afterwards called McAllister creek by the whites.

This story was written under many difficulties, and if any of the old settlers notice mistakes, regard them as the fault of memory and not intentional.

Esther Chambers

*The daughter of William Packwood, she crossed
the plains as a child in Colonel Gilliam's Company
in the summer of 1844. She was on Whidby Island,
staying alone with her child, when Colonel Ebey
was beheaded by the Northern Indians.*

Roy, Washington — June 3, 1982

My father, William Packwood, left Missouri in the spring of 1844 with my mother and four children in an ox wagon to cross the plains to Oregon. My mother's health was very poor when we started. She had to be helped in and out of the wagon, but the change by traveling improved her health so much that she gained a little every day, and in the course of a month or six weeks she was able to get up in the morning and cook breakfast, while my father attended his team and did other chores.

I had one sister older than myself, and I was only 6 years old. My little sister and baby brother, who learned to walk by rolling the water keg as we camped nights and mornings, were of no help to my sick mother.

The company in which we started was Captain Gilliam's, and we traveled quite a way when we joined Captain Ford's company, making upward of sixty wagons in all. Our company was so large that the Indians did not molest us, although we, after letting our stock feed until late in the evening, had formed a large corral of the wagons, in which we drove the cattle and horses, and stood guard at nights, as the Indians had troubled small companies by driving off their stock, but they were not at all hostile to us.

We came to a river and camped. The next morning we were visited by Indians, who seemed to want to see us children, so we were terribly afraid of the Indians, and, as father drove in the river to cross, the oxen got frightened at the Indians and tipped the wagon over, and father jumped and held the wagon until help came. We thought the Indians would catch us, so we jumped to the lower part of the box, where there was about six inches of water. The swim and fright I will never forget — the Indian fright of course.

I was quite small, but I do remember the beautiful scenery. We could see antelope, deer, rabbits, sage hens and coyotes, etc., and in the camp we children had a general good time. All joined at night in the plays. One night Mr. Jinkins' boys told me to ask their father for his sheath knife to cut some sticks with. When using it on the first stick, I cut my left-hand forefinger nail and all off, except a small portion of the top of my finger, and the scar is still visible.

On another evening we children were having a nice time, when a boy by the name of Stephen, who had been in the habit of hugging around the children's shoulders and biting them, hugged me and bit a piece almost out of my shoulder. This was the first time I remember of seeing my father's wrath rise on the plains, as he was a very even tempered man. He said to the offending boy: "If you do that again, I shall surely whip you."

A few days later we came to a stream that was deep but narrow. Mr. Stephens, this boy's father, was leading a cow by a rope tied around his waist and around the cow's head, for the purpose of teaching the rest of the cattle to swim. The current being very swift, washed the cow down stream, dragging the man. The women and children were all crying at a great rate, when one of the party went to Mrs. Stephens, saying Mr. Stephens is drowning. "Well," she replied, "there is plenty or more men where he came from." Mr. Stephens, his cow and all lodged safely in a drift. The company got him out safely, but he did not try to swim a stream with a cow tied to his waist again.

We could see the plains covered with buffalo as we traveled along, just like the cattle of our plains are here.

One day a band of buffalo came running toward us, and one jumped between the wheel cattle and the wheels of the wagon, and came very near having a general stampede of the cattle; so when the teamsters got their teams quieted down, the men, gathering their guns, ran and killed three of the buffalo, and all of the company were furnished with dried beef, which was fine for camping.

We came to a place where there was a boiling spring that would cook an egg, and a short distance from this there was a cold, clear spring, and a short distance from this was a heap of what looked like ashes, and when we crossed it the cattle's feet burned until they bawled.

Another great sight I remember of seeing was an oil spring.

Then we reached the Blue mountains. Snow fell as we traveled through them. We then came down in the Grand Ronde valley, and it seemed as if we had dried salmon, lacamas cakes and dried crickette cakes. We traded for some of the salmon and the lacamas cakes, but the crickette cakes we did not hanker after.

A man in one train thought he would fool an Indian chief, so he told the Indian chief that he would swop his girl, 16 years old, for a couple of horses. The bargain was made and he took the horses, and the Indian hung around until near night. When the captain of the company found out that the Indian was waiting for his girl to go with him, the captain told the man that we might all be killed through him, and made him give up the horses to the chief. The Indian chief was real mad as he took his horses away.

We went on down to The Dalles, where we stopped a few days. There was a mission at the Dalles where two missionaries lived, Brewer and Waler. We emigrants traded some of our poor, tired cattle off to them for some of their fat beef, and some coarse flour chopped on a handmill, like what we call chop-feed nowadays.

Then we had to make a portage around the falls, and the women and children walked. I don't remember the distance, but we walked until late at night, and waded in mud knee-deep, and my mother stumped her toe and fell against a log or she might have gone down into the river. We little tots fell down into the mud until you would have thought we were pigs. The men drove around the falls another way, and got out of provisions.

My father, seeing a boat from the high bluffs going down the river, hailed it, and when he came down to the boat he found us. He said he had gotten so hungry that he killed a crow and ate it, and thought it tasted splendid. He took provisions to the cattle drivers and we came on down the river to Fort Vancouver. It rained on us for a week and our bedclothes were drenched through and through, so at night we would open our bed of wet clothes and cuddle in them as though we were in a palace car, and all kept well and were not sick a day in all of our six months' journey crossing the plains. My mother gained and grew fleshy and stout.

Next we arrived in what is now the city of Portland, which then consisted of a log cabin and a few shanties. We stayed there a few days to dry our bedding.

Then we moved out to the Tualitin plains, where we wintered in a barn, with three other families, each family having a corner of the barn, with fire in the center and a hole in the roof for the smoke to go out.

My father went to work for a man by the name of Baxton, as all my father was worth in money I think was 25 cents, or something near this. He arrived with a cow, calf and three oxen, and had to support his family by mauling rails in the rain, to earn the wheat, peas and potatoes we ate, as that was all we could get, as bread was out of the question. Shortly after father had gone to work my little brother had a rising on his cheek. It made him so sick that mother wanted us to go to the place where my father was working. It being dark, we got out of our way and went to a man, who had an Indian woman, by the name of Williams. In the plains there are swails that fill up with water when the heavy rains come, and they are knee deep. I fell in one of these, but we got to Mr. Williams' all right. But when we found our neighbor we began crying, so Mr. Williams persuaded us to come in and he would go get father, which he did, and father came home with us to our barn house. My little brother got better, and my father returned to his work again.

Among the settlers on the plains were Mr. Zackriss, Mr. Burton, Mr. Williams and General McCarver, who had settled on farms before we came, and many a time did we go to their farms for greens and turnips, which were something new and a great treat to us.

Often the Indians used to frighten us by their war dances, as we called them, as we did not know the nature of Indians, so, as General McCarver was used to them, we often asked him if the Indians were having a war dance for the purpose of hostility. He told us that was the way they doctored their sick.

General McCarver settled in Tacoma when the townsite was first laid out, and is well known. He died in Tacoma, leaving a family.

After we moved out to the Tualitin plain many a night when father was away we lay awake listening to the dogs barking, thinking the Indians were coming to kill us, and when father came home I felt safe and slept happily.

In the spring of 1845 my father took a nice place in West Yamhill about two miles from the Willamette river and we had some settlers around, but our advantage for a school was poor, as we were too far from settlers to have a school, so my education, what little I have, was gotten by punching the cedar fire and studying at nights, but, however, we were a happy family, hoping to accumulate a competency in our new home.

One day, myself and elder sister and brother were carrying water from our spring, which was a hundred yards or more from the house, when a number of Indians came along. We were afraid of them and all hid. I hid by the trail, when an old Indian, seeing me, yelled out, "Adeda," when I began to laugh, but my sister was terribly frightened and yelled at me to hide, so they found all of us, but they were friendly to us, only a wretched set to steal, as they stole the only cow we had brought through, leaving the calf with us without milk.

My father was quite a hunter, and deer were plenty, and once in a while he would get one. So we did get along without milk. During the first year we could not get bread, as there were no mills or places to buy flour. A Canadian put up a small chop mill and chopped wheat something like feed is chopped now.

My father, being a jack-of-all-trades, set to work and put a turning lathe up and went to making chairs, and my mother and her little tots took the straw from the sheaves and braided and made hats. We sold chairs and hats and helped ourselves along in every way we could and did pretty well.

One day, while my father's lathe was running, some one yelled "stop;" a large black bear was walking through the yard. The men gave him a grand chase, but bruin got away from them.

My father remained on this place until the spring of 1847, when he and a number of other families decided to move to Puget Sound. During that winter they dug two large canoes, lashed them together as a raft or flatboat to move on, and sold out their places, bought enough provisions to last that summer, and loading up with their wagons, families and provisions, started for Puget Sound.

Coming up the Cowlitz river was a hard trip, as the men had to tow the raft over rapids and wade. The weather was very bad. Arriving at what was called the Cowlitz landing, we stayed a few days, and moved out to the Catholic priest's place (Mr. Langlay's) where the women and children remained while the men went back to Oregon for our stock. They had to drive up the Cowlitz river by a trail, and swim the rivers. My father said it was a hard trip.

On arriving at Puget Sound, we found a good many settlers. Among them now living that I know of was Jesse Ferguson, on the Bush prairie. We stayed near Mr. Ferguson's place until my father, McAllister and Shager, who now lives in Olympia, took them to places in the Nisqually bottoms.

My father's place then is now owned by Isaac Hawk.

Mr. McAllister was killed in the Indian war of 1855 and 1856, leaving a family of a number of children, of whom one is Mrs. Grace Hawk. The three families living in the bottom were often frightened by the saucy Indians telling us to leave, as the King George men told them to make us go, so on one occasion there came about 300 Indians in canoes. They were painted and had knives, and said they wanted to kill a chief that lived by us by the name of Quinasapam. When he saw the warriors coming he came into our house for protection, and all of the Indians who could do so came in after him. Mr. Shager and father gave them tobacco to smoke. So they smoked and let the chief go and took their departure. If there were ever glad faces on this earth and free hearts, ours were at that time.

My father and Mr. McAllister took a job of bursting old steamboat boilers up for Dr. Tolmie for groceries and clothing, and between their improving their farms they worked at this. While they were away the Indians' dogs were plenty, and, like wolves, they ran after everything, including our only milch cow, and she died, so there was another great loss to us, but, after father got through with the old boilers, he took another job of making butter firkins for Dr. Tolmie, and shingles also. This was a great help to the new settlers. The Hudson Bay company was very kind to settlers. In 1849 the California gold fever began to rage. So my father took the fever. I was standing by the fire listening to my mother tell about it, when my dress caught fire, and my mother and Mrs. Shager got the fire extinguished when I found my hair all off of one side of my head and my dress missing. I felt in luck to save my life.

In the spring of 1850 all arrangements were made for the California gold mines and we started by land in an ox wagon. We went back through Oregon and met our company in Yamhill, where we had lived. They joined our company of about thirty wagons. Portions of our journey were real pleasant, but the rest was terribly rough. In one canyon we crossed a stream seventy-five times in one day, and it was the most unpleasant   part of our journey.

After two months' travel we arrived in Sacramento City, Cal., and found it tolerably warm for us, not being used to a warm climate.

Father stayed in California nearly two years. Our fortune was not a large one. We returned by sea to Washington and made our home in the Nisqually bottom.

On April 30, 1854, I was married to a man by the name of G.W.T. Allen and lived with him, on Whidby island, seven years, during which time four children were born. We finally agreed to disagree. Only one of our children by my first husband is living. She is Mrs. L.L. Andrews of Tacoma, Wash. He is in the banking business. On July 7, 1863, I was married to my present husband, McLain Chambers. We have lived in Washington ever since. We have had nine children. Our oldest, a son, I.M. Chambers, lives on a farm near Roy. He is unmarried. Mrs. M.B. Wiley, our second, lives in Roy,

Wash. A.I. Chambers, our next son, is married and lives at Yelm station. Mrs. L.M. McIntyre, our second girl, lives at Stampede, Wash. We have two little boys at home. Have lost three within the last three years. We live a mile and a half southeast of Roy, Wash.

Now before I close I shall have to tell you I have lived here through all the hostilities of the war. Dr. Tolmie sent wagons to haul us to the fort for safety. My present husband was a volunteer and came through with a company of scouts, very hungry. They were so hungry that when they saw my mother take a pan of biscuits from the stove, one of them saying "excuse me, but we are almost starved," grabbed the biscuits from the pan, eating like a hungry dog.

I suppose you have heard of the murder of Colonel I.N. Ebey of Whidby's island? He was beheaded by the Northern or Fort Simpson Indians and his family and George Carliss and wife making their escape from the house by climbing out of the windows, leaving even their clothes and bushwhacking it until morning. I was on Whidby's island about seven miles from where he was killed that same night, alone with my little girl, now Mrs. Andrews. When one of our neighbors called at the gate and said Colonel Ebey had been beheaded last night, I said, "Captain Barrington it cannot be so, as I had been staying here so close by alone without being disturbed." Shortly afterward the Indians came armed, and one of them came up to me, shaking a large knife in his hand, saying "Iskum mike tahnass and matawa copa stick or we will kill you." I said to him, "I don't understand. Come and go to the field where my husband and an Indian boy are," but they refused to go there, and left me soon. I started for the field with my child, and the further I went the more scared I got, until, when I got to my husband, I cried like a child. He ran to the house and sent a message to the agent on the reservation, but they skipped out of his reach, and never bothered me again, but I truly suffered as though I was sick, although I stayed alone with a boy 8 or 9 years old.

And now, Mr. Editor, if you think my story worthy of printing, I hope you will pardon mistakes, as my limited education was only six months' schooling.

C.B. Talbot

The story of the first newsboy on the Pacific Coast.
He gives an interesting description of "the post office
of the plains" which he encountered on his
1849 journey to the West.

Tacoma, Washington — October 21, 1892

On the 4th of March, 1849, our family of six persons, father, mother, two brothers, myself and sister left home, near Monmouth, Ill., 'for the "far west." For a number of years my father had been making an ineffectual contest against the tax titles in that state, having settled with his mother on the prairie there twenty-two years before, and had a few months before quit-claimed his farm to the tax title claimants after years of litigations. To make a new home and to begin again was the aim he had in crossing the continent. He was, perhaps, like many of the men on the western border, fond of the air of change, and the chances of success, hidden in the haze of the future. From Massachusetts he had gone to Kentucky; from Kentucky to Havana, Cuba, making a successful and profitable journey home to Taunton. So his mother and self are soon again settled in the west, where he had made a good beginning. In this new venture, he hoped fortune might again reward his efforts, and so he made a start with us toward the setting sun.

Our early memories, it seems to me, are more fresh than later ones, and that March day, with its cold, damp air, the frozen ground, the "thaw" just then two days begun, the breezy woods, the hazy distance across the brown and bare prairies, seem as real as if it was but yesterday. At that time I was within a few days of my ninth birthday, and, being the oldest child, much of my time was employed soon in helping mother with the other children, the youngest brother a babe in arms, who had just begun to stand and walk a little.

On the evening of our second day's journey, at the Mississippi river, I saw a steamboat for the first time, and several years afterward I saw the first steamboat that ever disturbed the increasing circlets about the leaping salmon in the waters of the Columbia and Willamette. About that time I also saw the first steam sawmill and in 1871, I believe, the first locomotive on the Oregon & California line—though others had been in use at the Cascades and The Dalles several years before at the portages there.

Our journey was without event until one day in Missouri I saw my first black man. In all the slave states it was the custom for slaves to take off their hats on meeting any white person, and this old man, clad in a gray homespun linen shirt (about like coarse towels are made of) and blue jeans pants, barefooted, met me in the road, took off his old white wool hat and made an abject bow, almost to the earth. I had heard, thus early, of the devil and his dark ways, but no one had ever said a word to me about a negro or any likeness of him, as I recollect, but I was not long in making my allotment, and this man before me must be indeed one of his very children — and maybe the evil one himself. So turning, I ran frightened to the wagons, a good way behind, but it was sometime before I was completely quieted.

After a number of days through mud and rain we at last came to the Missouri river, where we were detained about two weeks waiting for our turn at the ferry, a small flatboat pulled by sweeps to cross its turbid breadths of swirling angry water more than a mile wide.

The dread of the trip over has often come to me since while listening to the lines of the old hymn:

"But timorous mortals start and shrink
  To cross this narrow sea,
And linger shivering on the brink
  And fear to launch away."

Our old boat was so heavily loaded that when one of the oxen changed his footing a little the craft began taking water over the gunwales and we were in much danger of swamping. Two men, however, got hold of the animal and put him in place. I believe we did not again cross a river on a flat boat, but by fording, swimming or on pontoons made out of wagon boxes, constructed especially for this purpose. In these we crossed the Platte and other rivers at the eastern end of our journey. This side of the Rocky mountains we had little need for them, most of the streams being small and in the dry season could be easily forded. We did not cross Snake river or the Columbia as many did, and so avoided much danger and loss — cattle and lives. On Snake river I saw one man lose his life swimming with the cattle.

Once on the western bank of the Missouri we began to form "trains" and "companies," to elect "captains" and officers who controlled the whole equipment, and in many cases sat as judges in all matters in dispute. Sometimes Judge Lynch meted out justice in swift and special manner. On the Platte river one night, opposite our camp, he held court and presently a man was chained up to a cottonwood and burned up. Sometimes a man would receive a good thrashing or an indefinite leave to quit the "company," which he was not long in doing, or the thirteenth bullet from twelve loadless guns sent some poor wretch to his doom in cases of extreme villainy. Whittier could have seen his "psalm:" "The best of now and here," in actual practice had he been among the '49ers, for I do believe that nothing short of the common good in men was so much seen as in the circumstances of the long and trying journey. But we also found many of the most recreant fiends that humanity ever owned. Escape was about impossible, and judgment swift and sure made the "way of the transgressor" (across the plains) "hard."

After we had been traveling a few days up the Platte valley, I had my first view of "horrid war," as General Sherman calls it. We were driving quietly along, when we met six pairs of horses, a blanket stretched between, on poles laid over their backs, and on each lay a poor wounded Pawnee Indian. The blood was brown and dry on their arms and bodies and an army of flies made more miserable the little life there was left in them. The ponies seemed to know the needs of their anguished and dying freight, as they stepped slowly and carefully along, preceded by the Indian leader, and followed at some distance by ten or twelve more, all mounted, painted and heavily armed with long, wood-stocked muskets, with flint locks, all over the wood stock covered with round-headed brass tacks in fancy patterns, shining like gold. Each was dressed only in skins of the deer, elk or buffalo, decorated with a profusion of beads and colored with brown, blue and red paint in many quaint patterns, and in the seams fringes of buckskin and red flannel. They were a gay but sorry-looking cavalcade, having nothing to say, passed by in silence. That day, in the afternoon, we entered the bounds of great cornfields, and when beyond these we went into their village, now deserted on account of the battle the day before with the Sioux tribe. As none of these exist now, I will describe it: There were from thirty to forty houses, built of prairie sod, each nearly alike, in this manner: Some had two, and some four central or high posts on which poles were placed on top. Lower down, about five feet high, a circle of posts about seven feet apart was set having poles on top as before. Each house was about thirty feet in diameter on the inside. All around the outside wall, at the ground line, was a raised earthen terrace, about ten inches high, having a log of wood on the inner side, about three or four feet from the wall. On this they slept and spread their blankets; and on the edge of it they sat. In the middle a fire is always burning, and in some of the houses we found the fires still burning, the occupants having fled, as all indicated, in haste. A hole about two and a half feet in diameter permits the smoke to go out. The poles or plates on the posts are closely covered with strong rafters, and on this brush is thickly laid, and above and outside turf about two feet thick is placed; the brush being covered with a thick coat of prairie grass. The door of the house — one only to each — being about three feet wide and four feet high. The river near by furnished water and its banks wood — and in the tops of the tall cottonwoods was the village cemetery, where the bodies were suspended in blankets or skins secured to the tree tops with leather thongs; so cheating the hungry wolves of their ready prey, if they were placed in the ground, as in that case they could easily dig them out.

We soon had the experience of passing through one of the model Nebraska cyclones. Although the country was then not named, the same general physical characteristics were at work then as now. We had camped in close order, our wagons forming a corral — in a circle — and outside of it our tents. Presently a bank of black clouds came up out of the west, and with it great sheets of glame and noise. All else was still. Now came the breeze, then the wind, then the hurricane — that scattered everything all over the prairie. Some of the wagons were overturned and the covers torn off, and the tents were everywhere. Now the rain descended, and in a few minutes the water was six inches deep; each little ravine was a river. In two hours the stars were shining brightly and blinking their saucy eyes at us from the eternal dome above. But such a sight! Not a dry thing upon, around or about us, and much of our belongings damaged and lost beyond repair; but at this time we were still rich in this world's goods and did not need them as much as later on.

At this point of our journey we were progressing finely, the grass was growing plentifully, our stock was in good condition, and beyond a few cases of dysentery, occasioned by eating buffalo and antelope meat, and errors of diet the general health was good; but this was not always to continue. In a few days, as we journeyed on up the south bank of the Platte river, cholera began to appear, and soon whole trains were halted by the roadside to bury their dead and wait for the sick to die. So rapid was this that a man would be driving his team one evening and the next would be dead. Camped for the night, the screams of dying in the painful cramps with which they were seized, could be heard all about us, for the wagons were traveling here, in lines six abreast, ahead and behind as far as the eye could see. It seemed for a week or two that half of the emigrants must perish. Every other tent was a hospital. Wives lost husbands and brothers and brothers wives and sisters, and drove on to the west alone. Some of these scenes of bereavement and destitution are beyond description, and no pen will ever tell the thousandth of the woes there covered by the sod or borne by sad and lonely ones beyond the view of men. Here my father was taken by the scourge; for four days hung in the balance. We had with us a good cow, and with the milk we mixed chalk. With nursing and a good doctor we were more fortunate than others, and after a delay of two weeks were again on the way, but had to get into a new "company," since our former companions had passed on. This was necessary, because the Indians had become, at times, impudent, and frequently took all the liberties they pleased, although we were so compactly traveling. We did not want to provoke them, as they perhaps outnumbered us, being then in the midst of the great Sioux nation, which at that time was supposed to be 40,000 strong. One day we fell in with a band numbering, it was supposed, about 3000, and it forms one of the most singular recollections of my life. The band did not make any pretense of being warlike, but were merely travelers from one hunting ground to another, but had their eye on the main chance, so they conceived the pleasant little duty of relieving us of 200 pounds of flour to each wagon—levied, they said, as a tax on all travelers through their country. We patiently stood still for three hours, and when they were through getting the flour we found they had gotten many other things—nearly all our wagon hammers and double tree bolts, and in some cases they had taken out the linch-pins from the ends of the wagon axles and we could not move the train until temporary ones were made. But aside from the unpleasant nature of their visit there was much to amuse and remember. In the first place they seemed to be in the best of good humor, their faces greased, the hair combed and painted with vermillion in the parting, the braids being nearly always pieced out with strips of red flanned braided in or knotted in the hair. Some wore tall dressed leather hats trimmed with beads and gaily colored feathers. Others were of fur or badger skin, trimmed with a wolf or fox's tail. Their garments were of buffalo and elk skins, and the newer ones were nearly as clean and white as paper. All were covered with beads and paint. Sometimes the fringes of beads would be half a yard long. They all appeared to be well fed and well clothed, and seemed to have all the necessaries of life in profusion. But how changed is all this now, fed on government beef and clothed in a few rags that they buy, beg or steal. I saw some of this same tribe of Indians last winter, but they were not the grand and happy men I saw forty years ago. When they finally gave the word to move the scene was amusing. Each pony had two long poles attached to its shoulders, and the rear ends resting on the ground. Across these, behind the horse, were cross sticks holding a buffalo skin hamper, into which the loose articles of the family were placed, and on the horse's back other things were packed on a saddle, made in the Indian fashion. These saddles have two horns, about a foot high, the rear and front being exactly alike, except that the rear one stands sloping a little more than the front. The horn of the Spanish saddle is of the same shape, but lower, and probably its shape is due to the Indian design. Each dog was harnessed, like the horses, with side poles, and, when the halt was made, the large dogs went first, and astride of the horse poles, and rested their loads on it, and then the smaller dogs, until they had nearly all their burdens laid on the poor horse. Some, however, laid down on the ground. When the march was resumed, the dogs waited until the horse started, then, they in turn, followed on in the most orderly manner conceivable, forming a picture amusing in the extreme. The squaws all rode astride like the men, and the smaller children, too small to ride alone, rode in the hampers behind the horses. The very small babes were hung to the saddles horns, in a long leather pouch, lashed in so they could neither move hand or foot, and the very young ones had their heads fastened so they could not turn them right or left. Each one of the men carried a musket, with flint lock—generally a pouch of tobacco and killicanick—and a thin steel tomahawk, the pole of which was usually formed into a pipe. The handle formed the stem, and had a bone, horn or stone mouth-piece at the end. Many had pipes made of a kind of red slate, with stems in the same way. Some of the tomahawks were made in the most handsome manner, inlaid with copper and silver. The Indian axes were much in the same shape, but had square heads or polls and were heavier, weighing three to four pounds. Many call these tomahawks, but such were never used as an arm of defence. Tomahawks are about like a common lathing hatchet, weighing about a pound, or a pound and a half. A few of these Indians had powerful bows, and quivers full of arrows. These they used for killing small game. An Indian of that day never discharged a gun unless it was needed, for powder was one of their most valued possessions, and for it they would sell anything they had. Whisky and tobacco came next, then blankets, trinkets and paints.

Much has been said of the vast herds of buffaloes and some discredit has at times been given the narratives concerning them. As for myself I believe I never read a story that could convey an impression of the illimitable number of them. On the great valley of the Platte at the time we were passing the eye could not reach the bounds of the vast herds encircling us. The distant hills, and wherever we looked, could discover a land of brown, gray and green, the brown being the buffaloes. They paid no more attention to our trains than they would to prairie grass, they would press before or behind our teams and pass between them. Sometimes they seemed shy, but not more so than cattle roaming at large. Frequently we stopped the wagons to let them go through. All of them were headed north and they were as persistent in their order of march as flocks of wild geese when flying their course. They usually travelled in lines, one after the other. In their main trails, which were worn down into the prairie sod a foot or more deep and were three feet wide, sometimes there would be five or six of these trails nearly parallel to each other—and for direction they were as straight as common roads. For the weeks we traveled in the buffalo country the "chips" formed our chief dependence for fuel. Where they were dry they burned well, made a hot, steady fire and our meals were soon cooked. To use them we dug a hole in the sod about eight inches wide and one or two feet long, and set the fry, stew and bake pans across the opening. Those who had camp-stoves used it as they did wood. Sometimes it got soaked with rain, then the cook's temper rose and the delays were dangerous. Fuel was sometimes carried along for many days at a time, and water was always carried in kegs and canteens; for, notwithstanding our guide books and guides, we frequently failed to reach fuel and water at night. In crossing the "Sublett Cut-off," east of Green river, we traveled three days and two nights without finding wood or water. The dust and sand it seemed never would end. Most of our traveling was there done at night. In hot midday we laid by. When about seven miles from Green river the cattle smelled the water and such an indescribable bellowing and running never was seen as that. Old foot-sore oxen that could hardly limp suddenly found out that they could run like a heifer. Their dry, parched tongues would hang out of their mouths a foot long, covered thickly with dust, many of their mouths bleeding, and panting for breath. Indeed, hundreds fell by the wayside famished, where the hot winds dried the flesh to their bones.

On the 4th day of July, '49, we camped by the shadows of "Independence Rock." To mention it is to bring to remembrance the face of a peculiar spot in nature. Few prairie schooner men "by the plains across," fail to remember it, as here the trains were converging on one road, through Devil's Gate and South Pass. The rock rises squarely out of the prairie, maybe 220 or 250 feet high, and as near as I remember it, its top inaccessible, but all around it, as far up as a man could reach standing in a wagon, inscriptions in paint and wagon-tar recorded the name and destination of famous men and women—

that is, in their eyes — at least they sought to make record there, high up, if possible above any other reach, the occupation, place of nativity, and date of birth of father, mother and children. In some instances messages were left inscribed there for those who were following on behind, telling them they were well or had been sick or some one had been buried. At once a post-office and monument! Could anything be more useful to the changing needs of man? After we had read as many of the inscriptions as possible, supper being over and twilight approaching, we had a wedding, and soon the sounds of the viol and horn floated out over the wilds, far into the night. We were strong and happy yet. None of the severer losses and privations had come to us.

The plains postoffice has been seldom described and a short sketch will answer. There being few returning rearward, and if any such were found it was not easy for them to find the persons addressed in the missives intrusted to them as anywhere from four to seven persons belonged to each wagon. Only the owner's name being written on the corner in most cases, with his former home and destination, many soon adopted a wider plan, naming each person it contained in bold letters on the cover. This was necessary since the teams were getting foot sore, many having died of alkali, or through sickness, or lying by for rest and recruiting the animals, the travelers got widely separated, even close relatives. So rather than trust the chances of the kindness of diligence of the returning they adopted the plan of taking a small stick a foot or two long, one end being sharpened so it would stick in the ground, and to the other or top end they tied their letter with a string, that the wind might not blow them away. Sometimes the stick was split between the bottom and top and opened and the letter placed in the crack. This left the writing flat and more easy to read the direction than when wound round and tied. Frequently several hundred of these would be set just outside the road, the captain or someone would read them to see if any belonged to his train. Each train had a name, as well as the wagons. Some of the inscriptions on the wagons were intended as much for a joke as any use that could be made of them, as for example:

William Stevens, Lucy, Jane and Jim

If you get through, don't wait for him.   Tucker's Train

From Sangamon, Illinois, to Oregon,

    March 15, 1849.

About this time people began to pile out all their extra loads, unable to haul them further through loss of teams. Here would be seen a pile of bacon 300 or 400 feet long as high as the wagon beds. If anyone wanted, they took it. If they had more than they could haul they left some. In these heaps were all manner of articles, such as would be found in a general store. The women and children began to walk now, and I should think fully half of them walked from the Rocky mountains to the coast. It was about here our family left the heavy wagon with all it contained, and from thence on we walked from seven to twelve or fourteen miles a day, as the teams could not be driven much, if any more.

In a few days, at 3 o'clock in the afternoon, we stood on the great divide, in the South Pass, looking down into the hazy purple of the west. That name was ever before; we could not see it yet. At noon we were in the land of grass and granite; at night fast descending into the valleys of dust, alkali, death, volcanoes, and eternal fields of lava. The night found us at Pacific wells—three large basins of clear water, twenty or twenty-five feet in diameter, seeming to be higher than the neighboring land, and encircled by a small mound. We tied lariats together and sounded them to a depth of about a hundred feet, but found no bottom.

For a time all went well until nearing the Green river and crossing the desert described before—but at the river—we encountered a ferryman who demanded about all the remaining money each wagon had—$8 or $10—but it was finally arranged, and Charon let us pass. There were several such grab stations. Someone would cross-lay a mudhole, or build a crib in some gully where it would take several miles of travel to get around it, charging a dollar, perhaps, and not infrequently the tourist hadn't the dollar, and then he traveled, as it was cheaper and sure.

At Soda springs, near Bear river, we found one of the wonders of nature—a great mound of soda, and springs of bubbling gas and cool water. Here we tarried for a day and did washing, baking, some blacksmithing, tire-setting, shoeing horses and oxen—for we shod the oxen, sometimes with difficulty, as their hoofs were worn too thin. In that case we made oftentimes rawhide leather boots for them, for our precious teams were more than gold to us, and we watched and cared for them as we did for children.

The footgear of men and women was also a matter of much concern in the later months of the journey. There were few persons who had a serviceable pair of shoes or boots. As soon as the teams began to die, all useless articles were abandoned and the people of every family could do nothing else than walk. Only the sick or aged persons could be indulged in riding, and many of these were often seen following on as best they could. Sometimes they would be several hours behind the wagons, but ultimately got in all right late in the evening, or far into the night when the day's march had been long. There might be seen at first persons wearing moccasins, but the soles were soft, so they would take a piece of green rawhide from some dead animal and make a sort of outside cover or sole, with a puckering string of the same material about the top, drawn firmly over a piece of wood until it got dry (three or four days was needed for this, perhaps,) when they were put on, though stiff and hard, they soon got fitted to the foot and were not so bad after all. But the feet would get sore and tender, and then were wrapped in any old cloth that could be found and cross-lashed outside with rawhide cords.

Here our Mormon and California journey-mates were separating their belongings from ours—brothers, sisters and friends were parting, since here the roads divide for the Sierras, or Cascades—the new home of saints and rest, or the land of gold and grain. The arguments of wise men about the sagebrush fires those nights have never been written in song or story, but hope is ever young, its fields are ever green, and each could see the other fool when his wagon tracks next morning went the opposite road. Most immigrants set out the line of travel on starting, and in most cases went to their destination without changing their minds; but the stories about the gold finds reached us as often now as once a week from returning mountain men who had heard the news from the west. For some time the excitement had been intense. When the Oregon road was reached nearly every man who started therein was marked down as simpleton or idiot, or, in some cases, not in best state of mind, since a man who could go to a place where there was no gold,—when on the other road was heaven and heaps of yellow ore—certainly a man was not right who would do such a thing. Yet the Oregonian here left the road to "bright jewels and the mine," and went down the middle of the other to smell the perfume of the apple and the pine. It was amusing to see the indecision of some. A man would talk with one party or the other, and after a start on one road or the other, a wild hurrah would greet him in the party he would join. As it was constantly being done, the chooser, arriving or going, and a new train laying aside to receive all such, the excitement was exhilirating—and served the purpose of real amusement, especially to those who had made their choice on starting months before. As soon as the required number of wagons, anywhere from ten to thirty, had been obtained, they at once elected a new captain and started on. It was here that the Mormons made sometimes a total wreck. Many of them started from the Missouri river with handcarts, but at this time nearly all them had been left behind the traveler hiring to or helping some emigrant for his fare. If it happened that his place fell on some Oregon team his lot in life was lost, for the leagues were long and score between Salt Lake and his lonely sack of scanty clothes. He was too tired to chase jack rabbits and grasshoppers, and cactus was not good eating. The Californians wouldn't have him—would not have any spies in their camp—when just about to enter the saints' rest. They did not rest much themselves, and his saintship usually rested just where he was, by his own fire in the sagebrush. Whether he had anything to eat was small matter to them, as long as he kept well away. The dread and fear they had of Mormons may seem strange—but events then and afterwards justified all that could be said or thought. Some of the escapes from the Mormons were more perilous than from Indians, and their robberies were always more certain and disastrous. In a few days we had some experience of it, and the victims were barely saved from death. We were traveling toward Snake river not far from Fort Hall, when two breathless horsemen arrived at our train front with tidings that their train of seven wagons was stopped and the men and women overcome by Indians. Thirty of our young men loaded their rifles and returned with the hunters (for they were returning from their hunt for game when they discovered the situation of affairs) and soon were at the seat of war. When they arrived they found all the men and women tied up but one woman who had a long cheese knife with which she had succeeded in keeping them out of her wagon front. Our squadron soon ran down and captured four Indians, with whom they returned to us, or waited till we drove up, for it was all over then. No one had been killed, but they were nearly frightened to death. Some had been cut and bruised a good deal. In the chase three white men were discovered among the Indians, and we afterward learned they were Mormons, who had been doing this business for some time, and this was one of their many raids for plunder. We tied the Indians up and led them behind the wagons for four days. Each night Indian dogs were heard around, but our train was then so large—eighty wagons—that they did not attempt to molest us. When the morning came, to let the culprits go, our drivers cut some good new whip crackers and put them on, and then formed a line about twenty feet apart and turned them loose, one at a time, and forty good men made their marks on them, and the blood run down their backs as if they had been cut with knives.

Not far from Fort Hall, one night we had a stampede. After that we knew what the word meant. The cattle and horses had been sent out at 4 o'clock, for we camped early these days, as our teams were thin and few, and most of them had been now left behind, dead. Our guard had just set the second watch when a shot was fired by one of them at what he supposed to be a wolf. The camp heard it and listened for signals, but not a sound was heard. Presently the four or five hundred animals came straight into camp, rushed through it and never stopped until they had run eight or ten miles. The guard followed, but at a distance and it was midday next day before they were all herded. Finally they were all together, but no man to this day can tell what started them. The Indians did it, but how they eluded the guards and what they were able to do to occasion such fright is an open question. Not a thing was seen but this wolf looking object. The night was starlight, and the grass was good but not high where the cattle were—only an open prairie, and a long distance to the hills or river. The very earth trembled at their running, and how the poor old beasts could run was a mystery to us all, for we could seldom drive them over ten to fourteen miles a day.

Numbers of the teams were getting so weak that they could not keep up this rate even, and the large train was soon dismembered, the travelers trying to class themselves, according to their animals, as to strength and numbers. Generally they became divided so that there would be not more than eight or ten wagons in a train. This was a feast for the Indians, for while they did not kill many that year, they took occasion to be impudent, and frequently stopped them and demanded gifts, which in most cases they got. From time to time they became more bold, and their success in these raids laid the foundation for the murders and robberies they committed in the next two or three years.

Nothing of moment occurred except the loss of our teams. Soon we reached Powder and Burnt rivers, and found the salmon thick, also service berries and wild currants, (black and white), great bushes ten feet high as full of fruit as in any garden. Grande Ronde valley is a great circle, ten or twelve miles across, in which the wild grass and oats was as high as the cattle's backs. The clear stream and blue of the mountains beyond, seemed a paradise indeed to such as we.

After a hard climb and descent among the odorous, green, stately pines of the Blue mountains, we found ourselves one evening not far from the present site of Walla Walla, and near the old Whitman massacre grounds. The Indians surrounded us and demanded this time nearly all we had — a supper for 200 of them, and all the flour, except thirty pounds to each of our seven wagons. After three hours and a half, we partially filled their emptiness, and the Hon. David Logan, then a member of our party, emptied his mother's preserve dish, that he was only to use when he got sick. Alas! for good intentions. Those tall, badger-skin hats nodded to each other over the jam jar, and, with each taste, they grunted; and, after grunting, the long fingers descended again for a new lift of the sticky ooze. David remarked that Uncle Sam would punish the villains for such behavior, but it was generally agreed that evening that he was too far away, and, perhaps, might never hear of it at all, as it then took nine months to get a letter back to him, though a year or two later Hon. Joseph Meek, United States marshal for Oregon, hung five of the same rascals at Oregon City.

As an excuse for stopping us they stated that our teams had been in their potato patch the night before at the old Whitman station. None of us had seen a potato vine or anything resembling one. The first notice we had of them was the placing of little white cloth on a stick supported by stones in the middle of the road, which we set aside. About a half a mile farther on we came to little "coulee" or box canyon, where there were rocks on either side that we could not get over. Here we were met and no help for us. After we were halted they jumped off their horses, came to some of the men, kicked them, got within five or six inches of their ears and talked as loud as they could in them, would want to trade knives, if one was shown them would take it, or took anything they saw. Old chief Otter Tail and his band did the work. Our wagon held the only family — all the six others belonged to single men, and the Indians seemed to take a special delight in teasing and insulting them, in all manner of ways they could invent. Their horses were standing thickly all round us, and they would ride right over the fires where we were trying to obey their orders when cooking supper for them. One of these horses kicked me that night, and as I trudged along on foot that 200 miles to Portland, and for ten months afterwards, I had a sore place on my ribs to remember him by, and I have not forgotten that glass-eyed spotted cayuse yet.

With the thirty pounds of flour, our family of six persons had to make the remaining journey, which required three weeks. Walla Walla to Portland in three weeks! Think of that, you men and women, who ride from Omaha to

Portland in a palace car in three days.

Arrived at The Dalles we sought to go down the Columbia, but my mother, being timid, the trip was abandoned. We again hitched up our poor old team, which at this time consisted of a mare, an ox and a small cow, and slowly drove to the summit of the Cascades, just south of Mount Hood. When we reached the summit it was quite frosty and ice formed heavily. It was November now and cold there, but no snow had fallen as yet. The weather was dry, smoky and cloudless. Descending Laurel hill into the Sandy we had an experience. It was so steep that a common wagon lock was of no use. Here we first discovered the proper use of a green fir pole. Each cut one and chained the top to the hind axletree when the train started. All arrived at the bottom in safety but poor old Mr. Clemmons. His pole broke and landed the whole chariot on top of his team's back. The old man viewed the affair with dismay. But time cures all things. Soon help was at hand, the food and blankets were lodged once more on wheels and he got safely on with the rest. Four days after that we camped by the house of Phillip Foster, near Clackamas river, and we all were now in the settlements of the Willamette valley. I remember his coming out of his cabin and asking if we were all well and if we wanted anything. We told him yes, and that we wanted all things — not the least was something to eat. He went to the house and brought out some beef and few potatoes. We still had enough flour for about three meals, but that night we had the supper of a king. Two days after that we arrived on the east bank of the Willamette, opposite Portland, on the 14th of November, 1849 — eight months and ten days from Illinois! That day it was still dusty, and in the afternoon it began the winter rain.

The immigrant, when he got into the settlements, was an object of pity, not of reproach, for all had trod in the same road. The "settler" last year was in the other's place, so the immigrant usually found shelter and a warm spot in some neighbor's estimation, and with it such help as he needed to again find his place in the world. If he had no money he had by his journey and hardships established a credit for his manhood and courage that stood for more than money. Such currency was the common coin of the time. Having extended to him the help he was a sorry wretch who betrayed the trust and failed to pay when he got the wherewithal.

The immigrants of '49 were more fortuate on arriving than those of succeeding years, as the male portion of the community, not sick or crippled, were in the placers of California. His services were sought, and well paid for. My father, in addition to the $1300 spent the previous year in getting ready for the trip, started with $350, but when he arrived he had left only 10 cents of actual coin. How little this was, will appear, when I state the wages current then. The very next day after arriving he went to work at $12 per day, and for some time was nearly all the time paid that sum, all in Spanish money — real silver. A year or two before wheat was made legal tender, but now the real stuff was plentiful. It was no uncommon thing to see a mule or a horse load of silver, being carried from place to place to pay debts due. The third merchant in Portland had four full barrels of silver standing opposite the back window of his store, within plain sight and reach of everybody, all winter, but it was not a sufficient temptation for any thief to take it. For that matter, we didn't have any thieves then. We had no locks on our houses, or anything else, and several years elapsed before I remember such a thing as thieving. If the silver had been taken, it wouldn't have been an hour until the culprit would have been caught. It also required a pretty good load of it to get through the day. For instance, eggs cost $3 apiece; dried apple pies, $1 each; apples, $1 to $2 and sometimes $3 each; fresh grapes, 75 cents to $1.25 per bunch; cocoanuts, $1 each; Sandwich Island squashes, $3 to $4 each; sweet yams, two to three pounds for $1; potatoes, $1 to $1.50 per bushel; cook stoves, $60; a bale of bed cord, $10; meal at hotel, $1.50 to $2; elsewhere, when not given, about $1; etc. With the silver was also a considerable quanitity of gold, Spanish doubloons, chiefly the property of gamblers. In some of their games I have seen a pine table break down with them, when covering it two or three inches deep.

On the return of the miners from California, in the spring of '50, gold nuggets came into use. They were of great size. I have seen a peck of them at a time, ranging from one to three inches in diameter. Some were half quartz, some solid gold. A neighbor of mine found one solid chunk which was worth something over $21,000. When these began to be brought home the silver-headed ones soon were as badly afflicted with the "gold fever" as any of the miners who were whetting their knives to dig out Pitt River Indian arrow-flints. Indeed, I knew one man — the proprietor of the Marquam Grand — who did this little act of surgery many years afterward, and he was not the only man who used his spare time on them. The Washington world's fair exhibit of nuggets wouldn't make a "grub-stake" for a miner of the old times of '49 and '50. The gold nuggets current at about $16 an ounce were soon displayed by the "slug" an eight-square shaped coin worth $50, and considering the large values of ordinary articles, were handy in their day; but as values decreased the minting of them was discontinued, and in their stead we have the $20-piece, which is about as unhandy now as the "slug" was then. About the time the "slug" was in its full bloom a barrel of dirty Chili flour was worth $50, and was imported into Oregon and sold at that price for some time. If we had to pay $20 for a barrel of flour, a double eagle would not be so unhandy, but we are using a coin four times as valuable (as applied to flour) as the "slug" was then.

The eight months had brought many changes. Starting with two wagons, four yoke of oxen; two span of horses, a mare and cow — the whole equipment costing thirteen hundred dollars — we had now arrived with the wagon bottom and wheels of the light wagon, one ox of the original team, the mare and cow, all else had been left behind. In two weeks the ox fell into a tan vat and died, and the fourth week the noble mare was killed by wolves not a hundred yards from the present site of Governor Pennoyer's mills in

Portland. The cow lived three years to bless our family board, and when she died our neighbors, knowing our loss, bought and made us a present of another, which was a neighborly custom then. With the hind wheels of the wagon and a yoke of hired oxen in the summer and autumn of 1850 my father for several weeks earned fifty dollars a day cutting and hauling piles to ships for the wharves at San Francisco.

Late in the winter of '49 he brought from Portland to Tumwater, near Olympia, $2000 for Captain Crosby, and afterward took up a claim on Chambers' prairie, where he planted a crop of oats, and returned to Portland for the family. Having paid $50 for a sailor and boat, we all took passage for the trip to the Sound. But when we landed on the west bank of the Cowlitz, a ready conveyance by canoe or batteaux could not be had, so he left us camped there while he came on to harvest his crop. The crows and other depredators had done it for him, so he returned to us, and once more, after a two months' absence and a short rest, returned with us to Portland, where my mother and sisters still reside.

When the *Oregonian* was first published I carried out the third number, and became the first and only newsboy in the northwest. Soon other papers were published and added to my list. When the steamer arrived I could deliver the latest news several days in advance of the weekly issue my own hands had rolled on the old Washington hand press. My gains, too, were good. One day I made $32. Not a single paper of any sort was sold for less than a quarter, and some a dollar each, and were sometimes five or six weeks old; sometimes two months old. Journalism then and now are two very different things. Soon I was enabled to attend school at the Portland academy, now a stable at the corner of East Park and Jefferson streets, Portland, a building constructed of pine lumber from the state of Maine, costing $175 per thousand. There were no sawmills here then. From this building, erected by thoughtful and loving men, several hundred of us passed to the lessons of life.

George Washington

Mr. Washington, born in 1817, tells the trials and tribulations of a "man of color" on the frontier during his westward emigration. He came to the Northwest in 1850 where he laid out the township of Centralia in 1872 on the line of the Northern Pacific.

Centralia, Washington — April 29, 1892

I am a native of Virginia, being born in Frederick county, within ten miles of Winchester, August 15, 1817. My whole life has been that of a pioneer, following the receding Indians until my final settlement in Washington territory, then almost unknown. At 4 years of age I moved with the family of James E. Cochrane to Ohio, settling in Delaware county, fourteen miles from the city of that name. Here, at first, the Indians were largely the majority; but in five years the county became somewhat settled with white men, and we moved to the northern part of Missouri, as far as had been penetrated. Five years latter we moved fifty miles further on the frontier. We then moved to Bloomington, Mo., where I was employed in Mr. Cochrane's gristmill and distillery, which he erected there. Two years were spent there, and two on the east fork of the Chariton river, where Mr. Cochrane built a sawmill. I then moved to Bloomington, Mo., invested in real estate, and built a brick house and owned property. A year later, with a partner, I rented a sawmill on the Missouri river in the Platte country, fifteen miles from the city of St. Joe. It was here that the state legislature passed a bill making me a citizen of the state, entitled to all the privileges and immunities of a citizen, except that of holding office. The case came up as follows: One Jeremiah Coyle bought a bill of lumber from me, giving his note in payment. When it became due he refused payment. A suit secured judgment and the amount was collected; but Coyle had me arrested, claiming that as I was a free man of color I had no right in that state according to law. The state was made plaintiff, and the case attracted great attention. Finally, coming before the legislature, it was shown my mother was a white woman of English descent, that I was free born and of good moral character, and I was made a citizen by special act.

The sawmill was destroyed by high water and I moved to Schuyler county, where I erected the first house ever built in Lancaster, the county seat, of logs, cut and hauled by myself. I afterward entered eighty acres of land at Fayette, Mo.

I bought a patent right for making whisky and secured machinery in Quincy, Ill., for making a barrel a day. While building the distillery in Lancaster, the legislature, then in session at Jefferson city, passed a bill prohibiting any man of color from manufacturing or selling spirituous or malt liquors. I sold out, and arriving at Quincy, Ill., found a bill had been passed by which any colored man entering the state to remain was compelled to give a bond of $6000 for good behavior, I left in disgust, and seeking out my old friend Cochrane we planned together to go to Oregon, then the least known part of this country.

On the 15th of March, 1850, we started for the Pacific northwest. I had four oxen and a wagon, and Cochrane had two span of oxen, a light buggy and a pair of Canadian ponies, the only kind in those days that could stand a trip across the plains. Before we started we pledged ourselves to stick together till the last. Our first halt was at Council Bluffs, Ia., on the Missouri river, where we arrived April 7th, completing the first 200 miles of our journey. We waited a month till the prairie grass grew high enough to support the animals, when our feed should have given out.

On May 6th we crossed the Missouri with a train of emigrants, our force consisting of fifty-six well-armed men, two old men exempt from guard duty, four women and five children. We followed the Platte river on the south side, at one time camping opposite Fort Kearney, crossed the south fork and went down historic "Ash Hollow," crossed the north fork, thence to Fort Laramie, and then shaped our course for the Black Hills. Later on we struck the "Sweetwater," as it was called, at "Independence Rock." The rock was then inscribed with names carved by those who had preceded us. We also visited the "Devil's Tattoo." In the course of our journey we crossed and recrossed the Sweetwater over a score of times. After making the last crossing, we went through the Rocky Mountain pass. We had no trouble with Indians or disasters, owing to constant watchfulness and care. In fact, our whole journey, though full of hardships, was uneventful so far as danger of life or loss was concerned. On one occasion, while yet on the Platte, we were nearly surrounded by a party of 600 Indians, half-starved and fierce, returning to their northern homes from an unsuccessful raid far to the south. Every man was at his post, fully armed, prepared to fight till the last. Our captain kept an unceasing patrol in front of our little band, watching every movement of the Indians, who, finding they could not frighten us into yielding them over our provisions and that we would certainly fight to defend what we had, drew off without bloodshed, and we went on our way unmolested.

One hundred and seventeen days of hard travel brought us to Oregon, our future home. Crossing the Cascades at Barlow's pass, we camped at Mr. Foster's house at the foot of the mountains. The train broke ranks at Oregon City, scattering in all directions. A year later Mr. Cochrane and I arrived at the Cowlitz river. The next year a boat was built and several families moved up the Cowlitz together. We landed at "Old Cowlitz Landing," crossed to the Chehalis river and pitched our tents not far from where the present Lewis county building stands in the town of Chehalis. In the fall of 1852, I settled where I am now, built a log cabin, cleared, fenced and sowed about twelve acres of ground. Indians were plentiful, but peacable, and I always maintained friendly relations with them. I sold my land with the improvements to Cochrane for $200, fearing it would be "jumped" on me by the rapidly incoming settlers. Mr. Cochrane moved here and took a donation claim of 640 acres, which I afterward bought for $3200. We ran an inn and ferry for travelers for several years. Mr. Cochrane died in 1859 and his wife in 1861. I buried these friends of a lifetime with sincere regret. In 1872 I laid out the present site of Centralia, on the Northern Pacific. I have accumulated property and money to the value of $150,000. I have a wife, one child and four step-children, and am a member of the Baptist church.

Chapter **2**

Up Sound Down Sound

William D. Vaughn

A nimrod of pioneer days, he did the hunting
for his 1851 wagon train. He built and sailed a log scow
on Puget Sound in 1854. Then seven years were spent
prospecting in the Cariboo mines. Also his account
of leading the lynching party that hung the
murderer of Andrew Byrd of Steilacoom.

Steilacoom, Washington — February 17, 1893

I was born in Carrol county, West Virginia, in 1831, and left that state in 1846 for Illinois, and stayed there one fall and winter. In the fall of 1847 I went to Missouri, from there to Louisiana, where I worked all winter, and then went to Mississippi and worked in the swamps all winter at lumbering. In the spring I took a raft to New Orleans. People were dying with the cholera every hour in the day. I went back to the Agoo river. The night after my arrival a trading boat tied up to the bank, and we heard there was a man on board with cholera. I and another man (a big Norweigan) waited on him until he died. The Norweigan said he had never been sick a day in his life. Before the next night I dug his grave. The following day I was down, as I supposed, with cholera. By using medicine they broke the fever and I recovered, but took chills and fever and had them for ten months, and was reduced to a mere skeleton. There were planters worth from $500,000 to $1,000,000 leaving for the north and putting their farms in the hands of negroes. While in Mississippi I worked for a man named Brown. In 1865, when in the mines in Cariboo, I saw this man's name as a guerilla. On the river it was said that every time his rifle cracked an officer on a steamer dropped. He stayed in the swamps and lived on game.

I returned to Illinois and stayed until my health got so that I could work a little, and then went to Missouri. From there I went Fort Leavenworth and began driving a government ox team of six yoke. I did this until fall (1850) and then was hired by a bridge company (Miller & Langlon), who were going to bridge the Platte river about 110 miles west of Fort Laramie. The year before this (1849) there was $60,000 made by a ferryboat at a toll of $10 per wagon. As the ferry could not cross wagons fast enough, some men took canoes and put planks across them and ferried people across on them. The ferryman bought the canoes for $1000 and set them adrift, after smashing them.

There were four men who came out ahead of us to build another ferry, bringing their winter's provision, tools, etc., with them. When we got there we found their cabin, built of green cottonwood logs. A large fire had been built against it, but, owing to the green logs, it would not burn. Everything was gone from the cabin, and we supposed the men were dead. We stayed here until it commenced to snow, living in a block house which we built of cottonwood. One day in walked these men, whom we supposed to be dead. They had been hidden back in the mountains in a hollow where Indians never came. Two of them — there were four — had been hewing logs some distance from their cabin when they saw the Indians coming. Hiding their guns under a log they went to the cabin and tried to get the Indians to leave them some provisions, but the Indians made motions to them to take the back track or they would get their throats cut. They were too glad to go. They walked a short distance out of sight and then did their best at sprinting. They hid in a cottonwood thicket until the next day, and then returned to look for the partners who were out hunting. They were close to the cabin when they saw their friends coming in with two horses packed with meat. They then all moved back into the mountains and hid until they saw our cattle tracks in the snow when they came down to us. They soon moved into their own cabin, a short distance away, and in plain sight, and continued work on their boat. The names of these men were: Joseph Falkner, John McGlaughlin and a man named Wiley, the other name I have forgotten.

I hunted all winter for my company; I had been hired as hunter and gunsmith, and when the bridge was finished I helped them finish their ferry boat. While these ferrymen were here they came up and wanted to take a hunt with me. I told them I knew where I could find plenty of buffalo. I took Miller's wagon and oxen and we went about twelve miles down the river and camped for the night. Next morning I and two of the men went hunting, and in the afternoon I killed four buffalo. I then told them to go back to the wagon and stay all night and bring it in the morning for the buffalo. They said they could not find the wagon. I then said that I would go and they could stay, as some one must be there to keep the wolves away. They were afraid to stay, but I told them to gather brush and build a fire and keep it going all night, which they did. I went back and in the morning returned with the wagon and took the meat into camp. After this the blacksmith wanted to go with me, and we went one morning when the snow was about a foot deep. We went about five miles from camp and walking up a ridge we saw on the other side a band of about fifty buffaloes. I took aim at a fat cow about 125 yards from me. He took one nearer. I don't know whether his shot took effect or not. I had knocked my cow down and went up to stick it, and she jumped up and took after me down the hill. I ran around a sage brush and she was just near enough to tear my coat with her horns. I ran and jumped a gully about eight feet wide and six deep. The buffalo fell into the gully and there I killed it. The blacksmith, who had run about 200 yards without looking back, now came up. Before I killed this cow I was afraid of nothing but Indians. I had a big buffalo hide which a wolf could not bite through. I would lie on this and cover myself with the other side of it. One night a big wolf came and pulled the skin (the buffalo skin, not mine) off my head. I shot at him with my pistol, for I slept with it and my gun under my robe. He howled, but was not killed. Sometimes it seemed as if there were a thousand wolves howling around me. On Christmas day, 1850, all the men went on a hunt. I loaned one of them one of my guns and one of my pistols. Late in the afternoon he came running in, saying he had killed an antelope. He had wounded it and then shot at it with a pistol and missed it; then he struck it with the gun and broke the stock off and killed it with the barrel. He wanted me to go after it, but I said he would not see that antelope again, as it would be eaten by wolves. Some of the men went back with him, but only found marks of where it had been devoured.

Emigrants were now coming through (spring, 1851), and I joined the ferrymen, but we could get nothing to do, as most of the trains passed on the north side of the river. So Falkner went to where a train was camped and asked permission to travel west with them. On receiving permission, he said there was a gunsmith (myself), who was also a great hunter, who wanted to go through. James McKane, chief of the train, said he wanted a man who could kill something, as none of the boys could get any game, so I was taken. The first day out I did not get any game, as the trains going through had driven it all back from the route. When I came in with nothing, McKane said: "I'm afraid you are like the others; none of them can kill anything." "Never mind, Uncle Jimmy," said I, "I will get something tomorrow." The next day I killed two antelope, and "Uncle Jimmy" said: "Well, I am beginning to think you are a hunter." From that day, as long as the game lasted, I kept the train supplied with meat. One day I was ahead of the train and about a half mile from it, when I saw an antelope about 150 yards from me, running. I fired, and its heels flew up over its head and it dropped dead. This was in full sight of the train, and two men rode up on their horses to get it, as I was reloading my gun; and asked me where I thought I had hit it. I said I thought somewhere near the heart. They found the ball in the small end of its heart.

When we left Little Sandy creek we filled our kegs with water, and an hour before sundown started for a sixty-mile drive across the desert to Green river. We stopped before sun up the next day to rest the oxen and let them graze on a little grass spot. I turned in for an hour's rest, when McKane roused me, saying there were four or five hundred antelope in among the cattle. Everyone was shooting, but only one antelope had been captured, having broken his fore legs. This was all the game that was killed by any one while I was in the train. When I got up the antelope were gone, so I went on about two miles ahead of the train and then turned off to the left and went about a mile. Here I saw six or seven antelope. I got up to within 180 yards of them and they started to run. I knocked one over with a broken thigh. It ran up to a little rise and let me get within 130 yards of it, and I killed it. The train had passed by this time and I called and a man came down and took the game in. About noon we reached the Green river and unhooked the oxen, which were nearly dead with thirst, their tongues hanging out of their mouths. We were afraid that in their eagerness for water they would drown themselves, but none were injured.

When we got into the Snake Indian country a band of Indians came galloping by, shaking their robes and wolf skins, and giving the warwhoop. The cattle stampeded and ran about two miles, killing one fine oxen and injuring two men slightly. I and a man named James Jackson now wanted to shoot at the Indians, who were on a sand hill about 300 yards from us. The older men told us not to, but we fired anyway, and knocked sand under the horses' bellies. The Indians then wheeled and left. We repaired damages and moved on, leaving one wagon, which was badly smashed.

Just before reaching Snake river we camped close to the timber and picketed the horses about a quarter of a mile from us. I picketed my horse, which I had got from the Indians some time before, trading a rifle for him, next to the timber. After supper we went to bring in the horses, and I found mine gone. I heard him whinney up in the timber and knew the Indians had him. We had seen sticks stuck up with bits of paper in them, saying, "Horses and cattle stolen here — look out for Indians" all along the road. Here we met four men with a lot of fine mules, who said the Indians had stolen two mules from them on a little creek a short distance ahead of us. When we reached this place we saw forty or fifty Indians on a hill a couple of hundred yards from us.

Two of them rode up within ten paces of the wagons, mounted on fine mules, which, from the description, we were sure were those stolen from the men who had just passed. Jackson and myself wanted to shoot both of them, but the older men persuaded us not to.

We now went on and crossed the "Barlow pass" into Oregon. This is the worst road I ever traveled; mud to the oxen's bellies, and all along the road we saw fine cattle dead. We often had to tie a tree on behind the wagon to keep it from running over the team. The first place we reached in Oregon was Foster's farm (October, '51). This looked very beautiful after our journey. The train had now been about six months on the road. I worked in Oregon until spring and then, with sixty-eight others, bought a fine brig worth $50,000 for $4000, as sailors could not be had to take vessels away. In the brig we went to Queen Charlotte's island, 150 miles north, in the British possessions, hunting for gold. We found nothing, and the majority voted to sail for Puget Sound. We set sail and landed at Olympia June 15, 1852. Olympia was then a settlement consisting of a few log cabins. We had had some trouble about the vessel, as some of the company had not paid their shares. So we now gave the vessel up to the man of whom we had bought it in order to pay the wages of the captain and sailors and the installments. I had paid up my portion, but got nothing back.

I now went to work on the Sound getting out piles and square timber. At this time there were only two ox teams on the Sound. In the spring of '53 I got a team of four yoke of oxen and went to loading vessels for myself, employing six men and getting $40 per day over expenses. When there were no vessels I logged for the Chambers mill, making about $20 a day. This was the first mill on the Sound on tide water. In the spring of '54 I built the first log scow on Puget Sound, using it to carry my team and to carry cattle to Whidbey island. The scow would carry forty head of cattle back of the mast. I carried Colonel Ebey's stock to Whidbey island. I moved the safe and other things belonging to the customs house, also, for the colonel. I beat a brig from Steilacoom to where Seattle now is. The captain said it was the first scow he ever saw that could beat him sailing.

In the spring ('54) I took a contract for a cargo, for a bark, of piles and timber for Albert Balch. He, meanwhile, was to go to Frisco, and return for it. On reaching Frisco he returned, sold his vessel, cargo and all, and left the timber on my hands. It was a contract without writing, as he said he "always counted his word good." I bought into a saw mill, at the same time laying east of Whidby island, on Tulalip bay. Lumber was $20 per 1000 when I bought, and it immediately dropped to $8. Had lumber, piles and timber remained at $20, I would have made $10,000 in a year, but the fall in price made me a poor man, as it used up all my cash, and all I had left was my scow and team. In a short time I sold out my mill and returned to Steilacoom with my scow and team, and turned the cattle on Fox island. In 1856 I went out with the first volunteers, under Captain Hayes. We crossed the Natchez pass in company with 100 regulars, under Captain Maloney. This made 200 men. We were to meet a company from Vancouver at the Wenatchee canyon. Just before we reached the canyon a man overtook us, who had been sent to tell us that there were 4000 Indians in the canyon waiting for us. Had we gone on not one of us would have lived to tell the tale.

We now came back to White river. Five of our men asked leave to go to Steilacoom. Their names were Robinson, Tidd, Miles, Moses and Dr. Burns. Miles and Moses were killed, and one got a ball in his head, but recovered. The others reached Steilacoom unhurt.

Next morning an express started for us. When they crossed the Puyallup river Dr. Burns saw them and crawled out from under a haystack and joined them and returned to camp. Some of our men went down one day to cut a footlog across the river a short distance from camp. The Indians fired on them and killed one man. They ran back to camp and called out a company, who went down and opened fire on the Indians. While we were fighting the express from Steilacoom wanted to return. They wanted ten men to guard them, and they wanted me among others because I was one of the best riflemen in the volunteer service. We got nine men and started. At Connell's prairie we found Connell, who owned it, about fifteen steps to the left of the road stripped entirely naked with a lot of wounds from a knife in his body, dead. The preceeding evening we had found McAllister, dragged off from the road, with a withe around his neck, lying between two logs. He was also dead. Farther on we found the body of a man named Miles close by the road. He had been shot and stabbed. All those bodies were naked. The next body we found was that of Abraham Moses. His horse had carried him out of sight of the Indians, and he crawled behind a log and died. The guard was looking in every direction now, and all were badly scared. Everything was, "Vaughn, look sharp." "Look here," "There," and everywhere. They all went under my orders and I made half look one way and half the other, telling them to tell me the moment they saw an Indian. When they got to Puyallup we all returned to camp. The men in this express were the worst scared set of men I ever saw.

After we had left camp on White river the boys fought all day, and in the evening returned to camp. I belonged with the packers, not with the soldiers, but Captain Hayes was anxious to get me with the scouts, on account of my shooting. Our next scout was to South prairie—fifty regulars and as many volunteers. We, the volunteers, were to cross at a lower foot log and drive the Indians to the upper log, where the regulars were. The Indians, however, ambushed the upper log and wounded two men, and then ran, so that the soldiers did not get a shot at them. I had been chosen first among the advance guard of expert riflemen. Sergeant Gibson was second. We heard the firing at the upper log before we reached ours and halted. I saw a mare and colt on the prairie ahead of us and while the company stood still I ran close to them and lay behind a wild rosebush, hoping the Indians would come out for them, but none came. We now returned to the regulars and found the wounded men, John Edgar and Mr. Perrin. We made a litter from the boards of a small cabin near by and carried the men to camp, five miles on a dark night, by torchlight. I could fill a whole edition of the *Ledger* with incidents of the war, but I will only give a few more particulars.

When the governor called for teams to haul freight and logs to build forts I put in three yoke of oxen and a wagon and went to hauling freight. At the end of a month I bought another wagon and put two teams to work. When we finished hauling logs for the fort at Connell's prairie we returned to Puyallup and camped. Next day the Indians fought 200 men there all day to prevent their building.

After the war I was three months trading in cattle and made $1050, and then I went to logging again. I loaded a brigantine with spars for China, making $10 a day. Then I took a government contract, building a military road from the Puyallup river to the White river, distance twenty and a quarter miles. I employed fifty-two men, and completed the same according to contract. I was two months and a half building the road and receiving for the work $12,331, clearing $1050. I then bought a ranch and improved it to the extent of $3200 besides my own work. Times began to get dull and little to do, and I had a big security debt to pay, and I saw I would half to sell property at half price to get the money. I saw two men from the Cariboo mines. They worked three months and made $12,000 apiece, and said they thought they would make $100,000 the next summer, and I concluded to go. Still I should not have gone if it had not been for the security debt. I sold property to pay the security and mortgaged the rest to get the means to go. I bought a pack train and started in the month of April, 1862. My money, pack train, tools and provisions amounted to $4000. I thought money made money, and I wanted to go full handed, and I would not let any of the boys know what amount of money I with me. I hid $400 on the side of the mountain, and calculated when I spent the rest of my money I would take that and leave. I prospected till my money was all gone but what I had hidden. I saw a place where I thought I would strike it, and I went to the $400 and got $20 of it and kept on the same way until the whole amount was gone. When I got within five miles of the mining town a man met me and offered me $1.40 a pound for all the provisions I had. I had a thousand pounds, but I would not sell. If I had sold and kept on packing, I could have made $6000 that summer. I camped and went down among the miners to see what I could do. I saw them cleaning up bed rock with a gold pan over half full of gold, and when I saw that, they could not have bought my provisions for $5 a pound. I went to work prospecting, and prospected faithfully for two years, when my money and provisions were all gone. A man showed me a claim that I could have taken $200,000 out of it, but there were fifty old miners told me that there was nothing in it. If we had taken it we would have had the richest part of the Diller and the Canadian claims, but it was not my luck. I was told one of the original owners sold out for a sack of flour, just before they struck it. The first claim we worked on we made grub a little while, but it gave out, then we run a tunnel into the mountain about 300 feet, and struck a little pay. It paid from $8 to $12 a day. We struck one little place, about two feet square, a low place in the rock, where we took out $68 one afternoon. One piece was worth $13 and some more over $15. We thought we had it sure, but it did not hold out. In the spring I went to prospecting on other small streams. We found another where we were making from $3 to $5 a day. There was quartz rock that run across the stream, and on the upper side in a place two feet square we took out $98. In other small streams we found coarse gold, but not enough to pay. I concluded I would try the mountains and go off a hundred miles or so where there had been no mining done, and see if I could find some new diggings. There was a man furnished us a lot of provisions if we would stake him off a claim. Some of the old miners told me I was not in the Rocky Mountains, and that if I went a hundred miles away I would never get back. I told them that if I never died until I got lost I would be older than Methuselah. Several parties got lost and almost perished. One man was an old mate of a ship that I was acquainted with. There was another mate with him and also two other men. They had compasses with them. The mate and I often laughed about it, and he said if they had had two more compasses they would have starved to death. There was another man found forty miles from camp where he had perished. He had written his name on his tin cup. There was another man started for a place ten miles distant and was never heard of again. We started on our long journey to hunt for new diggings and we went through the roughest country I ever saw. We had traveled about forty miles and came to a very high mountain. I concluded I would cross it and see what was on the other side of it. It took half a day to get on top of it. We started down the other side, and it was steeper than I expected. There were very few places we could walk. We slid down and held on to every little thing we could get a hold of until we got half way down the mountain. Then we came to a perpendicular wall of rocks below us, fully 200 feet to the bottom. Where we were the mountain was as steep as a house roof and there was danger of sliding off. My partner was nearly frightened to death. He said we would never get out of there. If we had got on any sliding rock we would have been gone. He cried, and I told him to be still and not get frightened. His name was Paul Emery. We laid on our bellies with our packs on our backs. I told him to hold on with his fingers and toes to everything he could get hold of, and we slid sideways a few inches at a time, I think we were half an hour getting 200 yards. We had to slide along that way for a quarter of a mile, and then we got to a place where we could walk. We went on down the mountain until we came to a creek and swamp. There we camped. He said I would never get him in a place again where he could not walk. That afternoon I killed a porcupine that weighed twelve pounds, dressed him, and the next morning we had him for breakfast. He was fat, and very good eating. That day we prospected some and killed three wild geese. We were glad to get them, for grub was hard to get. We kept on our journey until our grub got low. We had a quarter of a pound of flour and that much bacon. Since we had left the camp we had killed eleven ground hogs—some people call them wood chucks. They weighed from twelve to eighteen pounds apiece. We had eaten them all up. We hated to turn back, but we had to, for the want of something to eat. I knew I could go back a shorter cut than the way I went out. I depended on my gun and pistol for grub. We were four days on one mess of grouse. I had killed a little owl, and we got in sight of some ground hogs, and I told my partner to be still, and went up within thirty steps of its hole and waited for it to come out. I killed it. It was nearly half grown. I told my partner to skin the owl and ground hog and cook them as quick as he could, and I stayed there and watched for another, and killed one before he got that one cooked. I took the last one I had killed and went down to where he was cooking. Our dinner was about half cooked, but we took them out of the kettle and ate them up. We skinned the other one and put half of it on to cook. While it was cooking we cut down a spruce tree, cut off the boughs and made us a soft bed, and by that time the meat was cooked. We ate a few mouthfuls of that and lay down for a night's rest, which I never needed so bad in my life. Next morning we had our breakfast, rolled up our blankets, went down the mountain one mile and heard some more ground hogs whistle. I went on ahead and killed two of them. They were both big and fat. I told my partner that we would not go any farther that day, for we had plenty of meat to do us until we got into camp. We cut down another spruce tree, made us a bed and slept there that night. Next day we went on to the mining camp. When we got within two miles of the camp we met a man herding cattle. My partner asked him for a chew of tobacco, and when he got it he said he was all right. When we got into camp the saloonkeepers asked us to come in and take a drink in order to find out if we struck anything. As soon as they found out we had struck nothing they did not want to look at us.

There was a man whom I thought was a friend of mine. He had just taken out $12,000, I asked him for $3 to get some grub. He told me he did not have it, that he had put it in the bank. Then I pawned my rifle for $14 worth of flour, bacon and beans. I got a job of getting out some timbers for a tunnel. My partner went packing on his back for some of the merchants, as he was no hand with an ax. He was one of the best packers in the mountains. I got out the timber for the tunnel, got my money and redeemed my rifle, bought some grub and then went to prospecting again. I, with a man by the name of Johnson, took two weeks' provisions and started out. We got about forty miles from the mining camp and killed two caribou. They were fat and good eating. We built a platform of little poles, spread the meat over it, built a fire and dried it. What we could not pack we hid in a hollow log and plugged up the end so nothing could get at it, and went on prospecting. We made no more bread, but made flour gravy and spread it on our dried meat for our food, and prospected until it was all gone, and then came back to camp. Then I went out with another party, consisting of myself, James Mc-Cain and Ben Goodekuntz. We went about eighty miles through a very rough country. We found a little gold, but not enough to pay and then we returned. I went prospecting again with other parties and prospected hundreds of places that I won't mention. In the fall we formed another party of twelve men. Six of the men furnished the provisions while the other six did the work. The men that did the work were myself, James McCain, R. Sommers, Wilson, R. Dwather and Bingley. The men that furnished the grub I have forgotten their names except James Loran. We had thirteen pack mules and we were twenty-five days getting out. We took tools and other things to run a tunnel during the winter. That was the understanding when we started. Two of the men went back and got three head of beef cattle. We killed them and let them freeze for the winter. The company supposed that I would be foreman of the claim because I had been foreman of every company that I was in before the mines. Bingley and McCain knew that I would not start out there under any consideration except to run a tunnel. The other three men did not profess to be miners and did not want to say whether we should sink a shaft or run a tunnel. McCain and Bingley insisted on sinking a shaft. I had to give up for the other men would not say which we should do. We brought up a tail race two feet wide about a quarter of a mile. I wanted to make it five feet wide so we could run a tunnel from it, and then we widened out a place about twelve feet square and twelve feet deep to sink the shaft and turned the water off around us. It run off in the tail race; we had to cover it up to keep the water from freezing. We sunk about twelve feet and got twenty buckets of water for one of dirt. We burnt about forty cords of wood to keep from freezing to death and to keep the ice off the platform where we emptied our buckets. They all knew then I was right about running the tunnel. McCain wanted to start the tunnel then and wheel up a steep incline on plank. The other boys said it was too steep, they could not wheel there. McCain said Vaughn was the steadiest one in the crowd, he can wheel there. I said I guessed I wouldn't do it. McCain said if he was foreman he would make me do it. I was mad for two months before, but had said very little. I said you _____, if you think you can, just try it on. I dare you to lay the point of your finger on me. You have spoiled everything, and have thrown away our winter's work. He said nothing back. He bragged about being a fighter and that he never had a man hit him in his face in his life. I made up my mind he would never strike another if he hit me. I was wild mad. I cared for nothing. We had to saw out some two-inch plank and I was the only man in the crowd that could make cars, wheelbarrows and keep a saw in order. We puddled the shaft up and worked there until March, but the water beat us. Our grub was getting short. Vaughn bay was named for me. Surveyors named the bay after me. Lived in my house while they surveyed the bay which bears my name.

We were compelled to return to the mining camp, which was about eighty miles distant. We made us a lot of snow shoes and filled them with hides from the beef cattle. We were ready to start back and everything was covered with snow. Bingley and McCain wanted to take a nearer route. I told them all right, they could go that way and I would go the other way. The rest of the men said they were going whichever way Vaughn went. When our tobacco was about half gone we divided up the remainder. McCain did not use much tobacco and had two plugs more than anybody else. He gave me one and said he did not need it, and was very friendly with me. I knew he was afraid to trust his judgment to travel in the mountains. I told him we might strike some jump-offs that would be hard to get over. We started on the near cut and found some very rough places, but got through all right. One man that went ahead for an hour would drop behind. It was hard breaking the road. When we were within thirteen miles of the mining camp it was McCain's turn to go ahead. He said he could stand it and that he was going in ahead of all of us. I had showed him the way to travel. All the time before Dwather and I were behind, sat on a log and took a rest. I told him I would not be surprised if he got lost. He went on about two miles ahead and thought he was lost. He saw a grouse in a tree and shot all the shots out of his pistol, and the other boys shot all the shots out of their pistols at it and then they began to holler "Oh, Vaughn." I told Dwather not to answer them. We did not until we got up within 200 yards of them; then we answered them, and I shot the grouse they had been shooting at. We finally arrived into camp and all the men that had been working there wanted to go back and wanted the company to furnish grub again. The company refused. They said we had thrown away the winter's work. McCain said that we could go back and put in a wheel and prospect it quicker than with a tunnel. I told the company that we had done work enough if it had been done right to have opened the claim and drained it, and that we would have had no need of a wheel. That two fools had spoiled all the work. After that I went to work for wages for a month. Then there was a rich claim struck on Grouse creek. They took out $20,000 to the interest. They found the lead by running tunnels into the hill. There was a big flat down below where they thought the lead came out, and sent forty or fifty men prospecting for it. I took up a claim there and worked until my provisions were getting short, and sold a half interest for $100. We finished prospecting the claim, but there was nothing in it, and then took another one about a quarter of a mile from that. Six of us together sunk a shaft and struck the rim rock on the edge of the channel. Everybody thought we had a big thing. My provisions had given out again and I only had money enough to buy a beef head. I cleaned it and hashed it up, and put some salt and peeper on it and put it in a gold pan to cool. When I was hungry I cut a piece off of it and ate it. I done the same thing in two claims. Before that one was not allowed to leave their claim for more than 73 hours, or anybody could jump it. We were working hard day and night — three in day time and three at night — for if we stopped it would fill up with water. A man asked me if I wanted to sell my interest. I told him I would not take $1000 for it. I told him I was living on a beef's head and that if he would give me $100 I would give him one-quarter interest, as I wanted to get some provisions, so he took it and I bought $100 worth of provisions. It was cold weather and the two men on the windlass had to have a fire to keep from freezing. We tunneled fifty-one feet from the bottom of the shaft and widened out a place big enough to sink. The ground was so soft we had to have silk to set our posts on to keep the ground from settling overhead. The ground was what they called sediment. It was as fine as flour and full of water. We split out some piling and made a square frame and drove them around the frame. We kept them driven ahead of the dirt we were taking out. It was so fine it would come through cracks no bigger than a knitting-needle. Several old miners looked at it and said it was impossible to sink there. I was foreman of claim and named it and recorded it the "Tiger company," and it was a tiger too. I told the company that we could sink there. They said they could not see how it could be done. They said they would all work if I could show any plan that they thought would do. I told them we would have to let the tunnel and the shaft fill up with water, and that we would have to get a new whip-saw and saw out 10,000 feet of lumber, and that we would have to joint the piling and then break every joint and drive them double, and saw our frames so as to make everything true, and keep the piling driven six inches ahead of where we were taking out the dirt. There was one of the smartest surveyors with us that was in Cariboo, and he said he thought that plan would work, so we went to work and sawed out the lumber and had to drag it on the snow a mile, but we got the lumber all on the ground. The surveyor then said he thought he would pick out a place 100 feet from the shaft that would strike the channel. I told him it was very uncertain, that channels run crooked. He said he thought he could hit it anyhow, and that

-55-

it would save taking all the water out of the tunnel and shaft. We had to bring up a ditch a quarter of a mile, ten feet deep at the head of it, then we widened out twelve feet square and built a log wall to keep the dirt back. Then we turned the water off all around us and sunk in the center. We sunk down about four feet and struck level bed rock. The surveyor was beat. He said he did not want any more to say about it. I told them then that it would be better to make a pump. There was one old sailor with us who said the carpenters did not make the pump right. He said he could tell how to make it, but could not make it himself. I told him I would make the pump if he showed me how. I made it and it was the easiest working pump in the mines. We pumped the shaft and tunnel out, and then the surveyor surveyed it, and we sunk a shaft right down on the channel from the surface of the ground and my plan for the piling worked splendidly. There was sixteen feet of sediment that run the same as water and it was never known to be over five feet deep before. When we struck the channel there was three feet of gravel in it. We started the tunnel five feet to the cap overhead and the cap and the piling made it nearly six feet. We had to keep very near watertight overhead and on the sides down to the gravel and had to keep the piling driven six inches ahead all the time. One morning my shift was off. They came running to me and said we would lose the tunnel. I ran down and went down the shaft. There was a place where the sediment was pouring in just like water. We had a sixteen pound sledge and none of them could move the piling a bit. We had the hardest seasoned blocks we could get to keep from battering them. I told the boys to hold a block on the end of the piling. I took the sledge and every lick I hit they went in half an inch until I got the leak stopped. We struck a big quartz boulder three feet through and nine feet long. It laid in the center of the tunnel. There was so much crystalized quartz in it that it was almost as hard as a diamond. We had to sharpen our drill thirteen times to make one hole in the rock in which to put the blast. We got the rock all out and cleaned up the bed rock where it lay in the bottom of the channel. We then saw that there was no pay in the claim and gave it up. I had been working then over six months in the claim. I had used up all of my provisions and got some on credit and they were about gone.

I went up to the cabin and lay down on the bed to take a little rest, calculating after a little rest I would go out on some high rock where nobody would see and me and take my rifle and blow my brains out. Before I got ready to start my old partner, Dwather, came in and said he and his brother wanted to go out prospecting and asked me if I would go too. I told him I had nothing and said I didn't like to impose on them that way. He said that was all right, and if I would go he would furnish two horses and two months' provisions. That gave me a little life and encouraged me to go ahead and we started out to the place where we had wintered — the place where I wanted to run a tunnel and the others wanted to sink a shaft — about thirty miles from the mining camp. We got there all right and found a little gold in several places, but not to pay. We worked until our grub was getting short and then started back. We came back about thirty miles to a lake where we wanted to prospect a little more. I had made a canoe on the lake a year before that would carry eight men. The lake was eight miles long, and we carried our pack saddles and provisions in the canoe. It was all the horses could do to get through without anything. This was one prong of the lake. The main lake was forty miles long. Dwather's brother went in ahead of us and took the canoe up to the head of the lake. We prospected there a few days and then I went up to the head of the lake after the canoe. I left my rifle in the camp and took a big Colt's dragoon revolver with me. I got the canoe and was coming back, just rounding a point on the lake, when I looked back and saw a caribou coming behind me, traveling the same way I was. I got around the point and hauled the canoe up on the sand, and went back about thirty steps from the canoe and stood behind a big tree, with my pistol cocked in my hand. I heard him coming in the brush. When I thought he was close enough I looked around the side of the tree and he stopped. I shot him in the left shoulder and the bullet lodged in the flank on the right side. He fell dead. He weighed over 300 pounds. I had hard work to get him in the canoe. My partner wondered what I had as he was laying on his back with his feet sticking up. He thought I had some dry limbs to build a fire. It was the fall of the year and it was in fine order. I thought it was as fine eating as I ever saw. We skinned it and cut the meat in thin slices, built a scaffold, put a fire under it and dried it. We left the horses on a little prairie which had about two acres in it. We took the canoe and went to the lower end of the lake prospecting. There was some of the highest and roughest mountains on the edge of the lake that there was in the Cariboo country, and a good many favorable looking streams for gold. We prospected about a week and returned to camp. The sun was about two hours high and my partner said for me to stay at camp and fix up the things so as to be ready to start in the morning, and he would go back and get the horses. I thought he would be back in half an hour. He did not return at sundown and I thought he must be lost. I fired my pistol and called. I went out to the little prairie where the horses were and fired my pistol and called again and got no answer. It was now dark and hard to find my way back to camp. I was uneasy all night. Next day I took three days' provisions with me and started back the way we came to see if I could find the horses tracks, which I soon found, and in muddy places saw his tracks following them. He followed them the evening before until it got so dark he could not see, then he sat down against a tree and sat there all night. Next day he went back to the old camp, which was thirty miles from where we were camped. There was a big canyon five miles long and steep wall rocks on each side, and a nice little prairie at the head of it. There was good feed and the horses liked to range there. There was a bear got after them and they run into the canyon and the bear ran them through the canyon to flats below. We saw the horses' tracks side by side and the bear tracks between them. He seemed to be right after them. It was good traveling in the canyon, except a few places where there were jump-offs, straight up and down, five or six feet. We wondered how the horses ever got through without crippling themselves. They slightly skinned their legs and that was all. My partner thought the bear had got them and gave up the hunt and started back when I met him. He was tired out and nearly starved. I told him we would take a good rest and take another hunt. He said he thought it was no use, that the horses were crippled and the bear had got them. I told him the horses knew the way to come back off the flats to the head of the canyon. He said the mountain was so steep and rough he thought the bear had the advantage of them. I had my pistol and rifle with me and I said we would find the horses anyway, and that I would have the satisfaction of killing the bear. We went back and found the horses. They were not badly hurt. I never saw a man more surprised to find the horses in such good condition. He had some rope with him and we came about two miles and tied up for the night. Next day we went back to the lake to our camp. We packed up our things, put them in a canoe and I took them to the head of the lake and he brought the horses around. We packed up and came on into the mining camp. I got a job of work and he and his brother went to packing. Times were dull and I could get but half wages at the time. I worked for wages part of the time and prospected part of the time, and in the fall I started down (1869) which made seven years I was in the mines. I think there were about a thousand men prospecting that season who struck nothing. I thought I would not scratch another winter for my grub. I thought I would go where I could get something to eat. My clothes were a coat I had made out of an old blanket and my pants were patched with flour sacks. I had no money to stay at hotels. I had just enough to buy a little grub and sleep under trees along the road. I tried to save enough when I got down to the steamer to pay my passage, but I only had half enough. The captain told me I could go for half fare. I met a friend in Victoria and he let me have enough to buy a cheap pair of pants and shirt and I had 50 cents left. I went down to the steamer that Captain Finch was running from Victoria to Olympia. I told him I wanted to get passage to Port Townsend. I told him I had no money — that I was broke. He said: "That is not the way we do business, sir." I said: "Don't you know me?" He said he didn't and turned away. It made me mad and I would not then tell him my name. He knew me very well when I was shipping stock on his vessel and worth over $7000, but he did not know me when I was broke. There were hundreds of men came down from the mines begging their way all the way through. The manager of the Bank of British Columbia took a notion he would like to prospect and quit the bank. I met him just before I started down with a sack of flour on his back. I was told he was working in a tunnel for wages. There were some English officers went up in 1862. They had servants along to wait on them — even carried them water in the mornings to wash themselves. They intended the servants to dig the gold for them. They soon had no servants. Their horses were gone and they had to foot it down.

I saw a captain of a man-of-war that used to run on the coast here working in a tunnel, and his pants were patched with a flour sack. There were men of nearly all professions broke in the mines.

I saw a little sloop loading brick and I asked them for passage. They said if I would help load they would take me over to Port Townsend. I did so. The first man I knew in Port Townsend was Charles Eisenbeis, who used to live in Steilacoom. He asked me if that was me, and I told him it was what was left of me. He asked me if I wanted anything and I told him I wanted some dinner and a plug of tobacco, and that I wanted a job of work as soon as I could get it. He gave me my dinner and the tobacco and told me I could get plenty of work. A man just passed the door that wanted some men in a logging camp. He told him I was a good hand and wanted a job. I was hired and went to work. That was in November, 1869. I worked in camps until the next May. There were two young men that were working with me. I spoke of going prospecting in the Coast range mountains, and they wanted to go. We came to Steilacoom, bought two horses, packs and mining tools and started, and went from Steilacoom to Union City, on Hood's canal. We hired an Indian for a guide, and went up the Skokomish river. There were several crossings in the river that were very high. He said there was no danger. At two crossings I held on to the horse's mane to keep the current from throwing me down. The Indian guided us about twenty-five miles and then went back. We prospected all summer. There was plenty of game. We had grouse, deer and elk, and we killed two bears. In the fall we found some fine land on the other side of the mountains, about sixteen miles back from the tide water, on the Humptulips river. It was called the Half Moon prairie. We got some more provisions and tools, took them down the Chehalis river to Grays Harbor and hired an Indian to take them up the Humptulips in a canoe. One jam in the river we had to pack the provisions and haul the canoe over. We had to pole the canoe and in some places we had to get out in the water and pull over the rapids. We hewed out timbers for sills for our house. We had a three-inch auger and bored holes and in the sill, and put up poles for studding and rove out our weather boarding and built three cabins, and then came back to the Sound. I worked all winter in camps on the Sound, and in the spring we went back again. We planted a few potatoes and prospected until our provisions were gone then I came back and went to driving team for a camp, for Isaac Carson, who was then sheriff of Pierce county. We put in one raft where Higgins' shipyard now is. Carson then wanted me to go to Hood's canal, where he had a large amount of logs in the water on a little river, where they had a big dam and hoisted a gate to make the water drive them down the river. I went over and we got one raft out of the river, which was slow work. The logs were jammed up in piles. When we hoisted the gate there was not water enough to break the jam. It was five miles from the tide water to the dam, which backed the water up over half a mile. There had been a big camp there and there was a big lot of logs in the dam and nice timber around there. Carson wanted me to look at it to see if it would pay to start a camp. He said he would give me big wages and furnish the camp if it would pay. I told him every thousand he put in he would lose a dollar a thousand on it. I told him to sell if he could, and he done so. I bought the team and was to pay for it in logs. I went to my old creditors whom I was owing and told them I wanted to make a new start, and that I could never work it out by day's work. There was one house and lot which I mortgaged for $400, for which I had been offered $2000 in 1858. It was sold while I was in the mines and did not bring the price of the mortgage. I had another house that I sold for $1500, and held a mortgage against it that drew 2 per cent per month. I had pounded the mortgage when I went to the mines for $600, and it was sold and did not bring the $600. I had four town lots besides that were sold for taxes. It was in the time of the war and property was worth almost nothing. Before I went to the mines I sold one-half of my farm five miles from Steilacoom for $2150, and the other half I mortgaged to pay a security debt. It took it and the mortgage I had on the house to satisfy the security. I told my creditors I would give up everything if I could get a clear receipt so I could do business. They were all very kind but one, and that was J.J. Westbrook. The debt was for an old buggy I bought of him. I told him I hadn't the money at the time, and I did not want to go in debt, but he insisted on letting me have it on credit. I did not take it that time, and he came and offered it the second time on credit, and I took it. He got a judgment against me. When I came back from the mines I showed him all the receipts I had written out and said I would give my creditors all I had, and wanted him to sign one. He said he would sign it if all the rest did. I got all the rest to sign it and took it to him. He looked at it and said he guessed he wouldn't sign it. I concluded that he would not get in ahead of the rest of them, so I took the benefit of the bankrupt law, which cost me as much as the old buggy was worth. It was a good while before I made the money to pay it, but they were kind enough to wait on me. McCaw & Rogers got my trade to the amount of about $12,000 before I went to mines. They went my bonds for $10,000 on a road contract. The contract was for $15,000, and Henry Murray stood for the $5000. All the merchants made about 100 per cent on a big part of their goods at that time. I paid McCaw & Rogers $3 a piece for picks by the dozen; axes, shovels and other tools in proportion. When I got done with the road I paid them everything I owed them. I got some provisions on credit when I was working on my ranch, I don't remember how much. They went my security for $600 on one note and another of $400. They got the house and lot that was mortgaged for $400. P.J. Moorey lent me $600. I considered him the biggest loser of anybody. The rest of the debts were small. When I was making the government road Dr. Webb and Phillip Keach had stores, and they both wanted me to buy goods from them. They said it was not right to give McCaw & Rogers all the trade, and that they would sell me goods cheaper than McCaw & Rogers and give me all the credit I wanted. When I wanted to start a logging camp, after I had come back from the mines broke, I went to Keach and wanted to get some provisions on credit. He said he did not do a credit business. I tried Rogers and could get nothing. James Hughes let me have money to buy some timber, and I put the land in his name until I made the money to pay him. Clendenin & Miller had a store at that time and were strangers to me. Mr. Clendenin spoke to me one day and told me I could have all the supplies I wanted on credit, and then I started in to logging. I paid Carson for the team and managed to save about $1300. A man was fooling with a 44-calibre Winchester in my camp one day and let it go off, and the bullet struck the center of the thigh bone, half an inch below the joint, which crippled me for a long time. I was nearly blind for six months in my left eye. One of my fingers and two of my toes were paralyzed. I have not been able to do any hard work since.

When I got so I could work a little I started a gunsmith shop. I could not work more than a half hour until I would have to sit down and rest. I had plenty of work, all I could do. If I had sat down like a good many and said I could not work, I would probably be in the poor house to-day. I managed to work along at light work, save my money and put it out to the best advantage. I had been badly used all around. I took up a place on North bay, now called Vaughn's bay. I was the first settler on the bay, and it bears my name. That was where I bought the timber for my camp. The claim joined the timber land I had bought. John Brunemner took up the claim and said it would make a good farm. There was one acre that had some good trees on it. He wanted to cut the logs and sell them to me, and I bought them. He left the claim and went to British Columbia, and I took it up. I intended to have a little store and blacksmith shop and have a few boats to hire. It was a good range for cattle. I bought another piece of thirty acres joining it. It had some timber on it. I built a house and a barn and began clearing the land. When I was shot I had not moved from the camp. I paid $100 for grubbing stumps where the house and barn stood. I hired the other piece of timber put in that was joining. I was living on the place at the time. I lived on it four years and three months and worked a little, but was not able to do much. Several times I went out to work and had to take a stick for a cane in order to get back to the house. I found I could not do much there and I went over to Steilacoom and started a gunsmith shop and worked until the five years were up. I went to the claim several times and worked a little to make my time good. When the time came I went to Olympia to prove up. Brown, the registrar at the time, said my witnesses were not good enough. He said I didn't swear I lived on it five years. I told him I had lived on it four years and three months. I then went back and worked on it to make my time good until the five years were up. I told him I had got shot when I was working on the claim and I was not able to work at hard work; that I had gone to Steilacoom and started a gunsmith shop; that there was not one man in a hundred that had fulfilled the law as well as I had. He said again, "You don't swear that you lived on it five years." I could have got my claim all right if I had sworn the same as lots of others had done. I think I would have got my claim all right, but Brown, the registrar, was in the northern army and lost one of his legs in the war, and I was born in the south.

There was a fraction of ten acres which I paid $2.50 an acre for, where my house and barn stood. When I homesteaded the claim they offered to let me have the claim if I would pay $70 more. I thought he was a hard case and that I would wait until a new registrar was in the office, and then pay for it. When the new registrar took charge I did not have the money. A man named John Olverson asked me if he could live in the house while he built a house on his claim about a mile from there. I told him he could, but to look out for the place. I had a notice on the door about fire. He said he would do so, and if there was anything wrong he would let me know, and then he went and notified on it as a pre-emption. I waited until his time was nearly out to pay for it and prove up. I went back after his time was out and left the money at the office. He had no money to pay for it. When his time was up we had a contest, and he brought his daughter up and swore he had sold it to her for $30, and that she had taken it as a homestead, and I lost it. It was hard after all the work I had done and the money I had spent. It was the first time I ever knew that a girl could take up land.

I ran a gunsmith shop in Steilacoom, and rented a livery stable, which afterwards I bought, and now own, known as the Pioneer livery stable.

I left my home in 1846 and never went back. I have never seen any of my relatives until about two years ago; a second cousin paid me a visit. I have a brother in Atlanta, Ga., who is a Baptist preacher; two sisters and one brother in North Carolina, and the rest of my relatives are in Carroll county, Virginia. I would like to pay them all a visit, but I am getting old and feeble, and have poor health. I have had the la grippe the last two winters. When I was in the mines I had one shoulder broken and the la grippe has settled in it. I have not been able to put my coat on without help since last December. I worked four months on "perpetual motion." I got it to run over a minute on my first plan. I tried it on two more plans, but it failed to run. I am still well satisfied that I can make it run, but I have not got the money to go ahead without selling out some of my lots and my health is too poor at present to work at it. When my health gets better and property bears a little better price I intend to work at it once more. It is not for myself that I work at it for I have property enough to keep me the little time I have to live. I want to square up all of my old affairs before I die. I want to fix my grave and build a vault big enough for myself and a few relatives. I have always said, since I was 18 years old, that I did not want to be put under the ground. I do not crave any big fortune. If I had it I would just give it to the poor. All I want is just enough to leave my wife in comfortable circumstances and leave some for my poorest relatives.

Many interesting and striking incidents have come under my observation, and many have been experienced personally, since I have been on this coast, but I will refrain from mentioning but one other. It is concering the death of Andrew Byrd of Steilacoom, who was shot by a man named Bates.

At the time I was living five miles from Steilacoom on my ranch. Mr. Berry, who had bought and lived on part of my place, came out from town one evening about sundown and told me that Byrd had been shot and Bates was guilty of the dastardly deed. I tried to organize a company and go and hang Bates that night, but they would do nothing until morning. We all went to town the next morning and I called to see Byrd. He was still living, but was very weak. They would not allow me to speak to him, but to look at him strengthened the desire to see his slayer meet his just reward. I left the room with tears in my eyes, for he had always been a good friend to me. I had bought cattle and lumber of him, and had bought feed at his mill. I would sometimes tell him I did not have the money to pay for it, but he always said that made no difference, that I could have a $1000 worth if I wanted it. The more I thought of his untimely end the worse I felt about it, and I started out to get men to help swing Bates up. I found twenty men who agreed to hang him if Byrd died, but I wanted to string him up then, for it was plain that his intentions were to kill Byrd on the spot. Byrd died at 10 o'clock that night, and the next morning we adjourned to an old stable that stood near the jail. We put a pole out from the top of the stable, on which was fastened a big block and tackle. We took a big piece of timber, which we used for a battering ram, and tried the jail door, but we could not gain access. Steve Judson was then sheriff, and he braced the door on the inside. Philip Keach had taken a new ax up with him, and Thomas Headly took the ax and began to chop the door, but the door was so full of spikes that nothing was made by that effort. I then took the ax and placed it on the bolt which locked the door, and told Headly to strike the ax with the sledge hammer, which he did, and the bolt was cut in two. M.J. West was picking a hole in the brick with a crowbar, but I told him we would get the door open. I took the crowbar and pried off the casing the door was bolted to, and took the casing for a pry and broke it open. The door fell out toward the men, and Philip Keach had his arm slightly hurt. H.D. Montgomery made a rush to go past the sheriff, but he pushed him back. I then caught the sheriff by the arm and dragged him out the door, down the steps to the ground, and B. Dolbear got him by the other arm, and we held him, and the others rushed inside the jail. I was going to let the sheriff go, but the men told us to hold on to him and to take him down town, for they meant to hang Bates. While we were at work trying to get into the jail two lawyers were on hand, and they told us we would have to suffer for it. While we kept the sheriff down town the other men strung Bates up. When they were about to hang him he said he wanted to see old man Meeker, and tell him what to do with his property. He said he was willing to die if he could kill Dr. Spinning and Montgomery, brother-in-law of E.A. Light, and afterward the husband of Ellen Byrd. Bates was hung in the morning, and when I left town after dinner time his body was still hanging. Thus ended the life of one of the cowardly, dastardly fiends of crime which infested this coast a few years ago. Such punishment is rarely meted out to anyone in these days, and we all look at the prosperity of this grand country with pride. The strides we are making will be noted over the entire country, and we may expect as good and peaceable a people here as is to be found in any part of the world.

Captain J.G. Parker

Sent to the West in 1851 as an agent of the Gregory Express Co., Captain Parker recounts an interesting story about crossing the Isthmus at Panama. He gives a good account of early navigation on Puget Sound to 1881 including a tale of an exciting race between the steamboats Olympia *and the* North Pacific.

Olympia, Washington — February 10, 1893

In the spring of 1851 I left Detroit, Mich., for California. I intended to go on a sailing vessel via Cape Horn. Several sailing vessels in New York were advertised for that route, one for the isthmus of Panama and one for Nicaragua. Waited a fortnight in New York for the ship *Comet* to sail; she did not receive cargo fast enough to suit me, therefore I left New York on the initial trip of the fine side-wheel steamship *Illinois*, Captain Hartstein, for the isthmus of Panama. I came out as messenger for Gregory's Express company, the first express company established on the Pacific coast.

After a pleasant run of about eight days we made Navy bay, anchored abreast the mouth of the Chagres river and disembarked in the ship's boats. Landed at Chagres, a Spanish Indian village, represented by about 400 natives and Indians speaking the Mexican language, and 150 Americans and foreigners. It was their rainy season and the warm rain fell mildly, quietly, softly and steadily. The weather was excessively warm, so much so, that the natives had very little use for clothing, which consisted mostly of a hat and shirt.

The mode of crossing the isthmus of Panama at that time was to go up the Chagres river in bungoes (canoes) about thirty-five miles, to the village of Gorgona, then across by the mountain paths the balance of the distance to Panama, either by saddle animal or on foot. There was the usual rush and excitement of each passenger to get there first. Some enterprising Americans had succeeded in getting in running order a very small stern-wheel steamboat (the first that I ever saw), and I was exceedingly fortunate in being one of the favored few who were allowed to pay a monopoly price for the ride to Gorgona. This distance we made in two days, tying up at a small native village the first night, while some of the canoes that were heavily loaded were from four to six days making the same distance. The trip up the river was to me exceedingly novel and delightful. The scenery and climate were tropical, the foliage on the river banks was beautiful and alive with chattering parrots and monkeys. Some of our passengers interested themselves in shooting at alligators.

We arrived at the native village of Gorgona (the head of steam navigation for very light draft boats) at about 9 o'clock in the evening of the second day. Upon our arrival there, one of our passengers, Colonel Johnson, immediately hired a canoe and native crew, and started up the river for Cruces (the city of the Crosses), some ten miles further up the stream. He said he was in a hurry; that he was the first man ashore from the steamer *Illinois* and that he would be the first man to arrive at Panama. Some of the passengers went ashore and stumbled around in the dark. I laid down on my rubber express sacks and slept serenely.

On the following morning I was very agreeably surprised to recognize in my landlord of the "Hotel Casa Grande," (a one-story, one-roomed, thatched adobe hut) an old friend and acquaintance, Mr. White, formerly a prominent hotel clerk of Auburn, N.Y., and he entertained me in the most hospitable manner. At a late breakfast he informed me that two parties of our passengers mounted on mules had left that morning early for Panama. Mr. White noticed my impatience to start and quieted my nerves by furnishing me with a very handsome muscular mule and an excellent native guide, and bidding me a hearty "bueno dias," remarked: "You have the best mule on the isthmus and a No. 1 guide."

On account of the excessive amount of rain which had fallen, the trails from Gorgona were in a terrible condition. In my lifetime experience I have never seen any to compare with them. On the way over my guide cut side trails through cane brakes, and we floundered through innumerable swamps and passed numerous saddle and pack mules, hopelessly mired and abandoned by their riders and packers. Some of the poor animals were struggling for life, while others were lifeless animals and their packs abandoned.

Crossing the isthmus in 1851 was not what it is now, forty years later. I left Gorgona at 11 a.m. in a whole suit of good clothes. I arrived at Panama same day at about 5 p.m., and my clothes were all hanging in rags and ribbons. On the way over I saw nothing of the fellow passengers that had started ahead of me from Gorgona.

Approaching the city of Panama I met the editor of the Panama *Star*, accompanied by another gentleman, riding on mules, and astonished them by presenting them with copies of the New York *Herald* and *Tribune*. Two hours later Colonel Johnson was more than astonished when, as he came galloping into town, he heard the news boys crying: "Here's your extra Panama *Star*, arrival of the steamer Illinois and list of passengers."

My first experience regarding expenses of living on the Pacific coast was obtained at my first meal in the Lafayette Cafe, at Panama the evening that I arrived there. My dinner consisted of a slice of ham, a stale French roll, some butter suitable for axle grease, accompanied with a cup of wretched coffee. I laid a five-dollar gold piece on the counter. The landlord said that was right, swept into a drawer and gave me no change. Very politely I proffered him a cigar, he reached for it, but didn't get it. The next day I engaged board and lodging at a hacienda in the suburbs. The fare there consisted principally of fried plantains, tortillas, frigoles and chocolate.

There was no steamship at Panama ready for us to embark on for San Francisco. The *Illinois'* passengers and baggage came straggling across the Isthmus about a week later, and a large portion of the baggage was packed from Gorgona and Cruces to Panama on the backs of the natives; one native packed a small cooking stove from Cruces to Panama.

The city of Panama at that time consisted of a lot of dilapidated one story adobe buildings with tile roofs. The city was surrounded on three sides with a low adobe wall, the wall on the bay or water side having mostly crumbled away. Population about 3000, mostly Spanish, Portuguese, a few French and Germans; balance natives and Indians.

It was more than two weeks before a steamship bound for San Francisco made her appearance in the bay of Panama. On the same day one arrived from New York and one also from San Francisco. I went aboard the old original Pacific Mail side-wheeler *California*, Captain Budd. Both steamers were uncomfortably crowded with passengers. Here, I will state, the *California* was the first steamship that ever entered the harbor of San Francisco. Her destination at that time, on starting from New York in the fall of 1848, was Astoria, and the population at that time was about 1000. The *California* was one of a line of three steamships built by Howland & Aspinwall of New York to carry the United States mails from Panama to Astoria. The other two vessels of the line were the *Panama* and the *Oregon*. The *Panama* started from New York first, but put back disabled. The *Oregon* sailed next. She was commanded as far as Panama by Captain Forbes, a brother of A.B. Forbes, later agent of the Pacific Mail Steamship company. On our way up the coast from Panama we touched at several Spanish American ports, making the longest stoppage at Acapulco. The steamer remained at Acapulco the entire day and many passengers, myself included, availed themselves of the opportunity to go ashore. While strolling through the town with some comrades, we stopped to look on at a street gambling game. The proprietor was dealing Spanish or three-card monte. He tripped the ace, king and queen of clubs face down, and called for bets on the queen. I laid a $20 piece on the middle card and dropped my open penknife point down, pinning the middle card to the table. Turning the card over with the knife-blade still adhering, the dealer tossed his $20 to me and informed me that I could not play there any more. I had no desire to do so either then or since. There, several beef cattle were swam out to the steamer from the beach. A purchase rigged with lines was passed around their horns and thus they were lifted up and swung aboard.

After leaving Acapulco, the Panama or coast fever became prevalant on board and rapidly increased, causing an average of sixteen deaths daily, and during that time, every afternoon the steamer was hove to, to bury the passengers by the usual mode of service of sea burial.

On our arrival at San Francisco there was great excitement and a general rejoicing to meet friends and acquaintances and to obtain letters and the latest news. Flags were run up, salutes fired, and newspapers and letters were in great demand. My brother, E.H. Parker, came aboard to welcome me. He had left New York in 1849, came around the Horn in a sailing vessel, and was importing merchandise from New York and Europe. Among the pioneer names of prominent business men and firms that yet linger in my memory are Messrs. Jacob P. Leese, Macondray & Co., Dewitt, Harrison & Co., James Lick, Edward H. Parker, William T. Coleman & Co., Alsop & Co., Frank Godfrey, Case, Heiser & Co., Charles Mintern, Hussey, Bond & Hale, Nicholas Luning, Thomas H. Selby, Henry Haight, Forbes & Babcock (Pacific Mail Steamship company), Gregory's Express company, Isaac M. Hall, Ferris & Holman, Samuel Brannan, Clarendon Lamb, Tom McGuire, Parker house, Oriental hotel, Irving house, Sweeny & Baugh, of the Telegraph Hill and Presidio Point telegraph, G.B. Post & Co., Captain Charles Parsons, Charles Swain, Theodore Allen, Doctor Zeilie, James F. Hough, George Weller, Joseph Beach, Mat Scaring, Barney Johnson, John Clarke, Tom Battell, also Captain James S. Lawson, United States coast survey, who several years later had charge of the Puget Sound surveys and the United States survey schooner *Fauntleroy*. The captain is well and very favorably known from San Diego to British Columbia.

In 1851 San Francisco was represented by almost every nation and, to a great extent, all dressed in their native costumes. It was emphatically a cosmopolitan city. Everybody was busy, everybody seemingly in a hurry. Time was coin. Any laborer commanded $4 a day. Sailors were in demand at $100 a month, who had shipped in New York for $30. A number of vessels in the harbor were deserted and many sailors went to the placer diggings in the mining districts, where they averaged from half an ounce to an ounce a man. Board and lodging in San Francisco was from $100 to $200 per month. A large amount of business, wholesale and retail, was transacted in tents. Gambling games of all kinds were conducted openly in large tents, cloth and wooden buildings, reaching through from one street to another, and at night the gambling halls were brilliantly lighted and fine bands of stringed instruments were there under engagements at enormous figures. Those places were crowded nightly with representatives from the four quarters of the globe. Everybody made money easily and as easily let go of it. Sundays were observed by the closing of the principal wholesale and retail business houses and the community taking a rest, writing letters, going to church or to a bull and bear fight, horse races or a fandango.

In 1851-2 there were plying on the Sacramento river the steamers *Senator*, *McKim* and *Hartford*, followed years later by the steamers *Antelope* (Captain Poole), *Confidence*, *Thomas Hunt*, *Eclipse*, *Queen City*, *New World Chrysopolis*, *Nevada*, *Yosemite*, *Washoe* and the *Wilson G. Hunt*. On the Stockton route (San Joaquin river) were first the steamers

C.M. Webber, Urilda and *J.C. Bragdon*, followed later by the *Comanche, Helen Hensley* and *Kate Kearney*. The original fare on the steamer *Senator*, Captain Seeley, from San Francisco to Sacramento was $50. In later years when the fine steamers *Washoe* and *Chrysopolis* were competing for the trade the rate of passage was 25 cents. South of San Francisco, on the lower coast, the old steamers *Ohio, Sea Bird*, Captain Bob Haley, and the *Major Tompkins* were doing a good coasting business, followed later by the steamer *Senator*.

In May 1853, I left San Francisco on the steamship *J.C. Freemont*, which was then running to Portland, Or., for Olympia, Puget Sound, and Oregon. We had a pleasant run up the coast (six days) to Astoria. Instead of going up the Columbia river to Portland I left the steamer on the river at Rainier (French name properly spelled Regnier), a landing place on the Columbia, opposite the mouth of the Cowlitz river. The first acquaintance that I had the pleasure of forming in Oregon was that of S.G. Reed, Esq., of Rainier. Mr. Reed was a dealer in general merchandise there, and was then, as ever since, a genial, generous, enterprising man. Eventually Mr. Reed went in to business at Portland with W.S. Ladd, then a merchant there. I shall never forget Mr. Reed's numerous favors and his invaluable friendship.

Perhaps here it may be well to mention that the steamer *Gold Hunter* was the first ocean steamship that visited Portland.

In July, 1850, the first local or river steamboat that made a landing at Portland was the little side-wheeler *Columbia* (Captain James Frost) built at Astoria, then on her way to Oregon city. The *Columbia* was followed later by the steamers *Canemah* (Captain Hedges), *Black Hawk*, a propeller, the *Lot Whitcomb* (Captain J.C. Ainsworth), the *Multnomah* (Captain Fauntleroy, A.H. Steele, now Dr. Steele, in Olympia, purser). The side-wheel steamer *Fashion* (Van Bergen master, W.N. Hornton engineer) carried many emigrants and their outfits from the Cascades to Portland. The *Express* (Captain J.C. Ainsworth, George Hoyt, purser) was, I believe, the first stern-wheeler in Oregon and ran between Portland and Oregon city. The *Flint, Belle, Senorita, Mary Wasco, John H. Couch*, Captain Couch, and *Mountain Buck* were pioneer steamers of the fifties, running below Portland on the Willamette. The new steamer *Gazelle* (Captain Bob Hereford), exploded her boiler while lying at the wharf at Oregon City, above the falls. A very large number of spectators and passengers were killed and wounded. Mose Toner, the engineer, was considered the person to blame. He was not on board, but near by, and left that locality immediately for the woods and never returned. Captains Hoyt and Fease were also prominent and popular pioneer steamboat masters at that time, and as a whole the pioneer Columbia and Willamette river steamboat fraternity were a lively, agreeable and whole-souled party. The ocean steamships between San Francisco and Portland during the fifties and sixties were the *Gold Hunter, Oregon, Isthmus, J.C. Freemont, Sea Gull, Columbia*, Captain W.L. Dall; *America, Peytona,* Captain Nash; *Pacific, Brother Jonathon, Santa Cruz* and *Northerner.*

While at Rainier I had the pleasure of forming the acquaintance of Mr. Edward Warbass, who then had a store on the Cowlitz river. Hiring a crew of Indians and a canoe, Mr. Warbass accompanied me on my two days' journey, about thirty miles up the Cowlitz to what was then known as the Cowlitz landing. The first day's journey took us up to the forks of the Cowlitz and Gobar rivers. There we were furnished by the landlord of that then noted half-way house, "Hardbread's," with a supper for boiled salmon, potatoes, hard tack and herb tea. We retired early, and stretching ourselves out on our blankets that we spread over a dried cowhide on the puncheon floor, we were soon sound asleep.

Our next day's travel up the river brought us to the Cowlitz landing. There we were furnished by Mr. Goodell with an excellent supper and comfortable beds, which we heartily appreciated. On the following day, mounted on a fine mare that Mr. Warbass kindly insisted upon loaning me, I took the trail for Olympia, carrying with me Adams & Co.'s first letter express that was sent from San Francisco to the Sound, and in a fortnight after my arrival at Olympia established a regular express between Olympia and Portland which was continued for over a year, connecting with Adams & Co.'s express at the latter place. At that time, living between the Cowlitz landing and Olympia, were the pioneer settlers, Marcel Bernier, born in Oregon, Plumondeau; John R. Jackson, St. Martin; Joseph Borst, S.S. Ford and family, Frank Yantis and family, Antoine Rabbeson and M.R. Tilley and family. All the above parties had selected well-watered lands, and had horses, cattle and sheep grazing on the prairies.

Arriving in Olympia, wending my way among fallen trees and stumps, I dismounted at Sylvester's hotel, a log house on the corner of Second and Main streets. At that time Olympia was a small settlement, having a population of about 150, with an encampment of Indians on the west side of the bay. There were four stores. Several lumber camps were in operation in the immediate vicinity. The brig, *George W. Kendall,* was sailing on the route between Olympia and San Francisco. A.B. Gove was master, a brother-in-law of Hon. Elwood Evans, and a profitable business in spars, shingles, piling and square timbers was established. Later the brig *Kendall* was followed by the bark *Sarah Warren,* Captain Warren Grove. A weekly mail service, horseback and canoe, from the Columbia river to Olympia was first established in 1852 by Messrs. Yantis & Rabbeson, contractors. Edmund Sylvester was the original town proprietor of Olympia. Local transportation on the Sound was carried by canoes and sail boats. The people of Olympia were first regularly served by the sloop *Sarah Stone,* Captain Thomas Slater, plying between Olympia, Victoria, Bellingham bay and way landings. The custom house district was organized in Olympia in 1851 with S.P. Moses as collector.

The first newspaper, *The Columbian,* was issued on the 11th day of

September, 1852, by Messrs. Wiley & McElroy. The French Catholics built the first church in 1852. Then the Methodist denomination was represented by Rev. J.F. de Vore in Steilacoom. The Episcopalians were represented by Rev. Dr. McCarthy and Bishop Scott. The Presbyterians later by Rev. G.F. Whitworth.

When I arrived at Olympia, May, 1853, there were but a few board houses in the place, occupied mostly by the following named persons: Joseph Cushman, Esq., father of William H. Cushman of Tacoma, Simpson P. Moses and family, Captain S.W. Percival, A.W. Moore, P.M., J.M. Swan, Moses Bettman, Captain H.C. Hale and family, Milas and Silas Galliher and families, D.R. Bigelow, Isaac Woods, wife and brother Richard and John Woods, W.W. Miller, Patterson brothers, Offut brothers, J.K. Hurd, C.E. Weed, A.J. Baldwin, John Clarke, J.C. Patten, C. Ethridge, A.B. and A.J. Moses, Isaac Hawks and family and Edmund Furste. In the immediate neighborhood of Olympia, located mostly on their donation claims were Smith Hays, Ben Gordon, Andrew Cowan and family, Judge Gilmore Hays' family, Logan Hays and family, Thomas Prather, Captain C. Crosby, William Billings, A.J. Allen, Q.A. Brooks, Putnam Hays and family, David Chambers and family, Samuel Coutter, Andrew Chambers, Edwin Marsh, Frank K. Ruth, Gabriel Jones, Mr. Bush and family, John Kindred and family, Thomas Chambers, Samuel Ward, M.T. Simmons, Shelton brothers and families, Nathan Eaton, John Edgar and Thomas Linklighter. At that time Olympia was quite a smart village, and the community in general were all busy and happy.

In May, 1853, Steilacoom, consisted of a few small board houses, a couple of stores and an hotel. The hotel building was manufactured at New York or Boston and shipped out from there. The residents, so far as my recollection serves me, were Dr. Webber, Captain Balch, Mr. Martin and family, John M. Chapman, James Hughes and family and Philip Keach. L.F. Thompson was running the Sequalitchew saw mill and Frank Clark was then in his employ. William Packwood and George Schazer were then living on the Nisqually river. Fort Steilacoom had at that time a company of forty or fifty men. The Hudson Bay company, Dr. W.F. Tolmie, manager, had a trading post and station near the present site of Mr. Huggins' farm, the latter named gentleman then being chief clerk of the company.

The Hudson Bay company had two wooden steamers plying semi-occasionally between Nisqually, Victoria and British Columbia, the side-wheeler, "Beaver," Captain Swanson, and the propeller, "Otter," Captain Lewis. The "Beaver" was the first steamship that turned a wheel on the Pacific ocean, Columbia river or Puget Sound. She left the river Thames rigged as a brig and came out under sale, arriving at Astoria in 163 days. Soon after reaching Astoria Captain Horne, her first commander, steamed her around to Nisqually, then the Hudson Bay company's chief station on the Pacific coast, to the great astonishment of the native residents. She now lies hard aground, a wreck, on the rocks in the narrows at Vancouver, B.C.

It is believed that not a single person who came out on her in 1853 is still alive, and nearly all the company's officers, with a few exceptions, who received her on her arrival at the Columbia river, have passed away.

My first trip down the Sound, north, was in May, 1853, on the schooner *Rover*, loaded with lumber. Her crew consisted of two sailors, whose frequent pulls on a big brown jug resulted in my being obliged to take command after reaching the narrows. We followed the west passage of Vashon island until after dark. At the foot of Vashon island the Sound widened out to my view, the breeze was drawing free and I headed the schooner for the only light visible, distant about four miles across the Sound in a northeasterly direction. Crossing over I rounded the point, on which was a campfire, and hailed a man on the beach. He informed me that it was Alki point. Dropping the anchor and arousing the crew I accepted the invitation to go ashore in the stranger's canoe. It was then about 10 o'clock at night, and several of the residents turned out to greet us. Among those who were residing and engaged in business there were: Charles E. Terry, Dr. Maynard, S.W. Russell and family, Robert and Thomas Russell, George Frye, Hillory Butler and wife, the Holderness brothers and J.N. Low and family. There I learned that several parties, among whom were Arthur A. Denny and family, C.D. Boren, W.N. Bell and family and H.L. Yesler, had taken claims and were living up Duwamish bay, on the present site of the city of Seattle.

From Alki point I went to Whidbey island, on the sloop Sarah Stone, Captain Thomas Slater, and after a week's sojourning there returned to Olympia. Among the early settlers then at Port Townsend were J.G. Clinger, Captain Bacheler, L.B. Hastings, Captain Fowler, F.W. Pettygrove, Captain Frank Tucker, J.H. Van Bokkelen, and Albert Briggs. Around every settlement on the Sound were encampments of Indians. Generally speaking, the most of them were very independent in their conduct toward the whites.

At Scadget head, Whidbey island, Robert Bailey was fishing. In the vicinity of Penn's cove were the Crocketts, Samuel Hancock, Captain Robertson and family, Captain Coupe and family, Captain Barstow, Thomas Craney, Major Show, Samuel D. Howe, Captain Edward Barrington, J.M. Izett, the Ebeys and Robert and Nath Hill.

During the summer of 1853 the residents of Olympia received word that there was a large party of emigrants with ox teams, prairie schooners and horses near the confluence of the Snake and Columbia rivers, who, with great difficulty, were endeavoring to come to the Sound and willing to try the mountain trails. The citizens of Olympia and vicinity were desirous of extending a hearty welcome, and E.J. Allen called on me with a subscription list to raise funds necessary to cut a wagon road across the mountains by improving the Hudson Bay company's trail via the Natchez pass. The subscription then comprised the signatures of G.A. Barnes, Joseph Cushman and Moses Bettman, pledging $25 each. I persuaded Mr. Allen (now Major Allen of Pittsburg, Pa.) to be guided by my suggestions, to which he assented. Destroying his subscription list, I wrote a new one, headed it with $100 and sent him with it to Moses Bettman. Moses' pride was instantly aroused and down went his name for $200. George Barnes raised Bettman's $200 by subscribing $300, and Judge Cushman, not to be outdone by Barnes, subscribed $400. Captain Crosby also subscribed liberally, the amount I have forgotten, and Dr. W.F. Tolmie, then chief factor of the Hudson Bay company, also, which was greatly appreciated by all of us. Other residents in the vicinity donated provisions of various kinds and other necessary material, and a party of over fifty muscular young men from Olympia and vicinity fitted out with the supplies and equipments needed, commenced at Montgomery's on the eastern edge of the Nisqually prairie and cut a rough road across the mountains. Quincy A. Brooks and myself met the emigrants on the summit of the Cascades, near the Natchez pass. We were on horseback and attended by the celebrated Indian chief and guide, Quiemulth, Leschi's brother, leading a pack horse that carried our blankets and provisions. Among the party of emigrants that we met were: Charles Biles and wife, their sons David Charlie, Van Ogle, Asher Sargeant and family, Nelson Sargeant, Marion and sisters, Matt Baker and family, Isaac and Abram Woolery and their families and Himes and family. They were followed a couple of weeks later by another party, among whom were Isaac Carson, Rev. G.F. Whitworth and family, Mr. Boatman and family and the Wright brothers.

The first school house was built in Olympia in 1853 by the ladies of that place.

In the fall of 1853 Isaac I. Stevens, then recently appointed governor of Washington territory and superintendent of Indian affairs, arrived overland via Vancouver on the Columbia river, with his party of surveyors and engineers, then in the interest of the Northern Pacific Railroad company. The first legislative body of Washington convened over the store of J.G. Parker.

In the fall of 1853, Olympia becoming the capital of the territory, attracted emigration from many places, and the population increased quite notably.

In December, 1853, the following additional persons had arrived and were residing in Olympia and vicinity: Hon. Charles H. Mason of Virginia, secretary of the territory and one of the finest men that ever lived, Hon. Edward Lander, chief justice of the territory, Judge Monroe, associate judge, Judge Gilmore Hays, (who had crossed the plains from Missouri to California in 1849, returned home via the isthmus in 1850, and in command of a large emigrant train recrossed the plains with his family in 1852,) James A. Tilton, Elwood Evans, B.F. Kendall, Mr. and Mrs. Edward Giddings, Colonel William Cock and family, David Drewry, John Monroe, Captain A.B. Gove, Miss Gove, Major H.A. Goldsborough, Lieutenants Donaldson and G.B. McLellan, Captain U.S. Grant, who was then at Vancouver on the

Columbia river, Patton Anderson, United States marshal, Butler Anderson, J.C. Head and family, United States Attorney Clendenin and his wife, Dr. R. Willard, Benjamin Harnard, H.D. Morgan, John P. Hays, Alex Robinson and Dr. Lathrop.

The name of John Monroe recalls to memory the following incident that occurred in the fall of 1852: I missed him from our boarding house table, and was informed that he was in an adjoining room sick. I visited him after dinner and then called on his physician, who told me that John had typhoid fever. My reply to Dr. Lathrop was: "Doctor, John Monroe has the smallpox." And so it proved. We had Monroe moved to the old Thibault cabin and Messrs. Alex Robinson and Tal Bush, who years before had suffered from the disease, waited on him. A few nights afterward Monroe, while delirious, leaped out of his bed, and in his night clothes rushed out doors and ran into the bay. Of course, the cold water checked his perspiration and caused his death. Robinson and Bush laid him out, placed his coffin in a canoe, and Robinson and I paddled the canoe up the bay to the new burying ground, followed at a respectful distance by the mourners in a ship's row boat. I was in the stern of the small narrow canoe and Robinson was forward, but before we had gone half a mile I told Robinson that I would have to change positions with him and set to the windward of the coffin, as the smell from the corpse was unbearable. Robinson laid down on the coffin while I crawled over him and exchanged places. The grave was on a knoll near the beach, and six of us carried the coffin up the hill and buried it. I reeled back from the grave, feeling sick, faint and dizzy. That was the first case of smallpox that I ever heard of a white man's having on Puget Sound.

An interesting occurrence transpired near Olympia in 1855. I had a remarkably fleet riding horse, whose speed was known to none. A well-known business man in Olympia had a very fast saddle horse that he considered "ne plus ultra." He bantered me for a race and his proposition was accepted. The stakes originally were very light, but eventually increased to over $1500. The community in town and vicinity became greatly interested in the race and a large number of bets were made. At that time I was living about five miles from town, on Chamber's prairie, and guarded my horse closely, so much so that I had my rider sleep in the barn and keep the doors locked. The night before the race I was awakened by the sound of horses feet galloping near by. I went immediately to the stable and found the door unlocked. Lighting a lantern, I discovered my horse in a heated and steaming condition standing untied before an oats bin, eating freely, and my rider was in his bunk fast asleep. I immediately took in the situation, and two of us were immediately hard at work rubbing down the horse that had been stolen and raced at midnight with his competitor, as I learned several months later, and had been beaten twentyodd feet in a mile heat run on a straight stretch. We were on hand, though, the next afternoon, and on Bush's prairie ready for business. Such a crowd! Hundreds of people from far and near were there. Ranchers, farmers, townsmen and Indians came from fifty miles around, and bets were made of coin, horses, cattle, saddles and blankets. Everybody bet, and the excitement was intense. Finally time was called. The judges took their positions, and away went the horses. My opponent's horse crossed the starting line one length ahead, followed more closely to the first quarter, and were side and side on the second and third; but my rider had his instructions, and upon crossing the third quarter he leaned forward, and, with his whip in the air, gave a yell that would almost have petrified a Comanche Indian. Away went Bob from his competitor like an arrow from a bow, crossing the outcome amid the cheers of his many backers with a lead of forty-two feet. I have not bet a dollar on a horse race since.

The down Sound United States mails were first carried in 1854 by the American steam propeller *Major Tompkins*, Captain James Hunt and partner, John H. Scranton. The latter was considered to be the best single-handed talker in the territory. The *Major Tompkins* was shortly after wrecked while going into Victoria harbor, and was succeeded for the two years following, 1855 and 1856, by the iron steam propeller *Traveler*, J.G. Parker, master; William N. Horton, engineer. The *Traveler* was built in Philadelphia and brought around Cape Horn aboard ship in sections, put together again in San Francisco, and there purchased from Charles Pepters by Edward H. Parker. In 1855 J.G. Parker had her machinery taken out, and with the hull placed on board the sailing vessel *J.B. Brown*, Captain Mayhew, and shipped to Port Gamble, where she was launched, rebuilt and went into service on the Sound. This was the first steamer that navigated the Duwamish, White, Snohomish and Nooksac rivers. At the close of the Indian war in 1857 J.G. Parker sold the *Traveler* to W.N. Horton of Olympia. He chartered her to the Indian department, which used her for carrying officers and merchandise to the various Indian reservations. She was lost in March, 1858, off Foul Weather bluff, together with five persons, consisting of Captain Thomas Slater, T.H. Fuller, special Indian agent, George Hathway, John Stevens and a deckhand, name unknown. Two Indian deckhands succeeded in reaching the beach by swimming.

On my first trip up the Sound with the steamer *Traveler*, I landed the boat at the first wharf ever built in Seattle. All of my means having been invested in the boat and her fittings, I was about broke. Every man and boy in town came to the wharf to see the boat, and of course the community was greatly elated to learn that they would again have the United States mails regularly, and could travel by steam instead of canoe or sail-boat. I met Henry L. Yesler and told him of my circumstances and that I wanted some wood. "Well," he said, as he commenced whittling a big stick very fast with a big jack knife, "that is easily arranged. Go to the mill and tell George Frye to have the Indians wood you right up. Take all you want. Help yourself, captain, and pay for it when you feel like it." Yesler's was the first steam saw mill on Puget Sound, his machinery having come up from Massilon, O. On our way up to Steilacoom and Olympia that first trip, we steamed into Puyallup bay, as it was then called (later named Commencement bay), anchored off Swan & Riley's fishery, the present site of the Pacific mill, Tacoma, and there discharged a lot of salt, barrel heads, stores, cooper's tools and provisions.

In 1855 Indians were more numerous on the beach and waters of Puget Sound than gulls are now.

The steamer *Traveler* carried the United States mails between Olympia, Steilacoom and Seattle, and when urgent business demanded went to Victoria, Port Townsend and Bellingham bay. Victoria then consisted of the Hudson Bay company's station, in charge of Governor J.R. Douglas, chief factor, enclosed by a high stockade built in the shape of a large square surrounding the company's log warehouse, store and dwellings. The stockade, or fort, was guarded at the upper four corners with a turret offset, in each of which was a loaded cannon. There was one entrance, consisting of a very narrow gate, at which one of the company's armed servants was invariably on duty. Not more than six Indians were allowed within the enclosure at any one time, and they had to leave their blankets and arms outside the gate, which was near and facing the bay. Outside the stockade was a line of small one-story log dwellings that were occupied by the company's servants. The company also had an armed brig that frequently anchored in the bay under the range of the guns of the fort. Inside the fort were several cisterns and fresh water was obtained and distributed by filling barrels at a spring outside and the barrels then rolled over the ground to their destination. The store counters were so high and wide that all of the merchandise was kept out of reach of the Indian purchasers. Eternal vigilance was the absolute price of safety and security.

At Bellingham bay were Captain Paffle, Daniel Harris, Captain Henry Roeder, Edward Eldridge, Captain Utter and Colonel E.C. Fitzhugh.

The next steamer on the Sound after the *Traveler* was a little sidewheeler, brought on a ship's deck by Captain William Webster, called the *Water Lily*. She was quite frail and seldom went north of Steilacoom.

Early in September, 1855, the Indian war broke out. It was rumored that the Sound Indians were threatening the lives of the whites. A.L. Porter of Muckleshoot prairie warned the neighborhood settlers, and many of them went to the villages for safety. In October, 1855, the Indians on White river made a raid on the settlers, killing William M. Brandan, wife and child, Harry Jones and wife and George King and wife. The news of the murders spread rapidly and the alarmed settlers deserted their homes for the villages on the Sound. About that time the United States sloop-of-war *Decatur*, Captain Isaac Sterritt, steamed into Duwamish, now Seattle bay, and anchored. Her arrival was very opportune to the whites of Puget Sound. The *Decatur* was soon reinforced by the United States steamship *Massachusetts*, Captain Swartout. The United States revenue cutter *Jeff Davis*, Captain Pease, also rendered invaluable service.

A call for volunteers to organize into companies to fight the Indians was made by Acting Governor Charles H. Mason, and circulated from Olympia to Port Townsend. In Olympia no immediate response was made, until one day Judge Gilmore Hays rode into town from his home near by. He had heard nothing of the Indian murders. Being a very popular man, he was soon surrounded by the excited citizens. "Boys," said he, "this won't do," and picking up a pen, headed a call for volunteers with the signature "G. Hays." An hour later sixty names were signed. Two hours later a meeting was called and a cavalry company organized. At the first ballot for Captain, Judge Hays received fifty-nine votes out of the sixty, he being the only member of the company who voted for someone else. Judge C.C. Hewitt next formed a volunteer company at Seattle, and Colonel Isaac N. Ebey raised a company at Port Townsend. Captains Hennes, Maxon, Frank Shaw, Wallace and Charles Eaton also organized companies and reported for duty.

Block houses were hurriedly built in the settlements and patrol guards placed on duty. Adjutant-general James A. Tilton chartered the steamer *Traveler*, J.G. Parker master, and sent her to the Hudson Bay fort, Nesqualie, for arms and ammunition. None to be had. Then I was sent with the *Traveler* to Victoria with a requisition for arms and ammunition. About a half dozen cases of each were all the Hudson Bay company could spare, and we returned to Olympia. In conjunction with the United States military officials at Steilacoom, Lieutenant Slaughter, Captain Maloney and Colonel Casey, Fort Dent was established on White river on Pioneer John M. Thomas' present farm, and, down the river, on the Terry claim or farm, was established Fort Lander.

The *Traveler* transported most of the troops and all the supplies to and from each fort. To get the supplies up the rivers I had Mr. Bolten, who yet has his claim on the Sound just north of Steilacoom, build me a batteau, about sixteen feet beam by sixty feet keel. This batteau was loaded with military supplies and towed up the rivers to the forts. At Port Townsend, Colonel Ebey's company chartered the schooner *A.Y. Trask*, and the steamer *Traveler* towed her from Townsend up the Snohomish river and anchored just above the head of the slough that was then and there named, as also was the fort, after Colonel Ebey.

The Indian war lasted about a year. A number of men, women and children were killed, but as other pioneer narrators have given the details of the war in a very interesting manner, it is unnecessary for me to repeat the same.

One very dark night while steering the *Traveler* through the narrows, I noticed, what I supposed to be, two very large logs just ahead, and about thirty feet abreast of, and parallel with each other. As I had plenty of room I passed between them, when I discovered that the logs were large canoes, and filled with Indians that were lying in wait for us. The next instant the Indians had grappled on to our guards and were boarding us. Unknown to them I had a United States corporal and his guard of twelve soldiers aboard, who instantly turned out, and, with clubbed muskets, drove them off, several of them taking to the water like ducks. I called to the corporal to not shoot unless we drew their fire, and it was very lucky for Messrs. Lo that the soldiers were regulars instead of volunteers. The next morning, when the hands were washing deck they discovered several pools of blood and also four fingers that belonged to one of the first families of Washington. They had been cut off with a sabre that was swung by Assistant Engineer Girty. He struck at an Indian that was in a canoe holding on to our guards.

The volunteer forces under the command of Major Gilmore Hays, and the United States troops under command of Colonel Casey, routed the Indians and drove them over the mountains where the eastern Washington and Oregon military forces joined ours in putting the Indians to flight, and brought the war to a close.

In 1857 Hunt and Seranton returned to Puget Sound from California, bringing the propeller *Constitution*. They had a very rough passage up. She immediately commenced running between Olympia, Victoria and Bellingham bay, carrying the United States mails. Charles E. Williams of Olympia was purser. After several years' service she was converted into a sailing vessel and carried lumber between Port Gamble and San Francisco. The *Constitution* was followed in the winter of 1857 for a few months by the steamer *Wilson G. Hunt*, which was followed in the spring of 1858 by the stern wheeler *Julia*, Captain John Scranton; it being followed the same year by the side wheeler *Sea Bird*, Captain Wright, which was burned to the water's edge that winter in Victoria harbor. The *Sea Bird* was succeeded by the *Eliza Anderson*, which had nearly a monopoly from 1859 to 1868. In 1858 the fast side wheeler *Surprise* reconnoitered the Sound for business, but left shortly after for China, and there was destroyed by fire. The *Eliza Anderson* was commanded at different times by Captains Thomas Wright, D.B. Finch, W.C. Clancy, William Wait and David Wallace, Pilots John Suffern and Jimmy Wallace engineer. I have seen the *Anderson* leave Olympia for Victoria with her main deck crowded with cattle, her cabins full of passengers, cabin guards filled with sheep and her hurricane deck covered with boxes of fruit, poultry and other merchandise. The rates then were, Olympia to Victoria for passengers, $20; cattle, each, $15, and sheep, $2.50 per head; freight per ton, charged $5 and collected $10, and still "the old ark is moving along." At one time she was a mint for her owners.

G.A. Meiggs' tug boat *Resolute* was brought up, I think, in 1859, from San Francisco by Captain Pray, who was the pioneer in that line. The *Resolute* burst her boiler while towing a boom of logs in the Squaxon island passage. The explosion split the hull from stem to stern. Captain Tom Guindon, who was in the pilot house, was thrown up in the air, fell near the boom of logs, and had one of his arms and a leg badly broken. He was brought to Olympia in a canoe by the only other survivor, a deck hand, and some Indians. At my request he had Dr. A.H. Steele of Olympia attend to him. The doctor, being an expert surgeon, soon had him ship-shape again.

The next tow boat was the *Cyrus Walker*, Captain A.B. Gove, followed by the *J.B. Libby*, Captain Libby. The *Ranger no. 2*, a small side wheeler that was formerly running as a supply wood boat on the Sacramento river, and there owned by Jose Artega, was brought up by Captain John S. Hill and surprised the Victorians in 1858 by steaming into that harbor from San Francisco. Captain Hill was about forty days coming up, but eventually arrived there. She was the first general jobbing boat on the Sound. Her successor was Captain Hill's second boat, the *Black Diamond*, a small stern wheeler. In 1861 the Currys of Victoria placed the *Enterprise* on the Sound for a while, but she was withdrawn for the Fraser river trade.

In 1866 I was the lowest bidder for carrying the United States mails in steam vessels between Olympia and Victoria, and withdrew my bid from Washington by wire in favor of Messrs. Hale, Crosby & Winsor, who were to allow me an equal interest and to select a suitable steamer. But unfortunately, Captain Crosby had the high-pressure side-wheeler *Josie McNear* shoved on to him by the McNears of San Francisco, and steamed her up to the Sound. When I learned of the purchase I declined taking any interest or position whatever. The *McNear* had a long and very rough passage up, and arrived with the forward tube sheet of her boiler cracked. She was wholly unsuitable for the service required, and soon picked her owner's pockets in her efforts to compete with the *Eliza Anderson*, so the owners added a bonus of $40,000 with the *McNear* and traded her off to the Oregon Steam Navigation company for the *New World*. The latter boat soon financially swamped Messrs. Hale, Crosby & Winsor while competing with Captain Finch and the *Anderson*, and the *World* returned to the Columbia river. In 1869 the Oregon Steam Navigation company again put on the *Wilson G. Hunt*, Captain William Wait, which compelled the Wrights of Victoria and Captain Finch to build the then elegant side-wheeler *Olympia*, which arrived in 1870.

Then the Starr Bros. put on the side-wheeler *Alida*, commanded at different times by Captains Daniel Morrison and J.G. Parker, connecting at Port Townsend with the steamer *Isabel*, Captain C.E. Clancey, for Victoria. For a while the competition between the *Olympia* and *Alida* was strong, but was brought to a close by the Starr's paying a subsidy of $1400 per month to Finch & Wright. The *Olympia* was withdrawn and the Starrs took the "Olympia and Victoria" route and that business. The Starrs then had the steamer *North Pacific* built, at San Francisco by John Gates, commanded first by Captain Dan Morrison and later by Captain Charles E. Clancey and other now well-known masters. As soon as the *North Pacific* arrived the Starrs stopped the subsidy. Then Finch came on again with the *Olympia*, and a bitter steamboat struggle for the supremacy commenced in earnest. The boats were well matched as regards tonnage, models, fine lines, power and passenger accommodations; the "heft" of the owners' sacks being about equal.

The public was divided in the way of favoritism, the Victorians strongly favoring the *Olympia*, while most of the Puget Sounders backed the *North Pacific*. On preparing at Victoria for the second opposition trip up the Sound, both of the boats were ready for a grand trial of speed. They were beautifully decorated with their bright new colors. The thick black smoke poured out of the stacks, the pilots pulled their whistles simultaneously, passengers were hurried aboard, gang-planks were hustled in, the mates yelled their orders at the crew, the lines were let go and taken in, and the large and excited crowd of people that covered the dock to see the start, hurrahed with deafening cheers as the two boats left for Olympia and way ports. The *North Pacific* had the lead by about two and a half minutes, taking the circle course out of the harbor, while the *Olympia* started in pursuit, taking the cut-off between the buoys. At first the *North Pacific* seemed to be getting away from her rival, but she soon unaccountably slowed her speed somewhat, and the *Olympia*, then about a quarter of a mile astern, began to overhaul us.

I had just straightened out the *North Pacific* colors that had fouled the halliards, when there were cries of "Fire," "fire." Captain Morrison hurriedly gave me the wheel and rushed below. The passengers and crew were greatly excited. The between decks and hold were choked with smoke, and the chief and his assistants, Lon Cox and Sam Evans, were groping down below, lanterns in hand, to discover the origin of the fire. The dense, stifling smoke, soon reached the cabins, and many of the passengers were so alarmed that they rushed for life belts, and were ready for a stampede. In the meanwhile the mate, with his crew, coupled on the fire hose to the steam pumps, while some of the crew tumbled below with more lanterns, when suddenly Cox and Evans, greatly enraged, sang out simultaneously that they had located the fire, and then the air was turned from black to blue, with language that I do not remember ever hearing when I went to Sunday school. The origin of the black and intense smoke had finally been discovered and dispensed with. We soon learned the particulars. Only a moment before the *North Pacific* had left the Victoria wharf one of the *Olympia's* firemen, known as "Brick Top," was seen to jump ashore from the *North Pacific*. He had secretly gone into the hold of the *North Pacific*, opened the back connection of the boiler, and left the hanging doors braced open. That individual was in great demand on our boat for some time after the fire alarm. In the meanwhile the *Olympia* had gained on us so that she was close on to our starboard quarter, and going five feet to our three. But our crew rallied with a will, and though the *Olympia*, now the *Princess Louise*, was nearly abreast of us, the *North Pacific* picked right up, and as the smoke of additional barrels of pitch and resin rolled back from us into the face of Pilot Wait on the *Olympia* we steadily opened the gap, leaving her way astern, landing at Port Townsend wharf thirteen minutes ahead of our rival, amid the cheers of the people of that place. Soon after the advent of the *North Pacific* on Puget Sound, the steamer *Zephyr*, Captain Thomas

Wright, was plying between Snohomish city and Olympia. Other passenger, freight and tow boats, such as the *Phantom, Celilo, Wenat, Mary Woodruff, Chehalis, Addie, Ruby, Politkofsky, Favorite* and *Goliath* were plying the waters of Puget Sound.

In 1876 the Puget Sound Transportation company was incorporated, Thomas Macleay president, A.H. Steele secretary and treasurer, J.H. Parker manager, and built two boats, the Messenger, J.H. Parker master, and the *Daisy*, Captain Gil H. Parker, and purchased the steamer *Jessie*, Captain H.M. Parker, making a line from Olympia and adjacent waters to Mount Vernon, on the Skagit river, and LaConnor, on the Swinomish slough.

In 1881 a very spirited and strong competition was kept up for a season between the boats of the Puget Sound Transportation company and Starrs' line—the *Annie Stewart, North Pacific* and *Otter*—resulting in the Puget Sound Transportation company coming out victorious. In the fall of 1881 the Oregon Steam Navigation company purchased the Starrs' line and added some of its boats, the *Welcome, Idaho* and *Emma Hayward*. In the following year another company was formed, called the Washington Steam Navigation company, whose boats were the *City of Quincy, Daisy, Merwin* and *Washington*.

This carried us up to eleven years ago (1882), and the Puget Sound steamboat fraternity are sufficiently acquainted with the various steam boats, owners and officers that have since come upon these waters to resume my narrative, if they feel so disposed, and have not, with my readers, been killed by the task of reading these lengthy reminiscenses of your subscriber.

Captain John E. Burns

Captain Burns came around the horn in 1852. On Port Discovery Bay he helped build a small schooner, the A.Y. Trask, *launching it in 1854 which he claims was "the first seagoing American built vessel in the now State of Washington."*

Tacoma, Washington — April 28, 1893

Written from memory alone, this story, while possibly inaccurate in some minor detail, will, in the main, be correct and historically reliable.

In December, 1852, I sailed from Boston, Mass., for San Francisco on the clipper ship *Golden Eagle*, Fabens master, with a crew of six officers, thirty-two seamen and eighteen passengers. At this time of her crew there are now living at Port Townsend Captain Thomas Butler and James Keymes, and at Tacoma (or on board the schooner *Vine*) the writer. The ship was an extreme clipper, of a class not now built, and would "log" eighteen knots an hour. She was caught by the pirate Alabama during a calm and burned at sea during the war of the rebellion. Under all sail she was a picture of beauty of which no artist ever limned its equal.

All went well till off the Rio de la Plata, when a "pampero" stove her up forward, lifing her bowsprit from its bed, causing her to leak so badly we were compelled to 'bout ship for Rio de Janeiro, where, after eleven days and nights at the pumps, we arrived. While lying here four weeks for repairs we contracted yellow fever and a few days out thereafter buried at sea our fourth mate, Mr. Minor, of Salem, Mass., and instead of the "Land of Gold" we all (then young men) looked forward to, he went — whither? It was a sad incident for all of us. Coming up toward Cape Horn we began preparations that, together with the climate, drove fever from the ship, and our minds, as well. We "struck" skysail and royal yards and made all snug aloft by the time we were up to the Falkland islands. Then began the usual battle with the elements. Ice, snow, hail and all the delicacies of the season were encountered while doubling the Horn south of 60 degrees. In about four weeks, however, we had skysails and royal yards crossed, and under fair skies were plunging along toward our "terra incognito."

Without special incident we arrived at San Francisco about the 25th of April, 1853, where we, as did all others at that time, left the ship to commence the picking up of nuggets of gold. The first night ashore I paid 75 cents for a bunk with little bedding and big fleas. Next day I went out into the hills for nuggets, but found it out of season for the crop. I concluded to accept an offer to go to Puget Sound on the bark *Mary Adams,* with Captain William Webster, whose wife and daughter came with us. Mrs. Webster, now Mrs. Rogers, and Miss Katy are now living at Steilacoom, and are well known to all old settlers of Puget Sound. Miss Katy, then 2 years old, will, in the interest of history, pardon me for telling the fact that I was her nurse during the trip up, there being no girls to be had for that or any other service those days. There were on board several passengers who subsequently acted well their parts of the drama of civilization, then but begun. Many of them have since joined the great majority "over the river."

The writer remembers Daniel Brownfield, S.S. Irwin, Mr. Marr and son, James Keymes, John Tukey, John Cornish, Sprague Butler and "Old Chips," carpenter of the *Golden Eagle.*

Thirty days of fine weather brought us to the straits of Fuca. We first anchored at Soke, Vancouver island, and arrived at Port Townsend the same evening, May 30th. We, numbering about fifteen, made camp in Port Townsend, where the M.E. church now stands, and commenced cutting spars. We cut and hauled by hand, (no teams then) a cargo for the *Adams* off the present site of the town and in the vicinity of the present Lawrence street.

There were adjacent settlers as follows: Thomas Hammond, a Mr. Ross and Albert Briggs, who, with Pettygrove and Hastings, had families, and Charles Bachelder, Alfred A. Plummer, with about a half a dozen others, who were single. In Port Ludlow were J.K. Thorndyke and James Seavy, with families, and William T. Seaward without. They soon after began the construction of the Port Ludlow sawmill. This was in 1854. The settlements, in addition to the foregoing, were in Kitsap county. William Renton and Howard were at Apple Tree cove, where they built a small mill. They afterward finally located the present Port Blakely mills, after having one burned on Alki point by the Indians in 1855.

In Dungeness and Sequim, Clallam county, were George H. Gerrish, S.S. Irwin, Daniel Brownfield, John Bell, John Donald, Joseph Leary, Price Daniel Smalley, B.J. Maddison, Eljah McAlmond, Thomas Abernethy, Elliot Cline, John Thornton, Rogers and Charles M. Bradshaw, (late collector of customs.)

In Port Discovery were William Webster, John F. Tukey, James Keymes, John Cornish, Sprague Butler, Gallagher, "Chips," Benjamin Gibbs, Edward Lill, Tucker, James Allen, William Llewellen and myself, all single men. There was one white woman in Clallam county — Mrs. Bell. All these settlers located in the autumn of 1852 and the winter and spring of 1853, and were, till then, about all the settlers in the counties of Kitsap, Jefferson and Clallam. Island county had done a little better, having had more prairie land to attract settlement.

The length of this article will prevent giving all their names. Nearly opposite Port Townsend were the Ebey family, old man and wife, Isaac N. and Winfield, their grown children, and George, a nephew; Nathaniel D. Hill, Robert and Humphry Hill, William Engle, Samuel Hancock, Walter, John and Hugh Crockets, Captain Robinson, Captain Coupe, Captain Fay, Smith, afterward United States senator from Oregon, Judge Chenowith, Holbrook, Grennon and Thomas Craney, Edward Barrington, Mr. Alexander, Towers, Samuel Howe, John Gould, Charles Phillips, John Kinneth, comprising nearly all of the Island county settlers within dates given, and most of these with their families.

With the Indians numerous, troublesome and threatening, it did not at this time look very promising for a permanent settlement. In June was held the first territorial election, of which A.S. Buffington and myself were clerks. William T. Seaward and Daniel Brownfield were elected to the legislature, and nearly everybody else was elected to some office. July 4th was celebrated for the first time in that section. A "liberty pole" was erected about where Nathaniel D. Hill's drug store now stands. We constructed a temporary platform on which the orator declaimed. Alfred A. Plummer and myself led the celebration with a howling chorus of all the others, supplemented by some 500 to 1000 Indians "under spirit control." The water being bad we drank but little; still, strange to say, nearly everybody was "full." The festivities lasted nearly a week, during which time the greater part of the before named settlers took part. It was exceedingly "wild and woolly." Yet let me here say, seldom if ever were gathered together a more noble, stalwart and brave band of true men than was there assembled.

In December, 1853, James Keymes, William Llewellen and myself commenced the construction, on Port Discovery bay, of a small schooner of about fifty tons capacity. There being as yet no sawmill except Mike Summons' at Olympia (at Tumwater on Puget Sound), James Keymes and myself sawed, by hand, every foot of the lumber used in her construction (makes my back ache yet thinking of it). We often had to drop tools and stand off hostile Indians. However, after much hard, discouraging work, in August, 1854, we launched the first seagoing American built vessel in the now state of Washington. She was named by Captain A.Y Trask for himself, who presented her with her "colors" and a stand of small arms. Then and there was floated the first American flag on the first constructed seagoing vessel as above stated.

Illustrative of the times, and difficulties under which we labored, I may mention that our first anchors were of wood (crab-apple), weighted with large boulders, and our first suit of sail were two old ripped-up topsails from the ship *John Gosler*, and all our fastening we wrought from old iron and metal picked up from ships visiting the Sound for piles and timber at that time. Captain Trask is now one of the board of pilot commissioners for the state of California, living in San Francisco.

As this schooner served through the war of 1855-6, and that war being the pivotal center of all old settler stories thus far, I will follow up to its commencement with some of its history, hitherto unwritten — so far as the lower Sound counties are concerned, and with which this schooner was prominently connected.

We fitted out the *A.Y. Trask* as an Indian trader. Bought and mounted two nine-pounder guns and a brass piece on the "bitts," also small arms, ammunition and trade goods, at Victoria from the Hudson Bay company, who then represented the British government in British Columbia. After constructing, boarding, nettings and getting ready for sea, under a little private understanding with Governor Douglass, we cleared for port or ports in the Pacific ocean, and notwithstanding the fact of being under the American flag, we began trading, or fighting as the case might be, with the then barbarious savages of the west coast of Vancouver island.

Without describing in this article the various picnics we had with them, I will pass on to October, 1855. While at Steilacoom discharging oil, etc., from the preceding voyage, came the first news of the outbreak of the Indian war. My namesake, Dr. Burns, came riding into town hatless and breathless with the news of the killing of A.B. Moses and Mr. McAllister of his party up the Puyallup. At this time the wind was blowing a gale at southeast. We made sail at once, and before a howling gale made the run to Port Townsend before daybreak next morning, carrying the first news of hostilities down the Sound. Within the two weeks following, the *A.Y. Trask*, with the writer in charge, was chartered by the government to service throughout the war and until discharged.

A few words here of the organization of the territory for defense may be in proper sequence. The military was represented by some three or four companies of the Fourth United States infantry, who were at this time stationed at Fort Steilacoom, where the insane asylum now is, Vancouver, on the Columbia, and Walla Walla, east of the mountains, with detachments at Bellingham Bay and San Juan island. The volunteers, First regiment, embraced some eight companies in all, all organized west of the mountains, as I remember, in which were two battalions. The southern, from and operating principally in the up-Sound counties, was composed of one irregular and two regular companies. The northern, of which but little has hitherto been written, was composed of three companies, Captain Ebey's, Captain Smalley's and Pat Kanim's (Indian). Governor Curry of Oregon had a regiment, or part thereof, in the field in eastern Oregon.

The navy on Puget Sound was represented by the steam frigate *Massachusets*, steam sloop-of-war *John Hancock*, sailing sloop-of-war *Decatur*, United States surveying steamer *Active* and revenue cutter *Jeff Davis*; chartered and volunteer vessels were the schooners *A.Y. Trask*, *R.B. Potter* and steamer *Traveler*. This is substantially correct, if not entirely accurate. The Northern battalion, at first Captain Ebey's company only, but later on including Captain Smalley's and Pat Kanim's companies, then under command of J.J.H. Vanbokellen, with the rank of major, was the one but little written of hitherto. Being closely connected and personally acquainted with all its members, I will devote the remainder of this article to events and incidents connected therewith.

The *Trask*, on a dark and stormy November night, embarked Captain Ebey's command of about sixty-five men all told. The officers were: First lieutenant, Samuel Howe; second lieutenant, James Keymes; surgeon, Samuel McCurdy; orderly, Sergeant Vanbokellen (afterward major). The battalion quartermaster was R.S. Robinson. The file embraced nearly all of the names of settlers before mentioned. I may mention, the names of Charles M. Bradshaw (late collector of customs) and Hugh Crocket, now living at Puyallup, as two who are well-known here, who were among the "high" privates. The next day we arrived at Tulalip, near the mouth of the Snohomish river. We were ordered to blockade and hold the river until a fort could be built; so, preparing for the worst, we erected a barricade of four-inch plank around the schooner, which was fairly bullet proof. The planks we procured from a small mill then recently built and owned by Charles Phillips, John Gould and a Mr. Hall, on what is now the Tulalip Indian reservation. As soon as completed we got under way and worked our way over the mud flats into the river where Everett now stands. Thence up about a mile above the present site of Lowell to the junction of Ebey's slough (named for Ebey by us) where we disembarked the company, then anchored and moored the schooner mid channel, and held the river till the fort was built, some five weeks. Thus began the first settlement of the Snohomish country, Fort Ebey being the first building erected therein. After the completion of the fort I was ordered out to patrol the Sound, transport troops and supplies and keep off northern (British) Indians, etc.

The object sought in blockading the Snohomish river was to keep the Yakima and Klickitat Indians under Kanniakan from forming a junction with the kindred Sound Indians via Snoqualmie pass and river. The principal chiefs of the Sound hostiles were Ouhi, Leschi, Kanasket and Nelson.

The Trask served throughout the war, was with the Massachusetts and Traveler in the battle of Port Gamble. Was in 1857 sold to the British government, and while surveying in northern waters was lost in Chatham straits, thus ending her history.

In the summer of 1856 the northern Battalion moved up the river to Snoqualmie Falls, and one mile below erected Fort Tilton, and one mile above Fort Alder, (headquarters). In August the *Trask* was ordered to Snohomish river with supplies for the forts, which were then about out of provisions and stores, transportation being very difficult and only made by river and in canoes. John F. Tukey (now of Port Discovery) was sent as agent to get the supplies up the river. He went over to Holmes harbor Indian reservation and gathered up about 130 Indians with some thirty-five canoes. We loaded the stores therein, leaving the schooner in charge of the first officer. Tukey and myself started up the river with the goods. The Indians were sullen and ugly. While we were not afraid, we were a little nervous, especially at night. We got up all right after three days and nights poling and paddling, receiving a warm welcome from the hungry boys, who were eagerly expecting us. Tukey and I pushed on around the falls ahead of the supplies to headquarters, Fort Alder.

Here occurred a humorous incident. While a little raw considering the times and circumstances, I may be permitted to relate it. The boys were entirely out of food, except dry beans. Shortly after arriving at the fort, and before the arrival of the "grub" from below, dinner was announced. At a luncheon-table some twenty feet long seated in dignified sequence and order, at the head a major (Gouldsborough), thence down along its side, according to rank, some twenty or more officers, ending with Lieutenant George Ebey (the wag of the command) at the foot. Military etiquette prevailed to such an alarming extent that I began to feel somewhat nervous. The post chaplain invoked the divine blessing on ("beans straight") the dinner. Then occurred as follows: "Major Van B., may I assist you to some beans? Captain S, may I assist you?" and so on down to Ebey, at the foot of the table. He sat with his chin resting on his hands, his elbows on the table, with an ominous twinkle in his eyes, when the query, "Lieutenant Ebey, may I assist you to some beans?" came, the startling answer, "Nary a G___d___ bean, I thank you." Dignity was dished, if not beans, and in spite of the strongest effort at self-control, the dinner broke up, to draw it mildly, in confusion.

The battalion later moved through Snoqualmie pass, forming a junction with volunteers from Oregon. The command drove the Indians across the Columbia, and eventually, at the battles of Grande Ronde and Powder river, in eastern Oregon, under Colonel Shaw (called by the Indians "Pil Letate," red-head), in command of the brave volunteers, fought the bloody and closing battles of the war. Then and there ended, not only the Oregon Indian wars, but forever the power of the dangerous and dominant Indians of the northwest.

Then and thus began the permanent foundations of the young but vigorous civilization that has since blossomed to a perpetual fruitage in the great American northwest.

This article, containing as it does a great deal of historical detail, much of which will be new to present readers, is my excuse for its somewhat perhaps tedious detail.

W.W. Plumb

An 1851 emigrant relates the tale of his risky adventure horse trading by the roadside. In 1853 he was a customs inspector on Puget Sound.

Centralia, Washington

I have been a reader of the *Weekly Ledger* for the last year and have read a great many accounts of the trials and vexations and experiences of people while crossing the plains, and of the difficulties they encountered in settling in Washington and Oregon, and I finally concluded to give some of the leading points of my experience in crossing the plains and in settling at Olympia on Puget Sound.

I left Michigan City, Ind., on the first day of April, 1851, with a horse and buggy. I had the buggy very comfortably rigged out with good oilcloth top and curtains all around, and I had fixed them so I could button them down so I could place my things along one side of the buggy, take my blankets and lie down on the other, button the curtains down closely, and I had a comparatively pleasant bed room. The first day I traveled about twenty-five miles, and struck camp. Most people thought when I started I would never live to get through. They said when I went to camping out that I would not live long, but I thought I would make the trial while I was in the settled portion of the country. The next day I got into Chicago. I stayed there one night and all next day. It was snowing hard the next morning when I pulled out again. Nothing happened worthy of mention for several days.

I crossed the Mississippi river at a little town called Albany, in the state of Illinois. I traveled on a couple of days and overtook two ox teams driven by two young men. The next day we traveled on moderately. I concluded I would not go any faster than they did, as the roads were bad and it would favor my horse. Along in the afternoon there was a young fellow rode up behind us. He had a beautiful mare 6 years old, and as my horse was an old one I thought I would try and make a trade with him. He said he would not trade, that he had traded horses two or three times, and had been cheated so badly that he thought he never would trade again. Soon after this we came to a farmer's house and the men with the ox teams asked the proprietor how far it was to the next house. He told them it was three miles. They said it was farther than they wanted to drive that night and if they could get corn and hay from him for their teams they would stop all night. I spoke to this young man again and bantered him to trade horses. I wanted him to get down and examine my horse. I told him there was a chance for him to make up for some of his losses, as I would have to stand the share let me trade with whom I would, and that if he did not ask me too much boot I thought we could trade. He finally said he ought to have $10. The first thought that struck me was that he had stolen the brute, the next that maybe the horse would not work in harness. I told him I thought he was rather high in his price, and I asked him if she would work in harness. He said he did not know. I told him if he was willing I would put the harness on and try her, and if she would go I would give him the $10, and if she would not go I did not want her. He said if I did so he would not be responsible for any damages. I told him I did not ask him to, so he took his saddle off and I began putting the harness on. While I was doing that he said he would put the saddle on my horse and try her under the saddle. I told him he could do so. When I got his animal hitched up I took her by the bit, thinking to lead her around a little and see what she would do. The moment she started forward she flew back and began to rear. She tried to throw herself, but I finally got her stopped. He rode up to me and wanted to know if I was going to give him the $10. I told him no, that she would not answer my purpose. He then said he guessed he would go on and he put whip to my horse and away he went. I first thought I would get my gun and put a ball into him, but later I thought it was a good thing, for the animal he had left was worth a dozen of the other, even if she wouldn't work. I then didn't wonder that he complained of getting cheated every time he traded horses. The next morning I spoke to the man where we were stopping and asked if he had a yoke of cattle or steers that he would trade for my buggy, for the men whom I was with said if I could get a yoke of cattle to put with theirs, that I could put my things in their wagon, and we could take turns riding horseback, and come through together. The man where we had stopped told me that he had a cow and a four-year-old steer that he had broken to work together. We went down to the yard to look at the cattle and found his wife there milking. When he pointed out the cow to me his wife asked him if he was going to trade the cow off. He told her that she had been teasing him for the past two years to get a buggy, and said that I had a very nice one and wanted to trade it for a yoke of cattle. She flew in a passion and said she would leave the place if he traded the cow off. I told her to hold on and not say any more; that I wouldn't have the cow; that I never had been guilty of making a fuss in a family, and I was not going to begin now. I left the yard and went to the barn, put the harness on the mare and hitched her up to the buggy. I took her by the bit and started to lead her and she commenced rearing again. I finally got her started, patted her, rubbed her and talked to her, and got her so that she would walk a rod or two, and then she reared again. I kept on working in this way with her for I was satisfied that I could get along as fast as the ox team would any way, if she did not break the shafts of the buggy.

She finally got so, about 3 o'clock in the afternoon, that she walked along first rate. I then got my lines rigged and got into the buggy, and I was never more tired in my life, but from that time on for three mornings she would have spells of flying back and rearing. After the third morning I could hitch her up and she would travel right off. The men that were with me laughed at me, and told me that they were satisfied if the young man knew how well I had got her to work he would be back after the $10.

Nothing more of any note transpired until I got to Cainsville. There we had to get our outfits with which to make our start across the Missouri river. I found some men there who said they had been across the plains two or three times, and that it would be impossible for me to cross with my buggy. Here I found a man who had fourteen head of loose cattle, and he told me he wanted to get someone to drive them for him. He said if I would turn in with him and drive these cattle that he would furnish me with a horse and I need not do any chores or stand watch at night. He said he would board me and take my things through. I told him I had my outfit and provisions all bought. He said he would take them off my hands and pay me for them. He was all ready for a start, and I had no further use for my horse and buggy. I got an auctioneer to get into the buggy with me and we drove around through the principal streets, he crying off the horse and buggy at auction. It was only a short time till we got a bid of $257, and I told the auctioneer to let it go at that. The next day the train started out, and with it the man I was going with. We crossed the Missouri river and traveled about twenty miles. The next day we started on and it commenced raining, and we had the most terrific thunder and blinding lightning I ever saw. We got to the Elkhorn river that night and camped. It rained hard all night, the river was rising very fast and the ferryman was advising people to hold on, as the rain would soon stop and the river go down. But it kept raising more and more, and we were lying in camp, while the other trains would cross and go on. During the day I heard the man whom I was with, and a neighbor of his who was traveling with him, in conversation about turning back. I went to the man and asked him if he was going to turn back, and told him if he was I wanted to know it, so I could get in with some of the trains that were passing. His friend told me that he did not believe in men that had nothing to risk, urging men that had a good deal of property into danger and difficulty. I replied that I was not urging him into difficulty at all; that I merely asked him if he was going to turn back, so if he was, I could find other means of going on. The river by this time had got out of its banks and they wanted I should go over the river and see how things looked on the other side and come back and tell them what I thought about it. I told them they could go over as well as I could and see for themselves. They insisted on my going, so I started. It had been raining all this time and the river was rising fast. It rained harder at night than in the daytime. I went about a mile from the ferry, where a small branch came into the river. It was a very deep ravine, not more than twenty or twenty-five feet from one bank to the other, and they would have to take wagon beds and ferry across it, so I turned back. I had only gone a few rods when I met them. They had hitched up the teams and crossed the river and came on. We went out on the banks of the ravine and selected the highest spot of ground we saw and camped. We got two or three wagon boxes emptied and went to calking and fixing them for ferrying. Those that had tents struck camp and near morning the water got up so high that it run into some of their faces before they woke up. We all got up and went to work. We secured the wagon beds and everything else as well as we could, for it was still so dark we could not see only when it would lightning. We all got into the wagons and lay there till light of day. The river bottom was about four and one-half miles wide, and it was all covered with water. The women all burst out crying, and the men also. I saw and studied awhile. The coyotes, moles, snakes and mice came all around our wagons. The wind was blowing very hard up stream. I got mad and began to rip and tear at the men. I had often heard it said that profane language never did any good in the world, but after I had ripped and and swore at those men a while they began to calm down and wanted to know what they should do. I told them to take one of their wagon beds that was calked and put three men into it and let them have a blanket or sheet; let one take a paddle and start for the ferryboat, and the man that steered could keep quartering with the wind, and when they got a little too far down stream let the men hold up the blanket or sheet and the wind would take them quartering across. They got the ferryboat to come, and in it they took the women and children, tents and provisions to the other side of the river. The men on the ferryboat told them that they must go to ferrying their other stuff in the wagon beds; that they could not keep them any longer. The men aboard the boat said they were all bound for California. They said they had come up the night before and chartered the ferryboat to ferry themselves across, and they could not be detained, so we went to ferrying. Some of the time the water was shallow enough so that we could wade. We worked there nine days before we got the train over. In the meantime, while I was helping to ferry the man and his neighbor, whom I have mentioned before, made up their minds to turn back. The man I was traveling with began selling off his provisions while I was on this side of the river. When I got back on the other side I went to the wagon and found a sack of flour of 110 pounds and a sack of corn meal. My coffee boiler and frying pan were lying with those sacks of flour.

About this time there was a man came and looked in the hind end of the wagon and he saw that the things had been taken out. He asked me what I was going to do with those provisions. I told him I was going to take care of them. He said that they belonged to him; that he had bought them and paid for them. I told him that he would not get them unless he got them from under my dead carcass. I told him that the things belonged to me; that I put them in and took them out. The man came around whom I had started with, and he called to the man that was talking to me, and they settled the matter some way, I don't know how, but I kept the things. Then I had to hunt another way of traveling. There were a couple of men in the train whom I was slightly acquainted with in Indiana. They told me they were driving a couple of teams for a woman, and that they thought if I bought some kind of team to put on with her team that she would take me through. So I went and spoke to her about it. She wanted to know how much stuff I had to carry. I told her I would go and bring it up so that she could see just what I had. I went and packed my stuff up. The man whom I had been traveling with had a pair of cows that were broke to work, and he wanted to sell them, so I drove the cows up for her to look at. She and the men talked the matter over and agreed that if I would turn in what provisions I had and buy that yoke of cows and put on with her team, that they would see me through, and that I need not stand guard at night or do any other work. I was to let her have all the extra provisions I had. I bought the cows and yoke, etc. One of the cows had a calf the second day after I bought them. We killed the calf and started on the second day from that time. I was ahead of the teams and I met this woman's husband in the road. I was satisfied then that there would be trouble in camp from the fact that one of the men and the woman were sleeping together every night, so I made up my mind that I would have nothing to say to any one, either one way or the other. We traveled on and the second day the woman's husband came to me and asked if I knew anything about the matter. I told him I hadn't a word to say on either side; that I had made a bargain with his wife and those other men to take me through and that I didn't want to get into any muss; that I wanted to get through in peace. The next morning they tackled me for telling the old man. The old man was by and he stopped them immediately, and the next morning the old woman and one of the men tackled the other man's brother and accused him of telling the old man. The young man drew his revolver, cocked it, and told them that if either one of them gave him just one more word that he would kill them both, for they were not fit to live. The next day the young fellow wanted me to drive the ox team, so I took hold and drove that day, and the young fellows during the day made up their minds to turn the old man off and claim the teams. The men that were in the train came to me wanted to know what I knew about it. I told them that I would not have a word to say as long as I was obliged to travel with them, but, when I could get any other way to travel, then I would tell what I knew. I had in the meanwhile thrown away a good many things, thinking to lighten up the load, but these men gathered them up and put them into the wagons again, and of course that made the things theirs, not mine. We traveled along without much being said, until we got above Fort Laramie, then early one morning some of the men came to me and said that I must throw out everything of mine in the wagon that I could possibly spare. I told them I would throw out my things and they would pick them up and take them along as theirs. One of them said that if I didn't get and throw them out he would. "Well," I said, "don't let you and I quarrel. You get in and set out all of my things, my provisions and every solitary thing I have got in the wagon." "Well," he said, "I want the company to understand that I didn't turn you off." "Oh, no," I said, "you didn't turn me off, but you want me to throw away my things and then you pick them up and claim them for yours, and I furnish a team to help haul them. I don't propose to do any such thing," so I made him get in and set out all my things. I piled them up by the side of my tent and got a family to watch them while I went ahead. I found a man there that would take me in, and packed my things up there, and hitched my cows on with the other man's team. The second night the two companies camped close together and they got together and called the old man and his wife and the young man that had come through with her, and told the woman and the young man if they heard another word of complaint from her husband that they would set them beside the road to take care of themselves, and would not allow them to travel in the company at all. From that time things went on quite smoothly.

There was a great many minor difficulties transacted along the way, but it would take too much writing to give an account of all the vexations and trials that people had in crossing the plains. I got along very well till I got within a short distance of The Dalles, Or. After crossing the De Shute river up near The Dalles, the road that led to Barlow's gate turned to the left. After traveling on that a short distance I came to a family in camp beside the road. The man had been very sick but was getting better. He asked me if he could get me to help him, said he was getting better and wanted to get along. I told him I would help him, and his wife went with me and helped drive the cattle up and showed me how the cattle were yoked together, and I yoked them up and we started on. We got to Barlow's gate the next night just at dark. We stayed there all night. There were two other families stopping there, also a man on his way from Oregon to meet some friends that were coming on the plains. I sold him my horse, and I persuaded the men that were there to come back to The Dalles and send their families to Portland, Or., by water and let the men drive cattle loose over the mountains. I then came from The Dalles to Portland by water, stayed in Oregon through the winter and in the spring I started for Olympia. I got there about the last of May, 1852. I stayed around the Sound two or three weeks. I went to Tumwater and got work there on a mill. I met I.N. Ebbey and got pretty well acquainted with him. I had met him before. He was one of the county commissioners at that time. The men about Olympia sent me an appointment as justice of the peace, about the last of June. Ebbey's folks came across the plains the summer I did. I met him on Burnt river when I was coming across.

I worked around till toward fall. The people decided to have this part of the country set apart from Oregon, and this Colonel I.N. Ebbey was opposed to at that time. I speak from personal knowledge, from conversation I had direct from him.

I shall have to digress a little from what we are writing about and mention some other facts. A few days before the convention was to be held there was a ship in the Sound doing business under false papers. The collector of customs came to me and wanted that I should be deputized to go and seize the ship. Some of the men had deserted the ship and they let it be known that she was doing business under false papers. The collector of the port, Simpson P. Moses, deputized me to take the ship and sent me to Steilacoom and get some soldiers to assist me. I started for Steilacoom in the revenue boat with the men who had deserted the ship. We got a file of men, came back toward Olympia from Steilacoom, where the vessel lay at anchor for want of hands to move her. They were glad to see us coming. They thought we had captured the men and were bringing them back to work on the ship, but when the captain and mate found what my business was the captain was very hostile. I had had a little difficulty with the captain before.

He had employed some Indians to help get out his cargo of timber and then refused to pay them, and I had gone to him with the Indians to get their pay. The Indians had learned that I was an officer and so came to me and entered their complaint. He was very hostile when I first approached him but I took the matter very quietly and finally succeeded in getting him to pay the Indians, and as soon as he saw me aboard the ship he was terrible angry. I told him that if he wanted to stay aboard the ship he must go into his cabin and stay there. So he went down into his cabin. They had just been to dinner on board, and he ordered the cook to wash up the dishes and put them into a basket and take them into the cabin. When the cook started for the cabin I stopped him and told him I wanted the dishes. He said the captain told him to take them into the cabin. I told him that I wanted him to understand from that time on that I was captain of the vessel as long as I stayed there, and that I didn't want him to meddle with a thing about the ship without asking me.

There was a little sitting room on the deck of the vessel. I set the men that were with me to getting some fresh meat and potatoes that were on board, ready to eat. I went to cleaning the sitting room and found that there were two captains on board, an Englishman and an American. When I started to clean this room the American came to me and asked me what I was going to do, and I said that I was going to set a table there and have something to eat, and he said if you eat in that room I shall show fight. I told him if fight was what he wanted just to say the word and he could have all he wanted, and sent him down in the cabin with Captain Thomas, telling him not to let me hear another word from him if he didn't want to be set ashore. We got our dinner, and after that was over we hoisted the sails and anchor and started for Olympia. We run up as near the city as we could and cast anchor again. I then set the men to taking down the sails and stowing them away. The next morning I sent a note to the collector, saying that I would have to start the next morning for Monticello to attend a convention, and that he would have to come or send some one to take charge of the vessel while I was gone. The next morning he sent a man by the name of Hedge to take charge of the ship.

In the fall of 1855 our Indian war broke out — pretty early in the fall, too, and by my being a justice of the peace I had a good deal to do with the Indians and I was very prompt with them. In everything I said or did I let them know that I was a friend to them as long as they behaved themselves. I took a great deal of pains to settle their difficulties amicably with both parties.

The first call for volunteers was for three months' service. When that time expired they issued another call for six months, or till the war was closed. On the second call I enlisted on the 1st day of February, 1856, and soon after that time the Klickitat Indians, on the east side of the mountains, came over on the White river and got all the volunteers they could from the Indians on this side. They made a stand on what was known as Connell's prairie, and Colonel Casey started out with troops from Steilacoom, crossed the Puyallup river and camped at the foothills, where the road turned to go to Connell's prairie. He then sent a courier to Olympia to Governor Stevens, requesting him to furnish all the volunteer help he could. On the next day he gave orders for the company that I was in to be dismounted and go into the woods to Colonel Casey, but he allowed us eight men to stay and take care of the horses, saddles, bridles, etc. On the next day the teams were loaded with tents and provisions ready to start. Captain Thuness ordered myself and five other men to go as a guard for the wagons. We got across the Puyallup river and struck camp about eighty rods from Colonel Casey's camp. The next morning early we heard a gun fired at Colonel Casey's camp, and when we reached the camp we found that they had the chief of the Indians there, badly shot. He had sneaked up and hid behind a log and was just going to shoot the sentinel when he was discovered and shot through the shoulder. About 8 or 9 o'clock the captain informed me that I would have to go as an express messenger to Governor Stevens, and that I must go by way of Yelm prairie. I did not get started till about 11 o'clock, and he wanted me to get there by sundown. I had five loose horses to drive in front of me. I told him I would go, but that he must send some men to get me safely across the Puyallup river, which he did, and I arrived at Olympia that night before sundown. I was well loaded, for nearly every soldier had to send a piece of the old chief's clothing or hair to some of their friends. On my way to Yelm prairie, when I left the Nisqually plains where the road runs into the woods, I found five Indian tracks which were very fresh, and they followed down to the ford where they had to cross to come out on Yelm prairie, and I felt pretty confident they were not far from the ford when I crossed. The next day was Sunday, and on that day within ten miles of Olympia there was a man by the name of White, his wife and another lady started to where there was going to be a meeting held. But they did not hold the meeting, and they went to a house where there was a sick friend. When they started for home in the afternoon they had to pass a point of timber. The man was walking and driving the horse. There were five or six Indians rode out of the woods and scared the horse, and he ran away, leaving the man. Several of the Indians tried to head the horse, but they did not succeed, and the women escaped, but the Indians caught the man and cut him all to pieces.

We found out, by ranging around, that when there were Hudson Bay men living on the Nisqually plains, that the Indians would come in and camp near them and they would not let the volunteers know anything about it. Myself and three or four other volunteers went to Governor Stevens and told him that he must have those men arrested and taken in or we would shoot them the same as we would the Indians, and as soon as they were arrested the Indians left for the other side of the mountains. There were a good many Indians who told me that the Hudson Bay men advised them to fight. They told them they could just as well kill off what few white people there were here and then have their houses and stock.

As far as Colonel Ebbey is concerned in getting up a memorial, he had nothing to do with it. It was gotten up by a convention of the people. Colonel Ebbey told me himself that he did not want to have anything to do with it, as it would be unpopular at the time, and wanted the people to wait a year or two.

Chapter 3

Surrounded by Acres of Clams

Hugh Crockett

The story of the wreck of the ship Georgiana
*on Queen Charlotte's Island in the fall of 1851,
is recreated by one of the rescue party of the
ill-fated crew, who were being held for ransom by
hostile Indians.*

Puyallup, Washington — January 13, 1893

I have been asked many times to write a story about a vessel that was wrecked on Queen Charlotte's island in 1851. As I am one of a few that can do so from memory I have concluded to undertake it. It was, perhaps, in September, 1851, that the sloop *Georgiana* sailed from Olympia for the west coast of Queen Charlotte's island with twenty-four people on board. I will give below the names, as far as I can remember them, and follow them up to the close of their eventful lives: Captain Roland, Asher Sargent, Nelson Sargent, John Remley, Jesse Ferguson, Charles Weede, James Herd, Daniel Shaw, Samuel D. Howe, Mr. Colwell, James McAlister, Richard Gibbs, Benjamin Gibbs, Mr. McEwen, Sidney S. Ford, Jr., Pan Tucker and one Kanaka Tamaree. There were seven others whose names I have forgotten.

The sloop reached Queen Charlotte's island without anything transpiring worthy of note. Here she was driven ashore in a gale. Soon afterward a large number of Indians rushed on board, robbed the passengers of all they had and took the crew as prisoners. All of the provisions were lost and those on board were reduced to salmon, straight, for their food. Some days later the captain wrote an account of their capture on a slip of paper that he had in his pocket and gave it to a passing canoe which was on its way around the island. Captain Lafayette Balch, who had gone north, happened to meet the canoe and immediately put about and came down to Olympia with the news. Simpson P. Moses, collector of the Puget Sound district, who had just opened the custom house at Olympia, at once made arrangements with Captain Balch to go and relieve the captives. A requisition was made on Captain Will of Fort Steilacoom for a detachment of troops to accompany them. It was agreed that Lieutenant John de Mont with six soldiers, one corporal and eight volunteers, should go. The crew and forces consisted of the following: Lieutenant John de Mont, one corporal and six soldiers. The volunteers were Edward Sylvester, R.C. Far, G. McLaferty, A.B. Moses, Mr. Dulock, Dr. Johnson, A.M. Poe, V.S. Davis and Hugh Crockett, the writer of this story, Ship Carpenter Wilson, Sailor Gray and Sailor Jack, which are all the names that memory serves me with now.

The schooner *Damerescove* was fitted for the voyage, and everything was completed about the 23rd of December. When we sailed Collector Moses gave Captain Balch and Lieutenant De Mont a requisition on the Hudson Bay company at Victoria for $1500 worth of goods with which to ransom the men captured by the Indians, and also a suit of clothing for each man. The company kindly responded, so we got all we wanted. When we started on our voyage our captain made first for Fort Simpson, where we found Samuel D. Howe, the Gibbs brothers and McEwen, whom the Indians had allowed to go over to see what Captain McNeal would do for the party. Captain McNeal was powerless to do anything, as he had no vessel at the Fort to send, so Mr. Howe remained there until the arrival of the *Damerescove*. We stayed here for three days, as Captain Balch wished to bend a new main sail which he had made.

On the way up here a little incident occurred that is worthy of note. Sailor Gray got into a quarrel with the mate of the schooner and refused duty.

Gray was a very powerful man and it took the corporal and his six men to put him in rope yarns and lead him to the poopdeck, where the captain talked to him after which Gray begged the captain's pardon and went to work again bending the new sail. There were thirty or forty canoes around our craft all the time, out of curiosity. They had much to say about the row on board, and one of the chief men at the post came off and said that he wished we would not have such scrapes as it demoralized his Indians so. We told him it was inevitable as Sailor Gray wanted the ship and our captain did not fancy the idea of giving it up and walking home.

I think I must say something about the Indians here. Fort Simpson is built at the main town of the Simpshean's tribe, and they are one of the most numerous and powerful of the northern tribes. At Fort Simpson I saw more canoes at once than I have seen since. The people at the post said there were 700, many of them of the largest size. One hundred men could ride in some of them. The tribe on Queen Charlotte's island, where the Georgianna was wrecked, was the Hideat and they were all very strong and warlike.

We arrived at the place where they were the second day from Fort Simpson. When we hove in sight some of their men went up on a high bluff and stretched a red blanket for a signal. When we neared the place and fired a six-pounder, they soon let this pole fall. The head chief came on board. As it was not safe to anchor at this place, it was decided to go about five or six miles to the south, where the men were brought in large canoes, and where the negotiation was made with the Indians. The head chief was made to understand that the goods he received were given to him for what his people had done for our men. The men were all given a new suit of clothes, which consisted of corduroy pants, blue flannel shirt, Scotch caps, and coats with a hood. It was usually called Hudson Bay linen.

We lay all night at this place, and the next morning started for home, which we reached in due time without any accident.

As I have said above, I will now try to tell what has become of some of those men. Captain Roland was capsized and drowned in the narrows four miles below Steilacoom soon after his return. When his vessel was wrecked he lost every cent he had. Asher Sargent died a few years ago, after long suffering, with paralysis. Nelson Sargent was living the last time I heard of him. John Beinley went east of the mountains many years ago. I do not know what became of him. Jesse Ferguson is still living on his farm near Olympia.

Charles Weed lives in, or near, Olympia. James Hurd was in the butchering business, and, in trying to drive a vicious animal in the streets of Olympia, it attacked him and he lost his life. Daniel Shaw moved to Santa Barbara, where he died many years ago. Samuel Howe died at the sisters' hospital in Seattle after a long and painful illness. Many friends regretted his death, for he was a good man. He had filled many places of public trust, with credit to himself and satisfaction to the people. Mr. Colwell lives on Rock Prairie, about fifteen miles from Olympia; at least he did the last time I heard from him. James McAllister was murdered by the Indians at Connell's prairie, in the time of the Indian war in 1855. Thus ended a noble life. He was always in the front ranks, ready and willing to do his part, and his death was regretted by all who knew him. The Gibbs brothers know nothing of how Mr. McEwen managed to get sufficient funds with which to purchase a small schooner he was running on the Sound, and some time in 1858, I think it was, he was on his way from Utsalady to Steilacoom and as he was nearing the Nathan headland, at the entrance to Port Orchard, he was met by a large party of northern Indians. He had one man as helper, and a man and his wife as passengers. The Indians shot and killed all of them, took what they wanted and set fire to the schooner. He was a Scotch man, and had spent many years in the service of the Hudson Bay company. Kanaka Tamaree went to Victoria to live, and I do not know what became of him. Pan Tucker was murdered in his cabin at Port Discovery bay. His body was literally chopped to pieces. The perpetrators of this fiendish deed were never apprehended and brought to justice. I have just now thought of one more, Mr. John Thornton, now a highly respected citizen of Dungeness. Thus is told the story and whereabouts of all the men that went to Queen Charlotte's island in the ill-fated Georgianna in quest of gold.

As to those who went to their assistance: Captain Lafayette Balch ended his days in an insane asylum in California. He was an enterprising man and had accumulated quite a little fortune. Mr. Williams, the mate, disappeared, and I do not know what became of him. Lieutenant John Dement resigned his commission in the army soon after and went to Oregon City to live and went into business with a brother. He was going East and was on the ill-fated *Central America* when she foundered going from Aspinwall to New York. He saved his life by floating 24 hours on a hatch. Think he was not born to be drowned at that time. I regret to say I have lost all trace of him now. He was a good man and a universal favorite. Our soldiers all served out their time at Fort Steilacoom. I only know that two of them now live in this country. One of them, Murdy Fay, is a farmer, and doing quite well. The other's name is George _____. He has been blind for many years. Ed Sylvester was the proprietor of the steamer City of Olympia. He died several years since. R.C. Fay settled on Whidby island, where he died about twenty years ago. A.B. Moses was a brother of Collector Moses, and was killed by the Indians while coming in from Captain Maloney's camp. In 1855 Dr. Johnson went to Pacific county to live. I do not know what has become of him. A.M. Poe was taken sick and turned back at Cape Flattery. He died many years ago at San Francisco. Collector Moses tried to get both the war and state department to pay the expenses of this expedition, but as there was no money appropriated for such things they could not do so, so it went over until the first session of the legislature of Washington territory in 1854, which memorialized congress to pay the bill. Samuel D. Howe was in that legislature and was instrumental in getting up the memorial. Columbus Lancaster was our first delegate to congress, and he engineered it through and congress was pleased to make ample appropriations to pay all. Captain Balch received $5000 for his services. The Hudson Bay company was paid for their goods, and the volunteers all received $166 each.

Those Indians are great pirates. In 1856 they captured and burned a schooner called the *Susan Sueger*, in Queen Charlotte's Sound. They are different from the tribes to the south in that they are larger and their features are more like the Asiatic people. Many people think they are a cross between the Asiatics and the tribes on this side of the Behring Straits.

In conclusion I would say that I have written this story entirely from memory, and should a comrade or shipmate detect errors in it kindly attribute it to faulty memory and not to a desire to misrepresent anything. Remember this circumstance occurred over forty-two years ago.

Thomas W. Laws

An 1852 emigrant describes his trail experiences
and the terrible outbreak of cholera in that year.
Also an interesting story on hunting panthers and
cougars near Olympia, Washington in the 1850's.

Oakville, Washington — July 11, 1892

We crossed the plains in 1852, starting from Lawrence county, Illinois, in March of that year, bound for Oregon, we reached our destination after about eight months' travel, landing five miles below Fort Vancouver.

We crossed the Mississippi river at St. Louis. My father had four wagons and four yoke of oxen hitched to each wagon, making sixteen yoke in all. We had with us fifty head of stock cattle, the best that Illinois could afford; four wagons drawn by horses, which were eight of the finest horses that were to be found in Illinois in those days. We crossed the Missouri river at St. Joseph, and on leaving that place we left civilization behind us, and started out to breast the many dangers that awaited the emigrants who were crossing the plains.

When we reached Platte river we saw thousands of buffalo and antelope. We started out to try to kill some of the buffalo, and after having shot one decided that we wanted more and started for the band again. They evidently did not like our treatment and away they went in all directions, four of them running directly toward the train, and they went right over the wagons and oxen and dashed on paying no attention to the obstacles in their way. At that time there were about 300 wagons in sight of each other, and quite naturally the people were pretty badly scared, and for a time everything was in a wild state of confusion. We hastened about gathering up the things and found that no one had been hurt.

There were plenty of hares, or jackrabbits as some people call them, on the prairie. One day one jumped from the road and my father started after it on foot. It was a lively chase, and it is needless to say that the rabbit came out best. After that when we would see a rabbit we would call to father to come catch it, but the one experience had taught him that he was not fleet-footed enough.

We traveled up the south side of Platte river a long distance and crossed to the opposite side. In crossing Red river we found a quicksand bottom. My mother was driving her team across, when the wagon suddenly began sinking, and before a team could be got to the rescue the wagon was more than half buried. The outlook for the future was not bright about that time, and we thought we should be buried there in the river. But we had help soon, and came out all right, with the exception of a good wetting.

We traveled on, and nothing of much importance transpired until we reached a place called Wolf creek, by the emigrants, and across which they had built a bridge. The Indians had taken possession of it, and were camped there to demand pay from the emigrants or whomever might cross the stream. They demanded "$1, one wagon, one horse, 10 cents, one cow," but father told them he would not pay them, for the bridge had been built by white men and that they had no right to it. Upon receiving this information, there was a reinforcement on the Indian side, twenty big buck Indians joining those with whom the men of the train had been talking. In every direction could be seen hundreds of Indians but there were hundreds of emigrants also. A meeting was held among the whites, and it was decided that rather than to have trouble with them, they would pay, and told the Indians this, to which they replied "no." The men of the train then took charge of the bridge and told the wagons to come on, whereupon the Indians jumped for the first wagon. The oxen were afraid of them, and a man, one of the members of the party, went to the Indian and motioned him to stand back, but Mr. Indian made the same motion to the white man, indicating that they were going to have things their own way. The man drew back and "punched" the Indian under the ear, and to see the Indian roll over backward was a treat, and as soon as he got straightened on his feet he took himself away as fast as he could.

That night there were ten of our cattle stolen. The next morning a party of twenty men was formed and started to recover them, and soon came upon their trail, and in a short time found the cattle and brought them back. The next day a man was found where we had recovered our cattle. He was a trader and had been killed by the Indians.

We were glad to get out of that place, and made ready to resume our journey. Everything was peaceable until we came to Salmon falls on Snake river. The Indians on the south side of the river were hostile, and everybody crossed the river at Salmon falls. We were almost out of money and thought to save a little by swimming the river, which we tried to do, and lost two good oxen. So we gave up crossing at that point, and started down the south side of Snake river. We travelled two days from the falls when we were stopped by the Indians.

Our train by this time was getting small. Some of the party had left us and started for California. We had lost a great deal of our stock and were in no position to fight the redskins. There were at this time only seven men in our crowd, so we turned and went back to our old camping place. There we met our old friend, Mr. Morgan. He said to my father "We will go through in wagons or die." There were twenty well-armed men now in the party, and the next morning we made another start. The Indians were determined we should not pass, and while my father was talking with one of them, the Indian struck him over the head with his whip, and father then told him that they would go through or die, and they went through.

Two miles from this place we overtook three wagons of emigrants whom the Indians had held for three days. Their oxen were almost starved, but there were not enough men in the party to outdo the Indians, and they had been compelled to wait until help came. The Indians had given them to understand that if more white men came they would all be killed. Despite the threat, they were glad when they saw our train coming in sight. There were Indians to be seen in every direction. My father and Mr. Morgan were captains of our train, and they made preparations to get the people and teams all gathered together and move on. They decided not to interfere with the Indians if they would be allowed to pass on, which they were, and we got away from that place with no further trouble.

The trip across the plains remains a vivid picture to me and I shall never forget some of the suffering that we experienced, and of the marks of suffering left by those who had preceded us, in the form of hundreds of graves, which were in most cases shallow, and nearly all of which had been disturbed by wolves. The spectacle was appalling. The graves were not more than eighteen or twenty inches deep, and as the complaint that caused the majority of deaths was supposed to be the cholera, the dead were disposed of in the speediest manner. We were fortunate as we only lost one member of our party. But father was a pretty good doctor and we fared better than a great many others. At one time there was six of the family sick, but they all recovered. The suffering was terrible, and we could hear the sufferers crying to God to let them die, or asking to be killed so their suffering would be ended. To such the end soon came, and they were relieved. As I looked at the disturbed graves, miles away from civilization, I thought of the tragic ending of the lives of so many who had started out with a light spirit and strong body to make a home in the far west, and I offered a silent prayer to God, asking that we might be brought safely through. I was scarcely more than a child then, being about 14 years old, but I remember the desolation and suffering that was apparent on every hand.

We traveled on until our provisions were entirely exhausted, and we thought we should starve, but in the Grande Ronde we met a pack train. We sold three oxen for $50 and bought some provisions. We drove our cattle over the Cascades, and had many trials and difficulties which I will not stop to mention.

When we reached The Dalles we were entirely out of money, and had to get along the best we could. About this time we met a man who offered assistance in the shape of consolation, saying to father and mother not to worry, he himself had been in the same condition, only worse. He had been here since 1845. He helped us down the cascades, where we met another man, who proved to be a friend also, who helped us on down the river, and we landed at Vancouver, or five miles below, where we stayed through the winter.

That winter was a terrible one. Starvation stared us in the face, and there was nothing to be had but salmon and potatoes, the former selling for 25 cents per pound, the latter for $1.50 to $2 per bushel. We received $1 per day for our work. Flour was 25 cents per pound, and it took cash on the spot to get it at all. That winter we bought one beef at 15 cents per pound, one hog at the same price, and three hundred pounds of flour at the price named above.

In the fall of 1853 we came to Olympia, where father kept hotel until the next spring. We then went out about sixteen miles from Olympia, locating on Mina prairie, near Black river. In order to reach this prairie we had to cut our way through the thick underbrush and heavy timber, and we camped six weeks at this place, during which time our chief sport was hunting, and the chief game was panthers or cougars. There was one came to the camp and carried away a sheep that dressed eighty pounds. We had brought our old watch dog across the prairie with us — and a better, braver or more faithful dog never lived — and we took our guns and the dog and started in pursuit. We were soon rewarded, and came upon the beast all trim and ready for a fight. The dog waded in, and, after a hard battle, the panther was killed. It measured nine feet ten inches from point of nose to tip of tail. A short time after that one came into camp and killed a calf, which again took us out on a hunting expedition. The dogs put the beast up a tree, and there being four of us in the hunting party — my father, brother, a Dutchman and myself — we thought we could manage the affair nicely. We fired at him, which brought him to the ground, but not dead by any means. He gathered the old family dog in his mouth and began shaking him. My brother had a large heavy revolver which was loaded heavily, and he fired, striking the animal just at the butt of the ear, which made him drop the dog, and not being particular whether he got hold of the one who fired the shot, he made a drive for the Dutchman, who set up a howl, which at any other time would have been laughable. He cried to us to save him; that he was going to be killed sure, and the situation did look a little like he might be right, but before the animal reached him the other dog had taken it upon himself to lay the cougar out, and pounced upon him. We were afraid to shoot for fear of killing the dogs, so father began pelting him over the head with a club, which seemed to have but very little effect, if any. At last an opportunity came and my brother fired, putting four bullets in him before he finally gave up.

This is only one instance among many in our hunting expeditions both in crossing the plains and since my residence here. I have helped kill twenty-nine cougars since I came to this country, eight bears and forty wild catamounts.

When the Indian war broke out my father, brother and myself went as volunteers. We suffered many hardships, but came through all right.

While we have experienced many hardships and have been deprived of a great many things essential to make life pleasant, or even, at times, comfortable, we have the pleasure of looking over what was prairies of bunch-grass, now transformed into beautiful fields of grain, orchards of fine fruit and vegetable gardens that are not surpassed on this continent. Our rugged, jagged mountains, over which we passed, almost more dead than alive, are putting out minerals of all kinds, and we have only to look a little distance into the future to see our grand state of Washington second to none in the development of its natural resources.

Urban E. Hicks

An 1853 journey from Olympia to Shoalwater Bay by the U.S. Marshall and Thurston County Assessor taking the first census in Washington Territory. At their first destination they found 25 rowdy Oystermen gathering the native product for the San Francisco market, but "no assessable property not exempt by law or courtesy."

This being the centennial year of the discovery of Grays harbor, recently commemorated by railroad completion to that beautiful inlet to the Pacific border of this wonderful state, and duly celebrated by thousands of civilized inhabitants along the rich valleys and numerous tributary streams of the lower Chehalis, a short reminiscence of a lonely trip made by the writer away back in 1853, may not be uninteresting.

In September, 1853, I was appointed assessor for Thurston county. The territory then embraced by that county included all of what is now known as Mason and Chehalis counties, including Shoalwater bay as far south as Stony point.

J. Patton Anderson had been appointed United States marshal and sent to the coast ahead of Governor Stevens and party to take a census of the inhabitants of the territory north of the Columbia river and west of the Cascade range (there were no white settlers east of the mountains at that time) preparatory to the formation of a separate territory from that of Oregon, all of said territory being then included in Oregon territory, and had completed the census of the territory north of Thurston county. He came to Olympia and desired to go down the Chehalis to Grays harbor, and from thence along the sea beach to Shoalwater bay and the mouth of the Columbia.

As no one at Olympia knew anything positive about the number or business of the white inhabitants on the lower Chehalis and Shoalwater, the county commissioners — Sidney S. Ford and David Shelton, the latter still living, and for whom the town of Shelton is named — instructed me to accompany the marshal on this lonely trip, and report the number and assessable property of the inhabitants, if we found any. I think that no taxes were collected from them until long afterward, but the commissioners desired to know officially the character and occupation of all that might be found in that direction. I was the first official to visit that section, and, although people are not usually well pleased to receive a visit from the assessor, I was, however, smilingly received and royally welcomed by all.

We went out to the James' place on Mound prairie on the north bank of the Chehalis, and then engaged two Indians with a small canoe, just big enough to hold four persons, with our blankets, fry pan, tin pot, cup and a few small articles, small sack of flour, a few pounds of bacon, a few raw potatoes, a package of ground coffee and a little salt. With this outfit we launched our frail barque on the shallow rapids of the winding stream, each with paddle and pole as propelling power. The farthest settlement down stream was then known as Armstrong's saw-mill. From there on all was a wild wilderness of dense undergrowth lining both sides of the stream until we reached two bachelor shanties, one on the right and the other on the left bank, near the present town site of Montesano. Dan Scammon and _____ Porter had recently lodged on the bank near an open space a short distance back from the shore, and were endeavoring to hew out a trail onto higher ground. We encountered two immense drifts of logs and fallen timber in the stream before getting to Scammon's, one of which we carried our canoe around, but the other being nearly one mile in length, we were forced to leave the canoe and pack our traps around where the Indians, after more than a half day's delay, procured another canoe, no better than the first, when we again paddled onward. We traveled leisurely down stream, frequently stopping and going ashore to climb some prominent elevation to view the country, if possible. We used a hatchet to cut our way through the dense undergrowth, and blaze the way back to the canoe.

We found no more white settlers until we passed the small island at the upper end of the harbor, when we came upon a log house with a small outbuilding on a high bank just above the mouth of a good-sized stream and quite an extensive tide flat. Here we found Dr. Roundtree and family, with an old bachelor living nearer the mouth of the stream. The doctor seemed delighted to see us, as he had not seen or heard from any one up the Chehalis for many weeks. No other settlers were on the way and his nearest neighbor except the "bach," was on Shoalwater bay, more than twenty miles away. The doctor had frozen his feet the winter previous, so he said, and wore rags around them to shield them from thorns and sharp rock, but we suspected that shoe leather was scarce in those days. He would not listen to our going further that day and prevailed on us to stop over night. (I would not mention this but for what follows). That night two very hungry dogs got at our sack of provisions and ate up every morsel, even the raw potatoes. In the morning we started again on our trip minus all our supplies, which the doctor could not replenish from his scant larder, but before embarking I politely asked the doctor our bill for the night's entertainment. He fixed the sum at $2 each, which he regarded as quite reasonable owing to the scarcity of supplies and the long distance to market. (There are no clams on the bay.) I handed him a $5 piece which he quickly dropped into his pocket and looked for more, but finally said that would do; he had included the Indians also in the bill, which would have come to $6, but generously threw off $1 as we had been such entertaining company.

On arriving at Peterson's Point our Indian buried the canoe in the sand to prevent it being stolen and we proceeded on foot along a wide beach, one of the most beautiful on any shore, fifteen miles to Shoalwater. On the way we came across a large party of Quenoith Indians (I spell the name as pronounced), gathering kinnikapick berries, which grew in great abundance on the sand ridges near the beach, from whom we purchased a small quantity of very dirty rice and a piece of sturgeon. The Indians caught the fish in the surf. We reached the north shore of Shoalwater just at dark, foot sore and weary with our long walk over the hard beaten sands and through a long stretch of drifting sand more than ankle deep. We soon found a large pile of drift logs, which we set on fire and proceeded to cook the last morsel of our purchase from the Indians. The bay opposite was six miles wide, and the settlement all on the opposite side. Morning came and we watched the numerous canoes and small sailing craft going and coming from the oyster grounds on the other side, but none toward us. We hoisted a white blanket on a long pole and piled on sticks and logs to make as much smoke as possible, but no one seemed to notice it. All day long we lay there without anything to eat, and our Indians had to go more than a mile back from the bay to find fresh water, which they brought to us in a pint cup and frying pan. We couldn't go back, as the Indians from whom we had made our small purchase were perhaps gone from there, and showed an ugly disposition even while trading with us. There was no game except a few black ducks away out in the bay. I had a Colt's navy. Anderson had no arms. Even if we shot a duck there was no way of getting it so far out in the water. Night came on and we laid down with a distressing emptiness of stomach. Our Indians could stand hunger better than we could, and they had been lucky enough to catch a good-sized crab, which they stole off and cooked at another fire built some distance from us. I had fired my pistol a good many times, until ammunition was running out, and we had resorted to every possible means to attract the attention of those on the other shore, until we began to discuss the probable merits of Indian roast or broiled, but we had nothing on which to broil the Indian, and hence would have to depend on roast or raw.

Sunday came bright, calm and peaceful, and along toward noon I had succeeded in wounding a black duck in a shoal place, and by desperate running through water knee deep, captured it. We immediately plucked a few feathers, divided it in half, and each stuck his share on a long stick in the fire to scorch and remove a little of the raw fishy taste. A small sloop had been sailing around the bay for some hours previous, but seemed to purposely avoid our locality. Just as we were about to devour our roast duck, we noticed the boat heading for us, and we both shouted and jumped on logs, ran out into the water, waved bats and acted like crazy men, I know. We would bite off a piece of duck and yell at the same time. Soon the welcome boat came near enough to speak to us, and, when they discovered that we were white men, the two men aboard came ashore and assisted us on board with all speed. On board we found a few crackers and some cheese, and I have never tasted anything better or sweeter in all my travels. They soon landed us on the other side and when our condition was made known, every luxury the settlement possessed was freely bestowed and many apologies offered for not paying closer attention to our signals. They thought it was a band of Quinoith Indians, who were regarded as semi-hostile, especially toward the Chinook and Shoalwater tribes, who were engaged by the whites in gathering oysters.

About twenty-five white persons were residents of Shoalwater bay and vicinity at that time, most of them engaged in gathering the native oyster for the San Francisco market. Dick Hillyar and Job Bullard were the men who rescued us on the north barren shore near the ocean. The whites employed some 200 or 300 Indians, mostly from the Chinook tribe near the mouth of the Columbia, to gather the oysters, and liberally paid them in whisky and tobacco. Oyster beach was thickly populated with a roaring, rollicking crowd of drunken men and squaws, everything apparently being held in common among whites and Indians.

After feasting on oysters stewed, oysters fried, raw, roasted, fricaseed, broiled, baked, on the half-shell, whole shell and all, with copious draughts of salt-water whisky, we took an enumeration of the inhabitants, but found no assessable property not exempt by law or courtesy.

Here Colonel Anderson left me to proceed on to the Columbia, while I had to make the return trip alone with my two Indians. On the morning of departure I engaged a big Chinook chief to set me across the bay on the barren beach at Starvation camp; he possessed two beautifully fat, large, greasy squaws as wives, and a very large Chinook canoe, which he generously loaded with a crowd of drunken braves as escort and guard. He also owned a slave who did the steering, and whom he did not allow to touch whisky when he took a sail on the bay. We came near upsetting in the bay in a sudden squall of wind, but drawing up my butcher knife and cutting the sail-rope just in time saved us from overturning. The chief became very indignant toward me for cutting the rope, and I was compelled to knock or push him down into the bottom of the canoe and draw my revolver with a threat to shoot the first one that stirred. The steersman being sober, we made our landing safe. My two Indians were also very drunk, but by dipping water from the bay with my frying pan and liberally dousing them they soon sobered sufficient to stand up and receive my pack on their backs, together with a two-and-a-half gallon keg of whisky they had secured from the Indians on the bay. I allowed them to pack the whisky, as I was entirely dependent on them to get back home, but did not allow them to drink any on the way, as, indeed, they seemed to have sense enough not to do themselves. I got behind and drove them ahead on the trail. Near sundown, on our way up the beach, we again came suddenly upon the Quenoith savages, who were still gathering the Indian tobacco weed and berries. We would have avoided them had we not come upon them unawares, but to pass unobserved was now impossible, so we assumed a bold front and marched steadily and straight through their camp. They, however, smelt the whisky and followed after us. After coming about a mile this side their camp my two Indians stopped, laid down their packs and disappeared over the sand ridges to the right. Soon five stalwart fellows came up to where I was and demanded some of the whisky. I told them that it was not mine to give, but they disbelieved me. One big fellow with a long blanket around him attempted to steal the keg by sitting down on it and, on rising, lift it beneath his blanket. I rushed at him and pushed him off the keg, drew my revolver and told them I would die rather than let them have any of the whisky. I knew my only course was to appear as brave as possible, keep a very close watch of them, and let them know that they would have to scalp me before getting at the liquor. They offered to trade anything and everything they could give in exchange, but I knew that if they got a taste it was certain to end in a fight or a lively foot-race. They sulked about for a time and then went back to their camp, I thought, for reinforcement. They had but just gone out of sight when my two Indians came running up to me — it was then getting dark, a slight shower of rain began to fall — and motioning to me not to speak or make any noise they quickly gathered up our packs and touching me on the arm made me follow on a sharp trot over the sand ridges, through the lagoons, low brush and tall grass, in zigzag course, some quarter or half mile from the beach. We kept up the run as long as I was able to stand it, when we gradually worked our way back to the beach, the wind and rain dashing the waves or surf high on shore, running frequently up on to us in the dark nearly waist deep. We kept on up the beach for four or five miles, when I became totally exhausted. They led me out onto the low sand ridge, found a small hole or crevice made by the winds in the loose sand, stuck down two small sticks on each side the crevice spread a small piece of Indian matting over the sticks, made me crawl beneath so as to shelter my head and shoulders from the rain, and then laid down on my feet and legs to keep me warm.

Just at daylight we were up and on our way again as fast as we could travel. Arrived at Peterson's Point shortly after sunrise, dug up our canoe, quickly embarked and paddled out into the middle of the bay. During all of this time not a word was spoke by either of us, all being done by signs and as noiselessly as possible. While the Indians were digging up the canoe I gathered a small quantity of the beautiful blue-black sand which lay in shining ridges on top of the white sand on the point, the rain and early morning sun making it sparkle and glitter in beautiful colors. I had no thought of gold being found among it then, but learned afterward that considerable quantities of fine placer gold was washed from this sand.

After getting a good mile from shore my Indians began talking to each other in a low tone of voice, very slow and deliberate, and it was near noon before they explained to me in Chinook the narrow escape we had made. On ascending the Chehalis to nearly opposite the present town site of Elma my Indians left me in the canoe, and after about four hours' delay came back with three Indian ponies, led by hair ropes they used for bridles. We soon mounted, using our blankets for saddles, and took a trail up stream through the thickest of brush, jumping high logs, floundering down steep banks, across boulders and stony points, bruised and scratched by overhanging limbs and sharp rocks, until we reached the open country at the lower end of Mound Prairie. My Indians accompanied me to Olympia, and had many a story to tell of their journey to a far-off land in company with two "Boston tyees." I was pleased to meet one of these Indians not long ago on the reservation near Oakville, in Chehalis county, and, although he had not seen me for more than thirty-five years, he almost instantly recognized me and showed great joy at meeting me.

Colonel Anderson was elected the second delegate to congress from Washington territory, Columbia Lancaster being first. He never returned to the territory after his election. He was a general in the confederate army, was severely wounded, and died before or soon after the war closed. He was a splendid gentleman socially, of fine appearance, and most excellent company on a long jaunt of the kind described. He was a relative by marriage of General John Adair of Astoria, Or. I afterward assisted Anderson in completing the census of the territory.

Hon. Edward Eldridge

He left his wife and two children alone, when
he made a 500 mile journey, without a dollar in
his pocket, to Ft. Colville in 1855 in search of gold.
On his way back he encounters the initial outbreak
of Indian hostilities in Eastern Washington.

During the summer of 1855 reports reached the settlers on Puget Sound
that rich gold mines had been found in the neighborhood of Fort Colville in
the northeastern portion of the territory. At that time the only kind of
employment in which money could be earned by labor was in getting out
piles for the San Francisco market, working at the few sawmills then on the
Sound, or at the coal mine at Bellingham bay. As many of the pioneers of
Washington came from California, where they had had some experience in
gold mining, and as it was uphill work for settlers who were carving out
homes in the forest under the donation law, to procure money, without
which many of the necessaries and conveniences of life must be dispensed
with, the news of rich gold mines from which a pile (in gold mining
parlance) might soon be made, existing in our own territory, was hailed
with delight all about the Sound. No one who had means sufficient to live
where the benefits of civilization could be enjoyed, would subject himself to
the hardships and privations, saying nothing about dangers that must be encountered during the period it would take to make a farm from which a living could be obtained in the forests on Puget Sound. Hence nearly all of the
pioneers were poor and ready to avail themselves of any honest means that
would improve their financial condition. Rumors of Indian troubles east of
the mountains had also reached the Sound, but nothing definite or authentic
was known. Communication between the different settlements on the
Sound and with the outside world was almost dependent upon some one
having business at some other place who would carry letters or papers to
points along his route and carry any news recently heard to points it had
not yet reached.

The writer at that time was located with his wife and two infant children
on the north side of Bellingham bay, about a mile from the settlement at the
mouth of Whatcom creek. Having passed the winter of '49, mining in the
Yuba river in California, and knowing how much more rapidly money
could be made in a rich gold-mining region than in the woods around Bellingham bay, and knowing from experience the great benefit a little capital
would be to any settler on Puget Sound, I decided to give the Fort Colville
gold mines a trial.

Having been dependent on my own resources from the age of 13, and being of a roving disposition whenever I wanted to see any particular part of
the world, I never consulted the committee on ways and means as to how I

would get there. The only thing necessary in the premises for me to decide was, Shall I go or not? That once settled, the rest was plain sailing, for my experience had shown me the truth of the maxim, "Where there is a will, there's a way." To reach Fort Colville from Bellingham bay, by the then travelled route, was a journey of about 500 miles, and, as an illustration of how little judgment young men show in some of their actions, I will here state that at the end of July I decided to start on a 500-mile journey through an unknown region, work for a time in the gold mines and return within four months, as I was obliged to be back by the 1st of December if within my power to do so.

Two young men, James Houston and Barney Pender, agreed to go with me, but neither of us had a dollar in cash. The route from the Sound to Colville was by the Natchez pass, and the first place for us to reach was the town of Steilacoom, to which we had to go by water. As nearly every settler on Puget Sound at that time had to do his traveling by water, there being no wagon roads then to speak of, they all had a boat of some kind, and I happened to have a pretty good one. As all three of us were sailors, there would be no difficulty in making the first stage of our journey, so taking whatever we had that would be available on our journey, or in the gold mines, about the beginning of August we started. In looking back over the folly of starting on such a journey upon the meager information we had been able to obtain, I cannot but wonder how my wife every agreed to remain alone with our two children, the oldest not 3 years old, a mile from the nearest neighbor, in the then condition of the country. Four months was the shortest time she expected to elapse before she would see me, and during that time she had to rely solely upon herself in an Indian country, and yet she willingly consented to this in the hope of bettering our condition thereby.

Nothing particular occurred during the trip up the Sound, except the delay caused by sometimes taking the wrong direction, owing to the smoke that filled the air. On reaching the settlements at Seattle and Steilacoom, we found that a great many persons had started for Fort Colville, but that no direct news had been received from any of them, but that reports of gold being found were still coming in by way of Oregon. The rumor of Indian difficulties were also on the increase, and although nothing definite could be ascertained, still the rumors caused a feeling of uneasiness throughout the settlements. Upon inquiry we found that the persons who had started for the gold mines had been generally in parties of from three to six, each person riding a horse and having one or more spare horses with them to pack their outfit. As it was impossible for us to get even one horse, we decided to fall back on the natural means of human locomotion, and carry our outfit on our backs. In trying to obtain information concerning the route to Fort Colville, we went to Dr. Tolmie, who was then in charge of the Hudson Bay company's station at Nisqually. Upon hearing our intentions and the condition we were in, he used every argument in his power to induce us to give up the enterprise. He said there was no certainty about rich gold mines being found, and even if there was it would be impossible for us to get there without horses. He said we could not carry provisions enough with us; we would lose our way and perish for want of water. Besides there were large rivers to cross, which we could not do on foot. They were too deep and the current strong. But as experience is the only adviser that has any weight with fools, the doctor's advice fell upon deaf ears. We had started for Fort Colville, and to Fort Colville we were bound to go or know the reason why.

Thanking the doctor for his good advice, we told him we were bound to go, that we had roughed it a good deal in the mountains of California, and would thank him for such information as be useful to us on our journey. Finding that he could not dissuade us from going and knowing that two of us were countrymen of his (Scotch) and the other Irish, he cautioned us particularly about how to conduct ourselves with the Indians. He said there was trouble brewing among the Indians against the whites, and although he had not heard of any real difficulty having taken place yet, he knew the state of feeling that existed in the minds of some of the Indians, and he expected to heard of trouble before long. He said we might not see any Indians on this side of the mountains but we would on the other side, and insisted upon our telling them that we were "King George men," and that we had come from him. Here he told us the name the Indians called him, and which they all knew him by, and that they were going to Longbeard, the name the Indians had given Mr. Macdonald, who was then in charge of Fort Colville. He said some of the Indians were incensed against the Americans, and if we met any of them and said we were "Boston men" we might have trouble. He told us it would be almost impossible for us to keep the road without a guide, and cautioned us about crossing the rivers, particularly White river. The water was muddy, so that we could not see the bottom, ice cold, and the current very rapid, and liable to sweep us off our feet. He said each should have a good stick that would bear our weight, with which we could feel our way and not get out of our depth before we knew it, and we would find it a great help to rest on, if we felt the current getting too strong. He also advised us to have a small rope and tie ourselves together with it in crossing the river, so that if one should lose his footing the other two might be able to save him, which they could not do any other way.

After getting all the information we could concerning the gold mines, the way by which they could be reached, and the danger, if any, to be apprehended from the Indians, and being still determined to make the attempt to reach Fort Colville, the next step was to procure an outfit, which could only be done by selling the boat. I found a purchase in Phillip Keach who kept a general store at upper Steilacoom. He agreed to give me $30 for the boat if I would take it in trade. As it was trade I wanted, the bargain was made. Our outfit consisted of two sacks of flour, fifty pounds of pork, some tea and sugar, a double-barreled shot-gun, an axe, a pick, pan and shovel. Each had two pair of blankets, an overcoat and a change of clothing and a sheath knife. These, with numerous articles such as powder and shot, matches, soap, towels, etc., constituted a pretty large array to be carried on our backs, so that when we left the settlement and took the road for the Nisqually ferry, each of us had a load of over eighty pounds.

The prospect of adventure may seem pleasing and romantic to some minds in the early bloom of manhood, but an eighty-pound pack on the back will soon crush out all romance from the most ardent mind in existence. We could travel only a short distance with such a load without resting, so our progress was necessarily slow. It was about the middle of the day when we started and we made about eight miles that night and camped in the woods. Next day three men passed us on horseback, also bound for Fort Colville. We afterward heard that they were the last persons that left the Sound for the gold mines. We crossed the Nisqually river and reached Mr. Lemmon's ranch that night, where we were hospitably welcomed. Next day it was raining heavily and Mr. Lemmon advised us to stay with him that day, which we did. Here we decided to leave part of our load. Our two days' experience had convinced us that, although every meal we ate lightened our burdens, still we could not carry all we had, and we were satisfied that in the end we would have to throw some of our things away. So we thought it best to make choice now before we got worn out, and leave the things where we would have some chance of getting them again. We left our guns, pick, pan and shovel, our overcoats and a pair of blankets each, and kept nothing but our provisions, axe and half our blankets. Although we left those things with the expectation of getting them again, I will here state that we never saw or heard of them afterward.

Next morning was clear and bright, and we resumed our journey with lighter loads and brighter spirits, which, however, got somewhat dampened with the first crossing of White river. Different persons had given us different versions of its depth, but they all agreed that it had to be forded; that there were no boats, bridges or trees by which it could be crossed. Neither of us had ever crossed such a stream before, and as the water was muddy we could not tell how deep it was. As it would be useless to waste time in vain conjecturing, we got ready to wade across. With our axe we cut a stout walking stick for each, then taking off our clothes we had to secure them with our packs in such a way that we could carry them on our backs, holding them with one hand, while the other held the stick. The water was bitter cold, and the current very swift. The principal difficulty we found was from the boulders on the river bottom, some of them being too large to step over or around. Without our sticks we would have been compelled to throw off our packs and used both our hands to maintain our equilibrium, for it was almost impossible to stand on one leg in such a current, and if we lost our foothold we could never have regained it, and would inevitably have been drowned. But by planting the stick squarely on the ground I could rest on it and one foot, while I felt for a safe place with the other foot. Twice I thought I was gone, but by patience and firmness I recovered myself, and we all got across without any accident or the loss of anything.

Seven times we crossed the White river in this manner. The last white man we saw was Mr. Porter, who had a ranch on what was known as Porter's prairie. When we reached his place he was mounting his horse to go into the settlements. He tried to induce us to return with him, saying we would never reach Fort Colville; that the Indians would kill us sure; that they were after him; that he had kept his horse saddled night and day for the last fortnight, and that he was not going to stay there any longer. No feeling of danger or insecurity had yet troubled us, nor no desire to give up our expedition; so, getting all the information we could from Mr. Porter about the road and the rivers we would have to cross, we bade him goodbye and started on. We saw no other white man till we reached Fort Colville.

So far we had not seen a single Indian nor did we see any until we saw the Columbia river. We had been told that we would have to cross White river seven times, Green river twelve times on the west side of the mountains, and the Natchez river seventy-two times on the east slope.

At first we had been prodigal with our provisions, as the more we ate the lighter our packs become; but we soon saw that that could not be kept up indefinitely or we might find ourselves in the middle of the wilderness with nothing to eat, and no knowledge of where anything could be got. Before we crossed the summit of the mountains we had used up what few luxuries we had with us, and were living on flour bread and fat pork, which we ate raw, and found a good substitute for butter. We had three pairs of blankets, and by putting them together we could have one pair under us and two pairs over us, and in this manner after traveling twelve or fourteen hours through the day we could have as refreshing a sleep at night as ever we had in our lives.

We had no trouble about following the road until we were pretty well down the east side of the mountain. After reaching the Natchez river we found that our information of having to cross it seventy-two times was likely to prove correct. The pass is a narrow gorge and the river runs zigzag from side to side down it. At first we merely had to pull off our shoes and stockings to wade across, but as we descended and the river received many additions we had to take off our pants in order to get over. This had to be done so often and so much time was lost in dressing and undressing that we decided to remain on the left hand side of the river and not cross any more unless compelled to, as we could go on foot where a train of horses could not, and whether we lost the road altogether or not I did not intend to worry about it, for being a navigator and knowing the stars that are principally used in navigation and their position at the different hours of the night throughout the year, and having taken the bearings of Fort Colville from the maps before starting, so long as I could see the sun by day, or the moon, the north star or Aldabaran by night I had no fear of being lost so long as we had something to eat. In following down on the north side of the Natchez river we found, as the valley opened out, many roads or trails, made by horses, cattle, or sheep. Some of these we would follow until they ran out, or turned too far from the course we ought to follow, when we would leave them and head about northeast, which course brought us to the Yakima river. How I knew it was the Yakima was that we remained on the left hand or north side of the Natchez river when we crossed it last. The river we came to was lying about north and south where we struck it. Had it been the Natchez, the water would have been running north, while this water was running south. We were fortunate in reaching this river at a fish-trap which reached clear across it. It was sufficiently strong for us to cross on, and without it, I have no idea how we would have got across. It was about noon when we crossed. We had been thirsty for some time, so we stopped to eat our dinner and drink all the water we could, as we could not tell when we would get more. We had nothing that we could carry any water in. A fish would have been a great treat then, but we saw no human beings to get any from, nor were there any in the trap that we could see.

On leaving the river we traveled in a northeast direction and soon struck a large, well-traveled road, all the tracks of which seemed to be going one way. Had the tracks been both ways we would have followed the road one way or the other till we met somebody, but as all the travel on it was going one way, and that way seemed to be farthest from the course we ought to take, we decided to cross the road and keep on a northeast course.

We traveled all the afternoon on that course, the ground rising rapidly, but it was bare prairie ground, so that we had no trouble in traveling. That night was the first in which we suffered for want of water. Living on bread and raw salt pork will soon produce intense thirst. We traveled until it was quite dark in hopes of reaching water, but exhausted nature had to give way, and we had to stop and rest as best we could, without either fire or water. In the morning, as soon as daylight appeared we started on our journey without waiting for breakfast, water being what we wanted most. The ground was undulating but steadily rising. After traveling about three hours we saw some small timber and bushes, and on reaching it found water and a trail. We stopped there some time, and as the trail went nearly in the direction we wished to go, we decide to follow it and see where it would take us to. In a short time we reached the verge of an almost perpendicular precipice, and saw one of the liveliest panoramas spread out before us that the eye could rest upon. Nearly a thousand feet below us was a beautiful green field, as level as a floor, while a river that looked like a silver ribbon, extended from the north to the south in beautiful curves appearing no larger from where we stood that a man could jump across, and yet it was the Columbia river. Between the mountain on which we stood and the river the land was pretty level, both to the right and left as far as we could see, while across the river the land appeared in every imaginable contour and shape. Immediately in front of us the river must have been ten miles distant, judged from the time it took us to reach it after descending the mountains. While gazing on the scene before us we saw some objects close to the river, which proved to be Indian houses; and we also saw some moving objects, which were horses grazing on the plain. So far danger from the Indians had not troubled our thoughts, for since we left Porter on the other side of the mountains, about eight or ten days previous, we had not seen a human being. But now here were evidences of life, and whether we were to meet friends or enemies was now the question. Our provisions were getting pretty low, but yet if we had reason to think our lives were in actual danger, we could have retraced our steps and kept alive until we reached the settlement. But although we had heard rumors of trouble before we started, no one had any positive information, and to turn back now, after having come so far, without some information of some kind, was not to be thought of. Arms we had none except a sheath knife each, and an axe between us, so our safety depended upon meeting friends. Had we only known that Indian Agent Bolow, Mattice and several others had already been murdered not far from where we were, our thoughts and actions would have been very different from what they were, but we did not know that, and perhaps it is fortunate that we did not, for had we turned back we might never have reached the settlement.

The trail we had followed went down the mountain in a zig-zag direction, and concluding to go on and see what fate had in store for us, we began the descent. After reaching the bottom we could see nothing of the river or the object we had seen from the top. We started in the direction we thought they were in, and after traveling about an hour, we saw an Indian on horseback riding about. On seeing us he rode up to us, and we tried to talk to him, but could not make him understand. He soon galloped away, and in a little while returned with several others, all on horseback, and two of them had guns. We knew that whatever the feeling of the Indians might be, we were wholly at their mercy and that our safety depended upon our showing that we had perfect confidence in them and feared no danger. One of them could talk Chinook, and we made ourselves understood. After talking a little, they told us to go with them. On the way there was a perfect cavalcade of Indians on horseback, particularly boys riding out to look at us, as if we were some strange animals. On reaching the camp we saw about twenty houses of different kinds and sizes, and probably from 150 to 200 Indians, altogether. We laid down our packs and ate as if we were at home, and went down to the river to get a drink and wash our hands and faces, then came back to our packs. By this time the Indians had all mustered, and one who appeared to be the chief motioned us to sit down opposite him, while the Indians crouched and sat in a circle all about us. We knew then that if there was any truth in the rumors we had heard, that our fate would soon be decided, and although we felt a little nervous we did our best not to show it. We were put through a rigid examination as to who we were, where we came from, where we were going, and what we were going to do. We remembered what Dr. Tolmie told us and found his advice was of great benefit in disarming the Indians of any unfriendly feeling they may have had against us. After a long talk they seemed to be satisfied. We were very tired and hungry and we saw that the Indians had plenty of salmon and potatoes, which would be a great treat to us, after having had nothing but bread and pork for so long. On telling the chief that we would like to exchange some flour and pork for salmon and potatoes, he gave orders to the women and in a short time they brought us a fine salmon and a pot full of potatoes, both cooked. Delmonico, with all his sauces, could not prepare a meal that would have tasted sweeter, or gone down with a better relish that these Indians' salmon and potatoes did.

On inquiring about the road to Fort Colville, the Indians informed us that it was a long way up the river where it crossed, and that we could not reach it from there; that our best way was to go down the river to an Indian camp on the other side and get them to guide us part of the way, for there was a long distance to be crossed where there was no water, and where there was water we would not be able to find it, unless some one was with us who knew where it was. We spread our blankets down and went to sleep wondering whether we would wake up all right in the morning or not. But whatever our thoughts may have been, we were very soon unconscious of all trouble, and the next thing we knew the sun was shining on us, and the Indians were shouting, in their canoes, catching fish. We were now satisfied that we had nothing to fear from the Indians so, after breakfast, which was liberally supplied of salmon and potatoes by the Indians, we made a bargain with some of them who were going to the camp below in canoes, to take us with them. To the best of my recollection, we must have descended the river about twelve or fifteen miles, and on landing I saw the finest physical specimen of an Indian I have ever seen in my life. He was over six feet two inches in height, stout in proportion, and must have weighed 250 pounds. He appeared to be in the prime of life, and was the chief at that camp.

As the Indians we were with gave the new camp our history, it was needless for us to say anything. They seemed to sympathize with our apparently forlorn condition. Our principal concern was to make arrangements to resume our journey. As near as we could make out, it was three days' journey from where we were to where we would strike the road to Fort Colville, and that water was only to be found at two or three places in that distance, and that no strangers could find it. We made a bargain with the chief to send a guide with us and furnish two horses, as no Indian would go with us without horses. We would start about noon, and by traveling late, would reach the first water that night. Next day we would be traveling over sandy plains, but by the middle of the afternoon we would reach a plain trail, where the Indian would leave us and return. Following this trail we would meet an Indian returning who had left us two days before who would tell us how to go the balance of the way to the Colville road. For this we were to pay a pair of blankets, our ax and a portion of our flour. Our pork was done. We had given one blanket and a sheath knife for our passage down the river, so we had only a pair and a half of blankets between us and not over fifteen pounds of flour when we left the Columbia river.

The Indian and I rode one horse and my two companions the other. Our journey that afternoon was through what appeared to be the ruins of a mighty city, constructed in such ages and by such a race as produced the pyramids of Egypt. Great blocks of stone of every size lay in piles as if an earthquake had thrown down great towers or castles. In other places walls of rock were standing to great heights, built of blocks of stone placed on each other as regularly as a stonemason could place them. As we rode along I remembered reading of the ruins of great cities having been discovered in various places on the American continent, which proved that races far advanced in art and science beyond any of the races since the days of Columbus, must have existed on this continent ages ago, of whose history or fate nothing is now known. And the structures we saw that day was a proof of the truth of those discoveries, for here was plain proof of the work of man, but of far different men than the Indian I was riding with.

We reached our camping ground after dark, and started away again early next morning. During the forenoon our way was over a sandy desert, on which were some small alkali lakes. Occasionally we would see horse tracks, but every heavy wind would soon obliterate every mark, so that it would be impossible for a stranger to follow the way over the sands. Early in the afternoon we reached a tract of rocky iron gravel land, on which we could see a plain trail, and the Indian told us we were clear of the sand now, and that he would go with us a little further, and then he was going back. Soon afterward we reached a small running spring, and the Indian told us we would have no trouble now in following the trail, and the Indians that we would meet would tell us where to find water, and how to go. We were rather glad to be on our feet again, for riding on a bare-backed horse is not productive of much enjoyment, although we may have got over more ground in a given time. After getting our legs in shape again, we pushed on as rapidly as possible, for our packs were little encumberance to us now, and, unless we could reach some signs of civilization before day, our condition would not be a very enviable one. We continued traveling as long as we could see the trail plainly, and felt disappointed at not meeting the Indian we were told of. We camped close to the trail, so that if any Indian should come he would not pass us without our knowing it. We were just dozing off into sleep when we were awakened by a loud snort, given by the horse of the Indian we had been expecting to meet. It is doubtful which was the most scared, the Indian or us. To ride upon men right in the road asleep and no other sign of life around was a natural surprise to both horse and Indian, while we, not realizing at first where we were and what the noise was, were a little alarmed. We jumped up and the Indian was the first to speak, and asked in Chinook who we were. The Indian who had accompanied us with the horses told us the name of the Indian we would meet, also his own name, so when we told this to the Indian he got off his horse and talked to us, made up a fire and told us where we would find water next day. He traced on the ground the shape of a place we would come to next evening before dark, with high stone walls and pointed out the location of a spring and where we would find the road to Fort Colville. He then left us, saying he had to go till he got water for his horse. We continued on our journey next morning and had little difficulty in following the Indian's directions, both as to the road and in finding water, and about 4 or 5 o'clock in the afternoon we reached the place the Indian had described, which looked more like the remains of a monster castle than anything we had yet seen. We found a spring of fine water where the Indian represented it to be, also the trail leading up the hill that would take us to the road we were seeking. As our matches were almost gone and we had no other means of making a fire, we decided to make the rest of our flour into bread, for dry flour is not as palatable as bread of any kind, and as it threatened rain we did not wish to risk the chance of being unable to make another fire.

Next day I experienced one of those sensations we sometimes read of and that induces me to believe in a connection between the seen and the unseen, the visible and the invisible world. In the morning we ascended the trail that led out of the cavern or coulee, and in a short time struck a well-traveled road, but at that particular place it seemed to be at right angles to the way we ought to go. Like the road we saw on the other side of the Columbia, all the travel appeared to have gone one way. Had the travel been in both directions then we thought it might make little difference which way we went, as we would likely soon meet somebody. From the time we left the Sound we had always been expecting to meet some parties returning from Colville. Now the tracks we saw might be the tracks of those who had gone, or they might be the tracks of the people all coming back. We did not ask the Indian which way to go when we found the road, and the way the tracks were going did not seem to be the way to Colville. They were going too much south. Houston and I differed in our opinion as how we should go. I insisted that our road should head north and not south. He said he did not care how it headed, he was not going to follow those tracks until they brought him somewhere. As neither of us were willing to give way, we decided to divide what we had and each go his own way. Barney decided to stick to me. All we had now was a single blanket apiece and a little bread. We bid each other good-bye and set out on our different routes. We had not gone far before a gloomy foreboding of something wrong came over me. I tried to shake it off and feel cheerful, but it would not be shaken off. The further we went the worse it grew. I was unwilling to change our route, as I still thought I was right. Away in the distance we saw trees and so thought we would find water there, so I decided to keep on till we found water if there was any. But I soon became satisfied that I was in great danger of some kind, as I had experienced a similar feeling once before. While laying at a place called Roman bar on the Spanish main, loading a cargo of mahogany, boats were often capsized going in and out over a dangerous surf, and sometimes lives were lost. When our ship was nearly loaded a feeling similar to what I have been describing came over me, and the idea that I was going to be drowned took possession of me. For two days the feeling kept increasing, and on the third morning I felt so bad I could not eat any breakfast, although we had been away four hours in the boats getting a raft off to the ship before the sea breeze set in. The feeling of heart sickness was so intense that I made up my mind to feign sickness next morning so that I would not have to go in the boat. Half an hour after we had commenced work I was accidentally knocked down the hold by a log swinging loose, and was picked up for dead. It was almost a month before I was well. But the feeling I experienced before the accident I will remember to my dying day. Some being was watching over me and tried to warn me of my danger, but was unable to show me in what way the danger lay.

As we travelled on, this feeling became so intense that I became as well satisfied that great danger of some kind was hanging over me, as if I had been told by some one who knew all about it. It was nearly noon when we reached the timber and found a small running stream. We rested awhile, and although very hungry I could not eat. We started to go on the same way, as I wished, if possible, to discover from what source or in what form the danger threatened. But I had not gone ten steps before such an overpowering faintness, or heart sickness came over me, that I stopped and said; "Barney, I can't go this way; there is danger near us. I don't know what it is, but I do know that great danger of some kind is near us, and I won't go any further in this direction. We can turn back and follow Jim or we can find our way back to the Columbia river." He replied, "I'll go any way you go." We turned and retraced our steps, and in five minutes I felt like a new man, light as a feather. It seemed as if a heavy load that I could scarcely carry was lifted off my shoulders. We had not walked fast in the forenoon, but we almost ran going back. We soon passed the place where we struck the road in the morning, and before sundown we came to a spring by the roadside which looked exactly like a tub of water sunk in the level plain. It seemed to rise out of the ground on one side and sink on the other, and there was nothing to indicate that there was water near until you stood beside it. A flat stone on which was scratched the words, "Jim Houston, Thursday, 4 o'clock," was placed close to the water. He must have walked slow or waited, thinking we would change our mind and follow him, for it was not much after 5 o'clock then, and we had gone eight or nine miles before we turned back, so he could not be very far ahead. Knowing how badly he must feel all alone in the wilderness, we resolved to keep on till we came up with him, which we did as it was getting fairly dark. Of course, he was very glad to see us, for a man with but one blanket won't have a very fancy bed on the bare ground in the open air in the month of September, but three men lying close together with a blanket under and two over them can do some tall sleeping if it don't rain.

Everything in this world has to come to an end, and next morning our bread came to an end, and we started off, hoping we would find a dinner before night. A little after noon we came to the Spokane river, where there was a large Indian camp. No such event had every happened before with them — three white men arrive among them without a horse, without arms of any kind, no provisions, no nothing. It was almost impossible for us to make them believe that such was our actual condition. They insisted that we must have been robbed by Indians, and wanted to raise a big crowd and go back and whip them, and get our things back, but in the course of time they realized that we were telling them the truth, and they admired our courage. Nobody had ever done so before.

The Indians could not have treated us better had we belonged to their tribe. As two of us had worked in the gold mines in California, and we had told the Indians we were hunting for gold, they wanted us to hunt for it on their river, and show them how to find it. We stayed three days with them, prospecting up and down the river and in some gulches leading into it. We found the color in many places, but no coarse gold, nor anything that would pay to work, and as winter was approaching and the nights were getting cold, we knew that we had no time to waste in getting somewhere where remunerative employment could be had, or as far as I was concerned, of finding some way of getting back home. The distance to Fort Colville, the Indians told us, was about a hundred miles by the road, but they had a trail near the river which was shorter — about seventy miles. The Indians very kindly gave us some provisions and directed us on our way.

On the third day we reached Fort Colville and found our journey was made for nothing, our time wasted; that the reports from the mines were so discouraging that few of the parties who arrived there went any further, but started back by Oregon. Not one who came from the Sound had returned the way they came. This accounted for our meeting no one. We also were told by Mr. McDonald, who was in charge of the Hudson Bay company's establishment there, that he had heard rumors of trouble between the Indians and Americans, but all he had heard was only Indian rumors; that he had seen no white man yet who knew anything of it, but he was satisfied there was something in the rumors he had heard.

As both my companions were single men and all plans were alike to them, they decided to remain there through the winter, but I was obliged to return if I had to walk all the way back. After I had been at Fort Colville about ten days, I got an opportunity to return. Several parties were returning, but owing to the rumors of Indian troubles, some of them had been waiting for more company. Among them was a man who was not in good health. He had three horses and a quanitity of provisions, intending to work in the mines, but finding the mines were not what he expected to find and his health being impaired, he was going back to Oregon, and knowing my circumstances he offered, if I would help him to look after his horses, to let me have one to ride and furnish the provisions during the trip. I was very glad to accept the offer. There were about sixteen persons and forty horses in all. Our party was going down to purchase supplies for the mines and return. They owned most of the horses and had employed an old settler as a guide, who had been for many years in the Hudson Bay company's service, and who knew the country thoroughly. He was named Angus McLeod. I forget the date now, but it was some time in October when we started, and it was the intention of our guide, in view of the Indian rumors, to avoid the regular route as much as possible and travel over the best ground for the horses, although it might make a longer route.

Nothing of any importance happened for the first few days, but on the sixth morning two of the best horses were missing. They belonged to the party who intended returning. As no one would leave two horses without an effort to find them, and, as we did not wish to break up the party, we all remained, and for two days hunted in every direction for the missing animals, but neither of them could be found. McLeod was satisfied that they had been run off by Indians, or he would have found them. We kept a guard over the horses at night after that, for if we lost all our horses, we would have a long way to walk. On the third morning we resumed our journey, and it was either that forenoon or the next that we met the Hudson Bay company's train, bound for Fort Colville with their yearly supplies. There was one white man, a number of Indians, and fifty or sixty animals in the train. The clerk in charge of the train gave us a paper to read, which was a proclamation by Acting-Governor Mason of Washington territory, informing all persons that the Indians in eastern Oregon and Washington had broken out in open warfare against the whites, and warning all persons who had gone to the gold mines to remain in that region until further notice, as it was dangerous for small parties to cross the country to the settlements.

The nearest place we could reach for safety was the Hudson Bay company's post at Walla Walla. This was the fourth day since the train left that place, and a number of people were there then. The French-Canadians who were settled around were gathering in at Walla Walla. Our condition was not very flattering to meet an enemy. We were sixteen men, but not a gun of any kind; not even a pistol had any of us, nothing more formidable than a few sheath-knives and two or three axes. Some of the party wanted to return to Colville while some, of whom I was one, was anxious to go on. We agreed to stand together and a vote was taken as to what we should do, and it was decided to go on. On inquiring of the clerk if he had seen any Indians since he left Walla Walla, he said that they had seen two or three. They would ride up near them and as soon as they saw who they were they would ride off again. We were then within a few miles of where the train had crossed Snake river, and about 100 miles from Walla Walla, which we determined to reach as soon as possible. The clerk told us there was a canoe on this side of the river, which he had used in crossing, he told us where he had hidden the paddles so that we could find them, which we did on reaching the river. As there was but one canoe and it pretty small it took about two hours to cross everything. The south bank where we crossed was a very high bluff or mountain and while we were crossing we saw an Indian on horseback ride up to the edge of this bluff and sit watching us for a long while, then disappear. We had dinner before starting and intended riding as long and as hard as our horses could stand. We passed a small train with a Catholic priest going to a mission, but we did not get any more information from him. We rode till nearly midnight to reach a place the guide had in view where there was grass and water. There we stopped long enough to give the horses a good rest, keeping a bright look out all the time, as our guide said the Indians knew all about us, and if there was many of them near we might be attacked or at least an attempt made to run off our horses, and without our horses we would be at their mercy. We started before daylight and rode all day. Two horses gave out during the day and were abandoned, and about half an hour before sunset we reached Walla Walla and found it deserted. On the bank of the river we saw a number of powder kegs, which we afterward heard had been emptied into the river to prevent the Indians from getting them.

Our position was now getting to be serious. We were getting out of provisions. We wanted arms for protection, and we wanted some information as to why the fort was deserted, and where the people had gone. The fort was surrounded by a wall about ten or twelve feet high, built with mud bricks that had not been burnt. The entrance was by wood gates. They were securely fastened on the inside. I climbed over the wall and opened one of the gates to let the party in. We made a hasty search for letters or any notice that would give information, but found nothing. The dwelling house and store houses were all open except the merchandise store. Everything appeared as if a hurried departure had been made. The beds were just as people had got out of them. On the table dishes were standing as if a meal had just been had, and nothing removed from the table. No fire arms could be found, so we opened the merchandise store to see if any were to be had there. A number of guns were found on the floor, but the locks had all been taken off. Nothing could be found that was of any use as a weapon of defense, nor any ammunition. Everything showed that the fort had been abandoned that day, and the inference was that an attack was feared that night, and if such was the case, then the sooner we got away from the fort the better. As there was plenty of flour and bacon, we took what we needed and made a list of it so that it could be settled for afterward.

After everyone had gone out I was to fasten the gate on the inside and then climb over the wall, but before doing so I took the precaution to see that my horse was securely fastened, for I didn't want to be left in the lurch. My wardrobe was getting in a woeful condition, in fact, I was in rags, and almost barefooted, and at night and morning shivered with cold. Here was a storehouse with plenty of warm, substantial clothing, stockings, boots and shoes in it. I was determined to change my rags for a new fit out from top to toe, though all the Indians in the country should gather round the fort while I was doing it. So far as being afraid, or apprehending that I was

-123-

in any danger, I felt as safe and satisfied as if I was in New York dressing for a ball, and I took time enough to get a good article and a good fit of each kind. I tried on about a dozen pair of pants before I got satisfied, and the same way with boots. At last I got all I needed, and fasted up the store as well as I could. It must have been half an hour from the time I closed the gate, after letting the others out, before I got on top of the wall and saw my horse was still there. How I would have fared at the hands of Kamiakum or Pewpewmoxmox had my horse been gone, it is hard to say, but fortunately for me, he was still there, and from the way he whinnied when I spoke to him, he seemed to be as glad to see me as I was to see him. He was a good horse, and as long as I could stay on his back very few could catch me.

I took a long look from the top of the wall to see if I could get a glimpse of my companions, but it was getting too dusky to see far, and I could make nothing out that looked like life in any direction. I had been so absorbed in the business of changing my clothes that I did not look to see, nor ask any one what direction they were going to take. But I had sense enough to know that my horse could find them better than I could, and so mounting on his back I let him go his own road. He needed no persuasion. The road was level, and for a while he fairly flew, and it kept me busy to watch myself, for if I fell off his back, it is not likely he would stay till I got on again. After riding about five or six miles I saw some lights and found my companions camped and getting supper. They were beginning to wonder what had happened to me, but when I told them what had detained me they thought I was running a big risk. One man was on his knees praying. I laughed when they spoke of risk, and told them I was in no more danger then than if I was at home in my own house. I had confidence in my inward monitor, and firmly believed that I would be warned if my life was in danger. I afterward found out that had we gone on when that heart sickness came over me we would have met the Indians who killed Mattice and his party, and most likely we would have shared his fate.

I tried to cheer the party by telling them we were in no danger, but I thought I was saying more than I could vouch for, for although I firmly believed then that I could reach my home in safety, I might be the only one of our number that would do so. I said no more, especially when I saw that they did not take my levity in good part.

After supper a consultation was had. The nearest way to The Dalles was to follow the road down the river, but that would take us to all the Indian camps, with no way of avoiding them, and we had heard and seen enough to know that our safety consisted in keeping away from the Indians. McLeod's advice was to follow up the Walla Walla river to where some settlers were and find out whether the Cayuse Indians had turned against the whites or not. If they were friendly we were all right; if not, we could try and reach the emigrant (Mullen) road and try to reach The Dalles by it, or keep east to the Nez Perce country. After supper we started again to get away from the vicinity of Walla Walla in case an attack should be made on it. We traveled till midnight, then stopped and camped till morning, dividing ourselves into the watches, two of which could sleep while the other kept watch.

After breakfast next morning we started and traveled till noon, when we camped to recruit the horses. McLeod started off to visit some settlers' ranches not far from where we were, and while he was gone a French Canadian who was hunting for a stray horse came to our camp. He told us that Mr. Olney, the Indian agent; Mr. Sinclair, who was in charge of Walla Walla, and his family and all the settlers were camped not very far off, and that they were going to The Dalles. That afternoon we went over to where they were and camped near them. We told Mr. Sinclair of our visit to the fort, what we had done and what we had got, and gave him a list of the provisions we had, and I of the clothes, which I afterward paid Dr. Tolmie for. He was perfectly satisfied. Next morning we started for The Dalles. There were five wagons and a large number of horses and horsemen. That day the horse my friend was riding gave out and I had to give up mine for him to ride, and the rest of the journey to The Dalles I made on foot. I forget whether it was two days or three days that it took. Sometimes I was out of sight of the train, but always ahead of it. I did not want to court unnecessary danger, for if I got behind the train and anything happened to me, there would be no hope of any help; but if any danger presented itself ahead of the train, help would soon be at hand.

No casualty, however, occurred and the whole cavalcade reached The Dalles in safety. The town was in fact a military camp, both regular troops and volunteers preparing to take the field. Going into a hotel to hear the news I saw some newspapers lying round, and the first one I picked up was a copy of the *Pioneer and Democrat*, published in Olympia. I soon became interested in the editorial, which was a history of the Indian trouble, its causes, etc., and it contained a list of those known to have been killed by the Indians up to date. Conspicuous among these names appeared my own. I felt inclined to laugh at the idea that a man with the appetite I had at that time should be classed with the dead men, but when I thought of my wife, what her condition must be, the smile left my lips and I resolved to get this news contradicted as soon as possible. There were no telegraphs here in those days, no daily mail, and I knew there was no way of carrying the news to my home quicker than I could do it myself.

The free masonry there is among sailors enabled me to get from The Dalles to the Cascades and from the Cascades to Vancouver, but as it would be some time before a boat was going to Monticello I concluded to walk the rest of the way to Olympia. Most of the houses on my way were abandoned, the settlers, except at the most important points, having gathered together in block-houses for safety. Still I found a stopping place every night, where I was always very differently treated from what the average tramp would be today. The only persons I met on the road were parties moving from their homes to the block-houses, and they were generally escorted by two or three armed men. Two or three times I was accosted by such parties and asked if I was not afraid to be traveling alone on foot without any arms, as I was liable to be killed by Indians. My answer was that I was not afraid, and even if I was, I had to go to Olympia, and I knew of no other way to get there in my present condition than by pushing ahead. I saw no Indians, nor was I in any sense afraid. I had a firm conviction that I would get to Olympia in safety. I had the idea that if I was in great danger at any time I would get some warning—some premonition to put me on my guard, and so long as I felt no apprehension of danger, there was nothing to fear.

On the fourth evening I reached Olympia. I had been elected a member of the legislature and arrived in time to prevent a special election being called to fill the vacancy caused by my supposed death, the proclamation for such election having already been written. As the legislature would meet within a month, and as it might take most of that time to get to Whatcom and back with the then existing means of travel, and as I could get employment in Olympia, I decided to remain there, and found an opportunity of sending a letter to my wife. I afterward found that through the kindness of our neighbors she never saw the published account of my death until after she got my letter.

Many changes have taken place since then, but, thanks to the beneficent institutions of our country, I have now reached a condition when I can afford to smile at all the hardships and privations I have gone through in every quarter of the globe, both by land and sea, and bless the luck that induced me to cast my lot in the United States of America, and exclaim: Who would not love and fight for the country where it is possible for every man to raise himself from the condition I was in when I first saw the shores of America, to the condition I am in today.

Milburn G. Wills

An engrossing story of fighting Indians in the Yakima Valley in 1855.

North Yakima, Washington — April 18, 1892

In 1852, my father, James Wills, left Burlington, Ia., and made the journey across the country to Yreka, Cal., with an ox team. In the year following, on notification to join him, I, together with my mother, two brothers and two sisters, started on the journey, going from Burlington to St. Louis and thence up the Missouri river to St. Joe. We organized what was called the "Shelton-Weddle train," consisting of about sixty wagons drawn by brawny oxen. On the 4th of May, 1853, we crossed the Missouri river and entered immediately upon the hardships of a trip that was destined to occupy more than four months. From the standpoint of the usual experiences of those having crossed the plains, our trip was uneventful, though it was sufficiently spiced with incidents, and had hardships enough to make it thoroughly interesting. I was then a mere boy of 16, and did not fully appreciate the dangers to which our train was subjected. We had no actual engagements with the Indians, our company being sufficiently large to keep a check upon them, where smaller trains going over the same route a few days previous had suffered a great loss of livestock and very frequently some members of their parties. On September 10, 1853, we arrived at what was known as "Foster's," at the foot of the Cascades, in the Willamette valley, and finally located on "Dickey's Prairie," on the Molalla river, Klackamas county, near Oregon City, then the capital of Oregon territory, which embraced at that time the whole of what is now the state of Washington. My father then proceeded to make a home on a half section of land, taken up under the "donation act," a grant made specially for the benefit of early settlers.

I recall an incident that, I think, occurred in the spring of 1858. A missionary — I think his name was George Miller — settled in our neighborhood and began making a home.

He had a wife, and one child about 3 years old. The wife told her husband that on several occasions when he was absent, a big dog came around the house, and she wanted him to kill it.

So one day he was working near the house and took his rifle to watch for the dog. The woman was washing near the house, and the child started for the place where its father was at work, when all at once the woman cried: "George, there is that dog, shoot him." Just then the cougar, for such it was, sprang upon the child, catching it in the clothing at the back, and ran for the bushes, about fifty yards distant.

The father was paralyzed, momentarily, but suddenly grasped his gun and fired at the animal as it was making its last spring to get into the bushes with the child. Providence must have guided that bullet, for the animal fell dead in its tracks, and not a scratch was left upon the baby.

On one occasion, in the spring of 1855, William Bunton and myself went elk hunting on the Molalla river. We found no elk, but killed five or six deer and started to return to our houses. Resting by a big tree by the way side, we found in it a large hollow and Bunton inserted his gun and poked around in the cavity, when we were both greatly startled to hear a savage roar, and next to see the head and shoulders of a tremendous bear which had been disturbed in its winter quarters. Bunton dropped his gun and made a spring that would have done credit to an athlete. The bear went back to bed, but we were determined to rout him out. We figured around considerably before securing the lost gun, but finally drew it away from the hole with a forked stick; then Bunton took his stand and I threw rocks into the hollow until old bruin showed his head, when he got a chunk of lead that did the business for him. On finding out for a certainty the bear was defunct, we tried to pull him from his lair, but our united strength could not budge him.

Finally Bunton went and got his horse, and putting a rope around the neck and shoulders of his bearship, climbed upon his horse, and with a half hitch around the horn of his saddle he put spurs to the animal, and the bear came out, but the way that horse bucked and snorted when he saw what he had been pulling on would have tried the skill of the best Mexican vaqueros. The bear pulled down the scales at 500 pounds, net weight.

Early in the fall of 1855 the Indians in the northwest began a series of depredations upon the settlers in the sparsely settled regions of Oregon, which then embraced the now state of Washington. About the middle of October of that year, Governor George L. Curry determined to try and subdue the savage cohorts, and to that end issued a call for volunteers. A large number responded, and ninety-three of us from Klackamas county enrolled our names under Captain James J. Kelly, Company C, First regiment, Oregon militia volunteers. We started upon our campaign October 15, 1855, and after leaving The Dalles, it was found necessary to elect a new captain, as James Kelly had been promoted to Colonel. Samuel B. Stafford was chosen and Charles Cutting flag bearer, the other officers being, D. B Hannah first lieutenant and James Powell second lieutenant.

The organization being completed, we took to the field, arriving at Klickitat valley November 6, 1855. We had seen no fresh meat since leaving Portland, and the killing of a fine fat cow by one of our party was hailed with delight by all.

The Klickitat was then a veritable paradise for the little stock then running at large. The grass was over six feet tall and very dense. Striking camp the next day we crossed the Simcoe mountains and came to the beautiful Simcoe valley, now embraced in the Yakima reservation. On November 9th we made our way in the hills through which flows the Yakima river, then known as the "Two Buttes." Here the first active engagement of our campaign against the wily and wicked children of the forest occurred. Our advance guards, consisting of companies commanded by Captains Cornelius, Hembrie and Bennett, drove the Indians from their ambush in the brush along the river.

Being driven from their valley, they intrenched themselves in their rude fortifications upon the buttes. A howitzer was used in our first attempt to dislodge them, but the shots fell short and a charge was made upon the enemy by the commands under Major Haller and Captain Augur, assisted by a corps of volunteers, who charged up the rugged face of the mountain, forcing the Indians from their position and compelling them to flee down the opposite side of the butte in hot haste.

Finding that the whites were determined to force the fighting at short range, if possible, the Indians made no effort to assist the culmination, and kept a safe distance out of range.

That night we camped at the base of the buttes, near the river, and the first dawn of the next day disclosed the unwelcome sight of numerous Indians lurking about from place to place upon the butte, and to emphasize their presence they occasionally sent a stray bullet into our camp. An order was at once given to drive them from their vantage ground, and our command separated, one company going up the face of the hill and the remainder coming through the canyon between the two buttes.

Just as we reached the north side an Indian on horseback came at a breakneck speed around the bluff within fifty yards of us, and as he passed, Lieutenant D.B. Hannah jumped from his horse, and, taking good aim with his rifle, made an angel of that noble red man in less time than it takes to tell it. It was near the same place, on the side of the mountain, that I made the first notch in my "trusty rifle" by swelling the number of good Indians in the happy hunting ground.

A party of us went out, contrary to orders, to see if we could not have a little fun and reduce the number of our foes at the same time. Going to the top of the mountain, we were greatly annoyed by an Indian who, from the shelter of a large rock in the gulch below us, was trying to play a hand at our game. He would step out in full view and fire at us, and before we could bring to bear on him he was safely ensconsed behind his natural breastworks. Watching my opportunity, I slipped away from the crowd and rapidly made my way around the hill, out of sight of the pesky redskin. Unsuspicious of danger, he stepped out to try another shot at my comrades, but before he could get his gun in position I let him have one in the ribs, and, throwing his arms above his head, with a wild yell he gently passed into the spirit land. Years afterwards his skull was found by H.H. Adkins, who died recently at Yakima City, and it is now in my possession.

Having run the Indians from the hills, we started on the 10th of November to follow them up the Ahtanum valley, and, in company with Joseph Buff and an Indian guide known as "Cut-Mouth-John," I separated from the main body of our command and started around the mountains. We had not proceeded a great distance when our Umatilla guide called our attention to an Indian who was coming full tilt in our direction. The siwash rode rapidly toward us, and as I pulled the trigger of my gun, the horse I rode gave a sudden spring, throwing the muzzle of my gun in the air, where it discharged. Mr. Indian came up within a few feet of me, snapping an old Hudson Bay company's pistol, about two feet long, right at me, but it failed to go off, and our dusky foe when whizzing by, followed by my saddle animal and Cut-Mouth-John close behind. Our guide was riding a good horse, and soon overtook the fleeing savage. Placing the muzzle of his gun directly behind the shoulders of the Indian, our John pulled the trigger and blowed a hole in that redskin that a cat could crawl through.

Twenty-seven years after the event recorded I met Cut-Mouth-John in Pendleton, Or., and we had a great "wah-wah" about our campaign in the Yakima valley. Catching my own and the Indian's horse, and allowing Cut-Mouth-John to relieve the Indian of his scalp, we returned to the command. Our next stop was within two miles of the Catholic mission, in the Ahtanum valley. Several of our men, myself among the number, went up to the old mission, and arriving there, we found that some one had preceded us. A lot of devilment had been done, by whom it was never ascertained, and the place was deserted. Candles, crucifixes, beads and other Romish emblems were scattered in ruthless chaos all around, and vandal hands had worked irreparable injury to beautiful paintings and other decorations. A serious effort was made by our officers to discover the author of these impious outrages, and it would have fared badly with the offenders had they been discovered. We found about a ton of flour and a lot of dried camas and berries cached away, and, as we were then on half rations, these came in very gratefully to the Webfoot boys, who had learned to eat that sort of grub before leaving home.

On November 12th, while still camped on the Ahtanum, sixteen inches of snow fell, and on the following day quite a band of Indian horses were rounded up. The officers ordered the animals killed, and the mandates were obeyed.

Some of the most extraordinary exhibitions of bravery that has ever come under my observation, occurred on that same day. A scouting party composed of eighteen or twenty men, under Lieutenant Andrew Shephard of Silverton, Marion county, Or., and D.B. Hannah, were out reconnoitering at the head of the valley, when from 600 to 1000 Indians came down upon them. They were all on horses and had thrown themselves on the side of their animals, opposite our boys. They seemed thicker than any flock of black birds I have ever seen. The savages made a charge and our men retreated to higher grounds. The balance of our command, further down the valley, saw the dust and smoke and were ordered to the rescue. As the scouting party retreated, one Steve Waymire of Polk county, was shot through the fleshy part of the hips, and the way he did "squall" was a caution. George Holmes of Klackamas, was shot through the left arm breaking both bones to splinters. At this time the Indians were coming full tilt, yelling and firing their guns, and Holmes' arm was falling about from side to side, he having no control whatever over its motion. He dropped his gun, and being determined not to lose it, jerked his horse up, jumped down and got it and, remounting the animal, soon overtook the rest of the boys. Having informed them of the accident, a hollow square was formed around him and the wounded member lashed to his body so it would not fall around. He sat on his horse in a running fight for fifteen miles, and was not heard to give vent to even a groan. In the retreat Lieutenant Shepherd got after two wild bulls, and the Indians tried to cut him off from the command. The lieutenant jumped from his horse and fired at the savages near him and shot one of the redskins, who was tied to his cayuse. The Indian fell back, and the horse started through the sage brush, dragging his dusky master. Two other Indians, observing the fate of their comrade, ran their horses up to him, one of them jumping onto the horse of the dead Indian, while the other pushed the body up to him, and away they all went together. But Shepherd got away with the bulls. Holmes afterward went to San Francisco and had the bullet removed from its lodgement under his breast bone.

On the head of Simcoe creek we found the body of an Indian who had met his death in a peculiar manner. The bullet that laid him cold never touched his body, but had entered the mouth of his powder horn, exploding the powder and blowing an aperture into his side that you could have thrown a cat through, and blacking him from the shoulder down. He may not have been overly large in life, but his size when we saw him was tremendous. This occurred while Major Haller was cutting his way through the Indians, who had surrounded his command.

Having run the Indians to their mountain fastness, beyond our reach, we were ordered to return to the Dalles, and on the 16th of November started across the Simcoe mountains.

My horse gave out, and I sent word along the line to Adjustant W.H. Farrer, who rode back to me and ordered the men to kill my horse and put my saddle and blankets on the pack horses, at the same time telling me to get on his horse and ride to the top of the mountain, where I was to tie the animal to a tree and go on foot, and saying that he would see that my things got through all right. I think such men as General Farrer should never die. I followed his instructions, and tying his horse at the top of the mountain, set out on foot. On the night of the 17th I set my boots close to the camp fire and went to sleep, and on the following morning I found them burnt to a crisp.

The snow was about four feet deep on the summit, and I think it was the coldest weather I ever experienced. Nothing was left for me to do but wrap my feet in pieces of blankets, and I had to trudge along through the snow, in that biting cold until 12 o'clock that night, alone, for the command out-traveled me considerably and reached the Klickitat valley several hours ahead of me. On the 18th of November, 1855, we started for the remainder of the old Fort Klickitat, en route to The Dalles, and on the evening of the 19th Colonel Nesmith and all the other officers left us and went into The Dalles, leaving me commander in chief or corporal until orders were returned. These were received on November 21st, instructing us to come to The Dalles, and in a few days some of the boys, myself among the number, were granted a discharge. The discharge was granted to me November 26, 1855, as the following copy of a receipt I now have in my possession, from my captain, Samuel B. Stafford will show:

Dalles, November 25, 1855.

Received of Milburn G. Mills, one (1) saddle,

one (1) gun, one (1) powder flask.

Samuel B. Stafford, Captain Company C,

First Regiment, O.M.V.

On receipt of this I started for home on board a steamer running between The Dalles and Portland, arriving there in a few days and going to work on a farm, not expecting to ever be called back to the field of war again. But in this I was fooled.

Of course there were a number of interesting and exciting incidents during my first campaign not chronicled herein but the few I have mentioned will give some idea of the condition of the Yakima valley at the time of which I write, when there was not a white settler within a radius of 200 miles, extending from the Columbia river on the east and the Cascade range on the west.

General George L. Curry made the second call for volunteers February 22, 1856. I started out again under Captain William A. Carson, Company E, Klackamas county, with W.G. Moore, first lieutenant, William Mitchell, second lieutenant, George Reynolds, first sergeant and A. Holcomb, second sergeant. Leaving Portland March 3, 1856, we reached the Cascades on the 6th, and on the 8th we were ordered to The Dalles, arriving there late in the afternoon. On the morning previous to our arrival quite a number of freight teams started for Fort Walla Walla laden with provisions for the troops, and seventeen of our company, including myself, under Sergeant Reynolds were detailed to overtake them and guard them to Fort Henrietta. We did not reach them that evening, and as we had started with nothing to eat but flour and coffee, I killed a steer to stay our appetites.

The yearling belonged to Nathan Olney, and he should have been paid for it, but it is doubtful if it was ever reported. Next day our company caught up, and we camped about half way between John Day River and Willow creek. Early next morning some Indians made a rush on the guards and cut off about eighteen head of our horses, stampeding them. About twenty of us gave chase, following the Indians almost to the mouth of Willow creek, and came onto them in camp. The boys fired on them at long range and Mr. Depew shot and crippled a squaw, who fell, and jumped up, picked up her baby playing near the fire and ran into the willows along the creek. Part of our crowd went down to the creek and some to the Indian camp, while others waited on the hill to pick off the Indians as they ran. I was looking after the horses, and a comrade named Goshon asked me to look after the animals in his charge, as he saw a siwash in the bush.

He then crawled up and hid behind some grease wood within twenty paces of the willows, and had not settled in his position before an Indian, about thirty yards away, fired point blank at my head. The ball, or slug of iron, shaved off a lock of hair just above my right ear, and that member has been, though perhaps ornamental, a useless appendage ever since. Just as the Indian let drive at me, Goshen fired at him, and his aim was good, for the blood spurted all over the bush. We looked for him, but the Indian jumped into a pool of water, dyeing it with his blood and disappeared. We captured some of the horses and next morning visited the Indians' camp, burning all their outfit, but no savages were visible to the naked eye. We next went to Fort Henrietta on the Umatilla river, near where now stands the town of Echo, and thence to old Fort Walla Walla.

I think it was April 15, 1856, our company was camped on the Walla Walla river, when some seventeen of our boys went to the neighborhood of

Wild Horse creek and found thirteen head of cattle, two of which were very unruly bulls. We killed the two bulls that evening and the same night a messenger came into camp and startled us by the announcement that the commands under Colonel Cornelius and Colonel James J. Kelley, then camped in the forks of Snake and Columbia rivers, were in a starving condition — that if we could send beef cattle to them to do so at once. Captain Carson ordered us to cast lots and seven men were selected to drive the eleven head of cattle to the starving commands.

The only way to reach them was to swim the Snake river and drive the cattle through an Indian country. On the morning of April 16th a number of us went down to the river, which was about half a mile across and almost mush ice, where the Northern Pacific Railroad company's iron bridge now crosses at Ainsworth. We started the cattle and seven men after them, and our brave captain and I followed them. The captain and I got across safely with the cattle, but the other men landed on the same side on which they had started. We got on our horses and started for the suffering commands. Just imagine how cold the snow water of Snake river is in April, and after swimming through half a mile of it to drive a bunch of cattle six miles, with no clothing but an under shirt and a pair of drawers, running our horses to keep up with the cattle, the wind blowing chill enough to freeze the shirts on our backs till they rattled like paste-board, then the next morning to ride back and take the same dose in a spitting snow storm. But we did it, as Colonel James Kelley and T.R. Cornelius, who still live, can testify. That was the first time I saw Captain Hembrey. I warned him to be careful, as we had crossed a trail made apparently by at least 600 Indians, who had just gone along toward the Columbia river, about six miles below the point where the captain's command was crossing, and from their maneuvers I thought the Indians intended to cut the men off and capture their horses. As I had feared, the Indians caught him, and the gallant captain was immolated upon the altar erected for the sacrifice of thousands of other intrepid heroes who interposed their lives to protect their families and save this fair western land as a heritage to their children and children's children forever.

Returning to my command, I was detailed with twelve or fourteen of my companions to convey Samuel Price (now a brother-in-law of Senator Mitchell of Oregon) to The Dalles for medical treatment, as he was suffering from the mountain fever.

Reaching the John Day river, we found that stream very much swollen, and having no means of crossing, we camped for the night. The rain descended in torrents, and we bent willows and spread our blankets over them for protection from the storm.

The ensuing morning we began to construct a raft on which to convey the sick man to the opposite side of the river, which was deep, wide and swift as a mill race. On coming out of our impromptu tent a man named Geer caught his gun-lock on one of the willow poles and the weapon was discharged, the ball striking him in the left groin, and coming out at the hip.

We thus had two invalids on our hands, and one raft would not hold them. Seeing that immediate action was necessary, Jeff Miller and myself agreed to risk our chances with the river and go to The Dalles for assistance. Plunging into the stream with our horses, after some difficulty, we were fortunate enough to make the other side, and started rapidly for The Dalles, some sixty miles distant. We had gone but a short distance, when looking at a hill near us I observed something resembling a cougar or other wild animal, apparently sitting on its haunches watching us. With a boyish spirit I told Miller I was going to scare the animal and see it run. We had no guns being unable to swim the river with them, so I rode towards the animal unarmed. Getting within about forty yards of the supposed cougar, I noticed it dodge down behind the rocks, and, "smelling a mice," as it were, I turned my horse's head in the opposite direction and put cruel spurs into his flanks, just in time to hear wild yells issuing from half a score of dusky throats. (Jeff Miller is now a resident of Klickitat county.)

Sure enough it was "Injuns" and the "animal" on top of the rock had been fixed up as a decoy, which came very near doing what it was intended to do. When I overtook my companion our steeds were in a dead run, and then began a race for life. Having no weapons, we depended entirely upon the speed of our excellent horses, and the Indians, recognizing the superiority of our animals, sought to cut us off, but by dint of dodging in the canyons and over precipitous hills, we finally got out of their reach. (Paddy Miln, late clerk of the Umatilla Indian reservation, knows also of this ride.) Arriving at The Dalles without further incident, we endeavored to persuade several doctors to go to the relief of our disabled comrades, but the gentlemen refused to endanger their lives by making the trip. Fortunately for the sick men, a wagon train, guarded by troops, passed in the vicinity of the camp and they were brought to The Dalles, where, I am happy to state, they both finally recovered.

In a few days our command was mustered out of service, thus ending my experience as an active campaigner against the wily red men. These incidents can be recalled by many of my old comrades, among whom are Peter Leonard, who was shot in the leg in one of the skirmishes of the Indian wars above referred to, and Charles Stewart, who both now reside in the city of North Yakima, and are members of Multnomah camp No. 2, Indian War Veterans.

Little did I think in those days of the great future in store for the fertile Yakima valley, or that I would one day settle down right upon the ground over which I had trailed the aborigines, in a prosperous and growing city. But in 1879 fate or fortune directed my steps to Goldendale, in Klickitat county, Wash., where I resided about four years, filling the office of sheriff in that county, and finally drifting, after a residence of eight years in Pendleton, Or., to the great Yakima valley, where, with propitious fortune, I expect to end my days.

Christiana Corum

Girl of thirteen witnesses the death of her father while defending the family at the Middle Cascades Landing, on the Columbia River during an Indian attack in 1856.

September 11, 1892

Having read with great interest all of the old settlers' stories in the *Ledger* I wish to send you a few incidents of my experience in the early settlement of the west. I, Mrs. C.S. Corum, was born in Clinton county, Iowa, on the 31st day of March, 1843, and was the youngest daughter of George and Candace Griswold. In 1851 my father thought best to try his fortune in the far west. Our family at that time consisted of father, mother, three sisters, one brother and myself. My brother and two sisters not wishing to take this long journey, and having homes of their own, were content to remain where they were. In May father, mother and their two little girls Gennie and Anna (Eugenia and Christiana) started across the plains. Our team consisted of two yoke of cows and three yoke of oxen and one wagon well filled.

Here let me say, the cattle were traded off for five head of horses, and our load lightened by throwing away everything we could get along without before we reached our journey's end. We did not have any trouble with the Indians except in stampeding and driving our stock away. At one time they drove away all of the stock in the night. I can well remember with what fear we held camp the next day, as nearly all of the men went to look for the stock. Father struck their trail, and found them just as the Indians were trying to swim them over a river. As he was alone he began shouting and waving his hands for the rest to come on. The Indians, thinking the whole train was after them, fled, and he drove the stock back to camp. At another time, as we were preparing to camp, an Indian raised up on the opposite bank and shook a buffalo robe. The teams all took fright and ran away. Mother, being out of the wagon, our team ran over her hurting her shoulder, which gave her pain at times until her death. One man in the train was given to boasting of the good traits of his oxen. He would tell father that if he sang out "whoa" to his oxen they would stop at any time or place. One day he proved it. Some Indians came riding by the train on a run, and the teams stampeded. This man sung out "whoa" and his wheel oxen stopped so suddenly that it broke the yoke and the wagon ran over them. In all of this confusion the man cried out: "There, Griswold, I told you my oxen would stop."

We did not have hardships and privations in our train like some who were molested by the Indians, but a trip across the plains in early days with an ox team, is in itself a hardship enough for one to remember all of their life.

We reached The Dalles in October and went down the Columbia river to the Cascades, where father ran a saw mill that winter. We went to Portland in the spring and stayed until 1854, when he again returned to the Cascades, where he resided till his death. If we could have foreseen the terrible tragedies that afterwards took place here, we would have fled at once, but a wise Providence kindly veils the future from our vision, allowing us only to look back on the past scene of our lives, sometimes with pleasure and sometimes with sad regret.

Every one that has read the history of Oregon and Washington is familiar with the terrible deeds done by the Yakima and Klikitat Indians, and I shall only try to describe a part of the suffering at the middle cascades. The Cascades was applied to the upper, middle and lower landings of the boats. From the upper landing to the middle was a portage around the falls. The distance, two and a half miles, consisted of a plank railroad and had cars drawn by mules and horses. From the middle landing to the lower there was a wagon road, two and a half miles. At some stages of the water the steamboats landed at the middle landing, but most of the time bateaux were used. By these means all of the government and individual ammunition and freight was transported around the falls.

Father's occupation was transporting the freight. Captain Wallen, with the assistance of father's work hands and mill teams, had made a block house near our house, and several nights we stayed in it when the Indian excitement ran high. I have passed briefly over my life up to this time, as nothing transpired to mar the happiness of my childhood. But soon, ah! very soon, I was to take part in scenes that can never be obliterated from my memory.

On the 26th day of March, 1856, the sun rose over a happy and prosperous little village at the middle landing, but ere it reached its mid-day course, death and devastation reigned in our midst. As we were living at the place I shall try and describe some of the suffering here. Between the hours of 8 and 9 o'clock in the morning, when everyone was busy at their different occupations, the Indians attacked these three landings at the same time. At the lower landing the settlers were warned by a half-breed Indian, and all got in a boat and started down the Columbia river without any loss of life, and some only slightly wounded. The Indians burned everything that was left. At the upper landing they killed several, wounding some also. By all collecting at Bradford's store they held the place with great difficulty until help came from The Dalles. Here everything was burned. The blockhouse was situated on the bank of the Columbia river and was open to an attack on one side only. From this point the Indians began firing. Thinking it was only the soldiers firing off their guns, as they sometimes did, I walked out in the yard and stood talking to some others. Six bullets in rapid succession came over my head and about me, the last one striking a little boy by my side. He cried out, "I am shot." We then seemed to understand that we were in danger and went in the block house. By this time people had in every direction came flying in. They had taken all the soldiers to The Dalles but seven, and one of these was lying dead upon the hill in front of the block house and another one shot through the hip at the foot of the incline where they hauled the freight up, leaving five, with the assistance of the settlers, to fire the cannon and hold the fort. Mother was going to the spring for water, and came in with the bucket on her arm. Several came in wounded, but only one fatally, which was my father. He was shot in the knee while some distance from the fort, but reached it in time to sink down inside of the door. On seeing me first he said, "Is mother there?" I supported his head in my arms while mother took a black silk handkerchief from his neck, and also some of her clothing, and tried to stop the flow of blood, but alas! too late to save him. With the cannon booming over his head he sank quietly to rest.

Calm the good man meets his fate,
Guards celestial around him wait.

Everyone was at their post and the yells of the savages and the cannon's roar was kept up all of that day. For two days and nights mother and I sat on either side of our dead, and now, as I recall the scenes of those sad days spent in the blockhouse, tears dim my eyes. Often, before his death, father tried to persuade mother to take me (my sister being in Portland attending school) and go to Portland. She would tell him if he stayed she would also. He said he was needed here and he could not leave. Alas! for the brave man who would not desert his post. Alas! for his widow and orphan children. A pitiful sight, indeed, it was to see a German boy, who was shot down in sight of the fort, as he would raise his hands and beckon to the fort. The Indians seemed to delight in his suffering, and would shoot him with arrows to increase his pain. He died the first night and lay in sight of the fort until the third day. The Indians had piled cord wood on the soldier they killed on the hill, it was supposed, with the intention of burning him, but for some reason they did not. The one, who was wounded on the incline, crawled up the bank the first night and came into the block house. The second night towards morning the Indians ceased firing, and the third day they drew off to reinforce the upper and lower landings. They were seen crossing the river below the fort, and immediately the cannon was fired on them, but they were too far away. What a welcome sound was the booming of this cannon, for it seemed that therein lay our safety. Although it has been quite a number of years since I heard the firing of those guns, yet now, when I hear the report of a gun ring out on the night air my thoughts fly back to those nights of peril in the blockhouse. All of this time we were without food of any kind or a drop of water. The soldiers' kitchen was apart from the blockhouse, and during the firing no one dared to venture out. The third day soldiers came from The Dalles and volunteers from Portland and we were liberated. The greatest excitement prevailed, as the friendly Indians had joined the hostile band. Every family was leaving the fort. Tenderly laying our loved one to rest, we bade him a long farewell and went to

Portland. What sad news to convey to that sister — our father dead, and home and property damaged. A flatboat landed with 250 bushels of potatoes (at that time worth $2 a bushel) turned loose on the Columbia river, and as we floated down it seemed to me we were friendless indeed.

I must speak of some others that, like myself, saw the bullets fall thick around them. One man by the name of Murphy came riding over the hill on one of the horses cut loose from the cars. His brother, Jim, coming down on the railroad, saw the horse fall with him, as it was shot in the neck. He started to go to him, but he cried out for him to go back. Jim stood until his brother came up to him and they went into the fort together. Jim escaped unharmed, but the other was severely wounded in the shoulder. Three men came down on the railroad, and as they neared the fort the bullets became thicker and thicker. One man said: "See Jim run," and at the same time a bullet struck him in the shoulder. He being the last one, and as there was not room for one man to pass another on the railroad, he cried out to the one in front of him: "Run, Peter, run." Peter, who was a German, answered: "I can no faster run." "Well, then, let me run," said Jim, and he stepped aside and Jim passed him, and all reached the fort safely.

A few years after this time the fort and bank on which it stood slipped into the river, but the safety it gave the people at that massacre will never be forgotten. We reached Portland on my thirteenth birthday — the 31st day of March. I was placed in school with my sisters at the ladies' seminary. The following June my mother returned to the Cascades to settle up the estate, but there was not much left for us. (I am at this time trying to have my Indian depredation claims settled).

My sister was married in 1858 and died in 1863, leaving two boys. Mother died in 1877 in Prineville, Or. Myself, one brother and one sister, who is in Iowa, are all that is left the family that parted on the banks of the Mississippi in 1851. Ah! such is life.

I was married in the year 1860, and am the mother of six children. I have tried to write as explicit as possible, and will be pleased to see my father's and mother's names rank with the pioneers of the state.

Ellen J. Wallis

On the trip over the plains in 1852, she catches her dress on fire and has to continue the trip despite her injury. She and her husband were running the hotel at the Lower Cascades on the Columbia River when the Indians attacked in March of 1856.

Port Ludlow, Washington — May 25, 1892

I, Mrs. Ellen Jane Wallis, nee Mark, was born in Fleming county, Kentucky, on May 19, 1836, but was brought up in Mason county until 1850, when my people moved to Iowa, and there, on the 29th of December of the same year, I was married to Thomas McNatt. On May 1, 1852, having previously engaged our passage with a family named Nales, we left Agency City, Ia., traveling by the conventional ox-team, and were bound for the "far west," but we had not yet decided whether our destination should be California or Oregon.

By the 8th of the month we crossed the Missouri river, and found many emigrants encamped on its banks, as it was a sort of general rendezvous for travelers, and here parties were often organized. We joined one which was forming, consisting of about 100 people, whose worldly goods loaded some twenty-eight ox-teams. With this party we traveled as far as Fort Laramie. Nothing more worthy of note occurred on the way than a few stampedes of the cattle.

Dissatisfaction with our leader had crept in, and it kept growing stronger day by day, so, on arriving at the fort, our party agreed to disperse. We and our old friends, the Nales, agreed to travel on independently. In due time we pitched our tents by the Platte river, and here we encountered severe storms of wind, followed by hail and torrents of rain. All our efforts to keep our tents over us were unavailing, and we suffered extreme discomfort from exposure to the elements. Just after the storms passed over I was attacked with Asiatic cholera, and for twelve days was perfectly helpless; then I began to recover. On the night of the twelfth day of my illness Mrs. Nales retired to rest, apparently in her usual health, but in the night she, too, was attacked by this dreaded malady, and within two hours she expired. Her friends immediately dug a grave close by our wagons and buried her without delay; so all was over by daybreak.

Shortly after this we parted from Mr. Nales and joined another family named Sailor. Mrs. Sailor had been stricken with cholera a few days previously and her death left four little children motherless. These children I agreed to care for as far as we traveled together. Our route for some time after this was only too plainly marked by many fresh graves, such ravages had cholera made amongst the little bands of emigrants.

On July 4th we ate our dinner at Independence rock. On its face many travelers had recorded the fact that they had passed that way. Just after leaving we were treated to an unusually heavy hail storm.

From the Platte river to the Colorado desert our journey was exceedingly trying and very wearisome. We suffered greatly from the intense heat and from the alkali dust which enveloped us continually while on the move. The herbage became so dry and scant that our poor oxen were soon hardly able to crawl along. One after another they dropped down to die, until we had lost four yoke. In order to lighten them we had by degrees thrown away stoves, featherbeds, tents and every other article with which we thought we could possibly dispense. Before entering the Colorado desert we halted for two days in order to rest our remaining oxen and cut grass to carry with us for their feed. We encamped close by some other travelers who had stopped for the same purpose.

On one of these days the men had all gone to some distance for this grass, leaving us women, seven in number, alone in camp. During their absence a party of mounted and armed Indians rode up to us, threatening by signs that they would murder and rob us if we would not give them provisions. This we showed them we would not consent to, so one of them pointed his musket at my head and kept it so for several minutes, while I endured the agony of expecting my brains to be blown out any moment, and I dared not move. All the while the Sailor children clung to my skirts screaming with terror. Providentially, at this critical juncture, my husband, accompanied by other men, came in sight and for some unaccountable reason the savages gave a whoop, put spurs to their horses and soon disappeared from our view to trouble us no further.

Crossing the desert occupied about twenty-four hours. Several days after leaving it behind we were suddenly surrounded by a band of about 500 Indian warriors. They might have sprung out of the earth for anything we had seen of them before, and our alarm may be more easily imagined than described. These Indians were out on the war-path against some other tribe and were hideously decorated with an abundance of paint and sundry feathers, while they carried a great variety of weapons, including muskets, swords, spears, tomahawks and bows and arrows. They demanded a share of everything we had in the shape of food, and, considering their numbers, it is needless to say we were delighted to get rid of the 'braves' on such easy terms.

In the months of August we crossed the Rockies without adventure worth the recounting. When on the summit we hardly had parted with the setting sun on the west before morning was ushered in on the east.

At Fort Hall Snake river was crossed by us for the first time, and in order to avoid the lava desert which stretched along the north, we pursued our way on the south side, keeping as near the river as possible, and crossing numerous creeks which all emptied into this river. Our second crossing was just a little way above Salmon Falls. This crossing was the most difficult and dangerous of all the crossings on account of the great swiftness of the current. On arrival at the "Falls" we found a number of emigrants encamped and we were not a little glad to follow their example, as we were both fatigued and hungry. As soon as possible I had a fire of sagebrush (the only available fuel) made and I commenced preparing to cook supper. In the midst of my preparations I heard cries of, "You're afire! You're afire!" and then to my horror I discovered that it was I who was afire. Presence of mind deserted me and I rushed towards the river. As my dress was of cotton material I was soon enveloped in flames, but before I had gone very far my husband and some other men met and captured me. They succeeded in getting the flames extinguished and the burning clothing torn off, scorching their own hands severely in their efforts to save me. With my right sleeves (I wore double ones) came the skin from shoulder to wrist, and my right side from the shoulder to my waist was terribly burned. The arm was worse, however, as it burst open in many places when the doctor, whom we found among the travelers, tried to straighten it, so literally was it cooked. For twenty-four hours I was unconscious, but on reviving I suffered excrutiating agonies. For almost two years I was obliged to support my arm in a sling. I have little doubt but that I should have been burned to death had I not been wearing an underskirt heavily padded with wool, which effectually protected the lower half of my body.

In spite of my burns we felt it necessary to continue our journey as soon as our preparations were completed, for some preparations had to be made to enable us to cross the "Falls." The wagon beds were carefully calked to make them watertight, and the wheels taken off and packed in with the rest of the freight, and so were ready to be taken over the river. The best swimmers in the company took over a strong cable, each end of which was made secure on opposite banks of the dangerous stream. The wagon beds in their new capacity of freight boats were launched and guided across the current by means of the cable and the hands of the men in charge. The women and children were conveyed over in the lightest loaded of the wagons. Not the least difficult task was that of getting the oxen safe to the other shore, but it was at last accomplished. We and our friends got over safely, But on the following trip, a heavily-loaded wagon, which had not been well caulked, with two men and two boys in charge, filled with water and sank in mid-river. It happened so suddenly that no assistance could be rendered to the occupants, who were all drowned. We saw one boy's body washed over the falls. Their friends employed Indians to search for the remaining bodies and after a short time they were recovered and accorded a decent burial. This sudden and melancholy termination to four strong and hearty lives cast a deep gloom over every camp and roused our sympathies for the sorrowing relations who until that time had been only strangers; so completely "one touch of nature makes the world kin."

Saying goodby to Salmon Falls and our passing acquaintances, we now started by a new and heretofore untraveled way to find the old emigrant trail, from which we had deviated some time previously. This occupied almost ten days, as we rested every alternate day, while our guide went ahead to hunt a suitable road. Having struck the trail again, we proceeded on to Fort Boise, where we crossed the Boise river, and on again without accident or adventure until we entered the Grand Ronde valley, Oregon.

At the entrance to this valley we came upon a man lying by the roadside, apparently in an almost dying state. We halted to inquire in to his condition and circumstances, and as well as his failing strength would permit he told us his sad tale. He said his name was Ross, that he belonged to — I have forgotten where — and being rather delicate he thought a trip across the continent would benefit his health. Accordingly he engaged a passage by the orthodox conveyance of the day with a family who transported him to the spot on which he was then lying. Instead of improving on the way, he had gradually become weaker, until at last he was no longer able to wait on himself, and they, refusing to be further troubled with him, laid him out by the road, totally indifferent to what might be his fate. He begged piteously to be taken with us, and as we could not endure the dying creature to be left alone, my husband and I, who, like himself, had paid our faire for the journey, decided to give our place in the wagon and pursue our way on foot. He felt grateful for the sacrifice, the transfer was made and here we parted. Afterward we learned that he expired within twelve hours.

With the wagon we left all our earthly possessions except my husband's rifle, a change each of underwear, a canteen and tincup. Before leaving Grande Ronde valley we purchased from a relief party, which was sent out to assist emigrants, six pounds of flour for the sum of $6, and it was all they would let us have. We also bought some hardtack, a little salt and a few matches. With this generous provision we set off on our walk for the Dalles, a journey of several hundred miles. Occasionally my husband shot a squirrel, a rabbit, or a sage-hen, which proved a welcome addition to our humble fare. When night came we went to sleep under the stars without other covering than the clothes we wore and in the morning rose refreshed and invigorated for our usual walk of twenty-five or thirty miles, for what at first seemed very difficult soon became comparatively easy and rather pleasant. In this way we crossed the Blue mountains and so on toward the end of our pedestrian tour. The last two days were very trying as our provisions were completely gone and only one squirrel, or rabbit, I forget which, was bagged. To people whose appetites were sharpened by continued exercise, combined with the pure mountain air, and compelled by force of circumstances to tramp onward or die this was a real misfortune, and on the last day of our march we were almost fainting from want of food.

On October 3d we arrived at The Dalles, and after attending to the cravings of the inner man and resting for a short period, my husband engaged a passage for me on a raft going to the upper cascades; for this he paid $6. He helped drive a band of cattle to the same place, in return for which service he received his board. We got to the upper cascades on the 7th, and walked across the portage, six miles, to the lower cascades, where we remained until the 9th. On the 9th, at 5 o'clock a.m., we embarked on board the steamship Fashion, bound for Portland. The steamer was crowded, and for standing room we paid $6. The passage occupied the whole of the day until 9 o'clock p.m., and it was one of the hardest days in all my experience. About 4:30 a.m. we had breakfasted on a tin cup of coffee and a little bread, for which luxuries we paid $1, and this meal had to suffice until we reached Portland, as absolutely nothing was to be had on board. Want of food and absence of a seat made the day seem interminable. Nine o'clock, however, came at last and witnessed our arrival at Portland. We made our way to a hotel and soon were seated before a supper to which we did ample justice, and for which we expended the last dollar we possessed. On going out after supper my husband ran across an old school-fellow, W.W. Baker, who resided on the Willamette river six miles from Portland. He invited us to go with him to his home, which invitation, considering the state of our finances, we were only too glad to accept. Accordingly that very night we set off with him in a canoe, but we were not destined to get there as soon as we anticipated for a storm came on which compelled us to put in to shore. We took shelter in Wilder's mill, then not quite finished, and there spent the hours remaining before morning dawned. At daylight, the wind having calmed down, we returned to the canoe and at 9 o'clock a.m. we reached our destination, ready to enjoy the substantial breakfast soon spread before us by kind hands.

At this place we remained all winter. It was one of the winters which are still remembered for their severity, but through it my husband managed to make shingles enough to provide us with food. His health not being good here, we left in the spring of 1853 for Milwaukee, where we stayed for three months. From Milwaukee we went to Clatsop Plains, where we took up a claim on which we lived for nearly a year. In the summer of 1854 we moved to the lower cascades. Here, in the fall of 1855, in spite of the fact that we lived in constant dread of Indian massacres, we opened an hotel. Many times we were alarmed, and on one occasion we spent two nights in the block house. A neighbor of ours, one Captain Baughman, employed quite a number of Indians to row freight bateaux across the rapids to the middle cascades. These Indians always came to work early, but one morning, that of March 26, 1856, a day long to be remembered, contrary to their usual custom, not one put in an appearance; so the captain set off to the Indian village, about a mile distant, to investigate matters. On arriving in the village he found all the young "bucks" gone. The squaws said they had gone to the upper cascades, but Captain B.'s suspicions were now fully aroused, as before leaving home he had heard a report of a cannon at middle cascade, but had tried to make himself believe it was blasting of rock, as work of that kind had been going on. There was no doubt of it now. The Indians were bent on mischief. Before his return from the village, we at the hotel had heard of their rising from a man who, while driving his wagon across the portage, saw a band of them attack the block-house. He at once cut his horses loose from the wagon, mounted one of them and sped back to give the alarm.

My husband at once insisted on my immediate departure to a place of safety, if such could be found, so I took my baby, now Mrs. Poole of Ludlow, in my arms and ran as fast as I could about a mile down the river to a place where several families resided, hoping to escape with them. They had already been warned and were just about going on board a bateau as I joined them. Some of the women were in a most excited state. One in particular was helpless, yet none of them had heard the yells of the blood thirsty savages behind them as I had. When just ready to depart, the same man that had warned us at the hotel, and who had carried the alarm down the river, dashed up on horseback and ordered all our men on shore, except six to row our bateau, and threatened to shoot any one who refused, as his family and friends were, as he believed, at the mercy of the redskins. The men left with him, but as we learned afterward, they could not go immediately to the rescue of those in danger. With our lightened load we set off rowing down river, but a good breeze springing up we were enabled to hoist sail, and so made fine speed to Cape Horn. It was steamer day and at this point we met the *Belle* and the *Fashion* on their way to the cascades. We signalled them to stop, and having informed them of the Indian rising, we were all taken on board the *Fashion* and our bateau in tow. Both vessels turned and steamed as rapidly as possible to Vancouver. We landed before dark and with the least possible delay the *Belle* started back the same night with a company of soldiers for the scene of the massacre, for such it proved to be, while the *Fashion* conveyed us to Portland. Once in Portland the services of a company of volunteers were secured and the Fashion transported them to lower cascades to aid the soldiers in subduing the Indians. They landed between 6 and 9 o'clock on the morning of the 27th of March. On the way up, at Cape Horn, the Fashion picked up my husband, the men who had been taken from our bateau, and some others, about twenty in all. Just after I left my husband on the 26th, a Red river Indian who was friendly toward all the whites, came to warn him to flee, and told him the Indians' plans were to attack the upper and middle cascades first, murder the whites and burn everything they came across, then to treat the pale faces at the lower cascades to a similar fate, burn the buildings and finish up by killing our cattle and having a big feast. Their plans, except in the matter of killing all the pale faces were really carried out almost to the very letter. My husband was rather slow about acting on the friendly Indian's warning, so he came a second time to tell him that he was almost surrounded. This time my husband, with the men who had left us, and who were now in the hotel with him, thinking discretion was the better part of valor, took to the river to try to make their escape in a schooner, on board of which a good many of our effects were stowed away. Attached to the schooner was a bateau, and both were in a strong eddy. Finding it too lengthy a task to get the schooner out, she was abandoned, and all hurried into the bateau which they now cut loose. By this time a large band of Indians was within rifle range, and before getting clear of the eddy the bullets came whizzing thick and fast. One grazed my husband's head, cutting off a lock of his hair, which, like many pioneers, he wore long. Another grazed his wrist and the man who sat rowing beside him had one pass through his hip which crippled him for life. My husband sat on a keg of butter to row, and out of this keg were afterward taken no fewer than five bullets. Without further injury they succeeding in evading the savages and getting safe to the point, where they were picked up by the steamer.

After arrival of the steamers a battle was fought by the soldiers, volunteers and residents against the Indians. The latter were worsted, and fled from the field, carrying their dead and wounded with them. Only one soldier was killed. The soldiers pursued them for some distance. During the heat of the action some Indians were observed running horse races on the outskirts of the battlefield. Amongst these the soldiers sent some grape shot from a small field piece, which seemed to be effectual in bringing them to their senses. Soon after their return from the pursuit the soldiers, believing their presence no longer required, left en route for Vancouver, while the volunteers, reinforced by the residents, some of whom, including my husband, enlisted for a month, remained in the neighborhood to hunt up some Indians who had pretended to be friendly but who were seen in the engagement of the 27th. Sixteen of these were captured and hung immediately. The old chief himself did not hang until he was dead, but was cut down, put into his grave alive and then shot, as Indian allies were momentarily expected. He died as became a "brave," giving the warwhoop with his latest breath.

In the massacre sixteen whites, including one woman, were killed. One of the saddest cases of all was that of a boy who was riding to seek refuge at the block-house, middle cascades. The savages saw him and fired. The ball wounded him so that he dropped from his horse, but after reaching the ground he partially raised himself to beckon for assistance, as he was just a little distance from the house. This he did five times, and each time received an arrow in his body, sent with only too true an aim, for on the last striking him, his spirit took its flight. The arrows were forwarded to a museum in the east to be preserved as a momento of the massacre of 1856.

The blockhouse just spoken of was well situated to withstand a siege, as it surmounted a steep bank rising high above the Columbia and was open to attack on one side only. At the time of the massacre six or seven families had found shelter within its friendly walls and they, with the lieutenant and seven soldiers in charge, held it successfully against a large band of Indians. A few years later it, with the steep bank on which it stood, slipped into the river and were carried away by the current; so was an end put to its days of utility.

As our home was now completely destroyed and our dread of the Indians not much lessened, we went to reside at The Dalles. Here we stayed until 1858, when we again returned to the Cascades and again opened an hotel, which we built ourselves and in which we resided until my husband's death. This took place, after a lingering illness, on the 9th of May, 1861, and he was buried close to the garrison. During this period Indian scares were of frequent occurrence and many a night we sought and found protection in the blockhouse, but we never had a repetition of the terrible scenes of 1856.

I remained at lower cascades until 1867, when I moved to Seattle, arriving there on the 12th of March. From there I moved in April, 1871, to Port Ludlow, Jefferson county, where I at present reside, and where I met my present husband, William M. Wallis, to whom I was married on the 22d of January, 1881.

The facts I have given form but a slight sketch of my experience on the plains and western coast, and I can certainly vouch for their veracity.

Chapter 4

Conflict on the Sound

Urban E. Hicks

An overview of the 1855-56 conflicts
between the Indians and the recent arrivals
who had settled around Puget Sound

East Sound, Orcas Island, Washington — July 29, 1892

In the summer of 1855, gold placer diggings were discovered on the tributaries of the upper Columbia river, called the Colville mines.

Isaac I. Stevens, appointed and commissioned by President Pierce, governor and Indian superintendent for the new territory of Washington, was also instructed to make a preliminary survey for the Northern Pacific railroad across the plains; and empowered to treat with the Indians on the plains while crossing. With the Yakima and Clickitat tribes such treaty had been fully perfected, and Agent Bolland sent into their country to take charge and distribute annuities.

On receipt of news of the discovery of gold, several prospecting parties left the Sound country, going by trail across the mountains and through these tribes' territory. Stevens, fearing trouble with Indians not fully treated with, went back to the vicinity of the newly discovered mines to perfect peace with the wild men of the plains, leaving Hon. C.H. Mason, territorial secretary, acting-governor during his absence.

Major Granville O. Haller of the regular army had been sent out on the plains with a small detachment of troops to protect emigrants and co-operate with Stevens if necessary. About the 1st of October, 1855, word came to Olympia by pony express that Major Haller had been attacked and routed and that Stevens was in great danger. A messenger by the name of "Bill Tid" was dispatched from the commandant of the garrison at Vancouver to Olympia, the capital of the territory, conveying this news to Acting Governor Mason, with a request that he immediately muster a company of volunteers to accompany a detachment of regular troops across the Cascades, by the way of the Nachess pass, to rescue Haller and Stevens. News was also received that Agent Bolland had been killed and many of the prospecting parties waylaid and massacred, only a few escaping.

A company of volunteers was quickly recruited principally in and around Olympia and Steilacoom, with Judge Gilmore Hayes as captain. Colonel Casey of the regular army, in command of Fort Steilacoom, ordered out nearly the entire force, stationed at this post, under command of Captain Pickett (or Keys, I have forgotten which), and as soon as possible the combined troops started across the mountains.

The settlements west of the mountains were along or near the shores of the Sound, Olympia being headquarters with small villages at Steilacoom, Seattle, Port Townsend, and a few residents on Bellingham bay. Scattering settlements had been made along the valleys of the principal streams, the most numerous being those on on the Duwamish or White river, and a few on the Puyallup and Nisqually. South of Olympia the country was more settled, it being easier of access, but at the breaking out of the war the entire white population north of the Columbia river, I believe, did not exceed 5000. The Indian population was variously estimated at from 12,000 to 20,000. There was no settlement or at most but very few east of the mountains — none with families. No one, however, entertained any fear of the Indians west of the Cascades, as they were generally regarded as a cowardly fish-eating vagabond race but little above the brute, of whom 100 white men could whip a regiment. They were easily led into the vices of the white man, while imitating few of his virtues.

In 1853 congress made a small appropriation, and Lieutenant George B. McClellan (afterward General McClellan), commissioned to open a wagon road across the Cascade mountains north of the Columbia. Over this trail one train of immigrants came in the fall of '53, as did Governor Stevens and surveying party, but the winter winds and rains had nearly obliterated the trail in many places by 1855-6. This was the only open road or trail beyond the plains, or open lands, north and east of Steilacoom, with perhaps a short way opened on the Duwamish to the mouth of Green river, and a trail up the Puyallup.

Some uneasiness was noticeable among the better class of Indians, those who were hunters on the Upper White, Puyallup and Nisqually rivers, but the whites still had little fear of an outbreak. The Indians west of the mountains were divided into small tribes or bands, all more or less intermixed, but each claiming their own particular chief or head man, and each tribe using a little different dialect. The Nisquallys were, perhaps, the most numerous of the upper Sound tribes, those of the lower Sound being subject to frequent raids from the more warlike tribes of the north or British Columbia, were kept reduced in number.

The Hudson Bay company traders had invented a sort of combination of these dialects, mixed with Canadian French, called the "Chinook jargon" (Chinook being the name of the most numerous tribe at the mouth of the Columbia.) All the Indians had to learn this language as well as the whites, but as it contained words belonging to each and all, or nearly so, all readily acquired it. About 250 words composed the principal vocabulary and answered all purposes for trade and intercourse between whites and Indians — frequently among the latter alone. The chiefs, or head men among these tribes were well known to the whites. Satisfactory treaties had been negotiated with all these tribes, and no serious cause of complaint was known to exist. Governor Stevens and the commandants at the military posts were, perhaps, as much surprised at the sudden outbreak west of the mountains as were any of the citizens. Considerable effort had been made by humane and Christian people to ameliorate the condition of the poor creatures wherever possible, and the social equality displayed on the part of the whites generally seemed to satisfy their aspirations, it not being infrequent that invitations to eat at the same table with white families were offered, and game, fish and berries were freely exchanged for cast-off clothing, trinkets, etc., among the females as well as the males on each side. Many of the whites were nearly as poor in personal effects as were the Indians, and a community of interests appeared common.

Following the departure of the troops across the mountains, at the request of Acting-Governor Mason, Charles Eaton, who had married a squaw of the Nisqually tribe, organized a small company of the oldest residents, with James McAllister as first lieutenant, (McAllister could talk with the Nisquallys in their own tongue) to interview the tribes on the upper Puyallup and White rivers, with a view to ascertaining their status and prevent, if possible, their joining the hostiles east of the mountains. At the crossing of the Puyallup, by the Mullan road, Eaton left his main company in a small log cabin, and taking McAllister and Connell (the latter had built a log house and barn and fenced a few acres on the prairie between Puyallup and White rivers), went on, unarmed to show the Indians perfect confidence in their previous professions of friendship, to Connell's place, where a band of twenty had gathered as soon as the troops had passed. Leschi, one of the best hunters and most intelligent of the Nisqually, Puyallup and White river bands, who had been chosen by Governor Stevens as the chief spokesman among these bands, although he was never fully acknowledged as a chief by them, was at the head of the band at Connell's. Eaton and McAllister held a short parley with them in which they still professed friendship, and the three men started on the return to camp, accompanied by a friendly Indian from the band. The road or trail made a long detour through the timber this side the prairie, crossing a wide deep swamp. The white men followed the trail, but the Indians, by cutting across, could reach the further side of the swamp some time before the whites could get there. Just at this edge of the swamp the party was ambushed and McAllister and Connell killed, Eaton and the friendly Indians narrowly making their escape. The company heard the firing and met Eaton at the top of the hill beyond the cabin and thus saved his life. They took shelter in the cabin, which was quickly surrounded by a howling mob of savages and a furious assault kept up until dark. After dark two of Eaton's company crept cautious out, waded the Puyallup and proceeded with all haste to warn the people on the plains and valleys below, one going toward Steilacoom and the other toward Olympia.

On the second or third day after the departure of the troops, Stevens returned to Olympia, having made his escape east of the mountains by the aid of the friendly Nez Perces, bringing information that Major Haller had also escaped, after losing his baggage and animals and several of his men. "Bill Tid" was again dispatched with orders from Colonel Casey at Fort Steilacoom and Stevens at Olympia, to Captains Pickett and Hayes, in command of troops, to return. Tid made the trip of over 100 miles in less than twenty-four hours, overtaking the troops just beyond the summit. Much to the disappointment of the boys, they had to return, as the orders were peremptory.

Five of the Volunteer company obtained permission to come on ahead of the main company with Messenger Tid in return. A.B. Moses, sheriff of Thurston county, Dr. Burns, the company surgeon, A.B. Rabbeson, _____ Miles, an Olympia lawyer, Messenger Tid and one other, whose name I have forgotten, composed the party. On arrival at Connell's prairie (the next day after the killing of McAllister and Connell) they met the same band of Indians who had done the killing, stopped and had a short parley with them, not knowing what had occurred and not suspecting treachery, and rode on to the swamp before mentioned. In the midst of the swamp, water and mud being belly deep to their horses, they were fired upon by the savages. Moses shot through the body from behind, Tid hit in the back of the head by a bullet, but not seriously wounded; Miles' horse was either hit or threw its rider when he was overpowered and literally hacked to pieces. The others escaped without serious wounds. Moses rode about one mile further when he fell from his horse, was laid beside a log near the trail and left to die alone. He gave the Masonic sign of distress and begged for water, but none could be had. Rabbeson was also a Mason. Rabbeson, Tid and the other man abandoned their horses and took to the woods and brush. Dr. Burns spurred on a short distance when he, too, left his horse and crawled into the bushes. He was found three days later in a small haystack on the Puyallup bottom, his hands and feet terribly scratched and his clothing in tatters. Rabbeson and party crawled by night and hid by day and on the third day reached the settlement in a deplorable condition, having thrown away their footcovering to make less noise while traveling.

The day following the above incident the troops reached Connell's prairie and discovered that Connell's house, barn and fencing had just been burned, the embers still smoldering, and a party of Indians on the lower edge of the prairie on horseback. Pursuit instantly followed, running them across White river, where a stand was made and one or two soldiers killed. The savages were soon dislodged from the opposite bank of the river and chased for two days up Green river toward the foothills. A cold rain setting in, further pursuit was abandoned and the troops never returned to the settlements. It was never known how many Indians were killed in this first chase, as they either carried their dead and wounded with them or hid them in the brush. All of the above incidents occurred before the people of the valleys and plains were aware of danger. It was afterward learned that a small settlement on White river had been surprised and massacred, the women outraged, stripped, scalped and thrown into wells and cesspools, and the children cut in twain. About this same time Seattle was surprised and attacked, the presence of a gunboat saving its inhabitants from a probably wholesale slaughter. The Cascades, on the Columbia, was also surprised and attacked, and several whites killed. It was then learned that the Indians from British Columbia to the California line had been planning for some months to rise en-mass and exterminate the whites in all this vast territory, as it were, by one fell blow, but the unexpected return of the troops and too hasty action on the part of some of the more desperate bands frustrated their plans and gave the whites warning in time to avoid the blow.

News of the outbreak on the plains having reached Washington city, General Wool, commandant of the Department of the Pacific, was ordered to Vancouver to investigate cause and remedy. Wool was a major and Stevens a lieutenant in the Mexican war. A personal conflict occurred, while on the field of battle, for which neither every fully forgave the other. Stevens aspired to go to Congress from the territory of Washington, and Wool knew it. He made a pompous but superficial investigation and reported wicked injustice on the part of the whites against the Indians, coupled with speculative purposes. From this report the people of Oregon and Washington have never fully recovered. It has been the main cause of the refusal of congress to do justice to the pioneers. Stevens did subsequently go to Congress as delegate from the territory two or three times, but he could not fully overcome the prejudice created by Wool's report. They have both gone to a higher tribunal long since. Peace to their ashes. The publication in the *Ledger* and other liberal journals on the coast of these old stories of the recollections of the surviving participants in those scenes, together with the efforts of the Indian War Veteran societies of the northwest to preserve these stories in their archives for future impartial historians may remove the stigma cast by Wool through personal spite toward one man.

General Wool ordered the troops into garrison for the winter to await spring before prosecuting a campaign against the hostiles. This move was disapproved of by every one who knew anything of the Indian character and habits. The winter was the best time to pursue and punish them, but Stevens, being desirous of co-operating with the regular army, advised the settlers to fortify the best they could for the winter, and vigorous measures adopted in preparation for the spring campaign. Requisitions were sent to California and Oregon for supplies of all kinds, and Governor Curry of Oregon requested to lend us all the aid he could from the Willamette valley. The Oregon volunteers refused to be subjected to the orders of General Wool or come under United States army regulations, but Stevens required all Washington territory volunteers to take the regular oath. All friendly disposed Indians were gathered and placed on an island in the Sound, near Steilacoom, where they were fed and sheltered at government expense. Recruiting companies, gathering supplies and general preparations followed as rapidly as the weather would permit. Major James Tilton, surveyor-general of the territory, also a Mexican war veteran, was appointed adjutant-general of volunteers.

October 30, 1855, I was residing on a donation land claim on Chambers prairie, six miles west of Olympia. My wife had given birth to a baby the night previous. About 10 o'clock in the morning A.M. Poe, county auditor of Thurston county, came rapidly riding past my cabin door with the startling information that the Indians west of the mountains had broken out on the war path and were murdering the white settlers and families as fast as they came to them, and warning us to flee to town as quickly as possible. He was one of the escaping messengers from Eaton's party on the Puyallup. An ox team and wagon was procured and with assistance of neighbors my wife and baby were lifted into the wagon, bed and all, and hauled into town over a new road just opened. On arrival at town in the morning, great excitement prevailed. The settlers for miles around were fast crowding into the small village and every available shelter was sought to protect the women and children. Two and three families were crowded into one small room, and others found shelter in woodsheds and outhouses. It was then manifest how utterly unprepared the whites were for such an uprising. Men and women, with blanched faces and terror-stricken countenances, appealed to each other for help and protection. Unnecessary alarm no doubt, was felt, but the lack of arms or means of defense, the uncertain number of hostile Indians or their locality, the scattered settlements and restricted means of communication, all combined to present difficulties not previously anticipated.

A small home guard was quickly formed under command of Captain Isaac Hayes, brother of Judge Gilmore Hayes, picket sentries placed on the hills above town and every precaution taken to prevent sudden attack. Within a few days about two blocks of the town were stockaded by placing split logs, ten or twelve feet in length, on end close together, with convenient portholes and bastions from which to shoot, should occasion require. Every piece of firearm of any use was hunted up and loaded. Powder and shot immediately rose to fabulous prices. I bought a small Kentucky rifle, paying $40 cash, which did not cost at the factory above $6, and a Colt's revolver, second-hand, for $24, not worth $3. Arms and ammunition were very scarce, the Indians having bought up all they could before the war, as it was the habit of merchants and traders to sell to Indians hunters such supplies without reserve, as war was not dreamed of. They had also procured from the Hudson Bay company large quantities of muskets, powder and ball and sheath-knives without suspicion, perhaps.

After a time matters quieted somewhat for the winter. The farmers returned to their homes to look after stock and put things to rights; some fortified their homes and returned with their families.

February, 1856, the several volunteer companies being duly organized and equipped, a start was made for the spring campaign. Governor Stevens determined to establish a line of block houses along the McClellan or old military road before referred to, in which to house supplies, open communication across the mountains, and drive back any hostile bands that might have crossed to this side during the winter. It was known by this time that most of the depredations had been the work of the Yakima and Clickitat tribes whose home was east of the mountains. Comparatively few hostiles west of the mountains joined the eastern tribes. Had not the uprising been checked as above described, no doubt many more would have been drawn in. A kind of intermarriage had long existed between the tribes on the upper tributaries of the Sound and those across the mountains, and those engaged in hunting and trapping furs for the Hudson Bay company were superior in bravery and warlike skill to the clamdiggers on the Sound.

A company of sappers and miners was recruited for the purpose of reopening the Mullan road, erecting block houses, bridges, etc. Joseph White of Thurston county recruited the company, under the direction of Stevens, and was commissioned captain, U.E. Hicks, first lieutenant, and McLain Chambers, second lieutenant. We were assured of extra pay for this arduous and hazardous duty, as we had to go in advance of the main force to open the way. Our first camp was made on the Yelm prairie, from there we moved on to Montgomery's, where we entered the timber for the Puyallup crossing, and then on to Connell's prairie. At all of these places strong log houses were put up and the way opened for thirty or forty ox teams hauling provisions and supplies. A small guard was stationed at each place. Connell's being the last open place before entering the mountains.

Larger and more substantial structures were erected and a general supply depot established.

After completing the above depot, Captain White's company of "Pioneers" was ordered to proceed on to the crossing of White river to erect another blockhouse to guard the crossing. Captain White ordered me to take three men and proceed on in advance, as picket guard. The main company followed after, each man with ax, cross-cut saw or other suitable tool in one hand and his gun in the other. A yoke of cattle were also provided to remove logs when cut in two. On entering the timber, on the north edge of the prairie, a sharp declivity or bank was met, down which, some fifty or sixty feet, the road had to be cut sidewise. Up to this point no sign of hostile Indians had been encountered. We heard that a large force of Indians had attacked Lieutenant Slaughter of the regular army and Captain C.C. Hewitt of the volunteers, each in command of a small squad below us on White river, and that Slaughter was killed, the command routed, losing all their camp outfit and about forty head of horses and mules. On descending the hill above mentioned and proceeding a short distance further on, suddenly we came upon a large number of very fresh moccasin and mule tracks in the trail leading up the hill. With one of my men I walked up this trail to near the top to make certain that the Indians had gone that way. Not a sound or suspicious sight of any danger could be seen or heard. The main company was not yet in sight, and we walked back to the road to wait until our company came to the brow of the hill. As soon as they came in sight I gave the alarm. The words had scarce left my lips when a hailstorm of bullets fell around us. Fortunately none of us was hit at the first volley. Each instinctively jumped behind trees or logs, the nearest shelter, and a few moments after I saw a number of painted, almost nude red devils rise up from the brush and logs on the brow of the hill up which I had just walked to within, perhaps, less than twenty feet. The Indians could have easily killed and scalped us then and there, but they saw the main company advancing and had waited until all might be caught in ambush and then capture the whole company. They had posted sixty warriors, so we afterwards learned, a little farther on the road down another hill in the belief that when the attack was opened from the top of the first hill, which would then be behind us, we would run down the second hill right into the arms of those in ambush. But instead of running the way they expected, we took shelter right where we stood, or pushed back up under the hill from whence the first volley came. Three of my comrades were badly wounded, but none mortally, before we got out of there. At camp, about a mile away, some forty or more of our boys were in line just ready to go out on a scout, and as quick as they heard the firing broke and ran to our relief. On nearing the timber they saw the smoke rising up from the logs and brush on the brow of the hill and thought it was us firing down the hill at the Indians. The latter were so intent watching our movements they did not perceive the relief coming up behind them until the boys were right in their midst. Then there was a lively roar of guns for a few moments, when the Indians began to give way, which allowed us to regain the top of the hill and join our comrades. Had not relief came just as it did, the sixty braves posted further on, seeing we did not come to them as expected, were rapidly crawling up to us and in a few minutes would have overpowered and scalped the whole lot. The battle then opened generally along the edge of the prairie toward camp for a nearly a mile in length. It commenced about 8 o'clock in the morning and lasted until 3 in the afternoon. Only four white men were wounded in the battle. How many Indians were killed or wounded we never positively knew, one dead Indian only being found in a charge. They were finally routed, taking to the brush and timber in all directions. On going over the ground we found many marks of blood and trails where their dead and wounded had been dragged and either carried off or hid. There were about 250 Indans and 175 whites on the field. Judge Gilmore Hayes was commissioned major of the battalion, but, being a civilian with no experience in directing a battle, much confusion prevailed. Had a charge made by a small party of us been vigorously followed up all along the line but few of the enemy could have escaped. At the commencement of the fight several squaws were seen in the front ranks, frantically beating drums and yelling like demons to encourage the men. They thought the whites would not shoot at them, but the boys soon became tired of the noise and shot down a few of them, when the others got more quiet and hid. The bucks were nearly all naked or covered only with war paint, and their howls and whoops were almost blood-curdling at times, but their marksmanship was poor. H.W. Scott, editor of the *Oregonian*, was in the fight, being a member of Captain Swindall's company of Skookum Bay.

The second day following we again started out for White river, this time being accompanied by an advance guard from other companies. At noon of the second day of labor in building a blockhouse at the crossing we were fired upon from a high bluff on the opposite bank of the river and one of Captain Henner's company was severely wounded. We completed the blockhouse and returned to Montgomery's.

Two companies of Oregon volunteers having joined our forces, preparations were made to follow the Indians over the mountains, most of the companies being mounted and placed under command of Colonel B.F. Shaw of Vancouver, and in company with the regular troops started on the journey. Captain White resigned his commission as captain of "Pioneer Company" and I was promoted to his place, with Benjamin Lewis first lieutenant. Captain Swindall's small company and "Pioneer company" were left to guard this side of the mountains and scout for renegade hostiles among the hills and brush. Most of the Yakima and Klickitat warriors returned to their own country when they learned that the Oregon volunteers were entering it from the Columbia river side, leaving their west side allies to take care of themselves. These broke up into small parties and sought safety in dense forests and canyons along the foothills, from whence they would occasionally sally out, committing depredations and murdering those of the whites who had ventured out alone, or gone back to their farms to put in spring crops. Several white men were murdered by them, a well known farmer by the name of William White being thus waylaid and murdered on Chambers' prairie while returning from church meeting on Sunday, with his wife and a neighbor woman. The two women were riding in a small one-horse cart, White walking by the side. Six or eight Indians on horseback suddenly sprang out from a point of timber near the road and attempted to surround the cart, but the cart horse took fright and outran the Indians to the fort, thus saving the two women. Mr. White was overpowered, murdered, stripped, scalped and left on the prairie in sight of the fort. Only one plank of the cart bed was left on the cart when it reached the fort, on which the two women clung, one of whom held a small child in her arms and had one foot terribly mangled by the wheel. A man by the name of Northcraft, driving a wagon loaded with provisions for our camp, was waylaid on the Yelm road, horribly butchered and the team and provisions taken into the mountains.

We moved to South Prairie, where we erected another block house near the now famous Carbonado coal mines, but we were not then hunting coal; our business was with wild Indians.

While encamped on South prairie we made a scout up the foothills to near the snow line on Mount Tacoma, where we found one large ranch of the enemy, which we captured and burned, killing all except one buck and one squaw, who ran the full length of our file of guns and escaped. In this ranch we found many relics of the families massacred on White river — table cutlery, dresses, keepsakes, etc., together with one white woman's scalp.

From South Prairie we moved to the Tenalquot plains, where we built our last block house, and our labors as sappers and miners ended. About two dozen horses were procured, and I relieved those not mounted from further service. We remained in the field until August, when we were disbanded, by order of the governor, turning over all our remaining outfit to Quartermaster-General W.W. Miller at Olympia.

I returned to my little farm in the fall of that year, but in consequence of the loss of time and nearly all that I had accumulated, I could not recover, and shortly sold out, moved to town and went to work at my trade. Seven years afterward, following a somewhat prolonged correspondence with the third auditor, I was paid a small sum out of the government treasury for my services. In this I fared better than some of my neighbors, who gave or lost their all, and have not to this day been fairly recompensed. The pay finally allowed to the private soldier or volunteer was $18 per month and rations, and to commissioned officers the same as allowed the regular army, but no clothing. No extra pay was allowed to "Pioneer company." Many of the men in my company were more in debt for clothing than their pay amounted to. Much of the clothing furnished was rotten, shoddy stuff, for which three prices, at least, were charged above cost. Frequently a man would put on a pair of pants or boots in the morning and come into camp at night in rags. Our work was rough and most of the country through which we operated mountainous and rugged. Such clothing would not stand the wear. In the matter of provisions we were generally well supplied, but sometimes reduced to salt junk and hard tack.

Number of blockhouses and other buildings erected by the company, 9.

Number of miles of road opened and repaired, about 40.

Number of men in company at the highest, 47.

Time of service, 6 months.

Number of Indians killed or captured, *Kloneas*.

Pierce county, within the territory of which the principal center of the hostile forces was located, was mostly settled by Hudson's Bay company employees, half breeds, trappers and voyageurs, many of whom were living with Indian women. The town of Steilacoom was the county seat. (The city of Tacoma, where now reside, perhaps, ten times as many inhabitants as the whole territory then contained, was not dreamed of.) A large majority of the then residents of Pierce county were believed, not without reason, to be in sympathy with the Indians. The Hudson Bay company employees were inimical to the settlement of the country by the Americans. There was a dispute as to the boundary between the American and British governments, and should the Americans win the lucrative trade of the company with the Indians would be lost. Several such persons were suspected of furnishing aid and information to the hostiles. Leschi, the appointed chief of the Nes-quallies, before referred to, had surrendered upon return of his allies east of the mountains, and was held for trial for the murder of McAllister, Moses, and others before positive war had been declared. Some of the suspected white men were also held for trial by the military authorities in the field. Their friends employed lawyers — Frank Clark, Elwood Evans and others —

who applied to the civil authorities to arrest these prisoners from the hands of the military. Chief Justice Edward Lander called a special term of the district court at Steilacoom, and an order was issued from the court to the sheriff of the county, Stephen Judson, esq., to seize the prisoners from the hands of the military. The war had not yet closed, or at least peace and safety was not fully established. The governor, believing that such proceedings would greatly encourage the hostiles, and tend to prolong the war, in which opinion he was sustained by the entire volunteer force, proclaimed martial law over the county of Pierce, sent a company of militia from Olympia to Steilacoom, arrested Judge Lander on the bench and broke up the court. This action, of course, created intense excitement for a time, but a few days sufficed for calmer reflection and law and order soon restored. The suspected whites were held for a time and then released. Leschi was subsequently tried before the civil court in Steilacoom and hung by the sheriff.

In looking over the field at this distant day and viewing the wonderful changes that have been wrought out in one short lifetime—the populous and wealthy cities, the beautiful farm homes, wide roads, magnificent steamships, telegraph lines, and the iron horse now penetrating the same dense forests and shooting across the same cold, rapid streams where I once waded and wandered, I am lost in amazement, and the scenes I have attempted to describe seem but a dream. We were but few in number, poor in resources of defense, in a wild, rugged country and almost isolated from the world. I might add many other incidents—some laughable, some pathetic and others distressing—but my story is now much longer than I expected to make it. If I have interested the reader by depicting some of the labors, hardships and dangers encountered by the pioneers of the northwest my purpose has been accomplished. And what shall be said of the wives and mothers of those days of the anxieties, privations and fears endured and heroically sustained? God only is able to give just reward.

A.B. Rabbeson

Mr. Rabbeson relates the exciting time he had as an express courier on a harrowing ride from the Natches River to Steilacoom during the Indian Wars.

In looking over my diary as kept in 1855, I find the following account of a trip from Capt. Hays's camp, on Nachez river, to Steilacoom, as escort to Express Messengers Major Wm. Tidd and John Bradley. Believing that it may be of interest to your readers, I send you a copy: On October 30, Col. A.B. Moses, Dr. M.P. Burns, George Bright, Joseph Miles and myself, in company with the express messengers, left camp at the first crossing of the Nachez river, and traveled unmolested until we arrived at Connell prairie, in the White river valley, at 3 o'clock Wednesday evening. Here we met with a party of Klickitat and Nisqually Indians, numbering about 150 warriors. Having there discovered that Mr. Connell's house had recently been burned, we inquired of the Indians (they at that time showed no signs of molestation) who had burned the house, or if they knew how it came to be burned. They denied all knowledge of the cause, and declared themselves entirely peaceable, saying that their *tum-tums* were *hyas close copa Boston*, i.e., that their hearts were right towards the Americans. We talked with them a long time, asking many questions why they were there, and endeavored, as much as words would do, to draw them out and make them show their true position, they all the while making declarations of friendship. We then went to the place where we supposed they intended to camp and endeavored to purchase some moccasins from their squaws, and while there, we saw and conversed a while with their main chief, Leschi. In the meantime all the first Indians were gradually dispersing, but we did not know at that time where. We then mounted our horses again and proceeded on our route, about a half a mile, to a deep muddy swamp. There we received a murderous fire from these very same Indians, who had secreted themselves in ambush behind us. Col. A. Benton Moses received a ball, entering the left side of the back and passing immediately under the heart and came out through the right breast, going through the center of a letter in the breast pocket of his overcoat. Joseph Miles, of Olympia, received a wound in the neck which unhorsed him. He fell deep in mud, and was unable to regain his horse or get out without assistance. We directed him to take hold of his stirrup-leather, while we gather his horse's bridle, and then putting spurs to our horses we succeeded in dragging him out of the mud. We found that he had become so faint that it was impossible for him to mount his horse. He then told us to leave him and make our escape if possible, as there was no hope for him. All this time the Indians were pouring into us a continuous fire, not more than thirty yards distant, in which Maj. Tidd received three slugs on the head, which did not penetrate the skull. We were compelled to leave Miles, so we put spurs to our horses and rose about a mile and a half, when Col. Moses became so exhausted in consequence of his wounds that he could not remain on horseback any longer. We dismounted and carried him some 200 yards and hid him in the brush. We remounted and rode at full speed to the first crossing of Finnell's creek. Here we discovered another ambuscade, whereupon we dismounted and made a charge into the brush, three of us upon one side of the road and two upon the other. Each of us discharging the full contents of our revolvers and then using our sabers, completely routing the Indians, they not firing a gun. We must have killed quite a number of them, as none of us had to shoot more than ten feet, and several times we placed our revolvers against their bodies. Returning to Col. Moses for the purpose of making him more secure and comfortable, we took our coats and wrapped them around him and left him, having rendered him all the assistance in our power that we were able under the circumstances. On leaving him, his last words were: "Boys, if you escape, remember me." We returned to the edge of the bluff, going down Finnell's creek and discovered a large body of Indians on the opposite side of the prairie, that lay close by, but our number being so few, we did not think it advisable to risk another attack. All of us, with the exception of Dr. M.P. Burns took to the brush, but he kept straight on, declaring that "he would fight until he died." We considered it recklessness, but it was utterly impossible to persuade him otherwise. We saw him enter the timber on the opposite side of the prairie, and immediately heard the report of three guns and an Indian yell, and very naturally supposed that was the last of him. We kept in the brush and traveled until dark, and then stopped and held quite a consultation as to which course to pursue. Some were for returning to Capt. Hays' camp, others for making the settlements, but we finally concluded to make for the settlements, believing that we could get assistance to Col. Moses sooner. The weather was very disagreeable, rainy and dark in the fore part of the night and freezing in the after part. We all became so exhausted that we could not travel but a short distance at a time, sometimes up to our waists in water and at others entangled in the immense thickets of underbrush and fallen timber. While we rested, two of us would lay down on the ground and the other two on top of them. When the two underneath would get a little warm, we would change positions. At other times, when we would get to a hollow stump or tree, two of us would enter and allow the other two to lean against our breasts and blow the warm breath in one another's faces. About daylight we crossed the immigrant road, but dare not travel it for fear of discovery. We took a course as near as we could for the crossing of the Puyallup river, and struck the river at noon, about three miles above the crossing, then traveled down the river until we supposed ourselves opposite the upper crossing and went to the river, but found ourselves too far down. We here undertook to cross a large deep swamp. This was about two hours before sundown. On reaching the opposite side we found ourselves on the edge of Lemon's prairie, consequently we were compelled to remain in the deep mud and water until long after dark, all the while shaking with cold so much that our cartridge-boxes rattled like cowbells. About an hour from the time we first came there we saw two Indians approach close by and secret themselves in a small willow thicket. We supposed them to be spies, and could have taken them prisoners or killed them, but to do so we were afraid that we would have to fire a gun, and to escape without observation required much care and anxiety, having to scrape away the sticks and leaves from under our feet as we stepped until we were out of hearing. We crossed the Nisqually and took the immigrant trail direct to Steilacoom, and arrived at Mr. Tallentire's on Friday morning at 3 o'clock, all very much exhausted, having been three days and nights without food. George Bright became so much fatigued that it was impossible for him to travel any further, laid down and went to sleep, the rest of us being so weak that we could not carry him. On reaching the house we dispatched Mr. Tallentire and a friendly Indian, who was with him, in search of Bright, but he slept so soundly that their hallooing would not arouse him, and the dark being so intense, he could not be found until morning. After reaching Steilacoom we at once informed Lieut. Nagent of the above circumstances, who immediately detailed Capt. W.H. Wallace and command to the relief of Col. Moses. Two days after the body of Col. Moses was found by Capt. Wallace at the spot where left by us. The body of Joseph Miles was found some fifteen paces from the spot where he had been seen alive with a bullet wound shot through his neck, a large knife wound in the back and one through the breast, likewise sixty small penknife stabs in different parts of the body, showing that he had been tortured most fearfully. Some may inquire: What of Dr. Burns. He was found by Capt. Wallace, hid in a barley stack at Mr. Lemon's place in Puyallup bottom, and the time he had is best described by the following letter written by himself to Gen. Tilton:

To Adjutant General Tilton — *Sir:* Please contradict the report that I was killed by the Indians on Wednesday last. I killed seven with my own hands. They hunted me through the brush for one mile with dogs and lighted sticks, and every one who carried the light I shot. The only wound I got was a skin wound in the forehead from a buckshot. I lived in the brush on leaves, and shot an Indian this morning, for his dried salmon and wheat at Mr. Lemon's. Give my respects to Bright and Rabbeson, and let them know I am safe — only I had to throw away my boots and my feet are badly hurt. I lost my horse, instruments and medicine case. My horse was shot in the kidneys in the swamp where we received that murderous discharge of balls and buckshot. Please let Mr. Wiley say I am all right. I remain respectfully,

M.P. Burns,
Surgeon Capt. Hays's Command.

M.M. Ruddell

*The tale of a woman who journeys west
with her five children in 1850 to meet her husband,
William White, who had preceeded her. She relates the
details of his tragic death at the hands of
the Indians in the 1855-56 Wars.*

Olympia, Washington — December 9, 1892

I, with my husband, William White, and family lived in Grant county, Wisconsin, where we had a pleasant home. Mr. White, being in poor health, was told by the doctors that a change might benefit him, and advised him to come to the Pacific coast. Accordingly, in March, 1850, he started on the long, tedious journey across the plains. We received one letter from him while he was on the way, and after his arrival in Oregon he wrote us, the letter reaching us the following January. In it he told us that he was much better, and said if the family was with him he would make that place his future home. He also told us, if we decided to make the trip, what we should take with us and what to leave to make the trip as quickly and as comfortable as possible.

I decided to make the journey and join my husband in his new home, and in March, 1851, I, with my five children, the eldest of whom was a girl of 14 and the oldest boy 11 years of age, started on the way to our future home. There were plenty of men who wanted to drive the team, or help drive it, for their board across the plains. I engaged E. Titus to drive for me. We went as far as Iowa, where we stopped ten days to visit my father, brother and sisters. We were joined by my brother, A.W. Stewart; sister, M. Stewart and brother-in-law D.M. Ross and wife, who came through with me and my family rather than see me undertake the trip alone.

We arrived at Cainesville, where we were compelled to wait two weeks to lay in supplies, as this was the last place we could get anything of the kind until we crossed the mountains. It was now the month of May, and we had heavy rain, thunder and lightning storms, which lasted until we began to think we would have a continuous journey through that sort of weather. But we traveled on through mud and rain, and when we reached Elk Horn river we camped, stretched our tents and piled up brush on which to make our beds to keep out of the water. I have never heard of there being as much thunder and lightning as we had at that place. The water covered a stretch of ground six miles wide, with the exception of a small island which contained about an acre of ground, which was about two miles from our camp. The Mormons had a large ferryboat to ferry the people of the train to the island, and we were finally landed on it. There were about forty wagons in the train. We put up our tents, and I fixed a place for the children and retired myself, and was soon asleep. The driver and my brother slept in the wagon. I was awakened by a sharp peal of thunder, and never saw such lightning as there was that night, and which will never be seen anywhere except on the Elkhorn river in Nebraska. Every time I would move the water would find a new place to run, and the night was anything but pleasant. The loose articles lying inside the tent were floating about on top of the water. As we were tented on about the highest point on the island, there was nothing to do but for all of us to tumble into the wagon, which we did, and all soaking wet. The water was now up to the bed of the wagon. The men had staked the tent down so the things inside could not float away. The Mormons, who were doing the ferrying, were hunting ox yokes and chains, and threw the chains over the yokes to keep them from floating away, and swearing to keep their spirits up. We did not know but what we would all float off, and yet it was amusing to watch the performances that were necessary to keep things from getting away. It was a sea of water in every direction as far as we could see. There was no chance to cook anything to eat, and things looked very seriously at the time, but ere the day passed a ferry boat came to us, and took the women and children, with something to eat, and a part of a tent, to land. At night it rained as hard as ever. Ten or twelve people piled into the tent with the provisions, and they all took turns at resting. The pole of the tent had to be held all night to keep it from blowing over. All this time the men on the island were calking and fixing the wagon beds in which to bring the remaining things and the wagon wheels over, and finally landed them all, swimming the cattle across nearly the entire six miles, although there were places where they could wade. One of the men came very nearly being drowned in trying to make a horse swim, and finally, if I remember right, it had to be towed across.

About the 15th of May we started up the country and reached Loop fork, where we were ferried over in two canoes, one tied to the other. One of the wagons slipped over and sank, but was finally fished out, and there followed quite an interesting time drying the contents. The accident made Mrs. Smith, who owned the wagon, faint, and for a time everything was excitement in trying to bring her out right. Everything was finally made straight and we proceeded on our way, encountering nothing worthy of note until we reached a small stream, across which a brush bridge had been built by emigrants preceeding us. Two Indians demanded toll, but the captain of the train put the Indians under guard, and the next morning we crossed over and went on our way rejoicing.

While traveling up the Platte river we had plenty of grass for the oxen, but we had no wood. We had quite a merry time, and our company generally was good natured. On Sundays we lay by, and generally had preaching, and the day was mostly spent in singing, attending services, etc. At times our preacher was too tired to preach for us, but we always found our Sundays pleasant.

The man who was driving my team was sick for about three weeks, and during that time I did the driving, only when some of the company volunteered to drive for me, which I did not like to have them do, for they had their own driving to do, and helping me made it very hard on them. We had five yoke of oxen. I would yoke one team, Elizabeth one, William one and the driver one, and while he put them to the wagon we yoked the remaining team, which was put to the end of the tongue. At night we unyoked in the same manner. We all had our own work to do, and we did it without a murmer.

We had no serious trouble with the Indians. One day our company came upon some Indians who were in the act of robbing two young men. They had their guns pointed at them and were taking things from the wagon, but they left without taking anything with them. The men then traveled with us, but had previously been alone all the way. There was a company that passed us and repassed us nearly every day. They had horses to the wagon in which the family rode. The Indians stole their horses, killed one member of the company and wounded another and robbed their wagon. Their name was Clark. We were then traveling in the Mormon country and the Indians

-164-

often attempted mischief, but never seriously bothered us, although we were in holy terror of them all the time.

During this time I had no word from my husband. I had written him that I was on the point of starting, but had no means of knowing whether or not the letter ever reached him.

When we reached Snake river it was high enough to swim all the teams at once, and the driver could wade. So all the beds of the wagons were secured and we drove into the river, each driver holding his lead ox. I expected to have to swim, too, before we reached the other side, but we landed safely. We proceeded on with no event worthy of note until we reached the Grande Ronde valley. There we found a family who had been left by their company. Their mother was very sick and could not travel. She had a son, a young man, and a little girl, two little girls having died a few days before. The woman said to me in the morning when we were going to leave the valley, "You will not leave me, will you?" and I told her I would not, answering without thinking of the consequences. When our company came to talk it over they decided that provisions were too scarce to think of remaining. Mr. Rice, the son of the dying woman, said for them to go on and he would let those who would remain have horses so as to catch the train, so Dr. Spinning, Millie Stewart, Dr. Partlow, Lucretia Redding and my self stayed with Mrs. Rice. She died that day and we buried her, and started on to catch the company, which we did the next day.

Coming over the Blue mountaines it rained and the roads were very slippery. The men were compelled to hold the wagons to prevent their sliding around or turning over. We traveled on until dark, thinking to reach water, but found none. Our number was increased by one during the night, a bright baby boy whom we christened Charles Ross, being born to Mrs. D.M. Ross.

At Butter creek we met my husband, and I thought my troubles were at an end. He had two horses and a wagon, which helped us out wonderfully, for the cattle were almost given out. We arrived at The Dalles on the 15th of September, having been on the road six months. We had slept as best we could; had seats on the ox yokes, eaten from the ground, etc., and we began to think we would appreciate a home, be it ever so humble. Some of the company brought the cattle down the trail by the Columbia river, and the others came on a scow to the cascades, and there railroaded the things around the falls, and came down to Sauvie's island. Mr. White took a claim on the north side of the Columbia river, where we stayed through the winter, cleared five acres of ground and built a cabin, but which was overflowed, and we abandoned it, moving to Portland, where we earned a living by every one of us working as hard as we could. I kept boarders and sewed for the stores, and Mr. White teamed. We would have done well had we kept our health, but we all got sick, and we soon found that we could not live there. Dr. Spinning, Ben Spinning and some more of our old company had come to the Chehalis valley, and returned with glowing accounts, and they put us all in a boat and took us down the river to the mouth of the Cowlitz, and there we lay, trying to invent some way to get up the river, which appeared to be a very serious problem, but finally it was solved. We were landed in a cabin of Mr. Dilabaugh's, six of us shaking with the ague. Oh! what a time that was. I think it was some time in the month of September when we made our landing. Dr. Spinning, Ben Spinning and Mr. White all took claims on the Chehalis river, and built them each a cabin. The soil was rich and very fertile, but it was late in the year and we did not have much of a variety of eatables through the winter. The men killed a few deer, which helped us out. We boiled wheat, which was very good eating with our venison. In January the river raised and covered the whole prairie. The water was high enough to float the floor of our cabin, which stood three feet off the ground. The fire on our hearth was drowned out. We made a raft out of the puncheons, which kept us out of the water until Mr. White could go in a canoe to the home of Dr. Spinning and help them out. They had built a sort of scaffold and put their horse on it, and gave it the straw out of their bed to eat. The men took us to high land as fast as they could. The distance was about a mile, and it was a rather dangerous trip getting through the floating logs and brush, but we finally arrived in safety, and Mr. Davis kindly gave us room in his house until the water went down. Mr. White was not satisfied with a place that would overflow every winter, so he abandoned that claim and came to the Sound and took a claim about twelve miles east of Olympia, where we lived and did well until the Indian troubles of 1855-6, when we had to go to forts to live. We remained in the fort until spring, and some of the families thinking the trouble was over wanted to return, two or three families going into one house for mutual protection from the Indians. William Stewart and family, and Mr. White and family, were at the Eatons. There was preaching appointed at the schoolhouse for Sunday, so we put a horse to a cart and went; but the report which had previously been circulated, that Mr. Northcraft was missing, frightened the people and the meeting was given up. We did go to the home of Mr. Conner, who was sick at the time and who died in three weeks after this event, and after a short visit there started for home. On the way home the Indians came upon us when we were coming around a point of timber. One of them came so close to Mr. White before he showed his gun, that when he raised it and fired Mr. White caught the gun from the Indian's hand and fought with it. Our horse became frightened and ran away, taking us to Mr. Eaton's. Mr. White was walking by the side of the cart when he was attacked, and Mrs. Stewart and her baby and myself and baby were in the cart. The horse being large jumped to one side to keep the Indian from catching him, which nearly turned the cart over, and my sister-in-law was thrown on the wheel and her foot caught and the shoe was torn from it, and the sole was torn completely off the shoe. Her foot was seriously hurt, and she did not wear a shoe for two months. When we reached home there were two men at the house, Mr. Eaton and Mr. Berry, who had just returned from hunting for Mr. Northcraft. I begged them to go to Mr. White, but they had heard the firing, and instead of doing as I wanted they went to cleaning and fixing their guns, and would not, nor did not go to him, but prepared to go to the fort. I begged to be allowed to stay in doors, and Mrs. Stewart was so sick she could not sit up, but the men thought it was not safe to stay, so they fixed the cart so Mrs. Stewart could lie down, and put the children in some way and I on horseback. Mr. Eaton had a gun and a revolver, and he gave the latter to me and showed me how to use it, and said if the Indians attacked us he would fight until he failed, and then I must do my best with the revolver, and to not give up alive. Mr. Berry walked and led the horse, carrying also his gun and revolver, and thus we went to the fort that night. At the fort we found P. Northcraft with the corpse of his brother, but they were all so frightened that they would not venture to go to Mr. White. The next day they brought him in, and we buried him. Although the trial was great, yet we felt comforted that we succeeded in getting his body to give it a decent burial. Mr. Biglow took Mrs. Stewart, myself and the children home with him and kept us there until her husband and my son came home from the volunteer service, when we returned to the fort and remained there until peace was declared in the fall of 1856.

Martha H. Ellis

An 1852 Oregon Trail emigrant gives a good description of her overland journey, plus an interesting glimpse of Pioneer life on Puget Sound in 1853-54. She was a neighbor of William White when he was killed by the Indians near Olympia.

Olympia, Washington — August 21, 1892

A few weeks ago I received a copy of the Tacoma *Sunday Ledger*, and in the upper left hand corner was noticed the handsome offer of free tickets to the World's fair for the best old settler's story. Now, we all like free rides, but this is to be earned by the old settler in a way that is not in his way of doing things. Give an old settler a gun, a flail, a washboard, a skillet, or anything they are perfectly familiar with, and they are master of it, but the superiority of using the pen, is for them, bringing it down to a fine point. But the lack of energy to undertake anything, the pioneers of this state know nothing of, as the numerous readers of the *Ledger* can testify. Another peculiar characteristic of theirs is telling stories, true ones of course. If you have the time to spare, just ask an old settler some question about the early days of this country, and see for yourself. A trip to Chicago, only a few day's ride, with nearly all the comforts of home, the travelers of the present time, can have but an imperfect idea of. A journey across the plains forty years ago, required about six months' time while about six days is required to cover the same distance at the present time.

In the early spring of '52 we left the town of Albia, Ia., for the territory of Oregon, as this country was then called. Our train of four wagons consisted of David L. Phillips, son and two daughters, two families whose names I do not remember, but they went to California, so it does not matter, and my father, Joseph H. Conner, brother Milton, sister Jane and myself.

Perhaps a description of our private car would be interesting to those that have never seen the kind the emigrants used. It had heavy wheels, broad and deep beds, which were divided into two floors, the lower used for provisions and also things not needed for every day, and the upper used for clothing in daily use, and was general lounging place during the day and family bedrooms at night. It had a high, arched, canvas-covered roof. In the right-hand corner in the front was our water can and cup. Attached to the wagon bed at the back was the cupboard for victuals, dishes and cooking utensils, and what it lacked in height it made up in width and depth. It generally took four yoke of oxen to draw these heavily loaded wagons.

There was a great deal of sickness among the emigrants this year, as the cholera was bad. I remember one day of counting eight new graves where the dirt was not dry. Our train was very fortunate, only one teamster was sick for a little while, and Hulda Phillips and myself had the mountain fever and lost our hair but saved our scalps. By being in such a small party, ourselves as well as cattle fared much better. When passing through the country where Indians were not friendly, we would keep near a large train for protection.

There are many pleasant scenes and things to remember of that long journey as well as the many annoyances and inconveniences, but all things come to an end sometime, so after months of constant traveling we arrived at The Dalles. There father sold the oxen and wagon, and went down the Columbia to the Cascades in a canoe, where we got a pack horse for our traps and walked to where we made connection with a boat for Portland. There we stayed a week, then crossed the Columbia to St. Helens where we spent another week. Then hiring a team we started for Olympia, or, more correctly speaking, for Tumwater, where we again took a canoe, with which we finished our journey. Here we stayed another week, while Mr. Phillips and father were looking around the country for a good location for a farm. That being decided, we again packed in a wagon, with Captain Terrill for a driver, thinking this would be our last move, but it was not to be, for when we got to the place we found a tent up and Captain Hale in possession of the claim (which he afterward abandoned), so we went on to what is now known as the Hawk place, where a bachelor by the name of Fowler lived. There we stayed until father could look for another location and build a log cabin. Then we started on our last move — this time on a handsled. It being a short time before Christmas, we had plenty of snow. You probably can imagine the extent of our worldly possessions when all we had was moved in one load. In our cabin there was neither fire-place, window or door, and the last row of shakes of the roof were not on, but we were so glad to stop moving and to be by ourselves that we did not mind such trifles as those, but made a fire in the middle of the room, propped clapboards against the opening for the door, ate our supper, made our beds on the ground and went to bed, glad to think we did not have to move any more. When we awoke next morning our beds were covered with snow, but father went right to work and finished the roof the first thing. The shakes were held in place with long poles instead of nails. He made the door, the hinges and the latch, and the lock was a strong peg. A few days' work and the house was comfortable. The logs of the wall were hewed smooth and clap-boarded, the ceiling fixed with the same kind of boards, the floor made of puncheons, and the cracks on the outside chinked. All the timber used was carried on the shoulder from the woods, about a mile away. The fireplace and the hearth were made of rocks and the chimney of sticks and mud. All the furniture was home-made—bedsteads, table, benches, stool (we had one), washboard, washtub and washbasin. The last two were anything but pretty, being small logs dug out, but they served their purpose until we could get some from the store. With the exception of nails everything was on the place, and as soon as father was able to get the glass he made the sash for a window of twelve panes. Our clock was a post on the porch—good when the sun shone. Father was a carpenter, so was away from home most of the time, returning home Saturday nights. He built dwellings for David, Andrew and Thomas Chambers, and mills for Mr. Percival, Nathan Eaton and also one of the first at Tumwater. While working on the foundation of the latter mill he caught a severe cold, which resulted in a quick consumption.

The first flour we bought was $40 a barrel, potatoes $4 a bushel, but we never were out of bread, although we came very near it once. Our nearest neighbor was without bread for six weeks. The next spring we all made gardens and planted small fields of wheat and during the summer we had plenty of wild berries, beside wild game, which was plenty. I shall never forget that the first field of wheat, for we children had to be the scare-crows until the wheat got too high for the crows to pull up.

I must not forget to mention our first Christmas. We were told that Santa Claus would not be able to come to us Christmas eve, but would come on New Year's eve instead, and that we must go to bed early and go to sleep, for he did not want to be seen coming down the chimney. The next morning we found a doughnut made without sugar and one raisin in our stockings, and he had been so generous with mother, giving her a pan full. We obtained great satisfaction in looking at his tracks in the snow from the path to the chimney and back. We children had to depend on our labor for our toys, making for ourselves wagons, sleds, tops, bows and arrows, and what we could not make we did without. About that time father brought home a copy of the old *Pioneer and Democrat* with the chinook jargon in it. I never stopped studying until I had learned every word and also their meaning, from "Nika I" down to the last line, where the words were put into sentences, and I felt big when the Indians came, to be called on to interpret what they said. My brother thought it more fun to learn to sing and beat tomanamos. Chief Stehi and family, and a few other families, lived near our house most of the time, so we had ample time for practice.

The first summer here, that of 1853, it was decided we must have a school, so a log schoolhouse was built near Ruddell's, on Chambers prairie, and Dave Phillips was engaged as teacher. We lived six miles away. That was a little too far to walk twice a day, so I boarded with Mr. Phillips, and walked three miles every morning and every night, except Friday night and Monday morning, when I went and came from home. The next summer the district was divided, and school was held in a deserted cabin on our prairie. A few desks and benches were made, but the floor of dirt was left as we found it. The third year we had a good schoolhouse, of logs, of course, but we were used to that. During this time father had added a large and small room to the house, which had a rough plank floor. We had a cookstove and rawhide bottomed chairs, and also had a small orchard started. The first purchase in live stock was an Indian pony which cost $50. She was a treasure to us, and a good pack-horse when we wanted to go to mining town for provisions, gentle as she could be but with the failing of all Indian ponies—hard to catch. The next was a full-blooded Spanish cow that could discount a mule at kicking. Then three chickens, one apiece for us children, at least we claimed them, and the first chicken that died we had a first-class Indian funeral. Eggs at that time were $1.00 a dozen. The next purchase was a pig, but the best of all, a yoke of oxen and a wagon. It was then that my sister and I made our first appearance in town since our moving from it. There was great rejoicing among us children when we heard a cat mew under the house. Where she came from we never knew, but she stayed with us until she died of old age. The first three kittens, one apiece, were our special pets.

A bachelor who was greatly annoyed with mice persuaded sister to give her kitty to him, and he, to reward her for giving up her pet, gave her a pretty dress with trimming and a nice pair of shoes, so when a neighbor wanted mine I gave it up readily, but I did not get even thanks. It is an actual fact that cats were scarce in those days.

In February, 1854, my sister Alice was born. In the fall of 1855 the Indian war broke out, and after McAlister was killed we were warned to get to the fort as quick as possible, and we did so, leaving everything; but the next day our household goods and provisions were moved to the fort. There we remained in close quarters for a few months, but no Indians were to be seen in that part of the country, so we all moved home again, excepting those that lived too far away. Two or three families would live in the same house for mutual protection. Such was our case. Abijah O'Neal and Marcas

McMillan were away hauling provisions for the volunteers, so their wives and children lived with us. But we were not left in peace very long. First Northcraft was killed near the Yelm prairie, and two weeks later William White was killed near Eaton's. I shall never forget the day Mr. White was killed. That particular Sunday the Rev. J.F. Devore had an appointment to preach in our school house, but he considered it unsafe to travel, and so failed to come. But, not knowing that, a few went to church, among them Mr. White, his wife and baby, his sister-in-law, Mrs. Williamson Stewart, and baby. After learning that there would be no service, they decided to come and see father, as they knew he was sick. About an hour and a half before sundown they started for home. Their conveyance was a cart. Company gone, we children went to the barn to play, and after playing for awhile we wanted something from the house, and I went to get it, but it was frightened out of my mind, for I had just got into the house when we heard that never-to-be-forgotten war-whoop. All rushed to the porch and we saw six Indians, in war paint, crossing the prairie as fast as their ponies would carry them. I was told to go to the barn and tell the children to come to the house. I went, and was not long about it, either. The Indians rode around the field toward the house and halted within speaking distance. Father went out of the yard and spoke to them in Chinook, but their answer was in their own tongue. They rode off a short distance and held a consultation, then rode to the top of a high hill and five of them dismounted and they had another pow-wow; then, mounting, rode off toward McAlister's lake. When we first saw the Indians, Mrs. McMillan took down all the guns and carefully examined them, putting on fresh caps in place of the old. When the Indians were out of sight we all went to work. The guns were discharged and reloaded. Mrs. O'Neal, who never had handled a gun before, hit the target that my brother had placed on a large fir tree a short distance from the house. That tree was near enough to the house to be used by the Indians in an attack on us, but the best was done that we could do to protect ourselves. The first thing was to cover the window, before mentioned, so father, who was very weak, with the help of the women and my brother, got his work-bench securely fastened against the window; the smaller one was easily covered. Portholes were made on all sides of the house. We children carried into the house a good supply of wood and water, for we feared a return of the Indians after dark. Our nearest neighbor, Mr. Parsons, his wife, two sons and daughter, who had watched the coming and going of the Indians, came with their guns and axes to take their chances with us. About 11 o'clock, as we sat talking by the fire light, we heard someone call father by name. He started immediately for the door saying it was Mr. Eaton, but was held back as it was feared that it might be an Indian imitating his voice. Again the call came, and this time there was no doubt about it being Mr. Eaton. The men went out and there he was with ten men. They were cautious about coming too near until they knew who was in possession, we or the Indians. They told us of the murder of Mr. White

-171-

while on his way home. As they were going around the edge of a point of timber, he was walking by the side of the cart holding the reins when Mrs. Stewart said: "There is an Indian now." He turned and grabbed the barrel of the gun in time to prevent the shot from hitting him. The report of the gun frightened the horse, which ran away for home, leaving Mr. White in a desperate struggle with the Indian, trying to get the gun and protect himself, but before he could do that, eight more came out of the bushes. He fought hard, for his body was found 100 yards nearer home than where he was first attacked. Mrs. White, when she got home, wanted the men to go to Mr. White's aid, but they knew it was too late, and there were too many Indians. They thought it best to start immediately for Andrew Chambers' place where they left the women and children, got as many men together as they could, and started for our place. Four of them remained with us and the others went on to Captain Terrell's returning in the morning, when the most of them went the road that Mr. White had taken to get his body, and the rest of us took a shorter road through the timber. All of us were walking except father and my little sister. He also held the extra guns (for there were more guns than men), until we came to the timber, when we halted and planned what was best to do if Indians should attack us while going through the woods.

An Irishman, whose name I have forgotten, had me, a child of 11, walking by his side carrying a flint-lock shot gun, cocked, as he wanted it ready and handy to use when his own was discharged, so there would be no time wasted before he could shoot again. It is a wonder we got through that timber without that gun going off, for I neither looked at the gun or where I was walking, as I was looking for Indians. We got through without any alarm, and where we all could breathe natural again.

We stayed at the home of James Patterson until the new fort was ready to move into. It was never finished. Mr. Patterson's parents and brothers were there, too. There were just twenty-five of us, big and little, occupying two rooms. There were double bunks, one above the other. In these cramped quarters, just three weeks after Mr. White's death, father died. We lived in the fort all summer, and there being no more trouble with the Indians this side of the mountains, there was a general move of the families back to their homes, and with the little they had managed to save of their possessions during the war, went to work to improve their homes and make a living.

Long after the war was over, an Indian of the party that killed Mr. White, said that after sending the one that he (Mr. White) had wounded off in the care of two of their party, the rest of them rode over to our place, intending to kill us. But seeing so many women and children in the yard, they thought there must be men and that they were in the house and would shoot them if they came too near. Their riding to the top of the hill was to see if their comrades were all right. From this hill there was a fine view of the entire prairie.

Gradually the settlers recovered from the effects of the war and have done their best to help the development of their chosen state. Yet the newcomers call them "moss-backs." I wonder how much more they would have done, with the same hardships to contend with, than has the old pioneer.

James Longmire

*His wagon train was the first to cross
the Cascade mountains over Naches pass in 1853.
Mr. Longmire relates incidents on the Yelm prairie
during the Indian Wars of 1855-56 including the story
of the surrender and subsequent murder of Chief
Quiemuth in the offices of Governor Stevens.
He was the Indian's guard the
night of the murder.*

Eatonville, Washington — August 22, 1892

As I am one of the pioneers of Washington, in her territorial days, I will fall in line with the many who have already written, and attempt a description of our trip across the plains, and subsequent events. It may not be out of place to remind the newcomers of today that they have little cause for complaint of hardships and suffering as compared with those who made that long, tiresome journey thirty-nine and more years ago, through unbroke forests, over swollen streams, unknown and dangerous, over the desert with its scorching sun and blistering sands, exposed to warlike and hostile Indians, disease, and many other perils which you will doubtless perceive before the close of my narrative.

I started from our home in Shuwme Prairie, Fountain county, Indiana, on the 6th day of March, 1853, with my wife and four children, Elcaine, David, John and Tibatha. John, the youngest, was not able to walk when we started, but learned his first steps with the help of the tongue of our ox wagon while crossing the plains, holding to it for support, and walking from end to end while in camp evenings. John B. Moyer, a very finished young man who had studied for the ministry, but who was at that time teaching our district school, went with us; also Joseph Day, a son of one of our neighbors. I got a neighbor to drive us to Athica, the nearest town, where we took passage on the *U.S. Aiel*, a little steamer running on the Wabash river. Evansville at that time was a flourishing town of 4000 or 5000 inhabitants.

A shocking incident of our first start was the bursting of the boiler of the steamer *Bee*, twelve miles from Evansville, which caused the death of every person aboard. The *United States Aiel* took the poor mangled creatures aboard and carried them to Evansville, where they were met by sorrowing, griefstricken friends, who had sighted the signal of mourning displayed by our steamer.

-173-

From Evansville we took the steamer *Sparrow Hawk* for St. Louis, thence
by the *Polar Star* up the Mississippi river to St. Joseph. We were now upward of 2000 miles on our westward journey. There I bought eight yoke of
oxen and a large quantity of supplies and proceeded in wagons along the
river to Cainsville, now Council Bluffs, and camped. As it was yet too early
to start on our long journey, the grass not grown sufficient to feed our oxen
along the route, we decided to remain for several weeks and make some
preparations for another start. I bought a carriage and span of horses for
$250, which Mrs. Longmire and the children were to use as far as the road
would permit. I also got a sheet-iron stove, which, with utensils for cooking, only weighed twenty-five pounds, but which proved a real luxury, as
we were thus able to have warm biscuits for breakfast whenever we chose,
besides many other delicacies which we could not have had by camp fires.
For the stove I paid $12, though to us it proved almost invaluable. At
Cainsville I stood guard at night for the first time in my life, in company
with Van Ogle, who was also camped here, preparatory to going to Puget
Sound. It was dark one evening when I finished the feeding of my cattle, so I
could not see the person who spoke in a fine, childish voice, saying: "Is there
a man here by the name of Longmire?" I thought it must be a boy, judging
by his voice, and told him that was my name, whereupon he introduced
himself as John Lane, a man of whom I had often heard, but never had
seen — a tall man, well-built, with a smooth, boyish face, and fine squeaking
voice, much out of keeping with his great body. He invited me to his camp
near by, where I met his brother-in-law, Arthur Sargent, and his family.
After some conversation we made arrangements to continue our journey
together. While here we met a young man by the name of Iven Watt, who
was anxious to cross the plains. I engaged him to drive on my ox teams, and
found him an excellent help at various times when obstacles met us which
seemed hard to overcome. His friend, William Claflin, hired to Mr. Sargent
to assist his son and Van Ogle with Sargent's ox team. The time had now
come when we decided that there was grass for the cattle on the way and we
moved twelve miles below Council Bluffs to a ferry, where we crossed the
Missouri river, making our final start for the Puget Sound on the 10th of
May, 1853. We camped for the night about one mile from the ferry, where
we were joined by E.A. Light, now of Steilacoom, a friend of John Lane's.
Nothing occurred worthy of note until two days afterward when we
reached the Elk Horn river, where we found a ferry with only one boat, and
so many emigrants ahead of us that we must wait for two or three weeks to
be ferried over. A party of emigrants was lucky enough to get three canoes,
and while they were crossing we all went to work and made one more. By
this time they were across, so we bought their canoes, and with our own
proceeded to ferry our goods over the river. Here occurred an accident
which proved disastrous, and spoiled, in a measure, the harmony existing in
our little company of emigrants.

John Lane had started with some fine stock, among which was a thoroughbred mare of great beauty and very valuable, which he would not allow to swim with the rest of our stock safely across the stream, but with a rope around her neck, held by Sargent and myself on one side of the river and by himself and E.A. Light on the other side, would tow her across, which we did, but alas, dead! We landed the beautiful creature, after following Lane's instructions, and tried to revive her, but she was dead. Poor Sargent had to bear the blame, unjustly I think, and only escaped blows from Lane, whose rage knew no bounds, by my interference, but he left our party after begging me to go with him, and in company with E.A. Light, Samuel and William Ray, and a man name Mitchell, continued his journey. We regretted the loss of his beautiful mare and the unpleasantness between him and Sargent, which caused him to leave our party, for friends were few and far from home, consequently much dearer. But these friends we were to meet again, which we little expected when we parted.

Two hundred miles further on we came to Rawhide creek, a pretty stream with its banks bordered by graceful waving willows, cool and green. This was the last tree or shrub we were destined to see for 200 miles. Here we stopped to rest our now thoroughly tired, foot-sore oxen, and do our washing, which was not always done on Monday, much to the annoyance of our excellent housekeepers, who, at home, had been accustomed to thus honoring blue Monday. We had killed a few antelope along the road, which furnished our camp with what we thought the best steak we had ever eaten, and were fired with a resolve to secure a still greater luxury, in which we had not yet indulged. We had seen several small bands of buffalo, but with no opportunity of capturing any of them, so I selected Iven Watt, a crack shot, by the way, as my companion, and with our rifles on our shoulders, mounted my carriage horses, and with bright hopes and spirits high, started out to bring in some buffalo meat and thus further prove our skill as hunters from the Hoosier state. We left Mayer and Day to guard the camp, assist the women with the washing, and kill jack rabbits, game too small for us. We rode about fifteen miles to the north, when we came upon two buffaloes quietly feeding upon a little slope of ground. We dismounted, picketed our horses, and on all fours crept toward them till barely within range of our muzzle-loading rifles, when they saw us. We fired without hitting either of them, and they started toward us. We ran for our horses, which we luckily reached and lost no time in mounting, when the buffalo turned and ran from us across the level plain. Going on a little further we came to a ridge, or elevation, which afforded protection for our horses, which we once more picketed, and walking about a hundred yards came upon a herd of the coveted game, from which we selected a large bull, and commenced firing upon him. We fired nine shots apiece, but still our game did not fall. He would snort loudly, and whirl round as if dazed, not knowing from whence came the bullets, and not seeing us from our hiding place in the ridge of ground. Seeing our shots did not bring our game, I told Watt we were firing too high, and reloading we took aim and fired at the same time, but

-175-

lower and with effect. To our great joy the huge creature fell. Rushing back to our horses we mounted and hurried to secure our prize, which lay on the ground only wounded. Upon seeing us, he staggered to his feet and ran about a hundred yards, when he fell again. The rest of the herd, frightened at our approach, ran wildly across the plain with uplifted tails, and were soon out of sight. Seeing our buffalo could not run, I sprang from my horse, and taking fair aim at his head, fired and killed him, contrary to a theory I had heard that a buffalo could not be killed by a shot in the head. Again we secured our horses, and began to strip our game of his smooth coat, taking the hindquarters for our share, judging this to be the choices cut, which we were to put in a bag which we carried for the purpose. Little we knew of life and customs on the plains. In about fifteen minutes after we began our work we were surprised—yes, perfectly horror-stricken—to see about thirty big, hungry grey wolves coming rapidly towards us, attracted by the scent of blood from the dead buffalo. Nearer and nearer they came, till hearing a noise we looked toward our horses, only to see them running in the wildest affright, on, on to the north, in a directly opposite course from camp. We left our game to the wolves willingly, having no wish to contest their claim to it, and went in pursuit of our horses. We had intended to be in camp with our buffalo meat in time for dinner, and had set out in the morning without a morsel of food in our pockets, so nightfall found us hungry, tired, afoot, and miles—how many we knew not—from camp and friends, our horses gone and hardly knowing which way to turn. However, it was a starlight night, and fixing my eye on one bright star I said to Watt that we must take that star for our guide and go as far as we could that night. We went on, Watt complaining of hunger very often, until the sky became cloudy and we could no longer see our guide, when we sat down and placed our guns on the ground pointing toward the star that had been to us, so far, a welcome guide. The time we could not tell, as neither of us carried a watch, but it must have been far in the night. From the time of leaving camp, the many mishaps of the day and our extreme fatigue, it seemed an age. Soon all trouble was forgotten in deep sleep, from which we awoke to find the sky clear and our late guide ready to light us on our weary journey. We arose and started once more, neither stopping for an instant or turning aside for rock, hill or bramble, but kept as nearly as possible in a straight line, never forgetting our star until it grew dim before the coming daylight. Thus we went, still fasting, over a beautiful rolling country, till about 9 or 10 o'clock in the morning, when we climbed a steep bluff and below us saw the Platte river valley through which slowly passed a few straggling emigrant wagons. The very sight of them brought joy to our hearts, and also relief to Watt's empty stomach, for the first thing he did on reaching the wagon was to ask for food, which was freely given. I inquired the way to Rawhide creek, which the emigrants had left two miles behind them. Being so near our own camp I did not ask for food, but Watt insisted on sharing his portion with me, which I accepted, and must say relished after my long fast. We hurried back to the camp, where I found my wife almost frantic with grief at our long absence, thinking of course we had been killed by hostile Indians. Our friend Sargent was intending to continue his journey the next day if we did not return, but my wife was thinking of some plan by which she could return to our old home on the banks of the Wabash. However, when we told them of our narrow escape, even with the loss of our horses and game, grief turned to joy, and peace reigned once more in our camp.

After resting the remainder of the day we prepared, the next morning, not for a buffalo hunt but for a hunt for our lost horses. Mr. Sargent loaned us two of his horses, which we rode, and in case we did not return that evening he was to put two of his other horses to my carriage and proceed with Mayer, Day, my family and goods the next morning, we to over take them somewhere along the line. After making this arrangement we went back to the scene of our late adventure, where we found large herds of wild horses but never a track of our own, which, being shod, were easily tracked. We hunted till sundown when we came to a mound or hill, perhaps 100 or 150 feet above the level, with a circular depression or basin on the top of it, which we selected for our camp. Taking our horses into this basin we made them secure by hobbling them, took our supper, consisting of a cold lunch minus drink of any kind. We witnessed from our elevated position a grand buffalo show — fully 5000 scattered over that vast plain, many of them quite near the mound on which we stood. It seemed almost as far as we could see to be one vast herd of buffalo. We arose next morning and continued our hunt till the middle of the afternoon, when we gave up all hope of finding the lost horses, and taking a westerly course set out to overtake the wagons, which had stopped before night for our benefit. A buffalo hunt proved a source of joy as well as sorrow to our party for soon after camping for the night, Mayer saw two men, buffalo hunters, who, like Watt and myself, had been lost, riding our lost horses leisurely along the road. Going to them Mayer told them that the horses belonged in our camp. They said they had seen the horses on the plains, and knowing they had escaped from some emigrant train, caught them and gladly rode them into camp. They declined the $5 reward my wife and Mayer pressed upon them for the great service rendered. The previous day my wife and children had ridden in the ox wagon leaving our carriage to Mrs. Sargent and family in part payment for the borrowed horses, but the next day on resuming our journey she gladly gave up the cushions and comforts of the ox wagon for those of the car- riage, which was once more drawn by the lost horses.

Nothing further happened except the occasional killing of an antelope or stray buffalo, my desire for buffalo hunting not being fully satisfied, although I had vowed after my late adventure never to hunt buffalo again. Sargeant and I killed one about this time which weighed fully 2500 pounds, whose meat was so tough we could not use it. He was evidently the patriarch of a large herd. We crossed the Rocky mountains at South pass, according to instructions given in Horn's guide book for emigrants, which we had carefully observed during our trip. It gave minute instructions as to proper camps, roads, the crossing of streams, where to find good water and grass, and other information which we found of great value, as our experience afterward proved. Some days after crossing the mountains our party was increased by the families of Tyrus Himes, father of George Himes of Portland, Or., and Judson Himes of Elma, and Mr. Dodge, who settled on their arrival here, on Mima prairie.

All went smoothly till we crossed Bear River mountains, and, feeling some confidence with our own judgment, we had grown somewhat careless about consulting our guide-book, often selecting our camp without reference to it. One of these camps we had good cause to remember. I had gone ahead to find a camp for noon, which was on a pretty good stream with abundance of grass for our horses and cattle, which greatly surprised us, as grass had been a scarce article in many of our camps. Soon after dinner we noticed some of our cattle beginning to lag and seem tired and some of them began to vomit. We realized with horror that our cattle were poisoned, so we camped at the first stream we came to, which was Ham's fork of Bear river, to cure if possible our poor sick cattle. Here we were, eighty or a hundred miles from Salt lake, the nearest settlement, in such a dilemma. We looked about for relief. Bacon and grease were the only antidotes for poison which our stores contained. We cut bacon in slices and forced a few slices down the throats of the sick oxen, but after once tasting it the poor creatures ate it eagerly, thereby saving their lives, as those that did not eat it (cows we could spare better than our oxen) died next day. The horses were none of them sick. Had we consulted our guide before, instead of after camping at that pretty spot, we would have been spared all this trouble, as it warned travelers of the poison existing there. This event ran our stock of bacon so low we were obliged to buy more, for which we paid 75 cents per pound, and 50 cents per pound for butter, which we bought of Mr. Melville, one of our party.

We were joined at Salmon falls by a Mr. Hutchinson and family. Here we crossed Snake river the first time, a quarter of a mile above the falls. Hutchinson had a fine lot of horses and cattle, which caused him much anxiety, as he was afraid they would drown while crossing the river. There were a great many Indians here of the Snake tribe, and he tried to hire one of them to swim his stock, offering him money, which he stubbornly refused to do. Finally Hutchinson took off his overshirt, a calico garment, and offered it to him. This was the coveted prize. He took it, swam four horses safely, drowned one, then when he reached the opposite side quietly mounted one of the best horses and rode rapidly away over the hills, leaving us to the difficult task of crossing, which we did without further incident. We paid $4 for every wagon towed across the river. For 200 miles we wended our weary way, on to Fort Boise, a Hudson Bay trading post, kept by an Englishman and his Indian wife, the former being the only white person at the post. Here we had to cross Snake river again which at this point was a quarter of a mile wide. The agent kept a ferry and would not take our wagons for less than $8 apiece, which was as much again as we had been paying at other crossings. I tried to get an Indian to swim our cattle over, but failing, Watt proposed to go with them if I would, which seemed a fair proposition, and as they would not go without some one to drive them, we started across. Watt carried a long stick in one hand, holding by the other to the tail of old Lube, a great rawboned ox who had done faithful service on our long, toilsome journey. I threw my stick away and went in a little below Watt, but found the current very strong, which drifted me down stream. I thought I should be drowned and shouted to Watt, "I'm gone." With great presence of mind he reached his stick toward me, which I grasped with a last hope of saving my life, and by this means bore up till I swam to Watt, who caught on the tail of the nearest ox, thus giving me a welcome hold on old Lube's tail, who carried me safely to the shore. Only for Watt's coolness and bravery I should have lost my life at the same spot where one of Mr. Melville's men was drowned on the previous evening.

At Grande Ronde a happy surprise awaited us. Nelson Sargent whose father was in our party, met John Lane, who arrived in advance of us, with the welcome news that a party of workmen had started out from Olympia and Steilacoom to make a road for us through the Natchez pass over the Cascade mountains, ours being the first party of emigrants to attempt a crossing north of The Dalles, on the Columbia river. Lane waited at Grande Ronde while Nelson Sargent pushed ahead to meet his aged parents.

Our party was reunited at Grande Ronde. E.A. Light, John Lane and others who had left us at the Elkhorn river, met us and continued the journey with us across the Cascade mountains. We went fifty miles further to the Umatilla river, where we rested two days and made preparations for the rest of our trip. Lest our provisions run short, I bought, at a trading post here, 100 pounds of flour for which I paid $40 in gold coin, unbolted flour too.

We left the emigrant trail at Umatilla and with thirty one wagons struck out for Fort Walla Walla, now Wallula. Fifty miles further on was a trading post kept by an agent of the Hudson Bay company. Of him we bought lumber — drift-wood from the Columbia river — of which we made a flat-boat on which to tow our goods across, afterward selling it, or trading it, to the agent in payment for the lumber. On the 8th of September, at 2 o'clock in the afternoon, our boat was finished, and the task of crossing commenced. It was not a pleasant task, but by working all night, everything was safely launched by sunrise next morning except our cattle and horses. These we wanted the Indians to take across for us. Sargent was the only man who could speak chinook, but not well enough to make a bargain with the Indians, so we got the agent to hire them to swim our stock. Before they would commence the work they must be paid. We gave them $18, and they brought up twenty-five canoes, formed in line below the crossing, and we drove our cattle in the stream, and they swam to shore safely. Next came the horses. When they were about the middle of the river the treacherous Indians laid down their oars and made signs, which I understood to mean more money. Meanwhile our horses were drifting down stream, where high bluffs rose on either side, and they could not possibly land. Taking out my purse I offered them more money, and they at once took up the oars and paddled across, landing our horses safely.

The chief of the Walla Wallas was Pupi Pupu Muxmux, or Yellow Serpent, a very important person who rode, with the dignity of a king, a large American horse, a beautiful bay, with holsters on his saddle, and a pair of navy revolvers. He was a large, fine looking Indian, fully aware of his power as a chief, which was well demonstrated when we divided among our party some beef we had bought of him. It was cut in pieces varying from ten to twenty pounds, but it must be weighed. The chief went to Mr. Melville, the only man in our party who had scales for weighing, and taking them in his hand examined them closely, although he could not tell one figure from another. Then, looking carefully at the many faces around him, seeming satisfied with the scrutiny, he came to me, gave me the scales with a sign that I do the weighing, at the same time seating himself flat on the ground amongst us. I weighed, Lane standing by with book and pencil to tally. Every time a piece was weighed Pupi Pupu Muxmux would spring up, examine the scales closely, give a grunt which meant yes, and sit down; and so on until the last piece was weighed, Lane making settlement with him for our party. Pu Pu Muxmux was killed at the battle of Walla Walla during a four day's engagement in the spring of 1856 while trying to make his escape from the volunteers, who held him as a friendly Indian, to join his tribe, which he had represented as friendly, but who were really waging bitter warfare against the white settlers. A brother of this chief was hired to guide us to the Natchez pass.

I must not forget to tell you that at Walla Walla we saw the home of the noble Marcus Whitman. A log house covered with straw, held on by poles laid across the roof; a little garden and orchard were enclosed near the house, and a little further on we saw the graves of Whitman, his wife, and heroic little band who were massacred by the Indians some time before our arrival.

Our guide made a horse trade with Mr. Melville, in which he considered himself cheated, grew indignant and deserted us, and we were left in that strange country without a landmark, a compass, or guide, nothing to help us. We traveled on, however, to the Yakima river, which we crossed, and here lost by death one of our party, Mrs. McCullough, a relative of Mrs. Woolery, now one of Puyallup's esteemed citizens. Until this sad event she was the life, the sunshine of our party. Everyone loved "Aunt Pop," as she was familiarly called, but the death of her friend cast a shadow over her bright face, and made the remainder of our journey gloomy when we thought of the lonely grave by the Yakima.

Our next obstacle was a canyon at Well Springs, which seemed impossible to cross. From the Yakima river we had been followed by a band of Indians, who had kept our wives and children in perfect terror, but laughed and chatted gaily as they rode along. The tyees or big men were dressed in buckskin leggings, handsomely beaded, and breech-clouts, made of cedar bark. The sqaws were dressed very similiarly. Men and squaws all had painted faces. The squaws always carried the pappooses done up in the proper Indian fashion and hung to the horn of the saddle, which bobbed up and down in no very easy manner when the ponies were in full gallop.

At Well Springs we sent out men to find a better road, as we thought we were lost. The Indians, knowing from this move, that we were lost, got off their ponies, cleared a small piece of ground and marked two roads, one heading northeast, the other heading northwest, making dots at intervals along each road, the former having fewer dots than the latter. One of them, motioning his head in an upward and curving line, pointed with the other hand to the dots, saying at each one, "sleeps, sleeps," and at the end of the road, "soldiers," the only words we could understand, and really all the English they could speak. Lane said to me: "What shall we do?" I replied, "Let us take the road which has the fewest 'sleeps,'" which we did, going northeast one or two days, when we knew we had taken the wrong road. We had no compass, and would have known but little more if we had had one. We saw before us almost a perpendicular bluff, seemingly 1000 feet high, extending far away to the mountains. This we learned later was White bluffs, on the Columbia river. Here we camped for the night, ordering the Indians to camp at a respectful distance from us, which they did. We placed a double guard out, as we suspected they had led us to this trap in order to massacre our whole party. I really believe now that their intentions were good, if they could have told us so we could have understood them. The next day we retraced our way to Well Springs, where we had left our proper course. In due time we learned that our Indian escort meant to conduct us to Fort Colville, an English trading post, for the winter, thinking the snow on the Cascades would prevent our reaching Fort Steilacoom, where United States soldiers were stationed. Upon reaching Well springs, our followers left us, much to our relief. We were further encouraged the same night by the return of Nelson Sargent, who with others had gone in advance to look out a good road, with the glad news that after crossing the canyon a good road lay before us. Further, that they had struck the trail which the Steilacoom and Olympia company had blazed for the coming emigrants.

On the 18th of September, as well as I remember, we crossed the canyon, or rather traversed its length about a mile, which was the roughest traveling I ever saw, and came out on a beautiful plain. We traveled along Coal creek for two days when we came to Selah Valley on the upper Yakima, which we crossed, taking our course along Wenas creek, about ten miles, when we came to a garden, now the farm owned by David Longmire, which was kept by Indians of whom we bought thirteen bushels of potatoes, the first vegetables we had had since leaving the Rocky mountains—a real feast, though, boiled in their jackets, a bucketful making one meal for us.

Following Wenas creek to its source, we crossed over to the Natchez river, which we followed for four days, crossing and recrossing fifty-two times, then left it and started for the summit of the Cascade mountains, north of Mount Tacoma, which we reached in three days, finding fine grass and good water. Here we stopped for two days, giving our tired oxen a good rest and plenty of food, which they badly needed, for the rest of our journey. Three miles further on we came to Summit Hill, where we spliced ropes and prepared for the steep descent which we saw before us. One end of the rope was fastened to the axles of the wagon, the other thrown around a large tree and held by several men; and thus, one at a time, the wagons were lowered gradually a distance of 300 yards, when the ropes were loosened and the wagons drawn a quarter of a mile further with locked wheels, when we reached Greenwater. All the wagons were lowered safely but the one belonging to Mr. Lane, now a resident of Puyallup, which was crushed to pieces by the breaking of one of our ropes, causing him and his family to finish the trip on horseback.

At Summit Hill my wife and Mrs. E.A. Light went ahead of the wagon with their children, taking a circuitous trail which brought them around to the train of wagons, for which we made a road as we went. As they walked along the narrow trail, my wife before, they were surprised to meet a white man, the first they had seen aside from those in our party, since leaving Walla Walla. It proved to be Andy Burge, who had been sent out from Fort Steilacoom with supplies for the roadmakers, who had already given up the job for want of food, which arrived too late for them, but in time for us, whose stores had grown alarmingly low. No less surprised was Burge at meeting two lone women in the wilderness, who greeted them with: "My God, women, where in the world did you come from?" — a greeting rough, but friendly in its roughness to the two women who shrank against the trees and shrubbery to allow him and his pack animal to pass them in the trail, which was barely wide enough for one person. From them he learned of our whereabouts, and came to us, trying to persuade us to return to where there was grass and water for our stock, telling us we could not possibly make the trip over the country before us. Failing in this, he set to work and distributed his supplies amongst us, and returned to Fort Steilacoom, blazing trees as he went, and leaving notes tacked to them, giving us what encouragement he could, and preparing us, in a measure, for what was before us. For instance, "The road is a shade better;" a little further on "a shade worse," then again, "a shade better," and so on, until we were over the bad roads. We crossed Greenwater river sixteen times, and followed that stream until we came to White river, which we crossed six times, then left it for a dreary pull over Wind mountain, which was covered with heavy fir and cedar trees, but destitute of grass, with a few vine maples, on whose leaves our poor oxen and horses lived for seven days, not having a blade of grass during that time. I must not forget to mention the fact that in these dark days — seven of them — we and our half-starved cattle worked the road every day. We bridged large logs which lay before us, by cutting others and laying alongside, making a bridge wide enough for the oxen to draw our wagons across. Then all, except John Lane, E.A. Light and myself, left their wagons on account of their failing oxen, which they drove before them to Boise creek prairie, where there was good grass. Lane, Light and I arrived first; the rest soon followed with their cattle and horses. Four miles further we reached Porter's prairie, where Allan Porter, now of Hillhurst, had taken a claim, but who was at that time in Olympia. We again crossed White river, making the seventh time, and pushed on to Connell's prairie, thence to the Puyallup river, to the present site of Van Ogle's hop farm. Little did Van think then that he would ever raise, bale and sell hops on that piece of ground. We found the river low and filled with humpback salmon. We armed ourselves with various weapons, clubs, axes and whatever we could get and went fishing. Every man who could strike a blow got a fish, and such a feast we had not enjoyed since we had potatoes boiled in the jackets, but fish was far ahead of potatoes. John Mayer declared they were the best fish he had ever eaten. We had a royal feast. Some of our party were up all night cooking and eating fish. All relished them but Mrs. Longmire, who was feeling indisposed, but she fortunately got a delicacy — rare to her — a pheasant, which she bought from an Indian — her first purchase on Puget Sound.

The next day we moved on to Nisqually plains and camped at Clover creek, some 300 yards from the home of Mrs. Mahan, who, I believe, still lives there, and whose kindness the ladies of our party will never forget. On the 9th of October, the day after we camped at Clover creek, the men all went out to Fort Steilacoom to see Puget Sound, and during our absence Mrs. Mahan made a raid on our camp and took my wife, Mrs. E.A. Light, Mrs. Woolery and other ladies whose names I do not remember, to her home, where she had prepared a dinner which to these tired sisters, after their toilsome journey, was like a royal banquet. After months of camp life, to sit once more at a table presided over by a friend in this far away land, where we thought to meet only strangers, was truly an event never to be forgotten, and one to which my wife often refers as a bright spot on memory's page.

Before proceeding with my narrative I must mention the fact that I arrived in this country with torn and ragged pants and coat, my cap battered, with only one boot, my other foot covered with an improvised moccasin made of a portion of a cow's hide which we had killed a few days before. In this garb I was to meet a party of well dressed gentlemen from Olympia, who had heard of us from Andy Burge, led by Mr. Hurd, who had come out to welcome the first party of emigrants direct from the East over the Cascade mountains north of The Dalles. My garb was a sample of those of the other men, and when we were together felt pretty well, all being in the same fashion; but when brought face to face with well dressed men we felt somewhat embarrassed. But our new friends were equal to the emergency and our embarrassment was soon dispelled by copious draughts of "good old bourbon," to which we did full justice, while answering questions amidst introductions and hearty handshaking. This was on the 8th day of October.

On the 10th day of October, Dr. Tolmie, chief factor of the Hudson Bay company, stationed at Fort Nisqually, paid us a visit, asked us numerous questions about our long journey and arrival, treated us in a very friendly manner, but soon left, bidding us a polite farewell. In about three hours he returned with a man driving an ox cart, which was loaded with beef just killed and dressed, which he presented to us, saying, "Distribute this to suit yourselves." Not understanding it to be a present we offered to pay him, which he firmly but politely refused, saying, "It is a present to you," and it was a present most welcome to us at that time, and for which we expressed heartfelt thanks to the generous giver.

Leaving our families in camp, E.A. Light, John Lane and I, started out to look for homes. Having received due notice from the Hudson Bay company not to settle on any lands north of the Nisqually river, we crossed the river and went to Yelm prairie, a beautiful spot, I thought, as it lay before us covered with tall waving grass, a pretty stream bordered with shrubs and tall trees, flowing through it, and the majestic mountain standing guard over all, in its snowy coat, seemed a scene fit for an artist. Herds of deer wandered at leisure through the tall grass. It was good enough for me and I bought a house from Martin Shelton, but bought no land, as it was unsurveyed as yet, and returned for my family. Hill Harmon was in camp, waiting for my return. He had a logging camp on the Sound and wanted to hire my boys, John Moyer, Iven Watt and Will Claflin, (the last named had joined us at Fort Hall) who declined his terms, $85 per month, until they knew I could get along without them. Knowing the boys were needy, I told them to go, which they did, soon, getting an advance in salary to $100 per month.

We started for our new home, my wife and children in one wagon drawn by three yoke of oxen, which she drove. I went ahead with another wagon and four yoke of oxen. Our carriage had long ago been left on Burnt river, also the harness which we saw afterward on a pair of mules driven past us on the emigrant trail. Arrived "at home" we found a large number of Indians camped near by. About thirty of them came in to see us the first night to examine things new to them, which they did, expressing their surprise by grunts and guttural sounds which were Greek to us. We found but three white families for neighbors, Mr. Braile, a bachelor, Mr. and Mrs. Levi Shelton and Mr. and Mrs. Hughes, the latter now a citizen of Steilacoom. The following winter I took a donation claim, a portion of the farm on which I have since resided.

Late in the fall of 1853 Isaac Stevens, the first governor of Washington territory, arrived from across the plains in such sorry garb that Frank R.

Jackson, a pioneer, was loath to believe he was the newly appointed governor, a doubt which he openly expressed, and which the governor alluded to in later years laughingly, taking it as a better joke on himself than on Mr. Jackson. Governor Stevens also held the office of superintendent of Indian affairs, with instructions to make treaties with the Indians. I will write more particularly of the Nisqually tribes, whose chiefs were Leschi and Quiemuth, this being the tribe I was associated with more than the others. Matters went smoothly till the treaty in the fall of 1854. A council was held at Medicine creek, at the mouth of the Nisqually river, for the purpose of making this treaty, the terms of which are well known to every pioneer of the state of Washington. From day to day they met till the treaty was made by which the Indians were to recertain lands of their own choice, reserved from the public domain for them and their children as long as the tribe should exist. This seemed satisfactory for awhile, but emigrants coming in larger numbers the Indians grew jealous, incited, too, by persons unfriendly to the settlers, and began to appear less friendly toward us, frequently telling us the Klickitats were getting ready for war upon the whites, but assuring us the Nisquallys would never join them, would always be friends to the whites.

In July following the completion of the treaty, Quiemuth and Slugyi came to me complaining that the settlers did not give them enough for their work, saying in Chinook that the "Bostons" were bad people, but the King George men were good; that the latter had been here a long time and never stole land. Now the "Bostons" come and were fencing and stealing the land from the Indians. Slugyi, who could speak English, interpreted what I could not understand, which was nearly all of Quiemuth's Chinook. They finished by giving me the worst bemeaning I ever got. I tried to reason with them, saying the common people were not to blame, that the "tyees" had bought their land, the officials had made the treaty and they had agreed to it. Finding them unreasonable, I quietly took their abuse. When they had finished they got on their ponies and rode off. I saw Quiemuth once after this, when he was still growling about the "Bostons," but still called himself the "Boston's Tillicum." Notwithstanding these friendly assurances, we were greatly alarmed, but at a loss what move to make, as we did not want to leave our home unprotected, neither risk our own and children's lives by staying at home.

On the 10th of October, while my boys, Elcaine and David, myself and John Mollhigh, an Indian who often helped me with my work, were putting in rye about a half-a-mile from my house, where Mrs. Longmire and the two younger children were alone, at least thirty Indians rode up in company with old Stub, an Indian who had supplied our table with wild game since we first came on the prairie, a first-rate hunter, and an Indian who was friendly and honest, got off their horses, walked in the house with their guns and arranged themselves around the fireplace, crowding my wife and children to the back part of the room, the latter crying with fright, while their mother sat in deadly fear, not knowing what moment they would strike the fatal blow. Stub sat in the corner taking little part in the noisy conversation, which lasted about an hour. They made a demand for food in a rude impudent way, which was denied. They then got on their horses, after telling my wife in Chinook they were going to the Bald Hills on a hunt, and rode away, leaving Stub in his corner by the fire. After they were gone, my wife gave him some food in a tin plate, the best we had, which he ate in silence. Having finished his meal, he arose, went to my wife, laid his hand on her head and began to talk in a sad, mournful way. Not one word could she understand. Then he laid his hand on his own breast, then on the heads of the two frightened children, all the time talking and, as my wife thought, warning her of the fate of the white settlers and the horrible intentions of the Indians. He left silently, and this was the last time he ever came to our house. He went to the hostile Indians, was captured with Utsalawah, or Chuck-Note, as the settlers called him, about two months after the opening of the Indian war, taken to Olympia, put in prison in chains, where he killed himself by tying a strip of his blanket tightly around his throat. His companion was released later on, and lived till the summer of 1886 when he was laid to rest with his "tillicums" in a little burying ground about 300 yards from where my house now stands, the spot he had begged of me from year to year for his last resting place—almost since I had known him.

On the 11th of October 1855, the day after the Indians came to my house, I started with my family to Olympia, as we now knew there was no safety for us in our own home, which had already been under guard for two weeks. Our bachelor neighbors McLean, Chambers, Frank Goodwin and Mr. Perkins, the two former now living near Roy, in Pierce county, the latter at rest long since, came to our house for mutual protection, and kindly stood guard, taking turns, whose kindness we shall never forget. Arrived at Olympia I rented a house for my wife and children, put the two boys in school and returned to my farm, intending, with the help of John Mollhigh, to finish my fall work.

On the 20th of October Quiemuth paid a visit to Secretary Mason, who was acting governor in the absence of Governor Stevens, who had gone east of the Cascades to make treaties with those tribes which seemed to be leaders in the rebellious movements which we began to fear would end in a general massacre of the white settlers. Quiemuth assured Mason again and again of the friendship of his tribe, whereupon Mason told him to get his half brother, Leschi, and with their families, come to Olympia, where he would give them food and shelter. This Quiemuth agreed to do and returned to Yelm prairie for that purpose, but he had forgotten both his promise and his friendship long before his arrival, for no sooner did he meet Leschi than they took their families and moved as fast as they could to Puyallup. As the chief did not come the following day, Mason feeling somewhat alarmed for the safety of the white settlers, appointed Charles Eaton and twelve men, among them Connell, McAllister and George

McAllister, son of the latter, and a man named Wallace, to go to Puyallup and invite the chiefs to come to Olympia. I was to have gone but as I was four miles from the main road, they hurried on without me. Crossing the Puyallup river they went to where Van Ogle's farm now is, and sent a friendly Indian who had come with them from Olympia, to learn the whereabouts of the Indians. Upon his return he reported about 200 Indians having collected further on, with the two chiefs, Quiemuth and Leschi; also the Puyallup tribe. Hearing this, Eaton said it would never do to go further, for that meant war. McAllister and Connell ridiculed the idea, saying they knew those Indians well, and would go and have a friendly talk with them. Eaton replied that if they did go it was contrary to orders. Confident of success, they laid down their guns and, after buckling on their revolvers, started on what they meant as a friendly errand, with the two friendly Indians, but which proved their death, for in about twenty minutes Eaton and his little band heard the firing of guns, when Eaton said the men were killed and they must get ready for defense at once. They took refuge in a cabin which stood near, and fastened their saddle blankets over the open spaces between the logs, and filled a barrel full of water, in case the hostile Indians should fire the building. They then hid their horses close as possible to the cabin and declared themselves ready for battle, which began just before dark, a large band of Indians opening fire on Eaton and his ten men; one a friendly Indian who had returned with news of the sad fate of the McAllister and Connell, the other Indian having gone with the hostile tribes who were now fighting, sending bullet after bullet into the little cabin. One bullet struck Wallace, who, with the exception of being stunned, received no permanent injury except losing the upper part of one ear. The Indians tried to fire the cabin, but Eaton's band kept up such a constant fire they dared not approach near enough for the purpose, so set fire to a pen filled with wheat, which stood near, greatly helping Eaton by the bright light to see the Indians and take fair aim. Toward daylight the Indians drew off, taking their dead and wounded, also every horse belonging to Eaton's band. Assuring himself that quiet reigned once more, Eaton ventured forth with his men, crossed the Puyallup, left the main road, climbed a high bluff and made their way through the woods to the Nisqually plains, ten miles distant, thence to Olympia, leaving the bodies of McAllister and Connell where they fell.

On the same day the 28th of October, before sunrise, two Indians came to my house on horses dripping with sweat, and told Mollhigh of the terrible massacre on White river and the fate of McAllister and Connell, which Mollhigh afterward told me when I visited him. Mollhigh's wife and mother were camped near my house, but came at once on hearing of the massacre, and began to weep and wring their hands, and told me in Chinook to go at once or the Indians would kill me, which I did not understand. Mollhigh's wife told Mrs. Longmire afterward that I was the biggest fool she ever saw. During this excitement, Mollhigh continued his work, talking to the Indians, who were trying to persuade him to go and fight the whites. I noticed their excitement, which was greatly increased, when the thirty braves who had gone to the Bald Hills a few days before, arrived with their squaws, who were crying bitterly, which convinced me the news of the massacre had been sent them, and that I must get ready to leave, as the Indians were already grinding their knives and tomahawks on my grindstone, while they talked wildly and the squaws continued to cry. I fastened my revolver but left my gun in the house while I went after my horse. While looking for my horse from a high point which commanded a view of the prairie, I heard the sound of horses' feet, and stepping behind a tree I saw passing the two Indians who had brought news of the massacre, as I supposed, returning to Puyallup. Not finding my horse, I started home, but stopped at McLean Chambers', who lived where my house now stands, and who had already heard of the massacre. He begged me not to go back to my home, but I had left my gun and felt that I must have it. Finding I would go, he said I must take his horse, which I did, but while we were talking the same Indians I had seen while looking for my horse rode up, talked a few minutes and passed on. I believed I was the man they were hunting. Shortly I took McLean's horse and rode quietly home, to find it broken into, everything of value gone, every stitch of my clothing only what I wore, also my gun, which I looked for first on going into the house. Things of no value to the Indians were scattered over the yard, but not an Indian in sight — not even my trusted Mollhigh, who afterwards told me he went only to save my life. He told the Indians Longmire was a "cultus tillicum," and had always been good to the Indians, and not to kill him, but kill the "Tyees," the big men. They answered his pleading by saying if he did not come with them and help to fight they would kill him and "Longmire too," but if he would help them they would not kill Longmire. After long persuasion poor Mollhigh yielded, thinking this the only means to save either one of us, and went with the hostiles. He was true to me though, for after the war he came back and lived with me for years, always claiming that he saved my life.

Coming out of my house I looked carefully on all sides, with my revolver drawn, ready to fire at a minute's notice. I mounted my horse, which I put to a lively run, till I reached McLean Chambers, who at once took him and started for Olympia. The Indians had stolen my last horse, and I must now make my way to Olympia, twenty-five miles, on foot, which was not a pleasant trip alone. I walked over to Brail's, where T.M. Chambers now lives, to find his house deserted. He had left on first hearing of the massacre. I now concluded to go to Hughes, and get him to go with me, but dark came on, and hearing horses coming I dropped behind a pile of rails, which hid me from view. Soon I heard the peculiar hissing sound like "shee, shee," with which Indians always drive stock, and I knew they were stealing the last horses from the white settlers on the prairies. Arrived at Hughes' he and his family had taken flight. I hardly knew which way to turn, but finally decided to go to George Edwards', a former employee of the Hudson Bay company, an Englishman who still lives at Yelm station. I thought if he was gone I must take to the woods. Fortunately for me he and his wife, one of the Nisqually tribe, were at home, but thought it unsafe to remain in the house, so we went to the barn and spent the night. In the morning we started for Olympia, Edwards and I. I rode a horse belonging to the Hudson Bay company, known as old Roosh. Half an hour before our arrival word had reached Olympia from Dr. Tolmie, through Mollhigh's wife, that I was killed by the Indians the evening before. Much to my relief, my family had not heard the news when I arrived at home.

I met Charley Eaton, who was organizing a company of volunteers to go in pursuit of the Indians, bent on killing them all, else bring them to subjection. About sixty-seven men joined him, but on being sworn refused to take the oath, and deserted our ranks till only eighteen or twenty men remained in the company, which was called the Puget Sound Rangers. Charles Eaton was captain, James Tullis first lieutenant. The other officers' names I have forgotten. I enlisted and we started at once to scour the northeastern part of Thurston county and all of Pierce for hostile Indians and learn where they were collected. For several days not an Indian could be found, most of them having gone to White river to make a grand stand at Connell's prairie, where Qualchin met them with about 300 Klickitats from east of the Cascade mountains. Qualchin was the son of Auhi, chief of the Klickitats, whom he led to battle. Quiemuth led the Nisquallies, assisted by Leschi, and Kitsap the Puyallups. They were met here by companies commanded by Captains Henness, Gilmore, Hayes, White and Swindle; also one by Isaac Hayes. These were all volunteer companies. The Indians fought all the morning in ambush, the volunteers failing to draw them out into open battle. In the afternoon the volunteers, finding they could gain nothing by this method of warfare, resorted to strategy. One company was ordered to lie down on the ground, the rest to flee in confusion. The Indians, looking only at the fleeing volunteers and thinking the day was theirs, rushed madly forward with beating drums and wild warwhoops till they came within fifty yards of the prostrate volunteers, who suddenly rose and opened fire, the fleeing volunteers returning, firing as they came. A panic seized the Indians, who flung their drums and ran wildly not forgetting their dead and wounded, pell mell into the Puyallup river, swam to the other side, the volunteers following to the river bank, killing many as they tried to escape by swimming. Qualchin, not accustomed to fighting in the woods on foot, left for Yakima in disgust. The rest, left without a leader, and much reduced in numbers, scattered in small bands all over the country, stealing, burning houses and barns, killing the settlers and spreading terror everywhere.

The Puget Sound rangers in the meantime were attempting to hunt down fugitive Indians, all to no purpose, however, for not an Indian could be found. We became convinced they were getting information and assistance from friends, and so reported to Governor Stevens, who ordered the arrest of all persons suspected of rendering them assistance. Arrests were made of all men whom we suspected of harboring Indians. They were taken to Fort Steilacoom and and tried, but nothing could be proved against them, so they were released. After this the volunteers began to find Indians in small bands all over the country, whom they killed or captured, whenever found. However, depredations continued, and several more arrests were made, when Governor Stevens proclaimed martial law, to prevent persons suspected of aiding the Indians from returning to their homes, holding them as prisoners at Fort Steilacoom. Shortly after this move on the part of our worthy governor, some of the Indians surrendered and were placed on the reservation in charge of the Indian agent. The Puget Sound rangers were now discharged, and I made preparations to move back to Yelm prairie with my family, taking with me a friendly Indian named Peallo and his family, who camped near our house. We did not feel safe in our home, and Peallo and I took turns standing guard at nights; working with our guns beside us during the day.

The war had been going on now for nearly a year, and the settlers were tired and discouraged, and many of them living in blockhouses. One night when Peallo was standing guard he came to the door saying: "Mesatchee tillicums choco" (the bad Indians are coming). I got up, took my gun and went outside, when Peallo came to me, saying in Chinook: "If they do come I die with you." He lay down, putting his ear close to the ground, and listened a few minutes, but got up, saying he was mistaken. "It was the spirits, not Indians." But he was not mistaken, as examination next morning showed that horses had been fastened about a half mile from my house, on the edge of a swamp, apparently all night, the riders probably prowling near my house. When Peallo saw this he begged me to go to the blockhouse, saying we were not safe in our house. I told him I was not afraid. He then went to my wife and begged her to talk to me and get me to go to the blockhouse and not let her and the children be killed. On the second day after this we moved to the blockhouse, where we found Levi Shelton and family and Thomas Chambers, Sr., and family, besides five men to guard the commissary store, which was kept there.

About this time Governor Curry of Oregon sent a company of troops to our assistance under Captain Miller. Indians were still stealing horses and killing cattle. A band of these robbers were followed by Captain Maxon to the Mashel river, where the last one was killed.

Quiemuth and Leschi now separated, for what cause I never knew. The former grew tired of fighting and came to Ozha, a Frenchman, who lived on the Nisqually near the crossing of the Northern Pacific railroad bridge, and asked him to see me and see if I would take him safely to Governor Stevens, as he wanted to surrender and would risk his life to the governor. I told Ozha to bring Quiemuth to me after dark for if he were seen some one would surely kill him. I was glad he had surrendered as he was the only chief left on our side of the river whom we feared, but I hardly know why he came to me unless he thought as I was a friend of Governor Stevens it would make his sentence lighter. It was early in the summer of 1856 when he came one night with Ozha into my house unarmed, shaking hands with me and my wife as friendly as if he had not been fighting us and our friends for months and months. I got my horse and taking Van Ogle, George Brail, Ozha and Betsey Edgar, a squaw and friend of Ozha's, we started for Olympia, Quiemuth riding close to me, talking freely all the way, telling me if the governor did not kill him he would show me where there was lots of gold, as he knew where it was. It was a gloomy ride that night through the rain, and when we reached Olympia between 2 and 3 o'clock in the morning we were wet, muddy and tired. I awoke Governor Stevens and told him I had Quiemuth, who wanted to see him. He got up, invited us in, and ordered lunch, of which we partook heartily, being hungry as well as tired. Ozha, Van Ogle and Geo. Brail went to put our horses in the stable, while I remained with Quiemuth. The governor handed our prisoner a pipe of tobacco which he smoked a few minutes telling me between whiffs he thought the governor was a good man and would not hurt him; and that he was a good "tillicum." Governor Stevens offered me a bed, which I declined, as I was wet and muddy, and told him if he would give me a blanket I would lay down by the fire in the office. Blankets were brought for me and Quiemuth, and we lay down, one on either side of the fireplace, I being nearest the door. In the meantime, news of the chief's surrender must have been circulated, although I had intended it should be kept secret.

Governor Stevens left lights burning in the office, bade us good-night, and once more retired, and I was soon in a deep sleep, from which I was aroused by a great noise, I hardly knew what. I sprang up to hear the sound as of persons running out of the house, and to find the lights blown out. I saw by the dim firelight a man fall and heard a deep groan. I ran to the falling man and found it was Quiemuth, speechless and dying. At this moment the governor rushed in, saying as he saw the dead chief: "Who in _____ has done this?" I replied I did not know. "In my office, too," he added, "this is a club for General Wool." General Wool had opposed the policy of Stevens, and Governor Curry of Oregon, in the prosecution of the Indian war.

Before the governor reached the office I ran to the door, and by the dim morning light saw eighteen or twenty men outside the door. Never in my long and intimate acquaintance with Governor Stevens did I ever see him so enraged as he was that night, and justly, too, it seems to me, for even after all these years it kindles my wrath when I think of the cowardly deed. It was almost daylight, and the body of Quiemuth was left on the carpeted floor of the office till the coroner's inquest was held, which brought out the fact that Quiemuth had been shot with a pistol, the ball taking effect in the right arm and right side, which Dr. Willard, Sr., declared never could have killed any man. On closer examination he found the chief had been stabbed with a very fine blade, which had penetrated the heart, causing instant death. One, Joe Bustin, had been arrested during the inquest on suspicion. Elwood Evans, now of Tacoma, then a young lawyer of Olympia, conducted the prosecution, B.F. Kindall the defense, which resulted in the acquittal of Bastin, though many persons believed him to be the guilty party.

Quiemuth now being dead, Leschi was soon captured and sentenced to hang, but the execution was stayed, and Leschi returned to prison. Court again convened, when he was sentenced and executed near Fort Steilacoom. This ended the Indian war.

I must here mention that many prominent men condemned Governor Stevens strongly for proclaiming martial law, but his course was ably defended in the legislature, where the debates were long and stormy. I represented my county at that time, and approved our governor's action. Peace once more restored, the settlers returned to their homes to begin life anew, having been robbed of everything. My last horse was gone, but a few cattle were left. But with willing hands and bright hopes, the blessings of health and peace in our home, my wife and I took up our burden, and prosperity met us, so that when old age comes on we may rest in peace, waiting for the summons which calls us all to the better land.

J.W. McCarthy

A run-in with the assessor provokes a change
of the boundary line between King and Pierce Counties.
He relates his experiences during the Indian
Wars near present day Sumner, Washington.

Sumner, Washington — June 17, 1892

We left Lake county, Indiana, on the 18th day of March, 1853, bound for Oregon. Our train consisted of the following persons: George Belshaw, wife and three children; Thomas Belshaw and wife; Richard Parsons, wife and four children; Henry Parsons and wife; Stephen Martin, wife and three children; Thomas Conts and wife, Hiram Birch, Maria Darling, and the three brothers—F.A., M.Y. and J.W. McCarthy, I, the last-named, being then about 20 years of age.

Nothing of importance happened until we came within a few miles of the Mississippi river on the opposite side from Davenport, in Iowa, when suddenly all of our teams stampeded, most of them getting away from their drivers and breaking yokes and wagons. The oxen ran four or five miles before men or horses could stop them, leaping down steep precipices, where horsemen dare not go. A very amusing part of the affair was the upsetting of Richard Parson's wagonbox, which came loose from the running gear and went over endwise, catching Mr. Parson's wife and one daughter underneath like a flock of quails, and breaking and spilling bottles of painkiller and other medicines in the young lady's face and eyes, but doing no harm further than to make her eyes smart and the skin of her face peel off.

After recapturing our oxen and gathering up the wreckage, which, fortunately, was not great, considering that we were going through scattered timber, we moved on to the "great Mississippi." The next day we crossed the river at Davenport into Iowa, and lay by to repair damages and buy more cattle. Here two young men named Fayette Tech and Washington Martin joined our train. Nothing more of interest occurred until we reached Cainsville (Council Bluffs), where a young man, engaged to cross the plains to drive stock, killed his employer for his money, which was found in his boots the same night when he was captured. The money was in bank bills, and had a private mark that was recognized by the dead man's partner. The emigrants promptly tried the murderer and hung him on the nearest tree, putting him on a mule, fastening a rope round his neck and a limb of the tree, and then driving the mule from under him.

At the Missouri river the facilities for crossing were so inadequate to the needs of the emigrants that we were compelled to wait three days to cross. We finally got over, just at night, and drove a mile or so to camp. We had hardly camped and got supper when word came from the guard that part of the cattle were gone. Then came our first trouble with the Indians. Several of us young men seized our guns and started in pursuit. We soon struck the trail of the cattle and found that they were being driven away by Indians who had stolen them. Our little company, all young and fleet on foot, soon overhauled the redskins, who, seeing they were being pursued, left the cattle and fled. It being dark and the country strange, we thought it best to return with the cattle and let the Indians go. It was soon evident that we ought to organize and elect a captain for our company, which we did, and George Belshaw was chosen captain. Several days now passed before anything of note occurred, and then, one night, we camped near the Platte river, and formed a corral of our wagons, and got our cattle inside, when it grew suddenly dark, and a terrific rain and wind storm struck us, causing a regular stampede of the cattle, which ran wildly over men, wagons and everything else to escape the storm. The next morning search was made for the stock and all was recovered.

When we reached Fort Laramie we found there had been a disturbance a day or two previous, by drunken Indians and some white men. The Indians had fired a shot at the ferryman, which did no harm, but caused a big scare among the emigrants. The commander of the fort told the emigrants they would have to look out for themselves, as he had only fifteen men under him. So the emigrants, forty-five men in all, formed themselves into a company, and all were placed on guard one night; but everything quieted down the next day, and we moved on, and, on the 22d of September, we reached Oregon City, without any deaths in our train. There our company disbanded, some going up the Willamette valley and the rest, among them being my two brothers and myself, coming to Puget Sound, where we worked during the winter of 1853-54, paying $9 per week for our board. Wheat was then worth $3.50 per bushel, oats $2, potatoes $2, wild oat hay $60 per ton and barley $100; good cows $125 each, and American horses — well, there were none to be had.

During the month of February, 1854, Nathaniel Orr of Steilacoom, Robert Thompson, now of Tacoma; F.A. McCarthy, long since dead, and the writer took a trip from Steilacoom by way of what is now Edison, and past Nicholas Delin's sawmill, where Paulson's mill in Tacoma now stands. Thence we went up the Puyallup river by an Indian trail to Stuck river, and stayed over night with a discharged Hudson's Bay man, who had an Indian woman for a wife. We had bear meat for breakfast which the longer we chewed the larger it got. Leaving our host (with his bear meat) we went by trail up to where Van Ogle's hop ranch now is, and there Indian Tuapite (pronounced Too-a-pi-tee) invited us to dine with him, having a fine lot of potatoes roasted. We gladly accepted the invitation, and soon after resumed our journey, passing on our way what has since become known as Lime Kiln, near Alderton, and going on to what is now Orting. Thence we went, by Indian trail, to the upper end of Elk plain, where we were surrounded by a band of wild cattle, which one of our number put to flight by firing off his pistol. It was then nearly sundown, and no house near, and one man was so tired that he lay down on the prairie. He would probably have perished, too, in the cold, frosty air, if it had not been for the efforts of the others, who took him by the arms and forced him along to the upper end of Spanaway lake, where there lived a Mr. Gregg with a native woman for a wife. Mr. Gregg was not at home, and the Indian woman would not get us any supper until one of our party began to search for something to cook. Then she concluded to accommodate us, but our tired man had gone to sleep long before supper was ready. We slept in some straw in an outhouse, and next morning went to an Englishman named Dean and got some raw beef which we roasted for our breakfast and ate without salt or pepper. Then we returned to Steilacoom, all pretty well tired out.

On the 15th of the following April my brother and myself located claims near where Sumner now is. We had no roads; no means of getting our provisions, except by packing them on our backs or boating from Steilacoom to the mouth of the Puyallup, then up the river with three drifts to pass, at each of which we had to unload our canoes and haul them on the banks to the upper side of the drift on skids, something like what loggers use, then reload, and so on up the river to our destination, making a very hard day's work of it.

Some time in May the assessor of King county came around to see how much we were worth. He was also deputy supervisor of roads. In my absence he left a written notice for me to appear at 7 o'clock p.m. of a certain date at Porter's prairie, fifteen miles from my place and in an opposite direction from our outlet or place of trade. The result was we did not go, and some twenty or more of us were sued. We were summoned to appear before Squire Lewis on the lower White river. Mine was made a test case, as I claimed that I had not been legally warned, since 7 o'clock p.m. was an unusual hour to work the road. Therefore I applied for a non-suit, which was refused. Then I demanded a change of venue to Steilacoom, which was granted, forty days being the time allowed before the trial.

Meanwhile the legislature convened at Olympia, and the settlers on the northside of the Puyallup river, who were then in King county, petitioned to be stricken off from King and attached to Pierce. The writer took an active part in circulating said petition.

Just before the county line was changed, on the 7th of January, 1855, the writer was married to Ruth J. Kincaid, eldest daughter of William M. Kincaid, who owned the claim where the town of Sumner now stands. A justice of the peace came from Steilacoom to the house of R.S. More to perform the ceremony. The couple and their friends hired two Indians and their canoe to cross them over the river from King county into Pierce, the officer not being authorized to perform such ceremony in another county. This was the first wedding in the far-famed Lap valley of the Puyallup.

About the last of January, 1855, the legislature passed the bill changing the county line, making the fifth standard parallel the boundary between King and Pierce, thus ending the suit of King county against those who were set off. There are but few of those first settlers still living in that section, or even in this county. It may not be out of place, perhaps, to name those yet remaining. They are: Abraham Woolery, John Carson, Willis Boatman, R.S. Moore, the Kincaids (John F., William C., James F. and Joseph C., and Mrs. L.F. Thompson and Mrs. E.C. Meade) with their families, and myself.

To show the croakers and soreheads of the present day that they don't know anything about hard times or the privations of a new country, the writer will give a little experience in first settling the Puyallup valley. In the year 1855 he raised his first crop of wheat, tramped it out with his oxen, and cleaned it by making a wind with a sheet, two men swinging the sheet while another poured the wheat down slowly, the wind separating it from the chaff. The next trouble was to get the grain to mill. There was no ferry or bridge across the Puyallup river. The wheat was loaded on the only wagon in the neighborhood and hauled as far as John Carson's claim, where we were in the habit of crossing in a canoe, then ferried over the river in the canoe and carried up the bank. Next, the wagon was taken to pieces, loaded on the canoe and likewise ferried over. Then the wagon was put together again and the wheat reloaded. But it was still necessary, in order to get to mill, to drive over a new road which had been just cut out, and over which no wagon had ever been. When night came on we camped, let the oxen graze around while we got supper, then chained them to a tree and went to bed under the wagon-box. The next day we drove to the mill near Steilacoom, owned by T.M. Chambers. After the wheat was ground, we returned as we had come. When we bought flour, we had to pay $20 a barrel for poor, lumpy stuff that had come round the Horn. Salmon and potatoes were the staff of life, then.

In September of the same year, 1855, signs of an Indian outbreak disturbed the peace of our happy little neighborhood. About the 1st of October the Indians became very insolent and were decorating themselves with war-paint. Near this time a party of Indians came, whooping and making signs of war, to the house of William M. Kincaid, on Stuck river. Mr. Kincaid, his son John, a boy of about 17 years, his daughter Susan, about 15, and a little son 5 years old, escaped over a small alder log which lay across the river near his house, the boy taking the gun, and the girl carrying the little boy and fairly running across the river on that small log, while the old gentleman, not being good at walking so small a log even in the daytime, had to coon it across. They came running pell-mell to my house, saying the Indians were after them. P. Keach and Miss Martin, from Steilacoom, were at my house on a visit, and we had gone to bed, but having forgotten to load our guns, we were just getting up again to load them when in came the parties mentioned. The bursting in of my door by the Kincaids so excited me that I got my boots on wrong, and in loading my double-barreled rifle I forgot to put any powder in one barrel. By this time all had fled to a more secure hiding place in the woods. Mr. Keach and I came back shortly and got some blankets to keep the women warm, as the night was very chilly. The Indians did not come any farther than the river and did no damage at that time, even to the Kincaid house.

Not long after this two Indians came to my house. One of them had left a gun with me to mend, as I tinkered up guns for them some in those days. I had not touched his gun, thinking it not best under the circumstances, and, besides, I was busy with my harvest. He began to call me names and abused me for neglecting his gun. I told him to "shut up" and to go out of my house. He said he would not do it; that this was his "illehe," meaning his land. Being young and of Scotch-Irish descent, I was somewhat hasty tempered, and I at once seized a heavy stool-bottom chair with the intention of making the fellow go out of the house. He then drew a large two-edged knife of Indian make and made toward me. I was quite active in those days, and I instantly sprang and caught my double-barreled gun, which was loaded at the time, and had raised both hammers to shoot, when my wife put her hand on me and begged me not to do it. The Indian was running by this time. Had it not been for my wife's coolness I would have made a "good Indian" of him very soon. The neighbors then began to gather at a strong log house at night for protection. A few days later Isaac Lemon and A.S. Perham had some Indians digging potatoes. The Indians acted very suspiciously all day, and frequently strange Indians came and talked with them. They received their pay—some sugar and flour, the customary pay of those days—and took the articles to camp, made fires, and prepared their supper as usual; but when Messrs. Lemon and Perham, after having their own supper, went to the Indians' camp, they discovered that, although all was ready there for supper, not an Indian could be seen. The circumstance so aroused the suspicions of Lemon and Perham that they returned to their house, got their guns and hid in a large, hollow stump near by, to watch and see what was up. Very soon they saw an Indian slipping along half bent. They hailed him and he started to run. Mr. Perham, being very fleet of foot, soon overhauled him. The Indian had a loaded gun, which he said was not loaded, powder which he denied having, and a large knife. He made another attempt to run, when Mr. Perham struck him with his gun and "downed" him. This, no doubt, disconcerted the Indians in their plans, and thus delayed the outbreak for a while. Father Kincaid, learning of this affair, took his family to Steilacoom for safety, and two weeks or so later my wife and several others also went to Steilacoom.

About this time a party of rangers was organized, consisting of pioneers of Pierce and Thurston counties, among whom were McCallister of Nisqually bottom and Connell of Connell's prairie, near the present town of Buckley. Mr. Connell had an Indian woman for a wife, so it was thought the Indians would not kill him, and Mr. McCallister, who had also been on good terms with them, thought they would not harm him. There was a large camp of Indians on Connell's prairie, and the rangers went to see what they were up to. The company halted before they were within gunshot, and the two men named above started on to have a talk with the Indians, but as soon as they were near enough the Indians shot them down. The writer had some Indians working for him at the time, digging potatoes, and heard the shots that killed McCallister and Connell. He supposed, however, that the firing was done by hunters, though the Indians were shooting white men.

About this time the Indians attacked the settlers on White river and killed several, among them William Brannan, wife and child, a Mr. King and wife and a Mr. Jones and family. Mr. and Mrs. Brannon were horribly mutilated, and both she and the child were thrown into a well. Indian Nelson, who had been at Mr. King's house a good deal, and had become attached to the children, saved them by stealing them away, putting them in a canoe and sending them down the river by another Indian.

Lieutenant Slaughter and company and Captain Hays and company started across the Cascades by the Natches pass to quell disturbances on the other side, but the Indians were wide awake and were lying in wait for them in a narrow canyon, and no doubt both commands would have been massacred if orders to return had not been sent just before reaching the trap set for them. On their return they were attacked by the Indians of White river, near Porter's prairie, and they fought across the river all day, killing several Indians and one squaw who had come to rescue her brave. Soon after the battle across the White river the troops went to Connell's prairie and camped. The express rider, William Tidd, and several others, started for Fort Steilacoom. They had gone perhaps one mile when they were fired upon by Indians in a swamp near Connell's prairie, wounding William Tidd in the back of the head with buckshot and killed A.B. Moses and Joseph Miles. A.B. Robison, Dr. Burns and a Mr. Bright made their escape, leaving their horses and taking to the woods.

Learning that there was a large number of Indians camped on South prairie, the officers decided to attack them. The men were divided into two companies, one going one trail with Isaac Lemon as guide, and the other having A.I. Perham for guide taking another. It was intended that both companies should reach South prairie at the same time so as to cut off the Indians' retreat, but for some reason the company with Perham reached there considerably in advance of the other. While crossing a creek on a log, John Edgar and Perham were shot through the body by an Indian, who gave the alarm to the others and they all made their escape before the second company arrived. Edgar died after a few days, but Perham lingered along, and much to the surprise of every one, finally recovered.

The volunteers camped where Elhi now is. The guard had been on duty but a few minutes when he saw something slipping along close to the ground. He could not tell what it was, but concluded to fire at it. The object proved to be the hated Indian Tenascut, one of the sub-chiefs. He was wounded by the shot and was brought into camp. He began to order his men to surround the soldiers. One of them who understood what Tenascut said, shot him. In the spring of 1856, Mr. John Bradley and wife were plowing in a field not far from old Fort Montgomery, and were attacked by Indians with tomahawks and knives. Mrs. Bradley ran for the brush, while he ran to his house, calling on a Mr. Brown to bring his gun, but he did not hear him. Bradley reached his gate, and, as he went through, an Indian struck at him with a tomahawk, but hit the gate instead. They then rode away.

Some people of today may want to know why Mrs. Bradley was helping her husband to plow. This magnanimous government of ours, which held out inducements for people to settle up this wilderness and promised its citizens protection against the cruel savages, had pressed Mr. Bradley's oxen into government service, leaving him a pair of unbroken cattle to do his work with, which required two persons to plow. And to this day, for the most part, the government has failed to pay the pioneers for damage sustained during that war, and for services and property furnished to carry on the war. Oh! for shame, on our men in public places to neglect their duty to their fellow citizens on the frontier who have toiled hard and exposed their lives and the lives of their families to make the grand state of Washington.

Some time in the spring 1856 the good (?) Indians, as one of the men interviewed by the *Ledger* calls them, attacked and killed a Mr. White, father of Mrs. George Byrd of Fern Hill on North Craft, while returning from church on Chamber's prairie in Thurston county. Their families were in a wagon, and the horse took fright and ran, thereby saving the lives of the women and children.

Just about the same time the rangers were surrounded in a small log house on the Charles Bitting (now Van Ogle) claim. And all this time I was on my claim, near where Sumner now is, not realizing what danger I was in, though I felt, of course, not a little anxiety, and kept my gun and axe lying on the table at the head of my bed ready for use in case of need. One night I was awakened very suddenly by a tree falling on my fence, and, the first thing I knew I was out of bed on my feet prepared to fight. I picked up my gun, slipped to the door and listened through the key hole for any Indians who might be prowling around. All was quiet except for the heavy breathing of the two boys that were staying with me at the time. The next day, I think it was, a friendly Indian came and told me what the hostile Indians had done on White river, on the Brannan claim, and urged me to leave, saying the bad Indians would kill me if I remained. So the two boys and myself took our guns and blankets and started for Steilacoom. After going about a mile we met a Hudson's Bay man, who told us he thought it was nonsense to leave; that there was no danger. The Indian was still with us. He saw that we hesitated about going, and took hold of us and said we must go to Steilacoom, or the bad Indians would come and kill us. So we went on. When we got to the edge of the prairie we met a party coming out after us. Slaughter and company had returned to Fort Steilacoom, and Captain Hays' company was at John Montgomery's place at the edge of the prairie. Thus the Puyallup and White river settlements were left in the hands of the Indians, who burned and destroyed nearly every house and barn, and killed or drove off our stock. Two houses which had potatoes under them were spared, the Indians doubtless thinking they would get the potatoes for food.

Perhaps the writer ought to state here that he has recently been informed that, when the Indian war commenced, there were but 400 rounds of ammunition at Fort Steilacoom for the defense of this whole frontier country.

About this time Captain Wallace of Steilacoom organized a company, with S. McCaw and R.S. More as lieutenants. The legislature convening soon after, the company was put in the hands of R.S. More and quartered on the claim of Abial Morrison. There was also another company organized, mostly of Puyallup settlers, with John Carson as captain and William Boatman and O.P. Meeker as lieutenants. The quartermaster at Fort Steilacoom furnished us with ammunition. We scoured the Puyallup valley from one end to the other, destroying a quantity of dried salmon and a number of Indian canoes.

One very laughable incident occurred as we were charging on an Indian camp. One of the company fell into a hole of water up to his waist, and his gun went under water, but he jumped up, and, addressing his gun, in his characteristic way, said: "Well, old teakettle, I guess you're wet now." Of course everybody laughed, although we were expecting the Indians to fire on us at any moment, but he seemed as unconcerned as though we were chasing wild cattle. In our scout we captured one horse, which we turned over to the quartermaster.

The government was now gathering the friendly Indians on two islands in the Sound, near Steilacoom and Olympia, respectively, and was furnishing them with provisions. Thus some of the hostiles, who were getting starved out, were induced to come in, and still others were captured by the soldiers and volunteers and brought into Steilacoom and Olympia. One Indian was shot just as he was landed from a canoe in broad daylight by a brother of a man whom the Indian had killed. The Indian was told why he was shot. Another, the slayer of McCallister, was stabbed to death, though under guard (perhaps his guard was asleep) in Governor Stevens' office, between midnight and daylight. The Indian was supposed to have been killed by a son or son-in-law of his own victim. This was in 1856, just before the Indian war closed.

With regard to the head chief Leschi, despite the statements recently appearing in the *Ledger*, the writer believes, on the strength of other testimoney, that the Indian was really captured by the volunteers, and brought into Steilacoom. As to the fact of his subsequent trial for the killing of A.B. Moses, his conviction and sentence to be hung, all are agreed, though some at the time disapproved of the sentence, thinking that killing in war times is not murder. A young lawyer living in Steilacoom took it upon himself to defeat the hanging of Leschi, and got out a warrant for the sheriff and had him arrested on the plea that he had sold whisky to the Indians, and so the day for the execution went by. The governor then appointed another day and William Mitchell of Olympia was deputized to do the hanging instead of the Pierce county sheriff. Mr. Mitchell, thinking it best to prevent possible trouble, for there had been some talk of taking the prisoner away from him, brought a guard with him from Olympia, and got some more help at Steilacoom, and went to Fort Steilacoom. He took Leschi out about half a mile from the fort on the 19th day of February, 1858, and hung the noted Indian chief until he was dead, *dead*, DEAD!

After leaving my claim in October, 1855, I remained a while in Steilacoom, doing such odd jobs as I could find. Times being dull, with but little work to be had where it was safe from Indians, about the 20th of January, 1856, I went, with my wife, to Oregon, near Eugene City, and there got plenty of rails to split by taking cows for pay. I split 20,000 rails while there, traded my cows for oxen and bought two ponies. In the fall of 1857 my wife and I mounted our ponies, she carrying her babe of about eighteen months, and we drove our ten oxen to Steilacoom and sold them. It was a rough, hard trip for a woman. She was thrown from her horse three times on the way, either by getting into yellow-jackets' nests, or having her saddle turn, but, fortunately, neither she nor the baby were hurt during the trip.

On returning to Steilacoom I was hired to butcher beef by Messrs. O. and E. Meeker, who had a government contract to furnish beef for the soldiers at Fort Steilacoom. During that time the Frasier river gold excitement broke out, and, beef becoming scarce on the Sound, I went to Oregon and drove back a band of cattle for the Meekers. Afterwards, with John F. Kincaid, I bought a 10-horse power threshing maching, the first of note ever brought into Pierce county. We threshed 33,000 bushels of grain that season. The next year (1859) I moved my family to my claim on Stuck river, about half of which I still own.

In the following August an incident occurred, which, though amusing enough now, was deadly serious for the writer just then. Some Indians turned their horses into my pasture without permission, and when told to take them out, refused. I seized one of them by his long hair and jerked him down and applied my stogy boots to him pretty thoroughly. Soon, nearly the whole camp came running toward me with knives and hatchets, crying "Mewaloose, mewaloose" (meaning "kill"). I got hold of a piece of board about four feet long and used it vigorously for a few minutes, hammering five of them, they afterwards told me, and effectually scaring them out. My hired man and two boys were in the cowyard near by when this occurred, but took no part in the affray. The Indians soon got their horses out of my pasture. The next morning I wrote to the Indian agent on the reservation, telling him what I had done. He replied that if the Indians trespassed on my rights to "whip h____ out of them," which I thought I had already done. This ended my trouble with the Indians. Since then I have hired them a great deal for clearing land and picking hops, and they have given me good satisfaction.

In conclusion, may the writer express the hope that through the series of articles now appearing in the *Ledger*, the ties binding the old settlers shall be quickened and strengthened, and that a grateful posterity will ever cherish with kindly feelings the memory of those who received so many hard knocks and suffered so many privations to secure for them a heritage in this new but highly favored land. My present residence is near the shops at Edison, a suburb of Tacoma.

Mary Perry Frost

An 1854 emigrant, her father and uncle
were killed by the Indians on the overland journey.
During the Indian Wars she and her brother
tended sheep for the Hudson Bay Company and
were considered by the Indians to be
"King George Tilecums" or friends.

Hillhurst, Washington — July 1, 1892

How many times I have longed to put my story of the hardships, privations and troubles of pioneer life in print, but I have never before attempted it. I came here when I was a little girl but 9 years old. In the month of April, 1854, my father, Walter G. Perry, started with his family, consisting of wife and four children, from Garden Grove, Apanoose county, Ia., where he had a good farm and was considered a well-to-do farmer in those days for this far western country, but he was destined never to reach here.

After having traveled three or four months, we came to where the Indians had burned the grass along the emigrant road in order to starve the stock belonging to the emigrants. We were with a large train, under the command of Captain J.P. Coates, and when confronted by this situation, he thought it best to divide up into smaller squads, which course was adopted. The first train to start was called the Ward train, as it was composed of several families of Wards, all related, and it included all of the relatives, except one woman, who was with the middle train.

The captain gave orders for none to go beyond the burned district, or a place known in the guide books as Jeffries' cutoff. I will state here that we had guide books that had been published by some pathfinder, or trapper, describing every camping place, the distance between the watering places and all cutoffs and the names of creeks, etc. Each train had some of these books.

In cutting up the large train we brought up the rear with four wagons, consisting of four men with families and two young men aged 19 and 23 years. The men were Mr. Kirkland and family, including one young man, William Kirkland, and his son-in-law, Mr. Cox and family; my uncle, George Lake, wife and two sons, young men; my father, Walter G. Perry, and his family; C.C. Thompson, a young man, then about 20 years of age, and my father's teamster, Empson Cantrell, a young man aged 19 years or thereabouts.

Our last camping place where we were all to meet alive was at a creek, designated in the guide book as White Horse creek. I think it is in Idaho, and think it was then about the last of August, perhaps later. Starting on our journey the next morning we had traveled perhaps an hour when we discerned in the distance, to our left, Indians coming up out of a canyon in great numbers, the foremost ones being on foot, and who looked to be unarmed. They were followed by mounted Indians, armed with guns in sheaths made of deer skins. At this time a young lady, daughter of Mr. Kirkland of our party, was riding on horseback, ahead and apart from the rest of the train. Her horse took fright at the sight of the Indians, and, becoming, unmanageable, she dismounted and tried to hold the horse by the reins, but it jerked away from her. The Indians then surrounded and captured the horse, but Miss Kirkland made her way on foot to the train unharmed. After capturing the horse the Indians advanced on the train, and coming up squarely in front of the ox teams, held out their arms and stopped them, but appeared friendly and shook hands with the members of our party and asked for whisky, but were told that we had none. Thereupon they began to talk of trading with some of our party, and while my father was talking of trading a pistol for a pony they opened fire on us, shooting my father, my uncle, Mr. Lake and the young man Empson Cantrell, my father's teamster. Mr. Kirkland then called to his son to get their guns, which he did, and they then fired on the Indians, who retreated until out of range of the guns, but remained near, trying to stampede our stock, for several hours. It was finally thought that they wanted our horses, and it

-202-

was arranged to surrender them to the Indians if they would let us pass without further trouble, and when this was proposed by Mr. Kirkland the Indians readily assented. The horses were then turned loose, and the Indians were compelled to follow us several miles before they could catch them all.

When the Indians fired on us Mr. Lake fell dead, with the words, "I am a dead man." Empson Cantrell was shot through the abdomen, and after being shot asked my mother for my father's gun, which he snapped several times at the Indians, but it would not go off. He lingered in great agony until the following morning, when he died. My father was shot through the right lung, and lived until the evening of the fourth day, when death relieved him of his terrible sufferings.

The wagon that carried the shovels and other implements, known as the "tool wagon," was with the big train, and we had nothing with which to dig graves for the dead, nor did we care to stop to bury them right away, as we were afraid of another attack from the Indians. Hence we carried the bodies until the third day after the attack, when there was such a stench that we had to keep fires around the "dead wagon" to keep the wolves off. As the bodies had to be disposed of in some way, wooden spades were improvised with which a hole was dug and both bodies (Mr. Lake and Empson Cantrell) were buried in it. We overtook the big train on the afternoon of the following day and my father died about 10 o'clock that night, after having suffered untold agonies for four days, and begging many times to be killed and put out of misery. We dare not stop, and the jolting of the wagon was almost unendurable to him. He was buried on the following morning near the emigrant road.

On the day following our attack by the Indians, two Spaniards passed us, and in conversation stated that our men had shot two of the Indians, who were sure to die. I might say here that we never entertained a doubt but that the two men who led the Indians in the attack, were white men, as their manner, dress and talk indicated it. They wore good clothes, and had their hands and feet painted, which the Indians did not.

In about two or three hours after burying father we came upon the dreadful sight of the massacred Ward train, of which I spoke heretofore, they having gone ahead of the big train. Word of this massacre had been brought to the big train, in the following manner: The night previous to the terrible affair there were some horses stolen from the big train, and Alex Yantis, well known in Thurston county, this state, who died a few years ago on his farm near Tenino, was detailed to go with six others in search of them, and Edward Neely, now living on White river in King county, was one of the party. While tracking the horses they came upon the bodies of the men of the Ward train, who had just been slain by Indians, and could then hear the cries of the women and children. The Indians had stealthily crept up to within easy gunshot of the party while they were eating dinner, and had shot the men, after which they took the women and children to the brush to burn them, and it was at this crisis that the Yantis party came upon them.

As soon as they realized the state of affairs Yantis and his men charged upon the Indians and drove them from the wagons and undertook to rescue the women and children, but as soon as the savages discovered Yantis' meagre force they closed in upon them and they were obliged to retreat, after losing one of their number by a shot from the rifle of an Indian, with the despairing cries of the poor suffering captives ringing in their ears, imploring them not to leave them. But their numbers were so few they could do nothing but resort to flight to save their own lives. However, Captain Yantis was much dissatisfied with the cowardly conduct exhibited by two of his men, and as they approached the spot where the Indians had attacked the Ward train he was upbraiding them for not giving their support, when a nine-year-old boy, Neuty Ward, who had been left for dead by the Indians, heard him and recognized his voice, and asked if that was Mr. Yantis, whereupon they went to the little fellow, and, taking him in their arms, carried him away with them, this task falling wholly on Mr. Yantis and Edward Neely, as the other men wanted to leave him, stating that he could not live and that they would all be killed if they stopped to attend to the boy, and even undertook to leave them, whereupon Captain Yantis threatened to shoot them if they attempted desertion, which had the effect of keeping them together, but they would not help to get him away. However, by perserverance in this determination, they arrived safely at the large train with the boy, who recovered, and I have been lately informed that he is now living in Oregon.

Another of the Ward boys, William, a lad 14 or 15 years old, was shot with an arrow through his right lung, the point of the arrow going so nearly through as to cause the skin to protrude on the back, but he hid himself away in the brush until the savages had left, when he made his escape, walking to Fort Boise in this condition, which journey took him five days (during which time he lived on wild herbs and berries gathered on his route), where the arrow was abstracted by cutting to it from the back and pulling it through. He also recovered. These two make the only survivors of the entire Ward train.

I will here say that Empson Cantrell, the young man who was shot in our train, was a very nice young man, and had parted with a sister and two brothers at the California road, who were bound for California, and I do not know that they have ever learned the sad fate that befell him.

From appearances the Indians had attacked the Ward train on the same day that we were attacked, as the stench from the dead and mutilated bodies was terrible, but we stopped long enough to dig trenches and rude graves for the burial of our murdered companions. The women and children presented a most terrible spectacle, having been burned by the savages. After having performed this sad and sickening task we pursued our journey to its end without further incident of note, many going to what is now the state of Oregon, while we, with several other families, including Mr. John Meeker, the father of John and Ezra Meeker of Puyallup, and the Whitesels of Orting, made our way on to Puget Sound by the way of the Natchez pass over the Cascade mountains, which was a perilous trip. Very few undertook this route with wagons. In coming down the mountain sides the wagons had to be "snubbed down," as it was called, with ropes, which was done by making strong ropes fast to each wagon and taking half-hitches to trees, by which means they could be kept under control while going over the steepest places. This road was little better than nature left it, and was simply a route picked through the mountain wilds. Our course was down to the Natchez river, which we had to cross sixty-two times in one day. Here I had another bit of perilous experience. I, in company with my brother next older than myself, lingered behind the wagons to gather gum from the pine trees. After having crossed the river twice in succession and thinking we would not cross again soon we allowed the wagons to get some distance ahead of us, and when we started to catch them, to our surprise the river was between us and the wagons. As we could see no other way we set out to wade through the stream, which, although not very deep, had a strong current. My clothing soon became so heavy that I was unable to keep up, the strong force of the current throwing me down and carrying me from one boulder to another, to which I would cling as long as I could, but my strength was fast failing and I would have succumbed very soon had it not been that we were missed and my cousin, Arnold Lake, was sent to find us, which he did, in the condition described, from which he rescued me not five minutes too soon. My brother was slowly getting across, as he was older and somewhat stronger, as well as being clothed in a manner which did not incumber him so much in the water.

Pursuing our journey we came to what was then known as Bushelier lake (now Spanaway) and moved into the Bushelier cabin, which was built of logs and had no floor, door nor windows, and only half roofed over. This was sometime in October, 1854, our first rest after six long months of weary travel, beset with the hardships, grief and suffering of which I have stated, besides many minor trials incident to overland travel, not mentioned.

In this place, which we will call a house, we passed three weeks, during which time it rained almost all of the time, building fire and doing our cooking in the uncovered part of the house and sleeping and eating in the covered portion.

From here we moved to the donation claim, which my mother took at the time, on the south side of American lake, now owned by John and I.G. Murray, where we took up our permanent residence in quite a comfortable log cabin. Soon after this my oldest brother and myself were compelled to herd sheep for the Hudson Bay company to obtain provisions to sustain life, these being principally salt salmon and potatoes, with an occasional pan of flour. During the period of the Indian war here we were thus engaged, and our shield from harm was the statement that we were "King George tilicums" when questioned by the Indians, to which they would reply and pat us on the heads, saying that we were "Hias closh tenas telicums," which means very good little friends.

The agents of the Hudson Bay company were very kind in some instances, but if we could believe what the Indians told us, they were to a great extent the cause of the war. They said "King George tilacums" told them that the "Bostons," meaning Americans, were very bad people, and that if allowed to come here would take their country from them and take them away in a large black ship to an island from which they could never escape.

The history of the Hudson Bay company is that of apparent kindness to the natives, which, of course, was policy, their mission being trade and traffic with them. It is also very feasible that it was to their advantage to delay settlement in this section of the country as long as possible.

From being so much in the company of the Indians, seeing dozens every day, and herding sheep with or near them, my brother and I soon learned to talk the Chinook jargon (the common language between the whites and Indians) as well as our own language. I told them my father was a King George man, and the bad Indians had killed him while trying to get here, and how we had bought our liberty with our horses. It was a great wonderment to them how we got here, and not until the close of the war did I tell them that mother was a "Boston." She was always very kind to them, notwithstanding her loss at their hands, always gave them plenty of milk and traded butter for clams and oysters.

Throughout all our hardships we had plenty of milk, as we brought our cows through with us, but how we longed for bread!

During the most exciting times we would fly to a fort for refuge. We spent about two months in Fort Nisqually. On other occasions we went to Fort Steilacoom. It is a well-known fact by the old settlers that those Hudson Bay employees who had Indian women for wives lived on their farms unmolested so long as they furnished the Indians supplies and ammunition and kept them informed as to the whereabouts of the soldiers and volunteers.

Dr. Spinning and myself were talking only last week of the condition of affairs at that time, when Governor Isaac I. Stevens found it necessary to declare martial law throughout the territory, and a great number of this class of suspects were arrested and imprisoned at Olympia until the close of the war, which soon came after this step was taken.

After the close of the war we passed through nothing more eventful than the hardships incident to pioneer life in such a far away and sparsely settled country. I married Andrew J. Frost May 8, 1859, who came to the country ten years prior to my arrival. We have lived in this territory and state all of the time since, except four years, during which we resided in Mendocino county, California. We have now living six children, three boys and as many girls. We have buried two girls, one at 2 years of age, the other at 14. Our oldest daughter is the wife of Forest J. Hunt, who keeps a general store at this place. The oldest son and next younger living daughter are married and living in Cowlitz county, Washington.

I have had my share of pioneer life, and, although I shudder to think of the experiences and many perils we passed through, I have no desire to change my residence in the state of Washington to that of any other place on this earth, but I do have a yearning desire to go to the World's Columbian Exposition next year.

Alexander Vincent

Mr. Vincent arrived on Puget Sound during the Indian Wars of 1855-56. In Port Townsend he signed on with the "Northern Battalion" and encountered a few humorous incidents out in the field during his enlistment.

Port Townsend, Washington — July 15, 1892

I left the state of Missouri, destined for California. I arrived in San Francisco the 24th day of June. I went from there to Sacramento, where I worked in haying and harvesting. I returned again to San Francisco, where I took boarding and lodging in a private boarding house. The second night I slept in the house, the madame that kept the house robbed me of all I had, cleaning me out as clean as a whistle. I had her arrested, but could not convict her, there being only strong circumstantial evidence. She was discharged, and so was I.

It was now my business to look about for employment, and I begun to follow that occupation. As I was strolling about the docks I noticed an advertisement at the shipping office on the bulletin board which read: "A cook and steward wanted for the L.P. Forster, bound for Puget Sound." I shipped as cook and steward, and we were off for the Sound.

We had a very pleasant Voyage, excepting one incident which occurred between the cook and first mate. The mate wished me to make a duff. I told him I had no bag to make it in, whereupon he informed me that he would make me one, which he did. I went to work at my pudding. I put in a layer of flour, then a layer of dried apples, following with a layer of each alternately until the bag was filled. I tied the bag and put it in a kettle and cooked it for three hours. Thinking my duff was now about cooked, I took it out and emptied it into a pan, the mate standing near watching the operation. Out came dry flour and dried apples, just as I had put them in, and both the mate and I came to the conclusion that the duff was hardly eatable.

We arrived in Port Townsend about the 1st of December, and I begged to be released from the schooner and my request was granted. Upon going on shore I found the people excited concerning "war and rumors of war." They were expecting an attack from the Northern Indians every night, and forts and block houses were being built. I did not scare worth a cent.

I soon learned that there was man living here by the name of L.B. Hastings, with whom I had had a slight acquaintance in Illinois. I renewed my acquaintance with him and made his home my home. I was employed by him, and a friend of his, a Mr. Pettygrove, as their farmer, which occupation suited me far better than the one I had left when I left the schooner *L.P. Foster.*

I was soon induced to enlist with the Port Townsend guards, Captain Plummer being our commander-in-chief. I enlisted with the understanding that I was going to be a minute man, but as soon as I was placed upon the muster roll Captain Plummer, being a strict disciplinarian, ordered me in the quarters. He sent the corporal guard and marched me down to the blockhouse and ordered me on duty. The first gun that was fired was a good whisky cock-tail.

The next morning we reported for duty and were detailed to go to Point Wilson to build a block house as a lookout station for the purpose of keeping a close watch of northern war canoes. This block house never amounted to very much, as it was never finished. We remained in the block house at Port Townsend for about three months, until our enlistment expired. The native Indians in Port Townsend did not show any hostile disposition.

An Indian christened "Lord Jim" was a big Indian chief who ruled his tribe with a tyrannical hand. These Indians would now and then have a "black tamanous," and eat dogs alive. (This tamanous was a sort of religion to influence bad spirits on their enemies.) Lord Jim was the proprieter of several wives, and one day he had a sort of falling out with one of them. He got in a small canoe and started across the bay. The wind was blowing a gale. Lord Jim was never seen again. After his death his brother the "Duke of York," became the prominent chief of the Clallam tribe. He had two wives, "Jenny Lind" and the "Queen." The Duke of York was a fine, noble Indian, with many good traits and kindly disposed toward the whites. He was a friend to the white people and was respected by all who knew him. His remains lie in the Masonic cemetery and a monument erected by his friends marks his resting place.

Colonel Eby of Whidbey Island, who had a company of men stationed at the mouth of the Snohomish river, which was known as Fort Eby, now disbanded his company and returned to Port Townsend. Another company was being organized under the commission of Major Van Bokklenn, for six months' service, and we all went in and joined the battallion. We rendezvoused at Fort Eby under the command of Major Van Bokklenn, Captain Smalley and Captain Peabody. The latter had some northern Indians in his company.

Some time about the middle of March the command was ordered to proceed up the river. Our conveyance was in canoes, Pat Canen, the Indian chief, superintending the expedition. Arriving at Canen's house, we stopped there and visited what is known as Pat Canen's prairie and made inquiries as to the whereabouts of hostile Indians.

We proceeded up the river to the foot of Snoqualmie falls, where we all went to work building a fort, which was used as a commissary department. After remaining here a short time we made several scouting expeditions, moving at all times very cautiously, fearing all the while that we might be surprised by some hostile Indians.

The command was finally ordered to Snoqualmie prairie. After remaining there in a camp a few days we became quite restless, anxious to encounter some hostile Indians. We took up our march for Muckleshoot prairie. We were about ninety strong of white men and friendly Indians, under the command of Major Van Bokklenn and Captain Smalley. We proceeded across the country, crossed Cedar creek and stopped at Salal prairie. The next morning we resumed our march, and the following night camped at a lake where the hostile Indians had camped. The next day's march brought us to Green river. The river was very high, and we had some difficulty in crossing. Our provisions had given out, and our chief occupation the next morning was that of scratching flour sacks in the attempt to obtain enough flour to prepare something to eat. We forded the river without any serious accident.

We began ascending a hill, and when about half-way up we came to a halt. A controversy ensued between Major Van Bokklen and Pat Canen, the Indian chief, as to who would go in advance to the fort. Pat Canen mounted a horse, and Major Van Bokklen protested, but the former took the lead, whereupon the controversy became so heated that the Indians began to show hostile motives. They pulled the covers from their guns, and the whites immediately sought the off side of a tree for safety, having orders to fire upon the Indians if they made any attempt to raise a gun. They finally succumbed, however, and we marched on to the prairie.

In sight of the fort was a soldier herding horses. He noticed the Indians approaching, and supposing they were hostile, he turned about and ran as fast as he could to the fort.

Here was a company of United States regulars camped. Having a howitzer they were about to fire upon us, when they saw us in advance carrying the stars and stripes.

Here we camped for the night. The next morning we took up our march for Connell's prairie to join Colonel Hays, who was in command at the fort which had been christened Fort Hays. On arriving we learned that Colonel Hays had been attacked by the Indians. A pioneer company which was working at the river was first attacked, two or three of the company being wounded slightly. The firing was heard at the fort and a detachment of men was sent immediately to their relief. The Indians were driven back and made good their escape. About 10 o'clock in the morning the Indians again made their appearance about the margin of the timber. They gave the war-whoop and begun shooting at the whites. We returned the fire as soon as we had an opportunity. They remained in their position and continued their firing until 3 or 4 o'clock in the afternoon, when they dispersed. The next morning about 150 of us were detailed to go in pursuit of the savages, Colonel Hays and Major Van Bokklenn in command. We scouted about all that day and camped at night in a deep gulch, having discovered no marks of the Indians. The next morning Major Sueland and myself were detailed to return to the fort, and we started on our way. Each of us being unacquainted with the grouse, and hearing their lonely hoot, supposed it was the Indians hidden and that they were giving their signal to their fellows. As a matter of course we were pretty badly scared, but we got safely through and discovered before our journey was ended that the grouse was not at all dangerous.

When the command were ready to return to the fort they divided into small squads and returned the best way they could. One of the squads came accidently upon a camp of Indians. They opened fire at once, killing a boy, a man and two women, one woman making her escape. The killed were scalped after the Indian fashion.

The northern battalion remained in quarters at Fort Hays about a month, when we made another scouting expedition on White river, capturing four or five Indian horses. We then returned to Fort Hays without hearing anything about the whereabouts of any hostile Indians.

The northern battalion now received orders from Governor Stevens to return to Snoqualmie prairie, which was the headquarters of the battalion. Here we went to work to build Fort Aulder, which was situated near Snoqualmie river. Captain Smalley and his company built Fort Smalley at the south end of the prairie, which was located about a mile from Fort Aulder. The forts now being completed we were ordered to make a reconnoissance up Cedar creek, going over into the Yakima country. Arriving at the summit of the Cascades we camped for a few days. Two men were sent on as spies into the Yakima country to discover, if possible, where the Indians were camped. Major Van Bokklenn, with a party of three or four men, made the ascent through the Snoqualmie pass, during which journey he and his party lived on the inner surface of spruce bark. After a fatiguing journey, meeting with many hardships and encountering many dangers, they joined Captain Smalley on the summit.

We soon discovered that we could have a fight with the Klickitats if we wished it, but our provisions being exhausted and other things being against us, we decided not to insist on it.

We again returned to Snoqualmie prairie and lived at ease in the forts. Major Van Bokklenn now made out a general report to Governor Stevens, and a Mr. Crosby and I were detailed to carry it to Olympia and hand it to the governor. We made the trip in three days, and while there we had the honor of being interviewed by Governor Stevens. He appointed two gentlemen as topographical engineers to accompany us back to Snoqualmie prairie to ascertain whether a practical road, on which a military force, with cannons, ammunitions and provisions could move, could be built into the Yakima country. Upon their return and the receipt of their report the idea was abandoned.

Our six month's enlistment was now nearly expired. We remained in the forts making frequent expeditions in different parts of the country to discover, if possible, the whereabouts of the Indians. We began to come to the conclusion that there were no hostile Indians in the country, and as some of us were getting anxious for a little excitement of some sort, I, with Robert Smallman and Charlie Wheeler, concluded to get up a scare.

Quite a number of the boys were camped down by a creek, and we thought they would be the ones to work on. Several of the men in the fort were in with our scheme and had loaded their guns with blank cartridges. I and the two men above hid ourselves in the tall ferns in different places. Wheeler gave the war whoop and we began firing, the blank cartridges in the fort keeping good time with us. Our brave officers who were camped near the creek, thought that the whole Indian population had suddenly broken loose, and they were almost scared out of their wits. The funny part of the play was to see them running for the fort. Notwithstanding the fact that we were busy watching the officers get into the fort, allow me to say that the picture that old fort presented was one of the prettiest I ever saw, and one that I shall never forget. The men firing from the loopholes volley after volley, in a continuous manner, the smoke rising in a cloud from their guns, each second being joined by another cloud, made a sort of panoramic view that is past description.

The firing was heard at Fort Aulder, and they thought we must be having a real engagement of some sort, and a force was dispatched to our relief, but after discovering the real cause they returned to the fort.

Our term of enlistment having expired we disbanded, returning to our respective homes. Major Van Bokklenn took the oxen and horses to Olympia and turned them over to the commissary department and returned to Port Townsend.

The scare of the war having subsided I knocked about on the Sound, sometimes in logging camps, sometimes in the mills, until finally I took up a claim at Point Ringo. One day a large canoe of Indians came down and assaulted me. I repelled them and drove them from the house with an ax. Darkness was coming on and I made myself scarce, not caring to face them alone and singlehanded. I concluded I would abandon my claim, which I did, and returned to Port Townsend.

About this time a serious incident occurred. Colonel Eby was murdered by the Northern Indians, and his head was taken north as a trophy. Great excitement prevailed. A dispatch, by canoe, was sent to Governor Stevens, and he immediately sent officials to the scene. Meantime there was a canoe arrived from Victoria, which contained some Northern Indians and two half-breed boys, whose names were McDonald. They came for the purpose of purchasing an outfit for the Frazier river gold diggings. Their canoe and its contents were seized and destroyed by the excited crowd. Captain Fey, the Indian agent, being on the ground, prevented the crowd from massacring them on the spot. They were locked up in the block house, and the next day a meeting was called, over which Judge Chineworth presided. Excitement ran high, and the one question that everyone wanted answered was, what was to be done with the Indians? The cooler headed ones of the crowd suggested that they be returned to Victoria unharmed, which was done, as nothing of certainty that they had had a hand in the murder of the colonel could be proven. The head of the colonel was returned after two or three years by Governor Douglas to Eby's friends.

In the spring of '58 the gold excitement on the Frazier river attracted the attention of everybody on Puget Sound and in California. I prepared myself and went to the scene of the excitement. A large crowd of us stopped on a bar and prospected. Quite a number of Indians came among us. They were very impudent, and told us if we did not get away from there they would make us go. Several of them were knocking carelessly about my camp fire while I was preparing my dinner. They were saucy and ugly, and one of them pushed me to one side and spit in my frying pan. I felt a great deal like making a good siwash out of him, for I did not like that kind of seasoning at all.

The Indians on Frazier river became very hostile toward the miners there, and killed several of them. Finally we thought things had gone far enough and concluded we would stand it no longer and we went at them in earnest and soon had them cooled off.

The river became quite high, and again I returned to Port Townsend. In the latter part of the summer I got another outfit, and together with a man by the name of Foster, Tom Nickson, an Indian man and woman, and myself, we started in a heavily loaded canoe, bound for Frazier river. We went as far as Orcas island the first day, and at night we put into a small cove. We made a fire, prepared our supper and arranged ourselves for a good night's rest. The Indians slept in the canoe, which was anchored out in a short distance. Five or six Kanakas came in with a canoe and anchored for the night also. Our fire was burning pretty briskly, and we did not apprehend any danger whatever.

About 12 o'clock at night two large northern canoes containing about forty Indians each, made an entrance into the cove. They attacked my canoe and killed the Indians, and also attacked the canoe of the Hanakis and killed some of them. Pretty lively firing occurred for a while. Nickson and myself made our escape, going toward the top of the hill as fast as we could. We hid ourselves in a thicket, awaiting the events of the early dawn. Soon there appeared two or three individuals which we supposed were some of the Indians. We felt our blood fairly boil, but being alone, we thought best to remain quiet. Just at this moment there was a volley of musketry down in the cove where we had camped the night before. I said to Nickson, "now is our time to 'c'attawa.'" So we ran like two scared deer and descended into a small ravine and hid ourselves in the hollow of some logs. We now realized that we were exiles on Orcas island, on which there was not an inhabitant. I became tired in my place of concealment and told Nickson I would take a stroll down to the cove. I started, making my way through brush and over logs. Finally I came to a clear spot, and, looking a little ahead of me, I saw an Indian with a face as black as tar and a gun in his hand. I turned and ran a short distance, tearing along at a terrific pace, and then stopped and looked back, but did not see the Indian. I wondered what kept him from firing at me. I saw no way of finding out, so proceeded on my venturous way to the cove. Soon I encountered another Indian. This time I did not run, but instead I approached him and accosted him in the sublime language of the Chinook: "Mika tikey memalous copa mika. Pecotta? Yak halo wow-wow." He did not reply, for my Indian, whom I had been addressing with all the dignity I possessed, was nothing more than a black stump. Nevertheless, I considered it entirely too dangerous to proceed farther and returned to where Nickson was hidden.

The next thing for us to do was to get away from the island. We took a northerly direction, coming out at the Gulf of Georgia. We saw and hailed a boat, in which were two men. We told them what had occurred to us. They were bound for Victoria, but they took the scare and returned to Whatcom.

Whatcom was at that time in a booming condition, being chock full of miners, who were principally from California, and a wonderfully excitable crowd they were, too, and ready for any emergency.

A sloop was manned by a party of armed miners and they proceeded to the cove on Orcas island, with Tom Nickson acting as pilot, determined to avenge the wrong that had been done us. They learned that the Indians had made good their booty and had gone north. The last seen of them they were passing Point Roberts.

Chapter **5**

Revenge and Reprisal

E.A. Light

*Mr. Light, an 1853 emigrant, presents an
interesting story about the hanging of the Indian
Leschi. He then relates his experiences in 1862
in Idaho's Salmon River gold fields.*

Steilacoom, Washington – June 23, 1892

E.A. Light of Steilacoom started for this country from Lima, in north-western Iowa, a town which he himself laid out, and where he had built a mill. He says: "I manufactured a wagon while here – I used to say with a jackknife – the wood for which I kept in water for a year. I afterward assisted the blacksmith to iron it ready for us, and then painted it, striping it with a hen's feather. I afterward sold the running gear of it to Sherwood Bonney, in Steilacoom, for $175. I kept track of the wagon for more than twenty years, most of which time it was in use in the Puyallup valley.

In the fall of 1852 I sold out, mostly on time. On the 1st of April, 1853, I found myself ready to continue my journey to the far west. The party consisted of my wife, with a weak, sickly baby 2 years old, Charles Hadley, John Reagon (two young men who had worked for me a long time) and myself. We had five yoke of oxen, two cows, one Canadian pony, one heavy two-horse wagon (the one mentioned above), and one heavy one-horse wagon. We crossed the river and at night found ourselves on a broad prairie without a house in sight. We went on the next morning, and as we struck traveled roads at Cedar Rapids, we fell in with two men and their families by the name of Cook, who were on their way to California. I had known the men before, and we decided to travel with them as far as consistent. We found them very agreeable and were sorry when the parting came. They tried hard to induce me to change my mind and go to California, but I had started for Puget Sound and nothing could have changed my determination.

One afternoon a driving rain struck us. We were near a house and we laid over until the next day. The people were very hospitable, and that night insisted on my wife and I occupying a bed in their house, which we did. It was the last house we slept in for more than six months.

The next day we came to a stream where a bridge or boat was necessary in order to reach the opposite side. We concluded to make a bridge, as a fine grove of polars stood close by, and in a very short time we were landed safely on the other side. We passed on, crossing the Des Moines river where the city of Des Moines now stands. Near here we saw a farm house, near which was a herd of tame elk.

We journeyed through vast quantities of mud and water until we reached the bottom lands of the Missouri river, where we rested our animals about a week. We then arranged to cross. One morning early at Surprise Ferry, below Council Bluffs, while we were camped at the ferry, so as to be on hand early in the morning, I saw John Lane and Sam Ray, acquaintances of mine, going on the ferry with a train. I knew they had started for Puget Sound, so I made haste to find them, after crossing the river, and made arrangements to travel in their train. Here we reluctantly bid the Cook families good-bye and started with the train, bound for Puget Sound.

Before arriving at the Elkhorn river, Lane picked out a camping ground, and Sargeant, his brother-in-law, chose another. When we came to the place of choosing, Lane turned to his place, and I, with seven young men and two wagons, followed him. The others all went with Sargeant. We started for the ferry early the next morning, and found enough wagons waiting to be ferried over to keep the regular ferry busy for a week. We also noticed some people crossing in dugouts that some emigrants had made. We bought the canoes but had to wait a day for our turn to come. While watching the men operating the canoes we saw them, when empty, coming back for another load, run them under the current, and the men had to swim for dear life.

We at once made up our minds that there ought to be a deeper canoe. On the upper side of the river we saw a tree out of which we could make one, and all hands put to, and by the time we could use it we had it ready. Lane, the seven young men and myself had all our effects safely across in a short time, with the exception of a loss to Lane of a valuable mare. He had tied a rope to the animal and took the end across the river. He then had the mare pushed out into the current, and between the men at the end of the rope, and the strong current running over the rope, the mare's head was dragged under water and she was drowned. It was a sore loss to our friend, for the mare was a valuable one.

Lane struck out, leaving Sargeant, and the seven young men and myself followed. We had a train of six wagons. It was about four months before we again saw Sargeant and his party.

We guarded our stock well all the way up the Platte river, as we were in constant fear of the Indians. The hunters of the party procured more or less fresh meat. We noted several exciting races after buffalo.

After we had passed some 200 miles up the Platte river, just for a change in the monotony, we were treated to a genuine hailstorm, which came upon us without warning. I told Reagon to go on the pony with the cattle, which had all run in a huddle, and I doubled my three yoke of oxen that were on the big wagon, and Hadley brought the big oxen and little wagon on the other side, so we had our oxen between us, and we made them stand and take the storm. The wagons sheltered us a good deal, however. The other men unhitched their teams, and some of the oxen ran away, with their yokes on, dragging their chains after them. Some had got the bow off the near ox, and the off ox ran away with the rest of the yoke. When the storm was over they had great trouble in gathering up their paraphernalia.

After the rain and storm were over some of the cattle were found three miles away. We soon got gathered together and pushed on again.

This storm and several succeeding ones forced us to ferry some streams in my wagon box, which I had prepared for this purpose before starting out from home.

We soon began gathering firewood, as we were about to enter a stretch of country, about 200 miles wide, where there was no wood to be had. We in time had covered this uninviting strip of country, and had camped by good water and a nice grove of strees and laid over for washing. While here a hail storm came upon us. The most of the men were out on a hunting expedition at the time. I hurried nearly all the cattle in the center of the grove, and the others ran in themselves when the hail began to pelt them. I tied the lariats of the horses to the first tree I came to. The storm in its fury was soon fully upon us, passing near the horses, but the lariats being strong kept the horses, and the cattle, with a little persuasion from myself and another man who had come to my assistance, decided the best thing was to stay where they were. They wriggled about a little, but we managed to keep them within the grove, notwithstanding the severity of the storm, which proved to be much worse than the first one we experienced.

The cattle from the neighboring camps that had rushed by us went on, and when they reached the Platte river they plunged into it pell-mell and began swimming in a circle in the swift current. Some of them floated on down the river and gained the bank, but a great many were drowned.

There was a family camped in a sort of ravine when the torrent came rushing down the sides of the hill, sweeping their yokes and wagon, and everything with it, down the ravine. The family barely escaped drowning. Most of their things, except their provisions, were recovered, as they had lodged in some brush a little way down the stream.

A few days after this we were treated to some genuine fun. On the opposite side of the Platte river we saw two men in hot pursuit of a buffalo. When the animal reached the river he plunged in and swam across. His pursuers sent several bullets after him, but missed their mark. Our hunters grabbed their rifles and ran down to welcome the buffalo as he ascended the bank of the river, but he scorned their acquaintance and kept at long range, and the contents of their rifles did no more good than those of the hunters on the other side of the river, now casting wishful eyes toward their escaping prey. Lane was on horseback and got quite close, but the buffalo refused to wait for him. In the melee I had become somewhat excited and grabbed my doublebarrelled shotgun, which was laoded with buckshot, and ran ahead, thinking I might intercept the animal as he left the road, but I failed to connect. Lane called for me to "come on," as if I could keep pace with him and his game. While Lane stopped to load his gun, I kept a close watch on the game, and noticed that he turned a right angle back toward the road some distance ahead. I saw that Lane had lost his game, and motioned to him where the buffalo had gone. He started in pursuit and soon had him in view, and was close on him, when he again crossed the road, and going up close to an emigrant's camp, stopped and sat down on his haunches not ten feet from them. The man fired his pistol at him and shot him several times and he dropped over dead. The man's wife had fainted, and was lying apparently dead. She revived, however, and soon all hands were busy dressing the buffalo. My trip after the animal on foot was the subject of many a hearty laugh.

In a few days after this we were at Fort Laramie. After passing this point some distance, we one day met about 100 Sioux Indians, all mounted on horses, sitting as straight as so many cobs. Some of them could talk a little English, and relieved us somewhat of our fears. We then fully realized how utterly helpless we would be if we were attacked by these people. We felt that Providence was on our side, however, and that we should land safe on Puget Sound.

We soon saw the Platte river for the last time. We left the Black Hills behind us, and were passing ponds of alkali water near Sweet Water river. Near the crossing of this river is located the famous Independence rock, which is nearly covered with the names of travelers. Up the river a mile or so is the noted Devil's pass, where the Sweet Water river cuts a narrow channel through a mountain of rock and forms nearly perpendicular walls, up which lunatics have crawled to incredible heights to inscribe their names.

We agreed that we could get along very well without the light wagon, and a few days after crossing the Sweet Water we left it standing on our old camping place. We left it in good condition — cover and everything complete. We favored our cattle in every way we could. To the light wagon we had worked the finest yoke of oxen we had seen on the plains. In a few days after we abandoned the wagon it passed us with a span of mules drawing it.

The principal game in this section was antelope and jack-rabbits, of which we got our share.

In going through the south pass of the Rocky mountains, there was a gale of wind that we could scarcely make our animals face. It kept the sand and gravel rolling, and some of the lighter pebbles were picked up by the wind and blown with such force that they left a stinging sensation if they hit anything that had the sense of feeling.

When we reached Big Sandy river we found we were on a road which we didn't care to travel, so before crossing we struck down to the right, losing about a day's travel. On reaching Green river we found several of our party indisposed. Some of them did not regain their health until we reached the Bear river mountains, where we rested a couple of days. After our rest we went down into the valley of Bear river, where we arrived in the evening. The mosquitoes were so thick it was almost impossible to breathe. Our stock suffered terribly. From this river we caught some trout. In this valley the big black crickets were so thick for miles that they nearly covered the ground. The Indians gathered them, fried them and used them for food, so we are told. The night we arrived at Soda springs we didn't much like the actions of some Indians we noticed prowling around, and we had extra guards out, and there was not much sleeping done among us. We drank of the water from these springs, which had a very pleasant taste.

Here we parted with the seven young men who had been members of our party. They were going to California, and had accompanied us as far as practicable for them. We regretted to lose them from our train, for they were all educated, enterprising, civil young men, and hailed from New York.

Lane and his people, with our three wagons, turned into the road that led to Puget Sound and made very good progress on to Fort Hall and American Falls on Snake river. We passed on down Snake river to Salmon Falls, above which we crossed to the other side. We swam our cattle and horses and ferried our wagons. These falls are nothing more than steep rapids, or water rushing and foaming over rocks about a half mile, while the American is a perpendicular fall of the whole river.

The morning we left Salmon Falls we saw a drove of cattle, several hundred of them, going over the falls. The leaders got turned down the stream and the balance followed, and nothing could have stopped them. Some of the men barely escaped drowning. It was a terrible sight to see them rolling and tumbling over the rocks. All were badly injured, and many killed outright.

While on the north side of the Platte river our cattle got poisoned, and three of my oxen died. Lane also lost several cattle.

When on our way down Boise river we bought some red meated salmon from some Indians. It was the first we had ever seen. We decided unanimously that it was the best fish we had ever eaten. When we were almost ready to cross Boise river, we were encamped one evening, expecting to cross next day, when suddenly there was a noise as if bedlam had been thrown open, and the occupants were exerting themselves in celebrating the occasion. The brush between us and the place where the noise evidently originated obstructed our view, but knowing that the Indians were the cause of the proceedings we were very anxious. We were badly frightened and pulled a little distance away by a patch of brush, where we camped without any fire, and with the open prairie around us. All hands stood guard that night, but we saw no Indians. In the morning we found that one of their number had died, and that they had been working all night for his benefit by shouting and hammering on boards, which noise was supposed to frighten the devil away. Whether or not their demonstrations succeeded in keeping that dignitary at a distance I do not know, but they certainly kept us pretty well stirred up.

After crossing Boise river we were soon at Fort Boise, and here we ferried back across the Snake river to the south side. Two men and myself had crossed the river, and tried to induce the cattle to make a good landing. One of my large oxen had been poisoned, and was barely able to make his way, and we decided to keep him back and cross him in some other way. He was driven to one side, and the other cattle pushed into the stream. They made a

-221-

good and safe landing. The sick ox had seen the cattle make the landing and had entered the stream, and to our surprise came to the bank, where he would have died if we had not had roped and some way of getting him on dry ground and on his feet. He improved from this time on, and did me a good winter's work, and in the spring I sold the yoke to Hon. Henry Roder of Whatcom for $350.

We tramped on to the Malheur river, where we saw scalding hot water gushing out of the bank at the edge of the stream. We thought we must be pretty close to a hot place we had read about, and moved on. In a few days we laid by to do our washing, and we had to heat our water. We soon discovered that the stream by which we were camped had plenty of salmon in it. I had a fine five-tined steel spear with me, but the fish kept out of reach in deep water. We made a sort of a barrack out of brush and tied it firmly together and put a rope on each end and dragged the stream. I placed myself so as to catch the fish as they came down the stream, but they were so frantic in trying to escape the brush that was hurrying them on that they stranded on the sand at the banks of the river and the men kicked them out on dry land, and in a short time we had more than we could take care of for want of salt. We had great sport, and felt happy that we were journeying on toward the land of fish and clams.

We passed on over the hills, entering Burnt River valley, and on down into the Grande Ronde valley, where we met Nelson Sargeant of Olympia, who was on the way to meet his father's family and conduct them over the Natchez pass in the Cascades. We told him we would camp there until he came back, and we waited ten days. Indians were numerous. We had some interviews with them by means of gesticulations. We found trout in the stream near by, and had a good time in general, or as good as we could whilst in the place where we were surrounded by Indians.

Finally our old friends we had left at Elkhorn river rolled into camp, and we had a genuine old love feast, relating our experiences since we had last traveled together. The next morning we started on our journey over the Blue mountains, crossed Wild Horse creek valley and the valley of the Walla Walla, crossing the latter river at the point where Dr. Whitman's home was at the time he and his family were massacred. In due time we reached Wallula on the great river of the great northwest, where we were delayed about a week waiting for the ferry boat to be completed.

One afternoon the Indians put into a corral a band of wild horses. They would lasso one, blindfold him, array him with one of their primitive saddle-horse gearings, then they would worry him away from the yard when an Indian would mount him and pull a surcingle up across his knees which would effectually tie him to the horse, which would naturally make some wild breaks for liberty, and after becoming pretty well tired out the rider would pull the blind up from the horse's eyes, after which followed a great exhibition of leaping, jumping and floundering around, extraordinary in the extreme, and generally ended in a run, which continued until the horse was quieted.

Lane and myself again differed from Sargeant and his people about the best time and place to swim our cattle across the Columbia. We thought it best to cross where we were, and to do so early in the morning before the sun would be in our cattle's eyes. Although the river was wider here than further up, the current was not so swift. We made a bargain with Pew Pew Max Max to have a number of Indian canoes accompany our cattle and make them cross as straight as possible. The cattle reached the shore in good shape. The remaining cattle and the horses were taken further up the river to the foot of an island and successfully crossed over. We ferried everything across that could not swim. The Indians, after getting the stock half way across the river, ceased their efforts and refused to go further without additional pay. There was no alternative but to pay them what they demanded, as the sun was then shining in the cattle's eyes and they were turning and going with the current. More pay, however, induced the Indians to make further efforts, and they succeeded in landing all the stock, but some of them quite a distance down the river. I went after the stock, and while on the trip I came across a rattlesnake. I had not yet learned to love these reptiles, and I quickly dispatched him. That was the only venomous reptile I ever saw in this state.

We proceeded up the Yakima river, following an Indian trail, and crossed the river where the town of Prosser is now located. Pew Pew Max Max had gone on before us and had a beef dressed for us, waiting near where the trail left the river and went around through some small mountains. The beef was a good one and was bought at a reasonable price.

At this point we dug a grave and buried a man by the name of McCullah, the only one of our company that died on the journey. The funeral services were lonely and solemn, and the occasion was particularly sad. I carved his name on a board and placed it at the head of his grave. We had seen a great number of graves one and two years old, on the way, and especially on the north side of Snake river, where these lonely markers of former travelers where quite numerous. However, the whole road was a succession of graves. Probably no year had been more exempt from sickness and trouble with the Indians since emigration had begun than the year 1853.

After completing the sad rite of the morning, we continued on our journey on the Indian trail, reaching a pool of water, where we camped until the next morning. After traveling several miles we reached a place in the trail, which we concluded was impassable. It was unanimously agreed that it was best that Mr. Sargeant should go on and find out for a certainty whether or not the emigrants of Puget Sound had opened up a road by way of the Natchez river. We went back to the place where we had camped the night before, and camped again. I climbed to the top of a mountain and took a look over the valley. Below me lay the valley where the Yakima cities are now situated, but then barren of civilization.

Upon my return to camp I learned that some Indians had been there and had succeeded in making the members of the party believe that we should have taken a right-hand trail. The majority seemed in favor of going over to the other trail, and accordingly the next morning we set off on the right-hand trail, and after a hard day's tramp we found ourselves in a small valley on the banks of the Columbia river, where we camped for the night. I had seen the Columbia river from the top of the mountain and knew we would reach it soon, but did not know that the trail followed a rocky bluff along which no wagon could go, which proved to be the case. The women of the party generally believed it was a scheme on the part of the Indians to get us into this place and murder us, and consequently we spent the night in anything but a happy mood. Early the next morning we were on the move again, returning to our pool of water. When we reached that place Mr. Sargeant soon put in an appearance and reported the road as being cut up the Natchez river, which resulted in livening our spirits somewhat, and we determined to work our way through some way or other, following the ravines and gulches. We had at first thought it impossible, but came to the conclusion that "where there is a will there is a way." We retraveled our route and passed on, overcoming all obstacles by putting on more strength, rough-locking the wheels, etc., as the case required. We soon found ourselves fording the Yakima river the second time, and after following it a few miles we crossed Wenas creek and followed it for some distance. Rough-locking all the wheels, we let ourselves down the side of a mountain into the Natchez river, which, in following we forded sixty-two times over a rocky bottom.

This accomplished we left the terrible stream, for such we had come to regard it, and traveled through heavily timbered lands on quite an easy grade, passing up to the summit of the Natchez pass. In this place I measured one fir tree that measured more than 10 feet in diameter and 100 feet to the first limb, and which retained its full size well. On the summit of this pass I picked my first whortleberries.

The next morning early we started down the western slope, and after safely descending two steep slopes we reached a third, to look down which was enough to take the starch out of any living being except a pioneer. Our teams could not go down the first few hundred feet in the yokes, but unyoking them, we took them around singly on a sort of trail. We then rough-locked all the wheels and fastened a long rope to the hind axletree, the further end of which rope was wound several times around a tree, and by letting the rope out little by little, the wagons reached the place where it was level enough to again hitch the oxen to them. When my turn came I announced my determination of passing my team and wagon down without unhitching, whereupon there were many expressions as to my sanity. I was also called many undeserving pet names, and especially by an old woman who was in the train, who seemed to think she had a peculiar right to give vent to her surprise and indignation.

I had the men who were tending the rope wound round the tree take particular precaution about letting the rope out, and told them to keep the rope tight enough to allow the oxen to lean their weight in the yoke. After making everything secure, I started over the precipice, reaching the lower level safely, where I hitched my cattle, that had been taken down before, to the wagon, and moved on down the mountain out of the way of those who were to follow. The remaining ones on the top of the mountain decided to follow my example, and all moved down the side of the hill like clockwork, nothing happing until when Lane started down the precipice. From some mismanagement his wagon got away from him and went crashing down the mountain, where he left it until the next season. He packed his goods on his horses and we again took up our journey.

The Green Water river was soon reached, where we camped, and where we had nothing but fir and cedar brush for our cattle to eat. The next morning we moved down Green Water river, which stream we forded fifteen times, on a bottom of rolling boulders. On this tortuous route all our people preferred walking, as bruises and bumped heads had taught them that there was no certainty of the wagons always being right side up, the wheels passing over logs, roots and knolls made a seat in the wagon quite uncomfortable. On foot they followed the trail over some spurs of the mountain, and thus avoided some of the crossings of that river, which certainly was not to be regretted.

On arriving at White river we struck an open spot of gravel prairie at the foot of Mount Latate—a rock several hundred feet in height, with the form of a person's head on the top of it. The name Latate is the Indian meaning of head.

At this point we were met with a second supply of provisions from Puget Sound, which was timely indeed, for some of our people had begun to feel the pangs of hunger. The obstructions and delays by rains in the mountains, together with work that had to be done, had nearly worn our people out, and the meeting with these good Samaritans, with their hospitable donations gave us good cheer and renewed our ambitions and we started on feeling much better for the meeting.

In passing down White river, which we crossed seven times we encountered a fire, which had felled much of the timber, which was a great detriment to us as we had to remove it from our way, causing us considerable delay, besides being exceedingly dangerous from falling trees and limbs.

The crossing of White river was the most dangerous of any stream we had encountered, on account of the milky appearance of the water, probably caused by the continual grinding of the glaciers on the rocky, chalky, clayey surface of Mount Tacoma. We could not see the hidden rocks, and we were in constant danger while crossing the stream. Our cattle had fared badly without grass, and before we were all across Mud mountain some of the teams gave out and had to be taken on to where grass could be found, and after being refreshed with something to eat returned for the wagons. In ascending this mountain many of the teams were not able to take their wagons up all the way. Some were taken up by means of a pole, some chains and some elbow grease applied at the small end of the pole. This was done by placing the butt end of a long pole on the upper side of a small tree, the end projecting beyond the tree some four or five feet, to the end of which was attached a chain. At the same distance from the tree on the other end of the pole was fastened another chain. The ends of these two chains were fastened to a single leading chain, which was attached to the wagon. Several men would take the long end of the pole back and forth up and down the hill, some one being on hand to hitch the two chains alternately as they became loose. Each motion of the pole back and forth took the wagon up the side of the hill. While this operation may seem a little tedious, the reader will understand that we were then on our way to the far west.

Hon. James Longmier, John Lane and myself had better teams than most of the other members of our train, and we moved on, crossed Boise creek and camped on the prairie a day ahead of the rest. The following night we camped on Connell's prairie, the next on Finnell's prairie, and the next on the Puyallup river bank.

While in the latter camp we put my spear to good use catching hump-backed salmon, which made us a luscious feast, and which we all enjoyed. The next time we camped was on Nisqually plains, near Christopher Mahan's, from where we went to Steilacoom with one team, returning to camp on the 10th day of October, 1853, and for the first time saw a branch of the briny ocean.

The next day Longmier, Lane and myself accompanied Levi Shelton to Yelm prairie, where we stopped over night with John Edgar. (Edgar was afterward killed by the Indians.) Longmier returned home with Shelton, bought his place and resided there ever since. He has been a member of the legislature several times, has grown rich and is respected by all who know him. He has raised a large family, all of whom are married and prosperous.

Lane and myself went on to Olympia, returned the next day and moved camp to Byrd's mill, on Steilacoom creek. My first work was hauling potatoes for Lieutenant Slaughter, which occupation lasted several days, and for which I received good pay. From that place I moved into Steilacoom, occupying a house that Captain L. Bills had donated to our use, and which I gladly accepted. I was immediately employed as a carpenter, on trial, gave satisfaction, and was employed steadily at $5 per day.

Meantime Lane had been given a chance of furnishing several cargoes of square timber and piles, and cord wood for short storage and insisted on my putting in my team and going into the business with him, sharing the profits equally. I did so, and in a few days we loaded our household goods, and a few necessary camping tools, on a small scow, and set out on our first voyage on salt water, landing on the beach where the Pacific mill now stands, near the smelter, in Tacoma. The place was then a fishery, owned by John Swann and Charles Riley, the parties who had let the timber contract to us. They had a long building on the beach which they used as a home while fishing, and had given us the privelege of stopping in it while we were preparing ourselves a house. We landed just at dark, and, notwithstanding the fact that there were about 100 Indians of all ages and sexes camped near, the men assured us that our goods were perfectly safe in the scow, and, so after taking off our bedding and a few necessary articles, we decided to leave the remainder of them for removal the following morning.

There was a little anxiety about the goods, however, and about midnight Lane thought he would see if everything was all right. He meandered down the path along the beach, stepped down on the beach — not on an Indian, but on a skunk, which immediately went to work at his peculiar business. Lane neglected the scow, turned and came into the house. When he entered there was a general chorus inviting him outside, telling him to leave his clothing out if he returned. He did so, and while there was a breath of a suspicion as to what had happened him, we soon got reconciled to the inevitable, turned over and were soon fast asleep.

In a few days we had a comfortable house, for this climate, which we made from timber that was near at hand, by setting posts in the ground and using poles to nail the shakes and clapboards to, and having dressed puncheons for the flooring, with which our wives were well pleased. After making the necessary provisions for our stock, we, with Charles Riley and an Indian we had for a guide, marked out a trail quite direct to Dougherty's prairie. We camped in the woods all night, and the next day went on. We found some of our cattle with some wild cattle belonging to the Hudson Bay company. There were four bulls with them, which had frightened two halfbreed children, who had climbed on a high root to get out of their way, and about which the big, muscular fellows were pawing and bellowing frightfully. One of our men began shooting at them, and the wild cattle took fright and all disappeared. We soon had our cattle on the way home. It was not an uncommon thing for the wild cattle to frighten people, but I never heard of anyone being hurt by them. Lewis Measeley was once driven up a tree by them, about which they stood guard until late at night.

We did well in getting out the timber, and when we had finished I began building a house for myself and family, in Steilacoom, which I still own, and in which I have lived nearly all the time. The young men, Reagon and Hadley, who had crossed the plains with us, lived with us and they helped me with building. My lumber cost me $25 per thousand at the mill, and $5 per thousand to get it haulted in. We did all the planing by hand. I made the window sash by hand without the aid of a sawmill. When the house was completed it was said to be the largest in the territory. Hadley and I were two weeks in cutting down the trees that would reach the house. I removed the stumps from my lots, fenced them, and set out some fruit trees, some of which are still standing. In the spring of 1855 I rented Lafayette Butcher's hotel and took Henry Wilson as partner. We carpeted and furnished it throughout. We had a bar in the house but did not allow drunkenness, gambling, or disorder of any kind. We soon had all the business we could attend to and made a good deal of money.

About the time we opened this hotel the Indian war broke out. Many of our citizens were killed, business was almost suspended, and homes broken up, with the exception of a few families who were on friendly terms with the Indians, and which relations were sustained for a long time after the war had been raging, and hundreds of pioneers had been killed. Governor Stevens proclaimed martial law, sent a troop of soldiers and had the Indian sympathizers arrested and placed in the guardhouse at Fort Steilacoom.

Some lawyers got out a writ of habeas corpus to release the Indian's friends from the guardhouse. The district court was convened, Judge Chenoworth presiding. Governor Stevens sent Colonel Shaw, with his company of volunteer citizen soldiers, to the courthouse, which they entered, took the judge from the bench and the clerk from his desk and took charge of the books and records. These extraordinary proceedings satisfied the hostile Indians that they had best make themselves scarce, and to take measures to restore peace and quiet.

During the time I was in the hotel there was started in Steilacoom a paper called *The Puget Sound Courier*. It was published by Affleck & Gunn. I had considerable money invested in the enterprise, all of which I lost.

I had charge of the county auditor's office, justice of the peace's office, etc., and was considered a handy man all around. The women and children were gathered in the block houses at nights, and the men who were left in Steilacoom took their regular turns standing guard on the outskirts of the town. Sometimes Indians in war paint would be seen, but they were not so numerous as at some other points.

After running the hotel a year, Wilson and I sold out. About this time I received word from my attorney in Iowa that he had taken my mill property and farm back, and that it would be necessary for me to return there and straighten up affairs.

I immediately arranged for my family to stop with the family of Andrew Byrd, who, with several others, assured me that they should want for nothing during my absence.

On the 1st day of February, 1856, I sailed on the bark *Ork*, and was twenty-two days on the way to San Francisco, and arrived at that place a day too late for the sailing of the vessel bound for the isthmus. The steamers made trips only twice a month, so I had to wait in San Francisco two weeks. We then left, expecting to go via the Nicaragua route. We were met at sea by the steamer that was returning, and were informed that they were seized by Walker, the filibuster at San Juan Del Norte, who would not allow passengers to pass through the country unless they paid him tribute, and that they had proceeded on to Panama, and advised us to do the same, notwithstanding the fact that their passengers had had a riot at Panama and some were killed. However, we had no other alternative, and upon reaching the place were landed in row boats on the beach where a squad of soldiers were waiting to escort us to the cars, which were also guarded by soldiers. Here I took my first ride in a railway car, and looked upon my first locomotive. While crossing into Aspinwall I learned that only 300 of the 900 on board the train could take passage on the steamer awaiting us, as there were already more than 1200 aboard. The ticket office, baggage cars and steamer were inside of a yard that had to be entered by a small gate. I posted myself at the gate fully determined to be the first to go through, and to procure a ticket, but after my very best efforts, made within the bounds of reason and decency, I was about the fiftieth one to get my ticket, and after I had it I was lifted up and had to crawl back over the heads and shoulders of the compact, struggling mass of human beings. I rushed to the baggage car, procured a box and trunk, which constituted my baggage, and carried it to the steamer. I was to change steamers at Havana, in Cuba, and from there would go via New Orleans and up the Mississippi river.

Six hundred of our passengers were left in Aspinwall for two weeks. Most of the passengers who succeeded in reaching the steamer did so without securing their baggage, which in a great many cases was never recovered.

Havana reached, we went ashore. This was a fine harbor. Slavery in perfection was to be seen on all sides. Men were carrying loads like beasts of burden.

Near the mouth of the Mississippi river a terrible storm of wind, rain, thunder and lightning overtook us. It seemed that our ship would never stand it, but it did, and we passed up the river, by the forts, to New Orleans. Here we stopped two days. I took a look around the town. Saw Jackson's battle field, and also his monument. Took a look at the French graveyards, where the corpses were deposited in vaults, three in a row, generally one above another, in the wall that surrounded the block. Many fine and costly monuments were erected in the interior. I saw here many things that were new and of interest to me, prominently among which was the market place for slaves — the place where human beings stood on exhibition as merchandise, awaiting their purchase by such as would bid the highest price. I prayed that the curses of this cruel practice might soon be abolished, and that the dealers in such merchandise would meet their just rewards.

I took passage from here to St. Louis. In the state of Arkansas I saw plainly visible the path of a terrible cyclone. The devastation caused by this storm was something terrible. In the same state we stopped to take on wood. Negro slaves had charge of the sale of wood. In answer to questions they said they were satisfied with their condition; that they had no care nor anxiety as to their future, and that their master was a kind, humane man, and they would not leave him if they could.

When we reached the mouth of the Ohio river, imagine my suprise at seeing the city of Cairo, protected by enormous levees, standing where but a few years before there was a sea of water with brush visible here and there.

Near the same spot where the steamer *Corsair* had stove one wheel with driftwood, the steamer *Flying Cloud*, on which I was now traveling, picked up a piece of driftwood in one of the wheels, made several revolutions, and with the log threshed the wheel house into splinters. Of course the steamer was stopped as quickly as possible. The cracking and threshing of the wheel house had made a terrible noise, and the people rushed from their berths to the deck, all excited, some in their night clothes, some shouting, some praying. They were anxious to know if the boat was going to sink, and if it did, would it go down there, or could it be got to the shore. When they found that there was no danger of the boat going down, and that there was nothing damaged only the wheel house, they quietly returned to their berths, no doubt ashamed of their conduct.

The next morning we arrived in St. Louis. After mailing a daguerreotype of myself to my wife and looking around a short time, I continued my voyage on another boat to McGregor's landing, where I arrived safely one morning in time to take the stage for West Union. McGregor and Prairie du Chien were now both thriving places. One morning at breakfast an old man noticed me drinking cold water, and knew me. When it became generally known that I hailed from Puget Sound I was looked upon, as I was oftentimes afterward, as if I came from another world, and questions of all kinds, sorts and colors were asked me. There was a good load for West Union. We soon found that the most important thing to look after was some rails to lift and pry the stage out of the mud. The ride was slow and tedious. We changed teams, but did not reach West Union until after midnight of the next day. The next morning I set off for Lima, and gave my mother and other friends and relatives a big surprise. Times were quite dull, and there was not much prospect of selling property. I immediately went to work posting books for a merchant and to do some other writing for him. During the summer I repaired my mill and other property and took a contract to build a bridge across the river just below the mill. In the fall I had a siege of fever and ague, and was getting ready to quit the country. By New Years day there was three feet of snow on the ground and the weather was freezing cold, several people having frozen to death. I made up my mind I was through with that country for good, and disposed of my property again, mostly on time, and started for my home on Puget Sound.

I purchased a layover ticket for New York. I stopped in Belvedier, Ill., and went up into Wisconsin, where I wallowed around in the snow about two weeks. I was disgusted with the climate, and made another start. I found my trunks in Chicago, and rechecked them to New York city. I laid over again in Orleans county, New York, where my wife's people lived. I also stopped in Albany. When I was ready to resume my journey the river had become blocked with ice, and backed the water into the warehouses and the railroad track was so inundated that we had to go through Connecticut. My baggage had been soaked in the water, and many things I had were badly damaged. I had several valuable dress patterns for my wife, which I was trying to dry in a room I had rented for that purpose. The landlady kindly offered her assistance in ironing them and putting them up in good shape. She was anxious to do this for me, and when I offered to pay her she would accept nothing. Her kindness excited my suspicions, and, upon examination, I found that from three to five yards had been taken from each piece of goods. I said nothing but locked my trunks and kept mum.

A young man had noticed my name on the register and saw that I hailed from Steilacoom, W.T., and wished to accompany me on my voyage home. I felt a little suspicions, but he proved to be a good fellow. We looked about New York a good deal, and there saw some of the sufferings of the poor and downtrodden.

At last, after a two weeks' wait, the day for sailing arrived. Some of the passengers proceeded to get good and sick as soon as we started out, but my friend and I had taken a preventative in the form of loaf sugar with some oil of peppermint dropped on it, which we ate, and we got through all right.

On board the steamer was a man and woman who used to promenade the forward deck a great deal of the time. The steerage passengers took a great dislike to them. One day when they were out on one of their walks a sea struck the forward quarter of the bow which caused a great splash on the forward deck, and knocked both the man and woman down, completely submerging them. This brought out a shout of laughter from the passengers, and the nabob and his lady kept themselves in the background from that time on.

When we entered Graytown, the Yankee sailor boys manned the rigging of their ships and cheered us heartily, as did the crews of the other war vessels. They sent a boat to receive their mail, and we remained long enough for them to answer their letters. They gave us a rousing cheer as we left, and in good time arrived in Aspinwall and proceeded by rail to Panama, then aboard a steamer on the Pacific, which landed us at San Juan Del Norte, where we remained two days. I felt great sympathy for Walker's wounded soldiers, who were lying on boards and suffering terribly. When we left, two of Walker's men were discovered on the steamer. A boat was lowered and sent back with them, leaving them at a place a long distance from any habitation. Several of the soldiers were found afterward and were put ashore at Manzanillo.

On the voyage the steamer was on fire different times, but nothing serious happened but once, when several passengers were knocked down a stairway, breaking one man's leg and injuring others severely.

At San Francisco we took passage on the first steamer going north, which was the old *Oregon*. In passing over the bar of the Columbia we noticed the deck flooring, which opened and shut as the steamer moved back and forth. We decided to stay ashore in any event afterward rather than go on that boat again.

At Helens, on the Columbia, we engaged passage with three men in a skiff, who were going to Rainier, where we landed about midnight. We accompanied one of the men to his home, which was on the Washington side of the river below the mouth of the Cowlitz, the point from which we wanted to start the next morning. Our bed was a pile of hay in the corner of his cabin, our covering some old rags. Extreme poverty was here exemplified, but a king in his palace could not have been more hospitable, for he gave us of what he had, and did it cheerfully and willingly, depriving himself and wife in order to do so.

The next morning early we started for Huntington's hotel at Monticello, where we took breakfast, after which we started up the Cowlitz river, reaching Cowlitz after dark. Here we hired two ponies, at $10 each, to take us on to Olympia. The first day's ride was through Sanders' bottom, where for the greater part of seven miles we had to keep our feet drawn up along side the ponies to keep them out of the mud and water. That night we stopped with Sidney Ford, on Grand Mound prairie. We arrived in Olympia late in the afternoon of the next day, and immediately started out on foot for Steilacoom, where we arrived late in the evening. I found my family well, and they were glad to see me, which gladness was reciprocated.

Almost immediately I went in partnership with Andrew Byrd and his brother, and we built a grist mill on Steilacoom creek, but not until I had built me a house, which stood where the town of Custer is now situated. John Reagon and myself built the mill, with a little help on the machinery and gearing, and had it running in good shape by the fall of '57.

During the summer the notorious Indian chief, known among the whites by the name of Leschi, was to be hung at Fort Steilacoom. He had been sentenced for clandestinely inciting his people to horrid deeds of murder and the spoilation of property. Before this trouble there had been no trouble this side the mountains — in fact, all the following disturbances can be attributed to him and his secret work among his people. It is a pity and shame that there are men to be found today talking about judicial murder. They certainly have forgotten many of the losses, trials and privations of the people who were not Indian sympathizers in the memorable year of 1855.

On the day set for execution a steamer from Olympia brought Governor McMullen, Secretary Mason and other territorial officers, and nearly all the members of the legislature, and many citizens to witness the execution. Soon after their arrival came the hour for the execution. The time passed on, and no sheriff or deputy were to be found. Excitement and indignation ran high. Secretary Mason accused me of being accessory to the thwarting of the laws. I soon convinced him and all others present that he was barking up the wrong tree.

I soon ascertained that through the assistance and counsel of a lawyer (who was the only notary public in the county), the military officers of the fort, with the connivance and assistance of a United States commissioner, the county sheriff and his deputy, both of whom were more or less connected with the affairs of the garrison, and who lived just outside the military enclosure, had devised the scheme of arresting the sheriff and his deputy just at the hour Leschi was to be taken from the guard house to be executed. One of the lieutenants was made a deputy United States marshal, appointed by the commissioner, to arrest the sheriff and his deputy on a warrant issued by the commissioner on a complaint against the sheriff and his deputy, of selling spirituous liquor to Indians. The bogus marshal arrested his willing prisoners, as previously arranged, and sneaked off down town with them. The sheriff furnished the keys and he and his deputy were locked up. It is doubtful if history records a more dastardly offense than this, considering the fact that it was the perpetrator's sworn duty to protect the lives and the people of the country, instead of the outlaws and savages, who had waged warfare and destroyed lives, homes and property.

It is seldom that a more indignant crowd of people are found than that afternoon boarded the steamer for Olympia. I had the same feeling within me as did most of our citizens, and I was requested to draft a set of resolutions, and an indignation meeting was called for the next evening. The meeting was largely attended and I was elected chairman. The resolutions were unanimously adopted. They contained the name of each person connected with the preceding day's diabolical proceedings, and in general gave the opinion of the common public as to their actions. The most of the participants in this outrage are now dead, and I shall say let their names die with them.

I had business in Olympia and the next day went there on foot. I found the people indignant over the affair concerning the failure of the officers and some others were hung in effigy. It had become known that I had acted as chairman at the indignation committee and I was asked to state the sentiments of the people of Steilacoom, which I did. Immediately there was an act passed, the legislature convened the supreme court, Leschi was resentenced and the sheriff of Thurston county was ordered to select a posse of thirty men and to proceed to Fort Steilacoom, take Leschi from the guard house and execute him, according to the sentence of the court.

The plan was carried out. Leschi was hung near where my mill stood. Thus ended the life of one of the incitors of the Indian war.

I sold my interest in the mill to the Byrd brothers, and returned to Steilacoom to live. I was soon appointed postmaster, which position I held for about fifteen years, much of which time it was the only postoffice in the county. I had received an appointment, without any previous knowledge, of notary public, which office I held about thirty years, and for a long time I was the only one in Pierce county. After receiving the above appointment I received a commission as United States commissioner, which office I held for fifteen years.

I was made foreman of the first grand jury that ever sat in Pierce county, when we indicted a large number of men for living in adultery with Indian women. The least proved case of them all was tried and the defendant acquitted. A nolle prosequi was entered for the others.

While acting as United States commissioner, United States Marshal Huntington seized in Olympia a steamer owned by Jim Jones. He brought the steamer down and tied it to the wharf and put a keeper aboard. The next morning the steamer was missing. It was next heard of on the way to Mexico. The owner was found in San Francisco, brought back and committed for trial. This affair cost Huntington all he was worth, but he finally got another foothold.

I went into the stationery business, and attended to that together with a lot of offices of different kinds until 1862, when I got J.H. Munson to run the postoffice and store while I took a trip to the Salmon River mines in Idaho. With six other men I started. We stopped with Hon. E. Meeker the first night, and he sent some pack horses with us as far as they could go over Mud mountian. We stopped the next day at noon on South prairie, near John Fleet's, with whom I took dinner. Here we learned that some Indians had preceded us, and we could follow their tracks through the snow over the mountains. We crossed White river that evening, and started up a trail on the side of a hill. On ascending one of our horses lost his balance and went tumbling down the bank, first horse and then pack on top. He was not hurt, and was soon on his way again. That night we camped on Boise prairie, and the next morning dismissed the pack animals, and strapping about sixty pounds each on our backs we trudged on.

That night we camped where the snow was two or three feet deep. The next morning my brother-in-law and one of the others struck back for Steilacoom. The other three would have gone willingly if I could have been persuaded to do so, but I was determined to push on, and they stayed by me.

We manufactured a pair of snow shoes each and that day tried them. That night we camped on bare ground at the foot of Mount Latate. The next morning we waded Green Water river, put on our snow shoes and tramped up the river. We finally reached a log, which the Indians had used to cross the river on, and one of the men started across without removing his snow shoes, but slipped and fell into the stream. Another of the men started to wade with his snow shoes on, but fared almost as badly as the former one. Toward night we came to the river again, and here the Indians had felled a tree on which to cross. We crossed over and stopped for the night, building a fire in a large hollow tree, which gave us a fine warming and drying.

The next night we camped on the mountain where we, as emigrants, had let our wagons down, when on our way to Puget Sound. We made a fire on the snow, and left a hole, or sort of tent sixteen feet deep, where we had spent the night. We continued on over the Natchez pass, down the Natchez river, over the head of the Wenas, where we threw our snow shoes away. We crossed the Wenas on a brush bridge we built, and got an Indian to take us across Yakima river in a canoe. We passed the hills and ravines that had caused us to turn back, on a previous trip; passed the pool of water to which we had returned twice, ferried the Yakima again, and engaged an Indian to take us down the Yakima and Columbia rivers to Wallula. We then made a start in earnest for Lewiston. On the Tusha river we met an old man who told us of the battle of Pittsburg landing, which made General Grant a hero. At Lewiston I met John Scranton, the jovial, jolly steamboat captain of Puget Sound. Lewiston was a city in embryo.

In due time we arrived at Florence, in the Salmon river mines, after many trials and hardships. We started out prospecting and kept it up for two weeks. When passing one mine we inquired the name and was told that it was "Root Hog or Die," and thought the place well named. I had tired of prospecting and concluded to buy something that was already found. I accordingly bought a digging, kept it about ten days and sold it for more than I had paid for it, purchased a pony and started home via The Dalles and Columbia river. I arrived there with about as much money as I had taken with me when I started, and was out only about three months' time, but had learned a good many things about mines and miners.

About this time the Western Union Telegraph company began to establish a line from Olympia to Victoria, and was to have offices at paying points. In fact they had to have an office occasionally for the convenience of repairing, etc. Mr. Haines, the manager, came to Steilacoom, but failed to see any one except Messrs. Keach and Martin, who ridiculed the idea of introducing a telegraph business to the fir trees of the country between the points named. Mr. Haines returned and ordered the line constructed through between American and Gravelly lakes. I had not known anything about the visit of the manager, but as soon as I found that a line was being run through that part of the country I at once went to work to get it located through Steilacoom. I was informed that the route would be changed if the citizens would erect the poles on the three miles intervening between the line and Steilacoom, and would furnish an office and some one to attend to it for half the receipts. If this was done, he would send the necessary office fixtures and would send a man to stay two months to teach some one and show him the run of the business.

There wasn't a person willing, nor one that did give a cent toward the enterprise. I cut and put the poles on the line the whole three miles; dug the holes at my own expense, and John Latham and I, and I think one or two others, raised the poles and strung the wire. Sprague was sent to stay two months, but the office paid so much better than was expected that he was kept there.

In 1854 I was nominated for territorial councilman for King and Pierce counties. In King county the two parties divided the joint representatives between them and voted solid for their two men, and Pierce county voted the party ticket and elected the King county men and lost the capitol of the territory by one vote. I was run the next year for a representative of the lower house, but against my wishes, and I caused my defeat. About 1864 or 1865 I was again nominated in joint convention of Pier, Mason and Chehalis counties for joint councilman, but again defeated myself.

In connection with my other business I kept on hand some garden seeds, and among other things I bought were twenty-four hop roots, which cost in San Francisco $3. I set them out near my house, and they were the first hops ever seen growing in Pierce county. J.R. Meeker, father of E. Meeker, got some of my hop roots and set them out near Sumner, and they were the first hops planted in the far famed hopgrowing region of the Puyallup valley. This variety of hops proved a little too late for this climate, and, after a few trials, the variety introduced, I think was the same, or very nearly so, as is now grown in the valley.

Later I formed a partnership with Isaac Pinkus and Adolph Packscher, which partnership lasted about seven years, during which time we did a large business. We soon owned the Webber wharf, the Byrd grist mill property, the Sherwood sawmill property, in North bay, and the schooner Clara Light which we ran between North bay and San Francisco. I kept the books and attended to my offices, having six of the latter when I became a member of the firm. I was acting as county surveyor, county treasurer, United States commissioner, probate judge and postmaster. I got rid of the offices as soon as I could so as to be better able to carry on my business.

A short time after this Egbert Tucker, sheriff of Pierce county, wished to raise a company of Washington territory volunteers to garrison Fort Steilacoom, and asked me to take charge of his office, post notices for a new election, look after the prisoners, collect delinquent taxes and close up his business, which I did. Hon. Steven Judson was elected sheriff, and proved equal to the duties laid upon him. The jail was also the United States penitentiary, state prison and county jail, so we had everything in one, and some pretty lively times, too.

During the year 1863 Andrew Byrd was killed. A man by the name of Bates was around town, and he had spent nearly all the day behind the stove in my store. When it came time to close the store he went out, and the next morning he was on hand again and resumed his seat of the day before. I had noticed him and was a little suspicious, but paid no particular attention. I had stepped out of the store for a short time and was busy when someone rushed out, calling to me that Byrd had been shot in the postoffice. I rushed to the scene, but Bates had been taken care of and was safely behind the bars of the jail. Byrd had been shot in the lower part of the body near the groin. The wounds were pronounced fatal. Excitement was at its highest pitch, and I could see an undercurrent of will and determination that meant business to the murderer if Byrd died. He lived a day or two, and as soon as his death became known the town was full of men, and it seemed that those living at a distance had got there as if by magic, they made their appearance in such a short time. The crowd assembled at Keach's store. I was sent for and requested to go to the jail and interview the murderer. I did so. The man denied that anyone was accessory to the crime, but that he had killed the man of his own free will, and had meditated the deed. We returned to the place of the gathering and reported what the doomed man had said. They had a long rope, with a running noose, sledge hammers, picks and crowbars. Keach spoke and said: "Boys, you know your duty." They needed nothing further. They followed Keach to the jail. They commenced at the upper door. I had superintended the building of the jail and knew something of its construction, and I told them if they were determined to go into the jail they had best enter by the lower door, at which they flew beating with their sledges and hammers, all to no avail. They grabbed up a large square piece of timber and used it as a battering ram, but the door stood the test. I told them the best way, and the way of the least damage, was by removing the brick at each side of the door frame, which they did, and soon the door, frame and all was lifted out. The sheriff had placed inside one long, heavy, three-inch plank, secured the other end to the floor and was standing on it. The board came forward with a crash when the door was removed, and some of the determined men barely escaped being caught beneath it. The sheriff was armed, but he did not long remain so. The cell that contained the murderer was broken into and he was dragged out badly frightened. Some one cried out to give him a fair trial, whereupon I was appointed judge. I declined having anything to say in the matter, as he had acknowledged the crime, and the mob knew it. The man whispered to someone that he wanted to see old Mr. Meeker. A man was sent out on the road to watch for any soldiers that might come, and another dispatched for Mr. Meeker, who refused to come. In the meantime the rope had been placed about the man's neck, and about 100 men now lay hold of it and he was led to a barn, from which protruded the end of a pole. Over this the rope was thrown, and under it the man was placed, nearer dead than alive. He whispered to someone, for he could not speak audibly, that he wanted to see me. I went down to him and took down his requests in a book, and, as I was soon afterward made probate judge, I saw all of them carried out. When he had finished speaking I said to the crowd that he had nothing more to say, and in a moment more his body was swinging in the air. He showed no signs of life nor feeling after being lifted from the ground, and he was let down a corpse.

No one was ever punished for any part they took in this affair.

About a year after this event a reign of terror prevailed in the neighborhood of Muck valley. A man by the name of Gibson jumped a donation land claim belonging to Charles Wrens. The claimjumper was assisted in his dastardly work by a man named McDonald and some others who were in the same business. One day Wrens was on his way to Steilacoom when he was waylaid by three of the gang and was taken into the woods, tied to a tree and whipped well nigh to death, where he was left. This occurred about a half mile east of American lake. Wrens succeeded in getting away from the tree, but was so badly frightened that he was afraid to make himself known, and as soon as he was able he left for Victoria, where he was afterward joined by his family.

The other citizens were not so easily scared, and they combined and paid off the outlaws.

It became known that McDonald and Gibson were coming to town one day, and they in turn were ambushed near American lake by a crowd of the outraged neighbors. As the men were riding past bullets came flying past them. Gibson was shot two or three times, but not fatally. McDonald escaped serious injury. The horses were both wounded, but not seriously. Gibson stopped at the garrison to have his wounds dressed. McDonald came on into Steilacoom, riding through the town on a run to the stable, and sent a wagon after Gibson. He went out into the street and in a loud and excited manner told what happened. He came to the store and wanted a hat, having lost his in the retreat, and I gave him one, and told him he had best keep a little quiet, or seek a safe hiding place, and, above all things, to be careful of what he said. I went up to my home, acquainted my people with what had happened, and told them to give themselves no trouble on my account, and that I would come back safe. Armed men were to be seen coming in on the three roads, and before I got back down town I heard loud talk and guns were being fired. McDonald had said something that displeased the men, and one of them had called out "Kill the _____ _____."
McDonald sprung into Westbrook's saloon, running for the back door. Several shots were fired after him, but none of them struck him. Finally a charge of buckshoot from the back door of the saloon struck him in the side of the neck and he fell, and when I reached him he was dying, and in a manner he had always held he would die — with his boots on.

When the wagon returned from the garrison with Gibson the armed men took possession of it and started it up the hill again. When Gibson, who was lying in the bottom of the wagon, saw that he was being taken into the woods he sprung up and grabbed a pistol from the belt of one of the men in the seat in front of him, and began shooting at the men walking by the side of the wagon. He wounded two of them slightly, but bullets soon quieted him, and he was put out of the wagon by the side of the road and left there.

Some of the men who had a part in this affair were put to a little expense, but none of them were punished.

These proceedings in Pierce county and similar ones in King county no doubt had a salutary effect all over the territory.

Railroads and money now began coming to this country, and prosperity and increased population followed, and the pioneer was again introduced to civilization. He also met with the ridicule of some, who, with few brains and less sense, with great pomp on their part, try to make light of the "mossbacks," never stopping to think that it was the pioneer that made the cradle in which he is now being rocked, and that they had placed in the ashes the chestnuts they are now scratching out, and of which the pioneers are helping to dispose.

The incidents that might be narrated concerning the founding of this, the grandest and richest state in the Union, would make an interesting book instead of a newspaper article. I begun this summary of some of the incidents of my own life in response to a call from the *Ledger* and at the earnest requests of many friends. Many foreign incidents have necessarily drawn in the narration, and the story is more than double the length I meant it to have been, and I expect a good deal longer than the law really allows me. When we, who have passed through the hardships and privations of pioneer life begin to allow our minds to drift back over the years, the incidents all come to our view so plainly that it is with reluctance that we close our story.

For further details of matters of interest pertaining to this country, I would respectfully refer the reader to Hon. Elwood Evans, the Josephus of the northwest, to whom I listened a short time ago deliver in a masterly manner an address at Ocosta-by-the Sea. While at Grays harbor I visited Westport, on Peterson's point, by the ocean beach, and, in company with Hon. Edward Huggins, visited the old fort built by Captain Malonia of the regular army, in the year 1855, and which was garrisoned by volunteers under Lieutenant E.T. Jester, the Steilacoom jeweler. When this fort was built, thirty-seven years ago, the space intervening between it and the sea was a prairie. It is now covered by a dense growth of Norway pine and fir trees about a foot in diameter.

General A.V. Kautz

In a talk before the Alpine Club
the General tells about his first ascent of
Mount "Tac-Rainier" in 1857.

April 7, 1893

The assembly room of the Annie Wright seminary was crowded last night. The cause of this exceptionally large attendance was the announcement that at the meeting General A.V. Kautz, John Longmire and P.B. Van Trump would tell of their experiences in climbing Mount Tacoma. The entertainment for the evening was provided by the Alpine club branch of the academy. Judge Allyn occupied the chair. Secretary M.S. Hill read a number of communications from all over the country, received in reply to the sending of copies of Judge Wickersham's paper on the history of the name Mount Tacoma. All of the replies expressed a hope that the old Indian name may be preserved and the meaningless one imposed upon it by Captain Vancouver done away with. Among the senders of these letters were the following: The Albany institute, the Kansas State Agricultural college, both scientific and chemical departments, the Society of Natural History of Cincinnati, the Archaeologist of Allentown, Pa., the United Historical society of Utica, N.Y., the Franklin institute of Philadelphia, the American Philosophical society of Philadelphia, the Oneida Historical society of Utica, N.Y., Hon. W.H. Dall of the Smithsonian institute, the Scientific association of Meriden, Conn., the State library of Albany, N.Y., and the

Peoria Scientific association of Illinois.

Judge Wickersham read a letter from Colonel John Puget of the British army, the only living lineal descendent of Captain Puget, the discoverer of Puget Sound. It expressed a warm hope that the original name of the mountain might be retained.

The speakers of the evening were then introduced, General A.V. Kautz coming first. In his introductory remarks the general said of his paper that it was written a great many years ago for a magazine article. He had only received it the evening before from Washington, and it stood in need of several changes. He was at the time it was written a lieutenant at Fort Steilacoom, of which the proper Indian pronunciation was, he said, "Steelacoom," with a strong accent on the first syllable. The article was intended for persons who had never seen and probably never heard of the mountain. This project of climbing the mountain, which lay full in front of the camp, was the butt of all the wit of the officers of the fort, and "when Kautz goes up the mountain" became a by-word. The summer of 1857 seemed a propitious time for making the ascent. His brother officers, who had been lavish in offers to accompany him on his trip, began to draw out as the time for the undertaking approached. Finally he was about to make the attempt without any companion save the common soldiers and an Indian guide, but Dr. Craig came down from Bellingham bay on a visit at the time and resolved to go with Lieutenant Kautz. That summer Chief Leschi was in the guard house at the fort, awaiting execution for his share in the Indian war. Lieutenant Kautz had been urgent in trying to have him set free, so that the old chieftain, who at first rather expected to go as the guide of the party, gave the lieutenant all the information that he could as to the mountain, and advised his taking as a guide the Indian "Wapowatty."

At noon on July 8, 1857, the eight soldiers who were to participate were sent forward as the first division of the expedition with orders to stay at Wren's prairie, while the two others rode by way of Nisqually to pick up Wapowatty, the guide. The first night or two after, they came to the Nisqually Forks, where they found two salmon fishermen. These reported the overpowering of a band of fugitive Indians by a company of the Washington volunteers, who slaughtered them regardless of age and sex. The Mashel river, which he had seen fifteen months previous as a roaring torrent, was a sluggish rivulet of clear spring water. After leaving two of the soldiers with the horses in a camp the rest started on through the dark forest and dense underbrush, making ten miles a day for three days.

On the morning of July 15th they got above the cloud-line and could see the summits of Mounts Hood, Adams, St. Helens, Baker, etc., like icebergs in an ocean. Finally they got upon the saddle of the mountain—General Kautz and a German soldier named Drag. The hour was late, and remaining up there was out of the question without blankets or rations. The two then returned to the camp. Rations were running so low that a return to the summit was impossible next day and the homeward march was begun. In three hours ground was traversed that took ten to toil up. This was the eighth day out. The return trip was made without especial incident save intense suffering from lack of water. The men, when they reached the foot again, were unrecognizable from their sufferings.

Mr. Van Trump said: "I am much pleased to meet General Kautz here this evening, to whom belongs the honor of demonstrating that the mountain could be climbed.

"To others fell the honor of demonstrating that a man could stand on the very summit. To these, it was given to discover a system of glaciers equal, if not superior to those in Switzerland, and that there is a crater there in which it is possible for a man to remain all night." Mr. Van Trump then read from a manuscript. In the course of it he said: "The agitation in favor of the name Mount Tacoma ought to be kept up until the name "Rainier" is heard no more. As a landmark the grand old mountain was certainly named by the Indians. There are three main routes up the mountain, the south side, northeast side and west side. The Paradise route has two divisions, one of which General Kautz took." The speaker then hastily reviewed his many ascents of the mountain.

Mr. Longmire said that he had ascended the mountain but once, but that he probably knew more of the park lately laid off by the government than anyone else. He had been all round the mountain, except on the north. His main object in coming had been to ask the co-operation of the academy to get the remaining fourteen miles of road put through to Paradise valley, so that a buggy might get up there. Mr. Longmire then demonstrated that all of the ascents of the mountain would have to have Tacoma as their starting point, by detailing the distances. The approach from Seattle to Paradise park is 102 miles and from Tacoma sixty-three miles by road.

The following resolutions were then adopted, after which the academy adjourned, leaving the rest of the programme and the election of officers till the next regular meeting:

Whereas, It is expected that between 50,000 and 100,000 tourists will visit Tacoma this year, and it is believed that if proper arrangements were made a large number of them would visit the glaciers, mountain meadows, and even the snowy summit of Mount Tacoma; and, whereas, a county road is now completed to within nine miles of Longmire's springs, on the Nisqually, and dedicated to the springs; now, it is

Resolved, By the Tacoma Academy of Science and the Washington Alpine club jointly, that it is to the best interest of Pierce county that the road be at once completed to Longmire's springs, and the county commissioners are respectfully requested to complete it.

Resolved further, That a copy of this resolution be sent by the secretary to the board of county commissioners, to the chamber of commerce and to the Commercial club, and that they be and they are hereby requested to lend their aid and assistance to the better development of Mount Tacoma park before the summer visitors reach Puget Sound.

Hugh Crockett

*Hugh Crockett came over the plains with
the family of Colonel Ebey in 1851. He relates
the story of the beheading of the Colonel by the
Northern Indians and the causes that led
to this terrible deed.*

August 19, 1892

Having been asked many times to write an account of my trip across the continent and life on the frontier, I have reluctantly concluded to do so. Such a story should be prefaced by some of the reasons given that led to the trip. I will therefore say my oldest brother, Samuel B. Crockett, left home in 1844 and came across the plains in General Gilliam's company, that being the second emigration train that came to the Pacific coast. He, of course, wrote to my father what a nice climate was here and how healthy it was, etc.; and even before the discovery of gold in California we all wanted to come to Puget Sound. Then, after that great event, such glowing accounts came to us that my father and mother determined to come to this country.

He had three sons single and one daughter, and one son married. We got ready in the spring of 1851. Besides ourselves, our company consisted of James Cochran; and his son R.B. Cochran, afterward, for many years, a member of the Oregon state senate; the families of Colonel I.N. Ebey and Duley Ruddell. We all met by appointment at Centerville, Appanoose county, Iowa, about the 1st of April. From there we made our way to Council Bluffs, without anything worthy of mention occurring. Here several things delayed us. Mr. Ruddell had a little son that had a white swelling in one of his legs. He had been treated by a doctor by the name of Roberts, before starting, who had informed Mr. Ruddell that it would be necessary to amputate the limb, and, as the doctor was himself coming to Salt Lake, he met us here at Council Bluffs. We camped in the bottom, opposite where Omaha now stands.

In a few days the doctor came. When he got all ready to commence the operation, two strong men carried the little couch out of the tent. The poor little sick child didn't look like he was hardly worth saving. The old doctor took a common butcher knife and carpenter's saw and cut the boy's leg off. No one thought he would survive. But he lived through the operation and the succeeding trials of life, and the last time I saw him his weight was 200 pounds. He lives in Thurston county, and is doing well. His name is Steven Ruddell.

After this delay and the arrival of a steamboat with flour, about the 15th of May, all being ready, we crossed the Missouri river at the old trading point about seven miles below Omaha. The second or third day we came to a stream called the Papao, which was swollen so by recent rains that we could not cross it. While waiting and wondering what to do we were overtaken by another company, which consisted of three families and a married son or two. Their names were Richison. They had water-proof wagon boxes, made to use like boats. They offered to join us with the use of their wagon boxes to ferry across the streams. The offer was promptly taken and about two days was consumed in crossing. Everything had to be taken out of the wagons and carried over on these novel boats; then the wagons in the same way. The last night we spent here the Omaha Indians run off and killed some of our best work oxen. There was a large village of them near by, but redress was out of the question. We simply had to stand it.

The next obstacle we met was the Elkhorn river. The road that we were on led us to what was called the lower ferry. We found it impossible to cross here on account of the streams being out of their banks. They seemed to be three or four miles wide. After remaining here a few days we traveled up the river about twenty miles, where a half-breed, by the name of Fauton Nell kept a ferry, but there were so many wagons there ahead of us that we traveled about three miles farther up, where we found a place where the stream was in its banks. Here we had to resort to the wagon box boat again. It was rather a perilous undertaking, but at it we went. A strong man and a good swimmer swam across with a line in his teeth; then two wagon boxes were lashed together, the wagons unloaded and the tongue triced up with a rope and run on the boats and run across. It took one whole day to cross everything and load up again. We now found ourselves thirty or forty miles from the road and to find our way back to it was no small job, that part of Nebraska being so broken that it made it very difficult to travel without running into pockets. This we avoided by sending four or five men ahead four or five miles apart with flags to signal the train. One color said, "Come on," while another said, "Stop."

We had many streams to cross before we reached the road. Shell creek was very difficult to cross. It will be remembered that Nebraska is a treeless country, but we found a place where there was a bunch of willows on each side of this creek. These willows were felled across the stream from each side and covered with sod so that the train crossed over in safety. At last, after several days' travel, we reached the road again, where it crossed Beaver river, and here we met an unfortunate company that had had their cattle stampeded the night before by the Pawnee Indians. As we could not help them we proceeded on our journey. We learned afterward that they never recovered their cattle, and had to return to Council Bluffs to get teams to haul their wagons back, and wait until the next season.

The next stream we came to was the Loop fork. Some Mormons had kept a ferry here, but when we came they had abandoned it. We had to block our wagon-beds up about a foot. This was done by getting willow sticks and sawing them into foot lengths and lashing them to stakes under the bed. Now we had good weather and good roads so we could make good time. We had now lost about a month's time by high water.

Nothing of interest transpired until we reached Chimney rock. Here two births occurred within an hour or so of each other, and, strange to say, did not detain the train even for an hour. It was near camping time. Next morning the old doctor and the ladies decided that there would be no danger in moving, so we yoked up and started on our journey. The babies were both boys, "Bound for Oregon," where they are now honored citizens, 41 years old.

This route used to be the great buffalo range. Our boys killed all we could use. But now, as everybody knows, the buffaloes are things of the past.

When we reached old Fort Hall we learned that the Indians had given the emigrants ahead of us a good deal of trouble, which we found to be correct. About seventy-five or 100 miles below Fort Hall one evening they attacked us, and caused us to move camp, as we were in a place where they had the advantage of us. We had camped in the bottom, near Snake river, within gun-shot of the bluff, so we decided to move on up the bluff to the level plain. Next morning they came on us with increased numbers, and harrassed us for an hour or so, but finally they withdrew from the struggle, and we were glad of it. A few days after this we came to where the same tribe had done some of their dirty work. There was a train that had a man by the name of Clark in it. Mr. Clark was a well-to-do man, and was bringing thirty good mares with him. As feed was scarce where they camped one evening, Mr. Clark's son and his mother and sister started the drove on before the train was ready to start, in order that they might find some grass for them to eat. Mrs. Clark and her daughter rode in a buggy or carriage, while the young man drove the mares. After traveling a few miles they came to a grassy place, where they concluded to wait until the train came up. The young man went down to the river to angle for fish, and had only been gone a few minutes when the Indians came upon them and shot Mrs. Clark dead and wounded the girl, and after outraging her person in a horrible manner left her for dead. The young man, hearing the guns, rushed up to the bank to be shot like a dog. Then they ran off with all the mares, which were worth a large sum of money at that time. It is not hard to conjecture what a horrid sight met the eyes of the party in the train when they came up. The young woman was picked up and cared for and brought to Oregon, where she recovered from her injuries. Mrs. Clark and her son were buried where they were killed. After the train had moved on the Indians returned and disturbed the graves. Our people refilled them again. It was known at the time that the Indians killed, all together that season, about thirty people.

At a point about eighty miles east of old Fort Boise we were met by Colonel I.N. Ebey, who had come out in 1846, and whose family was accompanying us. It was indeed a happy meeting. He was an old friend of our family. My oldest brother, who had come in 1844, started with him, but stopped on the Umatilla, and did not meet us until we were in the Blue mountains. Here there was another happy meeting, as we had not seen him for seven years.

Nothing of interest occurred now until we reached The Dalles. From here there was no road and the rest of the way had to be made by water. This was accomplished by Mr. Ruddell, Colonel Ebey, my father and brother joining together in the purchase of a boat. It was a Hudson Bay company batteau. This one was big enough to hold five wagons taken to pieces, then all the baggage piled on them and the families on top. This was all right until we came to the Cascade falls. Here everything had to be taken out of the boat, the wagons put together and hauled around, and the boat let down over the falls with ropes. My brother was quite an expert at this business, as he had learned it in 1844. At The Dalles our crew was divided, Mr. Ruddell, Colonel Ebey and my two oldest brothers composing the crew that went with the boat; my two youngest brothers, Mrs. Ebey's brother, a young man by the name of Gritheay, who drove team for Mr. Ruddell and myself drove the horses and oxen down the trail near where the railroad runs now. The Columbia river trail was a rough and romantic sight then, and it is yet. A little instance happened to me there that is worthy of mention. One morning we failed to find one of our animals, a valuable mare. I told the boys that if they would start the drove I would stay in the neighborhood and, if possible find the mare. I looked all day without success. I was tired, discouraged and hungry, and quite late in the evening I heard a rooster crowing. With delight I started in the direction, climbing over logs and brush and at last came out upon a solitary Indian hut. A young Indian stood near by preparing a salmon for his evening meal. I said good evening to him. He nodded and grinned. I told him in English what was the matter, he grinned and said: "Wake cumtux, Boston wawa." I told him in English again that I wasn't from Boston, but I wanted him to tell me where that mare was. He grinned and repeated that "Wake cumtux, Boston wawa." Well, well, I said, you are a fraud, and as the sun was now fast sinking, I left him, this time by a trail that led me out to the main one. I did not go far before I saw smoke from a camp fire. I was not long in reaching it. One man alone had milked a cow and held some of the milk and thickened it by stirring in a little flour. He invited me to join him in the repast, which I gladly did. The man's name was Sam Maples, now an old and honored citizen of King county. I have not forgotten Sam Maples, although forty-one years have come and gone. It was now night and I slept under a tree; as I did not overtake my comrades with the lost mare, they stopped the drove to wait for me. Next day more Indians were met, and we asked about the mare, but none of them could tell anything about her until a pistol, single-barrel and almost worthless, was shown to them, and they were told that if they would bring her in that they should have the pistol. They went off and were only gone about an hour when they returned with the mare.

Our party that had gone down in the boat had unloaded and came back, about fifteen miles above the Cascades, and helped us to swim the cattle and horses over the Columbia. In due course of time the portage was made and the boat reloaded. The boat party and land party started for the mouth of the Cowlitz river, which we all reached in good time. Here Mr. Ruddell concluded to stop for the winter. Here, also, Urban E. Hicks, Mr. Ruddell's stepson, and Zephaniah Guthrey, stopped. Mr. Guthrey went to work for an old farmer by the name of Burbez, who loaded a schooner with produce, potatoes mostly, and started to San Francisco. Mr. Guthrey went with him. The schooner went out of the Columbia and was never heard of afterward.

Here we had to leave the horses and cattle and help to take the boat up the Cowlitz river, sometimes poling and sometimes pulling with a line or horse. About a week was spent in this way, when the landing was reached. We then returned for the horses and cattle, which we found all right, and drove them all up the trail. The party was all together once more and ready to proceed on the journey. The first day we came out as far as J.K. Jackson's. We found the string at his door latch on the outside, and made use of it. My father and mother slept under a roof after having slept in the open air for seven months. Mr. Jackson was well known as a generous and free-hearted man. Afterward he made an honored and efficient member of the first territorial legislature.

Nothing now of special interest occurred until we reached our destination, which was on the 5th day of November. Colonel M.T. Simmons came out and met our party, and being an old friend of my brothers, took us to his father-in-law's house, where we were kindly received, and where we rested a while from our long journey.

The next night after leaving Mr. Jackson's, a yoke of oxen that Colonel Ebey had bought at Cowlitz, strayed away and the next morning could not be found. It fell to my lot to go and search for them while the party moved on. I met two Indians and told them in English what was the matter with me. They shook their heads and said: "Wake cumtux Boston wawa." I knew now what that meant (a friend had told me), but by signs I made them understand. As they were on horseback they soon brought me the lost oxen. I got on now all right until I came to the Skookumchuck. The road crosses this stream close to where it joins the Chehalis river. The Chehalis at this point is a sluggish stream, while the Skookumchuck runs like an arrow and shoots into the Chehalis and forms a great whirlpool, into which it is said no man has ever been known to go and get out alive. When my oxen were about half way across the stream they took fright at some Indians on the opposite bank and started down the stream and came near to the whirlpool. I, too, went down to head them off and saved myself from going in by catching to a hanging willow. When I next looked across an old Indian had thrown his blanket and shirt to go in to save me. There was a large number of them living here, who now came around me jabbering in their own tongue. One old woman I understood by her nod and gestures to be congratulating me upon my fortunate escape. As I could not thank her in words, I did so in my heart, and now since forty-one rainy winters have come and gone, I do so still. That night I spent at the house of old Mr. Ford, who gave me plenty to eat and a place to sleep, and next morning overtook my company just as they were breaking camp.

Governor Stevens had a nephew drowned in the Skookumchuck or Chehalis whirlpool. He undertook to ford it where the Skookumchuck was swollen, and was washed down and drowned. His body was recovered several weeks afterward in some drift. The unfortunate man was beloved and respected by all that knew him.

Colonel I.N. Ebey had located a claim on Whidby island the year before, and through his advice we all went there and located our donation claims. The colonel and ourselves joined together and built a large scow to move in. At this time there was no steamer on Puget Sound. My brother and myself went down in the winter and built some log cabins. Colonel Ebey went with us on the first trip. Mrs. Ebey was the second white woman on the island, Mrs. William Wallace having settled at Crescent harbor in August the year before. Several weeks were then spent in building cabins, after completing which my two eldest brothers and myself started to return to Olympia for the rest of the family, and we had a hard time of it, as the south winds were blowing, which made it very difficult to travel against with that kind of a vessel. At last we reached a point about fifteen miles below Olympia. It was blowing hard at the time, so we tied up for the night. In the night our craft got adrift, and we were blown across the Sound, I think in a place called Skookum bay. In the morning we found our scow was left high and dry by the tide, and we went aobut 400 yards away to cook breakfast. While away an old raven went in our boat and devoured the last piece of salt pork we had, leaving us nothing but a few potatoes. It was not long before we got even with the raven. My brother had some strychnine in his chest and he fixed up a dose for him, and we had the satisfaction of seeing him turn up his toes.

As we were now out of provisions my brother concluded to take our canoe and proceed to Olympia for a fresh supply. George Allen and myself were left with the scow. We had no firearms of any kind. Mr. Allen went down to the beach and filled his pockets with stones, and said he would go hunting. He was not gone long before he returned with a fine grouse which I dressed and stewed, so we had a good feast from it. The next day my brother returned with a fresh supply of eatables and we made another start for Olympia, which place we reached without more trouble, and in due time returned to the island without any incident worth mention. It was very lonely on the island at first. We were 100 miles from a postoffice. My brother and myself spent the winter of 1852 on Penn's cove hewing square timber for the San Francisco market. About three months passed at one time without any boat or sail coming into our harbor. Late in February, one night, one of our neighbors, John Bartlett, came to our camp. He had been to Port Townsend. We asked him for the news — who was elected president? He told us, "Franklin Pierce." At this time there were only three counties north of the Columbia river. They were Clark, Lewis and Thurston.

In the spring of 1852 I went to Olympia to work for wages. I spent most of the summer in the neighborhood. That summer the Fourth of July was celebrated in Olympia for the first time. Hon. D.K. Bigelow delivered the oration, and Quincy A. Brooks read the Declaration of Independence. Governor Tanner was there from Salem, and Mr. Dryer, the proprietor and editor of the *Oregonian*, responded to a toast, "The Press." The next celebration that I attended was on Whidby's island, in a shady grove on Ebey prairie, in the good old-fashioned way. This was, if I remember right, in 1854.

In the winter of 1852 Colonel Ebey represented Thurston county in the Oregon Legislature, and he had Pierce, King, Island and Jefferson set off. I do not know much about the organization of any of them but Island.

John Alexander, John Crockett and Samuel D. Howe were appointed the first county commissioners, and Dr. R.H. Lousdal the first auditor, and myself the first sheriff. Colonel Ebey was present and assisted in the organization. We met at the head of Penn's Cove, in a little cabin, the residence of the auditor, Dr. Lousdal. The officers are all dead but the auditor and myself. It is but justice to say that Colonel Ebey secured the passage of a memorial to congress, asking a division of the territory. He was a faithful and efficient worker for the new country and met a tragic death at the hands of the northern Indians of British Columbia, who, about 1856, began cruising Puget Sound to barter and trade with the American settlers. They would come in large numbers in their large canoes, some of which were as much as 50 feet long and 7 feet beam, carrying as many as 100 men. They would go up to the head of the Sound and stay as long as it suited them, and then come down a distance and make another stop, and so on, until they were ready to go home, and then they would commit their depredations upon settlers near the shore. Some time early in the spring of 1857 there was a canoe stopped for awhile at what is known as Brown's point, just below Olympia. While they were there, there was a young man got into a dispute with one of them, and for some frivolous thing he shot and killed one of the Indians.

Later in the season there was another canoe went up the Sound and stopped somewhere for awhile. Returning, they stopped at Port Gamble. Some complaint was made against them, and the old steamer *John Hancock* being on the Sound at the time, the captain proceeded to Port Gamble to try to induce them to go home. But they were very impudent, and said they would go when it suited them to do so, and told the captain they were ready to fight him. The captain tried to get them to go, but failed, and then fired shot and shell into them, killing some and breaking up their canoes. He then took them all prisoners and took them to Victoria and wanted Sir James Douglas, governor of Vancouver island, to take charge of them, but Sir James claimed to have no jurisdiction over them, saying they lived in the Russian possessions (now Alaska), so all that our captain could do was to purchase another canoe for them and take them out a few miles and start them on their way home.

People who have studied the Indian character know that they never forget or forgive a real or supposed injury. They always retalitate, blood for blood, the unsuspecting and innocent being the sufferers. This time it fell upon Colonel I.N. Ebey. On the night of August 12th they landed a short distance from his house and stayed there all that day. The next day some of them went up to the field where he was at work and pretended that there was something wrong with their canoe, and tried to get him to go down to the beach and help them fix it, but he paid little or no attention to this.

His house had three bedrooms in it. They were occupied the night in question by Ebey's wife and little daughter, Mr. Ebey and two sons, Eason and Ellison, and George Corliss and wife. They had a very fierce dog which gave warning that something was around more than usual. Mr. Ebey went out at first but saw nothing and returned and went to bed again. It wasn't long till he was aroused the second time and went out again. This time two shots were fired at him, the second one taking effect. The ball struck him under the left arm, and two buckshot, one on each side of the ball, pierced his heart. While the Indians were busy beheading the dead colonel the other inmates of the house made their escape through a window. Mr. Corliss assisted his wife out first. There was a picket fence around the place and Mrs. Corliss in her excitement ran to it, setting her foot on a post, and leaped over it. Mr. Corliss assisted all the others out, he being the last to leave the house, all escaping in their nightclothes. Mrs. Corliss ran to the nearest neighbor's and gave the alarm, but before the neighborhood could be aroused the Indians had made good their escape, taking Colonel Ebey's head with them as a trophy.

I have always been under the impression that it was the Port Gamble affair that caused the attack on Colonel Ebey, but, in a recent conversation with Mr. Huggins, he assured me that it was the killing of the Indian at Brown's point, to which I have referred above, that brought on the attack. Mr. Huggins' word may be relied upon, for his long residence among the natives has enabled him to get at the real truth, when it was impossible to learn it in any way except by long residence and contact with them.

Colonel Ebey had living, at the time of his death, besides his own family, his old father and mother, one brother, two sisters and one niece, Mrs. A.N. Enos. They are all now dead but one son, Eason, and Mrs. Enos, who lives in San Francisco. Eason lives on the Nooksack river. Mr. Corliss and wife moved to California, where they were keeping a stock ranch, and one night some "greasers" (halfbreed Indian and Spanish), attacked them and brutally murdered them. Such is fate!

This tragedy threw a gloom over the entire settlement, and caused us to build stockades and blockhouses, many of which still stand. My brother and myself used to reproach ourselves somewhat for bringing our father and mother out to such an exposed country.

Captain Todd of the Hudson Bay company's steamer *Beaver* recovered Colonel Ebey's scalp in one of the trips they made, giving for it two bales of blankets. His niece, Mrs. A.N. Enos, told me only a few weeks ago that she has it at her house in San Francisco. I helped to lay his headless body in the coffin and to lower the coffin into the grave. Colonel Ebey filled many places of public trust. Before Thurston county was organized he was one of the county commissioners of Lewis county, and went from his place on Whidby island to the Cowlitz landing to serve on the board. John R. Jackson, spoken of above, and old Mr. Catlin, who lived at Monticello, with Mr. Ebey, composed the board. The distance he traveled was 180 miles.

This is not the only sad story that can be told of the northern Indians. Some time in the summer of the same year a schooner called the *Wild Pigeon*, about fifteen tons, sailed from Steilacoom wi.h five or six people on board for Port Townsend. I only remember one man, a German by the name of Schroder. She reached a point a short distance below the head of Vashons island early in the morning, where one of those large northern pirates overtook her; as it was only blowing a light breeze at the time, only one man was on deck steering. The Indians shot him and all the others as fast as they showed their heads above deck. When they had killed all the crew and passengers they plundered and burned the vessel, and in a few hours there was not a vestige left of the little craft.

A smaller schooner, I have forgotten the name, sailed from Utsalady. The captain and owner's name was McEwin. He was an old Hudson Bay company's servant. He had one man in his boat besides a man and his wife, as passengers. The same Indians met them near Rooky Point just south of Port Blakeley, and after killing all the people on board, set fire to the boat and burned her also.

Thus in a few hours eight or nine people lost their lives by these blood-thirsty Indians.

In Victoria, later, some local case was being tried and an old Indian was on the stand as a witness. The usual oath was administered to him, that is he was to tell the whole truth and nothing but the truth. The honest old "son of the forest" thought he was now obligated to tell about all the crimes that had ever come to his knowledge, and the foregoing is the story he told. He said he was in the canoe, but did not have anything to do with the work, as he was a slave.

It might interest some people to know how communication was had east before the Pacific Mail Steamship company's lines went into operation. As I have said above, my brother, S.B. Crockett, came across the plains in 1844. He arrived at Vancouver, on the Columbia, the 15th of October, and wrote a letter to my father in Missouri. He sent it by a Hudson Bay company's vessel, bound to the Sandwich islands. From there it went by a home-bound whaler to Providence, R.I. The letter reached its destination in the following June, eight months after it was written. Sometimes there would be a few men go back with pack mules, but only once a year.

I would like to say something about Indian troubles and the Indian war of

1855-56, but most of the events that happened then have passed into history. It is known that many of our best men lost their lives in that struggle. I will only relate one sad story. There was a fine young officer, a lieutenant of infantry, at the post where the asylum now stands. He went out with his command on White river, and one evening stopped in a deserted cabin and was shot through a crack in the wall. This occurred at a place that now bears his name — Slaughter.

We are sometimes asked if the Indians did not give us trouble before the war. In 1853 an Indian killed an old man by the name of Church. His body was discovered several weeks afterward. I was one of seven persons that held the inquest over it, but they are now all dead but Dr. R.H. Lansdale and myself. The Indian was caught, tried and hanged.

The pioneers of this grand state often have their feelings brought to arms by the sneering remark of new comers, who term us "mossbacks." They tell us how things should be done, and how they are done "back east." Sometimes I feel like telling them to go "back east" and be blessed. The pioneers that laid the foundation for the greatest state in the Union may not just suit the fancy of a "down-easter," but beneath the perhaps rough, uncouth clothing, there beats as true, kind and loyal a heart as has ever been imported on a palace car.

When the Union Pacific and Central Pacific railroads were completed, the pioneers of the state of California were given free transportation across the continent. Not so in our own state, which, in a few years, will abound as richly in its own products as does California. The government gave the railroad the franchise from out of the people's land, and the pioneers made it possible for the road to be built. Would it be any more than justice if the president of the Northern Pacific would pass the pioneers of Washington to Chicago during the Columbian exposition? Of course if he don't want to, as a small boy of today would say, he don't have to.

These scattered and disjointed statements have been jotted down entirely from memory, as I never kept a memorandum. If I have erred it is the fault of my memory, and I ask you, readers, to overlook the same.

Luzena Wallace

The widow of Ex-Governor and Delegate of Idaho Territory William Wallace provides an interesting glimpse of social life on Puget Sound in the 1850's. Mrs. Wallace claims she was responsible for the naming of Idaho Territory.

Steilacoom, Washington — September 23, 1892

Several of my young friends have insisted that I should contribute to the folio of "old settlers' stories" now being published in the *Ledger* for Sunday reading. I yielded when threatened with an interviewer to take notes of my narrative of disjointed incidents, and now recall some reminiscences of early life upon Puget Sound, illustrating how we got here a generation ago, who were the people, who were "old settlers," and some of their characteristics.

Myself a native of North Carolina, a resident of Illinois during much of my youth, an immigrant of Iowa, where I became wife and mother, an old settler of Washington territory, and one of the very earliest of the women who contributed by their presence to make American homes in the territory (now state) of Idaho. In all these changes no claim of heroism can be urged, nor can I ask regard "for the dangers I have passed." It is somewhat amusing to have noticed "old settlers" who must have been very young at the time they were making trips and observing incidents which now at an advanced age they recount with apparent pride and in great detail, as the recall incidents of "pioneer life," claiming consideration for "hair-breadth escapes" and hardships endured, many of which at the time disturbed not the tenor of life and by the parties themselves were treated as picnic pleasures. But as I did not come the 'plains across," those sisters will say I know nothing about what they endured, and I had an easy time getting here compared with their journey. I can answer, with the advantage on my side, I had rather ride in a dead-axe wagon, as I often did travel in early days in Washington territory, than to be sea sick an hour, either in steamer or sailing vessel, much less for a voyage of several days or weeks. But, enough of this. I followed my husband here at an early day, to the home he had prepared, when the country was a wilderness and but sparsely populated, whilst I was yet a young woman. And on my voyage hither I was accompanied by my only son, then 10 years of age. We came from New York by the Panama route, and from San Francisco in the good old brig Franklin Adams, Captain Collins, bound for Steilacoom, where my husband then resided. I have since lived in Washington city and Idaho, have made long visits to my early homes in Illinois and Iowa, yet I love no spot on earth like my little home on Puget Sound.

Pardon will be extended for referring with pride to the fact that I was born in Guilford county, North Carolina, on the identical spot where in revolutionary days the hard contested struggle occurred known in history as the battle of "Guilford Courthouse." From the old "North State" our family went to Illinois, I being in my ninth year. After a few years we took our march farther west to Iowa, making our residence at Mount Pleasant. At that place, upon the 3d day of February, 1839, I was married to William H. Wallace, who will be remembered by the old settlers as governor of Washington and first governor of Idaho, and as representing each of those territories in congress.

For many years, in fact in the early forties, when Oregon was attracting great attention in the then northwestern states, it was the constant desire of my husband to go to Oregon. Again in 1849 when the discovery of gold in California invited so many to the Pacific slope, he resolved on going to

-252-

Puget Sound, a desire increased by the belief that in my then poor health I would be benefitted. About that time he was appointed receiver of the United States land office at Fairfield, Ia., by President Zachary Taylor. During his term of office, which expired in 1853, on the election of President Franklin Pierce, he abandoned those notions for the time being, but after his term had expired, again he wished to "go west," and desired me to accompany him. I was extremely loath to take so long a journey, and all my family were unwilling, but I consented that he should come, and if he was satisfied, agreed that I would accompany him, if he would return for me. On the 1st of July, 1853, he started for Olympia, and upon his arrival there he thought it was the very place. When the tide came in during the evening, overflowing the lower part of the little town, rendering it necessary for the people to cross the street in canoes or boats, he concluded it was no place for him and he went on to Steilacoom, where he bought an interest in the townsite and determined to remain. He wrote requesting me to come, suggesting that my brother should go with me to New York, see me aboard the steamer for San Francisco, at which place he would see me on my arrival. Colonel Wallace urged my coming on the ground that the change of climate would probably restore my then declining health. Both father and mother strenuously objected to my undertaking the long journey, and at the prospect of a final separation from them. I concluded, however, to act upon my husband's advice and promised my parents that if the change did not prove beneficial my husband would return to Iowa with me. Father and mother, my sisters and only brother affectionately accompanied me and my son Willie, then 10 years of age, to New York city to take the steamer for San Francisco. On our way eastward we spent two days at Niagara Falls. We arrived at New York on Christmas day of 1854. Most of holiday week we spent in the great city sightseeing, visiting objects of interest, among which were the Crystal Palace, Central park, the city and state buildings, Barnum's museum and theaters. On the 31st of December I sailed for Aspinwall on the steamship *Northerner*. She is the same vessel which, on a voyage from San Francisco to Victoria on the 5th of January, 1860, struck a sharp pointed rock between Blunt's reef and Cape Mendocino, some twenty-five miles from Humboldt bay. In a few minutes she became a total wreck. Thirty-six lives were lost, among whom was Oliver P. Meeker of Steilacoom, brother of Ezra and father of Frank O. Meeker. On New Year's day 1855, we were out to sea, and I was the sickest of women; sicker than ever I was in my life, and from that dread sea sickness I suffered the entire voyage till I reached my home on Puget Sound. No hardship on the plains, no discomfort of land travel, except alone the dread of Indians and their malicious attacks, can compare with the actual suffering of the seasick voyager, for days and weeks, without any possible relief or retreat from persistent, protracted sickness, and the constant wish that the ship may go down and end your misery. I arrived at San Francisco in the latter part of January, 1855, and remained in that city till the 7th of March following, daily expecting my husband, who had agreed to meet me there. He, however, had failed to learn of my arrival, so uncertain and dilatory were the mails at that period; besides at that season of the year he was much absent from home, attending the terms of court. Having been informed on the Sound that court was being held in Seattle, Captain Collins landed me and my son at that place where I found my husband. While there we stopped at the hospitable residence of Hillory Butler. It was Saturday, the Seattle term of court had just closed, and that house was the headquarters of the bench and bar of Puget Sound, who were about to start that night for Port Townsend, where the next term of court commenced on the following Monday. On that evening we started for Port Townsend on the sloop *Sarah Stone*, Captain Tom Slater, then the passenger packet between Olympia and Port Townsend, by way of the Sound ports. The cabin of our packet was hardly larger than a stateroom; we had as passengers besides myself and son, Colonel J. Patton Anderson, the first United States marshal of the territory, and his brother, Butler P. Anderson, Major J.S. Clendenin, the United States attorney, Colonel Wallace, Judge Victor Munroe, Frank Clark, B.F. Kendall and Elwood Evans. It was a treat to hear those gentlemen telling legal anecdotes and cracking jokes at each other's expense. Of these attorneys, Elwood Evans, then but a boy in appearance, alone survives. The others have joined the great, silent majority, and the sloop herself, and her jolly master, Tom Slater, are no more. Myself and my son still live, and that first voyage on Puget Sound, attending court with my husband, will never be effaced from my memory. When we had reached Port Townsend my husband directed us to the hotel, but Evans said: "You're just from the east, and want more comfortable quarters than the hotel at Port Townsend will afford; come with me." On that he took me by the arm and escorted me up the hill to the lovely home of Mrs. Webster, now Mrs. E.R. Rogers of Steilacoom, who welcomed me most cordially, made my visit most agreeable, and during the week she gave myself and the lawyers a party, which we all enjoyed.

On the following Monday we crossed the Sound to Whidby's island, where, while Colonel Wallace and our party of lawyers attended court at Penn's cove, I made a most pleasant visit at the home of old Jacob Ebey, (always called old man Ebey), father of Colonel Isaac N. Ebey, then collector of customs at Port Townsend, whose tragic death I shall notice later. I made several acquaintances on Whidby's island. But two or three years had elapsed since its first settlement, yet there were several fine farms and most comfortable homes. All those old settlers were extremely kind and hospitable. That spring term of court was at a time when there was no steamboat travel upon the Sound, so when court adjourned we left Penn's cove in an open boat for Steilacoom. The other lawyers had found other conveyances up the Sound, but in our party was Mr. Clendenin and his wife, a late bride from Philadelphia. He was the attorney for the United States for the territory, a Pennsylvanian by birth, but appointed from Mississippi, through the influence of Jeff Davis, secretary of war, in whose regiment he had served in the Mexican war. The trip was very rough, and the first night we camped on Skagit Head. At that point there was a store and a shopping place kept by C.C. Phillips and a partner. Upon the next evening we reached our home at Steilacoom. This was about the middle of April. I had been on the go from the time of leaving Mount Pleasant in December, and was really glad to get home at last.

To illustrate the condition of things at the time of my arrival, as also one of the greatest annoyances or discomforts to which the old settler was subjected, I wish to refer to the vexatious disappointment of both my husband and myself in failing to meet in San Francisco, as had been our arrangement, if I consented to leave home.

When we were about to take passage in the sloop *Sarah Stone* for Port Townsend, and as I was going aboard with my husband, Captain John H. Scranton, owner of the *Major Tompkins*, which had been lost off Esquimalt harbor, on the 10th of February, previous, shook hands with me and was profuse in compliments upon my safe arrival. He told me how anxiously I had been looked for by the colonel and his friends. Said he: "More so than if you had been president of the United States." He said that on a business trip to Victoria, he and Colonel Wallace had stopped at Colonel Ebey's, on Whidby's Island, and there, by accident, picked up a San Francisco newspaper in which was announced the arrival of myself and son in that city. Said Mr. Scranton: "There was no sleep for either of us that night; both Colonel Wallace and myself walked the porch the live-long night, and the colonel was the most uneasy and anxious man to imagine." The fact was that both the colonel and myself had written letters regarding our meeting in San Francisco. Two letters had been addressed to him by express. One never reached him, the other was handed to him a year later at Olympia, when he was serving in the territorial legislature.

Late in the summer of 1855 rumors of an Indian outbreak east of the Cascade mountains became quite frequent, and commenced to excite alarm. The murder by Yakima Indians of miners on the way to the Colville gold diggings became known upon the Sound in the early fall. In October and November thè massacres on White river followed. Acting-Governor Mason called for volunteers. My husband raised a company, first designed for home protection, only two companies having been called to cooperate with the United States troops at Fort Steilacoom. The murder of A. Benton Moses and of James McAllister and Thomas Connell by hostiles of the White river and Puyallup bands, in the last days of October, led, however, to a different order of things. Regiments instead of companies were found necessary in the emergency. My husband's company (Company D, First regiment) was called into service in the field, and was ordered to march to the hostile country, to recover and bring back the bodies of the murdered Moses and Miles. Colonel Wallace had just returned from the fall terms of court at Port Townsend and the other places for holding court, when he commenced raising the company. As he had to travel in a canoe, I had not accompanied him. On his leaving home for the service, by invitaiton of Colonel M.T. Simmons, Indian agent, I made a visit to the home of the latter, on Skookum bay, to remain until my husband's return. I had been but a few days at the home of Colonel Simmons, when he was compelled to return to the Snohomish Indian reservation. The neighbors of Colonel Simmons, soon after his absence, became alarmed at the conduct of the Indians, and came to his house and advised our going to Olympia for safety. His family, accompanied by myself and son, started about sundown in little boats, rowing until midnight, when we landed at a point where the men made a big fire of logs, and when the women and children had thoroughly warmed, started on again, reaching Olympia at 4 o'clock in the morning, and stopped at the Pacific hotel, then kept by Colonel William Cock.

The bodies of Moses and Miles had been forwarded to Olympia for burial. Mrs. Moses was there at the time with her father (Judge B.F. Yantis) and her sister. The bodies were at the warehouse of the Kendall company, to which place I accompanied her to see the corpse of her late husband. A few days later I returned with her to Steilacoom and assisted her to pack her household effects to be removed to Olympia. She went there, but as a blockhouse had been built in the meanwhile at Steilacoom, I remained there until my husband should return from a hostile section, where his company was on duty. At the hotel in Steilacoom I met Allen S. Porter from Porter's prairie, one of the most outer white settlements. He had fled from his isolated home, followed by hostile Indians. After untold hardships he had reached Steilacoom, where he was then recruiting his health. He had been chased through the woods and swamps by the Indians until nearer dead than alive. After resting a day or two and getting well he again returned to the front, carrying the message from me to my husband, that if he did not return and go up to the legislature, of which he was a member, I would take the first steamer and return to Mount Pleasant.

At the blockhouse at Steilacoom it was the opinion of many that there was but little danger on the land side, as that approach was protected by the garrison and Fort Nesqually. Many, however, were of the opinion that an attack might be made from the water. One night there was considerable alarm caused by a great noise sounding like boats rushed up on the beach. We thought for sure the Indians were about to attack. While the men folks went out to reconnoiter, I went into my little room and watched my little son as he laid there asleep, then I looked at my gun hanging over the port hole, when I remembered that I had never fired a gun in my life; still I felt brave then, and if need be, I could shoot Indians as fast as anybody, if some one would only load the gun for me, for I knew nothing as to loading guns. I heard loud talk and running, back and forth as though upon the deck of a ship. I looked out the port hole.

I saw the masts of a ship right over my room. By that time our men were returning. On entering the blockhouse they said, "Ladies, don't be alarmed. It is a ship which has run upon the beach." It proved to have been a vessel of war coming up to Fort Steilacoom for the protection of the Sound country, and to overawe or punish the hostiles. Captain Webster acted as pilot, and he had run her on shore.

By the latter part of the summer of 1856 Indian hostilities in western Washington had sufficiently ceased to render travel upon the Sound comparatively safe. I therefore again accompanied Colonel Wallace on his trip to the fall terms of court. It was arranged for the steamer *Traveler* to make an excursion trip to Whidby's island. That boat was owned by Captain William N. Horton of Olympia, the well-known steamboatman and engineer, now deceased. Quite a party of Olympians came, including Captain Horton's eldest daughter, Mr. and Mrs. Edward Giddings, jr., Mrs. Wilson Osborne and several other Olympia ladies, together with Lawyers Evans and Kendall of that city. The part of the voyage from Port Townsend to Captain Robertson's, Whidby island, will never be forgotten. It was upon Sunday afternoon, the weather was rough and a high sea was on. The stern of the old *Traveler*, and perhaps a third part of her length, was entirely under water, and a number of times we had occasion to think that it would prove her last voyage. After much anxiety and many fears we finally reached our destination. Our trials and discomforts were more than compensated by the truly hospitable reception at the hands of Mrs. Captain Robertson, that kindest of hostesses, and her equally kind family. An excellent supper was quickly furnished, comfortable quarters were supplied for all. We received a most hearty welcome, and made a most agreeable visit.

That old historic steamer, the *Traveler*, a year or two later (March 3d, 1858) commanded by Captain Tom Slater, he who was master of the sloop *Sarah Stone* on my first voyage on Puget Sound, sunk while at anchor near Foulweather Bluff, at midnight, five of those on board meeting with a watery grave. Among those lost were Captain Slater and Truman B. Fuller, who had come to the Sound as purser of the *Major Tompkins*, and who was mail agent of the *Traveler*. She was a small iron propeller built at Philadelphia and brought around Cape Horn in sections. Captain John G. Parker, now of Tacoma, purchased her in 1855, and shipped her here from San Francisco to Olympia on the brig *J.B. Brown*. She ran for many months before the wreck of the *Major Tompkins*, between Olympia and Victoria carrying the United States mail. Captain Horton purchased her from Captain Parker and employed her as a transport carrying supplies to the Indian reservations, forts and block houses, and occasionally to carry passengers between the Sound ports. While so employed as a transport she was the first steamer to ascend the Puyallup, Duwamish, White, Snohomish and Nooksack rivers.

In August of 1857 it was arranged for me to accompany my husband to the court at Penn's Cove, on Whidby's island. He had business to attend to for Colonel Simmons, Indian agent, at the agency at Oak harbor, on that island, so he went ahead by canoe, leaving me to come down by the next steamer. At that term of court one of the sailors of the United States revenue cutter *Jeff Davis*, was tried and convicted for murdering a man at Port Townsend. The revenue cutter being there, Captain C. Pease of that vessel invited several ladies including myself, and also our husbands, who were in attendance on court, Mrs. Captain Robinson and Mrs. Captain Coupe, residents of the island, to take the trip in the cutter on Saturday to Port Townsend, spend Sunday at that place and return Monday. On Monday the cutter's boat returned, bringing also the lawyers, sheriff and prisoner. We landed at Kellogg's Point and walked from there to the residence of Colonel Ebey. While some of the gentlemen assisted the officers in securing the boat, Judge Henry R. Crosbie said to me: "Mrs. Wallace we will walk up the hill slowly, Colonel Wallace and the rest can soon overtake us." I accepted his escort. As we leisurely walked along we passed a camp of Northern Indians. A puff of wind caused their tent-cloth to flap, and I saw two or three big Indians sitting around with their faces painted. I at once exclaimed, "Oh, Judge, I saw Indians in there with their faces painted, and when the Indians paint their faces they mean fight." He laughed at me, and when the party came up he told the circumstance to them as a good joke at my expense. The crowd joined in the laugh, and repeated my words, "When the Indians painted their faces they mean fight." How sadly I recall the truth of my observation. On the third night after that perhaps thoughtless remark of mine, those northern Indians came to Colonel Ebey's house, shot him and then cut off his head and carried it to their northern home. On that fatal night the United States marshal, George W. Corliss, and wife were guests of Colonel Ebey. They were sleeping at his house when the Indians made the attack. Mrs. Corliss and Mrs. Ebey had been washing clothes that day; several Northern Indians had visited the house and insolently demanded provisions. Mrs. Ebey treated them kindly, and suspected no harm. The family and guests had retired for the night (August 11, 1857). The watch dog soon after alarmed the household by continued barking. Mrs. Ebey remarked to her husband that the Indians must be around the house, and that they would steal the washed clothes still hanging out. Colonel Ebey arose and went to the door. Mrs. Ebey slipped on her shoes, threw a shawl over her shoulders, and as she stepped out of her bedroom on the porch, the colonel was descending the steps off the porch. The Indians fired two shots at him; as he started to run they again fired, and he fell dead. The Indians then cut off his head, and having robbed the house they made their retreat, carrying off the head of the deceased colonel as a trophy of their fiendish malice. The sound of the firing awoke Marshal Corliss and his wife. They went into Mrs. Ebey's room, and having learned the condition of affairs, climbed out the window on to the porch, and while the Indians were engaged over the dead Colonel Ebey, ran to the woods. Mrs. Corliss, in her bare feet, made her way through gooseberry bushes and brush to the house of Robert C. Hill, distant three-quarters of a mile, where was staying Judge Crosbie, whom I have referred to in what he deemed a good joke about painted Indians. My husband and myself stopped that night at the house of

Hill Harmon, now of Steilacoom. He then lived on the island about one-half mile from Colonel Ebey. In the meantime a friendly Indian had been sent to Harmon's to give the alarm. Mr. Harmon and Colonel Wallace immediately went to Colonel Ebey's. They were the first to find the headless body of the colonel, in his door yard. Upon the next afternoon the rest of the Ebey family came from their hiding-places in the woods to Harmon's, almost exhausted from grief and exposure, where they were well-cared for. As for myself, I had become almost wild as my little son had not stopped at Harmon's, and I feared he might have been at Colonel Ebey's on that fatal night. Old Father Ebey's house was but a short distance from the house of his murdered son, Colonel Ebey. The afternoon after the murder he and his family were sent for to come to Harmon's, for safety. My son came along, to my intense relief. All remained at Harmon's until the fate of Marshal Corliss and wife, and Mrs. Ebey and their family, was ascertained, and their safety assured. I shall never forget the funeral. I went with Colonel Ebey's aged mother and the griefstricken sisters to the colonel's late house. I led the old lady by the hand to the coffin of her beloved son, for she was nearly blind. She said to me, "I cannot see him, I can only feel him." She then grasped his hand, and for some time talked and prayed. The funeral sermon was preached by one of the neighbors, then a Methodist minister, Joseph S. Smith, whom the island Indians called Sok-al-ee Smith on account of his tallness. He was a prominent lawyer, practicing in the territory. He moved to Oregon, was elected to congress from that state, and filled several other prominent offices. Corliss and wife escaped that memorable morning, August 12, 1857, to meet a similar fate in Lower California. On account of her health they moved to Las Cruces, Cal., and on the 16th of January, 1864, both husband and wife were murdered at their residence, and their house burned over their lifeless bodies. Who were the perpetrators of that awful crime has never been ascertained.

The scalp of Colonel Ebey was recovered in the fall of 1859 by Captain Dodd of the Hudson Bay company's steamer *Labouchere*. He presented it to Alonzo M. Poe, Esq., for a long time editor of the *Overland Press*, published at Olympia, for the relatives of the deceased. Poe gave it to Mrs. Enos of San Francisco, a niece of Colonel Ebey. In the fall of 1858, the old Hudson Bay company's steamer *Beaver*, on her annual trading voyage north, had stopped at a village of the Kake tribe of Russian American Indians (58 deg. 30 min. north latitude). There they heard that the band possessed the scalp of Ebey. Captain Swantson of the Beaver and Chief Trader Dodd then tried to buy it. They sent such word to the chief of the village. In a short time four large canoes filled with armed Indians came alongside the Beaver, and a dozen or more of their number had boarded her before their hostility was suspected. The decks of the steamer were then cleared for action, the guns run out, the armed canoes warned off under threats of being fired upon. An explanation of this hostile demonstration was demanded by the Hudson's Bay officers. The Indians replied that they had been advised that a demand for the scalp was nothing but a warning that the village would be attacked. The Indians, although disabused of the idea, would not listen to any terms as to the surrender of the scalp. In the fall of 1859, that sad memento of Indian perfidy was secured by a the Hudson Bay company for a large ransom in blankets and goods.

The murder of Colonel Ebey created an intense sensation throughout the country. The cause which prompted the dreadful deed was discussed, and the opinion reached at the time was that the Northern Indians (afterward ascertained to be of the Kake tribe) were part of a formidable war party then revisiting the Sound to avenge the killing of twenty-seven of their tribe, one of whom was a head chief, which had occurred November 21, 1856, at Port Gamble. Early in 1854 a northern Indian of the Kake or Stickene tribe had been wantonly murdered at Butler's cove, just below Olympia, for demanding of his white employer the wages due to him for labor. From that time the Northern Indians who came to Puget Sound to secure employment, on their return, to avenge that wrong would commit depredations on isolated settlements and murder solitary settlers and attack and kill small parties of whites traveling upon the Sound. The annual visits of those parties increasing in numbers and boldness, became alarming to the settlements. To drive them out, as also to punish those constant depredations, Commander Swartout, United States navy, commanding the steamship *Massachusetts*, then on duty in these waters, pursued a number of small parties of Northern Indians from the vicinity of Port Gamble on the 20th of November, 1856. At that place a large number of them were encamped. Commander Swartout used every effort to secure their peaceable withdrawal from American waters, before proceeding to extremities. They insolently defied his peacable messages, and all efforts having failed to secure their return to their homes, Swartout attacked their camp on the 21st, keeping up a fire on the village and woods adjacent, the whole of that day. The surviving Indians reported to him the death of twenty-seven, including one head-chief, and twenty-one wounded. Their huts and all the property of the Indians were destroyed. Their canoes all having been destroyed the survivors were received on the Massachusetts, fed and carried to Victoria, from which place a passage to their country was secured. Swartout flattered himself that the severe punishment by him inflicted would deter any further visitation to Puget Sound by those northern pirates. In that he was mistaken. The lamented Ebey forfeited his life according to Indian law, for that of the Kake chief killed in Swartout's battle with them at Port Gamble.

To return to my story. The night after Colonel Ebey's funeral, Marshal Corliss and wife, Colonel Wallace, myself and our son went over to Port Townsend in the cutter's boat, in company with Lieutenant James M. Selden, United States revenue service, and the other officers. Our husbands remained to attend court. On the next day, Mrs. Corliss and myself were put on board a Chilean ship, on which we were carried to Steilacoom. I spent next winter at Olympia, during the session of the legislature, of which my husband was a member. I there met with Mrs. Corliss. She was just becoming able to get about comfortably. She had never recovered from the effect of her trip that sad night through the woods when she made her flight to the house of Robert C. Hill, one of Ebey's neighbors on Whidby's island, now well known as president of a national bank at Port Townsend.

By this time population had increased, the white settlements were fast settling down to the routing of social life, and incidents or adventurous acts of life ceased to be worthy of mention. My husband was appointed governor of Washington in 1861, the same year elected delegate to congress. I accompanied him to the national capital. In 1863 Idaho territory was established, and he was appointed its first governor, and at the first election, elected delegate to congress from that territory.

I may refer with pride to my connection with the establishment of the territory of Idaho, at the expiring days of the session of congress, 1862-63. Quite a delegation was present at Washington City who favored the division of Washington territory, which then included all of Idaho and Montana west of the Rocky mountains, extending as far south as the northern line of California and Nevada. It was an immense region and contained the South pass, the great entrance of Oregon, Washington and California by the great immigrant route. The colonel was overjoyed at the assured passage of the bill, which he had in charge, and his friends who were assembled at his rooms joined with him in conferring upon me the high privilege of nominating the new territory. I answered: Well, if I am to name it, the territory shall be called Idaho, for my little niece, who was born near Colorado Springs, whose name is Idaho, from an Indian chief's daughter of that name, so called for her beauty, meaning the "Gem of the Mountain." Dr. Anson G. Henry, the surveyor-general of Washington territory, then on a visit to Washington City, was in the room. He clapped his hands upon his knees and said to me, "Mrs. Wallace, Idaho it shall be." The evening of the day upon which the bill passed, my husband came home and said: "Well, Lue, you've got your territory, and I'm to be the governor of it." A short time after the bill was signed, my husband was appointed its first governor, and at the first election held in the newly organized territory, he was selected delegate to congress, as I have above stated.

At the close of the session of congress March 4, 1865, we returned to Steilacoom, our old residence. My husband resumed the practice of his profession, I continuing to accompany him to court. He also served for several years as judge of the probate court of Pierce county. Our son, who had grown to manhood, married and made his residence at Washington City. Without any unusual occurrences to make a note of, husband and I lived happily and to ourselves until February 7, 1879, at which date he died, in the 68th year of his age, honored and respected by all his fellow citizens. The story of his eventful life, the story of an old settler, might be dwelt upon with great interest, but he was so well known that eulogy at my hands is unnecessary. One of his valued friends, a distinguished contemporary, the venerable Beriah Brown, referred to him and his death in this eloquent and appropriate language:

"We gather around his grave. We miss him now; we shall miss him greatly in the time to come. He walked among us well. All who knew him well loved him; all who met him trusted him. He did our common manhood honor, and we shall miss him sore for that there are so many who do not honor. Let all the noise and turmoil of the vain strife of life, in which for long he took boldly and bravely and truly his part, and did it well, be hushed about his marble form. A man has fallen at his post, we feel; a right, noble and true man. He has fallen honorably. His memory can but do us good. Let us cherish it. A death like this can long bear no bitter memories. The end was well as was the journey. Blessings and good will, from all good men, are garlands for his grave. It is a happy thing to die so. To go to one's grave with no man bearing a wrong of our infliction; with no lie, which we have fathered, living here behind us; to go in love, to go in truth. Oh! It is a thing to ask God for every day a man lives. May the example of the dead so preach to us. May we so live, true to the polar star of duty, that the living may say such words over us in truth, as we speak over our honored dead today. Take him to his rest; bear our true brother home."

> And if the ear
> Of the freed spirit heedeth aught beneath
> The brightness of its new inheritance,
> It may be joyful to the parted one
> To feel that earth remembers him in love.

Governor Elisha P. Ferry, one of Governor Wallace's successors as governor of Washington territory, the first governor of the state of Washington, as grand master of the Masons officiated at the grave and performed the beautiful Masonic funeral service in the presence of a large number of citizens of the territory, attending from Olympia, Seattle and various other towns of western Washington.

Since his death my life has not been so much the life of an "old settler." Its story would be but the story of every housekeeper and matron in the state, surrounded by the elements of home attendant upon an improved and advanced civilization. My parents and brother and sisters each and all have affectionately invited me to rejoin the home of my early days. My dear son, with filial love and affection, has insisted I should make his home my home and end my days under his roof, that he and his household may make my latter days more happy. Gratefully acknowledging these evidences of love, I have declined them, for here is my home. I have regained my health; I have passed the allotted three score years and ten, and thanks to Infinite goodness and to our salubrious climate, I am now in the enjoyment of perfect health, in the vigor of a green old age, happy and contented and entirely satisfied to live in the state of Washington until my summons comes to join my husband and other dear ones, who have gone before.

Chapter 6

Fraser River Gold Rush

Charles Prosch

He crossed the Isthmus at Panama in 1853.
In Steilacoom he started the second newspaper in
Washington Territory. He was the first to receive
and publish news of the Fraser River gold boom.

Seattle, Washington — May 27, 1892

It was on a warm, clear day in September, 1853, that the writer boarded the steamer *Illinois*, Captain Hartstein, from a wharf at the foot of Liberty street, New York city. Though by no means so large as some of the leviathans now plowing the waters of the Atlantic and Pacific, the *Illinois* was among the largest of the ocean steamers of that period. On this occasion upward of 1000 people took passage on her for the land of gold. About half of these were cabin and the balance steerage passengers, the two classes crowding the steamer to her utmost capacity. It was near sunset when she left the wharf and started on her ocean voyage. In the meantime clouds had gathered overhead, and the weather gradually assumed a threatening aspect. Night came on while slowly steaming down the bay, and soon thick darkness enveloped everything on land and water. Not caring to grope their way about the vessel in the dark, at the risk of coming to grief by violent contact with unseen chains or rigging, the passengers retired early, to dream of the kindred and homes they were leaving or the golden phantoms they were pursuing. All, save the officers and crew, were soon oblivious of their whereabouts or surroundings.

Daylight brought with it a surprise to all who had slept through the night. Instead of buffeting the waves of old ocean, as they supposed she would be doing before their slumbers ended, the steamer was lying quietly at anchor off Staten Island, with New York city in plain view. The first to issue from their berths were treated to a scene "not down in the bills." It seems that during the night, soon after coming to anchor, a vigorous search was instituted for stowaways, and it resulted in finding six men who, in their eagerness to get to California were prepared to take the most desperate chances on sea and land. No little courage was then required to brave the dangers, on the isthmus as well as on the ocean, which stowaways without money faced when they attempted to beat their way to California. These six unfortunates were ranged in line along the steamer's guards, while one of the sailors deluged them with salt water from the ship's hose. Having sufficiently cooled their ardor, the captain ordered them in a boat alongside to be conveyed to the shore, where they were left to find their way back to the city. Their daring deserved a better fate.

An hour or two later, breakfast having in the meantime been disposed of, the steamer was proceeding rapidly in the direction of Kingston, Jamaica, where she was to take on sufficient coal to last her to Aspinwall and thence back to New York. No sign of the threatened storm of the previous night was now visible, the sky was bright and clear and the air cool and refreshing. It was not until noon that we had any sea worth mentioning. Gradually it increased in violence until it began to shake the confidence of many who had indulged in the hope of resisting its influence. When the dinner hour arrived, a number of the cabin passengers concluded they didn't want to eat; others, myself among them, hastened to the first table. The fresh sea breeze, coupled with the motion of the vessel, stimulated my appetite to such a degree that I was too hungry to wait for the second table, though informed that it would be better than the first. At my side sat a man named Frankland, who soon became the cynosure of all eyes. The table at that time on the Pacific Mail company's steamers was equal to that of the best hotels, and this man set out to make the most of the feast of good things. Among the dishes on the table was a generous supply of roast chickens, about one for every four persons. Mr. Frankland's eyes took these in while seating himself. Hastily seizing his fork, he plunged it into the nearest chicken, transferred it to his own plate, and deliberately proceeded to dissect it while his neighbors waited for their share, expecting him to pass it to them. They waited in vain. Having cut up the fowl, he reached out and drew toward him such other dishes, as he desired to accompany the chicken. He had as yet tasted nothing. Having things now arranged to his satisfaction, he stuck his fork into a slice of the breast, but, while raising it to his mouth a death-like pallor suddenly overspread his countenance, his hand trembled, he dropped the fork and made a break for the bulwarks of the steamer. As he did so the people at the table, who had been watching him with feelings of disgust, gave vent to their pleasure by a loud burst of laughter. He was not seen again until we reached Kingston, three days later. The steamer remained there twenty-four hours. During this time Frankland lost no opportunity to atone for his protracted fast. Fortunately for him and others no more rough seas were experienced until we entered the Gulf of California, nearly three weeks later.

A lower stage of degradation than that which prevailed in Jamaica at this time it is difficult to conceive of. Much the larger proportion of the people are blacks, the oldest being emancipated slaves and the younger and middle aged their offspring. Among the children were many mulattoes and some octaroons, the latter in a few cases pretty enough to arrest attention anywhere. As the male passengers landed to stroll through the town they were waylaid by boys from 8 to 15 years of age, who vociferously solicited prostitution for their mothers and sisters. No shame was attached to this calling; it was considered perfectly legitimate, and considered in no way derogatory to the character of the people.

Many of the passengers, myself among the number, took advantage of the long stay of the steamer to extend their rambles to the country adjacent to the city. While the party with me saw much to interest them, nothing afforded them surprise and pleasure equal to the tropical fruits and flowers, of which there were many varieties unheard of and unseen before. In the course of our perambulations under a hot sun on dusty roads, as was natural, we became oppressed with thirst and sought to quench it at one of the dwellings by the roadside. A one-story cottage, surrounded by vines, flowering shrubs and fruit trees enclosed in a neat picket fence, presented an appearance so inviting that we hesitated not to lift the gate latch and enter the garden. As we did so a black woman with a smiling countenance appeared at the door of the cottage and invited us in to rest a while. She did not wait to be told that we were weary and thirsty. Bidding us to be seated, she placed on the table glasses and a large earthen jar of cool spring water. While we quenched our thirst she brought from a pantry dishes of nectarines, pomegranates, pears, oranges and bananas, all of which, she said grew in her garden, which covered less than two acres of ground. No seemingly happier creature than this black woman have I ever met. Her weight was all of 250 pounds, her skin coal black, and when she laughed she quivered all over like a huge mass of jelly. Harry Land, the smallest man in our party (he weighed not more than 100 pounds), indulged in an amusing flirtation with our hostess. She laughingly said she would not mind going with him to California, were it not that she was the mistress of a merchant in the city, who generously supplied all her wants. A very pleasant hour was passed in this cottage, when, on leaving it, we thanked our entertainer. She said she was glad we had called, because she was often lonesome and had enjoyed our visit very much.

On returning to the steamer we were treated to a spectacle entirely new to us. When we left her, in the morning, the work of taking on coal had not commenced. Now there were upward of twenty strong-limbed negresses carrying coal on their heads, in heavy tubs holding each one bushel, from the wharf to the steamer's bunkers. Going to and returning from the steamer the amazons marched in two files with military precision, chanting negro melodies unceasingly. Superintending the work, and seeing that none shirked, were four or five negro bosses. Loafing about the wharf, watching the women at their labor, was a gang of negro men, presumably the husbands of the coal carriers, waiting to receive the wages of the toilers. This scene continued without cessation through the entire night, which was illuminated by a full moon in a cloudless sky.

As the noise attending the process of coaling precluded the possibility of sleep on board, the passengers spent the time on shore.

The entire city was devoted to revelry; nobody slept or could sleep. Every public house was enlivened with the fiddle and the dance. No storekeeper would close his doors while there was a passenger ashore to spend a dime. The coaling there of the California steamers was an event of deep pecuniary interest to the natives and business men generally, and they made the most of it. Passengers were allowed a license which some shamefully abused. The people evidently feared to impose any restraint upon visitors, lest it would deter them from coming in future. The prodigality of many of our people during the night was proportioned to the license they enjoyed, and resulted in some of them having no means to meet the expenses incident to the journey across the isthmus. A military barrack and sentry boxes in the city and suburbs, with a half a dozen barefooted negroes in odd-looking uniforms, each carrying a musket, indicated the existence of some sort of authority. Its exercise was seemingly for the natives only and not for strangers. Amalgamation of races was a prominent feature of the inhabitants, pure white men being seen everywhere united to the blackest of negresses.

A curious sight we witnessed at Kingston was that of the numerous buzzards, tame as barnyard fowls, flying here and there in pursuit of garbage. With wings outstretched these foul birds will measure four or five feet. It is a penal offense to kill or molest them in Jamaica. Being protected by law, they have lost all fear of man, and will approach so near as to tempt him to strike at them with a walking stick, if he should happen to have one in his hand. There is a sanitary reason for thus protecting this foul bird. It is an excellent scavenger. It consumes offal and filth of every kind, the accumulation of which would breed a pestilence if suffered to remain and taint the atmosphere. The natives, being too indolent to remove the garbage, they leave the task to the buzzards.

Having finished coaling, the *Illinois* steamed out of the harbor of Kingston bound for Aspinwall. On the second day out a mutiny was threatened, not this time by the sailors, but by some of the steerage passengers, who thought they should have better fare than they paid for. The leader of the malcontents was a large, respectable-looking man of about 35 years, and he became the scapegoat in the affair. After Captain Hartstein had investigated the trouble, he was not only convinced that there was no just foundation for it, but also that it originated with this man. Quick to act in emergencies of this kind, he promptly ordered the man to be tied by the thumbs to the rigging, with his toes only resting upon the deck, in this position to remain until he promised obedience to the regulations governing the steamer at sea. An hour sufficed to bring the man to terms, when he was released, a sadder and wiser man.

Captain Hartstein, here mentioned, held a commission as a naval lieutenant, and was one of the most distinguished officers in our navy at that period. Hartstein island, located about midway between Steilacoom and Olympia on the west shore of North bay, is named after him. He it was who returned to Queen Victoria, under direction of an act of Congress, one of the vessels of the Sir John Franklin expedition, which was found adrift in the Arctic ocean by an American whaler and taken to an Atlantic port. On this occasion Hartstein acquitted himself with much credit, and for some days was the guest of the queen and lionized by all England.

After an uneventful voyage of three or four days through the Caribbean sea, we were safely landed at Aspinwall, an American town, the offspring of the railroad enterprise then in progress to connect the Atlantic and

Pacific oceans. Located on an extensive marsh, intersected with creeks and sloughs, it was the reverse of an invited townsite, and none were sorry to leave it, as we did before nightfall. Only about fifteen miles of the road was then built and used; the speed of the trains was some five or six miles an hour. We had not proceeded far before night set in, accompanied with a slight mist. While all were resting in fancied security near the end of the completed road the train came to a sudden stop, rudely awakening some who were dozing and starting all to their feet. On issuing from the cars and proceeding to the head of the long train, we learned that a trestle nine or ten feet high, just finished, had proved unequal to the weight of the freight cars, which crashed through the timbers, killing one man, wounding several others, demolishing several cars and scattering their contents. This compelled us to enter upon a long but not unpleasant tramp.

Leaving our baggage in the custody of the railroad agents, who assumed the responsibility for its safe transportation to Panama, in the morning early we started to foot it on a well-traveled road to the Cruces river. When we set out on our journey we were all more or less hungry, and there was no place in sight where we could break our fast. We were comforted with the assurance, however, that our road passed a number of farm houses, in any or all of which we could get something to eat. We soon verified this assurance by applying at a large log house some distance from the road. The occupants of the house, a middle-aged man and wife and several children, lost no time in preparing for us a breakfast which was enjoyed by all. It comprised bacon and eggs, bread, milk and coffee, more than we could eat and drink, for which we were charged 50 cents each. Later in the day we applied at another farm house for dinner, when our hosts bountifully supplied us with roast chicken, eggs, bread, milk, vegetables, etc.

Though we did not encounter the anacondas, troops of monkeys and flocks of parrots said to exist in Central America, we saw much to interest us. The district through which we journeyed contained very little timber and but few shrubs. All of the soil looked susceptible of profitable cultivation, though but little of it was cultivated. Several of my companions thought they would like to live there, provided they were not compelled to work.

About sunset we reached Cruces, where many of our fellow-passengers had arrived ahead of us. In this hamlet were two buildings called hotels, furnished with bunks and cots, and five or six barn-like structures which served the purpose of the less fastidious wayfarers. Few arose in the morning refreshed by their slumbers. An early and very poor breakfast awaited us before taking boats for a trip on the Cruces river.

These boats were flat-bottomed, capable of carrying from three to five tons each, and were propelled by stout ten-foot poles, in the hands of natives or negroes, whose only attire was a breechclout covering a few inches of the person. The boats had been loaded with baggage during the night, and the passengers found seats or resting places on the baggage. Two natives manned each boat, the starting of which presented a lively scene, as there was considerable rivalry in the matter of getting off first. In no part of the river traversed by these boats did the water seem to be more than three or four feet deep, and often it was reduced to twelve inches or less. As the water was too muddy to discern these shallow places before reaching them, the boats often grounded, when one or both of the boatmen would jump into the water and shove them off. This kind of travel soon became very monotonous and none were sorry when it ended, as it did in the afternoon of the same day. Once during the forenoon we stopped and went ashore for refreshments, when the boatmen obtained a much-needed rest. The boats landed us at a hamlet called Gorgona, where, after resting a night, we mounted mules and donkeys for the last and most amusing stage of our journey across the isthmus. A collection of smaller mules than those here presented for our conveyance has never been seen. Indeed, very few of the thousand or more comprising the band were larger than ordinary donkeys. When it came to mounting them many ludicrous scenes, which brought tears to the eyes of the spectators, were witnessed. Some of the riders had to mount three or four times before they succeeded in retaining their seats. Not the least ludicrous sight was that of a six-foot man mounting a three-foot donkey, and a number of the bipeds and quadrupeds were thus proportioned. How to dispose of their legs puzzled many riders. When the feet of the rider reached within two or three inches of the ground, his toes would collide with every loose stone by the roadside. Sometimes the roadbed was a mass of rock which had been traversed for many years by mules, who have a habit of stepping in each other's tracks until they wear holes six or more inches deep in the rock. When the forefeet of the mules we rode entered these holes our own feet would strike bottom with a violence that was anything but soothing. There were also broad and deep mud holes, in which the beasts would sink to their bellies, nor could they be extricated until the riders dismounted. Several frisky mules managed to dump their riders into mud puddles, then stood and wagged their ears in seeming derision of the unlucky equestrians. In short, it was more entertaining than a circus, and the unfortunates seemed to enjoy the fun as well as those who escaped mishaps. There were in the company ten women, all of whom bestrode their beasts like men. Before night we arrived in Panama, many of the steerage passengers bringing up the rear on foot.

The *John L. Stephens*, then a new steamer, was anchored off the city awaiting our coming. It was necessary to place the baggage and freight on the steamer before the passengers boarded her, and this consumed nearly twenty-four hours. In the interim checks were examined and staterooms assigned at the steamship office on shore. This delay afforded an opportunity to view the ancient city of Panama, and many availed themselves of it. One or two churches and government buildings, with shrubs and vines and mosses growing from the crevices in their massive stonewalls and roofs, could readily be believed to have witnessed the passage of two or three centuries. Crumbling stone walls and quaint structures which led the beholder to inquire what they were intended for or used, all testified to events and ages long passed and forgotten.

Signals from the steamer summoned us on board, and all hastened to the water's edge. There we found a score or more of naked natives carrying passengers on their backs through a hundred yards of shoal water to the ship's boats. As each boat in turn was filled with passengers it was rowed to the steamer, two miles distant. There was neither swell nor ripple at this time upon the water, as far as the eye could reach its surface was like a huge sheet of glass.

The paddles of the steamer commenced revolving the instant the last passengers reached her deck. Gradually the shores receded until, as twilight was merged into night, they faded entirely from view. Then the passengers proceeded to dispose themselves for the voyage before them, first visiting and locating their berths. For several days we were favored with a clear sky and unruffled sea. Everybody was happy in anticipation of a pleasant voyage to San Francisco. The captain of the steamer, Robert L. Pearson, was in full accord with his cabin passengers, and generously treated them to champagne in token of his pleasure at having so fine a vessel under his command. All went well until we entered the Gulf of California, when grief and terror took the place of joy and festivity.

About 9 o'clock in the morning of October 10th the first indications of the coming tempest were visible in lowering clouds, increasing wind and disturbed sea. Hourly the elements grew in violence until noon. A boisterous weather at sea always stimulated my appetite; I became very hungry before the dinner hour arrived. About noon I looked into the dining saloon to see what progress the waiters were making in setting the table. For such occasions vessels at sea have racks to hold the dishes in place, but no device then in use would prevent the dishes being thrown out on the floor as fast as the waiters put them on the table. Seeing how futile were their efforts, and despairing of obtaining dinner in the usual way, I went after the captain to inquire what he was going to do about it. Meanwhile the storm grew steadily worse. Clambering up to the hurricane deck there I saw Captain Pearson standing alone, looking with anxious eyes alternately to the clouds and the sea, as if to discern a ray of hope above or below him. He was enveloped in a rubber coat that reached his heels, and a tarpaulin that covered head and shoulders. The spray from the angry waves fell on and around him like heavy rain from the clouds. Approaching him, I asked:

"Captain, are we to have no dinner today?"

Looking at me a moment, as if in doubt of my sincerity, he exclaimed: "My God! can you eat in such weather?"

"Why, captain," I replied, "I am most famished with hunger."

"Then go to the steward," he said, "and get some biscuit; that's the best we can do for you now."

I found the steward in the pantry, and he told me to help myself. Filling my pockets with biscuit, I sauntered about the steamer while satisfying the cravings of hunger. Few of the passengers were astir; nearly all had sought their staterooms or berths or secluded retreats where they could without interruption give vent to their feelings. Amid the raging of the storm some were heard repeating aloud the Lord's prayer, while others in agonizing terror cried, "God be merciful to me a sinner!" The wind whistled, shrieked, screamed and roared by turns; the chains clanked and the cordage rattled; the timbers creaked ominously while the angry waters buffeted the ship on every side; broken dishes strewed the floor of the salon; hysterical women screamed and strong men trembled in the presence of the dreaded storm king. Men and women who never prayed before prayed then with a fervency and eloquence that would shame the formal and cold invocations heard in the sanctuaries devoted to the worship of the Almighty. A thousand people who never before bent the knee in supplication, many of them inspired with a terror new and hitherto unknown to them, thought it no shame then to kneel and humbly beseech the Master of the elements to rescue them from the great peril in which they were placed. All were sincere; it was no time for insincerity. At intervals one or two would venture outside in the hope of seeing a sign of abatement of the storm. Vain hope. Steadily the elements continued their warfare against the seemingly doomed ship, hour after hour, with apparently increased fury, while she groaned in a way that appalled the stoutest hearts. Not a few of her passengers momentarily expected to see the steamer succumb and, with every soul on board, find a grave in the turbulent gulf. Being asked, when the storm was at its height and the vessel trembled and creaked at every assault of the waves, what he thought of the danger, Captain Pearson replied:

"The storm and the peril are the worst I have ever experienced. It is now a question of endurance only. If the storm lasts long enough, the steamer will break up and sink, but I still have a hope that the steamer, being new and strong, will outlast the storm."

Night came at last, but with no hope for the despairing passengers, few of whom expected to witness another day in this world. At midnight the storm began to abate, and at daylight it had decreased sufficiently to inspire all with hope. By noon nothing remained of it but the recollection of the terror which all had suffered.

Three days more saw us safely landed at San Francisco, grateful for our narrow escape from a watery grave.

It was not my purpose to come to Washington territory when I left New York, nor did I expect to remain on this coast longer than one or two years. A residence of sixty days in San Francisco, however, reconciled me to a permanent home on the Pacific coast. The salubrious climate, favorable to health and comfort alike, just suited and soon decided me. To this day I retain a vivid recollection of the last hot, sultry, enervating and uncomfortable summer spent in New York city, and never have I desired to experience the like again. A grateful sense of the difference in the climates of the two sections has since then pervaded my whole being, and I have ever thought it better to live here in comparative poverty, or on the bare necessaries of life, then dwell where even great wealth and lavish expenditure did not exempt one from discomforts unknown on the Pacific shores.

In the winter of 1857-8, I made the acquaintance in San Francisco of Captain Lafayette Balch, the town proprietor of Steilacoom. He had a small water-power sawmill on Nisqually bay, a lumber yard in San Francisco, and three or four vessels plying between the two places, carrying lumber down and returning with merchandise. Steilacoom and Olympia were then rival towns; one had the territorial capital and the other wanted it. To boom his town and aid it in obtaining the capital, Captain Balch purchased and shipped to Steilacoom, in 1856, a press and type with which to publish a newspaper. Several printers had tried and failed to make the paper pay before I met him. He gave me glowing descriptions of the Puget Sound country and climate; its dense forests and majestic trees; its snow-clad mountains and grand bodies of water, in short, painted all in such rosy colors that when he asked me to come and publish a paper in Steilacoom I readily consented, though doing well at the time in San Francisco. The captain assured me that every want should be supplied whether the paper paid or not.

In February, 1858, accompanied by my wife and three sons, I sailed from San Francisco for Steilacoom on the brig *Cyrus*, owned by Balch & Webber, the latter a quasi partner only. Besides my family there were on board three passengers named John E. Burns, Charles Eisenbeis and William L. Cates. The first now claims Tacoma as his home, the second has grown rich at Port Townsend, and the last has long led an obscure life somewhere in Pierce county. A fair wind came up just as the lines of the brig were cast off. As we proceeded down the bay the wind increased to such a degree that the captain (W.H. Diggs) was afraid to venture out, and put about to anchor until the wind abated. Burns, who knew something of navigation, grew indignant at the thought of losing a wind that bade fair to carry us far on our voyage, and vigorously protested against the course the captain was pursuing. Diggs was finally prevailed upon to go to sea with two or three reefs in each sail. Thus handicapped the brig *Cyrus* went bounding over the waves at a lively rate, and soon left the harbor of San Francisco far astern, to the evident satisfaction of Burns, the mate, and all whose stomachs did not rebel against the rough sea and the bouyancy of the brig. The heavens wore a dull-leaden aspect; there were no drifting clouds, such as often indicated the approach of violent storms; the wind came strong and steady from the south, attended with a little rain at intervals. Such was the character of the weather for six days, during which period neither sun nor stars were visible.

During the whole time we had been at sea, Charles Eisenbeis was very sick. He came aboard the brig a rosy-cheeked beardless boy, the picture of health. On the passage he lost both color and flesh — became so pale and attenuated, in fact, as to excite apprehensions that he would not survive the voyage. Others on the vessel had been seasick, but their illness lasted only an hour, while that of Eisenbeis held on to the end of the passage.

On the morning of the sixth day, the weather being still cloudy and hazy, young Eisenbeis approached Captain Diggs on deck and asked, with a German accent:

"Captain, how much longer shall we be at sea?"

"I don't know," replied the captain. "Not being able to get an observation, I have been compelled to rely on dead-reckoning, and therefore cannot tell precisely where we are."

"Vell, how much longer you dinks we shall be at sea?" again he asked.

The *Cyrus* was a slow sailer and had never made the passage in less than three weeks, so the captain continuously replied:

"I think we shall be at sea two weeks longer."

"Ah, mein Gott!" exlaimed Eisenbeis, while a feeling of despair overcame him, "den I goes overboard!"

Fortunately he did not put in execution immediately his design to go overboard, though sufficiently desperate to do so. The thought of being subjected two weeks longer to such suffering as he had already endured was more than he could bear, and an attempt to end it by plunging into the sea would not have greatly surprised us. While he hesitated and meditated, a change in the weather was imperceptibly taking place. About an hour later the clouds on both sides of us lifed, the haze disappeared, and the shores of Fuca straits were plainly visible to all on board. Very much to the surprise of everybody, the captain included, we were speeding up the straits at a rate quite unusual for the brig *Cyrus*, notwithstanding the fact that her sails were still reefed. The wind with which we left San Francisco remained with us until Port Townsend came in sight. Not until then did it abate much in force. Eisenbeis indefinitely postponed going overboard, and lived to be twice elected Mayor of Port Townsend, where he landed soon after noon the same day. It is gratifying to know that he has prospered and is now the possessor of a handsome fortune. Captain Burns also landed at Port Townsend, which for many years was his home.

After landing some freight (composed in great part of bricks for chimneys) which was taken ashore from the brig's side in canoes, Port Townsend then having no wharf, we proceeded up the Sound toward our destination. Two days and two nights were occupied in sailing, drifting with the tide and towing by small boat. On the third day we reached Steilacoom, then a town of about 100 white inhabitants and a much larger number of Indians. It was now near the end of February, and the sun never shone upon a lovelier day, in Italy or elsewhere, than that on which I quit the vessel for my new home. Nor was this charming weather confined to one or two days; weeks and months elapsed before it changed, and then for three or four days only. During the last week in June refreshing rains visited us, but the sky again cleared within a week, and we had no more rain until

November. Thus I found the climate here much better than that of San Francisco, which some years before I thought was incomparably superior to that of the Atlantic states. This agreeable feature of Puget Sound had much to do with making me and mine contented in our new home.

My first step on landing in Steilacoom was to find a dwelling for my family and a suitable place for a printing office. These things disposed of, I lost no time in getting out the first issue of the *Puget Sound Herald*, which appeared March 12th, and which was then the second paper in the territory, there being but one other. Fortunately for my paper I was the first to receive and publish the news of the discovery of gold on Fraser river, which enabled me to boom not only Steilacoom, but all of Puget Sound. In less than ninety days from the first publication of this news, ten thousand people gathered in Whatcom, several thousand found their way to the mines, two hundred or more drifted to Steilacoom, while others sought temporary or permanent homes in Seattle, Olympia and Port Townsend. Several townsite proprietors became insane through excitement.

Captain Balch wrote to J.B. Webber, who held his power of attorney, directing him to deed to me two lots in token of his appreciation of my services, but at the same time refuse to sell to others at any price. He feared that by selling lots then at $200 or $300, their actual value at that time, he would lost their prospective value of $5000 or $6000 each. Other town properties pursued a similar course, and thus succeeded in driving away many who would otherwise have remained. But enough has been said on this score to weary the reader, and I will therefore bring the present sketch to a close.

A.W. Arnold

An indelible tale about starvation and sickness aboard a Frisco-bound clipper becalmed on the Pacific in 1851. Then Mr. Arnold tells of his experiences in the gold fields of California and the Fraser River.

San de Fuca, Washington — September 9, 1892

On the 17th day of November, 1851, at the age of 21, I bid my father, mother, brother and sisters good-bye and started on a journey to the Pacific coast. I had lived a quiet life on a farm in northern Indiana and did not realize what an undertaking the journey was. At that time there were but three ways to reach the coast, viz: by foot across the plains, around the horn by sail, and across the isthmus. I chose the latter route and made the trip safely, but not without dangers and hardships.

Entering the cars a few tears were dropped in memory of familiar fast receding scenes. By rail and steamer I arrived in the city of New York, without incident worthy of note, where I purchased a passage on the steamer *Brother Jonathan,* then running to Chagres. I went through the usual course of seasickness, having quite a rough passage across the Gulf stream. After being six days out the steamer ran into the harbor of Kingston, on the island of Jamaica. There we found summer only six days from winter weather. Natives were nearly naked and tropical fruits were abundant and cheap. The object of the steamer's calling here was to procure coal. The supply was put on board by native women carrying a bushel basket full on their heads at each load.

Two days more of pleasant sailing and we were at Aspinwall. Now all was bustle and confusion in getting baggage and embarking in the natives' boats for the shore. Here an incident occurred that was not down on the bills. One of the passengers becoming crazed, seized a sledgehammer and began beating out his brains. The tool was taken from him, though not in time to prevent his head from being badly cut and bruised. What became of him I never heard.

Each one was busy providing means of transportation up the Chagres river, and enthused over the novelty of the situation, together with the tropical climate and scenery. Several of us procured, for a consideration, the services of a couple of natives with a boat to take us to the head of navigation at Gergona or Cruses. After procuring sufficient provisions for the voyage, we set out among the armada of boats, some with only four, while others contained thirty passengers. Sailing over our heads and lighting on the overhanging branches along the river banks, apparently without fear, were innumerable birds, the more conspicuous being the pelican, which proved a tempting mark for those supplied with fire arms. Ten miles up the river, we camped for the night, at a native town. The inhabitants, I should judge, comprised a cross between the Mexican and African.

During the evening the natives entertained us with the candle dance; this consists in forming a circle of youths and maidens with a number of candles in each hand, the greater the number the better, and hopping, jumping, wriggling and twisting in the most ridiculous shapes possible. The more outlandish the posture the more stylish the actor was termed. Some of our youths took part in this dance, not that they were so charmed with the music, ah, no! It was the same old charm that captured Adam.

As the water in the river here was of sufficient depth to admit of using the oars, we had a pleasant day's journey. Camping at night on the river bank where there were a few convenient trees and some native huts, we made up for the sleep lost the night before. The next day we entered a stronger current where the natives had to propel the boat with poles, and to lighten the boat we went with a pilot through the woods across what the pilot said was a neck of land expecting the boat to meet us in the evening. For this favor we had to stop that night on a rocky bar without supper. The next morning the boat came along and we soon had breakfast cooking. We stuck to the boat that day and at night camped in a large canvas lodging and boarding house. This was a two-story arrangement with a great number of bunks made by nailing canvas on poles. Men and women tired and exhausted, turned in without undressing, to sleep for all there was in it. Early the day following we arrived at Gorgona. There were mules to be hired here, but I had to husband my means and walk to Panama. The roads were bad, as it was raining nearly all the time, and my boots gave out, so that I threw them away, and walked the last six miles with bare feet.

In Panama there was great excitement caused by many of the passengers having bought through tickets from a company that had no boats on the Pacific side. Some turned back to prosecute the company, while others bought passage on a steamer line then expected, belonging to another line. Tickets on that line were held at a premium, and were above my means.

The bark *Cabarga* lay in port, advertised as a No. 1 clipper ship, bound for California. I, with about 100 others, purchased tickets on her. After a few delays in getting on board wood, water and provisions, we set sail. A brisk wind was blowing from off the land, which was very acceptable, as the farther we got out to sea, the more likely we would be to get wind that would help us on our way.

We left Panama on December 13th and the breeze continued for eighteen hours so that we made an offing of 400 miles. The wind then died out and the sea became as smooth as glass. For three weeks we lay floating about with the sun almost directly overhead. There was no shade from the sails and the heat was intense. The salt beef that was given us was full of maggots, and the bread was impregnated with blue mold. One after another was taken sick until there were but eight well persons among the passengers.

Death now commenced its work, and persons apparently well at sundown, would be put in a sack by 10 p.m. ready for burial in the morning. In seven days there were fourteen dumped in the sea as food for the ever-present sharks. It appeared like the cholera or yellow fever that had attacked the ship. There were many complaints about the food and some attributed the sickness to that cause.

To add to the horror of the situation, we were put on an allowance of a pint of water a day, and persons burning up with fever would swallow that without taking the cup from his lips. This could not last. The captain of the vessel was deaf to all appeals for water or healthy food, and would make fun, or laugh, when a person would crawl on his hands and knees to the quarter deck and beg for water.

One evening I saw a man crawl in that manner from the forecastle and beg for a glass of water. The captain told the steward to give him some. He gave him but an inch in a glass. He thanked the captain, then crawled back, when the captain laughingly remarked that he guessed that was the last water he would want, and so it was as the next morning he was passed over the vessel's side.

This was getting to be more than human nature nature could stand.

Unless there was help we knew the end must soon come. If there was no water on board except what the captain said there was, and no other food but what he was furnishing us, then there was nothing to do but die.

The eight of us that were well talked the matter over, and came to the conclusion that we would know what there was in the ship or get killed trying to find out. Knowing the authority that the master of a vessel at sea is clothed with, we armed ourselves as best we could, and went to work. We first tore down the partition between the main hold and the store room, where, to our joy, we found fifty-four barrels of flour and three large casks of water. We then raised a portion of the floor out of the main hold, and found six half-barrels of molasses. This settled the matter about food, and showed the inhumanity of the captain.

We had hoisted up the beef, when our man on watch warned us that we had been discovered. As soon as possible we replaced the plank in the floor and stood on them, when the captain, first mate and four sailors came running down the stairs. The captain and mate each had a revolver in hand. Our side comprised an Irishman named Malone, an American from Wisconsin named Fox, a stowaway that had been in the Mexican war that we called "Panama Jack," one Canadian, two others, whose names I have forgotten, and myself. Three of us had pistols, three had knives and two had bottles by the neck. Malone had a bottle only, but, arms or no arms, I don't think he cared for the whole ship's crew. He was a large, powerful man, and all sand, as will be seen hereafter.

The captain, seeing the beef on the floor, his first words were addressed the sailors, saying, "Men, put that beef back." Not a word was spoken by us, knowing that they could not get the beef back while we were on the plank, and as the sailors made no move, our courage rose, thinking we had only to deal with the captain and the mate. The captain then addressed us, saying that it was mutiny, and that his men should have nothing more to do with the ship, and he hoped we would all go to hell. We told him that it was not mutiny; that we were dying for want of wholesome food and water; that there was an abundance on board and we proposed to have it. After a wordy war, he said that he would give us navy rations, that being all we could claim. We hired a man to make the flour into light biscuit, and a change of diet, and healthy food did wonders in bringing the sick from their beds, and reviving the spirits of the passengers in general. The rations were to be given out every morning, and as I was appointed to receive and distribute them, I found I had no pleasant job. I would go to the cabin and ask the captain for our rations, and he would order me off the quarter-deck. To get even I would dare him to come down on the main deck. There was one man that was burning up with fever and he begged me to get him some water. I had a tin tube that I used to carry papers in, one end of which had a bottom. I tied strings to it and lowered it in the cask and filled two bottles for him. The captain saw him with them and asked where he got them. He refused to tell. "Then," said the captain, "I will make you tell or hang you to the yardarm." He ordered his men to take the man on deck, which they did. The captain went below and got a pistol and returning, asked him if he would tell now. The answer was no. "Then up you go," said the captain. "Men, put a rope around him." As they attempted to do so, he falteringly said: "I suppose if I must." "Not a word out of yez," said Malone. "I would like to see him hang a man to the yardarm here." That ended it. The captain beat a retreat to the cabin and was seen no more that evening.

It is strange what thirsty men will drink. I saw a fight one day over the dirty briny pickle in a keg of codfish tongues. We had now been out three weeks, and had made no headway except for the first eighteen hours. The A No. 1 clipper ship was transformed into a bark on the start. The rigging, the sailors said, was rotten, and they were afraid of wind. Finally, one morning, there were indications of wind, and it appeared that the captain shared their fears, as he ordered the light upper yards, with their sails, brought on deck. The wind came, and, as it increased, all hands were kept busy taking down the yards until there was nothing but the masts and the main yards left. A sail was raised on the mizzen mast, close to the deck, and with that and a close reefed jib, we ran for nearly two days. Some of the passengers were frightened almost out of their wits. One Irishman would pray and swear by turns.

Lying in an upper bunk next to the deck, I could look through the hatch and see seas apparently fifty feet above us. As the wind abated, sail was again made, but as the wind was nearly all the time dead ahead, we made but little progress. After about eighteen days of this kind of sailing, the captain said we were abreast of Acapulco. The wind being favorable for making that port, the ship was headed that way to get a supply of water. We were all delighted at the prospect of once again getting our feet on land, where we could get a change of food. We entered the harbor, one of the best in the world, it being completely land-locked by high mountains. There we found plenty of food at reasonable prices. Money being scarce among the inhabitants there was quite a competition for our trade. The change in use then among the Mexicans was cakes of soap.

As it took my last dollar to buy my passage on the *Cabarga*, I sold my watch for $4. We lay there four days, when the casks of water being filled and hoisted on board we again made sail. There was now almost a continual breeze, though nearly all the time dead ahead, so that our progress was very slow. After being eighteen days out the reckoning showed that we were not half way from Acapulco to San Francisco. As our water would not last if used in abundance, we were again put on an allowance. No fresh supply of provisions was brought on board, but we didn't care for that as long as the flour and molasses held out. From this place to San Francisco we had but two deaths, and there was nothing else transpired worthy of note.

There were some things occurred on the passage that were amusing, notwithstanding the serious predicament we were in. There was a sort of an exhorter, or one-horse preacher, on board, who took upon himself the responsibility of praying for the whole ship's company. There were also some who kept up their spirits during the worst, and would sing songs, and, if they could get anyone to furnish the music, would dance. One of the passengers, who had come through a severe attack of the fever, felt so rejoiced that he got out his violin and commenced to give us the "Arkansas Traveler," with its variations. Hearing this, the preacher came running down from where he had ben trying to console a departing spirit, and with a look of holy horror on his countenance, said: "For God's sake, men, what are you doing? Here is a man just over your heads about to draw his last breath." The mate of the vessel, a hot-tempered man, who happened to be standing close by, said he had something to say about what was permitted on board, and that one thing was sure, and that was, he had stood his praying long enough; that the men needed any recreation they could get, but if he kept on with his prayers and talk there wouldn't be a live man on the ship in a week. "I have seen enough of it," said he, "and if I see any more, the sharks will have a live man to chew on for a change." This was too strong talk for the preacher, and what praying there was after that was silent.

There was a tall Irishman on board, who would fly in a passion at nothing, and would slap a small inoffensive person in the face. He did this several times, when it was proposed to put him through a course. A little Jew that he had slapped the day before was put up as a stool pigeon for him to try it on again. His intructions were to get into the same argument, and if he saw the Irishman make a move as if going to strike, he, the Jew, was to hit him the best lick he could. The passengers then that were in it, placed themselves in two rows from the quarter-deck to the bottom of the stairs, knowing that would be his line of retreat after the battle opened. Sitting on the edge of the quarter-deck the dispute commenced between the two and had not gone far before the Irishman made a motion to strike. The little Jew saw us ranged in line to his elbow, and before he was hit got one in on the Irishman's mug that surprised him; although not so much as the next lick from Malone. Kicks now came thick and fast until he was allowed to pick himself up at the bottom of the stairs. He was a peaceable passenger the balance of the voyage.

When we seized the prisoners on board the ship, and during our war of words, the captain said that if we had not wasted the water and provisions there would have been enough for the voyage. I told him he was a liar. "Who said that?" said the captain, turning and facing us. Malone stood beside me, raising his hand to my shoulder said: "This young man; and he will tell you so again if you want to hear it."

On March 2, 1852, after passage of seventy-nine days, we arrived in San Francisco, and here I witnessed the saddest sight of the voyage. It was to see a German lady walk on shore among entire strangers, leading by the hand a little girl of 7 years, her sole companion, having lost her husband and two children on the passage.

At San Francisco I found it took $1 to get a meal, and that being 100 cents more than my pocket-book contained, a friend paid for the meal and my passage to Stockton. As he was going there, we went together. At the hotel where we stopped the landlord had a lot of four-foot wood which he wanted sawed in two and split for the stove, for which he was willing to pay $5 a day. I worked four days until the job was completed, paid the borrowed money and started for the mines in Tuolumne county, via Knight's Ferry. The country around Stockton was flooded with water, so that I had to proceed to French camp in a boat, where I struck the road on high land.

I stayed at the camp over night, thinking I could walk to Knight's Ferry, on the Stanislau river, in a day. Shouldering my blankets and taking my carpet sack in my hand, after a hearty breakfast, I set out. After walking about eight miles, my feet commenced to burn and soon to pain me so that I sat down and pulled off my boots to investigate. I found blood blisters as large as a quarter of a dollar on the bottom of my feet. The rain was coming down so that the tree afforded little shelter. The situation was anything but funny. I took a pin and let the blood escape, but that was little relief. While thinking what was best to do I saw a team coming and going the way I wished to travel. As it came up I showed my feet to the teamster and got an invitation to get in and ride. Arriving at the ferry boat late in the evening I was allowed the privilege of spreading my wet blankets on the ground floor inside of a canvas house for $1. This teamster, having only a part of a load, offered to take me as far as he went free. Here I was in luck, as my feet were so sore that I could hardly put them to the ground. Having been so long on board ship all the hard flesh had come off, leaving nothing but thin skin on the bottoms of my feet.

On the 9th of March, 1852, I found myself in Camp Saco, Tuolumne county, California, where the miners were as thick as bees in a hive. There was a great call for workmen, and as soon as I could use my feet I commenced my apprenticeship at mining, for $5 per day. When I left home father gave me $197. This I had to scheme as best I could to get through. I was fortunate in that I did not experience a sick day from the time I left home until I arrived in the mines. I had worked hard all my life, and thought if work would obtain money I could get it, but I soon found that steady employment was not be had in what was called the "diggings." I soon purchased a claim and commenced mining on my own hook. I made a little money, and as father's circumstances were rather cramped I sent it to him. This was a mistake on my part. I soon needed the money, as the water to work with gave out and I had to seek for day wages.

I got employment for three weeks, when my employer's claim ceased to pay. I then went to prospecting, but found it hard to find ground that would pay. However I secured several claims for the winter's work, and commenced on them as soon as the rainy season set in. For a time I did very well and commenced to get ahead, but soon was taken sick with the smallpox. Unfortunately I had sat on a jury beside a man that was taken sick with the disease, the next day the man died.

The terrible winter of '52-3 had now set in, the equal to which has not been known since. Flour rose from $10 to $100 a barrel, and board to $21 a week. I could not get strength enough to work and had to pay $21 a week for fourteen weeks' board. After the water gave out in '53 I heard that a company that was building a ditch up in the mountains above Sonora wanted workmen. I shouldered my blankets and went up and got work as a carpenter at $120 a month. I worked for that company until they bursted up, owing me $1204 of which I never received a dollar. Other workmen would go to Sonora every month or two, draw their wages and "blow it in," while I stayed in the mountains, where I did my own washing, etc., so as to save every cent possible, and get a home stake. Hearing our company had bursted we all packed our blankets and went to Sonora. That night the city burned. For three weeks I worked at carpentering and then returned to Camp Saco, no better off than when I left. I worked there a few months, then sold my claim and moved to Dom Pedro's Bar, on the Tuolumne river. I worked there for wages, in a river claim. The next spring I moved to Indian Bar and worked for a company at carpentering, working on pumps and wheels. The next year I worked at Bar, mining. I had a small stake and four of us formed a company and put in a dam and flume, turning and securing 800 feet of the river bed. Damming, turning and fluming the river was a perfect success, as far as the work went, but a freshet in the mountains one day swept everything in the river. Again I found myself nearly penniless.

I was disgusted with California, so were my partners, and we concluded to leave the country for some other clime. Arriving in San Francisco we saw a bark advertised to sail for Puget Sound. They also wanted men to work in the mill at Port Madison, as the vessel was going to that port for a cargo of lumber. They agreed to take us there for a consideration, and after we had worked there for six months they would give us a free passage back, provided we wished to return. This was in November, '57. We accepted the terms offered, and after a passage of twenty-three days on the bark *Charles Devans*, Captain Adams, arrived at G.A. Meigs' mill. About the first person I spoke to proved to be an acquaintance that I supposed was in California. It was Captain Guindon.

We went to work there and worked until the following spring, when news came that gold had been discovered on the Frazier river in British Columbia. Thinking that here was a chance to be first in new diggings, we chartered the schooner *Rover*, Captain Hicks, to take us to Fort Langley on that river. We could find but one person that could pilot us to the river; this was Charles Bachelder. He said that he had been there in the Hudson Bay company's employ. As we were going to an Indian country, we ransacked the mill towns for arms, not knowing but we might need them. Four of us that came from California together had navy revolvers. As there were nine going, we found five more, among which was one rifle and one double-barreled shotgun.

As we intended to proceed up the river from Langley in a canoe, we went to Port Gamble to purchase one and get what supplies we could, that we might want. We found there a fine large canoe, for which we paid $100. We had brought a chest of tools from Madison. This we lashed in the canoe, and after roping the canoe so as to tow it stern foremost, we started for Port Townsend. Here we were fortunate in finding some rocker irons, picks and shovels. We also laid in a three weeks' supply of provisions and a few blankets, and trinkets for Indian presents and barter. We lay there over night, and in the morning set sail. This was early in April of '58. Rounding Point Hudson, the breeze, already fresh, grew stronger, and, as we passed Point Wilson, it was blowing a gale. The wind was fair, but too strong for canoe towing in a rough sea. The captain ordered us all below and closed the hatch, as the seas commenced to board the schooner, and, worse than that, the seas would nearly throw the canoe on board. Fearing it would get broken, or do some damage to the schooner, Captain Hicks told us that he would have to cut it adrift, unless we chose to get into it and paddle away from the schooner. He had no more than said it than four of us stripped off everything but shirt and pants, and each grabbing a paddle sprang into the canoe. The captain cast her adrift and we now, in the true sense of the song, were left to "paddle our own canoe." This we soon found we could do without the least danger of swamping. Putting her head quartering on the seas she would bounce over them like a cork. We, being abreast of Smith's island, started for that place to make a harbor on the lee side.

Making that place we were picked up by the schooner, and as the wind died away the water became smooth. We enjoyed a meal of boiled salmon prepared by the captain's wife, a native. We now had fine sailing to the mouth of the Frazier, or to the mud flats near the mouth, where we brought up. We lay on them during one tide and skirmished for the mouth of the river, which we succeeded in finding in a tide marsh.

Hoisting sail, with a fair wind we glided along in perfectly smooth water, admiring the foliage and scenery along the river bank. We proceeded thus for a number of miles to where the river forked. Not knowing which fork to take we dropped the anchor, thinking that we would have some opportunity of ascertaining the channel that would take us to Langley. We had been at anchor but a few moments when an Indian in a small canoe was seen moving along the opposite bank of the river. Thinking that we could procure the desired information from him, nine of us manned our canoe and gave chase. Being experts with the paddle and having a fine canoe we gained on him, though it was evident that for some reason he was trying to avoid us. All at once the Indian disappeared, and we soon discovered the cause was that he had entered a creek coming into the Frazier at a right angle. Into this creek we went, determined to overtake him if possible. About 200 yards from the creek's mouth it made an abrupt turn to the right, where we found that, instead of catching the Indian, a whole tribe had caught us. The canoe had such headway that we could not stop, though we ceased to paddle.

Directly in front of us were at least thirty Indians with guns cocked and leveled at us. Though each of us carried a revolver we dared not move, as they had the drop on us. The canoe carried us to the bank of the stream, and within ten feet of the muzzles of their guns. Talk about hair standing on end and flesh crawling, this was my first experience in that line. There was not any show for us if they chose to open fire. Not a word was spoken for a few seconds, when, as they held their fire, our interpreter told them about our business, and proposed to give a blanket to one of them if he would pilot us to Fort Langley. To our relief they raised their guns saying they thought we were northern Indians coming to attack them. They proved to be friendly, and one willingly entered the canoe, and we returned to the schooner, hoisted sail, and as the breeze had freshened, we were soon speeding along toward the fort.

Our river fork proved to be caused by an island, so we had our scare and trouble for nothing. Although it was not funny at the time, we had many a laugh, in telling of our feelings at the time the guns were leveled at us. We made Langley soon after noon, and came to anchor between the fort and a large Indian ranchera on the opposite bank of the river. The Indians swarmed around us, nearly filling the river with their canoes.

As we wished to purchase something we could not find on the Sound, a Mr. Walker and myself went up the fort. The Hudson Bay company's houses were surrounded by a stockade or high board fence. As we neared the gate two Indians came out, one of whom appeared to be pretty well geared up. He had slung to his side a large army sword, and, seeing strangers before him, he drew the sword and attempted to charge us. He had advanced but a step or two when I covered him with a revolver. Seeing the situation the other Indian sprang forward and pinioned his arms and led him away. We then entered the stockade, where we found nearly all kinds of business carried on, even to making axes. The officers at the fort proved to be affable and obliging, showing a willingness to assist us in any way in their power. What we were most in need of was a whipsaw. We were unable to procure a new one, though they gave us one that had been used, which we made answer our purpose. The Indians were very anxious to trade with us, but not wishing to offend the traders at the post, we declined their offers and gave them a few presents. Having procured a pilot to take us as far as the territory of his tribe, which reached we parted with the schooner and proceeded up the river, sailing when there was a breeze and paddling when there was none. Having a fair wind the most of the time, we made a good day's run, but as evening approached a light rain or mist set in, which caused us to seek early camping quarters. While looking along the bank for a suitable place to camp, we heard a terrible uproar of voices, which our pilot said was a tribe of drunken Indians that were likely to give us trouble if we attempted to pass them then. Wishing to avoid, as far as possible, any difficulties with the Indians, we came to a halt and camped in an alder thicket. We soon had our tent spread and supper cooked. We were a little uneasy about the condition of our arms, and while considering the propriety of firing them off and reloading them, our pilot came in, saying that he saw Indians among the trees watching us.

Thinking we might wish to use our guns before morning, we fired them all off, making nearly sixty reports. We then reloaded, and putting two men on watch, to be relieved in three hours, turned in, but there was no sleep for me. I worked hard for a couple of hours trying to sleep; but gave it up, and, calling one of the watch in, I took his place and stayed on watch nearly all night. We were not disturbed, and our pilot said that the Indians were scared by the report of, as they supposed, so many guns. These Indians knew nothing of a gun that would shoot more than once. Early the next morning we passed the rancher's, finding all quiet. Arriving at Fort Yale our interpreter found that an old schoolmate had charge of the fort. He gave us all the information he could respecting the river, the dangerous places we would have to pass, etc. Proceeding from here to the foot of the little canyon we camped, and prospected for several days in the river and in the creek, but found nothing that would pay. Two of us then proceeded through the little canyon and found paying ground, on what was afterwards called Sailor's bar. We then returned and succeeded, by making several portages, in getting our canoe and outfit through. We now went to work sawing lumber to make rockers. After making three we commenced mining. We made $15 a day to the man on this bar, but others coming in so fast we were compelled to move to a new place, where we staked off a claim, determined to hold them and not be run out again. We had a little trouble with the Indians at a large rancher's, but pacified them by a present of a couple of blankets. At 4 p.m. we set one rocker and washed out $64. The next day we got $124. The river was rising about three feet every twenty-four hours, and the pay became less. We named this place Madison bar.

The Indians began to be troublesome, and, if they found a man alone, would take his kettle of beans off the fire and sit down and eat them up. There was one large Indian that persisted in working close to where my rocker sat. When Walker would lay his pick down he would pick it up, and Walker would have to wait and could not keep me supplied with dirt. I remonstrated with Walker for allowing him to do it. He said he did not wish to have any trouble with him. A few moments after, Walker again laid his pick down when the Indian grabbed it and put it on his shoulder, the handle pointing behind him. I sprang for the handle and gave a quick jerk, planting the Indian on the ground on his head and shoulders. He picked himself up and started down the river, muttering something and shaking his fist at me.

I concluded there would be trouble, and kept a lookout for him. Walker had to go down and get dinner, so that I was left alone. As the dinner hour arrived, I started down to camp, taking the shovel along for a weapon provided I should meet the Indian. I soon saw him coming with a large knife in his hand. As we neared each other I took hold of the shovel handle with both hands, intending to cut him down unless he got out of the trail. He got out, not only of the trail, but left the diggings. A few days after this Walker and I were sitting on the bar near our tent, when two shots were fired at us, the balls passing near, striking in the water. Having our revolvers on, we sprang up, dodged in the timber and ran for the place we thought the shots came from. We found no one there.

Finding our provisions getting low, five of us started for a fresh supply leaving what we had and the claims in charge of the four remaining. Arriving at Langley, we showed our $900 in gold dust to the employees of the fort. It was the first they had seen of any amount. We made as quick a passage to the Sound and back as we could. On arriving at Yale we found about 1500 miners there, waiting, on account of the high water.

The Indians were killing nearly all that ventured up the river, as we found bodies every day floating down with their heads cut off. Something had to be done. How numerous the Indians were we had no way of finding out. A meeting was called and it was agreed that two things must be done at once; one was to disarm all the Indians about Yale, and the other was to raise a company as large as we could find arms for, which should go through the canyons, and if occasion required, kill all we could. We at once commenced disarming the Indians. They kicked at first, but soon gave in. How many guns we got in all, I never heard. We had thirty muskets besides many knives in our tent. These guns we tagged with the owners' names, to be returned after they became good Indians, and gave them in care of the Hudson Bay company. When we came to take stock of rifles to fight with but sixty could be found. The Indian guns we tried, but found them worthless. However, sixty men were ready with their guns and were soon on the march up the river. They passed through the canyons uninterrupted. Many Indians were seen looking down from the high rocks, but they did not care to attack so large a force. At the head of the long canyon they found a large camp or ranchera. While the riflemen were sitting down consulting what they should do next, a Frenchman came running out from the brush, his face covered with blood from a scalp wound made from an Indian's musket. He said that his partner was killed. Two Indians soon came running out, but they lay down on sight of the whites. This opened the campaign. Crossing the river about forty "good" Indians were left at that place, and from there to Yale about as many more. There were no more men seen floating down the river after that. The Indians who were left were so cowed that they would beg, but dare not steal.

As soon as the river commenced falling, the miners began to ascend. Every day we would see canoes, blankets, sacks of flour and all kids of mining outfits that would float, coming down. To see men swimming and drowning was an every day occurrence. Near the head of the long canyon I found a man by the name of Smart. He was an acquaintance and came from Port Madison. He said he had been there two weeks and had seen fourteen men drowned. It was the worst place in the river, and was called the large whirlpool. We made a portage there, and stayed over night. A few hundred yards above there we were through the canyon and out of dangerous water. We went up as far as the mouth of Thompson's river, and getting no prospects that would justify working, we turned about and started back to prospect some places we saw in the canyon.

It is the safest way, in running down a swift stream, to turn and land with bow up stream. This we attempted to do above the large whirlpool, but found the current so swift that we could not turn. I sat in the bow with a coil of rope in my hand, and as the canoe neared the rocks I jumped; striking my feet on a slippery rock, they went out from under me precipitating me onto the river. I struck my face on the rocks, and cut my eye badly. I held on to the rope, though my eyes were blinded with blood. I found myself going with the canoe, but fortunately my breast came in contact with a rock, so that I held the canoe until she swung in shore but a few feet from the rapids. I could not see, but I could hear those in the canoe singing out for me to hold on. As soon as the boys got out of the canoe, they lifted me out of the water, washed the blood from my face, and proceeded to Smart's tent, bandaged my eye with some bacon and cloths. The boys said that they would not leave until I could see, as a man needed both eyes to travel that river. We lay there three days, then came on down, stopping now and then to prospect, but finding nothing that paid. The claim that we left was worked out when we returned, and as our provisions were again pretty low, and winter approaching, we concluded to pull out for the Sound.

There was one laughable incident occurred at Yale, while we were taking the arms from the Indians. We had a guard to watch, to see that while some were in the Indian tents taking their arms, others did not run to the brush and take weapons with them. Captain Guindon, to whom I referred before, was there, and on watch. We had just come out of a tent, where we had secured some muskets, when I saw Guindon raise his pistol and fire at an Indian that was running from the tent we had just left. The Indian fell to the ground with, apparently, something in his blanket. We were on top of him before he could get up, and found that he had a loaf of bread.

We returned to the Sound, and again went to work for G.A. Meigs. I worked in the different mills on the Sound until 1865, when I married and settled down on Whidbey island, where I am now living and have a family of six children.

I have here placed before you part of my experiences of more than forty years on the coast, and more than thirty on Puget Sound. When I came I found it a wilderness, peopled by numerous tribes of Indians and a few whites. The only way of making a living was by working in the sawmills, or, Indian like, feeding on clams, venison and potatoes. For fifteen years there was no perceptible change in the situation. It was only on the completion of the Northern Pacific railroad that the emigration began to set this way, and we are fast becoming a populous state. Towns no sooner have a birth than they become cities, some with already more than 50,000 population. And why is this? It is simple enough. In this state, which has an outlet in this Puget sound basin, we have everything that was required to line the Atlantic coast with cities from Maine to North Carolina. If all things were made for a purpose who can imagine what a picture this inland sea will in the future present. Think of the magnitude of these waters. All the navies of the world could be so secreted that not a spar could be seen by people traveling by the regular route of steamers running between Olympia, at the head of the Sound, and Victoria on the Straits of Juan de Fuca. Looking back across the continent, we can see another cause for the increased immigration here. Uncle Sam's maelstrom-like crucible, into which has been passing the surplus human products of nations, is filling up and pouring over the Rockies, astonishing the world with the fruits of its amalgamation, and causing the crowned heads of Europe to behold with vague apprehension its approaching overflow. And why? Because they see a monument of liberty raised by a freedom-loving people, antagonistic to their forms of government. It was commenced by our revolutionary heroes and finished by those of the rebellion, and, if I mistake not, on its summit our children will see Columbia stand, the world's dictator.

In 1875, after being twenty-four years on this coast, I visited the old folks at home. I found them all alive and well, father, mother, four sisters and a brother. To them I was an entire stranger. From a youth of 21 years I had become a gray-haired man of 45.

Urban E. Hicks

The Fraser River gold boom
graphically described by one who was there.

East Sound, Orcas Island — March, 1893

In the spring of 1858, soon after news reached Olympia that gold placer mines had been discovered on Fraser river, Gallatin Hartsock, John Forbes, Thomas B. Hicks and the writer formed a party, purchased a chinook canoe, loaded it with provisions, mining tools, etc., and set out down Sound for the new El Dorado. Our canoe was a splendid specimen of Indian architecture, twenty feet in length, made from a large cedar tree, nearly new and decorated with a long prow like a swan's neck, the edges of the prow studded with small marine shells, having the appearance of beads, and gaily painted vermilion on the inside. It was well stanchioned with ribs and thwarts and as tight as a drum. Four well made, light maple paddles and a large canvas sail constituted our propelling machinery, which, with a favorable wind and good muscles, buoyed by hopes of shining dust lying just beyond, only awaiting our arrival to be gathered into long purses, fairly skimmed us over the bright shining waves of the sea. We watched the receding shores, as we moved along, on each side of us like a flying panorama. We chose paddles rather than oars because we could hug shores closer against strong currents, and all could sit facing the direction the canoe was going. We found it much to our advantage in this respect, as ascending the rapid currents of the river and in making sharp turns around projecting rocks and rugged promontories. I had been employed in the *Pioneer and Democrat* newspaper office for some time previous, and owing to the hardships and exposures endured in the Indian war campaign of 1855-6, had not fully recovered, which, together with close confinement in a printing office for more than twelve months, had reduced me in strength and flesh very much, and I hailed with delight the opportunity of outdoor life again and an open sail on the broad salt waters of the Sound. And here let me say that the trip of about five months I was in the water more or less nearly every day, frequently up to my neck and shoulders in the icy waters of the Fraser river, yet I caught no cold nor felt an ache or pain, and never enjoyed better health.

Not any of us had more than a limited experience in the handling of a canoe, but my brother Tom, who had been in the custom house employ under Colonel Isaac N. Ebey, was pretty well acquainted with the various channels and numerous islands of the Sound, and he assumed command of the craft and did the steering. Hartsock was my wife's father, Forbes was a brother-in-law and two brothers formed the party. Forbes took the bow of the canoe, Hartsock, being a large, stout man, was seated in the center, the writer just behind him, and brother Tom in the stern.

We skirted the east shore of the Sound all the way down, touching at Steilacoom and Seattle, (Tacoma was not then thought of), and passed through the canoe passage east of Whidby island, out into Bellingham bay, and arrived at Whatcom about the 1st of June, 1858. Here were camped about 2000 miners, in tents and log huts, around the mud flats and debris of the remains of an old saw mill and timbers of tramways and broken wharves used by the Bellingham Bay Coal Mining company. Every conceivable kind of small sailing craft lined the shore and filled the offing, and a roaring, rolicking, rough and tumble scene met the eye on all sides.

I have been asked to explain why so many miners were at Whatcom in the early discovery of gold on Fraser river.

Nearly all of them were from California. Steamship and sailing lines advertised to carry passengers from San Francisco to the gold fields, but only landed them at Victoria. From thence they had to make their way as best they could across the gulf to the mainland, some fifty or sixty miles, to Fraser river, and thence up the river for at least 100 more before reaching the gold fields. There was no trail on land up the river at that time, though a wagon road was afterward opened as far as Port Hope, I believe, which required some years to construct. An effort was made to build up a rival town to Victoria on the American side of the boundary line, and Bellingham bay was the most feasible point. A small trail was cut from the bay to Fort Langley on the Fraser river, over which many miners packed their outfits, and then trusted to luck to get up the river. One or two small stern-wheel steamers were running on the river as far up as Port Hope. Many purchased canoes and other small craft from the Indians on the bay and among the islands and made their way up the river by way of the entrance or mouth.

Whatcom, at the time we reached it, was a busy place, built up mostly of canvas tents where large quantities of miners' supplies were promiscuously piled, while others were constructing log houses, and one small brick structure was put up about 14 x 16, which still stands to mark the spot around which most of the business then centered. But little was doing toward permanent improvement, as all seemed bent in getting out of there as quick as possible for the mines. The city is now about the third largest on the sound.

Many were returning from the mines badly busted and forlorn, while as many more were going on utterly oblivious to the warnings and woeful stories of hardships and disappointments that had befallen those who were returning. We, like others, paid no heed to the warnings but determined to push on, and after one day's rest again pulled out from shore for the mouth of Fraser river. I verily believe that had we met the last white man who had been to the mines on his return and had he told us not to go, we would have gone on, for we had started for the mines and we intended to "get there," sink or swim, bust or no bust. We skirted along the shores of the bay until we found our way into the Nooksack and thence into the gulf of Georgia. Our first night out from Whatcom we attempted to camp on a sand spit at or near the mouth of the Nooksack, and not knowing the state of the tides in the gulf, we came near getting swamped in the quicksand before getting afloat again. While we were wading and floundering through the treacherous sands, in pitchy darkness, with a roaring surf in our rear and a howling wind in our faces, trying to get our canoe into deep water again, a party of belated stragglers, like ourselves, who were not far distant, on a kind of raft made of drift logs and old sawmill slabs, stuck fast in the sinking sands and, surrounded by the howling phosphorescent waves, struck up the old familiar song:

"Ain't you mighty glad you got out of Whatcom,
 Got out of Whatcom, got out of Whatcom,
Ain't you mighty glad you got out of Whatcom,
 Down in Bellingham Bay?"

Well, yes, we were glad to get out of Whatcom, even though we were in such a predicament. And I have many times thought since of the circumstances and the narrow escapes we made on that and many other occasions during the trip.

The next day we made the long pull of twenty miles, or more, across the gulf to Point Roberts. The sun shone down on us with a scorching heat. Long rolling waves made our canoe swing from the crest of high mountains of water down into deep valleys, and all of us paid more or less tribute to old Neptune while keeping up a steady stroke with our paddles. The tide and currents were against us, and late in the evening we arrived, tired and

worn out, on a beautiful narrow beach, on the east side of the long penin-
sula. It had a small stream of cold water trickling down among the rocks
and a cool shade of arbutus and white willows lined the beach. Instead of
rounding the point, as we should have done, we were only too glad to get
ashore and rest our tired limbs and quench our burning thirst. Brother Tom
and John Forbes generally slept in the canoe, while old man Hartsock and
myself bunked ashore. Just at daylight next morning the old man and I were
aroused by the shouts of the boys for us to hurry aboard. The tide had
receded, the wind suddenly arose and the canoe pounding on the rocks,
threatening destruction at every wave. We had to wade out waist deep to
get to the canoe, got in and pulled with all our might to get out of the way of
rocks, when we encountered a heavy, chopped sea, the waves like hay-
cocks, which our canoe could not ride but plunged through, filling it almost
full, and for a few minutes threatening to engulf us among the rocks and
whirlpools, which it would have been impossible to survive. However, we
rounded the point and beached the boat just in time to save it from sinking.
We hurriedly unloaded, built a fire and proceeded to dry out as fast as
possible. Our flour was in sacks and was the self-raising kind, being
manufactured and mixed with cream soda, as most all flour for miners was
then made. The warm sun soon appeared, and by evening we were all right
again. We pulled out and entered the mouth of the Fraser river just about
sundown.

The English authorities at Victoria had stationed a small gunboat in the
river just above the mouth for the purpose of collecting a mining tax from
all Americans seeking to trade or mine on the river. Of this we had been
warned and its location accurately described by those returning, and we
resolved to dodge the tax if possible. Chance favored us with a brisk breeze
up stream. The tide was also with us, and about dusk we hoisted sail, pulled
out into the broad stream and plied our paddles vigorously. When about
opposite the gunboat we were hailed and ordered to come ashore, to which
we paid no attention. A loud threat, accompanied by the rattling of chains
and rumbling of gun carriage on deck, informed us that if we did not stop
we would be fired upon. We told them to shoot and be _____ if they
wanted to, that we had good American powder and ball, and it was a game
that two could play at. The commander ordered a ship's boat lowered,
manned with a crew of sailors to overhaul us, but we laughed at them. They
pushed out lively after us, but our craft soon left them far behind, and we
escaped. The tax was $5 per quarter for each miner or trader. We passed
Fort Langley the next day on the opposite side of the island, and saw no
more tax-gatherers until long afterward. A good many Americans paid the
tax, but we never paid a cent. A namesake of mine came around in the fall
trying to collect this tax. I argued him out of it. He claimed that the tax went
to maintain the Victoria police, not one of whom were on the river at that
time. I pointed out to him that had it not been for Yankee enterprise these
mines would probably have never been discovered; that their discovery

brought the country into notice and greatly augmented the trade and wealth of the town of Victoria; that the American miners needed no police protection or interference; that we were abundantly able to take care of ourselves, and that we did not propose to pay tax for the maintenance of a few British marines at Victoria. It was a shame, if not robbery, to compel the poor miner to pay a license to mine before he had discovered whether there was anything to mine. Not one in a hundred who reached the country was able to find half the amount it cost him to get there.

On reaching the first rapids in the river we came to a large ranch of Indians camped on a low island or sandbar. The whole camp was on a platform erected near the middle of the river, about ten or twelve feet in height, where they lounged and slept, to get above the immense swarms of mosquitoes that rose from the surface of the water in clouds that fairly darkened the sun and stifled the breath. I have seen mosquitoes on the Mississippi bottoms, but nothing to compare with the swarms we encountered on Fraser river. We had to carry a brush in each hand, and at every stroke of the paddle brush the face and neck, and yet the blood trickled down each side of the neck from the ears and our faces were swollen from the bites and stings of these desperate insects. At night we generally camped near a large drift, which we set on fire and then got into the thickest of the smoke, covered head and ears with our blankets and managed to sleep a little.

At the first ranch of Indians we hired the son of the chief to pilot our canoe, who assumed command, and by his knowledge of the currents and eddies we made much better progress than we could without him. He was followed in a small canoe by his two wives, who, at night time, camped near us. We were lucky in getting this son of a chief for a helmsman, as he was well known by all the Indians on the river, and his presence saved us from molestation and annoyance. The Indians of Fraser river are of a brighter color, much more intelligent and brave than those of the Sound country. They gave the miners much annoyance by theft and robbery. Several whites were massacred below Port Hope, and above there were white miners and Chinese were waylaid, killed, their heads cut off and bodies cast into the stream. In this hostile attitude they were evidently encouraged by old Hudson bay trappers and employes who had settled among them. They looked upon the "Boston men," or Americans, as enemies to their race, while the English, or "King George men," were regarded as friends. My brother Tom and I had fought Indians before, and we could all talk the jargon or chinook language pretty well; hence we knew how to deal with them and they generally let us alone as soon as they made our acquaintance. We were five days going up the river. The same distance I afterwards made in one day coming down.

When we arrived at Port Yale we found at least 5000 miners camped just below the mouth of the great canyon, through which it was almost an utter impossibility to push further with canoes or any kind of craft. Still hundreds would try it, only to meet with disaster and death. Large canoes and boats would be caught in the whirl, be upended and disappear, only to be seen again miles below all in splinters. It reminded me of the sight I had seen below at Port Hope. But few were engaged in washing the gravel and sands of the shore, but between Port Hope and Port Yale both sides of the stream were lined pretty thickly all along with men of every nation and tongue, busily at work with rocker and "long tom," digging into the banks and washing the loose sand and gravel of the various bars and shoals of the rapid stream. The water was icy cold as it came rushing down from the snows and ice caps of the far north. The principal bars that were being mined between Port Hope and Port Yale, fifteen miles in extent, were Puget Sound bar, Emery's bar and Hill's bar, the latter being just across the river from Port Yale, and the richest bar on the lower Fraser. Apparently every inch of ground where a prospect could be found was claimed between the above named ports, and to go further was out of the question with us. After some consulation we decided to drop back down to Puget Sound bar, a majority of the claimants on that bar being from the Sound country. We located claims at the head of the bar, the water of the bar being eight or ten feet deep at that time. We built a comfortable log cabin, and brother Tom and John Forbes took the canoe and went into the freighting business. No steamer then plying on the river could make the rapids from Port Hope to Yale, hence all goods and supplies had to be transferred to small boats at Hope and towed by long ropes around the most dangerous and rapid places. They each made $5 a day, taking a full day to make the trip up and then coming down in less than forty minutes.

Soon after we located, the miners of the bar held a meeting to elect a new bookkeeper or "alcade" of the bar, the one first chosen having resigned and left for home. Through the personal friendship of Joseph Foster of Seattle, who had been a member of the legislature of Washington territory from King county, the writer was chosen as bookkeeper. I had never been in the mines before and really knew nothing of the duties of the office, but Foster made a majority of the boys believe otherwise and I was chosen by nearly a unanimous vote. Soon after this Billy Ballou started an express route on the river and gave me the agency for the bar. The two offices enabled me to make enough to keep up expenses until the water fell so that we could commence washing the sand and gravel on our claims. In California the heads of bars were always found to be the richest, and when we succeeded in getting the first pan of dirt, and it panned out about six bits, we could have sold out for $5000, but we felt sure of a much larger sum. A small portable sawmill was running on the bluff opposite Yale, where we bought enough lumber, paying $100 per 1000 feet, to build a forty-foot current wheel to raise water for a sluice. This wheel we set on two large flatboats, for which we paid $450, and after about two months' steady work we got our sluice running. We employed two sets of hands and ran night and day. I ran the night shift and Hartsock the day force. We paid $4 per day and $5 per night and board. The first run of about forty hours we took out about $900, which enabled us to square up all our indebtedness and lay in additional supplies. We took in another partner, which enabled us to hold five claims in one body. Each claimant, by rules of the bar, was entitled to hold twenty-five feet up and down the bar or bank, and running back into the hills indefinitely.

To illustrate how luck runs in a mining camp I will state an incident: The boys were in the habit of coming up to our cabin in the evening to get their mail, learn the news and "swap" stories. I had practiced a little in making "machine" poetry, or mining songs, and occasionally would offer one for the evening's entertainment. One of those jingling rhymes seemed to please a poor, simple fellow who held a claim a short distance below us, and he proposed that if I would give him a copy of my song he would give me his claim. The transfer was duly made, and in a few days after I sold the claim for $100 cash, and the parties who bought it within two weeks took out over $2000 in small, round dust, which they discovered in a pocket or hole near the main bank, which had previously been covered with water, and where no one thought of looking for more than mere color. We did not take out much more than this from all our claims, and I returned home at the commencement of winter with just about as much as it had cost me to go and come.

Another incident will show "miners luck." One day I got a pot of badly burnt beans outside our cabin door, along side of which the main trail ran, and over which hundreds of miners were coming and going. About noon I noticed a poor fellow come stumbling along. As he passed the pot of beans he stopped and looked earnestly at it, and then looked all around to see if anyone was near. When he saw me he moved a little further off and again stopped and looked at the beans. I went up and asked him what he wanted. He weakly, and half hesitatingly, asked me if he might have those beans in the pot. I told him he could, and at them he went like a hungry wolf. I watched him for a few minutes as he stuffed the black and badly burned grub down his throat, and ordered him to hold on. The poor fellow was half scared through fear that I would take them away from him. I invited him inside the shanty, warmed a pot of coffee and set out a hunk of bread and some cold boiled ham and bade him pitch in. I then saw that the poor fellow was nearly starved. He had been away up Thompson river, had run out of grub, was nearly naked and barefooted, and was trying to make his way back the best he could. He had come from San Francisco, where he had been the head bookkeeper in a large wholesale grocery establishment, and was a young man of fine education and social standing at home. As we needed additional help just then, I gave him a job shoveling tailings during the night run, out of which he made enough to get a good pair of boots, better clothing and pay his passage by steamer to San Francisco. There is so much, if not more, distress, hunger, want and poverty to be seen right in the midst of a mining camp than anywhere else on earth, and my experience taught me that it is not, as a general thing, the one who dips the precious metal out of the ground that gets the best share, but rather the saloonkeeper, gambler and trader.

The upper Fraser was no doubt richer in gold deposits than the lower, but the whole seemed to be placer, as no quartz leads have been discovered that would pay working. The gold was float gold, difficult to save, requiring large quantities of quicksilver and the best of apparatus to catch and save enough to pay for labor and expense in mining. Most of the lower bars and mining camps soon fell into the hands of Chinamen, thousands of whom remained for many years, and are still employed in many places from Port Hope to the headwaters of all tributaries.

The Indians, as before stated, gave the whites much trouble and annoyance at the outset, until finally two companies of volunteers, of 100 men each, were organized, armed and equipped, who marched in parallel lines on each side of the river and cleaned the Indians completely out, burning their ranches and winter provisions wherever found. The Indians caught and dried large quantities of salmon, upon which they subsisted during the winter. These salmon dry-houses had very much the appearance of old Missouri tobacco dry-houses, tons of salmon being hung up under long sheds, which, when set on fire, would create a blaze that could be seen and smelled for miles around. This raid was gotten up entirely by the American miners, without waiting to consult the British authorities, and was over before it was fairly known in Victoria. Governor Douglas of Victoria afterward came up to Yale with a small file of marines, but peace had been restored, the volunteers returned and disbanded before he got there.

Among the noted personages at Yale along about this time, was the notorious Ned McGowan, of vigilante notoriety in San Francisco. I had just read his pamphlet, detailing his narrow escapes and hot pursuit by the vigilant committee of San Francisco, and curiosity lead me to take a trip up to Yale one evening to see him. He was the king of gamblers and thugs of the Pacific coast, and a more repulsive looking wretch was not to be met with anywhere. I came near being shot at for my timidity in trying to get a good look at him, as I was mistaken for a vigilante spy just from San Francisco. The failure of a pistol cap, perhaps, saved me from becoming another one of his victims.

As before stated, I returned home at the commencement of winter, coming down as far as Langley in a canoe, and there engaging passage on a small stern wheel steamer, owned by one of the Wrights, who charged us $10 each for passage to Victoria. The boat had been condemned by the British authorities at Victoria, and as we were crossing the gulf we met the little propeller *Blackhawk*, who threw a letter of warning on board to the captain, whereupon about thirty or forty passengers were transferred to the *Blackhawk* and the remainder of us were taken back to Langley. The captain refused to refund our passage money, and as there was no legal redress we had to pocket our loss. A clear case of downright robbery. After waiting a day or two at Langley the old Hudson bay steamer *Otter* came up with a quantity of coal for the gunboat referred to, and after unloading took on board about 250 passengers at Langley for Victoria—passage, $5. We were all crowded on the upper deck, without food or shelter, and the deck covered with coal dust. She steamed down to the mouth of the river in the evening and found the water so rough at the bar the captain decided not to risk it until the weather was more favorable. He anchored just above the first island in the river and remained all night in howling wind and freezing cold. The only warmth we could get was around the smokestack, and much scrambling, pulling and hauling took place among a lot of desperate men to hold and retain a place near the stack. A dozen bloody fights was the result before daylight. We were becoming desperate and an impromptu meeting was held by the miners, a committee instructed to interview the captain and demand that he either proceed to Victoria or take us back to Langley where we could get something to eat. He decided to cross the sands at all hazards, and for the second time I thought the bottom of the sea was my destiny. But the *Otter* was a very staunch built boat, and although we struck bottom several times before getting into deep water, she finally made Victoria about 10 o'clock at night, landing as dirty, ragged, frozen and hungry a set of mortals as was ever seen. We had been about forty hours without anything to eat or fresh water to drink, and many were so numb with cold they could scarcely walk.

In Victoria I disposed of my dust at $14.50 per ounce and took passage on a small sloop called the *Blue Wings*, Jimmy Jones skipper, for Olympia, paying $13 passage. We made the run from Victoria to Olympia in twenty-three hours, about the fastest trip that had been known by sail up to that time.

Hartsock, Forbes and brother Thomas remained on the river all winter, the two former returning in the spring, bringing but little with them, and brother Tom has remained on the river ever since. All of the party are still alive, and I verily believe the trip added years to the life of all.

Henry Beckett

Mr. Beckett caught the Fraser River gold fever in Cleveland, Ohio in the summer of 1858. He sailed around the Horn on the Herman *studying human nature and drinking in the beauties of Mother earth whenever he was in port.*

Orting, Washington — March 3, 1893

The summer of 1858 found the writer in Cleveland, O. All at once we were electrified by the news of the discovery of gold on Frazer river, British Columbia. The fabulous accounts outrivaled the palmy days in California. The flaming posters met one's eye in all parts of the city informing us that two steamers would leave New York August 20th for San Francisco, by way of the Isthmus of Panama. The fever struck me hard—so hard that I resigned the position I held, sold my goods and chattels, took passage at Cleveland on one of the lake steamers for Buffalo. On this trip I experienced a fearful storm. The steamer pitched and labored so hard that every one on board thought it would founder. The captain ordered the crew, and as many of the passengers as he could get, to heave part of the deck load overboard, which eased her, so that she rode out the storm in safety, losing only a portion of her cargo and having three of her crew disabled, and arrived at her destination twenty-four hours behind time. I took the Erie railroad and arrived in New York too late to obtain passage on either of the steamers that left on the 20th. So eager was the rush that bonuses of $100 were freely offered to the lucky ones that had tickets, but they refused to sell. The disappointed ones stood at the wharf and saw the steamers pull out completely jammed with passengers. Instead of waiting ten days, as we expected to do, we found they were about to establish a new line of steamers. The pioneer ship of the new line, *Herman*, was to leave on the 24th of August, to be afterward followed by the *Washington*. All old New Yorkers will remember those two steamers, which were built in New York in the year 1848 and cost $600,000 apiece, and which for ten years carried the United States mails to Southampton and Bremen. The democratic administration of that day, with the usual plea of economy, gave the carrying of the United States mails to a rival foreign company, so that the boats had to be taken off and laid up to suffer the fate of the splendid Collins line. That was protecting American interests with a vengeance. On the 24th day of August the steamship *Herman* pulled out from the dock at North river, drawing twenty-six feet of water, amidst the booming of cannon and the hurrahs of thousands of people who had congregated to see the steamer and their friends off for the golden shores of the Pacific. In sailing down the bay I was familiar with all the surroundings. The flat shore of New Jersey, the beauties of Staten island, Fort Hamilton and New Utrich stood out in all their beauties. Fire island passed and most of our passengers felt the swell of the ocean for the first time in their lives and began to realize what seasickness was.

There were but few passengers on deck to get a sight of the last land to be seen as we were leaving New York, the highlands of Nevesink. The next day found us well out to sea, steering south, with few on deck or attending meals. Second day out all passengers were ordered to muster on deck and show their tickets. The captain had neglected to do this in the lower bay, which was usual. The ship was searched from stem to stern. The muster showed 629 passengers, thirty-two stowaways and 120 crew, a total of 781 souls, which was the greatest number up to that time, that had ever been over that route on one ship. The captain treated the stowaways with great humanity. He told them they had no business on that ship without tickets, and that he would punish them for their audacity by leaving them in Rio de Janeiro, 5000 miles from home. He never put his threat into execution, but carried them right through to San Francisco at a loss of over $3000. A more hetrogeneous set of humanity it would be hard to find under any circumstance. Almost every nation of Europe was represented, also every state in the Union, Canada and the West Indies. Almost every trade and profession had a representative. The captain flattered us by saying that to take us all round we were the finest lot of passengers he ever saw on the *Herman* and he had been captain of her for a number of years. Almost all of us were between the ages of 25 and 40. There were only forty-one lady passengers.

A long voyage at sea is a splendid place to study character. There was the German, ever smoking and telling us how much better all the flowers and fruits of Germany were than any other country. The excitable Celt, always ready to back up his argument with muscle, the clanish Cornish men, who kept aloof from all the rest, the pompous Englishman, who paraded up and down the deck and felt so self-sustained, the plug ugly and Bowery boys of New York, who thought they could overawe the quieter ones by saying: "Don't you smell the blood on my boots?" These were of the same stripe, who in the war became bounty-jumpers and whom the vigilant committee in Andersonville hung. We whiled away our time as well as we could, some by dancing at every opportunity, and that was almost every evening, some by card playing, some by reading, and some of the most interesting time was spent in debates between the fire-eaters of the south and the free-soilers of the north, but without bitterness, although we used to love to dress them out just for the fun. A very prominent person among us was a man who styled himself the Rev. Dr. Tyler, who used to preach to us Sundays and to tell us what miserable sinners we were, and the great necessity we had to be redeemed from the wrath to come, and how God planted his footsteps on the seas and rode upon the storms, all of which took well. He thought no one knew him on that ship, but there was a man from Sandusky, O., by the name of F. Ford, who knew him well, and who said the doctor belonged to that set of intriguing, smooth-tongued fellows who persuaded weak-minded women that their husbands were not proper affinities for them. In other words, he was one of a sect called at that time "free lovers." The woman with him, and who passed as his wife, was the wife of a respectable man in Sandusky. She took all the money she could obtain, and Tyler borrowed of her husband all he could, and they left the husband almost destitute with four small children. We came to the conclusion that his spiritual teachings came from a corrupt fountain, and we had no use for it.

We had been out about twenty days when the first fight occurred. Everything had been pleasant up to that time. The steerage passengers were not allowed soft bread, and the few plug-uglies that were on board made a raid on the bakehouse and took all the bread they could. The baker showed fight, but they overpowered him and would have thrown him overboard, but some of the hands belonging to the ship came along just in time to save him. The captain put the leaders in irons. The next day at breakfast another of the dead rabbits threw a cup of hot coffee in a sick man's face. A man from Kansas cleaned him out, and when he got up he drew a knife and slashed Kansas five bad flesh wounds before they could capture him. His friends, the plug uglies and dead rabbits, drew their knives and revolvers, but they were overpowered by superior numbers. Kansas was put in the doctor's care and was about the first case he had had since we left New York. Mr. Plug Ugly was handed over to the captain, put in irons, and the captain was notified that if he was turned loose among the passengers any more they would heave him overboard.

This day we saw the first sail since leaving New York. We had sailed over 4000 miles and our hearts were made glad by one of the most beautiful sights to be seen on the ocean — a full-rigged clipper ship under full sail, with a fair wind, with stunsils, topgallant and sky scrapers set, bowling along at the rate of twelve knots an hour. At quite a distance she ran up a signal that she wanted to speak to us and wanted to get our latitude and longitude. Our captain sent some seamen up in the rigging with a long blackboard, with the information written on it with chalk. The captains spoke through their trumpets. She swept down on us like an ocean bird set free, with the stars and stripes flying at her mast-head, bound for Boston. We gave her one rousing cheer as we passed her, and soon left each other.

About this time there was a great deal of dissatisfaction with the steerage passengers about their food and the way it was cooked and served; so much so that the captain promised them that after we left Rio he would see it righted and that allayed the bad feeling for a time. Early in the morning, the twenty-sixth day out from New York, we crossed the equator with the sun straight over our heads. For a number of nights it was so warm below deck that the passengers laid up on deck so thick that they were in the way of the deck hands working the ship, one Englishman yelled out at the top of his voice, "Blast my heyes, hopen that 'ole so hi can git ha breath of hair." The next day we saw land for the first time since leaving New York. When the lookout cried "Land" we yelled like demons. It has been said by Italians, "see the Bay of Naples and die," but they never could have seen the bay of All Saints, Rio de Janeiro. Many travelers speak of the beauties of New York harbor coming in from the sea, which, in summer time, with the pretty cottages painted white with the green Venetian blinds, surrounded with trees and flowers, is a great contrast to the many ports of Europe, with their dull approaches. In viewing Rio from the sea it makes one think of the elysian fields of a Mohammedan paradise, with the beautiful girls, which, they say, were made to tempt the youth and torment the men, left out. The first striking object that catches the eye is Sugar Loaf mountain, which was considered so steep that no one could be found to ascend to the top of it, until some Yankee bluejackets accomplished it and to the great annoyance of the port officials left the American flag flying at the top. All was done in a joke, never thinking they would take it so to heart, as to offer two rewards, one to the person who would climb up and take the flag down, and another to the person who would identify those who dared insult them by raising a foreign flag, in such a place. But the flag remained there until it was destroyed by the elements in defiance of all rewards. In the background of the Sugar Loaf mountain the land rises gradually to quite high hills covered with the loveliest of tropical productions, consisting of orange groves, cocoanut trees, coffee and bananas, interspersed with evergreens and tropical flowers and flowering vines enlivened by birds of beautiful plumage. It is a scene to enchant the eye and mind. The first conspicuous building that came to view was the great fort with its frowning port holes and guns, one of which they fired ahead of us as a warning to heave under the guns of the fort, so they could examine our ship's papers and give her a permit to proceed to the upper bay. Such is the red tape of Brazillian officials, even in times of peace, so unusual in American ports.

The next place of interest after leaving the fort was the coaling station on a small island. We proceeded on up the bay, cast anchor, the city of Rio on one side of us and another small city on the other, with Signal hill towering up in the former, with a panorama of beauty in the back ground. After casting anchor we were surrounded by a fleet of small boats, some of them containing government officials, who informed our captain that only 100 of our passengers would be allowed on shore at one time. A number of us had already made arrangements with the boatmen to take us ashore for a York shilling apiece, when the captain ordered us not to leave the ship until we had received passports duly signed. That was the custom there any time they took a notion to enforce it, and caused such a bad feeling that the captain guaranteed for our good behavior, but the officials demanded that we leave all firearms on board ship, and, also our pocket-knives. We asked the officials what they took us for, and if they thought we were a lot of pirates. Finally they agreed to let us all go ashore at once, which gave great satisfaction. In less than one hour most all of us were ashore.

We got into a quarrel with the boatmen, who took us as soon as we landed, as they tried to impose on us by charging double price. Some of them paid it rather than have trouble. The party I was in refused to pay more than we agreed. We offered him that and he refused to take it. We put the money in our pockets, pushed some of the boatmen aside and walked off.

I afterward learned how it was they refused to let us all ashore at once. In 1849 a number of clipper ships had put in there on the voyage to San Francisco. Just at that time the government had held out great inducements to emigrants from the British Isles, large numbers of them had congregated in Rio and were claiming that the government had acted in bad faith, trying to send them to a remote province among hostile savages instead of a province where some of their countrymen had already settled to the number of 60,000. I think the emigrants had just cause to complain. It resulted in a great riot. They overran the emperor's palace, which had the effect of making him abandon it for one he built out in the country a few miles from Rio, and also took possession of Signal hill, where there were some cannons mounted which commanded the city. Almost all English speaking men that happened to be there at that time took sides with the abused emigrants, the British admiral interceding in the interest of his people, and the city of Rio.

The Brazilian government paid the emigrants' fare back home, which ended the riot ever after and they were very shy of letting too many foreigners ashore at one time.

Once ashore we had the opportunity of looking around and seeing the city in detail. Although it is the oldest and largest city in South America, and a place of great commerce, there was not a wharf along the entire waterfront. All ships lay out in the bay a long distance riding at anchor. It was a sight to see 300 to 500 strong negro slaves, each one marching with a sack of coffee on his head, putting it in a flat-bottom barge, then pulling out to the ship and hoisting it aboard by hand. In wandering around we came across a few of our fellow passengers quite drunk. That being a sugar country, good, pure rum, as mild as milk, was very cheap—only 2 cents per drink—and some of the boys were drunk before they knew it.

It was now getting late, so late that we had to seek lodgings for the night, which we procured at the Hotel de France by paying 50 cents apiece in advance. The man who showed us the beds took us up several flights of stairs, along a number of dark gloomy halls until we reached the top story, which contained a number of good rooms and beds. The walls of this building were from three to four feet thick, with heavy thick bars of iron running perpendicularly across the windows. It was built in the old Portuguese, or Moorish style, giving it the appearance of a jail. We had been in bed but a few minutes before we felt that we had been bit by millions of fleas. We got out of bed, struck a light, turned down the clothes, when we found the sheets so black with fleas that we thought of the plagues of Egypt. It was impossible to sleep, so we whiled the night away telling yarns and drawing our likenesses by the shadow on the wall.

Leaving the hotel at dawn we came across an American named Boston Joe, who was doing well keeping a hotel and store combined.

We visited the navy yard, where we found one vessel on the stocks building. Her keel had been laid over twenty years, and from the slow progress they were making it looked as if it would take twenty more years to finish it. Thirty white men, chiefly English, were working in the machine shop. They had lost eight of their party by yellow fever. We visited the churches and other public buildings where we saw a number of oil paintings and works of art by the old masters. They are extremely religious on Sunday mornings. The churches have an awe inspiring effect with sculpture and gloomy look and with the niches of the walls filled with the departed saints, which the churches seem to possess in abundance. They are devoid of all nice, soft seats which are found in our churches of today. Most of the worshippers bring a small mat which they lay on the flagging stones to kneel on. Five priests officiate at mass, which they make as solemn as possible. Brooklyn is called the "City of Churches." Rio may well be called the "City of Churches, Convents and Monasteries." They are found in every part of the city, but it looks bad to see so many fat, sleek-looking monks eternally begging instead of working, but I guess they find it easier. The heads of the church are very indulgent to the members of their church, who attend the circus and bull baiting in the afternoon and the theater in the evening.

We called on the American consul to obtain information about things in general. He treated us very kindly, told us it was one of the poorest places for unskilled labor, but if any of us were engineers and made up our minds to stay in the country we could do well. The emperor, Dom Pedro II, paid Rio a visit. He traveled in an old-fashioned Virginia traveling carriage, six small horses attached, with an escort of cavalry. He attended mass in what is known as the "Emperor's chapel," which is lavishly decorated with gold leaf. It put me in mind of Laura Kean's theater on Broadway. After mass he held a reception at which every one who wished could have audience with him. He was a fine-looking gentleman, a countenance beaming with fatherly kindness and love. His plain republican manner greatly endeared him to the masses. He was always received by firing a salute.

We had been ashore four days when we thought it was about time to visit the vessel, which had gone to the lower bay to coal, where she was taking on 3000 tons. Arriving at the island we found about 200 slaves, who were chanting an African dirge, or song, with a large tin rattle, which one of them shook while the chorus was sung tramping in single file, each with a basket of coal on his head, which he dumped in the hold. Although some of these slaves had been on the island over twenty years — in fact, every since they were stolen from the coast of Africa, they appeared happy and contented. Two of them got into a fight and the overseer took the rattle away from them and took the fighters into an inner court and punished them. They then became sullen and morose. The vessel was so dirty with coal dust that it was disagreeable to stay on board, and the officers informed us it would take three or four more days to coal her, so we concluded to go ashore again. Just as I was leaving the boat a man came running to me and said he was from Cleveland, O., and wanted to know if I knew him in Cleveland. I told him I did not. I saw he was troubled and asked him what was the matter. He said one of the second cabin passengers had stolen his wife and was keeping her in his stateroom and would not let him in to see her. I told him she must be very willing to be stolen or she would not stay with him. He said that was the worst part of it; that he wanted to get her out of the ship, but could not do it. I advised him to let her go. The poor fellow declared that he loved her so that he could not do so. He had been to the captain, who refused to put her ashore against her will, to obey the Portuguese officials as long as she was under the American colors. The poor fellow was in a sad fix. I told him to come ashore with me to the consul's office and we could soon fix the matter. Arriving there and telling that officer the facts he issued a writ on the captain to produce the woman in his office at 10 o'clock that morning. The woman was produced, as per order, and set free, going away with her husband, just the same as ever. When we sailed they were still in Rio.

Nine of us went aboard the steam ferry boat across the bay with the purpose of visiting the coffee plantations. There were about 200 passengers on the boat, but what a contrast to the people on such a boat in the states! There was not a newspaper among them. One or two were reading a book. The ladies were all closely veiled, so that it was impossible to see their features. To look at them one would suppose they belonged to some Turkish harem, or to a bygone age of the Moors, when they held sway in Portugal. I saw only one good looking native lady, and she was the emperor's daughter. The others I saw unveiled were very much lacking in female loveliness. In steaming across the bay we ran close alongside the United States frigate *St. Lawrence,* with the stars and stripes flying. All the Americans on board were filled with patriotism. We rushed to the side of the boat and gave a rousing cheer, which was responded to by the blue jackets from the rigging. She was a splendid specimen of naval architecture, was manned with a fine crew and well officered, and a pride to the nation. When we cheered the other passengers thought we were crazy.

Arriving in the little town we started out in the country, which looked fairly well cultivated. We saw some magnificent cocoanut trees in full bloom. Orange, lemon and lime trees, combined with flowers and vines, made a most enchanting scene to behold. The sides and tops of quite high hills were covered with coffee trees. We wandered on, drinking in the beauties of nature, not noticing how far we had gone, when we began to feel hungry. Suddenly we came to a nice creek in which a negro woman was standing, nearly naked, up to her knees in the water washing clothes, which she did by raising them up as high as her head and bringing them down on a large flat rock as hard as she could. We stood looking at her wondering if that was the way good old Mother Eve washed Adam's shirts. She looked up and seeing us gave a yell that made the hills ring. She hurried up a private road that led to the planter's house, yelling all the time. We followed, but she arrived before us. As we neared the house we saw a great commotion. A tall dark looking man, with a skin like parchment, stood amongst them and was surrounded with negroes of both sexes and all ages, armed with all kinds of weapons, and there were more appearing all the time. It was easy to see that the whole plantation was aroused. We attempted to approach him, but he kept gestulating and waving his hands toward the road and crossing himself. We retired for some distance, one member of our party advancing, making signs that we were hungry, holding up money showing that we were going to pay for it, but it was impossible to obtain anything. We picked a few oranges to eat, and retired, the negroes following until we reached the main road. We came to the conclusion that we had seen all the plantations and Brazilian hospitality we wanted to. After walking several miles we came across what we thought was a milk ranch. A man was milking: we made signs to him that we were hungry, but with no better success. Tired and hungry we trudged back to Rio.

A most laughable scene occurred on one of the streets. One of the crew belonging to the United States frigate *St. Lawrence* had deserted. The commander offered a reward for his return. He was captured by six Brazilian soldiers, who were marching him along the street. He did not walk fast enough to please one of the guards and he pricked him with the bayonet. The sailor wheeled around as quick as a flash and knocked him down.

Speaking of soldiers, their system looked very odd to us. Some regiments are made up of blacks and whites, all colors and all heights. Their crack regiment was picked men, all blacks, and made a fine appearance.

After we got back to Rio we found out where we missed it. If we had gone to a priest, for a fee he would have given us a pass that would have secured us against any troubles. The good old padres are very obliging and plastic. A large number of the crew belonging to the frigate got leave to come ashore. We fell in with them and had a good time. They fairly hugged us and treated us like brothers. New York papers were the greatest present we could make them. They had been on the station two years and were eager to return home. Some Italian girls were singing and playing the tambourine on the public square. We paid but little attention until they began singing "Columbia, the Gem of the Ocean," and other national songs, which nearly crazed us with joy. Never music or song sounded sweeter, not even "Shandon's Bells." The girls reaped a good harvest, as the boys gave liberal.

The business part of Rio is very flat, and the sanitary condition very bad. Extremely narrow streets, that is most of them, and no system of sewerage, at least that was the condition at that time. It is no wonder they have yellow fever, the way they invite it. All the filth was put in large tubs, which were carried on the heads of the negroes to the edge of the bay and thrown in, so that at low tide the bulk of it lay festering in a tropical sun. Even the bedding and clothes of fever patients they throw out instead of burning.

The national songs, the lavish treatment of the boys belonging to the St. Lawrence, and the thought that this was our last day in Rio, as our captain had posted notice that we would sail the next day, made lots of us a little reckless. The city gendarmes, with their short swords, were very officious and mean. They never missed an opportunity of snatching your pocket knife out of your hand and striking it on a wall and breaking it. Their annoyance and the natural prejudice of Americans with any colored race put in official position over them, brought on quite a number of collisions, our boys generally coming out best, but nothing very serious occurred. Quite a large number of us had spent the evening at a hotel, kept by a German. We had had a good time and expressed a desire to go to bed, as we had engaged our beds early in the day. To our great surprise he told us where we got our eat we could get our sleep. That made the St. Lawrence boys mad, for we had been invited there. The German gave some of the boys the lie, they took it up, knocked him and his son down and started to clean out the place. His wife ran out, gave an alarm which brought down on us the gendarmes. We overpowered them and escaped to the water front, obtained boats and left for our respective ships, where we arrived all right, and found the ship in fine order for sailing.

The signal gun was fired, warning us all aboard. A few had been in the lock-up for their good behavior, but the day before the United States consul had got them all discharged so that they would not be left behind, but a few were left, arriving four months later on the ship *Visurgis.* We steamed down the bay, and by dark were well out to sea. The next day there was the usual amount of sea sickness and few to meals. In a few days all were well and as hungry as bears. The dull routine of life on ship gave me a reflective mood on the part of observations I had had in Brazil. We had just left a country as large in area as the United States, with fabulous resources of agriculture, cabinet and woods, and mineral untold along the foot of the Andees, and only a few hundred miles back along the Atlantic ocean was thinly settled, the interior a perfect incognito, inhabited by savages, without any railroads, although there were a few miles being constructed. That was a deep scheme of the British government in 1820, after Dom Pedro's father and uncle had exhausted their resources fighting for the crown of Portugal, the British fleet interceded on the grounds of humanity and carried Dom Pedro's father to the Portuguese colony of Brazil and made him emperor. That act, with the usual spirit of British merchants to push trade, supported by the British fleet, which always supports an admiral of the south Atlantic fleet who resides in Rio, made Brazil what she was. With the wise policy of subsidies paid to her steamers for carrying the mails, which are frequently officered by ex-officers of the British navy, coupled with the niggardly policy of the democratic party, in power at that time, which destroyed the Collins line of steamers, the only opposition line the Cunarders ever feared, gave Great Britain the upper hand. What had our farmers done to the government of the United States that British merchants could buy our wheat, ship it to England, convert it into flour, send it to the Brazils and undersell us? Echo says because our government neglected to insist that the United States should be treated as well as the most favored nations. Why was it that the mails for the United States were carried from Rio to England, from England across the Atlantic to New York, always in English bottoms? Echo says because our government refused to pay a few thousand dollars per annum for one or two steamers to run south on the west coast of South America as far as Valparaiso, calling at the important ports, until they connected with our line to California at Panama; also one or two steamers going as far south on the Atlantic side as Montevideo, calling into Rio and other important ports, until they made connection with our steamers at Aspinwall. The government may have saved a few thousand dollars, but our people lost millions by the trade they would have built up. Then our people down there ask why it is that the English have such a preponderating influence. These are the causes I have mentioned. The people of Bazil have overthrown the empire and established a republic. I hope it will flourish and become one of the great nations of the earth, but I tremble for the masses, who are steeped in ignorance and superstition. With these comments I bid adieu to that subject.

We got along fine and rapidly approached the cooler latitude. Two little memorable scenes took place. Several wrestling matches were going on at different times. One of the coal passers, who weighed over two hundred pounds, was champion, until a little Irish girl, called Margaret, challenged the champion. She was so small along side of him that we all thought she was only in fun. She told him to come on. He put both hands on her shoulders and she took him by the arms, asking him if he was ready. He said he was, and she took both legs from under him as quick as a flash. He went down so hard that the deck fairly shook, and the noise awoke Mr. Rogers, our chief engineer, who was so mad he rushed on deck, caught one of the passengers who was jumping around him with delight, and slapped him in the face. The young man was on the muscle and soon gave Mr. Rogers all he wanted. We expected to see part of the crew take it up for Mr. Rogers, as one watch was on deck. They all rushed up, and the passengers also at the same time, many of them drawing their revolvers. Mr. Rogers, who was very quick tempered, saw his mistake, apologized and went below.

Instead of the bill of fare improving, as Captain Caffadey had promised, it got worse every day, until the crisis came. When the cook furnished for dinner coffee and hardtack, some of the waiters were very insulting and soon got what they little expected. Over 300 of them fell into line, about four abreast, went and cleaned out both cooking galleys of the dinners that were intended for the officers and crew. The captain was furious. He ordered all the steerage passengers on the main deck and the cabin passengers below, but no one obeyed. He threatened to put the leaders in irons. They told him to go to h____; said they would put him in irons and put Captain Paterson in command until we reached Valparaiso, where there was an American consul. Then he tried to address them, saying he felt for them in his bosom. They answered him by saying that if he thought he had a lot of poor European emigrants that he could treat like hogs he was fooling himself; said they were Americans and knew their rights, and had all of him and his d____d promising they wanted. They hooted and yelled and demanded that Captain Paterson should be allowed to address them. It might be well to state here that Captain Paterson was an American captain of great experience in the clipper line that ran between New York and San Francisco. At that time he was acting as first mate of our ship. At Panama Captain Caffadey was to leave for New York and bring the *Washington* around the way we came, and Captain Paterson was to take command of the *Hermann*. Captain Cavendy (that is the proper way to spell his name) was a Swede by birth, and had been commander of the *Hermann* for a number of years and was a good seaman. His family resided in Brooklyn. Captain Paterson came forward to address the mutineers, as Cavenday called them, and was listened to with respect. He told them there was plenty of provisions on board of good quality, that an reasonable person ought to be satisfied with, and that they could not expect to be fed like cabin passengers on a voyage of 100 days. The passengers complained that the cornmeal mush was served nearly raw. It was not the quality they complained of, it was improperly cooked, so they would not eat it, and sometimes lacking in quantity. The conference had good results. The passengers were ordered to form messes, ninety in a mess, appoint four committeemen to each mess, whose duties were to keep order, see that the food was properly cooked and cleanly served, demand civil conduct from the waiters, and put a stop to the dirty practice some of the waiters had of wiping the tin plates on the seat of their pantaloons. At the request of the passengers the captain wrote out a bill of fare for one week, twenty-one meals, showing just what the ship allowed each meal. The plan worked like a charm, as only one complaint was made by any of the committeemen the remainder of the voyage. At one meal hard tack and coffee only was served while the bill of fare called for butter or molasses or dried apples — the committee complained to the captain, and he told them to send the purser to him. They went to the purser's room and found him sleeping. It made him mad to be disturbed, and he attempted to slam the door in their faces. One of them put his foot in the door which burst the hinge off. The purser called them bad names, got his revolver and threatened to shoot. The committee drew theirs and told him to shoot away. Captain Paterson, who was on deck, hearing the rumpus, came forward, told them to put up their revolvers, sent the purser into the captain's room and in a few minutes butter was served. All the trouble was caused by the dishonesty of the purser and storekeeper, who were leagued together to cheat the passengers out of their rations, so that they could sell them in port. I was informed that they sold $800 worth in San Francisco. This is an old trick of army contractors. A little hanging would put a stop to it.

It got so cold that all warm clothes were in demand. Passengers with overcoats on huddled close around the smokestacks to keep warm. One man came to me with a very serious look and asked me how much colder I thought it was going to get, and where we were going, and saying, do you know we are on the other side of the sun, look at it? I explained matters to him and he became satisfied. In nearing San Francisco he came to me and told me how glad he was to be on the right side of the sun again.

The cry of land made us rush to see it. We were entering the Straits of Magellan. The low flat coast of Patagonia could be seen. It was very cold. The engines slowed down as we put our way up the straits. We got a good view of Patagonia. It looked as if it would make a pasturage for cattle or sheep. We made soundings often, arriving at the first anchorage we spent the night. Next morning we pulled out slowly, making for the next anchorage. There are only three in the straits, from ocean to ocean. Terra Del Fuego, or Land of Fire, was in full view, with her snow-clad hills and volcanic mountains. The coast shore scenery changed greatly from that we had passed. Instead of low and flat it was very mountainous and rocky, with the perpendicular rocks coming right down to the edge of the water.

Moss and a few scrub trees relieved the barren look. This part of the straits, next to the Pacific, are very circuitous and narrow, so narrow that in the distance it looks as if there was no passage, but as it is approached that idea fades away. Soundings were made for anchorage where we should spend the night. The next day was a repetition of the day before. At night we anchored at Port Starvation, which obtained its name justly, for a whole ship's crew perished there. The Chileans have a convict settlement there. A brig of war, belonging to them, lay at anchor, which had just discharged a lot of convicts. They called it Fort Gallant at that time, but I am inclined to think it was known as Punto Arenas, a fortified place at this time. No place in the world could be found that would be easier to fortify so no vessel could pass it. Whether the laws of nations would permit one of the high roads of commerce to be closed would be a question not yet solved. The next morning at 4 o'clock we pulled out with the hopes of making the Pacific ocean before dark, as the mouth of the straits is a terror to all navigators. We were doomed to disappointment, for after running sixty miles in the gale that had threatened broke in all its fury. It would have been the height of folly to have tried to make the ocean in the face of such a gale. Everything was made taut and snug. The steamer turned round and arrived at Fort Gallant all safe. We anchored under the lee of a mountain for shelter, and the winds their revels kept for two days and two nights, when the weather moderated. In the forenoon the savages swarmed round our ship in their canoes. One of the "Dead Rabbits" threw a large glass bottle, striking one of the Indians on the breast, wounding him severely, which made the Indians very hostile. The "Dead Rabbit" was punished, and the captain told him that he had ought to be handed over to the Indians, so they could make a lunch of him, as they are all cannibals. They rowed around the ship so close and acted so hostile the captain made motions to them to go away. The two cannons we carried were loaded and the crew was armed, as far as the firearms went. The steps were raised and a strong force posted to see that they did not climb up the chains and gain the deck. The passengers had firearms of their own and knew how to use them. I could not see much danger, but the officers told of several vessels that had been captured and the crew made a feast of, and they said they did not want the decks begrimed with blood if they could help it.

The following summer, 1859, they attacked a ship, but by good use of the ship's cannon they drove them off, killing a number and sinking some of their canoes. The British sent a brig from the Faulkland islands with a lot of missionaries. The Indians received them very friendly, and as soon as the vessel left they made a feast of them. When the vessel returned, in about a year, they felt pleased, thinking they would have another feast. Our captain gave them a box of hard tack and some beef and tobacco, as they kept hollering "beef, beef, backy, backy." The passengers gave them a lot of clothes, and it was laughable to see them put them on. One squaw had two pair of pants tied around her neck, and letting one pair down her back, the other down her breast. We told the ladies they had ought to give the poor creatures some clothes, which they were ready to do, going to the side of the vessel to throw them down into their canoes. When the Indians raised up the ladies saw they were attired in the same costume that Adam and Eve wore before she sewed the fig leaves together. The ladies left very suddenly and gave us fits for the joke we played on them. In the afternoon the Indians became so numerous the captain made motions for them to go away, and finally they left. Some of the petty officers lowered a boat to go ashore to obtain some cold water, as we were drinking warm condensed water, the condensers being too small for such a crowd, so that a drink of cold water was a great treat. We asked the captain to please let us have a boat to go ashore. He consented, warning us to keep together and on no account go far from the shore or out of sight of the vessel. He let us have a nice metallic life boat. Everyone made a rush to go in the first boat, as some of us were to bring the boat back so that others could go. The boat was jammed so full there was not standing room, and it was impossible to do anything. Just at this time the boat with the petty officers returned, reporting that it was impossible to make a landing. Our first mate was looking over the side and saw the condition, ordered us all out of the boat and the boat hoisted back into the davits. It was a great disappointment to some of us as we wished to go ashore in Patagonia. The commander of the Chilean man-of-war was paying our captain a visit and trying to make a bargain with our vessel to tow him out of the straits, but they could not agree as to the price. The sequel proved it was a good thing for us they did not agree. The crew of the man-of-war's boat was busy amongst our passengers trading Patagonian lion skins, when nine of us went down the companion way to see their boat, which was in charge of the dingey boy. We offered him tobacco and money to let us have the boat to go ashore with. We very unthoughtedly took it by force, pulled out from the ship and up the straits, intending to try and land on a small island. Only four of us knew anything about managing a boat in such a sea, with the current running swift against us. It was a whaleboat and steered with an oar. A young man from Detriot was steering. One of the boys could not handle the sweep, so two of them took hold of it and broke it in two, when the boat swung around the broadside to the sea, which broke over her, nearly filling her with water. The passengers were watching us, expecting to see her swamp every minute. Captain Paterson was in the rigging calling through the trumpet for us to come back. Some wanted to go back, but the majority of us decided to make one more trial. We had baled the water nearly all out of the boat, and brought her head to the wind when the boat steerer sung out "Pull away!" By constant bailing we kept the water down so that it seldom got more than half full. We finally succeeded in landing. Birds flew up so thick they darkened the air. On the island we found a spring of delicious cold water and nearly foundered ourselves drinking. We also found one wigwam. It is almost a misnomer to call it that, it was so poorly constructed. It contained two large Indians and one large squaw. We agreed that she belonged to the woman's rights party. These savages are considered the finest race of savages in the world. We got down on our hands and knees and crawled into the wigwam to warm ourselves by their fire, which was about a hatful. They also had forgotten to dress. The squaw put out her hand and began crying: "Backy, backy." We gave her some tobacco, which pleased her much, and retired. Some of the boys had forgotten what the captain told us in the morning, and now that we had taken a man-of-war's boat by force we were liable to be punished for it. Some of the boys wanted to stay longer, but we noticed all at once Indians up among the rocks watching us. As soon as they saw that we had seen them they kept out of sight. I guess they were calculating what a good supper we would make for them. On this island a whole ship's crew had perished. They erected a post, split the top, fastened a boat in it, and cut their names with their jack-knives. I thought of that beautiful song which says, "And the shrill winds whistle around the mariner's grave."

As it was getting late it made us think we had better be going to back to the ship. We pulled out in the straits, when, lo and behold, what should we see but a large boat belonging to the man-of-war with twenty men in it armed to the teeth. We stopped, held a council of war, and decided as they were coming up after us we would turn back and let them chase us around the island, knowing when once we were out in the straits, with the wind and current with us, we could make our vessel before them and escape. We pulled around the island but they did not follow us, but lay in waiting for us. We saw it was all up with us.

When we came near them, they shot alongside our boat, boarded us, took us all prisoners quicker than you could tell it and took us down to the *Hermann* to get their captain. When the boat got alongside the gangway I took up the hawser and threw it on the steps; one of our passengers grabbed it, pulled up the boat close to the steps and four of our boys jumped out. I prepared to jump but one of the sailors pushed me back, and another cut the rope which caused the boat to drift down and beat against the ship. I signaled to one of the passengers to drop me a rope. He responded. I grabbed it and climbed on deck, they holding the other four prisoners in the boat. It appeared that when the commander was ready to go back to his ship the boy told him we had taken the boat by force, and he felt very much annoyed by what he chose to call a great insult and theft. He signaled the brig to send up an armed boat and declared he would give us twenty-five lashes on the bare back, so we would respect a man-of-war boat another time. Our captain apologized to him, said he was very sorry it happened and that we had done it unthoughtedly. We also apologized; that is, five of us did. Finally, when he found out that there were only four left in the boat, he told us to pay for the oar we had broken, which was $16. We failed to raise the money, so the captain gave him one out of the ship, which settled it.

As soon as it was light enough to see a ship's length we pulled out to make another attempt to reach the Pacific ocean. We thought then that if the

Spanish discoverer, Vasco Nuñez de Balboa, saw it at the Straits of Magellen instead of at the Isthmus of Panama he would have named it "Angry Waters." We made good headway all day. The wind began to freshen at noon, increasing steadily until night, when it became a terrific gale, and found us right in the mouth of the straits, near the Terra del Fuegan shore. It was about here that the United States vessels got so disabled in 1848, when they had to put into the first port to refit, and also where the English man-of-war was lost with all on board, except three. At 8 o'clock the gale had become a hurricane. When I went on deck the ship appeared to be in the same place as it was at 6. Out of all the passengers I was the only one on deck. I sat down on the seat clinging for dear life. Captain Paterson and two quartermasters were lashed, and also both men at the wheel. I heard Captain Paterson say for them to tell Mr. Rogers to get up more steam. In a few minutes he sent word for God's sake to make her go a mile, if possible. Mr. Rogers sent back word that she was carrying all the steam he could get. She was pitching and heaving. She would be on the top of a wave, then go down, end first, and make you think that was the last time. I had seen a gale off the coast of Newfoundland when every stitch of canvas was taken out of the ship, "ashburten" and the passengers fastened below. I had seen the ship *Oswego* lay rolling in the trough of the sea like a tub, with her top masts and yards gone, but that was a nice zephyr alongside of this. The gloomy outlines of that inhospitable shore could be seen through the flashes of lightning. Peal after peal of thunder resounded amidst the ringing of the ship's bell which sounded more like a funeral dirge than anything else. But the gallant ship laughed at old Neptune showing a temper, and went right along. Sitting where I was I soon found I was in a very dangerous place, Captain Paterson saw me sitting there and called out for me to go below, saying that was the place for me unless I wanted to go overboard. I yelled back that I was afraid to move. He told me to get down on my hands and knees and crawl along the deck, which I did. I went as far as the mainmast, saw Captain Cavenday lashed to the mast and said, "Good evening, captain." He replied. I said, "This is an awful night." "Yes, too rough for you to be on deck," he said. Just then a cross sea struck the ship, stove the wheel house into splinters, carried the seat where I had been sitting overboard, and filled the decks full of water. I was thrown against the bulwarks and very nearly drowned. It threw the beef cattle out of a pen six feet high right among the steerage passengers; threw a number of passengers out of bed and hurt a few. A pile of trunks that were stacked up went down with the crash. The ship staggered, reeled and trembled; arose like some leviathan of the deep, shook herself and plunged ahead with the water rushing out the seuppers. As soon as I could gather myself together and spit the salt water out of my mouth I started to go below, but found it impossible as the passengers were panic-stricken and were rushing on deck. The first one I met I asked where he was going. He raised both hands up, saying: "Oh, man, she is split?" I tried to pacify them as well as I could.

Pandemonium reigned supreme. Some were sprinkling themselves with holy water, some wringing their hands, some crying, some praying very fervently. One in particular who was a pretty hard Christian, promised the Lord if He would save just this once he would never swear or lie any more as long as he lived. He very soon forgot all about it and swore he never prayed at all. Such is poor, weak humanity. A great many never got out of their berths, although I am told by some of them, who used to spend more than half their time in their berths, that there was ten feet of water in her hold, and it was a question whether she would float until morning, and they had better get out and try and save themselves. They said they would go down in her in preference to becoming food for the cannibals. When I went on deck again I noticed the deck hands were putting the beef cattle back in the pens and the gallant ship was still on her course, all of which tended to allay the excitement. Few slept that night and remarked they never again wanted to suffer the horrors of such a night. Morning came at last, and was a pretty sight for us. The storm had spent its fury and the ship had come out of it all right, with the exception of one wheelhouse being mashed to pieces and quite a lot of seats carried overboard with the supports. The whitecaps on the top of the waves, the sea gulls, and Mother Carey's pigeons flying, with a few albatross in the distance, made a pleasant picture. The ship's carpenters very soon made necessary repairs and gave the ship her old look.

One of the grand sights to be seen off Cape Horn was the comet that appeared at that time. In no part of the world was it seen to such advantage as it was there. It was very brilliant, with a tail fourteen million miles long. I did not measure it — astronomers said it was. It appeared to reach right across the southern hemisphere.

An aged man died and was buried at sea, which cast a gloom over us for a short time. But one of our lady passengers, thinking it was a pity to go into port with one short of our original number gave birth to a fine boy, which made up the complement again. We passed by the island of Robinson Cruso, but did not call. Nothing of importance occurred until we arrived in Coronel, a coaling place for all steamers coming this way. It is in southern Chile. The coast is rather flat here, the beach raising very gradually so that a ship has to lay out quite a distance in an open roadstead as there was no wharf. This would be a good place to land an army under cover of their own guns. As this was our last coaling place, after filling the coal bunkers they stored quite a lot on deck, which was used first. These coal mines are owned by the richest woman in the world. I have forgotten her name. The mines made her her riches. The coal here is very soft, and often ignites on shipboard by spontaneous combustion, which occurred twice on the way up to San Francisco, but by the free use of pumps and hose, with great exertion we subdued the fire both times. This coal is mined by Scotch miners, common labor performed by Chileans. This is quite an important place, and has a fine agricultural country surrounding it, producing everything that is produced in the temperate zone, and it certainly has a fine future. After coaling here we had a fine run to Valparaiso, where we stayed two days. This port is open to the sea about one-half, and is protected by a sea wall. Two or three streets along the water front form the business portion of the city. The dry dock and warehouses give it a substantial look. The residence portion is built in terraces right to the top of the hills, which are very steep. The streets are named after the yards in a ship. In walking over the town where the United States steamship Baltimore boys were attacked, we received this polite salute: "Come in here, you d____d Yankee filibustering sons _____!" We found quite a number of Americans here who had started to go to California, but the inducements there at that time were so good they remained in the country, claiming they had just as good times as they ever had in California. Here we found the same influence that gave the British a preponderating influence in Rio. Their lines of steamers were running into every port of importance. This was the first time since leaving New York where we had seen an American newspaper. Here we found the New York *Herald*, giving an account of the discovery of gold at Pike's peak, and the San Francisco *Bulletin*, giving an account of the Frazer river being overrated and overdone, and stated that the disappointed miners were returning by the thousands, which was a sad disappointment to us, but we did not fully realize it until we landed in San Francisco some weeks later. If we had arrived before the mail in Valparaiso we should have obtained over 200 passengers, but as it was we only got a few.

The Chilian girls are very partial to American and European men and never missed an opportunity of showing it. The city, from the seaside, is very easily fortified. A powerful battery planted on the southwest point and another on the other side of the roadstead commands the whole inner harbor and as far out to sea as modern cannon can reach, so that an enemy coming in from the sea would be continually under fire. We once more put to sea after our short stay in port, steering for Panama bay, which was our last calling place. Smooth seas and bright skies made the trip very pleasant. The south Pacific and equatorial portion swarmed with marine life. The whales spouting, porpoises tumbling and playing, makes a pretty sight. We passed a boat drifting on that great waste of waters, with birds flying in and out. The captain refused to slow down the engines and lower a boat so that we could go and examine it, for we felt sure it contained some dead mariners, but he said it would do no good. After a pleasant run we came to anchor at the Island of Toboga, Panama bay, and found we were nearer to New York than we had been for many weeks. Panama makes a pretty appearance, with her rich tropical growth of orange and other trees. The British warship *Spitfire* lay here, and for recreation the crew were catching sharks, and had just towed a large one ashore. The writer had the misfortune to fall overboard and came very near being devoured by one. Just as he was about to make the fatal bite a sailor thrust a harpoon into his body, which diverted him from his purpose. After laying here two days we proceeded on our voyage. In crossing the Gulf of Tehuantepec it was very rough, which made the ship roll considerably, although she drew twenty-six feet of water when she left New York. The coal and provisions were now nearly exhausted, which made her very light.

Only one sad event occurred on the run to San Francisco. One of our quartermasters, a fine seaman, died of Panama fever. Never did the burial service sound more solemn or impressive than it did on this occasion, when his body was committed to the deep until the sea shall give up the dead. We arrived in San Francisco after a voyage of ninety-six days. A more disappointed, crestfallen lot of men it would be hard to find. This was in the fall of 1858, just one year after the financial panic, when the Central America went down with $2,000,000 on board, which was followed by the failure of the Cincinnati Trust company, and the suspension of specie payment by all of the banks with the exception of the Chemical bank of New York city. The winter of 1857-58 will never be forgotten by the men in New York and Brooklyn who went through it. The almost free trade policy of the democratic party had resulted in overstocking the country with foreign imported goods and caused the closing of nearly all of our factories, and the utter ruin of thousands of business men. The country was drained of its hard money to pay for foreign imports, and $1000 of some of the state bank's paper bills, which was called money, would not purchase a one horse load of flour. Fourteen thousand families were receiving coal, blankets and other aid from the cities of New York and Brooklyn. Laboring men and mechanics, when they could get employment, received the noble sum of from 50 cents to $1 per day. Thousands that came to this coast at that time came here in the hopes of bettering their condition and getting away from the terrible depression of the east. But changing from the east to San Francisco at that time did not improve our condition. The emigrants were coming in across the isthmus, also overland, and were pouring in on every boat that came from Victoria or the Sound, coming from the over-stocked and over-rated mines of British Columbia. Every hotel and boarding house was full of hard up and destitute miners and immigrants. Professional men fared the worst. They had not been accustomed to rough it, and it went very hard with them to become dishwashers, housemaids and peddlers. The four Vanderbilt steamers were laid up. The Pacific Mail company charged high fares. Thousands sent back home for means to pay their fare back. Large numbers lived on one meal a day. Others found a precarious living by bumming on their friends and lunching in the saloons. Quite a number committed suicide or died from unknown causes. The spring of 1859 brought a great change. Things improved greatly. The idlemen scattered in every direction and every one found employment at something. This year was memorable in the annals of Chinese emigration. Messrs. Coleman, the great democratic leader, and Merchant were running a line of clipper ships to China and brought over a load of coolies in defiance of the state law, which prohibited it. Mr. Coleman made a test case of it, and the supreme court declared the law unconstitutional, which opened wide the doors for

Mr. John. The unsettled Spanish grants, drouth and large ranches were considered a curse in California, but those things were very insignificant in comparison with the invasion of the Chinese, which turned our boys out of nearly all light work, made loafers out of them and filled the state prisons. The effect on the girls was still more pernicious, for it drove them in great numbers into immoral lives. It is no magnified story to say that the Chinese prevented hundreds of thousands of whites from settling on this coast, because they did not want to compete with coolie labor.

California is a grand and great state with fabulous resources, but the writer had, when back east, obtained a government work entitled "A Natural History of Washington Territory," written by George Gibbs. All old settlers remember him as being interested in the United States topographical survey, and living about five miles this side of Steilacoom. The equable climate, rich valleys, inexhaustable timber, plethoric fisheries, untold mineral resources, which, in speaking of coal, he says: "It will be found at some future day more, or less, all the way from the White river to Bellingham bay," with commercial harbors, only equalled by the Mediterranean sea, caused me once more to think of casting my lot in Washington territory. After a visit through Peteluma, Santa Rosa, Healdsberg, Cloverdale and other places, viewing the country which for two years had suffered drouth, made it look as if the destroying angel had passed over it, decided me, and in the fall of 1864 I took passage on the brig Josephine, with wife and four children, and bid good-bye to San Francisco. We had a fair passage, only one heavy storm, when she shipped a sea that drove the crew into the rigging, partially filled the cabin and nearly washed your humble servant overboard. We had two young men as passengers, who were sick all the way up, and said they only wished they had the man who wrote the song "There is Life on the Ocean Wave, a Home on the Rolling Deep," and said if they could only kill him they would die happy.

The twelfth day out we sighted Cape Flattery and were driven off by head winds, but finally made the harbor of Victoria, where we discharged a large portion of the cargo, consisting of flour and other merchandise for the Hudson Bay company. We lay here several days, which gave me a chance to view the place. The government offered me 100 acres of land, fifty for my wife and ten for each of my children if I would settle in the colony, but I did not see it that way. We left Victoria and reported in Port Angeles, as that was the port of entry at that time. The custom house and the officials comprised the place then, with the exception of a large number of Indians camped there. About one mile back stood a solitary log cabin which was deserted. The parties who built it had become disheartened, the wife first leaving; the poor man stood it two weeks and then joined his wife. Such is the power of woman. Next we put into Port Townsend, where we lay five days, a north wind blowing all the time. Had to edge out from the wharf to keep the vessel from knocking to pieces. Finally beat up the Sound against head winds, anchoring off Steilacoom, forty-two days from San Francisco.

Steilacoom at that time looked as if her spirit had departed. The sidewalks were rotten, streets not graded, houses dilapidated and weatherbeaten, but her people sanguine of a bright future. In a few days after landing in Steilacoom L.F. Thompson, state senator, invited me to accompany him to his home in Sumner, where I was very kindly entertained by his worthy wife. After viewing the valley from the reservation to the foothills I settled on what is now my present home, within one mile of the town of Orting, being the first settler to take up a pre-emption or homestead claim in this region of country. There had been four donation claims taken by D.E. Lane, Henry Whitesell, Mr. Headley and Daniel Varner, the two latter not returning to their claims after the Indian war.

When I take a retrospective view of the past the changes that have take place are, indeed very great. Steilacoom was the hub and county seat where we obtained our mail and got our blacksmithing done by the venerable pioneer, Peter Ringwest, who is yet making the anvil ring and singing the old Virginia songs. Natt Orr built and repaired our wagons. Mr. Rogers, who built the first brick building in Washington territory, so it is claimed, can still be found in his store. Also Fred Esinbier. All old pioneers; also the sage of Steilacoom, Mr. Salter, who still sticks to it that Tacoma will never amount to much, but says just wait until the great Oriental & Pacific railroad is built, of which road Mr. Salter is president, and then Steilacoom will boom as the terminus. Last, but not least, is one of the live men of that day who lived at Steilacoom. Stephen Judson, who was sheriff of Pierce county some eight or ten years, and represented us in the legislature several times, of which he is now a member, all of which offices he filled with credit. He was always a friend of Pierce county, and his clarion voice will be heard in the house against the division of old Pierce.

Steilacoom plains at that time were very thinly settled. Lands could be bought for $2 or $3 per acre, or acquired by pre-emption by squatting on them. The timber lands had no value. Our nearest school was at Sumner. For twelve years I drove an ox team to deliver what produce I raised, and got my milling done in Steilacoom. It used to take three or four days to make the trip, and once I could not get home for ten days on account of high water.

The first Fourth of July celebration I attended I think was in the year 1866. We swam our horses across the south fork of the Puyallup river. It took us three days to celebrate it. We had to follow trails, and it took one day to go ten miles, one day to celebrate and one day to get back home. We were like Mark Tapley: "Doing it under difficulties." Such was life in western Washington.

Sixteen years ago the Northern Pacific built its road to Wilkeson, which changed the route of travel and made Tacoma the hub instead of Steilacoom. There is a change from the old to the new, with the probability of a greater change within the next thirty years. The old settlers are fast passing away, Orting losing four within a few years.

Chapter 7

Northwest Wanderings

Governor Eugene Semple

Searching for adventure and wealth,
he walked from Umatilla Landing on the
Columbia River to the gold fields of Idaho in 1864
wearing a fine new pair of Wellington boots.

August 5, 1892

Being the recipient of an invitation from your office to furnish for publication incidents of pioneer life in the great northwest, I hereby hand you a short account of a journey I once made from Portland, Or., to the placer mines in the Boise Basin in Idaho. These circumstances do not relate to crossing the plains, for my journey to the Pacific coast was made at a time when it was possible to come by steamship, but the incidents of life in Washington and Oregon before the advent of railways and telegraphs were almost identical with those of earlier days, and often involved quite as much hardship.

I arrived in Portland, Or., in the fall of 1863. Portland was then a city of less than 6000 inhabitants, but it was the commercial emporium of the northern country, and was the outfitting point and the winter rendezvous for miners and adventurers who sought the placer mines of Oregon, Idaho, western Montana, Washington and parts of British Columbia. It was a very lively place, especially in the winter, and vast numbers of miners who assembled there at that season were engaged in spending the money they had earned during the summer in the mountains. Many of these men were veritable Counts of Monte Cristo, and spent money with such a princely hand, and told such wonderful stories of adventures in the wilds, and contests with Indians and outlaws, that nearly every spirited young man who came to the country was moved to abandon more sober undertakings and hie himself to the mountains in search of sudden wealth and fame.

In the spring of 1864, being then not much more than a boy, I yielded to adventurous impulses and started for the then prominent mining region, known as the "Boise Basin." I had to go by steamboat from Portland to Umatilla Landing in Oregon, a distance of about 170 miles. Umatilla Landing at that time was a bustling business town with a population of probably 2500, living in tents, flimsy houses and adobe huts. I waited at this place about ten days for an opportunity to go forward under favorable circumstances, but at last was compelled to undertake the journey on foot. I was very green in the ways of the west at this time and to this circumstance is due most of the hardships I was compelled to submit to on this journey. I was not flush and my choice of means of travel was limited to the least expensive. I endeavored to obtain employment on a pack-train, but my slight build (I weighed 135 pounds) did not indicate that I could lift the heavy loads with which the pack animals were saddled, and so my applications were rejected. A number of packers offered to give me employment in a more subordinate capacity, but I had seen younger parties of the trains subjected to hazing by the packers, and as I was·heavily armed and not possessed of a pacific disposition, I foresaw endless difficulties in that role, and so concluded to adopt the perfectly independent way of going on foot.

Accordingly on the 1st of April, 1864, I left Umatilla Landing for Bannock City, a distance of 300 miles, on foot. The first twelve miles was over a burning sage brush plain. I had on a red flannel shirt, part of my fireman's uniform, and an expensive pair of Wellington boots, besides, of course, some other articles of apparel. In this first tramp over the hot sands my feet were swollen, and, owing to the friction of the heavy boots, the skin was removed from heels and toes. I did not understand the proper method of slinging a pack and carried it in the most wearisome way; consequently at night I was very tired and sore. The day had been extremely hot, but the night was cold, my blankets being covered with a heavy frost in the morning. I rolled over at daylight, but was too sore and tired to arise from the hard bed I had selected in the midst of a thicket. When the sun came out hot, however, I was glad to escape from the covering of the blankets. That day I occupied ten hours in going six miles. At that point the trail left the Umatilla river and ran over bunchgrass uplands for fifteen miles without water, and I concluded to undertake that on a day by itself. I could not wear my heavy boots owing to the swollen condition of my feet, and so the next day I made that fifteen miles in my stocking feet, carrying my pack and my boots, which altogether weighed sixty pounds. In the mean time, however, a miner overtook me on the road and showed me how to arrange the pack so as to carry it with utmost ease, and so I got along pretty well, making the fifteen miles long before sundown. I was at a place called Swift's encampment, where is now, I believe, the city of Pendleton, Or. I here endeavored to trade my Wellington boots, which had cost $14 in Portland, for a lighter pair, without success. A man there, however, who appeared to desire the boots and who understood the necessity of my case offered me $6 for them, which I was glad to take. He was very much elated at the good bargain he had made and after a while began to describe to those in the room that the boots were just what he wanted, that he was engaged in building a dam across the river and those boots, being waterproof, would enable to him to work to greater advantage. In fact he said that but for obtaining these boots from me he would have been compelled to send to Portland for a pair. He then concluded to try the boots on and found that they were much too small for him. I offered, thereupon, to rescind the bargain, but the bystanders, who considered that the man should suffer the consequences of the hard bargain he had driven in their purchase, insisted that the agreement should be carried out. I purchased a lighter pair of boots and continued my journey that night. After leaving Pendleton the trail ran right along the crest of the high ridge and the wind became so swift that I could not stand against it, so went down into the valley again, and selecting a camping spot put up for the night in a thicket of underbrush. I traveled alone most of the time, because other men who traveled on foot were stronger and more experienced than I was and carried less weight, consequently made better time than I could. They went totally unencumbered, except by their arms, and would make twenty-five to thirty-five miles a day, aiming to reach a station or pack-train encampment at night. I found out afterwards that the pack-train men were always glad to entertain an armed man, furnishing him with supper, blankets and breakfast for the additional assurance of his presence, as the entire route was through the country of Indians who were more or less hostile and committed depredations upon whites whenever they could do so with impunity. The trail was also frequented by highwaymen, who would shoot a man from ambush and examine his pockets afterwards, instead of using the traditional method of ordering a man to stand and deliver

As I was traveling through a country unknown to me, was alone most of the time, and could not make the long stages that those of greater experience could, I was compelled, most of the time, to camp by myself. As a measure of precaution I avoided lying down until after dark, and then shifted my position to the extent of half a mile or a mile, as circumstances dictated, generally endeavoring to get into some bushes, behind an abbattis of sagebrush, or in an open space covered with gravel or small stones, so that I might have notice of the approach of an enemy. In this instance, when darkness came on, I ignored the preparations made by daylight and advanced about a mile to some thickets I had observed before dark. I felt safe in this retreat because I was armed with the latest improved weapons, understood their use very well and only wanted to guard against surprise. During the night a shower of rain fell and then it turned quite cold, so that the blankets in which I was wrapped, being wet from the rain, afterward froze quite stiff and in the morning I was sealed up very much like a silk worm in his cocoon. It required severe contortions to relieve myself from the predicament, and reflecting upon the helpless condition that a man would be in if attacked under such circumstances, I would never afterward roll up in blankets even in hotels of a mining town.

From Swift's the trail led up the valley of the Umatilla river to the agency of the Umatilla Indians, thence over the Blue mountains to the Grande Ronde valley. The mountains were white with snow and extensive groves of pine and tamarack trees covered their tops, while in the valley the trail was through sage brush and over light ashy soil that rose in dust at the disturbance of my footsteps and mixed with the perspiration that was forced from every pore by the intense heat. In consequence I longed hour by hour for the cool mountains that showed up ahead and made forced marches to reach them. I camped at their foot and rose early the next morning so that I might reach the shady groves before the sun became too hot. The trail led straight up the mountain side, and I went along it fast enought, at the start, for I could see the top just ahead of me. But, alas! when, after many spurts and rests, I reached the apparent top, there stood another mountain, greater than the one I had just conquered. And when I mastered the second one, a third appeared, and then a fourth one above the third, and so on until I was almost exhausted. It was more than "Ossa on Pelion." To my disheartened vision, "Hills o'er hills and Alps on Alps arise, and mountains piled on mountains to the skies," but at last I reached the snow only to find that it was rapidly being melted by the sun, existed only in patches, and between was mud and slush and slippery rocks. After floundering through and over these for an hour or more I sat down to rest at a point where I could overlook the valley for miles. In the bird's eye view thus obtained the sage brush and grease wood looked quite green, the bunch grass on the ridges had a fresh yellow color, the clear waters of the river sparkled in the sun, as they wandered from side to side and doubled in horseshoe bends, while the fringes of deciduous trees on the banks waved gracefully in the warm spring wind. An Indian encampment of many lodges occupied a bend in the river, and near by the women were engaged in drudgery while the "bucks," arrayed in gay-colored blankets, stood like statues near by or moved majestically about their habitations. A herd of ponies were grazing on the plains at one place, and at another place a similar herd were being hustled by half a dozen mounted Indians, who executed a great many difficult maneuvres, and kept the herd moving, first one way and then another, without any apparent object. Dreamy curls of smoke arose from the lodges, from the agency buildings and from the camp-fires of a wagon train whose animals were picketed on a piece of bottom land.

In the foreground were the pines and tamarack, around and under foot was the snow. In the background was a black forest whose yews and hemlocks and fleecy-pointed firs covered the hills and lined the canyons, away! and away! and away! until my imagination turned back upon itself in despair of conceiving its dreadful extent.

I had been muttering as I passed along the slushy trail, and a keen ear might have caught the sounds of an occasional solitary oath, or even a fantastic group of them, as I plunged into some depth of mud hidden beneath a crust of snow that seemed to offer a secure footing, but when this scene burst upon me I was fascinated, and lingered over it, and bethought me of "what fools we mortals be" when we trust our sense or count upon the realization of our hopes.

I had to presently move on, but, before doing so, I stood upon a fragment of basalt, and while the ooze and water trickled from my broken boots, recited to the winds and trees from Washington Irving: "He who has sallied forth into the world, like poor Slingsby, to seek his fortune, finds too soon how different the distant scene becomes when visited. The smooth spot roughens as he approaches, the wild spot becomes tame and barren, the fairy tints that lured him on still fly to the distant hills, or settle upon the lands he has left behind, and every part of the landscape seems greener than the spot he stands on."

I had to move as fast as I could over the slushy trail in order to reach Lee's encampment, a celebrated hostelry at the summit of the divide, before night, as I did not consider it prudent to camp on the snow. This hotel, which was then kept by A.B. Meacham, a gentleman who afterward rose to great prominence and was wounded by the Modoc Indians at the time of the murder of General Canby, was a great log structure with a dining room and assembly room on the ground floor, and an immense dormitory under the rafters. There was a very large fire place which was kept piled high with logs in the assembly room and around it was a crowd of the determined looking men who constituted the Pacific coast type of that day. All were heavily armed and more or less taciturn, it being considered safer to use one's eyes and ears, than one's mouth, in such a mixed assemblage. People were strangers to each other, and used all the precaution of guerrilas. Nobody knew what the other fellow's name had been in the states, and it was dangerous to carry an official envelope, lest someone should shoot you on the theory that you were the bearer of a requisition. The guests around the fire pulled their hats over their eyes, swung their pistols into handy positions and "said nothing to nobody." The next morning everybody was alert at the "peep o' day," and immediately after breakfast the crowd strung out along the trail. I was among the first to move, as I was anxious to reach the Grande Ronde valley before night. I failed to do so, however, and had to camp in the snow. The night was bitter cold and the darkness was intense, so I did not sleep very much. If I had not been so green on the frontier I might have used the snow banks as a protection against the cold. The wild animals, whose quite fresh tracks I had seen during the day, did not come near me in the darkness, and nothing else happened, so at the earliest dawn I was ready to move forward and did so at a very brisk pace, as that was the only way to get warmed up. I reached the Grande Ronde valley about 10 o'clock, having wasted more than an hour admiring its beauties from the top of the last hill before I finally turned my back on the snow and rushed down the steep trail into the sunshine of the low lands.

From this on the journey was somewhat monotonous. The trail was merely spaced with weary marches and punctuated by solitary bivouacs until I reached the foot of the Bannock mountains. Here I relieved myself of all impediments and resolved to reach the town of Placerville in one more day. There was no difficulty in this, and I registered at the principal hotel before sundown. I had less than $15, and three of them had to be put up for supper, bed and breakfast. I was very tired, and retreated to the dormitory or "bed house." The beds were narrow ones, arranged in long rows up the attic. Some time in the night I was awakened by a man getting into my bed. I reminded the gentleman that he was in the wrong place, but he very positively assured me that he had made no mistake, and that if his company was not agreeable to me I could move away. In the next instant, however, he had changed his mind, his ears having heard the click of my revolver. This ominous sound produced commotion in all parts of the dormitory and many another weapon was gotten out, but when the nature of the disturbance was understood they hooted the intruder as he rapidly retreated, commended my action in a few emphatic words and went off to sleep again. This episode was much talked of next day and gave me a favorable status with the aggressive part of the community. In other words, I had had the very best kind of a "send-off." At that time the Boise basin contained a number of rich and populous camps. There was Placerville, Centreville, Bannock City and Pioneer City. Money was easily obtained and much of it was spent on cards and whisky. Every night and all day Sunday the saloons were crowded with heavily armed men, and it was not an unusual thing to have "a man for breakfast" — i.e., wake up to find that some one had been killed during the night. Lawyers were well paid, the minimum charge for any service being $10. Fees for an appearance in court began in the hundreds and ran into the thousands. At that time postage from "the states" to Oregon points via Panama and San Francisco was 10 cents on each half ounce. There were no mail facilities in that part of Idaho, and Wells, Fargo & Co. charged a dollar for each letter from Portland. With this tariff in force the love letters that under ordinary circumstances gave such delight to the average youngster, became like white elephants. You dared not stop them and it bankrupted you to receive them.

I spent the open season in the Boise basin and migrated with the crowd to the "webfoot" country when the snow began to fly. My intention was to go back in the spring, but I never did. I went up on foot and came back in a four horse wagon.

A year or two after my return to Portland I was engaged in a dispute with a gentleman in regard to the distance from Umatilla to Bannock City. I maintained my views with vigor and finally the gentleman remarked, "Well, young man, you appear to be so positive about this thing that I would like to know the source of your information." I replied: "By George, sir, I stepped it!" The gentleman immediately gave up and treated the company.

C.P. Ferry

The Duke of Tacoma tells about his early days
as a "drummer" in the Idaho gold fields and the
rivalry between Tacoma's new town and the old town.
He also gives the history of General McCarver
who was responsible for the Northern Pacific
Railroad making Tacoma its terminus.

I am very much interested in the pioneer stories, and hope that they will be continued. There are many yet to be heard from who could write interesting narratives which will be very much more interesting when the pioneers shall have passed away. I shall not contribute my share until I return to America, but realizing the interest which is taken by almost everyone in the most trivial incidents connected with the early settlement of the eastern states and cities, I should like the early settlers of Tacoma to furnish incidents in their lives in the infant days of the city of Tacoma. There might be many repetitions of the same incidents, but told from different standpoints, and with the blurring influence of time in different degrees, they would be of interest even now. I find that incidents which I thought at the time would never lose their vividness, are becoming misty in my memory. Even several very narrow escapes with my life, in my early travels in Idaho, Washington, Oregon and California — incidents the memory of which made me shiver in the night for years afterwards, have lost all the sharpness, and in some cases the details are almost forgotten. I will spare you recital of them now, but will mention an incident of which a well known gentleman of Seattle is the hero, which will give you some idea of the experience of business men selling goods in Idaho and Washington in the early sixties.

The word "drummer" was not known in those days. There were four persons, all, I believe, partners in the houses which they represented, besides myself, who made a two months' trip twice a year to sell goods and make collections. The four men were from San Francisco. Ike Huntoon of Puget Sound and John Huntoon of Boise City were two of them; the others are dead. I was from Portland. We went by boat to Wallula, from there to Walla Walla by stage, and from there by mule or horse to different parts of Idaho — some of the trips 300 miles, with not a roof to cover us the entire distance. Highwaymen abounded, and one of them ornamenting a tree could occasionally be seen. There was no mail route, but letters and gold dust, the latter the currency of the country, were carried until roads were made by pony express. Expressage was therefore 10 per cent.

Profits on our goods were enormous, 100 to 200 per cent, but 10 per cent was too much to pay for expressage, so we brought our gold dust down on horseback, ten to twelve weary days. At the start the packers received $1 per pound for freight from the Columbia river, and for a long time 50 cents per pound, so, as they received their pay in gold dust, they had large amounts to take into the settlements. For mutual protection several packers would frequently make up a party, with probably some of the interior merchants who had gold dust to carry, and I used to sometimes join one of the parties. On one occasion there were seventeen in the party — Baily Gatzest of Seattle, who was then a partner in a house at The Dalles, was one of the party. Every man had his cantinas (small pouches hanging on the horn of the saddle) filled with gold dust, and in addition we had two mules packed with the article. I had over $40,000 in dust. I do not remember how much the total in the party was, but it was enough to tempt the cupidity of a small army of highwaymen. We had no fear for our lives, it was our property we were concerned about. We were all heavily armed with revolvers, and shotguns cut short, the latter loaded with buckshot. At places on the road where there was brush (there was no forest, except for a short distance), we rode with arms drawn, stock, lying across the left arm, ready for instant use. At night, with treasure in a pile at our heads we slept in a circle, in our blankets, with revolver and gun at side, cocked, ready to shoot at any point.

At noon one day we struck a brush shanty, occupied by an emigrant family who had just come across the plains. They gave us a wonderful meal for the plains. They had, I remember, all kinds of preserves. They told us there was a new crossing the Payette, where there was a stopping place, something to eat and all out doors to sleep in, and which was a shorter route. We traveled until dark over trackless plains, until we were too fatigued to travel farther, without finding any signs of man and made camp, which, in this case, meant simply setting trail ropes on our horses and spreading our blankets on the ground. We had not a mouthful to eat. Some-one shot a prairie chicken, but it wasn't half a mouthful among seventeen healthy men. At a very early hour in the morning we broke camp. We had a desert of about thirty miles, if my memory serves me right, to cross, without water, and what was more important, without food. At this distance we knew there was a brush shanty. Being old stagers we did not suffer for water, as we filled our canteens at the river the night before.

After travelling over a treeless, sandy desert in the hot tropical heat for ten hours, not having eaten a mouthful for twenty-six hours, we began to think that something to eat was the most important thing in the world.

The pace traveling horseback on a long ride is at best a quick walk, but encumbered with two pack mules, each laden with about 200 pounds of gold dust, and each horse carrying from thirty to forty pounds of dust, besides rider, (a most cruel load), our progress was necessarily very slow. Hunger, after thirst, (I have experienced both to a suffering degree), is king, and when we were within about one hour's ride from the shanty, the pace of those in the lead quickened until the entire cavalcade was on the double quick, each one thinking that those behind would stay with the treasure, until the last ones, thinking only of something to eat followed at the same gait the almost famished procession. I had as good a horse as money would buy, and I was not the last. It was about 4 o'clock in the afternoon when the last man arrived. We were terribly hungry. We were famished. There was nothing in life at that time for us but something to eat. But the shanty could only accommodate about eight persons for a meal, and this with tin cups and plates. We would have traded plates of gold and cups of choicest Sevres at that moment for the bacon, bread and coffee with which we were to be served. To the fact that only about one-half of our number could be accommodated at one time at the table, was due the early discovery which was made by one of the second tableites, who exclaimed: "Where are the mules and the treasure?" Consternation existed in camp for a few minutes. An informal roll call showed that every one was in camp except Baily Gatzest and the mules. Four hundred pounds of gold dust on those mules and only one man to guard them against possible highwaymen.

There was a rush to the horses, but it is a remarkable fact that only those who had drawn the second table went to the rescue. A half hour afterwards the mules, Baily Gatzest, the treasurer, and the guard entered in triumph, saluted with honors by the first table — having dined. I always had a great respect for Baily G. ever since. I would support him for governor or senator, even if he is a Seattleite. He is a safe man.

At the risk of being tedious I want to say something which I deem important, and which I would like very much to think would influence legislation. I said we had no personal fear. Why? In that country everyone carried a revolver which he used on the slightest provocation. No one was hung for killing a man fairly. A thief was hung on the spot. What was the result? Murder upon murder, upon the slighest provocation. In Idaho City I always slept in a bullet-proof room to be protected against stray bullets. It was simply gentlemanly to be cool under fire. A gambler I knew was fired on by a butcher from behind a house. The gambler was on horseback. He was a dude, only they did not know that expression there, and even in that wild miner's camp, he wore kid gloves. He very cooly and deliberately took off one glove and commenced returning the fire. Finding the fire of the other fellow behind the house rather hot, he backed his horse into the open front of a saloon, still firing. The bullets coming rather uncomfortably thick in the saloon from the other fellow, the barkeeper drew his revolver on the dude, who, between two fires, was forced, which he did very cooly, to retire. To protect my treasure in this country I carried a revolver, and on the road at other times, even in that country, I never carried one.

I was one time given until 6 o'clock (it was then 4) to give a man acquittance of a claim of $2000, which I had against him justly. From being a very rich man he had become, from gambling, poor and desperate. I had secured $2000 of his goods, bought from other parties and unpaid for, on which he had expected to get the cost to gamble. He was a gentleman, nothing rough about him. He had been on the most friendly terms with me, but the reign of the revolver was absolute; he intended coercing me. At home I would have shuddered at the idea of bloodshed. What did I do? The meeting was in the street. I asked him to wait a few moments and I would show by my memorandum book that he was mistaken. I returned with my open book of accounts in my one hand, a derringer, cocked, in my other hand, which I kept in the pocket of my linen duster. He saw the derringer and the account, and was convinced that he was wrong.

When I landed in San Francisco in 1859, I was full of the fear of earthquakes. We had been at sea twenty-eight days and my appetite was enormous. This was long before the days of the Palace hotel of San Francisco, but after the seafare, of which I will write you at another time, the table was delicious. I ate until I could hold no more. I still cherish fond recollections, after thirty-four years, of that hotel on Jackson street, then in the heart of the retail part of the city. I had never been to sea before, and consequently I was very unsteady on my pins. My cousin Billy and I slept in the same room. In the night I was awakened by a great commotion. I sprang out of bed and went to the window. The building was rocking in a very uncomfortable manner. I steadied myself by clutching the two sides of the window. The uproar was terrible. I could think of nothing but earthquake. I thought the end of the world had come. Billy was resting quietly in bed. I thought he was overcome with fear. "Billy, this is terrible!" I said. "What is terrible?" he asked. "The earthquake," I replied. "Earthquake be d___d! Come to bed you d___d fool, it is only a fire." I had been accustomed to fires and returned meekly to bed.

Anyone who knows what a rumpus the volunteer firemen of San Francisco could make, might be excused from thinking there was an earthquake. I remained only a few days in that city, but my credentials being exceptionally good, I was offered a position as bookkeeper by McClelland & Co., at $150 per month. My head was set on the north, so I started on the brig *San Francisco*, of about 300 tons, for Portland, Or. We were out nearly a month. On the way up the Columbia we met the steamer *Eliza Anderson* on her way to Puget Sound. She had been built of Oregon fir at Portland. As she is still in service, or was a short time ago, she furnishes good proof of the quality of our fir for ship building. Were you aware that the flag staff on the Windsor castle, the residence of the queen of England, is of Oregon fir. Speaking of steamboats reminds me that in 1859 I had a friend who was purser on the steamer *Multnomah*, the only steamer running on the lower Columbia between Portland and Astoria. I relieved him several times, and have made the trip from Astoria to Portland without a passenger and the entire freight a barrel of salmon. For that matter, I have traveled over the Northern Pacific railroad from Tacoma to Kalama with not a passenger, and I was a deadhead, Holt the conductor, and I used to kill time talking of Tacoma's future greatness and of liars generally. There were many people who lied about Tacoma in those days. When I landed in Portland in 1858, it was a very rough looking place, with a population of less than 2000, but it was the metropolis of the northwest, and all lines of travel centered there. If a person wanted to go from Puget Sound to San Francisco he was obliged to go to Victoria and take the steamer, when it arrived from San Francisco, sometimes several days late, and go to Portland, and after remaining there two or three days, possibly, proceeded by the same steamer to San Francisco. Sometimes the steamer would go to Portland first and then to Victoria—Portland had important jobbing houses even then, buying directly from the factories of the east and England. I obtained a position as bookkeeper in one of them, H.W. Corbett's, and I know that his credit was as firmly established in New York city as that of any merchant on the Pacific coast today. Profits were large and interior merchants, though slow, were sure. Remittances very often came in the shape of country produce, and generally in very crude shape. Butter packed in shoe cases was rather stylish. There were three small wharves and one wharf boat. Colonel John McCracken had the wharf boat, and if my memory serves me, he accommodated all the river steamers with it. There was one public school, which stood on the present site of the Portland hotel.

There never was a more punctual school in the world. Josiah Failing, one of the solid merchants, was a director, and took great interest in the school. He had a fine chronometer watch and it was kept with the sun. No matter what business was on hand, as the time drew near for the school bell to ring, he had his watch out, and if it did not ring on the second, the principal was asked to explain. But Josiah Failing was a kindly soul and I do not think his strictness was very severe.

The theater in Portland of those days was a very little better than the old theater at Tacoma, but strange to say, a year or two afterwards we had wonderful stock companies who remained months at a time. The wonderfully accomplished Julia Dean Haine was among the number. Edmond Kean and his wife, formerly the celebrated Ellen Tree, on their way from London to Victoria on private business, appeared for two nights. I have watched the career of those stock companies, and, strange to say, nearly every one of the actors became stars. In those days you could count the stars of the theatrical world on the fingers of your two hands. Somewhat later the Pixley family, who had been living at Olympia, came to Portland and remained a year or two. Annie Pixley was pretty but was an awful stick, and was guyed every time she came on the stage. I never could understand how she became so successful. On the contrary her younger sister, now Mrs. McCracken of Portland, was exceedingly clever and a great favorite. If she had continued on the stage, she would undoubtedly have made a great success.

The only way of crossing the river at Portland there was by a one-horse, or rather one-mule ferry. Scarcely anyone lived on the east side then, so that rapid locomotion was no object.

There were very few railroads then on the Pacific coast. The only ones I have any knowledge of was one around the Oregon City falls, and the other around the Cascades. They were operated by mule power. All the goods for the upper country, as east of the mountains was called, were hauled by wagons across the portage at The Dalles. Freight and passage were extremely high. It is truly related that plows for the Indians on the Indian reservation near Idaho were shipped ready for use, and then measured "over all," and that the freight on a plow from Portland to Lewiston exceeded $100. The steamboats were small affairs, and were said to pay for themselves every trip. I was on the steamer *Mary* on one occasion when there was not room enough for the passengers, except by sitting on the deck (there was no rail), and letting their feet hang over the side. When well loaded it was impossible for some of these steamers to pass such places as Priest rapids without the assistance of passengers and crew. I have seen nearly 200 men on a rope, pulling the steamer over these rapids. I was secretary and purser of one of the companies. They used to have sail vessels on the upper Columbia. With Captain Gray, father of Mrs. Tarbell of Tacoma, in command, I came down the Columbia at high water on a sail vessel at almost railroad speed. In the early days at Portland we had one mail a month, which arrived from San Francisco by steamship. The arrival of the steamship was the great event of the month. It meant news from home, news of the world; it brought results of shipments of the month before, and many other things which the people of the present, who growl because they don't have their mail delivered every morning on time, cannot understand. The steamer fired a gun on reaching the wharf, and no matter at what hour of the night she arrived, the entire population was around, and every one rushed to Wells, Fargo & Co. and to the postoffice for their mail, and then waited until their name was called, or, if not called, returned home, many of them with sad hearts if no expected letter came, to wait wearily for another month, perhaps to again be disappointed. Steamships and sailing vessels frequently ran aground in reaching Portland, but they were generally large vessels. In the days I write of the steamers and ships were very small, and yet they often ran aground in the river. This is not the reason the old Oregonians give for this often occuring with the steamers. Prices of nearly everything fluctuated rapidly in California those days. A short supply of onions would sometimes send the price up to $10 or $12 a bushel. Other things were subject to the same raise. Captain Dall of the steamship *General Wright and Columbia*, was a speculator. A mercantile firm in Portland were friends of his. Potatoes, wheat, bacon and some other products of the country would rise greatly in the San Francisco market. The steamships would get ashore in the river below Portland, Captain Dall with his gig would proceed to Portland, leaving mail and passengers to arrive some hours after. On his arrival a courier would start up the Willamette valley and buy enough of the articles wanted to load the ship. When the mail came in and shippers tried to ship, they found all space engaged. Experiences of this character made the few farmers of the Willamette valley extremely cautious about selling. Banking on this knowledge, Dave Logan, a dry humorist and one of the brightest criminal lawyers Oregon ever had, made a bet that he would visit every farmer between Portland and Salem, some fifty miles, and offer each one $5 per bushel for his wheat and not be able to buy a bushel. It was in the winter with the roads a quagmire, when, accompanied by the other party to the bet, he started on horseback. Covered with mud from head to foot, their horses reeking with perspiration and covered with mire, they approached the first farmer's house, and after a little preliminary talk Dave commenced on the wheat question.

Wheat was worth 75 cents per bushel, but he commenced by offering $1, gradually rising to $5. He repeated this programme at every farmers. There were not many on the road, but he did not get a bushel of wheat. There was scarcely any emigration into Oregon at that time, and though I was a mere boy, the editor of the *Oregonian*, a very caustic writer, gave me the benefit of a column article on my arrival, writing a stinging article on the importation of Indiana office holders, which state had her full share at the time. I am a "Hoosier" and — it has just struck me for the first time why it was that I came to the outer edge of civilization, thousands of miles from home. It is in the blood.

I first landed at the present site of Tacoma (at Old Town) in 1867. The only convenient way of coming from Portland to the Sound at that time was by steamship to Victoria and from there to Steilacoom, Seattle and Olympia by steamer, at a cost of about $75. There was no outlet by land from the bay except by a trail from Carr's house to the prairie, and a road from the little mill at the head of the bay, where the bridge crosses Puyallup avenue, for hauling lumber to the Puyallup valley and to Steilacoom. The mill cut, I believe, about 500 feet of lumber per day; when there was a demand. When I was with the Tacoma Land company, I sold the mill irons of the company for $10 to Van Bibber of Elhi, and Van thought I charged him too much. Carr's and General McCarver's families were the only ones on the bay except the family at the mill. General McCarver's family lived in a cabin on the shore in "Old Woman's gulch," it was afterwards called, in the ravine below the site of the new hotel. You have published an account of our arrival at our first visit, so I will not repeat. I must, however, tell you a fish story: The general's cabin was within a few feet of the water. Every day at certain times one could in a few minutes, without, hook, line, net or any other device, catch enough smelts to feed a city. Pursued, I presume, by some large fish, thousands in a compact mass would rush towards the shore, and hundreds of them be forced upon the land. You had only to stand at the edge of the water with legs apart, and with open hands throw them on the beach far enough so that they would not flop back, to secure as many as you wanted, and more too. We left the bay by wagon. No steamer landed there at that time. I paid $18 extra to be landed there. My wife and self went by canoe from General McCarver's to the old mill, and remained there over night. The mosquitoes were simply terrible. In the morning we were taken by lumber wagon to Steilacoom, where we took the boat. We were thus, beyond doubt, the first passengers landing by regular Sound steamer, and the first to leave by land. I have believed in Tacoma ever since. I did not move there until the terminus was located in 1872. Everything was then very primitive. The grand primeval forest covered the entire site of the present city, except a few acres at Old Town.

A short time afterward the entire forest from near the exposition building to, I think, about Sixteenth or Eighteen streets, about 800 acres, was slashed and burned. It was a heavy forest, and the trees falling in every direction, interlaced in every form, often forming almost compact masses of boughs and trunks twenty to thirty feet high. There were no roads, only an imperfect trail, but the night the slashing was set on fire I went from Old Town alone to see the sight. It was a grand sight to see those seething, whirling, eddying, gorgeous masses of flames fed by the inflammable trunks and arms of thousands of prostrated giants. I was an enthusiast on Tacoma then, and I think that the hour I stood and looked at the sea of flames was one of the most satisfactory of my life. I saw in the myriads of fantastic shapes the flames assumed, dwellings, business houses, churches, schools, factories, steamships, ships of many countries, an active, grand, far-reaching commerce, a beautiful, grand city, the peer of any — the realization of what I had hoped for for many years. All of the small population of Tacoma were enthusiasts. People of the present day do not understand the feeling. Every man's hand was raised against the infant town, and lying about it was the custom. So every one in Tacoma, even the women, were always in arms.

I remember Mrs. Hosmer, late wife of Theodore Hosmer, then manager of the Tacoma Land company. She was one of the most charming, cultivated ladies that I ever met, coming direct from city life, where she had been surrounded by luxury and friends, she was so imbued with the spirit of the coming city, that, gentle as she was on all other subjects, she would indulge in great indignation when Tacoma was unjustly attacked. Hosmer carried his tomahawk in his hand at all times. When I first went to Tacoma there was no wharf except the mill wharf, and there was no road to the beach.

There was a large amount of building commenced at Old Town when the terminus was located, as it was supposed the railroad would come to Old Town. It cost $2.50 per thousand to haul lumber from scows, one or two blocks, because of the difficulty of hauling from the water. General McCarver was made road supervisor so as to control funds to best ends, and I was the actual supervisor, without pay, however. Then McCarver street was not exactly a county road, but we stretched a point, and I made a grade from the water in three days which knocked the $2.50 per thousand hauling. There was only a steep difficult path to the mill wharf. I raised a subscription of $9 and Ackerson of the mill donated refuse lumber, and I built a pair of steps of which every one was proud. These were the first street improvements in Tacoma. General McCarver and Dolph Hannah built a wharf at the foot of McCarver street. When Jay Cook "busted" things were very flat, but I, among others, was holding on, hoping for better times soon. I had a fine business in Portland which my partners were running, but I wanted something to do while waiting. When the wharf was finished I proposed to the owners to take it on shares. They were only too glad, because they could not afford to hire anyone. My highest dividend for one month was $30. I was paying my servant $25. It was tough handling those big lines from steamboats, and the guying was awful, as I knew every one nearly who traveled in those days. But I stuck to it until I could do better. I jumped from there into a place at $150 per month. The Northern Pacific railroad company was so poor they had to cut expenses. The land department, with Colonel Wheet and Van Schroder, and the Tacoma Land company, with Captain Hatch, was costing $600 or $700 per month. They asked me if I would do all the work at $150. I said yes.

I worked sixteen to eighteen hours per day. I am sorry to say including Sundays. While I was running the wharf I opened a real estate office, and hung out a big cedar shingle with my name on it. A gentleman from the east offered me $10 for the shingle, it being the first real estate sign. I received one consignment of goods, about $200 worth, consisting of green and dried apples, from John Myers of Oregon City. How I did wrestle with that consignment! It took me two or three months. I used to report sales, but I was awful glad to have an occasional Oregon City man come around, so that he could report to Myers that the goods were really on hand. Taking the lines of a steamer from Seattle to Olympia one day, I saw Carl Bosco, a clever magician, with whom I was well acquainted. "Going to stop and show?" I said to Carl. "No, it won't pay," he answered. "How much will you take for your house and stop off?" I asked. "Twenty-five dollars," he replied. "Get your traps off," I said; and thus I found myself the manager of the first show in Tacoma. Louis Levine was standing by, and proposed a partnership, which I agreed to. We hired a little, rough, one-story building, corner of First and McCarver streets, for which we paid a small rent. We could not have hired music if we wanted to, which we didn't. We were our own door keeper, ticket seller, stage manager, property men – in fact, we had no expenses except for seats. I think, after paying everything, we divided $20. That was my last show experience, flattering as it was. How many people know that the first bank of Tacoma was started at Old Town? It was Jay Cook's bank; that is, he backed it.

His two nephews, Del and Pit Cook, came out to run it. By special arrangement I made the first deposit. They opened temporarily in the mill company's store. When Jay Cook failed, Theodore Hosmer, who is their uncle, advised them to pay all depositors in full, which they did and quit business. When I commenced work at "New Town" I bought a house and moved there. It was the first full two-story dwelling house in Tacoma. There were a few two-story buildings, but they were used for other purposes besides dwellings. The buildng stood on a leased lot on the alley just back of the opera house. It was on the outer edge of civilization. It was about twelve feet wide by twenty-four feet long, with a shed in the rear. It was valued at $400, and I traded the owner 160 acres of land now in the city of Seattle between Lake Union and the water front. I presume it is worth big money now. The house was originally one-story, but the owner raised the roof and put one-inch boards on top, then battened over the cracks, which was all that held the upper story in place. I never saw an extremely heavy wind in Tacoma but once. I do not think there were more than twenty houses in Tacoma, and the wind had a clear sweep. There were probably half a dozen trees standing on the town plat which had been cleared, and the wind twisted the branches off of these as though they had been pipe stems, and whirled them through the air. I lay in bed in the upper story of my house, wondering how long the top story would last and whether it would be safer on the first floor or where I was. With hatchet and saw I built a platform in front of the house. The boards were planed and I felt quite proud of the addition. I send you a rough etching in keeping with the building, which I have made from memory.

The county seat and metropolis of Pierce county was Steilacoom, and to get there we had to take a road which led to Old Town, and when we reached a point five or six blocks from the water, somewhere near the intersection of McGarver street and Tacoma avenue, took the back track on the Steilacoom road, which, back of New Town, followed the section line, which is now the dividing line between Ferry's Second and Ainsworth additions. Going and coming this route made an addition of about four miles to the trip to Steilacoom, and every one had to go to Steilacoom more or less often. A road through my central addition on Eighth of Ninth street to a point in which is now my second addition, would save us the four miles. That was before the company employed an attorney at Tacoma, and I attended to all matters before the county commissioners. They laid off a country road, I think it was on the line of Seventh street, at my request, but gave me no money to open it. The Old Town people were against us and would not help us. Ezra Meeker had been appointed road supervisor in order to secure a good road from Tacoma to the valley, and he needed all the money, and more too, to accomplish that. Finally he let me have all the road money I might collect from those persons whose taxes I paid, and my own taxes, to me on this road. I owned at that time about 220 acres, which is partly covered by Central and Ferry's First and Second additions. I paid taxes for all the Portland owners of real estate in Tacoma, about 100 acres, part of which was the celebrated "Nigger tract." This looks like a big concession, but it was not. I could not do anything the first year but save the money, but in a year, with two years, I accomplished the work. I had just $36 I think, and that would not build the road, but I was bound to cut off that four miles.

The timber was not very thick on the route, in fact, there was quite an opening and swail about N and Eighth, I think. I made a contract with two men to slash all the timber on the route, and at the edge of the swail dig a well two or three feet deep, where we got delicious cool water (I am not sure but there was a little spring there which was opened) for the $36. I then invited every man, woman and child in town, and it didn't take long to do it, to meet at the well on a certain day to a road picnic. At the appointed time everyone in town was on hand. We got axes and shovels from the Northern Pacific Railroad company. Every place of business (I think there were five or six) closed. We closed the Northern Pacific and Tacoma land office. Every team in the city was there, to handle the logs in short lengths. These teams consisted of Cogswell's entire livery stable (one team), and the buggy team we used for driving to Steilacoom, belonging to the Tacoma Land company. I do not think there was ever such unanimous, enthusiastic work done by any town. Men, women and children worked as though their lives depended upon it. We stopped at noon for a splendid lunch which the ladies had prepared. After lunch, thinking, I supposed, that I had not worked as hard as the others, they called on me for a speech. I told them that their work of the day would pay them in the saving of time and fatigue, but that many of them would get their great reward in the memory of that day, when, in years to come, they traveled over the same route on a handsome street, lined with fine houses. Enthusiast as I was, I made this statement, only because there were a great many young children there who were likely to live a good many years. But every one was enthusiastic, and some one immediately got up and moved, that, as one day would not finish the work in good shape, that the entire town turn out the next day and finish "the Ferry cut-off." This was unanimously carried, and every one turned out the next day, and the road was finished.

The Northern Pacific railroad company in those days and before, was the only hope the northwest had for development, and yet, strange to say, every man's hands were raised against it and its terminus, Tacoma, and none were so bitter as the people of Old Town. The causes were serious. Before the terminus was located every one conceded that the terminus would be the great city, because it was expected that the railroad would be built over the mountains immediately. That the railroad was not commenced from Tacoma across the mountains, instead of the useless four years road to Portland, we must thank Portland influence. Portland should raise a monument which should endure forever to one of her former citizens, now a good friend to Tacoma, for if it had not been for his influence the road would have been commenced at Tacoma across the mountains, instead of to Portland. Who can doubt what the result would have been? There could have been no strong rival to Tacoma. Portland would have lost much of her prestige in 1871, and even if the road had only been completed at that period across the mountains, what an impetus it would have given immigration to the interior. There is not a city on Puget Sound which would not have been more important than it is today, and Tacoma would be a grand city. This being the feeling at that time, the towns failing to get the terminus were naturally dead against the railroad, and commenced their work of destruction against Tacoma. It was supposed and was the arrangement between the company and General McCarver, "the founder of Tacoma," that the road should come to Tacoma, which was Old Town. This was undoubtedly the intention of the company at that time, but unfortunately when the surveys of the city were commenced it was found that ten acres about the corner of North E and Seventh streets, (which would, with the gulch from the mill, have been the commencement of the business part of town) belonged to some other parties and myself. There was a log shanty at about that location belonging to me, where they established engineer headquarters. As soon as they made the discovery that someone else would have property in central location, they moved the headquarters to the corner of Ninth and Pacific, which was then a skunk cabbage swamp, where a small board shanty was built. What facilitated this was that one of the commissioners had been a steamboat captain on the Mississippi, and one of the reasons he had for choosing Tacoma was that it reminded him of Natchez, which is on a bluff. So changing the center to a place where there was a big bluff did not scare him. That it was a great mistake there is no doubt. It divided the energies and exertions of the people, and in many ways it hurt the town for years. Every passenger brought by rail being taken direct to the wharf by boat, had the impression that Blackwell's hotel, the depot and a few shanties was Tacoma, and that there was no place to build a city except under a big bluff and on the mud flats. Even at the present day it is a disadvantage. To the fact that every building in Seattle could be seen from the water, and that every passenger that landed there for years past had to pass through her narrow and therefore crowded streets is due much of her prosperity. The contrast with Tacoma from under the bluff was decidedly in favor of Seattle. Old Town was therefore hot against the Northern Pacific and New Tacoma.

Another great grievance was a road along the beach. Hosmer and myself lived at Old Town because there was no place to live at New Town, when C.B. Wright made his first visit to Tacoma after the terminal was located. I was opposed to a road on the beach, because it would disconnect the two ends of what should have been one town. Dolph Hannah was the champion of Old Tacoma interests. Dolph persuaded Mr. Wright to consent to the beach road. I heard of it about 6 o'clock in the evening.

A consultation with Hosmer resulted in my starting for Blackwell's hotel on the wharf at 7 o'clock, as Mr. Wright was to leave early next morning. There were only two ways of reaching the wharf from Old Town, by the beach or by boat. I could not find a boat, so had to tramp. The tide was sufficiently low on going to allow me to reach the hotel before 8 o'clock. A fifteen minutes' talk with Mr. Wright gave me instructions not to permit the road. The railroad company had felled the timber along the bluff to build bulkheads, and much of it lay as it was cut across the beach. The tide had rose so that it was impossible to follow the beach the entire distance. Many times I had to scale the bluff, grope my way over fallen timber, through ferns far over my head, occasionally tumbling into a hole several feet deep made by the uprooting of some huge tree. It is, I believe, about one mile and a quarter from the old Blackwell hotel to Hanson's mill. I was about four hours making it, and arrived fagged out, covered with dirt from head to foot, with clothing torn and bleeding hands and face, at about midnight. That was not the last of the road. Dolph and I were good friends, but when I represented the company before the commissioners, we had several hot tilts over it. After the road was completed between Kalama and Tacoma, the Northern Pacific, nor any person connected with it, did anything for Tacoma, and yet she had the odium of being the pet of the railroad company. For many years this was very injurious. The few people at New Town, the so-called "pets of the company," were bitter against the company because they did nothing. I presume that it is almost forgotten that Railroad street was intended for railroad tracks, and that a track was laid to a point in the street where Gross Brothers' store is on Ninth and Railroad streets with the intention of landing passengers in town instead of on the wharf. This was never done, and gave great cause for complaint. There used to be a mail route between Old and New Town. Ira Cogswell was the contractor at,

I think, $300 per year. The Old Town people raised a row, because they claimed that the Northern Pacific was obliged to and did not carry the mail to Old Town. General Sprague was superintendent then, and made the contract with Cogswell for the company.

Speaking of General Sprague reminds me of an incident of those days of which he was the hero. Poverty and economy controlled the Northern Pacific at that time. Holt was station agent at Kalama and ran out as conductor to meet the train from Tacoma, when the other conductor doubled back to Tacoma. I think there were only two locomotive engineers. At any rate a boat load of cattle were landed at Kalama to go through and meet the boat for Victoria at Tacoma, but there was no engineer. General Sprague was equal to the emergency and mounted an engine and brought the train through on good time.

I have never seen any statement in regard to the first water works. They were located in Old Town. General McCarver and Dolph Hannah put up the money to build them. I had one share of stock, I believe, to qualify me as director. General McCarver was president and I was secretary. I don't remember whether Dolph had an office.

My water rent was $1 per month, I think, and I had free water for my salary. The reservoir was situated on McCarver street, opposite the general's house, near Fourth street, I think. It may be there now for all I know. The pipes were wooden, bound with hoop-iron, and they used to do a good deal of free sprinkling when the street was laid out. We had no schoolhouse in New Town, but there were a number of children who were anxious to attend school. We had no money — not a dollar — to build with. McGraw, Walker and myself were school directors. "Skookum" Smith, who was always ready to do Tacoma a good turn, told us he would let us have the lumber on credit, until we could raise the money. This would have made it very easy to build a one-story building, but the Masons wanted a lodgeroom, and the directors being Masons, we concluded to build a two-story building and finish the upper story for a Masonic hall. It was a great responsibility, for the next directors might refuse to pay for the building, and the building would cost $900 — a big sum of money then.

I do not know where that schoolhouse was located, unless it was where the Emmerson school is now, but the reason I doubt it is that it seemed so far away from the town, which was nearly all between Seventh and Ninth and A and E streets, as near as I can remember. The schoolhouse in all its ugliness was a monument of progress considering the time, greater than the most costly edifice that Tacoma will ever build. Miss Jennie McCarver, now the wife of Thomas W. Prosch of Seattle, was the first teacher, and she was a very good one.

I do not think any one would accuse Fife or Fife's hotel of political ambition, but when three stores represented the business of Tacoma he worked hard to be made postmaster. Fife had never been postmaster before, and had never been in any business where there was no profit, so, as the salary was as nearly nothing as could be, he charged a fair profit on postage stamps. Customers not being accustomed to paying profit on stamps, naturally kicked. The matter was referred to the postmaster-general.

The first gas made from Washington coal was manufactured in the Tacoma land company's building, I think in 1875. It was on a very small scale, but the result, when communicated to Mr. Hosmer, in Philadelphia, by myself, created great interest in Northern Pacific circles. Sproule, who was hung in British Columbia a few years ago, took up a coal claim not far from the original discovery claim of Gale. Governor Ferry and myself took claims, which are now, I believe, worked by the Central Pacific people. Sproule explored all that country. I was chief clerk for the Northern Pacific land department and Tacoma Land company at that time. Our office stood on the present site of the theater. It was out of town. Sproule brought me several specimens of coal one day, which he said came from my claim. Among them was a small, smooth piece which had evidently been worn by being in a stream of water for a long period.

It was much heavier than the other samples. I took the samples to P.G. Eastwick, who was a coal expert. Under his direction I bought two clay pipes at Fife's store and placed the two kinds of coal in the bowls — sealing them with clay. There was a roaring fire of bark in the office. On this I placed the two pipes. In a few minutes that gas was burning, the first gas in Tacoma, from the stem of one. From the other there was no gas. On breaking the pipes we found in one a perfect piece of coke, the form of the bowl of the pipe; the first coke manufactured from Pacific coast coal. The coal in the other remained just as we had put it in, except that it had beautiful peacock colors, perfect anthracite. Worn by water as it was, a piece not an inch square, it would have been difficult for Sproule to obtain it, besides which he had no purpose to serve in deceiving me. I think he had searched my claim to do me a service, for he was under great obligations to me. I had at one time the absolute power of going on to his claim, the Smith and Fife tract, and taking possession legally, and he could not have helped himself in any manner, and he knew it. This is unwritten history, the particulars of which will probably never be given. There were only four persons, two besides Sproule and myself, who ever knew anything of this. Another and myself still live; the other two are dead. With this knowledge on Sproule's past, I do not see why he should have desired to deceive me. I therefore feel quite sure that pure anthracite coal will be found at some point in the country drained by the stream which cuts the Central Pacific mine in two.

It will no doubt be news to nearly all Tacoma that the first Tacoma fourth of July celebration was held by the Indians at the reservation. All Tacoma was invited. For some reason, for which I have never had explanation, they invited me to preside. This was quite an honor. All the speeches except some feeble remark by the president, were made by the Indians. Peter Stanup was then quite a young boy, but he interpreted the speeches with marked ability for one so young and inexperienced. There was a splendid dinner prepared under the care of the agency at the expense of the Indians. The Indians had a separate table.

Writing of first things reminds me that I lately bought a book of charts and engravings published in Paris in 1795. It relates to the voyage of Captain J. Mears in 1786 and 1787. I do not think that there are many persons who know when and at what time the first vessel was built in the north Pacific ocean. This book gives that information through an engraving. It shows a small vessel at the moment of launching. The British flag floats at the stern and on a house adjacent. One white man is on the deck and two officers are standing on the ground, surrounded by numerous Indians, most of them sitting Indian fashion on the shore. Indian canoes and two ships are off shore. Below it is an inscription in French which, freely translated, means:

"A vessel on the northwest coast of America, seen when launched at the entrance of Nootka. It was the first vessel which was constructed in that part of the globe." So at the entrance to Nootka sound (a very fine map of that part of the country being in the same book) the first vessel was built. An engraving of the straits of Fuca shows that the vessel built was a light-draft schooner, tender to the ship, to be used probably for entering shallow harbors.

When I commenced this letter it was for the simple purpose of trying to induce the old settles to write up early days in Tacoma, on the lines of the early settlers' stories, and insensibly, almost, I have wandered off and written about many things I had determined to keep until I was ready to write more fully covering more ground. I hope this letter will call out letters from many old Tacomans. Has anything been done with the old Carr house? When it is destroyed it will be a source of regret that it was not preserved. Better delay some park improvements and make it a feature of the parks, which would grow in interest as the years pass by. The cost would be trifling, and the neglect indefensible on any ground. If the city was to duplicate the original log house alone (Mrs. A. Carr has a photo of it) at the exposition, making it Tacoma headquarters, and lining its walls with large photos of present buildings, the object lesson would repay the cost many times over.

I have recently read in the *Oregonian* that the channel above Portland is to be improved to Oswego, about six miles above. I presume that even old Portlanders know that Portland was not always the head of navigation. The brig *Francisco*, on which I landed in Portland thirty-four years ago, was partly owned by Captain Smith of Portland. He was an eccentric old Yankee. We arrived at night, and the next morning at 5 o'clock the old captain was in my stateroom and within half an hour he knew pretty near every detail of my life, and had hired me to act as freight clerk in discharging cargo. When I had finished discharging the cargo, the captain asked me if I could tally lumber. I told him I thought I could. I knew I could learn, and he engaged me to go with the brig to Oswego. There was a small sawmill there, but the business being unprofitable, the mill had shut down, and we were to take all the lumber, good and bad, in his yard.

I studied lumber measurement in the evening with the kind-hearted, honest proprietor, and commenced talking with him next day, and as he had to make allowance for all lumber not perfect, and as the old gentleman was very honest and liberal, the lumber tallied out with a handsome margin in San Francisco, which gave the captain a high opinion of my ability. Before I had completed the work I found that the captain's curiosity had done me a good turn. I had made out the ship freight bills, and my handwriting, when H.W. Corbett's bill was presented, attracted the attention of his bookkeeper. Inquiry led to the information that a leading merchant of Portland had known me from a boy. Mr. Corbett wanted a salesman. I received a letter asking me to come as soon as possible, and that is how I know that the brig *Francisco*, in 1848, was the last sail vessel to go above Portland. When the old captain handed me $5 per day for my work I thought my fortune would be soon made. That was before the war, when $500 per annum was pretty good pay in the east.

The following letter from C.P. Ferry, now in Geneva, relates to General McCarver, who, as the letter shows, had much to do in making the history of Tacoma what it has been:

No. 2, Rue des Alpes,
Geneva, June 2, 1892.

President, Chamber of Commerce, Tacoma
Dear Sir:

I send as a present to the chamber of commerce a crayon portrait of the father, the founder of Tacoma, General McCarver. It is a splendid likeness, an enlarged copy of an ambrotype.

Had the general lived until the present day, no man would be so highly honored by Tacomans as he, but there are few to whom the name now means anything, and it is a pity, for there is not a man who has come to Tacoma to make his home, who loves the place, or has prospered in it, who does not owe a debt of gratitude to General M. McCarver. But for him Tacoma would not have been made the terminus of the Northern Pacific railroad, and a village might exist where now stands our beautiful city.

General McCarver was well known all over the Pacific coast, and from the year 1867, when he laid out the town of Tacoma, his name was almost synonymous with Tacoma with all who knew him. He was no ordinary settler or government hand, whom some railroad company or speculator found in possession of an eligible site for a town and made well off by purchasing his interest, but a man of sagacious and of broad views, a founder of cities, one whom all citizens of Tacoma may now and hereafter honor as a man who founded the city, not only as a means of making money; but to assist in building, as he believed, the great city of the Pacific coast.

He had, it would appear from his history, an intuitive knowledge of points which would make cities. He bought real estate in Chicago in 1835 and lost it in litigation many years after. He bought the site of Burlington, Ia., and founded that place. In the fight between Benicia and Sacramento, when Benicia was the capitol, he cast his fortunes with General Sutter and Sacramento. In the early days of Oregon he laid off a town near the mouth of the Willamette river, in opposition to Portland. It was the correct place, as the millions of tons of freight and hundreds of thousands of passengers carried by boat up the river, by steamships to Portland and then back again by boat to the Columbia, and vice versa, will testify. He started from my house in Portland, Or., on horseback, to find the terminus of the Northern Pacific railroad, which we hoped would be constructed from both ends at the same time. The Sound country was almost a wilderness in those days and there was only a foot trail into Commencement bay. The strategical position of Commencement bay on the map had, of course, caught his attention, and he decided immediately on visiting the bay that was the place he was looking for. He immediately bought Mr. Carr's interest at Old Town, the only settler on the bay, and took up a homestead, with his cabin in "Old Woman's Gulch," embracing a considerable part of the present city. He brought his family there, and there I visited him with my wife—his daughter—shortly after. Carr's cabin and his were the only ones, but he and the family were as contented as though they were living in a palace and he was sure of securing the Northern Pacific terminus. There were a number of Indians on the bay, and it was from them at that time I learned the name "Tacoma," a name which I gave afterward to the town. I think Seattle people called the mountain Tacoma in those primitive days.

General McCarver was a man of untiring energy, and from that time he left nothing unaccomplished to induce the Northern Pacific to make its terminus on Commencement bay, and devoted all his time, energies and money to that end, and it was only through his unselfishness and efforts that the Northern Pacific railroad was induced to make its terminus where it did, for the early stockholders of the Northern Pacific were a greedy lot and wanted it all.

General McCarver acted for the Northern Pacific and persons interested in the company, in obtaining subsidies and buying land, without recompense, and as a proof of his unselfishness it is only necessary to say that all the present townsite then owned by the Northern Pacific and Tacoma Land company, except that owned by the Northern Pacific under its land grant, was obtained by or through General McCarver, and yet when the city was laid out by the Tacoma Land company the general had not reserved one lot for himself, notwithstanding that his homestead was a part of the new city. I think it was after the general's death I called the attention of Mr. Hosmer, then in charge of the Tacoma land company at Tacoma, to this matter and he succeeded in having two lots deeded to the estate on Pacific avenue, worth at that time $200 each. The consideration of his services and interest in the location of the terminus by the Northern Pacific people is best known by the fact that the first telegram by the commissioners appointed to fix the terminus, giving the decision as to location, was sent to the general at Tacoma. I had the pleasure of opening and reading it to the family.

The city is so new that little interest is felt in the early history of the place, but it will not be many years before everything connected with the early times and of the man who founded the city will be sought for with interest. His romantic and eventful life as a pioneer in Illinois, Iowa, Oregon, California and Washington should furnish many interesting incidents.

Such men as Captain J.C. Ainsworth, a relation by marriage and life-long friend of the general's, Dolph B. Hannah, and others who knew him for many years under many circumstances, ought to be invited to contribute all they know of his life; not only the bare history, but incidents which, though unimportant now, will be of interest hereafter.

In this connection I think it would only need a hint from you to the amateur photographers to have photos taken of many old land marks of early days; land marks rapidly disappearing under the march of improvements, which will be of value hereafter.

Yours very truly,
C.P. Ferry

P.B. Van Trump

Mountaineer Van Trump relates
many incidents about the majestic mountain
Tacomans called Mount Tacoma and
Seattleites called Mount Rainier.

April 14, 1893

The following paper was prepared at the special request of the Academy of Science and the Washington Alpine club by P.B. Van Trump and read at a joint meeting held recently:

Mr. President, Ladies and Gentlemen: I was both pleased and surprised by the invitation to be present here this evening and to address you, presumably on the mountain theme: pleased because the invitation was to give me the opportunity to meet for the first time, at their joint session, the members of the Academy of Science and the Washington Alpine club, and pleased, too, because of the implied compliment, for it certainly is a compliment and an honor to be asked to address such an audience; and surprised as well, for after all that has been written on the subject of the mountain, after all the stories of the ascents that have been told and re-told, after the varied discussion that has been obtained relative to the mountain, and especially after all that I have written about it, for I have been a public scribbler on the mountain subject at frequent intervals for twenty-two years past — after all this, I repeat, I supposed that in the estimation of the public the theme had become hackneyed and threadbare, and that a repetition of the old story on my part would seem to a Tacoma audience more wearisome than a thrice told tale. I am much pleased to meet and be able to make the acquaintance here tonight of General Kautz. To him belongs the distinction — and you gentlemen of the Alpine club, if you have acquired the true mountain spirit, will not fail to consider it an enviable one — of having been the first one to explore the south slope of the mountain, the first to demonstrate the feasibility of ascending our great peak, and the first to show that there existed within the borders of our country a bona fide and magnificent glacier, a fact unknown up to that time to scientific men, or doubted by them. The era of General Kautz's mountain exploit was a decade prior to the time that Seward turned his statesmanlike and prophetic glance toward the territory of Alaska, with the practical idea of acquiring it for the United States, and it was unknown at that time that Mount St. Elias (that still unconquered giant) had a stupendous system of glaciers. It fell to the lot of other mountain climbers following in Lieutenant Kautz's footsteps, to prove that man is capable of reaching the very pinnacle of Tacoma's hoary summit, of penetrating its crater, hitherto unknown, and even of slumbering on its inner smouldering rim; to them, too, fell the lot of proving that our territory possessed not one or two glaciers, but a grand system of them, not inferior in grandeur, perhaps, to those of the far-famed and classic Alps. As I am not sufficiently experienced in public speaking to address you in an extempore speech, I have committed to paper what I have to say, and as I cannot help thinking that a repetition in detail of any of my previous published mountain accounts would be wearisome, I shall make some reflections on the naming òf the mountain, allude to a few features of past ascents, describe the several lines of ascent, give some mountain anecdotes, some advice to climbers by the more dangerous lines, and conclude with some remarks on the mountain as a great health resort.

Notwithstanding the distant, and calm and reposeful grandeur of our great mountain, it is curious to note how provocative it is of contention, dispute and rivalry. When, in the far and dim past, the red man, the primitive dweller on the showers of the waters of Whulge, gave to the name "Tacobet" the meaning of "The Nourisher," he gave or builded wiser than he knew, for not only is the mountain — or the perpetual snows of its lofty summit — the source of those hidden fountains which form the numerous fertilizing rivers, about which our worthy and pioneer citizen, Hon. Elwood Evans, has so eloquently spoken, but it has been, and is, the "nourisher" of a tense and bitter contention between two great cities whose buildings, and spires, and temples and shipping are today mirrored in the glassy and placid waters which of old reflected only the shadow of the forest primeval, the shape of the passing cloud or the great white form of the majestic Tah-ho-ma. And this contest and rivalry exists not only between these two cities, but between the old settler elsewhere and the innovating newcomer. Had

Shakespeare's prophetic vision extended down to these later times and to these distant shores, he would doubtless have modified his remark about the triviality of a name. The near future gives no promise of a cessation of the conflict over the mountain's name, or that the bloody hatchet of nomenclature will be buried. Had our great peak been placed on the classic spot where the fabled throne of Jupiter lifted its summit toward the sky, and ancient Athens and Rome had bitterly contested over the naming of it, what wars would have raged, and what heroic conflicts would have taken place!

Still other Homers and other Virgils would have immortalized their names in sublime epics on the theme. Possibly there is among our people some poet who will yet rise equal to the occasion and the theme, or some modern Dean Swift may yet give us a poetic tale of two cities or the battle of the names. Which of the two great factions in the state, founded on a name, is to finally succeed, the Rainier faction or the Tacoma faction? By what name is our mountain to be called for all time? By what name is it be known in history, in story and in song? This is a very interesting question and it is one which ought to be agitated by this club and by this society till a majority of the people of the state, and till the governmental powers that be, are in favor of abolishing the name of Rainier. The argument in favor of Rainier has, indeed, the canon or rule of discovery on its side, of English discovery but it should be remembered when it is claimed that the distinguished Vancouver discovered the mountain, that it had already been discovered and named by a people who had so long resided beneath its sublime shadow that their origin was hidden in the dimness and mystery of the past. Long generations before, the Indians had beautifully and significantly named the mountain Tacobet, the nourisher, or source of waters, and Tahoma, the rumbler and thunderer, whose peculiarly cloud-capped summit had, from time immemorial, foretold to him the changing weather, and in whose rivers and streams, fed by its everlasting snows, he had for centuries caught the silvery salmon. The Indian was the rightful owner of the sublime mountain and of the country it so grandly dominates. We have robbed him of his birthright. Let us honor him for retaining, let us at least do him the justice of preserving the name with which he so appropriately christened the mountain. Many of those who object to Tacoma and Tahoma claim that the Indian never had a name for the mountain. Even so able and intelligent a writer as Editor Scott of the *Oregonian* long since claimed that the Indians never called the mountain Tacoma or Tahoma, that the modern so-called Indian name is the name invented by Theordore Winthrop. In a recent issue of the *Oregonian*, in reply to an inquiring correspondent, he reiterates this assertion, notwithstanding the fact that he must have read, in his Tacoma exchange, Judge Wickersham's able and exhaustive letter on the subject, in which he furnishes accumulative Indian testimony to the fact that they always had a name for the mountain, and one with a particular and appropriate meaning. The editor of the *Oregonian* is strongly prejudiced in favor of Rainier. Human prejudice is more difficult of eradication or change than ignorance, and educated ignorance is the most inveterate. How ridiculous is the assertion that the Indians had, and have, no name for the mountain, when we know that the Indian has names for the most trivial objects in nature. Wouldn't it be unreasonable to suppose that this grand and imposing object, in relation to which he has so many legends and superstitions, was ever nameless to him? Would any scholar assert that the mountains which are known in classic literature as Olympus and Parnassus were "nameless forevermore" among the ancients, and that their names were the invention of writers and poets? Would any literary critic claim that the Scotch highlander could have had no name for some of his favorite mountain peaks, and that Scott invented the names of Benledi, Benvenue and Ben Lomond when he immortalized those speaks by the beauty and magic of his descriptive verse? As well assert that the Indian never had names, and expressive ones, for mountains that he venerated and ever gazed on with awe and superstition. When time shall have long rolled its ceaseless course, when the present shall have become an epoch in the far distant past, when the history of our people and our state shall have become ripe and full of years, then will our great mountain be classic in history, in story, and in song, just as many a peak, far less grand, in the old world is classic. How important, how appropriate then it is for us to give our mountain a name that will stand the test of time and meet with the approval of coming generations; that we should endeavor to supercede a name that is not significant, that only perpetuates the name of a mere individual, a man who was not great, who was not in sympathy with the theory of our government or in touch with the genius of our people. I was never in favor of the modern English and American practice of naming rivers and mountains or any sublime object of nature after individuals. Had Captain Gray anticipated Vancouver, as he might have done in entering Puget Sound, he would have discovered the mountain and would doubtless have named it for Washington. What appropriateness or significance would there have been on either side in thus naming it? Better for us and the coming generations to perpetuate that name by enshrining his memory more loyally in our hearts, by more closely following his wise teachings, and by modelling our political life on his patriotic example. We are wont to admire much that was sublime, and beautiful, and grand in Greece and Rome. Why not follow their design in nomenclature? Is it not supposed that the ancient Greeks and Romans revered their teachers and lofty intellects as much as we do our great men? But when did they name a great river or great mountain after Plato or Socrates, after Cicero or Caesar? Could any people venerate their seers and teachers more than the ancient Hebrews venerated Abraham, Isaac and Jacob? Their history tells us of Mount Sinai, Mount Zion, Mount Hermon, Mount Tabor, and, best of all, Mount Olivet, or Mount of Olives, but not of a Mount Abraham, a Mount Isaac or a Mount Jacob. The names of ancient mountains, except those whose etymology has been lost, express something that pertained or appropriately belonged to them. Just so Indian names for natural objects are significant and appropriate.

Although the commission or bureau on geographical names appointed by the late administration adopted, or rather confirmed, Rainier as the official name of the mountain, I believe the time is not very far off when public opinion will demand a rescinding of this decision, just as public opinion sometimes demands and effects the repealing of a law or the changing of a constitution. My own preference as to a name for the mountain is the Klickitat form of the Indian name — Tahoma. The meaning that the Klickitats are said to attach to the word is very appropriate, as any one who has ever heard the muffled thunder of the glaciers will admit. The meaning that is ascribed to Tacobet or Tacoma is probably more beautiful and poetic.

It would take quite a volume to record all the discussions, the anecdotes, and the sayings, wise and otherwise, humorous and vindictive, that have grown out of this rivalry and contention over the two-named mountain. Several anecdotes occur to me that may be new to the audience. A gentleman from the east had landed first in the City of Destiny. Someone, no doubt an obliging real estate man with an eye to business, had been showing the newcomer and supposed capitalist around the city, and finally called his attention to Mount Tacoma, and expatiated him on its grandeur and beauty. When the gentleman had gazed for some time with pleased and appreciate eye at the majestic peak, he turned to his companion and said, "Now show me, please, where Mount Rainier is," and he seemed quite surprised when the speculative dealer in municipal dirt informed him that they were one and the same mountain, only viewed from different centers of civilization.

Late in the summer when Cleveland was running for his first term, I was an eye and ear witness to the following anecdote:

The political caldron was boiling pretty lively at that juncture and politics were like "razors in the air." The overland passenger train had stopped a few moments at Yelm. A gentleman, apparently just from the east, was on the rear platform of the last passenger coach, taking in the sublime view of the mountain that Yelm affords. An old settler of Yelm, a granger, crossed the track near the train. The gentleman on the car platform said to him: "Tell me, sir, is that mountain yonder Mount Tacoma?" The old settler straightened himself up, and, with an offended air, sharply answered: "No, sir! That is Mount Rainier in this latitude." As the train started the gentleman waved his hand deprecatingly and called back: "See here, my friend, it is evident that you are a Cleveland mossback." This is the first instance to my knowledge of the mountain being dragged into politics. By the way, the commission that decided to retain Rainier as the official name of the mountain was appointed by the republican administration. It will be remembered that the first official act of Cleveland was to rescind the action of the late administration on the Hawaiian question. May there not be among the large number of democrats in the state, who are anxious to serve their country, enough advocates of the Indian name, when supplemented by all the republican opponents of Rainier, to send a long enough petition to Cleveland on the subject to induce him to reverse the decision of the late administration's board on geographical names? If this could be effected, it would be dragging the old mountain into politics to some purpose.

On one of my annual trips to the mountain I camped with my party one evening at Mishell prairie, on Mishell Henry's place. There were three parties camping near together, one from Seattle, one from Tacoma and one from Yelm. In those days all parties to the mountain passed through Mishell prairie, and every one camped on Henry's farm. His granary supplied grain and his mow hay for the horses, while his well-stocked garden furnished vegetables for the hungry tourists — consequently Henry "put money in his purse." After supper on this occasion the three parties got into a long discussion over the name of the mountain. Finally it was agreed that Mishell Henry should settle the dispute. He was called into camp, and one of the Seattle gentlemen asked him to tell the company the real name of the mountain. Henry had a shrewd eye to the main chance, and knew that his customers represented both sides of the mountain question, and were equally good pay. Stalking slowly into camp, he stood for a moment looking judicially from one party to the other, and then, gravely sweeping his arm in the direction of the mountain, replied: "Taka name Lanier-Tahoma." This solution of the knotty question was laughingly acquiesced in by the disputing parties. Herein is a suggested solution to the two warring name-factions in the state. If Seattle and the old settlers won't give up Rainier, and the Tacomans and the newcomers won't give up the Indian name, why not compromise on shrewd Henry's compound name, Rainier-Tacoma, or Tacoma-Rainier?

There are three lines or routes of ascent of the mountain so far developed: One by the south side of the mountain, one by the northeast side, and one by the west side. It would probably be more correct to say that there are two lines of ascent on the south or Paradise side of the mountain, the line followed by General Kautz in 1857 and the one originated by General Stevens and myself. General Kautz ascended, I think, on the left or west side of the great Nisqually glacier, starting from the lower extremity of the glacier, Stevens and myself starting from the head of Paradise falls and ascending the mountain a little west of due north, on the divide between the Nisqually glacier on the left or west, and the Cowlitz glacier on the right or east. In the long interim between 1870 and 1884, several attempts were made by mountain climbers to reach the summit by the north side of the mountain, but they were all unsuccessful. One season George B. Bayley reconnoitered the north side with the intention of making the ascent, but his experienced eye told him that an ascent from that side in a southerly direction was impracticable, so in 1883, in compliance with my advice, he, in company with James Longmire and myself, climbed to the summit by the Stevens and Van Trump route of 1870. In 1881 F. Fobes, in company with two companions from Snohomish, tried the oft-essayed north ascent, but failed, like their predecessors, to scale the precipitous north face of the mountain, so they returned to permanent camp, but not to their homes, disheartened, like their predecessors; but they passed around to the left or eastward, crossing the Carbon river glacier and reaching the ridge between the Carbon glacier and the White river glacier. They climbed this ridge till they got above the most dangerous and thickly crevassed portion of the White river glacier; then descending the side of the ridge they got on the White river glacier itself, and after some difficulty, and some narrow escapes, reached the summit of the middle peak by this line.

The third line of ascent is on the west side of the mountain, and was marked out or decided on by myself in exploring expeditions to the west side in 1889 and 1890. In August, 1891, Dr. Riley and I made the ascent by this line with the intention of reaching the summit of the north peak. After a long, arduous climb, made so by deep, new-fallen snow for the last 1000 feet; we reached the base of the north peak and passed some distance up its eastern slope, but by reason of extreme fatigue and on account of night setting in, we had to abandon the north peak to climb to the crater of the middle peak to spend the night there. As a rule, a night spent in the crater begets a desire to descend without delay to lower terra firma. He who for one night becomes the guest of the grim spirit whom the Indians fable to be the genius loci of Tacoma's summit, usually rises from his steamed and sulphur-fumed couch on the following morn with a heart not nearly so courageous as on the evening before, nor so full of ambitious dreams of daring mountain enterprise.

The for the nonce forgotten charms of the nether world reassert themselves, and his paramount desire is to seek the flowery mead or lovely park in which his distant and well-stocked tent is pitched. The exception to this rule, in my experience, was the night spent in the crater by Bayley and myself in August, 1892, after we reached the summit by practically the line climbed by Dr. Riley and myself in 1891. This night (in 1892) was the least disagreeable of the four nights I have spent in the crater. There was for once practically no wind, and the morning broke calm and beautiful. Our spirits were as buoyant as on the day before, and we were full of desire and determination to master the long coveted, but to us hitherto elusive north peak. We did reach and explore the summit of the north peak, as my narrative twice published has shown. When Dr. Riley and I were on the east slope of the north peak's summit, we particularly examined the approach to it by way of the White river glacier, and we were of the opinion that the summits of the north and middle peaks can be reached by the northwest line of ascent easier than by the west side. I have not been on the north side of the mountain and have never tried the northeast side, but I am of the opinion that the most difficult and possibly the most dangerous line of ascent is by the west side. The element of danger will be to the true mountain climber an added zest, rather than an element of discouragement. In the "Lady of the Lake," fierce Roderick Dhu, disguised as a common highlander and acting as guide to Fitz James, lost in the mountains, asks the knight why he trusted himself in the mountain fastness when the outlawed Roderick, or one of his retainers, might compass his death, Snowdoun's knight replies:

"A warrior thou, and ask me why!
Moves our free course by such fixed cause,
As gives the poor mechanic laws?
Enough, I sought to drive away
The lazy hours of peaceful day;
Slight cause will then suffice to guide
A knight's free footsteps far and wide—
A falcon flown, a greyhound strayed,
The merry glance of a mountain maid;
Or if a path be dangerous known
The danger's self is lure alone."

The supposed impracticability or the known danger of a route to the summit of any celebrated mountain peak is a successful "lure" to the ambitious mountain climber. The old line of ascent by Paradise valley and Gibraltar has been so often traversed, has become, so to speak, such a beaten track, that the ambitious climber will hereafter often try the west-side route. To those not professed mountain climbers, who may want to essay the west-side route, a little advice or a few suggestions might not be amiss. Establish permanent camp as near snowline on the main mountain as possible. Before leaving your tent for the final ascent, see that it is securely pinned down and well anchored to surrounding rocks or trees. When starting on the ascent do not overload yourself. A pack that is light at starting will become wonderfully heavy at 12,000 feet. Have on an all-wool suit of underclothing, and outside clothing fairly warm. Carry two good blankets as far as temporary camp above snow line. This temporary camp should be made at some suitable point at an elevation of at least 10,000 feet above sea-level—better 11,000 feet. Take to this camp at least three days' provisions, and it would be better to take a four days' stock, to allow for a possible detaining storm. When starting from the upper camp on final ascent, roll your coat, which is all the better if flannel lined, in one good blanket; take enough simple provision to last two days (thinking always of possible detention), being sure to have some Leibig's extract of beef in the proportions of one jar (ordinary size) to each two persons; carry a canteen well filled with water before leaving camp. One drawback to the ascent by the west side is the scarcity of running water above snow line. Do not, if you can at all avoid it, eat snow or ice to quench thirst; it will most always produce colic or cramping pains. Carry a generous piece of chocolate, and occasionally let a small piece melt in your mouth. It will allay thirst and is nourishing. Be sure to have a good alpenstock, seventy-five feet of three-eighths rope, an ice hatchet, a compass, smoked glasses or green goggles for the eyes, and steel caulks in your shoes and a supply in your pack, to replace lost or broken ones. Do not fail to provide the seventy-five or 100 feet of rope mentioned. In case of losing an alpenstock down a crevasse in which it lodges, one of the party can be let down to recover it. I have been let down into a large crevasse to regain an alpenstock that had lodged on a deep shelf of the crevasse. The rope which I carried last summer saved Bayley from a probable lingering death in the huge crevasse into which he was hurled at the end of his fearful slide, almost from the brow of the mountain on the west side. Had we used the rope, as we should have, at the point of greatest danger, he would doubtless have been saved the fall, saved many days of torture, and would not today have three broken ribs. The mountaineer, after long experience without mishap, like the unharmed veteran railroad man, gets careless or acquires an oversweeping confidence in his own skill, and then an hour comes when disaster overtakes him.

When you commence the descent of the steep and dangerous places, let your leader plant his alpenstock firmly in the snow and tie one end of the rope firmly to the staff low down near the snow, and then let the rope hang full length down the line of descent, the leader getting a firm footing and bracing the upright staff. Now let each of the other mountaineers, in turn, take the strand of rope and carefully descend the length of it. Then the leader hauls back the rope, letting the one end remain fastened to the lower end of the staff, and then with the other end takes a half hitch or sailor's bight around the top of the alpenstock, and lets the double rope down the mountain side. Then he takes in one hand of the lower strand of the rope and descends like his companions, but of course only half as far. When at the end of the double strand, he pulls on the strand fastened to the top of the alpenstock till it comes out of the snow and slides down to him. He again repeats this process until he reaches his companions; and these operations are repeated till the dangerous declivity is passed. I much prefer this method to the Alpine or Swiss plan of the company being constantly tied together when climbing or descending. It is slower, but it is safer. The leader is always braced and looking out for a slip or fall on the part of the man descending. In the other plan some man may fall unseen, and his sudden jerk and strain on the common line, at a danger point, may cause all to lose their footing. The alpenstock is the mountaineer's sheet anchor, and he should never be without it on the mountain side. Twice I saved my life by a dexterous use of it.

Volumes almost have been written about Mount Tacoma as to exploration, mountain climbing, prospecting, etc., and as an object of sublime beauty and grandeur, but it seems to me it has not been considered enough as a grand health resort. Comparatively few will climb or want to climb to the summit. Hundreds can visit it in search of health, to regain lost appetites, to strengthen weakened muscles, to recuperate or regain lost energy, to awaken and revive torpid livers, to forget aching, ailing physical self, to forget, for a time, the business, the toil and the cares of life; to drink in the strengthening, revivifying ozone of the mountain air at the line of perpetual snow, or high up on the glacier or rocky mountain spur where it sweeps down in taintless and magical purity from the icy dome of Tacoma. Let the banker, or merchant, or clerk, or minister, who in summer is a victim of dyspepsia, who has lost energy, life and vim, whose liver is torpid, and to whom all the uses of life have become "stale, flat and unprofitable," flee to the mountain in July or August; and after a few weeks spent at the snowline in rambling, climbing and exploring, in eating drinking and sleeping (for then he will eat, and eating and sleeping will for once at least, seem to him to be the very business of life) my word for it he will return to his home and business, or calling, a new man; a man with newer and brighter views of life, and with better hopes of heaven. To the man who suffers with asthma, to him who is a sufferer with nasal catarrh, or catarrh of the head, a sojourn in the parks of the mountain, in July or August, will be of great benefit. A cold contracted in the low country soon yields to the influence of the pure mountain air at a high altitude. But a man with organic disease of the lungs, he who has passed the incipient stages of consumption, and has a tendency to hemorrhages, should never attempt high mountain climbing. To the mountain climber, to the tourist, to the botanist, to the scientist, to the hunter, and to every lover of the beautiful and the sublime in nature, the slopes and peaks of Mount Tacoma offer a wide and varied field of study, of occupation, and of pleasure.

Rev. Myron Eells

Born at Tshimiakain Mission (near present day Spokane, Wa.) in 1843 to the Missionary Cushing Eells, Myron describes his early life on the frontier and his later years as a missionary to the Indians.

August 12, 1892

When I was at the centennial celebration at Astoria last May, some persons questioned my right of being called a pioneer or of wearing the pioneer badge, because I never crossed the plains as other pioneers did. At that time Hon. M.C. George of Oregon, in a speech, said that he did not know whether he had the right of being classed among the pioneers, because he remembered but little about their hardships and really suffered but little, as he came when he was a year and a half old. I acknowledge that I was obliged afterward to say that I came when I was a year and a half younger than he was. Nevertheless, the pioneer societies have been willing to acknowledge me as a pioneer. When I look at my life of nearly fifty years I find I have been along with the pioneers, and I think myself that I am one kind of a pioneer, at least—a pioneer baby.

I was born at the Tshimakain mission station among the Spokane Indians at Walker's prairie, Spokane county, Washington, October 7, 1843, my parents, Rev. C. Eells, D.D., and wife, having come in 1838 as missionaries to the Indians. Hence I feel as I might at least be classed among the old settlers. Still I wish to vary my story, or a part of it at least, and tell partly, not how the west seemed to an easterner, but how the east seemed to a westerner.

We lived at my native place until 1848, when, on account of the Cayuse war, we were obliged to leave it, and for ten weeks remain at Fort Colville, under the protection of the Hudson Bay company. I shall not narrate the incidents of that war, as I bore no part in them, and as I have written some of them in a book entitled "History of Protestant Indian Missions on This Northwest Coast," as they have gone into other history, and as my father has recently written out his recollections of that time. After the Cayuse war was mainly over, as it was not thought to be safe for us to continue among the Indians, seventy of the volunteers went north as far as the Spokane river, where we met them in the summer of 1848, and they escorted us to the Willamette valley. This journey to The Dalles, from whence we went by water, I made not on foot or in a wagon, but on horseback, riding my horse alone, without being tied on though only 4 years old. Portland was nowhere then, there being only a few houses there, two or three I think. At least, as I was asleep it was not thought necessary to wake me up to see it, and so I lost that view of the future metropolis of Oregon, and passed on to the real metropolis, Oregon City. As the gold mines of California were discovered about this time, everything was very high, and it was hard work to get much to eat, as we came out of the mission with almost nothing. We went to Abiqua, where we remained five weeks, and then to Salem, where father and mother taught school in the institute, as it was then called, the beginning of Willamette university. For a time it was bread and molasses for breakfast—black New Orleans molasses—molasses and bread for dinner, and bread and molasses again for supper for variety. I was once told that I was lucky to have had bread, as many pioneers did not get that. But in those days I have heard my father say that he was never without flour or tea in the house, though when in the Spokane country he always had to go from seventy to a hundred and fifty miles to mill—Colville or Walla Walla—and pack all the flour on horseback. The tea, however, did not benefit me much, as I have never drank a cupful of tea or coffee in my life.

At Salem I first went to school, a pioneer scholar in that institution, but in 1849 we moved to Forest Grove, where my parents taught in what has developed into the Pacific University; and in 1841 to Hillsboro, where we remained until 1857, when we returned to Forest Grove and made that our home until 1862, when we moved to Walla Walla. Those were the days of horse stealing, and my brother and myself slept by ours all summer. One night at The Dalles when moving, we were awakened in the night by the barking of our dog, and a man rode up. When we asked him what he wanted he said plainly that he was hunting horses. Undoubtedly he was, but he concluded those were not the ones he wanted, just then. When at

Walla Walla we lived on the old Whitman mission, and we intended to keep them in sight. Father generally watched them. One day they went out of sight into the bushes on Mill creek. He started after them immediately, went where he had last seen them, then on the road, across the creek and through all the bushes to the open country beyond, listening for them as he went along. They were neither to be seen or heard. Returning through the bushes he again listened, and at last heard a little rustle, when he turned to the place and found them all and a man on one of them. He had managed to keep them very still when father first passed, and their noise was very slight as he returned. "Is—is this your horse?" said the man. Father said it was. "That—that man sent me after them and said they were his," said the man. "What man," said father, but the thief could not tell. In the meantime he slipped off and went away. Some said father would have done better if he had caught the man and lost the horse, rather than to have lost the man and saved the horse. But father was not armed, and the thief motioned as if he was, and father was so glad to get the horses that he did not think it best to take too much effort to capture the thief alone. All that summer we put our horses in our corral every night, and my father and myself and our little dog slept by them until fall, when we finished a stable, where we could lock them up.

That fall father and I went to my native place, the first and last time I ever visited it, since we left it in 1848. From the Snake river to the Spokane river we were two days traveling, and we saw not a person, white man or Indian. I imagine it is different now.

In 1865 and 1866 were the days of the vigilance committee. I was not a member, as I was sent that winter to school, my last year at college. I presume I would have been in it had I been there. If any old settler in your columns would write a history of that as fully as T.J. Dimsdale has done that of Montana, I think he would get the prize and go to Chicago next year free. I often wonder why some one has not done it, for I presume it is safe now to tell the story. Even Colonel F.T. Gilbert, in his large history of Walla Walla, keeps mum about it, as well as all other writers. I was there only at the beginning and the close.

The first man—a horsethief—was shot on our place, across the Walla Walla river, not much more than half a mile from our house. His name was Sanders. He lived about two miles from us. I heard the shots, but thought nothing of them until afterward when he was found in the bushes. It seemed hard as he left a family, but he was undoubtedly very guilty, and his brothers-in-law, who were members of the vigilance committee, took care to see that their sister did not suffer. The captain as was supposed, of the whole organization, William Courtney, lived about two miles from us; in fact we were surrounded by vigilantes, and they were good, brave, determined men. They waited for the law to do what it ought to until long after patience ceased to be a virtue, and then they went to work. The courts would sometimes convict, but the blacklegs elected the sheriff, and if it was winter and the rascals had nothing to live on, they would stay till spring and get out; but if it was summer they would stay a few weeks in jail and then say good-bye to it. For a time it seemed doubtful whether the vigilantes would win or not, for there were about 400 on each side, and the blacklegs had spies among the vigilantes; but after a time a new organization was made by them of men who could be trusted, and they quietly went to work, took one man out of bed and hung him, then hung six or eight more, and soon about seventy-five of the worst blacklegs left the valley, and it became safe for honest men to walk the streets of Walla Walla in daylight, which had not been the case for some time previous.

That fall I went away to school, but said I would not come back without a revolver. I did not, and have the revolver yet. That summer my brother and I slept with a loaded shotgun on one side of our bed and the loaded revolver under our heads. I well remember the last man that was hung. It was after my return home. He came to the house and wanted to stay all night, saying that he had been there about the time of the Whitman massacre. My brother was away at that time and father had to go soon after he came, for he had engaged to deliver an address that evening some six miles distant. Only mother and I were left. While I was attending to the chores I gave him some lectures about the massacre which had been recently delivered by Rev. H.H. Spalding, and he read them. At night we had a long talk about the massacres, for I hoped to get some new items about it, but I learned nothing except what was in those lectures. At night I gave him my room and bed and went upstairs to sleep, but first—I never knew why except on general principles, for I did not then mistrust him to be a thief—I went in, locked my trunk and also took my revolver, leaving, however, the belt and a sheath knife in the belt. The next morning after breakfast I went off to take care of some horses. He went into the room and stayed sometime and then left before I returned as my mother told me. While I was gone I began to think, and wondered if there was anything there that he could steal, and could think of nothing he would probably take except that knife. As soon as I went home I went and looked to see if it was there, but it was gone, although the belt was left. I missed nothing more until Sunday, when I found that he had taken a silk handkerchief from my Sunday coat. I was lucky to lose so little. I afterward learned that previous to this he had had a row in a camp, stolen some things and burned the camp, and that soon after he stayed with us the vigilantes ordered him to leave the valley, but he would not do so. Then they marched him out, but in a short time he was back again, and the next thing that was known about him was that he was found hung. He was believed to be a spy, sent by the blacklegs to see whether it was safe for them to return or not. They found it was not.

In the fall of 1867, I was on the petit jury, but returned home every night—six miles. One day we had a case before us of a white man named William Swayne, who had sold liquor to Indians. The evidence was very clear—in fact, his lawyer threw up the case when he found how clear it was.

It was late when the case was concluded, and the judge, Judge Wyche, said he should be sentenced the next morning. The next morning there was quite a frost, and when I got up, about 5 o'clock, some one knocked at the door, and when I opened it, who should come in but this same man. I knew him in a minute, but did not let on that I did. He also knew me, but he did not let on that he did, but he did not know what I thought of doing. He was nearly chilled through, having stayed by our haystacks the coldest part of the night, and could not have gone much farther if he had tried. I soon got mother up, and a young lady who was staying with her, there being no other persons about the place, but did not tell her who he was. As soon as I could leave I ran up to a neighbors, John Glenn, about three-fourths of a mile distant, and asked him to come and help me. He did so, and as soon as I was ready I took down the shot gun from over my head, and told him he was my prisoner; that he was convicted of selling liquor to Indians the day before. He said yes, but was not sentenced. I told him that the judge said he was to be sentenced that morning. He said: "Don't shoot," and gave up entirely. While I was gone he told mother that he knew me — that he had got into a bad snap and that his lawyer had advised him to leave. It was after conviction and the bondsmen did not consider themselves held any longer, and before sentence, so the sheriff was not as careful as he ought to have been. I left him guarded while I did my chores, and after breakfast I put him on a poor horse, got on my best one, marched him back and delivered him up to the sheriff. At noon his lawyer, named Stevens, came to me and wanted to know if I arrested him, and I told him I did. He wanted to know if I did not know that I was liable to arrest for taking a man without a warrant. I told him I did not, but told him that I knew that all those who had helped the murderers of President Lincoln to get away, were punished, and thought this was a parallel case on a small scale, as I knew all about the case. I told him, however, that I would see the judge and tell him about it, and see what he had to say. Then Mr. Stevens changed his base suddenly, and said: "O, no, you need not see the judge at all, and if anybody makes you any trouble I will defend you." But I did go and see the judge that night, and he said I did right and allowed me $5 for it. No one ever troubled me about it, but I always remembered that lawyer. All he wanted was for me to pay him some money to keep him quiet.

I graduated at Pacific university in May, 1866, in the second class which ever graduated from that institution, and the first one that ever held any public commencement exercises. Then I went to Walla Walla and carried on the farm for two years. President S.H. Marsh, D.D., of that university once said to me that I was born and brought up on this coast and had obtained my education here, and was a pretty good specimen of an Oregonian, and that what I still needed was to go east and become an American. In the summer of 1868 I determined to do so, having decided to study for the ministry. Rev. J.E. Walker, now of China, went with me — both green Oregonians — but we helped each other, and so probably kept out of some snaps in which we otherwise might have got caught. We went by way of the isthmus. Having never been in any place larger than Portland, then a place of less than 8000 people, we naturally felt uneasy when our first jump was into San Francisco and our next into the little village of New York city.

I left Walla Walla July 28th and visited in Oregon till August 19th, when I sailed from Portland on the *Continental*. When we crossed the bar at the mouth of the Columbia it was very smooth, so I was not really seasick on the whole trip. We stayed at San Francisco nearly a week waiting for a steamer, and put in the time sight-seeing at the Mechanics' fair, Woodward's gardens and every other prominent place to which we could go where something good might be learned. I had made up my mind that my eyes and ears were to be open. A log was on exhibition at the fair from Washington territory which was 48x32 inches, and forty-eight feet long, containing 3584 feet. A pretty small log by the side of some that will go to Chicago, but they thought it quite a show. In San Francisco I heard a pipe organ for the first time in my life, but did not like it at all. It seemed as if there was too much style put on; too much of the use of thunder for the worship of God; but after I had heard them for three years and came back to the cabinet organ in church, it sounded very flat for a time, but now I am glad often to get the use of one of them.

We left San Francisco on the *Colorado* August 29, and soon heard lots of swearing and did lots of thinking about the way we were treated — second cabin. The law, hung in a conspicuous place, said that double berths, as far as men were concerned, should be occupied by members of the same family, but while Mr. Walker and I had bargained for single berths in the same room, we found ourselves in double berths with entire strangers, in different staterooms. The law said that double berths should be four feet wide, but ours were only three. The law said that each passenger should be allowed fourteen superficial feet, and we were allowed six and a half. We went to look at the ship and berths before buying our tickets, but the berths were re-numbered after we bought them. Our food, too, was not all "mother's cooking," beef, squash, cucumbers and the like, often so full of pepper that it covered up all the bad cooking. We had some good green corn one day, but when I asked for more I had to wait a long time, and then it came, but it was raw and had apparently been put into the water after I had asked for it and taken out so it was hot but raw; potatoes were red, what we called "hog potatoes" at home; meat on an average was half raw — some entirely cooked and some entirely raw; cornmeal sometimes mixed with water, not cooked, just like I had fed to the chickens at home; milk apparently chalk and water with very little chalk, warranted to keep in any climate; and bread generally sour, but I managed to eat it by putting plenty of sugar on it; but even now as I think of it I can almost taste it and remember how at last I came to have a disgust for bread and butter and sugar. I was glad I had not been accustomed to grumble at the cooking at home, or my conscience would surely have troubled me.

At Panama I visited the old cathedral, a with a few persons kneeling here and there on their pieces of carpets, and with its tombstones sacred to the memory of distinguished persons. There were a large number of natives around the cars who wished to sell ice water, lemonade, cookies, wines, curiosities and the like. One old darkey woman, whose cookies I had been looking at, as I was leaving took hold of my coat-sleeve and said: "My dearest love, what can I do for you?" I felt much like saying "Get out!" but at last concluded to get myself out. Others also were quite affectionate.

From Aspinwall we sailed on the *Arizona,* and our accommodations were better, we two chums having single berths in the same stateroom. The food, too, was a little better. On the Pacific side, tharwozplenteuvit suchazitwaz, here itwazgudenufwottharwuzuvit. The second Sabbath out a couple of young men came around with tracts to distribute and we got considerably acquainted with them, though they belonged in the first cabin. The next Sabbath they said it was our turn to distribute them. I had never done such a thing in my life, and dreaded it, but they seemed to say we must, so I concluded to dash ahead, and really found it very pleasant business. Most of the passengers had almost no reading and were hungry for anything. One wanted something different, as he had that the previous Sabbath, and one wanted something much larger, but only two (United States soldiers) refused them, and that very quietly. The great trouble was we did not have enough – 125 tracts for 340 passengers. It proved to be very pleasant business.

Arriving at New York we determined to leave the city as soon as possible, because we had heard so much about the pickpockets, and then return and see the sights after we had learned the ways of the world. Before leaving, however, I called on Mrs. Dr. James, a sister of Mrs. G.W. Somerindyke of Walla Walla, to whom I had a letter of introduction. I took out my pocket-book and gave her the letter, then put the book back again. During the coversation we talked about the pickpockets, and I was told so much about them that I put my hand up to my pocket to see if mine was there, although I had put it there but a short time before. Only twice, however, did I ever feel uneasy or was I molested while east. Once when I was in Hartford, where I had been a year or two, I was walking rapidly down Main street, when some man came out of a side street, put his hand on my shoulder and muttered something which ended with "shick." I knew what he wanted in a minute. He wanted me to think some one was sick there, then to go there and be robbed. I said nothing, turned my head just enough to see that I really did not know him, and walked on. His hand fell from my shoulder, and he looked very sheepish when he found himself left there. Once I was in Buffalo and was walking from the depot to the wharf half a mile or more, when it seemed to me from appearances that I was in the worst part of the city. I met a policeman and asked him if that was the way to the wharf. He said it was, and just then a man jumped up from his seat with the others on the sidewalk and said he was going there, and would show me the way. I did not like his looks, but the policeman looked at him, and then at me, and said: "He will show you the way." That was a recommend, and I went with him, but I liked him worse and worse. He repeatedly offered to help me carry my things, but I determined to hold on to them. When we were nearly to the wharf, he said, "I shall only charge you 25 cents for this." I said nothing, and thinking whether I would pay it or not. Soon he said, louder, "Do you hear me!" I said, "Yes." I would not have paid him a cent had I felt at home, but I was a stranger, for the first time in that place, and concluded it might be best to give it to him. When I did so, he told me that the steamer would not leave for sometime, and that I might go over to a saloon where he was going and wait till the steamer should go. I did not go, but gave him about as cold a shoulder as I ever did to any man in my life, and I think he realized it, for I never saw him more. But I always blamed that policeman for sending me off with that fellow. These are all the incidents of that kind I ever experienced, though I have traveled nearly 70,000 miles since I left Walla Walla in 1868.

At Worcester, Mass., my mother had a sister living, but although the hotel where I stayed the night was not fifteen minutes' walk from her house, it was nearly noon before I found her, though I had her address, owing to my ignorance and greenness and the crooked and curious streets, some of which seemed to be built along the old cow-paths. I had a time also learning to burn coal. A young man helped me to build a fire one Sabbath morning. I then went to church, came back and my fire was out. I took out all the coal, put in kindlings, as I had been shown how to do, also coal, and started it. The kindlings burned, and then the fire went out. I tried again the same way, and with the same result, only with blackened hands, even if there was nothing else blackened. I gave up for the time, wrapped myself up in my overcoat and quilts, and shivered. Several said my stove was a poor one, so in two days I changed it and tried again, but it smoked until all the kindlings were burned, when it went out. I waited two days more, when I got some help, and succeeded, but was not so successful in keeping the fire for it went out twice that day, but I had learned how to build it.

That winter was spent in study, visiting all the factories, such as Colt's armory, Sharp's rifle factory, sewing machine works and everything else of note in the city of Hartford. At first I felt as much alone as a person could for Mr. Walker had gone to Maine to study, for there was hardly more than one person there of whom I had ever heard, and I felt as if I were in water up to my mouth, which was sometimes coming in, and only could get breath enough to live on, but I lived through it. The students, too, were about as much surprised to see a person who had come from Washington territory, who knew anything, as if I had rained down.

The next summer, during vacation, I went to Williams college commencement, then on to Dr. M. Whitman's home in New York state, and then to Niagara falls, Ohio and Illinois, visiting relatives. Returning I went south as far as Memphis, when I took the railroad through by Atlanta, Chattanooga and Bull Run to Washington, Baltimore, Philadelphia and New York, West Point and Hartford, stopping to visit the most prominent battle fields. At first I felt nervous when I went south alone, among those who had such a bitter hatred to the north, but I kept my own counsel, and remembered my father's advice when we parted, "Be cautious among strangers."

The next vacation I went to Maine, Boston and that region, and so tried to get acquainted with my own country and become an American.

In 1871, having finished my studies, I returned west on the Union Pacific railroad, stopping along to see the country. When I went to Salt Lake City among the Saints, I felt a little nervous again, having heard so much about their secret work with strangers, but I escaped their clutches, and at last came to the conclusion that a person might safely go where he would if he behaved himself.

I first came to the Sound in 1871, on a visit, over the old stage line from Monticello to Olympia; then went to Boise City, Idaho, where I preached until 1874, when I came to the Skokomish reservation, where I have since resided.

But this is too long already and the bulk of my life among the Indians has gone into my "Ten Years at Skokomish," so I will omit this part.

My writing of books and pamphlets began somewhat in this manner: In 1875 I was asked to write out for the Philadelphia centennial an account of the Skokomish Indians. I did so. Among the questions was one about their traditions concerning the deluge. I became interested in seeing how widely that tradition was scattered among the various Indian tribes. Being asked to deliver the address before the college societies of Pacific university, in 1876, I took that as my subject. Professor J.W. Marsh was interested in it, and asked me about the general religious belief of the Indians, and when hearing their principles, said they were much like those of the old Romans. I followed out that idea, trying to learn all I could about the main principles of their religion among all the Indian tribes of America. The result was a paper on "The Worship and Traditions of the Aborigines of America; or Their Testimony to the Religion of the Bible," which was read before and published in a condensed form by the Victoria Institute of London, or Philosophical Society of Great Britain, and in an enlarged form in the *Washington Magazine* of Seattle. Among other books that I read at that time was Rev. W.H. Brett's "Mission Work in Guiana" and when reading it the thought flashed into my mind, why might not the story of mission work among the Indians on this North Pacific coast also be written in like manner, as the material was here, only needing to be worked up. I asked Rev. Dr. Atkinson of Portland if he would write an introduction to it, if I would write the book, and he said he would and did, and the book was written and others of various kinds have followed. Hence I find in looking over my life that it has been much of a pioneer life, although I am not an old man. When I march among the pioneers I find now but few in the ranks ahead of me. When I think of Walla Walla, I find that those are called pioneers who went there no earlier than I did in 1862. When I am asked how long I have been on Hood canal and reply, "eighteen years," the answer comes, "how long?" And when I look among the old settlers I find only eight men or families who were here then who are still here; and when I look among the Congregational ministers of Oregon, Washington and Idaho, I find that there are only three now preaching in the ranks, who were here when I began my work. Some others are living who have left the business, and some others who were preaching here twenty-one years ago, are still preaching elsewhere, but only three of my predecessors are still at work here, and none of them are pastors of churches.

Epilogue

Milburn G. Wills of North Yakima was last evening awarded the *Ledger's* prize for the best old settler's story, the prize consisting of two round-trip tickets to the world's fair at Chicago. The judges were Judge J.W. Robinson, Colonel L.S. Howlett and John R. Reavis.

Mr. Wills' old settler's story was the second one of the series, and contained an account of how he swam the Snake river in the spring of 1856 to carry food to the garrison of soldiers on the other shore.

The time of making the award was changed till night, so as to be made when the exposition management awarded the "Old Settler's" medal. Judge Robinson made a brief address in awarding the *Ledger's* prize, the awards being made in the office of the management, where the old settlers had gathered.

Judge Robinson said:

"By reason of the liberality of one of our distinguished citizens and the business enterprise of the management of one of the leading journals of the Pacific coast, a few months since a prize was offered for the best "old settler's story," and in response thereto more than forty persons have contributed, and the same have been published from week to week in the *Ledger.* To determine this question Colonel Howlett of North Yakima, Hon. John R. Reavis of Spokane and myself were selected. The difficult duty of deciding with so many excellent stories will be fully appreciated upon a moment's reflection and you will not be surprised that the verdict is not unanimous. The judges readily agreed that all were exceedingly interesting and well written, but which one of all the forty was the best? This question has received our most careful and conscientious consideration, and I have been chosen to announce the result, but it has been suggested that it would be proper for me to say a few words to you before doing so.

"Certainly these gatherings of the old settlers are full of interest to all, but the thoughts that must come to you at such an hour must bring more sorrow than joy, and yet I presume it is not all sorrow. Here and there the sunlight of pleasing recollections must break through the clouds. You have been spared by a kind Providence to witness and enjoy very many of the rich fruits, the possibilities of which you and your associates created. But while tonight you gaze backwards and live over again the trying ordeals of pioneer life, recalling this and that hardship, remembering as if it were today, a thousand thrilling incidents and perilous adventures, turning here and there to drop a tear upon the sacred grave of one who, perhaps less fortunate than yourselves, sleeps yet along the line, and as you recall in part what you have endured, with all the sufferings and sorrows your hearts must go out in gratitude to Almighty God that you have been spared to witness your present surroundings. And you no doubt feel proud — as you justly should — that as such pioneers you were made the instrumentalities through and by whose energies, deprivations and bravery the foundation has been laid for the grandest commonwealth over which the stars and stripes every floated. Brushing aside all the sorrows and shadows of the past, standing for the present surrounded by this magnificent audience, no small percent of which is made up of your honored sons and daughters and their respected children, within this grand building, where are exhibited the products of brain and muscle, the equal of those in like institutions in other states, upon which has shown the light of culture and civilization for more than a century, within a city whose speedy and substantial growth, whose commercial and business relations, whose steady development of so grand a variety of American industries and with so large an increase in its citizenship within so brief a period, proclaim it everywhere the most marvelous city of the nineteenth century — with these inspiring surroundings, with these practical living results of your handiwork, you can feel confident that your lives have not been spent in vain and that 'there is a divinity that shapes our ends rough hew them as we may.' Your neighbors and friends from motives of love and gratitude may erect over the grave of the pioneer a shaft of marble that will withstand the blasts of storms, but their own labors laid the foundation of state and thereby left a monument to their memory more lasting than any made of marble slabs.

"Happy indeed must be the thought that you have lived to see this wonderful development. It was my good fortune to stand near the desk of President Harrison in the White house on November 11th, 1889, when, as the executive of this great nation, he and the gifted Blaine issued the proclamation by which the territory of Washington, named after the father of his country, shot out upon the broad sea of statehood to enter into a meritorious contest among a sisterhood of more than forty empires. And this is the monument that civilization dedicates alike to the memory of the pioneer and of Washington.

"Two of your committee, Colonel Howlett and Mr. Reavis, decided that the story written by M.G. Wills is the best of the series, and Mr. Wills therefore secures the prize. But while having implicit confidence in the literary ability and judgment of my associates, I am unable to concur in their conclusion, and in my humble judgment the letter of James Longmire entitles him to the prize, and I therefore record my vote for him.

"And now on behalf of the committee and the *Tacoma Ledger*, I wish Mr. Wills and his companion a safe and happy journey to the world's fair and hope and pray that the lives of all of you may be joined to each other, and this grand state for years and years to come, and that the record of your troubles, trials and privations, as evidenced by these interesting letters, be preserved in a more enduring form than in the scattered pages of a daily journal."

A COMPLETE CONTENT LISTING
OF MYRON EELLS' SCRAPBOOKS

Volume 1
- The Old Settler; lyrics to the song
- Advertisement of the *Ledger* telling of the contest, inviting those who came to Washington by wagon to write the paper an account of their trip. Prize to be given to best, and all to be published by the *Ledger*. All the following articles are from the *Tacoma Ledger*.
- Adam Matheny's Experiences in the war following the Whitman Massacre; April 8, 1892.
- Incidents of the Indian War in the Yakima Country in 1855; M.G. Wills; April 15, 1892.
- F.W. Brown's lonely trip from Portland to Willapa in 1854; April 17, 1892.
- An old timer who was on the Frontier in Ohio seventy years ago; George Washington; April 29, 1892.
- How they swam the Snake River; C.D. Wilcox tells story of trip in 1847; April 29, 1892.
- Hon. Edward Eldridge describes his trip to Fort Colville in search of gold in 1855; May 6, 1892.
- Crossed with McCauley; a boy of seven who came along to show his father the way; June 3, 1892.
- A.L. McCauley of Dayton tells the story of his journey in the summer of 1865; May 13, 1892.
- Urban East Hicks had several skirmishes with Indians on the plains; May 27, 1892.
- A frightful journey from Olympia to Grays Harbor in 1883; an extract from a private letter, dated Feb. 25, 1883, by J.W.P.; May 20, 1892.
- Mrs. Ellen Wallis tells the story of her trip across the plains; May 20, 1892.
- R.B. Harrison's story; a narrow escape from drowning and a narrower one from slaughter by the Indians; June 10, 1892.
- Charles Prosch of Seattle tells the story of his trip to this coast by steamer in 1853; May 27, 1892.
- A daughter of Wm. Packwood, crossed the plains in 1844; June 3, 1892.
- Merril Short crossed the plains to Wash. in 1853; June 10, 1892.
- Three stories of settlers who came over in 1851 and 1852; June 17, 1892.
- E.A. Light crossed the plains in 1852; June 24, 1892
- Story of Mrs. Mary Perry Frost's trip overland; July 1, 1892.
- Urban E. Hick's story of a journey to Shoalwater bay in 1853; July 1, 1892(?).
- James Gleason's trip from California to Washington in 1878; July 8, 1892.
- Mrs. Lucy Woodard crossed plains in 1853; July 8, 1892(?).
- Alex. Vincent finds fun fighting Indians; July 15, 1892.

Volume 2

- Andrew Frost came in 1844 and saw the murderers of Whitman hanged.
- Hester E. Davis came in 1852 – her party was blinded by heat and tortured by thirst.
- Thomas W. Laws saw rough times both on the way and after his arrival.
- Lieutenant Urban E. Hicks tells the story of early Indian massacre.
- C.P. Ferry came by Panama and had a pointer on Puget Sound.
- General McCarver was well known as the founder of Tacoma.
- Governor Eugene Semple walked from Umatilla Landing to Idaho, starting in a fine pair of Wellington boots in 1864.
- Rev. Myron Eells was born in the Northwest in 1843, driven to the mountains by the Cayuse war, later a missionary among the Indians.
- Hugh Crockett came over with Colonel Ebey and family, and later tells the story of the murder of Colonel Ebey, and possible reasons.
- Major C.M. Barton, secretary of the state Senate, sets story straight as first-born white child in Oregon Territory.
- James Longmire tells of buffalo hunting, and of the surrender and subsequent murder of Quiemuth, brother of Leschi.
- J.B. Knapp had adventures with Indians while crossing the plains in 1852; his wife died near The Dalles.
- A.C. Morse came overland in the spring of 1850; tells how four murderers were arrested and how vigilantes handled them.
- A.W. Arnold suffered abuse on a sail journey around the Horn; tells of later experiences in the gold mines of California and on the Fraser River.
- John Flett took part in the transfer of the Umpquas to the Grand Ronde, and tells of tragic scenes of the trip northward, including the murder of an Indian prophetess.
- Sherwood Bonney tells sad story of summer of 1852; and of menace by Indians while fighting cholera in the Snake River Valley.
- Mrs. Martha H. Ellis' story of her trip overland in Spring of 1852 and how her first house was built, and how she carried a gun in the Indian War.
- Luzena Wallace relates experiences of a lawyer's wife in early days of Western Washington; she named the state of Idaho.
- Mrs. M.K. Overman tells sad story of settlers who came in 1852, of a cemetery in every camp, and of a jack rabbit who saved an ox's life and kept the whole party from starvation.
- Al R. Hawk and family crossed plains in 1852, witnessed cholera trail, had many perilous experiences in the Rapids, and a fall from fright that resulted in the death of Mrs. Hawk.
- William R. Downey's family came across plains in summer of 1853. Three of his sons served as volunteers in the Indian War of 1855.
- Old Settlers Day at the Exposition; list of settlers who wrote stories for the *Ledger*.
- Old Settlers' Prizes (one awarded to John McLeod, another to Milburn G. Wills).

- Milburn G. Wills awarded the *Ledger's* tickets to the World's Fair.
- George W. Burford tells how he crossed the continent in 1852.

Volume 3
- M.P. Dougherty came to Oregon in 1843 and to the Sound in 1850; September 30, 1892.
- Massacre at Cascaes, story of Mrs. Christiana Corum; September 11, 1892.
- Horse thieves routed, incident of A.F. Sawall's trip across the plains; September 11, 1892.
- J.B. Knapp's vivid recollections of the terrible summer of 1852; October 14, 1892.
- Story of C.B. Talbot, who came across the plains in the year 1849; October 21, 1892.
- Story of Hon. Eldridge Morse; October 28, 1892.
- Mrs. Nettie Hallenbeck's story of life in Michigan, Nebraska, and Washington; November 4, 1892.
- Mr. C.C. Bozarth's thrilling narrative of his ox-team adventures; November 25, 1892.
- Founder of Aberdeen, Samuel Ben tells of his experiences at Grays Harbor; November 25, 1892.
- Mrs. White's journey across the continent to her husband; December 9, 1892.
- Story of John Flett's death; December 16, 1892.
- T.O. Abbott's book, a compilation of all laws affecting real property in Washington; December 16, 1892.
- Rev. A.J. Joslyn's experiences in crossing the plains in 1852; no date.
- Walla Walla Battle, four days of hard fighting with the Indians, winter of 1855; October 28, 1892.
- Hugh Crockett tells the story of the rescue of the crew of the *Georgiana*; January 13, 1893.
- Walla Walla Valley; some of the memorable events in the history of the valley of many waters; February 5, 1893.
- Captain J.G. Parker's recollections of early days in the Sound country; February 10, 1893.
- William D. Vaughn, the nimrod of pioneer days in Washington and Oregon; February 17, 1893.
- Henry Beckett of Orting, caught the Fraser River gold fever in 1858; March 3, 1893.
- W.W. Plumb of Centralia tells his story, across in the plains in 1851; no date.
- Story of John E. Burns, came around the Horn to California and then to the Sound; April 28, 1893.
- Story of Clinton B. Ferry; no date.
- Story of Alfred Miller; May 21, 1893.
- Story by Urban E. Hicks; May 14, 1893.

- Story of James McAllister; March 24, 1893 (2 copies).
- Story of the early climbers of Mt. Tacoma; April 7, 1893.
- P.B. Van Trump relates anecdotes of ascents of Mt. Tacoma; April 14, 1893.
- Story of Joseph McEvoy; May 28, 1893.
- Washington's early Capitols; March 31, 1893(?).
- Reminiscences of U.E. Hicks; no date.
- Story by R.B. Rabbeson; a terrible ride from Naches River to Steilacoom, in *Oregonian*, July 16, 1886.

INDEX

Laws, Thomas W.   100-104
Lee's encampment (Meacham)   323
Lemon, Isaac   196-198
Leschi   9, 13, 14, 17, 151,
    158-159, 160, 185, 187-190,
    192, 200, 232, 240
Lewis county, Oregon Territory   8
Lewis, Squire   194
Light, E.A.   63, 174, 175, 179, 217-239
Linn, Lewis F.   3
Llewellen, William   82-83
Logan, David   36-330
Longmire, James   173-192, 226, 239
Lord Jim (Indian)   208
Lousdal, Dr. R.H.   248
Lovejoy, A.L.   6
L.P. Forster   207

McAllister, James   9-19, 23, 24, 49, 97, 151
    170, 186-187, 197, 255
McCain, James   53-54
McCarthy, J.W.   192-201
McCarver, General   22, 331-342
McCarver, Jennie   337
McClellan, George B.   150
McCracken, John   328
McGlaughlin, John   46
McGowan, Ned   295
McKane, James   47
McLaferty, G.   97
McLeod, Angus   122
Major Tompkins, ship   257
Maples, Sam   245
Mary, steamer   329
Mary Adams, bark   81
Mason, Charles H.   76, 186-187
Massachusetts, steam frigate   75, 84, 260
Mayer, John   183
Meacham, A.B.   323
Meek, Joseph   36
Meeker, Ezra   234, 253, 334
Meeker, J.R.   236
Meeker, O.P.   199, 253
Miles, Joseph   49, 152, 159-162, 197, 256
Miller, Jeff   134
Miller, George   127
Miller, W.W.   158
Miller and Langlon, bridge builders   45-47
Mishell, Henry   347
Mishell prairie   347
Mollhigh, John   185, 187
Mondesh   11-19
Monroe, John   73
Montesano, Washington   105
Montgomery, H.D.   63
Mormons   34
Moses, Abraham Benton   49, 97, 152,
    159-162, 197, 200, 255, 256
Moses, S.P.   69, 92
Mount Latate   225, 234
Mount Rainier (Tacoma)   19, 157, 239-241
    342-351
Muck Valley   237
Mullan Road   155
Multnomah, steamer   328
Munroe, Victor   254
Munson, J.H.   234

Natchez Pass (Cascade Mountains)   71-72,
    111, 150, 205, 224-225, 234
Natchez river   114, 159, 182, 205, 223, 224
Navy bay, Panama   64
Neely, Edward   203
Nell, Fauton   243
Nesmith, James W.   4
Nickson, Tom   212
Nisqually, Fort   9, 184, 206
Nisqually Indians   10
Nisqually river   184, 185
Nisqually Valley   10
Northcroft, Mr.   157, 166, 167, 171
North Pacific, steamer   78-79
Northern Pacific railroad   335, 341

Oak Harbor, Washington   257
O'Fallon, Thomas   7
Olympia, steamer   78-79
Olympia, Washington   48, 69-73, 86,
    93, 103, 153, 166, 168, 191, 233,
    248, 253, 261
Orcas Island   212
Oregon city, Oregon   127
Oregon Spectator   5
Oregonian, The   39, 330
Oregon volunteers   128, 157
Ork, bark   228
Orting, Washington   316
Osborne, Mrs. William   257
Otter, steamer   70, 295
Ozha   190-191

Pacific Mail company   66
Packwood, William   20-25
Panama   65-66, 270-271, 276
Panama bay   313
Panama Star   65
Parker, Captain J.G.   64-80, 257
Patagonia   307-309
Pawnee Indians   27
Pearson, Robert L.   271-272
Pease, Captain C.   258
Pendleton, Oregon   320-321
Penn's cove   71, 247, 248, 254, 257
Perham, A.S.   196, 198
Peterson Point   106, 109
Pettygrove, W.F.   6
Peu Peu Mox Mox   124, 180, 223
Phillips, C.C.   255
Phillips, Dave   170
Pioneer and Democrat, newspaper   170
Pioneers Company   155
Placerville, Idaho   323-324
Platte river   45-47
Plumb, W.W.   86-94
Plumondeau, Mr.   69
Poe, Alonzo M.   97,153,259
Point Roberts   290-291
Point Wilson   208
Port Angeles, Washington   315
Port Discovery, Washington   82
Port Gamble, Washington   248, 283
Port Townsend guards   208
Port Townsend, Washington   59, 71, 81,
    207, 254, 274
Porter, Allan   183

-371-